W9-BLT-203

continued . . .

SYNCHRONIZED SORCERY

A Witchcraft Mystery

Juliet Blackwell

BERKLEY PRIME CRIME
New York

BERKLEY PRIME CRIME
Published by Berkley
An imprint of Penguin Random House LLC
penguinrandomhouse.com

Copyright © 2021 by Julie Goodson-Lawes
Excerpt from *Bewitched and Betrothed* by Juliet Blackwell copyright © 2019
by Julie Goodson-Lawes

ISBN: 9780593097953

First Edition: July 2021

Printed in the United States of America
1 3 5 7 9 10 8 6 4 2

To Maddee James,
for the friendship and the artistry

SYNCHRONIZED
SORCERY

Chapter 1

"I'm worried about Oscar," I said, twisting in my seat as I tried to get settled. The San Francisco–bound flight was still loading passengers, and the newest arrivals were doing that crablike shuffle down the narrow center aisle that was unique to modern air travel.

The aisle seat to my right was occupied by a polite Parisian woman whose headphones discouraged conversation, at least with this chatty Texan. Fortunately for me, sitting on my left, by the window, was a sexy psychic named Sailor.

Even though we in economy class were jammed elbow-to-elbow into cramped spaces with inadequate leg room, I didn't mind. I would have happily rested in Sailor's lap all the way from Paris, so enamored was I with my new husband.

Husband. I still found that hard to believe.

"And exactly *why* are you worried about Oscar?" Sailor asked with the strained patience of a private school headmaster. I gave him credit for refraining from rolling his dark, beautiful eyes.

Sailor had been less than enthusiastic that Oscar, a shapeshifting pig and my ersatz witch's familiar, had accompanied us on our honeymoon. There was a reason I had invited Oscar along, of course: I had promised to help him search for his mother, who suffered under a curse that had turned her into a stone gargoyle. It's a long story, but the upshot was that I spent my honeymoon traipsing around Europe, checking out gargoyles adorning castles and cathedrals and manors, and mediating between the two most important fellas in my life—who had a habit of vying for my attention.

"How is he going to get home?" I asked.

"I would imagine the same way he got to Barcelona, to Paris, and to Budapest, as well as every other destination on our mind-bogglingly complicated honeymoon itinerary." Sailor intertwined his long, graceful fingers with mine, and I took a moment to gaze at our interlocked hands. The crystals in my antique druzy engagement ring sparkled, and our matching wedding bands—wrought of tiny intertwined vines of silver—gleamed in the overhead lights.

"Hey, wife," Sailor said in a low, grumbly voice. "Remember Prague?"

"*Prague*," I breathed, closing my eyes.

"And the turret room?"

"The *turret* room," I repeated, blushing at the memory of the beautiful, round room at the top of the medieval castle, with its ancient stone walls, plush window seat, and tall windows looking out across the red-tiled roofs of Prague. Not to mention what all had gone on beneath the down comforter in the turret's king-sized canopy bed.

"Not easy cleaning up all those rose petals you manifested." Sailor gave me a barely-there smile and a smoldering look, and for a moment I forgot all about Oscar and the hustle and bustle of the boarding airplane. He continued, "Or that tapas bar in the market in Barcelona our first night?"

"What about last night in Paris, in that little bistro with the carousel on the corner . . . ?" I sighed. "I loved everything we saw, and ate . . ."

"And ate, and *ate* . . ."

I laughed. Having spent several weeks touring Europe, I truly understood the phrase "the honeymoon period." It had been a glorious, romantic, blissful adventure to start our new life as a married couple. We weren't *technically* married, at least as far as the law was concerned, because my friend Bronwyn had not been able to get licensed in time to officiate, and Sailor's several-years-in-the-making divorce had not yet been finalized. But our handfasting, held in a redwood fairy circle, had been witnessed by our closest friends and family and sanctified by the woods-folk. We would legalize our union at city hall eventually, but regardless, ours was a true marriage in my witchy book.

"It was a *great* honeymoon," I said.

"It was. Would have been better without our porcine companion, but otherwise . . ."

Sailor let out a soft "*oof*" as I poked him in the ribs.

He chuckled. "All I'm saying is that it would have been nice not having to explain the presence of our 'pet pig' everywhere we went. I thought that poor bellboy at the *Parador* in Spain was going to run right off the parapet."

The *Parador* was a tenth-century Moorish fortress turned castle turned hotel, perched atop a hill overlooking the city of Tortosa and the Ebro River. We stayed at a number of wonderful old castles in our travels, and the experience never lost its charm. Each and every one had made me feel like a princess. Except for the annoyance of lingering ghosts haunting those stone walls, but that was par for the course for me. My paranormal skill set does not include the ability to communicate with spirits, but they tend to sense my presence and often reach out. It's disconcerting for me, and I can only imagine how frustrating it must be for them.

"It's hard to believe we're heading back to real life," I said. "I guess this means the honeymoon's over. Shall I start to nag you now?"

"I think it's required. And I'll start scratching and making weird bodily noises."

"Please don't."

"I won't if you won't."

"Deal."

We kissed and sealed the deal.

"I wonder how Calypso has handled things in my absence . . ." I said. "I sure hope Aidan is doing better."

My last encounter with Aidan Rhodes, the head of the San Francisco Bay Area's magical community, had been horrifying: He had been covered in blood from terrible injuries sustained in a fight with a demon, wounds that required the kind of treatment modern medicine could not provide. I forced myself to take a deep breath and concentrate on the positives: Aidan was now under the care of my grandmother's skilled colleagues near Michoacán, Mexico, his recuperation aided by drawing upon the energy of the salt caves. Or at least I hoped so. Aidan and I did not always see eye to eye on things, but he understood my complicated past in a way few could, and had become a true friend.

"Your grandmother told us last week that he's healing well, so it shouldn't be too much longer," said Sailor. Unlike me, Sailor carried a cell phone, which had made it possible for us to enjoy the occasional FaceTime with friends and colleagues while we were in Europe. "And just think: In the meantime you get to fulfill your egomaniacal ambition to be the Grand Poobah of Bay Area witches."

"I have no such ambition," I scoffed.

He raised one eyebrow.

"I'm serious. I have *no* desire, none at *all*, to be a Grand whatever-you-said. I have no interest in being in charge. Really." I could hear that I protesteth a mite too much and added: "I do think I might handle certain things better than Aidan, but that's not the same thing as wanting to take over."

"Sure about that?" Sailor looked amused.

"Positive." I paused. "It's just that . . . running the San Francisco Bay Area magical community seems like a job for a woman."

Sailor raised his eyebrow again. "Resorting to sexist arguments now, are we?"

"No. But there's a reason the vast majority of witches are women," I said. "It's an energy thing. I simply think a woman should be in charge, that's all."

"Well, that's good, because it seems you've inherited the job."

"*Temporarily* inherited the job. I'm just filling in, remember." I sighed. "The worst part is there's always a lot of bureaucratic paperwork, and people wanting me to fix things all the time."

"Repeat after me: 'I'll see what I can do.' Works every time."

I laughed. "I'll keep that in mind."

"And just for the record: When you *do* become the Bay Area's Grand Poobah, I'll be happy to fulfill my obligations as First Gentleman. I imagine there will be a lot of cocktail parties involved. I'm quite partial to a lovely platter of canapés."

I ignored that. "*Anyway,* I can't wait to see Selena, and Bronwyn, and Maya, and Conrad, and all the others. . . . I wonder how business has been."

"Didn't Bronwyn say your grandmother's coven has been helping out at the shop?"

"She did, and that's what worries me," I said with a smile. "What do you want to bet there's not a sparkly garment left on the racks? Those old women are a flock of magical magpies."

Most of the passengers had finally finished stowing their luggage and taken their seats, and the flight attendants began one last sweep through the cabins, shutting the overhead bin doors and soothing nervous fliers. I was reaching for the in-flight magazine in the seat pocket in front of me when the medicine bag I always wore around my waist started to hum.

I looked up to see a late arrival burst onto the airplane. He was of average height and weight, with an olive complexion, dark eyes, and longish near-black hair, approximately my age. He wore a gleaming gold earring in his left ear, but otherwise there was nothing especially remarkable about him, certainly nothing to explain the sudden conviction that I knew him from somewhere. I wondered whether I might have met him years ago in Germany when I visited my father—a visit I could still only vaguely recall. If this fellow were somehow connected to my father, he might very well spell trouble.

Our eyes locked as he proceeded down the aisle. He was some form of magical practitioner, I would bet my boots on it.

My heart started to pound, the tingling at my waist still issuing its warning. Not that it was all that unusual for me to encounter another witch; after all, there were a lot more of my ilk walking around than most cowans—

nonmagical folk—realized. But there was something about this mystery man that put me on edge.

He averted his intense gaze as he passed our row. I craned my neck to follow his progress down the aisle, but there was nothing more of note: he proceeded to the rear of the plane, stowed his bag in an overhead compartment, and took a seat, disappearing from view.

"Everything okay?" Sailor asked, following my gaze. He didn't miss much.

"Sure," I said, and shook my head as if to clear my thoughts. By now the aircraft door had been shut, the flight attendants were in the aisle doing a choreographed dance demonstrating the use of seatbelts and flotation devices ("in the unlikely event of a water landing"), and the pilots behind the cockpit door were spinning up the engines as they prepared the airplane for departure.

"Why do flight attendants always demonstrate how to put on a seatbelt?" I asked. "Is there a person alive who doesn't know how to operate a seatbelt?"

"Hard to imagine, but once it's a rule, I guess they're compelled to tell us." Sailor glanced at me. "Feeling antsy?"

"A bit. As anxious as I am to get back, it will be hard to return to real life."

"We have a lot to do," agreed Sailor. "But we're very fortunate, all things considered."

"Oh, I agree," I said. "Still. It's much more fun to travel and be waited on in restaurants and sleep in castles than to go to work and do laundry and pay bills."

"Can't argue with you there. Among other things, we need to address the living situation, you and I."

"And Oscar."

"And Oscar," Sailor agreed in a weary voice.

"Poor guy still hasn't found his mother, despite all those gargoyles we saw. I wonder if he'll ever stop looking."

"All in good time, as your grandmother Graciela would say."

"She also says: 'Just 'cause you put your boots in the oven don't make 'em biscuits.' I never figured out what that meant, either."

He chuckled, and as the plane taxied into position on the runway I tried, without luck, to catch another glimpse of the mystery man. So I gazed instead at Sailor's hand, intertwined with mine, and wondered what our return to "real life" in San Francisco might hold, and how Sailor and I, as a couple, would transition from our glorious, carefree honeymoon back to real life, with all its cares and responsibilities.

The plane's engines roared as we started down the runway and picked up speed, the rumbling of the wheels suddenly going silent as we lifted off of European soil.

"What is *that*?" I asked eleven hours later as we circled San Francisco, preparing to land.

"What 'that'?"

"*That* shape, down there," I said, pointing at a brightly lit rectangle in the dark expanse of the bay waters below us. Sailor and I had exchanged seats halfway through the flight, so now he had to lean over me to look out the small window.

"Must be a cargo ship of some kind," he said.

"It's too big to be a cargo ship—look at it in comparison to the others. It looks more like an island, but which could it be?"

"It's not Alcatraz, that's for sure," said Sailor, and our eyes met. Not long ago we had survived a series of harrowing encounters within the walls of the old federal penitentiary on the island. Both of us preferred not to be reminded of those experiences.

I knew there were other islands in San Francisco Bay: Angel Island, Yerba Buena Island, Station Island, Belvedere, Alameda, plus a few lesser-known rocks poking out of the water. But none of them resembled what I was looking at.

"Besides," I said. "Why would a cargo ship be lit up like a Christmas tree?"

"All good questions," said Sailor, wrapping an arm around me and giving me a hug. "Perhaps you could look it up on the Internet, if you ever learn how to use the computer. So, how does it feel to come back to the City by the Bay?"

"Truthfully? Like coming home."

"Even though it's not Europe?"

"Do I sound silly?"

"Not at all," Sailor continued. "It sounds like you love where you live, and your friends and community. I'd say you're very lucky."

"*We're* very lucky." I laid my head on his shoulder and gazed out the window as we flew past the city, skirted the bay, and finally set down on the soil of my adopted state.

I was coming home to good friends and family. To my Haight Street vintage clothing shop, Aunt Cora's Closet, and to the temporary (I hoped) role as the head of the San Francisco Bay Area magical community. I was returning with scads of gifts for everyone, a few spellcasting items and souvenirs for myself, and one disappointed familiar. As well as a mysterious fellow passenger, a dozen rows behind us, who might just spell trouble.

My medicine bag had continued to hum throughout the flight. The man with one gold earring might be out of sight, but he was most definitely not out of mind.

Chapter 2

I searched for the mystery man upon arrival, but as we passengers crowded into the aisle to retrieve our various items and file off the plane, I couldn't find him among the throng. Neither was I able to spot him in the resident or nonresident passport lines, nor as we collected our checked bags and headed to customs.

"Who are you looking for?" Sailor asked.

"Are you reading my mind?" I asked.

"I wouldn't read your mind even if your thoughts weren't so well guarded. It would be too much of an invasion of privacy. But it doesn't take extrasensory abilities to know when something's bothering my woman."

I shrugged. "There was someone on the plane who looked . . . familiar."

"As in a witch's familiar?"

"No. Just . . . familiar."

It's probably nothing, I told myself. Just some weird bit of random déjà vu.

Except that, in my world, weird feelings were almost

never "nothing." When I adopted San Francisco as my city, I acquired not only a new world of friendship and community but a region rife with magic and murder. Besides, my medicine bag had tingled a warning—and my medicine bag rarely got it wrong.

"Speaking of familiars," Sailor said, after we cleared customs. "Oscar just texted me. He said to tell you he's tracking down a few final tchotchkes in the airport gift shop. And that he's hungry and to remind you that they sell See's Candies at a stand in the arrivals area."

"Oscar *texted* you?"

He nodded.

"Oscar has a cell phone?"

"Apparently."

"Since when does Oscar have a *cell phone*?"

"I guess that clinches it," said Sailor with a chuckle as we walked along the nondescript corridor that led out of the terminal's restricted area. "You are officially the last person on earth—or the last *creature* on earth—without a cell phone."

"Oh, look! There's Maya!"

I spotted one of my closest friends in the crowd, waving. Maya was in her midtwenties, petite and strong, and wore her braided locks decorated with beads. She worked at Aunt Cora's Closet and was a student at the San Francisco Academy of Art, and though she possessed a first-rate mind, she seemed to be in no particular hurry to graduate. Maya was one of my most levelheaded friends, who had come into my magical world with a healthy dose of skepticism. She was open to new ideas and unexpected realities, but wasn't sure how far she was willing to go with the whole witch-type deal.

Jumping up and down beside her, clapping her hands, was Bronwyn, another dear friend who also worked with me at the shop. Bronwyn kept her own herb stand and, while I ran around town tending to other business, pretty much helped run Aunt Cora's Closet alongside Maya. Bronwyn was a proud fifty-something, full-figured Wiccan, who tended toward gauzy purple outfits and wildflowers, such as the garland of yellow dandelions currently adorning her wild mop of graying hair. Bronwyn was a dues-paying member of the Haight Street Welcome Coven and had no trouble at all with my witchy ways.

The sight of the eager smiles on the faces of these dear friends flooded me with emotion. Not so long ago, in what now seemed like another lifetime, I came to the City by the Bay at the suggestion of a drunken parrot named Barnabas in Hong Kong. I had arrived alone and friendless, and hadn't expected my situation to change. I had long since accepted that I was a solitary soul, fated to travel my path alone.

And just look at me now. I was newly married to a wonderful man, and two amazing women—more cherished sisters than good friends—were welcoming me back to my adopted Bay Area.

The hugging went on for a very long time.

"Have we got everything?" Bronwyn asked, as we started for the exit doors. "Fingers and toes all accounted for?"

"Let's hope so. Any more luggage and we'd have to hire some pack mules," Maya teased.

"Don't complain," said Sailor as he pushed the over-laden luggage cart. "Half our suitcases are full of gifts for you all."

"I would expect nothing less," Maya said with a laugh.

As I looked around to be sure we hadn't forgotten anything, I caught one final glimpse of the Mystery

Man with the gold earring. He was standing near the exit to Ground Transportation. As our eyes met, he tipped an imaginary hat in my direction, smiled, and slipped out the door.

I'm no clairvoyant, but I had the distinct impression this would not be the last time I laid eyes on that man.

"How's everything at Aunt Cora's Closet?" I asked as we headed toward the multistory parking garage.

"Great. Well, except there is one thing. . . ." Maya hesitated.

"What is it? Is something wrong?" I asked, alarmed.

"Nothing, really. Just that I did my best, I swear I did, but there's still a pretty big pile of laundry that needs doing," said Maya. "I honestly don't know how you manage."

"Laundry," I said with a sigh. "*Yay.*"

It was official. The honeymoon was over.

Bronwyn talked animatedly all the way back to Aunt Cora's Closet, filling us in on what had happened in our absence, while Maya skillfully navigated the crowded city streets and added clarifying comments here and there.

My heart again filled with emotion when we turned onto Haight Street. The neighborhood had become a true home.

Although it was well past closing time, the windows of my vintage clothing store, Aunt Cora's Closet, were brightly lit, and a crowd was milling about near the door. And . . . was that singing I heard?

"What in the world?" I asked, climbing out of the car. The strains of an off-pitch rendition of some song I didn't recognize assailed my ears.

"It's a welcome home party!" gushed Bronwyn. "We're doing karaoke!"

"It was *supposed* to be a surprise," murmured Maya, giving Bronwyn a sidelong look. "But, and I say this with all due respect, your grandmother's coven isn't great at following orders."

"I'd be shocked if they were," I said with a chuckle.

"Everyone is so excited to see you!" said Bronwyn. "They couldn't wait!"

"And I, them," I said, though a part of me longed for a hot shower and my soft bed. It had been a long trip, and my old pal, jet lag, was beginning to make itself known. It probably didn't help that I had watched back-to-back movies on the plane instead of trying to sleep. I rarely had such uninterrupted time to hone my popular culture references.

I opened the shop door and was greeted with the familiar, beloved aroma of fresh laundry and the sachets of lavender and rosemary that I hung around the place. Clearly the herbs had been replenished in my absence. No surprise there; the shop had been chock-full of witchy women: my *abuela* Graciela's entire coven, whom I referred to collectively as the Aunties, visiting from Texas. They were a veritable United Nations of the elderly West Texas witch population: Viv, Rosa, Caroline, Winona, Kay, Betty, MariaGracia, Pepper, Iris, Agatha, Darlene, and Nan. Graciela made it a perfect thirteen, a lucky number for us magical folk.

The sales counters were covered with a tower of homemade cookies, cakes, and muffins, as well as an assortment of libations. I am a solitary witch, but having attended a coven meeting or ten, I had learned that witchy gatherings were always accompanied by plenty of great baked goods. I noted with relief, however, that there were no cupcakes among the treats. I had recently developed an aversion to beautifully frosted "fairy cakes" as the result of a series of encounters with a maleficent baker named Renee. Another long story.

Baby, baby, don't get hooked on me
'Cause I'll just use you then I'll set you free
Baby, baby, don't get hooked on meeeeeeeee

Near the dressing rooms an informal stage for the karaoke singers had been created with plywood and wooden packing crates. Upon spotting us, Rosa and Viv interrupted their duet. "Lily! Sailor! Welcome home!"

I waved back, and asked, "What are they singing? I don't recognize that song."

"It's by Mac Davis, a country-western singer. Big hit in 1972," Bronwyn's boyfriend, Duke, a retired fisherman, explained. "Welcome back, Lily."

"Lily!" I heard, and was swiftly embraced by my mother, Maggie Ivory. She and I had a difficult past, but we had made a lot of progress in healing it, and her hug was as comforting as a soft warm towel after a dip in the frigid bay. "It's so good to see you."

"You, too," I said, and meant it.

While Sailor lugged our suitcases in and stowed them in the workroom, I reveled in greeting my many friends: several members of Bronwyn's Welcome Coven; a few Haight Street neighbors; our "gutter punk" friend, Conrad; and Maya's mother, Lucille, and several of the seamstresses who worked for her. Sailor's cousin Patience Blix nodded at me coolly, which was more than I expected. My friend Hervé Le Mansec, a hoodoo practitioner, gave me a big hug, and his wife, Caterina, greeted me politely. Caterina did not like me very much, probably because I was in the habit of calling her husband in the middle of the night to ask for his assistance in investigating one murder or another. Even Carlos Romero, the SFPD homicide inspector was there, chatting with Patience. Carlos had become a friend over the course of far too many of those murder investigations.

Everyone talked at once, sharing stories and peppering us with questions to the background strains of septuagenarians warbling, with off-key enthusiasm, to the Greatest Hits of the 1960s and '70s. To my surprise, my notoriously private new husband took out his cell phone to show off various photographs of our travels, a crooked smile on his lips as he lifted his eyes and met my gaze from across the room.

This is how it starts, I thought. *A lifetime of shared memories.*

"How are you, Selena? I missed you!" I said to my young charge, who was in the sullen-teenager phase. At least, I hoped it was a phase; it had been going on for so long I thought it might never end. Still, Selena was slowly starting to show signs of a greater maturity, and I saw a bit of my young self in the awkward, lonely, powerful young witch. "You didn't say anything when we FaceTimed last week."

She shrugged but gave me a shy smile.

"Here," Selena said, awkwardly handing me a rolled-up sheet of sketching paper. As a trio of the Aunties crooned, "*Billie, don't be a hero, don't be a fool with your life / Billie, don't be a hero, come back and make me your wife . . .*" I unfurled the scroll to find a drawing of a mermaid drifting amidst a swirl of blues and greens, rather like an underwater version of van Gogh's *The Starry Night*. The mermaid's long green hair obscured her face, and she floated in a prone position, her arms limp at her sides. The image was strangely beautiful, yet decidedly melancholy.

"Is she asleep, and just drifting along with the tide?" I asked. It never occurred to me to wonder if mermaids slept, but if they did it made sense they might do so like whales or dolphins, simply floating in the water.

Selena shook her head. "She's dead."

"She's . . . what?"

"Dead," Selena repeated in her typically flat affect. "That's why she's floating like that."

"Oh," I said, not sure how to respond. "Was it . . . did you have a vision?"

"Mermaids die, you know," she said. "No one lives forever."

"Well, that's true enough. Thank you, Selena. This is beautiful. I love it."

A squabble broke out near the karaoke machine, there was a brief lull in the music, and then Fleetwood Mac's "Go Your Own Way" started up.

"Oh, I know this song," said Maya's mother. "My, that takes me back. . . . So, where's Oscar? I thought you'd pick him up at the kennel on your way home."

Among my friends, only Maya and Bronwyn knew Oscar was a magical shape-shifter. It made it awkward to live with the fiction that he was an ordinary miniature Vietnamese pig, at least as "ordinary" as a pet pig could be in San Francisco.

"Um . . . first thing tomorrow," I said. "They were already closed for the day."

"Conrad, dear, have you checked out the snack table?" I overheard my mother ask Conrad. "I made your favorite."

"*Cowboy* cookies?" replied the Con. "Thank you, Mrs. I. You're so thoughtful."

"It was my pleasure, dear," my mother said, patting his arm. "You're too thin; I like to see you eat."

Witnessing their easy exchange, I felt a spurt of jealousy and was disappointed at my reaction. As Bronwyn always said, love must be shared, not rationed. But a small part of me was still a scared little girl feeling the sting of maternal rejection. By the time I was eight years old, Maggie had come to fear my magical abilities and suggested I go live with Graciela, and when I was a teenager, she tried to force the magic out of me at a disastrous snake revival. My history with my mother was so fraught that I supposed it would take a while to put it all to rights.

I excused myself to drop my purse in the store's workroom, which was separated from the shop floor by a heavy brocade curtain. The area doubled as a break room and a laundry room and was furnished with a green Formica table and chairs, a small fridge, an electric teakettle, an extensive collection of Bronwyn's homemade tea mixes, and a jumbo-sized washer and dryer. Most vintage clothing was too delicate to machine-wash, so the most expensive garments were outsourced to a green dry cleaner and the rest were handwashed in the two deep utility sinks.

Maya joined me. "I really am sorry about all this laundry, Lily. We tried to keep on top of it, but you know how it is when the shop gets busy. The Aunties tried to help, but after a second load of whites got mixed up with some red 49ers T-shirts and everything came out pink, I told them I would handle the laundry and, well, it got to be too much."

"Land sakes, you had your hands more than full just running the store and wrangling the Aunties!" I said. "I appreciate everything you and Bronwyn did while we were gone. I'll get started on the laundry tomorrow, no worries. Looks like Sailor's already added our stuff to the pile."

A splash of color within the mound of soiled clothing caught my eye. "Speaking of pink . . . What's this doing here? This needs to be dry-cleaned."

I pulled what I thought at first was a richly beaded evening gown from the pile. But as I held it up, I realized it wasn't a gown at all. It was a costume. A mermaid costume, to be precise, complete with an ornate tail with scales created by swirls of beads and spangles and nautilus designs. This was no homemade or store-bought Halloween outfit inspired by a Disney character.

I held it close to sense its vibrations. The garment sparked in me that special sensation that only came from old, antique, and vintage clothing. I closed my eyes. What was that I was picking up? Water? Salt? Something . . . oceanic? Maybe that was simply my imagination running riot. It was a mermaid costume, after all.

"Where did *this* come from?" I asked.

Maya shook her head. "I'm not sure . . . to tell you the truth, I hadn't noticed it. What do you think it is?"

I spied Selena skulking behind Maya.

"Selena, do you know anything about this costume?" I asked. "Is this what inspired you to make the drawing of the mermaid?"

She shook her head.

"Are you saying you don't know where the costume came from, or that it didn't inspire your drawing?"

"Both," she said, then added, "I'm hungry," and headed back toward the cookie tower.

"It certainly appears old," I mused, inspecting the costume. The needlework was detailed and very fine, the "tail" was covered in thousands of faceted beads, and delicate seashells had been woven into the net sleeves. "There's no label, but it's the right era for Elsa Schiaparelli. And it's her pink."

"She has her own pink?" Maya asked.

"Schiaparelli was an Italian designer," I nodded, as Bronwyn and Conrad joined us in the workroom. "She was arguably the chief rival to Coco Chanel."

"Did she design mermaid costumes?" asked Bronwyn.

"I don't know about that," I said. "But hot pink was her signature color."

"I wish *I* had a signature color," Bronwyn sighed. "But I can never decide between purple and teal and sunflower yellow, so I usually just go for rainbow."

"Dude, way to problem solve," murmured Conrad, munching on a cowboy cookie.

When the karaoke enthusiasts took a break to soothe their dry throats with a round of margaritas, I brought the costume to the shop floor and held it up. The crystals, beads, and sequins shimmered in the overhead lights, sending out a spray of tiny rainbows that landed on the vintage merchandise, the food, the partygoers.

"Everyone, can I have your attention for a moment?" I asked. "First of all, thank you for the best welcome home party of my life. Actually, the only welcome home party of my life, now that I think of it, but that's neither here nor there. Second: Does anyone remember where this mermaid costume came from?"

"A few of us went to garage sales while you were gone," Iris suggested. "Maybe we bought it at one of those?"

"Do you remember buying it?" I asked.

"I don't remember a lot of things these days," Iris said. "Probably on account o' not enough fish oil."

"That's true," Agatha confirmed. "You really should add more fish oil to your diet, dear."

"Maybe a homeless person brought it in," Maria-

Gracia suggested. "Occasionally they stop by with something to sell."

"A homeless person with a vintage mermaid costume?" Caroline said skeptically.

"It could happen," said Betty.

"Maybe a sailor dropped it off! A sailor from a faraway country!" said Kay, her thick tortoiseshell glasses making her eyes appear almost comically large.

"A faraway country?" Rosa said. "You mean like Denmark, home of Hans Christian Andersen's *The Little Mermaid*? That's a made-up story, you know."

"You're so cynical," Kay said, pouting.

There was a pause while we all admired the level of artistry of the costume.

"I wonder if it might have come from the attic," Lucille suggested.

"What attic?" I asked.

"The attic that spans our buildings. Didn't you know? They're twins, constructed at the same time by the same builder." Lucille had the shop next door, where she designed, and her talented seamstresses produced, modern—and machine-washable—reproductions of vintage designs sized to fit today's larger, healthier women.

"I didn't even know there *was* an attic," I said, a bit unsettled by the thought. "I assumed there was some space under the eaves, but not that it was usable space. I've never heard anyone up there."

"I don't imagine you would have, Lily. The attic is only accessible from my building," Lucille explained. "It's always been locked, and as you know our landlord doesn't come around much. He did go up there the other day, though. Said he needed to clear out some of his late mother's things. Hadn't had the heart to deal with them before, poor man."

Our landlord, Khalil Singh, had never seemed like a "poor man" to me, but rather a shrewd businessman. But as I knew only too well, when it came to our feelings for our mothers, all bets were off.

I made a mental note to ask Singh about it tomorrow, and set the odd, and beautiful, costume aside for the moment. I wasn't sure why I was so preoccupied with it; the vibrations felt in equal parts disturbing and enticing. It put me in mind of the stories of siren songs, those seductive tunes that charmed sailors before luring them to their deaths.

"Do you have an update on Aidan?" I asked my grandmother, who was humming along as the karaoke singers, vocal cords refreshed, launched into ABBA's classic "Dancing Queen." Graciela and I had spoken by phone last week, but I had learned long ago that, when interacting with my grandmother and the Aunties, it was best to talk in person.

Graciela's dark eyes had always seemed to me as old as the earth, and now were even more so. She hesitated before answering, which worried me, then said: "He is on the mend, Lilita. It has not been easy. The salts are helping."

"Thank the goddess for the power of crystals," I said, stifling a yawn.

"The power of *salts*," said Graciela.

Any witch worth her salt—pardon the pun—knew the power of the deceptively simple white crystals. We created salt circles for safekeeping and protection, and to cast spells. We could even call on lesser demons and trap them within a salt circle or a triangular Seal of Solomon. Here in San Francisco we were bordered on three sides by saltwater, which explained some of its mystique; and during the incident on Alcatraz the salts of my lachrymatory had helped to protect us from a disaster threatening not only San Francisco but the entire Bay Area.

"Did·you see your father when you were in Germany?" asked Iris, her glasses magnifying her rheumy blue eyes.

"I'm sorry?" I asked, startled by the question. I had what folks in the Bay Area called a "complicated" relationship with my father. As in, he had abandoned me and my mother, and then his ambitions had led him to be in thrall to a demon. In my experience, anything having to do with my father was bad news. "Why would I have seen my father?"

"She's wondering about the prophecy," said Darlene, and suddenly I found myself encircled by elderly witches.

Chapter 3

"We thought you might have asked him if he had another child, and where that child might be," explained Pepper.

I opened my mouth but no words came out, only another yawn.

"She means another child besides *you*," clarified Rosa. "Because of the prophecy."

"Yes, I realize that but . . . do we even know for sure this is a thing . . . ?" I asked.

Not long ago the Aunties had matter-of-factly told me of a prophecy involving my coming to San Francisco, presumably to lead the magical community in opposition to a supernatural threat. And as if that weren't enough, the Aunties then said it was possible the prophecy applied not to *me* but to my alleged half sibling, a brother, the existence of whom was news to me.

I glanced over at my mother, Maggie, who was now busy rearranging the cookie tower. A former small-town beauty queen, she was not a practitioner and had been no match for my magical father. I wondered whether she knew that he might have had a child with another woman, and if so, how that would make her feel. Then again, it had been a very long time since he left us, and she knew she was well rid of him.

Still.

The thing about my grandmother, and her twelve coven sisters, was that this kind of potentially life-altering information—such as ancient prophecies and the like—was often mentioned off-the-cuff, as casually as placing an order at the Coffee to the People café down the street.

"But to answer your question, *no*," I said. "I did not see my father."

I was going to have to deal with him, and with my alleged half brother—*and* the prophecy—at some point, but that was for a later time. At the moment all I was good for was bed.

As happy as I was to be reunited with friends and family, the jet lag was slamming into me hard, creating the surreal feeling of not knowing what time it was, accompanied by bone-deep weariness and a zombie-like sense of being asleep while still awake. It wasn't quite nine o'clock at night, but according to my internal clock, it was five in the morning.

Just as I started making excuses for slipping out of my own party, Bronwyn handed me an envelope. "Oh, Lily, I almost forgot: Calypso sent this note for you."

"I was wondering where she was," I said.

"She couldn't make it tonight. Poor thing's been swamped handling Aidan's business on top of her own, as you can imagine."

I *could* imagine. Calypso was also still hosting all twelve of the Aunties, plus Graciela and my mother, at her large farmhouse in a forest glade near Bolinas. Calypso was a powerful and wise woman, but that was a lot for anyone to deal with, magical or not.

I opened the note: *Hello my dear Lily! Welcome back! I'm so sorry I can't make it to your party, and even sorrier to ask you to come meet me at Aidan's office as soon as you return, but there is sooo much to discuss and it really cannot wait. Blessed be, Calypso.*

"She says she needs to see me as soon as I get back," I said to Sailor, who had joined me in saying goodbye to some well-wishers.

"Meaning right now? Sure it can't wait for morning?"

"Calypso wouldn't ask if it weren't important."

"No rest for the weary, as they say," he said with a wry smile. "I'll drive you."

"That's really not necessary," I said.

"It's late."

"Sailor, we talked about this on our last night in Paris, remember?" I said in a low voice, not wanting to air our couple's issues in public. "I'm a grown woman *and* I'm a witch. I've taken care of myself for a long time. Also, we've been joined at the hip for several weeks now. It was wonderful, but a little space might do us good."

He gazed at me a long time before giving a barely-there nod. "All right. If you really want to go see Calypso now, I'll stay here and start a load of laundry."

I let out a long sigh. "All I *really* want to do is fall into bed—into *our* bed. But since I foisted this on Calypso in the first place, I feel like I should go."

He touched my cheek tenderly. "So run on over there and take the reins from her. Then come back and crawl into your bed with your man. He'll be waiting."

"That sounds mighty tempting indeed. Thank you."

He gave me a kiss goodbye. It felt strange to leave him, after weeks of being together every minute of the day.

It wasn't quite so easy to extricate myself from my still-partying friends and family, but they understood. As I was leaving, Graciela reached out and gently grasped my arm. "*Bon courage, querida.*"

"You're speaking French now?" I asked with a smile. "I should think Spanish, English, and Nahuatl would be enough for anybody."

She didn't answer, seemingly concentrating on the floor. I looked down at her hand, the prominent blue veins, the paper-thin wrinkled skin stretched taut. Graciela refused to admit her actual age, but it occurred to me that she was very old indeed . . . which meant we might not have her around much longer. My heart hurt at the very thought. I loved her. I needed her.

I felt a surge of energy, and heat, akin to a sunburn, on my arm.

"Graciela, *estás bien*?" I asked her if she was all right.

"*Sí sí, por supuesto.*" Of course, she said. "Just keep your wits about you, *niña.*"

I nodded, hugged her, and squeezed my medicine bag for strength.

Leaving the warmth of Aunt Cora's Closet, I slipped out into the foggy night, walked around the corner to the driveway I rented for a small fortune, climbed behind the wheel of my vintage Mustang, and headed across town to the wax museum at Fisherman's Wharf.

No one was staffing the ticket booth. That was odd.

Usually Clarinda attended the little kiosk and seemed to like nothing better than to give me a hard time. I spied a battered paperback romance novel lying facedown on the counter, so I assumed she was around somewhere.

The wax museum stayed open late to take advantage of the tourist trade, and since the front doors were unlocked, I went on in. Climbing the sweeping floating staircase, I hurried by a display of waxen political figures, all the while suppressing the shudder I felt whenever I walked through these halls. Mannequins and I did not get along. I appreciated the artistry involved in their creation, and was under no illusion that they were alive or anything, but . . .

To my mind, the lifelike sculptures seemed like poppets: too ready to be inhabited, and controlled, by a powerful practitioner.

There were a few customers wandering around the themed exhibits, couples admiring historical figures, and several young people snickering and teasing each other in Dracula's cave. Everyone but me, it seemed, loved the Chamber of Horrors.

The door to Aidan Rhodes's office was ajar. That was odd, too. Aidan's office was under a general protection charm and a cocooning spell, which kept most passersby from even noticing it was there, much less gaining access. A key part of the enchantment was keeping the door closed.

Perhaps Calypso was less rigid about such things.

I paused, searching for signs of Noctemus, Aidan's familiar. No doubt the long-haired white cat had gone with him to Mexico. The imperious feline and I didn't get along all that well, but I was happy to imagine her by Aidan's side, giving him the special kind of silent support and comfort that could only be offered by a beloved animal companion, especially a familiar.

"*Knock knock*," I said as I pushed the door open. The office was dark. "Calypso?"

I flipped on the light.

And froze, stifling a scream.

Chapter 4

A man was slumped across Aidan's desk, sprawled on the blotter.

In the mellow light from the amber wall sconces I could see that he was balding on top, his shiny pate fringed with long platinum-blond hair, and his olive complexion had a decidedly gray tinge.

The long hair partially obscured the man's face. I didn't think I knew him but couldn't be positive.

Maybe he isn't dead, I thought. But . . . he sure *felt* dead. I didn't sense any kind of aura, didn't feel any dynamic vibrations at all. Still, this was another area in which I was far from expert.

Could be he was just taking a nap. In a weird position. On Aidan's desk.

Stroking my medicine bag, I slowly approached him.

"Hello?" I said, my voice shaking. "Sir? Are you hurt?"

I jumped as a bat, emitting a high-pitched screech, flew past me. The bat landed on the bookcase, hung upside down from one of the shelves, and folded his brownish-gray wings over himself. I heard a lark-like trilling.

"Well, hello there, little fella," I said, regaining my composure. "Fancy meeting you here."

It trilled again, as if in response.

Why was there a *bat* in Aidan's office?

I approached the man on Aidan's desk, still feeling for vibrations. Nothing. Reaching out a shaking hand, I gently pressed the side of his neck. No pulse. The man was not yet cold, but he was definitely dead. It seemed as though rigor mortis had set in.

I blew out a long breath, stroked my medicine bag, and closed my eyes for a moment of solemn reflection. I was certain now that I did not know this man, but the loss of a life made me sad. And frightened.

Should I yell for help? Flee? Pull a fire alarm?

My eyes searched the shadowy corners of Aidan's self-consciously Victorian office. Was anyone else here? I was a witch, not a psychic, and would not necessarily sense the presence of another person, even if that person intended me harm. And though my supernatural abilities were growing, I was more a concentrate-alone-at-home-while-brewing witch, not a grapple-with-a-murderer-in-Aidan's-dark-office witch.

Could whatever happened to this man be linked to Clarinda's absence from the ticket booth downstairs? Was she all right? And where was Calypso, who had asked me to meet her here?

Aidan's office, though dimly lit, didn't have a lot of potential hiding places. Besides the mahogany desk, the desk chair—which was occupied at the moment—and two leather wing chairs for guests, the office held a crowded bookshelf, currently sporting a trilling bat, and a comfortable reading chair next to a standing lamp with a fringed Tiffany lampshade. That was about it.

I focused on the door that opened onto an octagonal chamber, which Aidan had specially designed to increase magical powers. Inside the chamber was my lachrymatory and the salts I had used to defeat a demon's minions on Alcatraz, not long ago. They were powerful salts, born of suffering and grief.

I placed my hand flat against the closed chamber door and concentrated. Calypso wasn't in there, I was sure. I knew her vibrations well, and I would sense her.

And if there *were* a murderer in there, he wasn't going anywhere. There was no other exit from the chamber. I dragged a chair over and jammed it under the doorknob. *Would that be enough to keep someone inside?* For good measure, I picked up a heavy paperweight from Aidan's desk, just in case I needed to conk someone on the head.

I chanted a quick spell over the doorknob, though I had no idea how well it would stick, and, heart hammering in my chest, turned back to the dead man.

My medicine bag hummed, and I felt a sudden, intense squeezing on my arm, in the very spot my grandmother had touched me.

Someone was watching me.

"What's going on?" A man stood in the office doorway, backlit by the bright lights of the museum floor.

I held up the paperweight as if to throw it. In truth, I wasn't much of an athlete and was unlikely to hit the broad side of a barn, but the intruder had no way of knowing that, and besides, the paperweight was the only weapon I had.

"Woah!" he said, holding up his hands in surrender, and I got a good look at his face.

It was the Mystery Man from the plane.

His gold earring glinted in the amber lighting and he spoke with a very slight accent I couldn't quite place, though it sounded vaguely eastern European.

"I apologize if I startled you. I was supposed to meet Aidan Rhodes. Is he here . . . ?" His gaze fell to the man slumped over the desk, and his eyes widened. "Is that him? What happened? Did you . . . ?"

"That isn't Aidan. And no, I didn't. Who are you?"

"I had an appointment with Mr. Rhodes."

"Mr. Rhodes hasn't been here for some time. With whom did you make the appointment?"

"With . . . a woman. His secretary, maybe? I didn't think to ask her name. I made the appointment quite some time ago, as I was led to believe that Mr. Rhodes was a very busy man." He gave me a charming smile, apparently not particularly disconcerted by the body on the desk. "Look, I know how it is, dealing with dead bodies on your desk. I'll just leave you to it, come back another time."

"Hold it right there, pal. Who are you, and what did you want to talk with Aidan about?" I asked.

"I'm afraid that's rather personal."

"You can tell me. I'm filling in for him while he's gone."

"Is that so?" He looked doubtful, his gaze sweeping over my vintage dress and Keds and my no-doubt haggard appearance after the long transatlantic flight. He, in contrast, looked fresh as a daisy, as though he had showered and changed before coming. "You were on my flight."

"Sure about that?"

He seemed to relax. "You recognize me as well as I do you," he said, sounding more confident now.

His vibrations were guarded, making him very hard to read. A lot of cops, veterans, and practitioners main-

tained that kind of guard. I didn't think he was dangerous, but I couldn't be certain. Was he as hapless as he
had at first appeared? Or might he have killed the man
at Aidan's desk, gone to the men's room to wash his
hands, and returned after realizing he had forgotten
his pet bat?

This is the kind of world I live in.

"You pretended to tip your hat to me," I said. "At
the airport."

"You kept staring at me. Thought maybe we had a
thing."

"Seriously?"

He shrugged and flashed a crooked grin. "What can
I say? I've got that boyish charm thing going. Women
check me out."

"Not this woman. I was on my *honeymoon*."

"Were you, now? Then perhaps you shouldn't be
flirting with strange men."

"I was most certainly *not* flirting, what an
egomaniacal—"

"You most certainly were, madam, I—"

The bat trilled loudly, interrupting our exchange
and highlighting the absurdity of two strangers bickering about nonsense in the presence of a dead man. And
a bat.

"Is that your bat?"

"My what?"

"Your. Bat." I enunciated.

"Certainly. Not." He replied in kind.

I sighed. "Oh, never mind."

Clarinda suddenly appeared in the doorway.

"Hey, what do you think you're doing?" she said to
me. "You can't just waltz in here without a ticket, you
know."

I had once helped to save Clarinda's life. She had

thawed toward me for a while after that, but apparently the Ice Age had returned.

"Where were you earlier?" I demanded. "You weren't in the ticket booth."

She smiled up at Mystery Man. He wasn't all that good-looking, but I had to admit there was something intriguing about him. Clarinda's expression soured when she turned her attention back to me.

"Geez, I was in the freaking *bathroom*. Excuse me for having a bladder. Security was supposed to keep an eye on things. Like a person can't go to the *bathroom* for a few minutes. With the kind of hours I work?" She finally noticed the body on the desk, and stilled. Her mouth gaped open. "What the hell?"

"Do you know him?" I asked.

She shook her head. "No, I mean . . . I sold him a ticket, I guess. I recognize the weird hair. It was a while ago. What did you do to him?"

"I didn't do anything to him," I said. "I found him like this. Where's Calypso?"

"She didn't come in today," said Clarinda. "Needed a break, or whatever. I tried to cancel her appointments, but I guess I missed a few. So is he . . . ya know?"

I nodded. "I was about to call the police."

"I'll just be running along, then," said the Mystery Man.

"Ditto," said Clarinda.

"No one is going anywhere," I said, grabbing a handkerchief from my dress pocket to pick up the phone. Mustn't inadvertently obscure a murderer's fingerprints. "The police will need to speak to both of you."

The Mystery Man started backing away. "I had nothing to do with this."

"Me, neither," echoed Clarinda.

"They'll want to speak with y'all, anyway. Hey, don't—," I called out as the Mystery Man took off, with Clarinda hot on his heels.

I raced to the door in time to see the two of them hurrying down the stairs.

"*Clarinda!*" I yelled. "Where do you think you're going? I know where you live!"

Actually I didn't, but I knew where she worked—*here* at the wax museum. And she seemed always to be here, stuck like a veal in that little ticket booth.

A few curious tourists turned to look, but otherwise my words had no effect.

"*Dammit.*"

I returned to Aidan's desk and placed a call to my old pal in the SFPD homicide department, Carlos Romero. I knew his cell number by heart.

"Great party, Lily. Colorful. Makes my family's get-togethers look positively tame."

"Thanks, Carlos, but I'm afraid I'm not calling about the party. I found a body."

"Already?"

"I'm not kidding."

There was a pause. "Where are you?"

"Aidan Rhodes's office, at the wax museum."

"Are you safe?"

"I think so. There are people around. Sort of."

"Go be with people. I'll send the nearest unit and will be there as soon as I can. Don't touch anything."

"I haven't."

"You're holding the phone right now, aren't you?"

"Okay, I haven't touched *much*. A paperweight. Oh, and a chair. I used a handkerchief for the phone, but I don't have fingerprints anyway, remember?"

"I remember. Just . . . get out of there and go some-place safe. I'll find you."

"Okay."

The bat trilled again as I hung up. Its fur was reddish-brown, its broad black ears pointed forward, and its leathery wings were long and narrow. Its shining black eyes were so huge they were almost cartoonish. A very long pink tongue flicked from time to time.

"Are you a familiar?" I asked. It sang back. I approached slowly and held out my hand. It didn't flinch. If the bat was the dead man's familiar, then the victim was likely a practitioner of some sort.

I glanced down at Aidan's appointment book. Written in a hand that did not belong to Calypso was an appointment for today, at this late hour, with one Dragomir Ivory.

Dragomir Ivory?

Ivory was *my* last name. My father's last name.

The dead man had to be in his fifties. Far too old to be my father's child.

The Mystery Man from the airplane, the one who said he had an appointment right now with Aidan Rhodes, was not.

I gazed at the empty doorway.

Had I just met my half brother?

Chapter 5

"*Dragomir*? What kind of name is Dragomir?" I asked the next afternoon at Aunt Cora's Closet.

I was annoyed, jet-lagged, and decidedly on edge. I had gotten a late start this morning and had spent much of the day catching up on my least favorite thing, aside from murder and laundry: business-related paperwork. Receipts, quarterly taxes, workers' comp . . . it never seemed to end. In between yawns I had sketched the broad outlines of last night's events for Conrad, Maya, and Bronwyn.

"Actually, I sort of like that name," said Bronwyn. "'Dragomir' sounds like something out of *The Lord of the Rings*, doesn't it?"

"Apparently it has Slavic roots," said Conrad, staring at his phone. Conrad was tall and gaunt, with shaggy sandy hair. He was an addict who had recently gotten sober, helped in part by my special brews, but had not been able to find a job and so continued to live on the streets or in nearby Golden Gate Park. Accord-

ing to Bronwyn and Maya, while I was on my honeymoon Conrad had shown up every day to guard the
store or to help with whatever needed doing.

Now that I was spending much of my time running
around the Bay Area scouting out clothes for the store
and fighting demons and whatnot, it occurred to me
that another pair of hands in the shop might be a good
idea. I placed a protection spell on the store's front
door every morning, but it wasn't foolproof, and enough
odd things had happened that I didn't like to leave anyone tending the shop alone.

Maybe I should offer Conrad a job. If my math was
correct, Aunt Cora's Closet was doing well enough that
I could afford it.

Conrad continued, "According to this, 'Dragomir'
means 'to whom peace is precious.'"

"Huh. Well, I certainly hope old Dragomir lives up
to his name," I muttered. "Otherwise, he might just . . ."

What was I thinking? That the Mystery Man had
killed the dead guy on the desk, mistaking him for
Aidan Rhodes? And would that mean that I, or Calypso, or one of my friends, was next? Could he have
been looking for something?

I didn't trust him, even *before* I learned that he
might very well be my brother.

Half brother. The son of our entirely untrustworthy
father, who had attached himself briefly to my mother
in the dusty West Texas town of Jarod, and then moved
on. Given the way things usually went with me, not to
mention the prophecy involving me or my brother, I
doubted our sibling relationship would be a smooth one.

Last night at the wax museum, while waiting for the
police to arrive, I had called Calypso and was relieved to
hear that she was alive and well, at her home in Bolinas.

"Gracious, Lily," Calypso said, "I assumed you'd

come by *tomorrow*, not the very moment you got back!"

"I thought it was urgent. Anyway, I found a dead man in Aidan's office."

"You found a . . . what? Oh, no, you poor thing! Are you all right?"

"I'm fine. This ain't my first rodeo, you know. Unfortunately." I had stumbled across a body or two in my day. "I'm calling because a stranger was here a few minutes ago. European guy, who spoke excellent English. He said he had an appointment with Aidan, which was written down in the agenda. Did you make it for him?"

"No, but Clarinda was taking appointments."

"What about a bat?"

"A what?"

"There's a bat in the office."

"It's not mine." There was a beat. "Is it a familiar?"

"I'm not sure. Could be; it seems pretty comfortable with people. Anyway, I should warn you that you'll probably be hearing from the SFPD soon. I'll have to tell Carlos Romero that you've been working in Aidan's office."

There was a long pause. For many of us who color outside the lines, interactions with the authorities were anxiety producing, if not panic inducing. Over the course of several murder investigations I had become friends with Carlos Romero, but even so, in his official capacity as a homicide inspector he still occasionally incited hyperventilation.

"Yes, of course you must," Calypso said finally. "A man has died."

"I'm sorry about this, Calypso—"

"It's fine, Lily. The police would have found out about me eventually, anyway. Thank you for letting me know. It's not a problem."

I put down the phone, worried. One reason I didn't like phones was because I couldn't feel the other person's vibrations through the device. A landline was better than a cell phone, but not by much.

Then I called Sailor.

"I knew I should have driven you," he grumbled.

"You couldn't possibly have foreseen something like this."

"I'm a psychic, remember?"

"Not that kind of psychic."

"Anyway, I'd rather be by your side," he said in that low growl that made my stomach flutter.

"I know, and I appreciate it," I said. "But your presence would just complicate matters. Besides, I don't like you spending time around the SFPD."

"You and me both."

Sailor and Carlos had a fraught history, and though they had come to tolerate and respect each other, and Carlos had stood up with us at our handfasting, they were not exactly pals.

Then the police arrived, and I spent a very, *very* long time talking to Carlos Romero. I gave him a minute-by-minute account of what I had seen and done, then hesitated for a moment, unsure whether or not to tell him about Dragomir Ivory, who might or might not be my brother. Finally, I did.

"How is it you don't know if he's your brother?"

"Complicated family history."

"So tell me, does this alleged brother take after your dad or your mom?"

Carlos had dealt with my father before and didn't have much good to say about him.

"Same father, different mothers. And I've had exactly one interaction with my alleged half brother, so I honestly don't know if he has any kind of relationship to my—our—father, magical or otherwise. Assuming, that is, we are in fact related."

"Okey dokey," Carlos said, jotting something in his well-worn notebook. "Gotta say, Lily, you do live an interesting life. So let me get this straight: You don't know if your brother's your brother, and your husband isn't really your husband."

"Sailor *is* my husband, in every way that counts. We just haven't filed all the paperwork yet."

"Yeah, well, I'm a cop. Take it from me: Paperwork matters. All those pesky laws and statutes, and what-not," he said with a grunt.

Thinking about it now, I wondered: Had Carlos found out anything about "Dragomir Ivory" since last night? Or about the victim, such as who he was and why he was in Aidan's office? Most importantly, had he been murdered, or might there be another explanation for his death?

"Hello? Earth to Lily," said Conrad, bringing me back to the present. "He might just . . . what?"

"Hmm?" I asked.

"You, like, stopped talking in the middle of a sentence."

I was standing at the counter in Aunt Cora's Closet, my friends looking at me as if I had taken leave of my senses.

"Oh, sorry, jet lag again," I said with a jaw-cracking yawn. Not to mention I had been up half the night with a dead body and the fine fellows from the SFPD.

"Poor dear, you're dead on your feet," Bronwyn said.

Just then the bat, which I had kept in a box behind the counter, woke up and flew around the store, swooping and screeching and trilling. Luckily there were no customers in the shop at the moment, but Bronwyn, Maya, and the Con shrieked and ducked in surprise.

The critter alit on an antique Edwardian ball gown I had draped high on the wall as a decoration and hung upside down from the fragile taffeta. I cringed, enough of a vintage clothes connoisseur to worry that the little creature's claws might shatter the silk.

"Forgot to mention that I found a bat at the scene of the crime last night," I said.

"Awesome!" said Conrad. "*Dude*. I love bats. They eat, like, tons of mosquitoes, and the Con does *not* like mosquitoes."

Carlos had given me a pained expression when he spied the creature in Aidan's office, but when I told him it might be magical he suggested I should take care of it unless I wanted him to call animal control. Carlos didn't really believe in magic . . . and yet, he did.

When I brought it back to the apartment, Sailor teased me about being a stereotypical witch, walking around with a bat in the dead of night.

"What are you going to do with it?" asked Maya, looking concerned.

"I don't know. I couldn't just leave it there."

"He's a cute little guy," said Conrad. "Like a little cartoon character come to life."

If the bat were indeed the dead man's familiar, then I hoped it might be able to tell me what had happened. Unless it was simply the victim's exotic pet. Or the killer's . . . ? Or, what did I know; maybe the bat was a part of something Aidan had been doing before he was injured, and the poor little guy had been hanging out in the wax museum, forgotten and neglected.

The bat's pink tongue stuck out and its huge eyes gleamed, as if interested in our discussion. It took flight again, and landed on Conrad's head. The Con grabbed it and flipped it into his arms to cradle it.

"I like him," said Conrad. "Can we keep him?"

Bronwyn, mixing teas behind her stand, chuckled. "Maya's parents took Loretta-the-dog when Lily brought her home, and I took Beowulf-the-cat before that. I guess this one's for you, Conrad."

"I'm not sure that's a good idea," I said. "After all, we don't even know how to care for a bat. What do they eat? How do they drink?"

"The Con is *on* it," Conrad said, using his free hand to scroll through his phone. "This site is full of information. Looks like he needs an enclosure of some kind. *Dude.*"

Those phones are veritable fonts of information, I thought. Maybe I really should consider giving in to modern life. One of these days.

For the moment, I needed to concentrate on the tasks at hand. But my mind kept returning to the dead man, slumped across Aidan's desk. What had caused his death? I hadn't seen any blood or obvious wounds or marks. Could he have died from natural causes, a heart attack or a stroke? Or something more insidious, like poison? And who *was* the poor man? Did his potentially untimely demise have anything to do with the sudden appearance of Dragomir Ivory, my purported half brother?

And if the man who called himself Dragomir Ivory really was my half brother, then what would that mean for me, for the prophecy, and for San Francisco? No doubt about it, I needed to consult with my grandmother's coven and wring all the information I could from Graciela and the Aunties while they were still in town.

"What time does the coven usually show up?" I asked.

"Oh, they weren't planning on coming in today," said Maya. "Since you're back, they figured they weren't needed here at the shop."

"As much as I love them," said Bronwyn, "it's a wee bit calmer around here with just us. Feels almost like old times, doesn't it? A certain bat excluded, of course."

"Well, you have a point there," I said. "Are they at Calypso's?"

"I don't think so," Maya said.

"Last I heard they were planning on going to Napa for a wine-tasting jaunt," said Bronwyn.

"Wine tasting?" I asked.

"That's what they said," said Maya.

"They didn't invite *me* to go wine tasting," I said, a whining note in my voice.

"I imagine they thought that since you've only just returned from your European tour, you might have a few things to tend to right here at home," said Bronwyn with a smile.

"*Hmpf.* I suppose so." As much as I had missed my home and my friends when I was abroad, now that I was back in San Francisco I kept thinking about the cities and castles of Europe. Seems I was having trouble changing gears. Especially now that I had stumbled onto a body just a few hours after my feet touched California soil.

Carlos was right. I was a magnet for magical mayhem. A hotspot for hinky homicide. A . . . portal for pandemonium? That was a frightening thought.

"You want me to text the Aunties?" asked Maya. "See what's up?"

"No, thanks," I said with a sigh. "They should enjoy their wine tasting, and anyway I imagine I'll hear from them soon enough."

"They'll be here tomorrow morning at nine," said Bronwyn. "I scheduled a staff meeting before we open. Thought it was a good idea to get you caught up on everything. I figured it's best to have the Aunties all in the same room, or someone may think somebody else picked up the gowns at the green dry cleaner's or signed for the delivery of the laundry detergent."

"That's putting it mildly," Maya said, and I realized that my absence, coupled with the "help" provided by the Aunties, had created a lot more work for my friends than I had anticipated.

Aunt Cora's Closet is your shop, Lily, and your responsibility, I scolded myself. *Time to get back in the saddle, like a good store owner.*

"That's an excellent idea," I said. "Thanks for thinking of it. And again—thank you all, for everything you did so I could enjoy my honeymoon."

"Happy to help," Bronwyn said.

"And *very* happy you're back," Maya added with a grin, then retied her new Parisian silk scarf around her locks. "You really didn't have to shower us with so many gifts."

"It was my pleasure, and the least I could do."

"Sorry to tell you this, Lily," said Conrad. "But it seems bats eat and, um, 'excrete' a lot both in solid and liquid form about twenty minutes after they've eaten . . . that's a hell of a digestive system. Says here: *Hence, the enclosure floor will fill with bat waste in the form of liquid poop, solid poop, and urine. It will require regular cleaning.*"

"Great," I said. Not that I had any kind of an enclosure fit for a bat. Assuming he was a regular bat, that is, and not a familiar. But how could I tell?

"Also," Conrad continued reading, "it says that bats can be domesticated and playful with people, but it greatly reduces their life expectancy. In the wild they can live thirty years, but as a pet more like five."

"Well, that's depressing," I said, looking at the creature. "Poor little fella. He looks like a big-eyed little puppy, but with leather wings. I wonder . . . does it say anything about whether a domesticated bat can be safely released into the wild?"

"Not sure. Lemme look it up."

Meanwhile, Maya was scouring the Internet for references to one Dragomir Ivory. "He doesn't have much of a digital footprint, Lily, that much I can tell you. I could probably find him on the flight manifest if I did a little hacking, but I don't see any point in that, since it won't tell us much except his name and flight information, and you already have that. He's not on social media, at least not under the name 'Dragomir Ivory.' That's a moniker that sticks in one's mind. Hold on." The computer made some clicking sounds. "Hmm, this is interesting. He's listed as an author on a couple of articles on higher education in Romania. Isn't Sailor's family from Romania?"

"A very long time ago. They migrated to Spain generations ago, long before coming here. So Dragomir's involved in higher education? You mean, as in college?"

"Yeah," said Maya, showing me the references on the computer.

I read: *College Leadership in an Era of European Union Unpredictability; Careers in a Changing Era: How Higher Education Can Fight the Skills Gap and Prepare Students for a Dynamic World of Work; Success at Scale: Strategies for Improving Outcomes for Underserved Students.*

"Those look pretty . . . academic," I said.

"I think you mean 'boring,'" Maya agreed. "But they're translated into several languages, so perhaps they're useful."

"Hey, everybody: I've decided something," Conrad announced.

"What's that, Con Man?" Bronwyn asked.

"I'm gonna call this little dude Winston."

"Why Winston?" I asked with a smile.

"After my main man, Winston Churchill. Little dude looks wise, doesn't he?"

"That sounds perfect, Conrad," I said. The bat's wide-eyed gaze looked more surprised than wise to me, but I was going to let that one go. "But we don't know for sure if it's a he or a she, do we?"

"Yeah. Maybe it should be Winona," Maya said. "I imagine Auntie Winona would be honored to lend her name."

"Good point," Conrad said, consulting his phone. "I'm on it. Not that I imagine he or she would care about our gendered names. That's, like, a human obsession. I bet bats are way beyond that kind of thing. You know, totally evolved."

"What a nice way to look at things, Conrad," Bronwyn said.

"Hey, Lily, you okay?" Maya asked quietly. "You seem kind of distracted today, and that's not like you."

"I think I'm having trouble making the adjustment back to real life," I said. "Plus jet lag, and I didn't get much sleep last night. Ignore me." Maya was right, though: I was feeling edgy and grumpy. I needed a distraction; filling out government forms was just not making the grade.

My eyes alit on the mermaid costume. I hugged it close to feel its vibrations, closed my eyes, and thought of Selena's drawing.

"Hey, by the way, I did a little research on mermaid costumes," said Maya. "I've found lots of references to Disney-inspired Ariel getups, and some Etsy offerings. Also lots of shell bras, which, I must say, sound mighty uncomfortable."

"Shell bras?" Conrad asked. "*Dude.*"

"But what I was really hoping to find was some kind of mermaid-dressed swimmers, like they had in old movies and stuff? Wasn't that a thing, back in the forties or so?" Maya addressed this last to Bronwyn, whose eyebrows shot up.

"Maya, my dear girl, I may have been on this earth during the Summer of Love, but just how old do you think I am?"

"I wasn't implying that you're old enough to remember live Busby Berkeley shows," Maya responded with a chuckle. "I just thought that since you're the one most familiar with San Francisco, maybe you had heard of a place where that might have been a thing. Like, I don't know. . . . Maybe the Tonga Room at the Fairmont? Doesn't that seem like a place that might have mermaids?"

"The Tonga Room has a floating tiki bar and an indoor rainstorm, but I've never heard of any mermaids," Bronwyn said.

"I couldn't find any mermaid references to the Italian designer you mentioned, either, Lily," Maya said.

"Elsa Schiaparelli."

"Right. She designed a few mermaid dresses, but those simply hug the body, they aren't actual costumes. Though you're right, it's definitely her pink. I also found a fascinating article about Esther Williams, who starred in huge synchronized swimming shows back in the day. The swimmers wore elaborate outfits, including mermaid costumes."

"I've always wondered whether there might be more to the fairy tales about mermaids," Bronwyn said in a dreamy voice.

"In what way?" Maya asked.

"I don't know. But now that we know about widdle piggies like Oscar, I was thinking maybe there might be more to it. Selkies, sirens, the like . . . there are so many stories about creatures of the sea that I thought maybe . . . ?"

Bronwyn had clearly forgotten that Conrad wasn't in on Oscar's true identity as a shape-shifter, so I caught her gaze and put my finger to my lips. Fortunately the Con was too engrossed by his phone to notice.

"I mean . . ." Bronwyn said, chastened. "I miss that little guy something fierce, don't you?"

"When's the little piggy dude coming back?" asked Conrad, looking up from his cell phone.

"Any time now," I said.

"There are lots of myths about fabled sea creatures," Maya, our resident skeptic, said. "But mermaids existed only in the imagination of lonely—meaning horny—sailors who had spent months on the high seas. Which, if you think about it, is kind of weird. Then again, so are synchronized swimmers dressed as mermaids, if you ask me."

From above our heads came the sound of hooves on the wooden floor, and all three of us looked up.

"Oscar's back!" Bronwyn said.

"Awesome, dude," Conrad grinned. "I missed that little guy. I still don't understand why you had to put him in a kennel, though. I would have taken care of him."

"He needed the piggy socialization. Anyway, Sailor must have gone to get him and come in the back way," I improvised. I was getting better at lying, a necessary skill given the life I lead, but I still wasn't good at making all the parts work and was even worse at remembering what I said to whom. I should probably work on that.

Maya glanced at the mint-green clock on the wall. "It's almost time to close, anyway," she said. "We'll finish up down here if you want to go see him, Lily. Right, Bronwyn?"

"Of course we will! Run along and greet your little Oscaroo!"

"Thanks, y'all. What would I do without you?"

"*Dude*," said Conrad, handing Winston-the-bat to me with a few further instructions on his care and feeding.

I carried the bat up the stairs that led from the workroom at the back of the store to my neat but compact apartment. As I opened the door at the top of the steps, I heard Oscar and Sailor bickering in the kitchen.

"Do I look like a short-order cook to you?" grumbled Sailor. "You'll eat what's served."

"That's not the way we do it around here," Oscar replied, outraged.

"Yeah, well, there's a new sheriff in town and—"

I hurried into the kitchen and interrupted Sailor before he could finish that sentence. This did not bode well for the domestic bliss I had been hoping for.

Chapter 6

"Oscar! It's so good to see you!" I said, setting the bat on the shelf, where it immediately flipped over to hang upside down.

"What's *that*?" Oscar demanded.

"A bat."

"Why?"

"It's . . . I found it at a crime scene. Anyway, when did you get home? I was worried."

Oscar made a dismissive wave with one oversized hand and gave me a pained look. "I'm a travel guy, mistress. You gave me the cloak, remember? No jet lag for *moi.*"

That might also be due to the fact that Oscar spent most of his day snoozing, I thought but did not say.

"Speaking of your new bat," said Sailor. "I made him a little house today."

He led me out to the terrace, where a cedar box was attached to a post. It was flat with an open slit at the top, and looked similar to a large mailbox that might hang on a wall.

"A bat box? I can't believe this! You made this, just today?"

"I found the plans online. I wasn't sure we wanted him in the apartment." He ducked his head slightly at my reaction. "Surprised to learn I know my way around a hammer?"

"I guess it's never really come up. I had no idea you were talented in woodworking."

He gave me a wink. "I like to keep a little mystery in our relationship."

"You are a treasure," I said, picking a pear for Winston from one of the miniature fruit trees I kept on the terrace. "A *mysterious* treasure. I am confident that life with you will never be boring."

"*You're* the one who trips over bodies and brings bats home in the middle of the night."

We shared a smile.

"Listen, I have to run but I'll be back in an hour or so," said Sailor. "I'm getting together with Patience. She says she has a proposition for me."

I raised my eyebrows in mock disapproval. "It better not be an indecent proposition."

This was a joke between us. Once upon a time I had been jealous of Patience's beauty and brash ways, but when I summoned the courage to confess my feelings to Sailor, he had laughed and made sure I felt very secure indeed. And though I once would not have thought it possible, Patience and I had since become friends. Mostly.

"Want me to pick up some takeout on the way home?" Sailor offered.

"Pizza!" said Oscar.

"I wasn't asking you," Sailor grumbled, and Oscar again looked outraged.

I sighed. If the three of us were to live together in

peace, we were all going to have to make some adjustments.

"Bronwyn said she bought some groceries for us," I said. "Why don't I make us a nice dinner? I haven't cooked in a blue moon."

"Tater tots?" Oscar asked hopefully.

"You spoil him," Sailor said.

"No, she *doesn't*!" said Oscar.

"Nothing wrong with a little kale," declared Sailor. "Do you good."

"You stay out of this!" cried Oscar.

"That's enough out of both of you," I intervened. "Oscar, if you help me make dinner then you can help decide the menu. Sailor, go see Patience, and when you get back we'll have a nice family meal together, all three of us. A nice, *quiet* family meal." Oscar and Sailor scowled at each other, then Sailor gave me a quick kiss and grabbed his keys and helmet.

"Back soon," he said.

"Don't let the door hit you on your way out," Oscar muttered under his breath as Sailor left. "So, what's with the bat?"

"I was about to ask you that."

"How would *I* know?" Oscar's green eyes, the color of bottle glass, were so big they reminded me of Winston's. "First Sailor, now a bat? I mean, it's better than that cat you brought home once, but it's gettin' pretty crowded around here, mistress, I gotta tell ya."

You're not wrong, I thought. "I'm wondering if the bat could be a familiar. I found it at the scene of a suspicious death last night."

"*Another* murder? I thought Sailor was kiddin' about that."

"Unfortunately not," I said. "And that's not all. It happened at Aidan's office."

"Maaast— I mean, mister *Aidan's* office, mistress? That could be seriously bad juju. Might leave a residue." Once upon a time, Aidan had been Oscar's master, before giving him to me as my familiar. I had since freed Oscar from his obligations to me and to Aidan, so that he could live his life as he chose. To my delight, Oscar wanted to stay with me. But it wasn't a lifetime commitment, and now that Sailor had moved in . . .

"I found Winston there," I said. "If he *is* a familiar, then the victim must have been a practitioner, right?"

"Probably. Unless somebody gifted it to him to watch over him for some reason. Maaa-ister Aidan gifted a dog familiar to a cowan once. So what?"

I blew out a long breath. "I don't know, I'm thinking this through. If the victim was a practitioner, then Aidan should have a record of him somewhere. Maybe in the Satchel?" The Satchel was where Aidan kept documents pertaining to the magical community, including the names of people who owed him favors. Why hadn't I thought of that last night? I should have grabbed the Satchel before the police arrived. Now Aidan's office was a crime scene, and I doubted Carlos would be willing to hand it over.

"The *Satchel*?" Oscar breathed. Aidan's Satchel struck awe into the heart of my familiar.

"I'm wondering if Winston here could tell us what happened last night, seeing how he was a witness. Could you ask him about it?"

Oscar gaped at me, wide-eyed. "How'm I supposed to do that?"

"I thought maybe . . . you know. Familiar to familiar?"

"It's not like there's a secret handshake or anything, you know."

I really didn't. The world of the familiars was foreign to me.

"Could you give it a try? Please?"

"I hate to break it to you, mistress, but your Oscar here is no run-of-the-mill familiar. Not your average ol' magical frog, cat, or crow, you know."

I grimaced. I was reminded daily that Oscar was not an average familiar. For one thing, he almost never did what I asked him to.

With a big sigh, he leaned down so that he was eye to eye to the bat, which was hanging upside down, its wings wrapped around itself in what looked like a protective gesture.

"What's your name, kid?" Oscar demanded in a gruff voice reminiscent of an old detective movie. "Who do you work for?"

Winston stared at him.

"Oh, a wise guy, eh?" Oscar raised a fist and made a menacing face. "You better talk, see, or I'll . . ."

"Oscar, don't scare him!"

Oscar sighed, dropped the tough guy act, and shrugged. "Sorry, mistress. Doesn't look like he's gonna crack."

"That's it?" I asked. "That's the best you can do?"

"What can I say? He ain't talkin'."

"Well, that's certainly giving it the old college try."

"Your standard familiar won't just come out and admit it, ya know, 'cause most cowans get all freaked out about it." Oscar padded across the black-and-white-checked kitchen floor and opened the refrigerator, then let out a sigh and shook his head. "You shoulda let Sailor pick up Chinese food or something. There's nothing to eat in this house."

"Bronwyn said she shopped for us."

"The whole icebox is full of *vegetables*."

"She's on a health kick lately," I admitted. "But she also left a plate of brownies, if I'm not mistaken. . . . Oh. . . ." On the counter, under the glass cake dome, a blue plate held nothing but a scattering of dark brown crumbs. "I'm surprised you didn't lick the plate."

"I'm huuuungry," Oscar said, swaying a little as if in imminent danger of fainting.

"Personally, I could go for a home-cooked meal," I said. "What with all those hotels and restaurants we ate in the past few weeks. How about—"

"Mac 'n' cheese?" Oscar volunteered. "Say what you will about 'merican food, nothing says 'welcome home' like a big ol' bowl of homemade mac 'n' cheese."

"Well, mac 'n' cheese it is, then," I said, and Oscar grimaced, which was his form of a smile. As I gathered the ingredients, I decided to cook a side of cornbread in my iron skillet, which would make the place smell like home, and a mess of garlicky greens from the fresh vegetables Bronwyn had generously bought. That should satisfy all three of us.

Winston had eaten the pear I gave him, so I gave him a little more and, cognizant of what Conrad had told me about the digestive habits of bats, placed him in his new bat box on the terrace. I left the door open in case he would rather come back in with us or do . . . whatever it was that bats do.

Dinner was almost ready by the time Sailor returned from his meeting with Patience. He seemed preoccupied, and rather than ruin our first meal back with talk of some new Rom drama, I did my best to keep the dinner table conversation focused on the state of Aunt Cora's Closet and a discussion of who was going to do the grocery shopping. But keeping the peace between Oscar and Sailor was no easy task. Oscar kept whining about the lack of carbs in the fridge and on the menu, while Sailor complained that Oscar was a spoiled slob who expected someone else (me) to clean up after him, and repeated that there was a new sheriff in town (Sailor) and that certain gobgoyles (Oscar) had better get used to it. Oscar, meanwhile, asserted that he was here *first* and that the immutable laws of "firsties" meant I should take his side.

Personally, I wanted both of them to pipe down and/or to go away.

Maybe it was the jet lag.

Maybe it was the dead body.

Maybe it was the fact that the brother I hadn't known existed appeared to be in town, and I had no idea what he wanted but was willing to bet that whatever it was, it wasn't good. I was sure his presence would complicate my life, one way or the other.

"It's called respect," Sailor lectured. "R-e-s-p-e-c-t."

"Gold star for spelling," Oscar replied. "Here's one for you: You can kiss my scaly green a-s—"

That did it. A box of white ritual candles flew off a high shelf, my crystal ball spun on its bejeweled and filigreed base, and my Book of Shadows lifted itself up and smacked back down on the kitchen counter.

Sailor and Oscar fell silent and stared at me.

"*Enough*," I said. I rarely lost control of my temper—and my magic—anymore, but I was at the end of my rope. "Sorry, but I am one tuckered witch. I'm going to bed."

I got up in the sacred quiet of the early morning and carried my mug of steaming coffee out onto the terrace. The air was cool and mysterious with San Francisco's famous fog, and laden with scents of earth and herbs. A garden like mine is essential for a brewing witch. Bronwyn had tended it well in my absence, and the soil was moist, the herbs were thriving, and the vines had grown. While I was nowhere as talented as Calypso when it came to botanicals, I knew my way around a garden. The deep green vibrations, the rich loamy earth, the cycle of growth in the spring and rest in the winter, centered me and reminded me, always, of the miracle of rebirth and re-creation.

I checked on Winston in his new house. He was hanging upside down, his wings folded over his body. He appeared to be sleeping, though I wasn't sure how to tell. I refilled his water dish and left a fig and a few pieces of apple.

"Hello?" I whispered, in case he really was a familiar and could understand me. "I'm sorry about your human. I don't know if you want to stay with me, but if you do, you're welcome here. If you can, let me know what you need. Otherwise, I'll just bring you fruit. I assume you can find insects on your own."

What happened to familiars when their people died? Graciela had taught me that in the Mexican tradition, it was said that people's *tonallis*, or animal spirits, were born at the exact same time as them, and died when they died. Did that hold true for a witch's familiar? Would Winston sicken without his "master" on this earthly plane?

Going back inside to the kitchen, I poured myself another cup of French roast and sat down to make a to-do list, complete with bullet points:

- *Figure out who the dead man is/who killed him if he was murdered*
- *Figure out the prophecy/is my brother a killer?*
- *Keep San Francisco's magical community together/ask Carlos for the Satchel and when*

*crime scene will be released/make sure octago-
nal room is cleansed*
- *Get Aunt Cora's Closet together/do paperwork/
bookkeeping/pay taxes/check stock*
- *Finish laundry/personal and professional*
- *Figure out mermaid costume*
- *Figure out Bat*
- *Witch stuff*

"Witch stuff" was an admittedly broad category. For
most people, coming back from a trip meant going
through the mail, paying the bills, doing the laundry.
But for a witch like me, it entailed a host of other
catch-up activities: the care and feeding of my medicine
bag; carving amulets and pentagrams from the wood of
a fruit tree; and harvesting ingredients for my spells,
such as herbs and roots, which then needed to be dried
and processed prior to use. I also had to find the time to
assess the suitcase full of items I had picked up during
my travels: the vial of water from the Tiber River in
Rome, a tallow candle from a private chapel in a Châ-
teau in the Loire Valley, several ferns I collected in the
Spanish Pyrenees. I rarely knew what I would use the
items for prior to their calling to me, but just knowing I
had them on hand gave me a satisfying sense of plenty.

Sailor emerged from the bedroom. He was dressed
in a T-shirt and jeans and was freshly shaven, but his
hair was still adorably ruffled, as if he had forgotten to
comb it. He kept grumbling that he needed a haircut,
but I enjoyed running my fingers through his locks.

No doubt about it, my husband cleaned up good, but
I preferred him like this: when I could see a trace of the
little boy he must have been, getting up in his pj's and
watching cartoons. Or whatever it was Rom kids did.
Sailor did not like to talk about his past.

"Hey, husband," I said softly, after we exchanged a gentle kiss.

"Hey, wife."

I smiled. "I wish saying 'spouse' wasn't so awkward. I'd rather refer to you with a gender-free word."

"I dunno. The plural of spouse must be 'spice,' right? I like that." He grinned. "How do you say it in Spanish?"

"'*Marido*' for husband, '*mujer*' for wife. Officially, it's '*esposa*,' '*esposo*.' I suppose you could say 'espos-x,' like they say 'Latinx,' but it's still awkward as a newborn filly."

"Is that last one a Texan expression?"

I smiled. "Not sure if they say it, but my mom does."

"It was good to see her, and Graciela, and the Aunties."

"They like you."

"They have excellent taste."

"Nah, they're just easily swayed by your motorcycle jacket."

"Will they be around today?"

I nodded. "They're supposed to come by and catch me up on what happened at Aunt Cora's Closet while I was gone."

"That looks like quite a to-do list," said Sailor, peeking over my shoulder. "Anything I can help you with?"

"Not so far, unless you can tell me something about the dead man."

"Get me something he was wearing, and I'll try."

That was something else I should have thought of while I was waiting for the police. Land sakes alive, a person would think I had never been on the scene of a suspicious death before.

As Sailor went to the counter to pour himself a cup of coffee, I watched his muscles move under his jeans and T-shirt, feeling my now-familiar attraction to him but with the newfound understanding that we were now married. *Mine. All mine.* I realized anew that this was the rest of my life: waking up with Sailor, exchanging kisses and small talk over coffee.

I remembered the actress Betty White once said that before marrying someone you should be sure their manner of chewing doesn't bother you. So far, at least, I loved the way this man chewed.

He leaned back against the counter, holding my gaze and blowing on the steaming mug. I felt desire rise in me. Maybe the to-do list could wait . . .

I heard a loud, low belch, the blankets in the cubby over the refrigerator rustled, and Oscar's head popped out.

"G'mornin'! What's for breakfast?"

Sailor glared at him.

I added an item to the list: *Keep Sailor and Oscar from killing each other.*

"Fix yourself some cereal," I suggested. "Unless . . ." I looked at Sailor. "Would you like me to make something for us?"

"Sure, *Sailor* gets whatever he wants," Oscar said, and jumped down to the floor. He continued in a falsetto, "'Would milord Sailor fancy a stack of Belgian waffles, mayhaps? Just let me run and churn some fresh butter.'" Oscar waggled his head. "Meanwhile, it's 'Oscar, you're just a gobgoyle. Fix yourself some dry cereal.' *I* see how it is."

Oscar pulled himself up to his full height and strutted through the kitchen in high dudgeon, heading toward the bathroom.

"Good work, wife," said Sailor.

"Don't you dare laugh at him," I warned.

"Much as I would love to put that overly familiar familiar of yours in his place, I have a few errands to run. We need toothpaste, and I'll grab a few more groceries. Also, Patience set up a meeting with a potential investor to go over more details about this new business venture." He shrugged on his motorcycle jacket. "What are you up to today?"

"The usual. What's this business Patience is proposing?"

"It has to do with Silicon Valley tycoons. It's a little complicated, and I'm not yet sold on the idea, so I'll fill you in when I know more. And anyway, I was thinking, now that I have a rich wife—"

"Rich? Who's rich? Comfortable at best."

"Rich enough to afford an apartment and a shop lease in San Francisco. Anyway, I thought maybe I would be a househusband. Cook and clean, find a new apartment . . ."

"Do what, now?"

"Be a househusband?"

"I'm on board with that part. What came after that?"

"Cook and clean?"

"A little further."

"Find a new apartment?"

"Bingo."

"We've talked about this, Lily. There's not enough room here for you, me, and the pig."

"He doesn't take up that much room. He sleeps in a cubby in the kitchen, for heaven's sake. I know you need your space sometimes, which I'm totally okay with, but that's why you kept your apartment in Chinatown." Sailor's psychic abilities and practice were most successful in quiet, calm, meditative surroundings. Aunt Cora's Closet was almost never quiet, and I had to admit that my apartment wasn't either, especially not when Oscar and I were at home. "I think we just need to get used to each other's rhythms and habits, work out the kinks."

"I think that's a little optimistic," Sailor said. "For instance, Oscar's probably going to be in the bathroom for a while—the other night when you traipsed off to find a dead body, he staked out the bathroom for a full hour. I finally broke in and found him taking a bubble bath."

"A *bubble* bath?" The visual of a gobgoyle surrounded by bubbles made me giggle. "I wondered where my good bath salts had gone."

"You laugh now, but just wait until you need to pee and have to go downstairs to the shop bathroom." He leaned down to give me another kiss, smelling of coffee and my homemade oatmeal-honey shaving cream. "Anyway, of course I won't make any commitments without you, but I thought I'd at least scope out the possibilities, maybe narrow down our options. Even before I saw your list, my extrasensory abilities told me you wouldn't have a lot of time for house hunting."

The clockwork in my old Bavarian cuckoo clock started to hum, and the little bird popped out of the little door to chirp eight times.

"True. But we really do need to talk about this more, Sailor, because there are a lot of variables in play. I wouldn't be up for a long commute, for example. But right now I have to get showered and dressed. Staff meeting downstairs at nine."

"Aw, shucks, so sorry to miss it," said Sailor unconvincingly. "Staff meetings are just about my favorite things."

Chapter 7

Sailor was right: Oscar monopolized the bathroom. By the time he finally emerged, enveloped in a cloud of steam, and ostentatiously poured himself a bowl of cereal, I was running late. I jumped into a quick shower and towel-dried my hair, dressing in my favorite style: a vintage pastel-peach cotton sundress from the early sixties, matched with a sunny cardigan and a pair of aqua Keds. I had opened my apartment door to go downstairs to the shop when I heard voices chatting in the workroom: Bronwyn, Maya, and . . . Oscar?

I found the three of them sitting around the jade linoleum table in the workroom, the brocade curtain drawn for privacy from the sales floor. Oscar was holding forth, a smudge of powdered sugar on his snout. A telltale pink bakery box held half a dozen donuts.

"So, as you leave the rest stop on the highway there's this sign, see?" said Oscar. "And it says in several languages: Have a good trip! *Buen viaje! Buon viaggio! Bon voyage!* And then in German: *Gute fahrt! Gute* fart!" He repeated the punch line, tears running down his grizzled muzzle at the sheer hilarity of the word 'fart.' "'*Fahrt*'! Like 'fart'! Get it?"

Bronwyn and Maya laughed, though I imagine they were more amused by Oscar's telling of the story than by the actual joke.

"Lily!" said Bronwyn, rising to give me a cinnamon-scented hug. "Good morning! Oscar called and requested a dozen donuts. Seems I erred in purchasing too many vegetables."

I gave Oscar the side-eye. He looked away, the picture of innocence.

Maya and I shared a hug as well. It was so good to come back to these friends who had become family. My family. My town. My home.

Did Sailor really want to move? I loved living above my shop. I loved my terrace and its mature garden. I loved the black-and-white-checked floor in my large kitchen, where bundles of herbs and roots hung from thick beams overhead, and a pot of basil sat by my moon calendar. I loved the big tub in the old-fashioned tiled bathroom, the charming bedroom, and cozy living room.

But it was true, the apartment was not large. Sailor was a big man, and it wasn't out of line for him to want a bit more elbow room. Driving across town to his Chinatown apartment wasn't going to work as a daily plan, unless he wanted to use it as an office.

But did he even *need* an office? What was Patience's business proposal? Last time Sailor got involved in the psychic business for profit, things went south fast. Graciela always counseled me not to "borrow trouble" by worrying about things that might not ever happen, but still.

As Oscar mowed his way through the remaining

donuts, we chatted companionably, catching up on one another's lives. Bronwyn spoke of her grandkids and Maya of her mother and what was going on at the Academy of Art. They told funny stories about Graciela's coven, a spat over an American flag bikini, and the time Kay lost her glasses and after a forty-five minute storewide search Conrad found them perched on Darlene's head. And Bronwyn mentioned that Carlos Romero had taken Patience out on a date.

"*My* Carlos?" I asked.

"I wouldn't call him *your* Carlos, Lily; after all, you're a newlywed!" exclaimed Bronwyn.

"I didn't mean it that way. I just . . . wow. How did it go?"

"We were hoping you might be able to find out," Maya said.

Bronwyn let out a sigh. "Don't you just love all this romance in the air?"

"I thought that was just the smell of the lavender sachets mistress makes," said Oscar.

As the conversation died down, I picked up the mermaid costume. "I just can't understand where this thing came from."

"One of the Aunties probably picked it up somewhere and forgot about it, or it came in with some of the other items and we didn't notice," Bronwyn said sensibly.

"Very likely," I conceded. "There's just something about it. . . ." What was it? Not sinister, exactly, just very specific and . . . odd. Salty. I shrugged and continued: "You know how I am. And you don't see mermaid costumes every day, certainly not vintage ones."

"Wait," said Oscar, and nodded at the costume. "You're talking about *that* thing?"

"Do you know something about it?" I asked.

"Yeah, sure. I put it in your suitcase."

"You did *what*?"

"I put it in your suitcase."

"You—when? Where? I don't understand."

He smacked his muzzle again, wiping jam and powdered sugar from his chops. "What, am I not speaking English right now?" Oscar waved his big hand and gave a world-weary sigh. "I don't know what language I'm speaking anymore, on account of *le grand tour*! Like that old movie, *If It's Tuesday, This Must Be Belgium.* You ever see that one? I love me some Suzanne Pleshette. They don't make 'em like that anymore."

"Oscar, you *are* speaking English but I'm confused—*you* brought the mermaid costume here?"

"Sure. Who'd you think brought it?"

"I didn't know. That's what we've been trying to figure out."

"Where did you get it, Oscar?" Maya asked, cutting to the chase.

"A guy."

"A guy."

He nodded.

"Could you give us a few more details?" I asked.

"Dragon guy."

"A 'dragon guy'?"

"You mean like a real dragon? Dragons are real?" Bronwyn asked. "I knew it!"

Oscar laughed. "Nah, dragons ain't real. Not anymore, anyhow. Be cool if they were, though."

Bronwyn looked disappointed. "What about werewolves?"

"I hope not," Maya said. "Gobgoyles are challenging enough."

"You should meet some of my relatives," Oscar agreed with a hoot. "Now *there's* a pack of loons."

"Oscar, please," I said, trying to get this conversation back on track. "Where did you meet this dragon guy?"

He cocked his head. "Budapest, I think. Or . . . Barcelona, maybe? I think it was a *B* word. Anyway, he gave me a package and asked me to bring it back here."

"Haven't you ever heard not to take packages from strangers?" asked Bronwyn.

"He didn't seem all that strange. Not any more than most people, anyway. You humans are an odd lot."

"True enough," said Bronwyn with a sage nod.

"By 'dragon guy,' do you mean he was dressed like a dragon?" I persisted.

He gave a raspy chuckle and looked at Maya. "Dressed like a dragon, *hoo-whee*, this one here's got an imagination, amiright?"

"Was his name Dragomir, by any chance?" asked Maya in a wry tone.

"That sounds familiar. Sounds like 'dragon.'"

"Yes. Yes it does," I said. "And did the dragon guy tell you why he wanted you to take the costume?"

He shook his grizzled head. I let out a long sigh. I adored my familiar, but sometimes I wanted to wring his scrawny neck.

"I figgered it had to do with you and the shop. You know how you are about used clothes."

"*Vintage* clothes," I couldn't help but correct him.

"Don't sell yourself short, mistress. Maybe your reputation precedes you all the way to Berlin."

"Think hard, Oscar. Was it Berlin, or Barcelona, or Budapest?"

He shrugged. "One of the *B* places. Like I said."

"What did he look like?"

"Who could tell? Y'all look alike to me. He was regular. Anyway, I'd love to sit and chat, but I'm not really a meeting kind of guy. I got things to do and places to pee. I mean, people to *see*! Ha!"

Brushing the powdered sugar from his lap, Oscar bid us farewell with a deep bow and a flourish.

"He obviously had a grand time!" said Bronwyn. "Oh, it's so nice to see him. And to hear all his *stories*!"

"The Angels and Devils night in Sitges sounded amazing," said Maya, chuckling. "Sounds like Oscar ran with the devils."

"Of course he did," said Bronwyn. "Everyone knows the devils are more fun at parties than the angels."

"Hey, before the coven arrives," I said, "I wanted to ask you both: How would you feel if I hired Conrad to work at the shop?"

"Funny you should mention that," Maya said, glancing at Bronwyn, who nodded. "Bronwyn and I talked about suggesting it to you. Assuming, of course, that you can swing it financially. We think it's a great idea."

"We do indeed!" Bronwyn confirmed. "He really has been such a help, and a nice presence in the store. Also, it's sort of like when Duke hangs around—I think it makes some men feel more comfortable in what's often seen as a woman's venue."

"Perfect. I'll ask him today, then."

"Oh, listen," said Bronwyn. "Sounds like the Aunties' bus!"

At the blast of air brakes, we emerged from the workroom to see the Aunties' converted school bus pulling up outside the shop's front windows. It still amazed me that Aunt Agatha, citing better eyesight than the rest of the coven members, had managed to drive the huge contraption all the way from West Texas. And that the old behemoth hadn't broken down. Might be some magic at work, there?

Just then Conrad appeared and held the door open as the Aunties filed into the store, everyone talking at once, and enveloped us in the usual flurry of hugs and kisses, giving exclamations and descriptions of the wine tasting and how Viv insulted a sparkling-wine maker by insisting that true champagne came only from the Champagne region of France, and then Rosa mistook the tip jar for a spit jar, and then Pepper and Winona and Darlene wandered away from the tour group and got locked in a private wine cellar.

"*I* didn't think it was so bad," murmured Darlene. "After all, we were in there with kegs of wine."

"I told you, that wine isn't ready yet," said Pepper. "It's like you don't even *listen* to the tour guides when they discuss the wine-making process."

"Hey, where's my mom?" I asked, realizing she wasn't among the thirteen women.

A couple of glances were exchanged.

"*Dude*," said Conrad. "Lily, your mom's awesome."

"Maggie decided she wanted a morning alone," said Nan.

"She finds us a bit much sometimes," said Maria-Gracia. "But then, who could blame her?"

"I think it was the wine cellar incident that put her over the edge," said Caroline.

"No, it was the tip jar incident," Viv said, glaring at Rosa.

"Anybody could have made that mistake," Rosa said guiltily.

There wasn't room for all of us at the workroom table, so we arranged folding chairs in a half circle on the shop floor. Bronwyn, Conrad, Maya, and I sat behind the display case and counter, and the coven members squeezed in between the ruffles and crinolines and poodle skirts.

Bronwyn, showing her savvy, had hidden two dozen donuts from Oscar and now handed the pink boxes around, to a chorus of appreciative *oohs* and *aahs*.

We chatted about new items and various sales that had taken place while I was away.

"I can't believe that spangled pantsuit sold," I mentioned.

"Oh, *I* bought that one," said Betty.

"What in heavens are *you* going to do with a spangled pantsuit?" asked Nan.

"I wanted to be prepared," said Betty. "After all, you can never find a spangled pantsuit when you need one."

"Anyway, *m'ija*, your store is still standing, and you made money while you were gone. That is enough about that," Graciela said. "We have more important things to talk about."

I glanced at Maya and Bronwyn and Conrad, and decided it was better to be open.

"Is this about Deliverance? You're going to try to get rid of her?" A while ago I had gone up against a fierce and terrible demon-like elemental creature named Deliverance. I hadn't taken proper precautions to protect myself, and part of her had taken up residence within me. Sort of. I wasn't clear on where she actually was, only that she occasionally reared her head with a ferocity that was almost overwhelming. The determined but gentle Ashen Witch was my usual guardian spirit, and she and Deliverance were not particularly compatible.

"For the moment," said Graciela, "we think it's best if you keep her."

Iris whispered: "The prophecy."

"How can Deliverance help with the prophecy?" I asked.

"We're not sure she can," replied Viv. "But we've been sensing an imbalance here in the Bay . . ."

"I keep seeing a *torana*," said Rosa. "A very vivid *torana* keeps appearing in my morning tea leaves."

"What's a *torana*?" I asked.

"It's from the word for 'bird perch.' It's also referred to as a *vandanamalikas*," explained Caroline.

"Essentially, it's a gateway," said MariaGracia. "In the Jain architecture of the Indian subcontinent, they were quite common."

"Okay . . ." I said. "But we're not on the Indian subcontinent. So how is it relevant . . . ?"

"They also appear in China, where they're called *paifang*," said Iris.

"In Japan, *Torii*," said Viv. "In Korea, *Hongsalmun*, and in Thailand, *Sao Ching Cha*."

"And, of course, *Pylon* is the Greek word for a monumental gateway," Nan said.

"In the ancient Egyptian religion, the *Pylon* mirrored the hieroglyph for 'horizon,' which depicted two hills between which the sun rose and set," added Darlene.

"Right," I said, trying to keep track of what everyone was saying and put it together in a relevant fashion. "But I'm still not understanding what this has to do with me."

"It's symbolic of re-creation and rebirth, *m'ija*," said Graciela. "The images have been appearing to us in reference to the prophecy."

"But . . . I thought we vanquished the threat to San Francisco during the encounter on Alcatraz," I protested. I knew Renee-the-cupcake-lady was no longer a threat, at least not for the moment. But if this was a much larger, existential thing with an imbalance or some kind of portal . . . *Ugh*.

"A threat such as this is not a single prong but a many-tined fork," said Rosa.

"I'm sorry?"

"It's not a one-and-done," Caroline clarified. "Doesn't work like that."

"But . . . there was an *earthquake*," I insisted, as if I could talk them out of it. "There were *casualties*, not to mention a heck of a lot of property damage to one of the most popular attractions in the National Park Service. You're saying there's more to come?"

"Like we've been saying, we're sensing some kind of opening, and an imbalance of some sort," added Kay.

"What kind of 'sort'?" I asked.

"We're working on that," said Rosa. "I should read your tea leaves."

"Haven't figured it out yet," said Winona. "But I could use the pendulum on you."

"We'll get around to it," said Viv.

"All in good time," agreed Kay, as the others nodded.

"What you really need first is a good tarot reading," said Graciela. "But Rosa's talents are running more to tea leaves lately, and Kay has her chakras blocked ever since the incident at the Exploratorium."

I decided it was probably best not to inquire as to the details of that incident. Instead, I said: "Patience and her aunt Renna are both gifted in tarot."

"*Bueno*," said Graciela, with a nod. "You go get yourself a reading, Lily, and let us know what it reveals. Then perhaps we could draw down the moon, and read your tea leaves and the pendulum. See if we can figure this out. Because the coven can't stay here forever, *m'ija*. Eventually, we have to leave you to take care of things on your own."

A shiver ran through me. Graciela's coven had orig-

inally come for a brief visit, then decided to stay and
help with the Alcatraz adventure, then delayed their
departure again to participate in my handfasting with
Sailor. They were no doubt anxious to get home to
West Texas, which meant their reluctance to leave suggested something big might be on the horizon.

"Okay, I'll get a tarot reading. But for the meantime,
you're telling me I need to be on the lookout?"

"For now it's best if you keep Deliverance with you.
Just make sure to keep her in hand."

"Oh, sure. 'Cause that's simple."

I took my list from my dress pocket, set it on the
counter, and added another item:

- *Figure out existential threat to SF.*

Chapter 8

After announcing they were off to Muir Woods for more sightseeing, Graciela's coven departed as noisily as they had arrived, the ancient school bus belching diesel exhaust as it rumbled down Haight Street.

I turned to Conrad. "Hey, I wanted to talk to you about something. You've been spending a lot of time here at Aunt Cora's Closet, and—"

"Dude. The Con's making a nuisance of himself? I'm sorry."

"No, Conrad, it's not that, I—"

"It's just that it's harder now, since I've gotten sober," Conrad said, hanging his head. "A lot of my old friends still use, so I don't want to hang around them, and it's sort of hard to know what to do with myself."

"Conrad, I—"

"I'll just sweep the sidewalk, and then get out of your hair."

"*Conrad*," said Maya in a firm tone. "Stop talking and listen. Lily's trying to offer you a job."

Conrad froze. "A what?"

"A job," I said.

He stared at me, and then Maya, and then Bronwyn. "For serious?"

"For very serious," I said. "We *like* having you around. And your presence is valuable."

"*Dude*." He collapsed back in his chair. "I, like . . . I've never had a job before."

"Never?" Bronwyn asked.

"Well, I used to help old people by mowing their lawns or cleaning out their garages, and sometimes they paid me, but that wasn't exactly a job, and it was a long time ago."

"Then it's high time you had one," said Bronwyn, reaching over and squeezing his hand.

He nodded, and his Adam's apple bobbed. "I mean, I'm sober . . . but I'm still an addict."

"We know that, Conrad," said Maya.

"And where better than here for your first real job?" said Bronwyn. "Why don't we show you the ropes?"

While Bronwyn and Maya walked the Con through the shop's daily routine, I spent a long time on the phone with Calypso discussing the business end of Aidan's work with the magical community. It consisted mostly of the standard stuff: bureaucratic snafus, complaints because the city required fortune-tellers to be licensed, and a couple of issues that needed to be addressed with the mayor. I was not looking forward to that last one. Witchcraft and politics don't mix, at least not in my mind. Aidan saw it differently, and I supposed he was being realistic: None of us could duck the responsibilities of policy and public service these days.

"Inspector Romero said Aidan's office was still considered a crime scene," said Calypso. "And we're not allowed back."

"That's what he told me as well," I said. "I'll let Clarinda know that I'll be working out of Aunt Cora's Closet for the meantime, in case anyone has urgent business. I just wish I had thought to grab the Satchel while I was there, and maybe his appointment book."

"I'm glad you didn't," Calypso said. "I believe that's considered 'tampering with evidence.'"

"Only if the police find out. . . . But I suppose you're right. It's just difficult to know what steps to take at this point."

"Would you like me to come into the city, so we can go over everything in person?"

"Why don't you enjoy a little downtime? You've been holding everything together while I've been gone, not to mention hosting a houseful of visitors. We can get together after the police release Aidan's office and review everything." I paused, then added: "So, how's my mother doing?"

"Maggie seems fine. She's reading on the porch at the moment, with a cat in her lap, no less. Would you like to speak with her?"

"No, I don't want to bother her. Just say hi from me."

"I will. And please give my best to Inspector Romero when you see him. He's clearly a special man. Very different from my last experience dealing with the police department."

"I'm glad to hear it," I said. "I couldn't agree more—he's pretty special."

As if I had conjured his presence, upon hanging up the phone Carlos Romero walked into the shop. He wore his usual "uniform" of a thigh-length black leather jacket and khaki pants. Carlos was a good-looking man, only a little taller than I. But he had a way of holding himself that commanded respect, no doubt due to the fact that he had been a homicide detective for many years. He had seen a lot of the seamier side of life; perhaps too much.

After exchanging greetings with Bronwyn, Maya, and Conrad, Carlos asked to speak with me in private. I led the way into the back room, and we took seats at the jade green linoleum table. A pink bakery box held a few leftover donut halves.

"Donut scraps?" I offered.

"Don't mind if I do," he said, choosing a maple-frosted old-fashioned.

"Sorry it's just the leftovers. The coven has already been here this morning."

"No problem. I try to stay away from donuts, just to mess with the stereotype, but the truth is, I haven't eaten this morning."

"Tea or coffee with that?"

"No, thanks. I've had way too much coffee this morning. Haven't slept much."

"Work?"

He nodded and finished off the donut.

"I'd be happy to make you something more substantial, Carlos. It's no trouble. Eggs and toast, maybe? You need to take care of yourself. None of us are as young as we used to be, you know."

"Unlike me, *you* look younger with each passing day, Lily. Marriage must agree with you. Anyway, thanks for the offer of breakfast, but I'll take a rain check." He pulled his notebook out of his back pocket. "Got an ID on the stiff."

"Have you been watching cop shows recently?"

"All detectives talk this way."

"You don't."

Carlos smiled. "His name is Marcellus Tinley. Ring a bell?"

"Never heard of him."

"Medical examiner isn't ready to rule the death a homicide," he said, his tone thoughtful.

"What did he die of?"

"Drug overdose. We found a hypodermic needle beneath the body, tested positive for heroin and fentanyl. Still waiting on the tox report. Possibly accidental."

"Oh. But you don't think it was an accident?

"Seems odd to me. Nobody associated with the wax museum remembers seeing the guy there before, and Aidan Rhodes has been out of town for a while. So why'd he break into Rhodes's office and decide to shoot up? That's assuming it was an accidental overdose, of course. Anyway, we're still looking into it. He's local, from Treasure Island."

"Treasure Island, like the book?"

"Yes, and like the attraction at Disneyland. But it's also the name of the island where the East Bay span of the Bay Bridge meets the San Francisco span."

"Oh, that's right. I've seen the freeway exit signs. But I thought the bridge crossed through Yerba Buena Island?"

"It does. That's the island Mother Nature created. Treasure Island's the man-made island next to it."

"People *built* an island? Why?"

"For the World's Fair, I think, a long time ago. Just before World War Two broke out. I don't remember the details of why, or even how; before my time. I do know it was a naval station for a while."

"So what's on Treasure Island now?"

"As far as I'm concerned, it's a no-man's-land," said Carlos. "There are people out there, of course, and lots of rumors about developing condos and the like, but nothing's come of it so far. Lot of problems to overcome, like ease of access and egress, and soil contamination from the old military post. Anyway, any idea why this Marcellus Tinley character would end up at Aidan Rhodes's office?"

"Not a one."

"Tinley was in rigor mortis when you found him, which means he'd been dead at least a few hours. According to Clarinda, she canceled Aidan's appointments for the day because Calypso wasn't able to come in. We've looked at the security footage, but no one in particular looks suspicious, and with all those tourists in and out all day . . ." He shook his head. "What about your purported 'brother'?"

"What about him?"

"He been in touch?"

I thought about what Oscar had said: that Dragomir gave him the mermaid costume when we were in a-European-city-that-starts-with-a-*B*. But I saw no reason to mention that to Carlos until I knew more, such as whether that mermaid costume had anything to do with the suspicious death. Which reminded me: I should ask Sailor to "read" the costume, see if he could pick up on any vibrations that had eluded me.

"No, I haven't heard from him," I said.

"We're still trying to track him down."

"You think he had something to do with this?"

"You tell me."

"What I can tell you for certain is that I'd never met the man before last night. I'm not even sure he *is* my brother. He could be some criminal using his identity, for all I know."

"All *I* know is that one Dragomir Ivory was allegedly at the scene of a possible crime, and that he took off for parts unknown. Clarinda was no help, by the way, other than to say, several times in fact, that he was 'a hottie.' Anyway, I gotta shove off. Let me know if he contacts you."

"Will do. Carlos, when do you think the scene will be released? Aidan will be out of town for a while still, and I'm supposed to be tending to his business."

"If you had any sense at all, you'd stay away from Aidan Rhodes, his office, and his business—whatever that may involve."

"I know how you feel about Aidan," I said. "But I made him a promise. And someone's got to keep the magical folks in line. If I can't get access to his office, would it be possible to get a few things?"

"Like what?"

"There are some research books, and a satchel with some documents in it, and an agenda with appointments scheduled. Also, if I could get an article of clothing from the deceased, Sailor could try to 'read' it, maybe offer some clues to help your investigation."

"Help my investigation, huh?" Carlos said, clearly skeptical. He blew out a long breath and rubbed the back of his neck. "I can't promise anything, but I'll see what I can do."

"Thanks." I let out a long sigh.

"Glad to be back, eh?"

"Words fail me."

"What did he say?" Bronwyn asked after Carlos left.

"Not much," I said. "But he thinks the death seems suspicious."

"Oh, that's such a shame. But actually, I was wondering if he said anything about his date with Patience?"

"I forgot to ask!"

"Jet lag again?" Bronwyn asked.

"I suppose so," I said.

I looked around the store. Maya was going through the hanging garments, checking that each was on the appropriate rack, Bronwyn was inspecting her herbs for freshness, and Conrad was wiping down the large dressing area mirrors with my homemade vinegar-lemongrass spray. Everybody, it seems, was busy working—except me, the store's owner. So much for "leading by example." I took a seat at the counter, opened a file, and began plowing my way through more paperwork.

But I kept thinking about what Carlos had said, and when the shop was free of customers, I asked: "Have any of you heard of a man named Marcellus Tinley?"

Maya, Conrad, and Bronwyn shook their heads.

"Carlos says he's from Treasure Island," I said. "Which, I know now, is an artificial island. Is it just me, or does it seem weird to build an island?"

"I think it was for the World's Fair, wasn't it?" suggested Maya. "Like, right before World War Two."

"I know a fellow who lived out there," said Bronwyn. "I met him while doing some canvassing for Greenpeace. We had drinks out on his deck . . . this was years ago, of course. The view was breathtaking, but otherwise the island's name makes it sound a lot more romantic than it really is."

"I'm still stuck on the fact that they built an *island* just to hold a fair."

"That was back in the day when men—and I use that word on purpose—used to love to see if they could chop down the biggest tree or do things like create an island in the middle of the bay," said Bronwyn. "Just to see if they could accomplish it, I suppose. It led to some great feats of engineering, but it's far too man-versus-nature for my taste. In Wicca we believe in working in concert *with* nature. And we would *never* chop down a thousand-year-old tree."

"Dude," the Con said with a solemn nod. "I love sleeping under trees. I totally get it."

"Bronwyn, are you still in touch with your friend who lives there?" I asked. "Do you think he would talk to me?"

"I imagine he'd be happy to talk to you, but he moved to Berkeley a little while ago. He was convinced the island was making him sick."

"The island itself?"

"The navy used to clean the ships that carried atomic bombs at the old naval yard there," said Bronwyn. "Some areas still have dangerous levels of radioactivity. I know real estate developers keep talking about building condos and what all out there, and certainly the views are stunning, but as far as I'm concerned, the whole place is a bit . . ." She shrugged.

"Rundown and creepy," said Maya in a matter-of-fact tone. "I drove around there once, just out of curiosity. There are a few small businesses, a pretty marina, and a winery . . . but no two ways about it, it's a strange place."

"Not surprising for an artificial island," said Bronwyn, looking through her old-fashioned paper address book. "It was created for what was officially called the Golden Gate International Exposition, in part to honor the engineering marvels of the Golden Gate and Bay Bridges, which had both been recently completed. From what I heard, after the fair there were plans to build an airport, but when war broke out in Europe the island was turned into a military base. Here he is: Eugene Leimert. I'll write down his contact information for you, Lily. But why are you interested in talking with him?"

"I was thinking that given its relative isolation, Treasure Island might be the kind of place where everyone knows everyone," I said. "Maybe the victim's neighbors, or your friend Eugene, could give us a clue as to what he was doing in Aidan's office."

Bronwyn shared a glance with Maya. "Possibly. But . . . I don't mean to be nitpicky, Lily, but shouldn't you leave this to Carlos to investigate?"

"Oh, I intend to. My to-do list is far too long at the moment."

"Uh-huh," said Maya, unconvinced.

"Not to mention," I continued, "Carlos said the victim died from an overdose. They found a needle."

Conrad shook his head and said in a somber whisper: "*Dude*."

"That seems odd. Why would he have gone to Aidan's office to shoot up?" asked Maya.

"That's what's bothering me. And Carlos. Calypso has no idea who he was. Clarinda, the woman in the ticket booth, remembered he bought a ticket earlier in the evening but didn't recognize him, so presumably he wasn't a friend of Aidan's. I suppose he might have needed a fix and happened to find the door to Aidan's office unlocked, but . . ."

"That's not likely, is it?" said Bronwyn. "I mean, given that it's you, and he had a bat."

"Dude, that reminds me: What's up with little Winston?" asked Conrad. "And little Oscaroo?"

"Sailor made a bat box, and we put it out on the terrace. I don't want Winston to go cold turkey in the wild if he's used to being a pet, but the whole digestive thing made me a little nervous about keeping him inside the apartment. And I imagine Oscar'll be down soon to enjoy his lovely new pillow. Thank you for that, Bronwyn."

While we were gone, Bronwyn had sewn a new silk cover for Oscar's shop bed, the old purple one having gotten a bit ratty. This one was chartreuse, peppered with tiny yellow diamonds.

The little bell over the shop door tinkled as a pair of

young women came in and started flipping through the clothes on the sale rack. On their heels came a middle-aged woman with a teen whom I presumed to be her daughter.

"Okay, Conrad, time to man up and do some laundry," Maya said. "It's not for the faint of heart or weak of biceps, let me tell you. Step right this way."

Conrad followed Maya through the burgundy curtain into the workroom and listened intently as Maya showed him how to categorize garments into machine-washable, hand-washable, and dry-clean-only, and how to inspect each one for signs of needed repairs. Then she demonstrated how to sort the machine-washable items into piles by fabric and color, which machine settings were appropriate for each pile, and how much detergent to use.

I had always known Maya was intelligent, but only now did I realized how much she had learned about clothes, and their treatment and care, since she had started working at Aunt Cora's Closet. No doubt she had done research on her own, because she now seemed more knowledgeable than I, as she explained to Conrad that clothes made from nylon had to date after 1939, when the fabric was first introduced, while zippers were not mass produced until after 1935. She also showed him a few of the "tells" for genuine vintage, including designer labels and novelty buttons.

Maya handed Conrad a bag of recently acquired clothing and said: "Now you try."

"Dude," Conrad said. "It's not like doin' the regular laundry, is it?"

"Nope, it's a little more complicated," Maya said.

"I'm impressed," I said to Maya when she came back to the shop floor. "You're a natural-born teacher. How did you learn so much about clothing?"

"Mostly by listening to you for the past couple of years. And then there's the Internet."

As much as I hated to admit it, I had to hand it to the Internet. A research trove.

We all worked side by side for a while, answering a few customer questions. The two young women thanked us but left empty-handed, while the mother bought her daughter a fringed leather jacket and a spirit bottle, which I make to encourage creativity and calm. I was watching them leave when I heard Conrad speaking to Maya.

"It's just that sometimes these feelings come up, and they're really hard. I never used to feel my feelings, I just tuned out, went on a different wavelength, you know what I'm saying? Got high and didn't feel much of anything. Sometimes I wish I could feel that numbness again."

"Did you call your sponsor?" Maya asked.

Conrad nodded. "I do, every time I have those feelings. I really am doing okay about not using, it's just these feelings. I mean . . . *duuuuude*."

And then I watched Maya do the least Maya thing I could think of: She gave Conrad a big hug.

They stayed like that for a long moment, their arms wrapped around each other, eyes closed. I looked at Bronwyn in surprise, and she smiled. We both bent our heads over our work—Bronwyn tending to her tea blends while I plowed slowly through the stack of paperwork on the counter—and pretended nothing was happening.

I also made a note to myself to brew for Conrad to replenish the supply I had left him with while I was away. I couldn't force him to stay sober—no amount of magic could—but since he had made the decision himself, the botanicals helped his resolve.

The laundry under way and the shop again free of customers, Maya opened the computer and dove into more research on Treasure Island.

"Here are some photographs of the fair," said Maya. "Including something called Sally Rand's Nude Ranch on the 'Gayway.' I'm guessing 'gay' didn't have the same connotation back then."

"I think you must be right," said Bronwyn.

"I'm a little shocked, though," said Maya. "I mean, nude performers at the fair? Why do I always think those were more innocent times? Check out this photo."

She turned the computer around so we could see an image of smiling young women in cowboy hats and boots lined up behind a fence, the wooden slats strategically placed to cover their chests and hips.

"Wow, you're right, that seems pretty risqué," I said.

"Oh, and this is disturbing," said Maya. "Look: There's a Nazi flag pictured here."

"A what?" I asked, coming closer to look over her shoulder.

"It says here that there was a 'cavalcade of flags' from all over the world," said Maya.

"World War Two hadn't started yet," Bronwyn pointed out. "The Nazis were the recognized government of Germany, and that was their flag."

"Interesting," I said.

"And disturbing," said Maya. "It goes on to say that the Exposition was meant to demonstrate the city rising from the challenging era of the Great Depression, employing out-of-work architects, engineers, craftspeople, and artists to create a magnificent pageant of the Pacific."

There were more photos: giant towers built to look like elephants, and walls topped by stone carvings of chimeras and gargoyles. I wondered whether this would send Oscar on another wild goose chase, if he heard about it.

"Apparently it was a big deal that the fair was so 'electrified,'" Maya added. "From San Francisco and Oakland, Treasure Island was meant to appear to be 'a floating city of lights.' Oh! Listen to this, from an article dated in late 1939: *A dramatic turn of events tonight at the expo: a worker fell from the scaffolding surrounding a three-story tower, and an eight-year-old girl, sopping wet from a dip in the bay, rushed up to him, laid her hands upon him, and he was healed.*"

Chapter 9

"Eight is pretty young for a faith healer," I mused. "Was it part of a show? Some kind of entertainment?"

"Not according to these articles. The little girl's name was Shirley Mangicaro, and apparently she became quite the sensation. Also, there's something here about an actual mermaid mixing in with the synchronized swimmers . . . and on an entirely unrelated tangent, here's an article on Esther Williams," said Maya.

"Was she at the fair on Treasure Island?" asked Bronwyn.

"No, but she sometimes performed in a mermaid's costume, so she's been on my mind," said Maya. "Listen to this: *She eels through the crystal blue water in a rosy-red bathing suit or splashes in limpid magnificence in the gaudy water carnival.* I wish *I* could write like that. Next to this, my prose is positively wooden."

"Oh, I bet that's not true. When can I read your latest?" I said.

Maya had been involved in a long-term project to

collect stories from elders in the community, people from all walks of life. She took the occasional hiatus, but had recently accepted an offer from a local public radio station to present some of the recordings on-air.

"I was thinking," Maya said. "The more I look into this Treasure Island thing, the more I'd like to find some elders who might be able to tell me something about it."

"That could be a challenge," Bronwyn said. "Given it was so long ago."

"But maybe someone who went to the fair as a child? There are probably some of those folks around, somewhere. I wonder if little Shirley Mangicaro is still alive?"

"Now *that's* something my old friend Eugene might be able to help with," Bronwyn offered. "As I said, he lived on the island his entire life, until he moved to Berkeley. Perhaps he has some names for you."

"That's a great idea, Bronwyn," said Maya. "Thank you."

I checked my watch. It was only eleven in the morning, but I felt like taking a nap and was having a hard time focusing on the forms I was supposed to be filling out, never mind the bookkeeping. When a young woman came in looking for the perfect vintage dress, I was more than happy to be distracted.

"Do you think it's weird to wear a dress like this on a first date?" she asked, emerging from the communal dressing room and smoothing the flared skirt over her hips as she studied her reflection in the three-way mirror. The deep blue outfit dated from the 1940s, with a polka-dot bodice and a matching bolero jacket. It suited her perfectly, not just in style and color but in energy.

This is one thing I love about old clothes: They absorb the vibrations of their wearers and reflect them back to us. Happiness, of course, but also more negative emotions, which can be grounding: Righteous anger can help a current wearer with ambition and determination; even grief can make a wearer coping with sorrow feel understood by reflecting the depth of her emotions back to her.

"I think you look stunning, but then, I'm an old married woman," I said, surprising myself with my own words. When I first opened Aunt Cora's Closet, I felt barely older than the college students who frequented my store. But it had been an eventful few years; I had seen a lot, experienced even more, and learned about myself, my past, and my powers. "Let's check in with a younger cohort. Maya and Conrad, what do you think? Is it too much for a first date?"

Maya shook her head in an emphatic no. "Nah. You look amazing."

"*Dude*, anyone intimidated by you wearing that isn't worth your time," said Conrad. "I say let your fashion light shine."

"My sentiments exactly," I said.

"Sold," the woman said with a laugh.

We spent another half hour finding the perfect pair of gloves, jewelry, and even a darling pillbox hat; apparently, she had taken Conrad's advice to heart. I rang up her purchases, folding the dress carefully and placing everything in one of our Aunt Cora's Closet reusable tote bags. "Good luck on your date. Come back and tell us about it!"

"I will, but only if it goes well," she said with a smile as she left. "This was fun. *So* much better than the mall, and cheaper, too."

"And more environmentally sound," mentioned Bronwyn. "Did you know that clothes make up a good part of most landfills? Our obsession with new, cheap clothing is spelling disaster for our planet."

"I didn't know that. But now that you mention it, it makes sense." The woman added with a smile: "That does it: I'll be back, even if the date is a disaster."

After she left, I turned back to my paperwork with a sigh. A rustle of paper in my pocket reminded me of the lengthy to-do list.

"*Ugh*," I moaned.

"What's wrong, sweetie?" asked Bronwyn.

"Nothing really, but I'm overwhelmed with too many things to do, I don't want to do any of them, and my body's still on European time," I whined. The worst part was, I knew I was whining and still couldn't stop.

I had just returned from a glorious honeymoon, for heaven's sake. I owned a thriving business and worked with my best friends; I had a community of supportive friends and family, a gorgeous husband, and a terrific familiar; and I had my health. Other than having found a dead body in Aidan's office, I had literally nothing to complain about. But I was complaining, nonetheless.

"You know," Bronwyn said, "when we find ourselves unhappy when there's no real call for it, our subconscious may be trying to tell us something. Do you think that might be it?"

"I dunno," I said with a shrug. Great. I sounded as sullen as Selena, without the excuse of adolescence.

"Dude," Conrad said from his perch on a ladder, where he was changing a burnt-out lightbulb in the ceiling. "It's like a great philosopher once said: Listen to the Force."

"Maybe you need some fresh air and sunshine to reset your inner clock," Maya said. "It can be hard to settle back into work routines when you've been away for a while."

"I bet that's it!" Bronwyn said. "Take the afternoon off, Lily. Go for a walk, or maybe take a nap."

"I couldn't do that," I said. "You all are here working, and I just got back from a vacation for heaven's sake."

"We're eminently bribable. Buy us lunch and we'll call it even," Maya suggested.

"I'd happily watch the store for the afternoon if somebody bought me lunch from that new Cambodian place down the block," Bronwyn said. "I tried their crispy rice salad the other day and it is to die for. I just happen to have the takeout menu right here. Who's with me?"

"Count me in," Conrad said.

I smiled. "You really wouldn't mind?"

"For an order of their Nam Khao? You're on."

"You know, it's probably not on your to-do list," said Maya, looking up from the computer. "But I just found an address for the dead man: 182 11th Street, Treasure Island. Now that Conrad's here and an expert on the laundry, and Bronwyn's willing to watch the front of the store, what say you and I take a little trip to the island? See what we can learn about Marcellus Tinley and synchronized swimmers?"

I hesitated for the briefest of moments.

"Bronwyn, money for lunch is in the register. Order whatever tickles your and Conrad's fancy. Maya, we'll grab lunch on the road. Let's go."

Maya volunteered to drive, so I handed her the keys to the Mustang and we headed east on the Bay Bridge, crossing the span that connects San Francisco to Yerba Buena Island. But rather than going through the tunnel, as usual, we took a left exit off the freeway and followed Treasure Island Road. It was a gorgeous day, and I relished the stunning view of San Francisco off to our left.

The classic Mustang easily handled the road that clung to the side of Yerba Buena Island until we reached a causeway connecting the natural island to the artificial Treasure Island. There was a marina on the right, half-full of sailboats and small yachts, and farther along a low brick wall announced we had reached the US Naval Station. A large administration building had been built in a sweeping curve, with the smooth art deco lines of the 1930s.

"Hard to believe someone built an entire *island*," I said. "I mean, why not have a world's fair in one of the lovely neighborhoods on solid ground?"

"Like Bronwyn said, I think there was a sort of 'do it to see if we can' mentality back in the day," said Maya. "I read they dredged the dirt from the shoals of Yerba Buena Island, and had to cart it all the way out here. But they filled in areas of lower Montgomery in San Francisco proper, too, remember? Every once in a while, someone still digs up an old ship when they excavate for a new building or dig out a basement."

"I tell you what, you are from a fascinating part of the world."

"You're from here now, too, you know," Maya said.

"I like to claim it, that's for sure. But I'm not really from here, and my accent always gives me away."

I left Jarod, Texas, in the rearview mirror when I was only seventeen and had never had any desire to return. But lately my childhood home kept coming to mind. Maybe it was because the Aunties and my mother were in town, speaking in a comforting Texas twang. Maybe it was pure nostalgia. Or maybe I now had the strength to face a few personal demons.

Whatever it was . . . maybe I wasn't completely done with my hometown.

"Anyway, so far Treasure Island doesn't look so

bad," I continued as we progressed down Avenue of the Palms, studded with palm trees and stretches of grass. And everything paled in comparison to that stunning, unobstructed view of the San Francisco Bay all the way to Marin, the Golden Gate Bridge, the city, Angel Island, the hills of Marin, and Alcatraz.

As usual, my eyes lingered on Alcatraz a little too long. What was it with me and islands lately? I could only hope my experiences on Treasure Island would have nothing in common with those on the cursed penitentiary island.

"Can't beat the view, that's for sure," said Maya.

"Just imagine it with the orangey rays of the sunset coming through the Golden Gate. It must be even more amazing."

"It kind of goes downhill from here, if I remember correctly," said Maya as she turned right onto a smaller street. "I don't know much about the island's history, other than what we read back in the shop. There used to be a museum, but I checked and it's closed. No sign whether the closure is temporary or permanent."

In contrast to the meandering slopes of Yerba Buena Island, Treasure Island was large, flat, and rectangular, with few trees or bushes to interrupt the monotony. The streets ran straight and met at right angles in a grid pattern. Once we left the water's edge, we entered a more industrial area, passing a number of nondescript, flat-roofed buildings, many of them numbered: Building 496, Building 372, Building 234.

"Are these buildings mostly warehouses?" I asked.

"I think so. I know there are some businesses out here, and maybe the navy still has a presence? They still have signs up, anyway. According to the Internet, there's at least one winery, but I think it's near the marina."

Two very large buildings had been constructed as if

they were the spokes of a wheel. A smattering of cars in the parking lot attested to the presence of employees, but there were no signs to indicate what went on within. There were plenty of big rigs that appeared to be out of commission, and dozens of shipping containers were stacked on otherwise empty lots. Several cyclone-fence-enclosed empty lots sported the distinctive placard indicating radiation: a black dot surrounded by three spokes against a bright yellow background.

Built with the angular lines of 1930s- and 1940s-era architecture, many of the buildings were cordoned off with bright orange barricades or temporary fences, their windows broken or boarded up. Numerous road signs, barricades, and orange arrows directed drivers along detours, the construction projects seemingly abandoned halfway through. Most of the old docks and wharfs dotting the bay were falling apart.

Across from a well-manicured athletic field was a small grocery called the Island Cove Market. A tall, potbellied man in a Harley-Davidson T-shirt watched us go by, his head following our slow progress. He glowered at us, his beefy arms crossed over his chest as though willing us to leave. I looked away and noticed the water faucet on the athletic field was marked with a skull and crossbones.

"So what do you think of the place?" asked Maya.

"I know you and Bronwyn tried to tell me, but I kept picturing something like that casino in Vegas, or a Disneyland version of a pirate's lair. But despite the skull and crossbones signs, this is more . . ." I trailed off at the sight of another cyclone-fenced lot, devoid of anything except weeds and broad puddles of standing water.

"Like some apocalyptic zombie movie?"

"Sort of," I said with a chuckle. "I mean, of course

it's not as bad as all that. But it does have a rather abandoned feel to it, doesn't it? It's a study in contrasts: hot tubs with incredible views, the beautiful Avenue of the Palms, followed by abandoned buildings with broken windows. But I suppose a lot of cities are like that. Some areas are fabulous, and then you take a turn and suddenly it's a different story. Like Oakland: I didn't realize how nice it is until someone showed me around."

"Here's the place I found on the Internet, Aracely Café," Maya said, pulling over to the curb. "I could get used to the parking situation here, that's for sure. When's the last time you parked right outside a restaurant in downtown San Francisco?"

I was glad not to have to use my parking charm; I always felt vaguely guilty about taking someone else's parking space. I tried to make myself feel better by targeting gas-guzzlers, but it was still wrong. I sighed inwardly. Now that I was part of a community, it was harder to use my magic for personal gain.

We had a scrumptious lunch on Aracely's verdant patio, sharing plates of fried Brussels sprouts with a green onion remoulade; a burrata, squash, and onion tart; and a slice of olive oil and lemon cake with mascarpone cream for dessert. All in all, a meal to rival any café in the city. The friendly waitress could not tell us much about the World's Fair, but did warn us away from the areas with radiation contamination. The museum was closed at the moment, she confirmed, then suggested we check out the winery, and pointed out the magnificent views. Other than that, she did not seem inspired to suggest we visit anyplace else on the island.

Upon leaving, we drove around neighborhoods full of flat-roofed, two-story buildings that might have once been military barracks. A playground was cordoned off with yellow caution tape.

"Do you suppose it's closed due to the radiation, like our waitress suggested?" I asked. "Or are monkey bars simply considered too dangerous for kids nowadays?"

"Hard to say," said Maya. "But there's nothing quite like an off-limits playground to put one in mind of the end of the world, is there?"

Near the water on the east side of the island, we drove past a motorcycle repair shop. A man who had been hunched over a workbench straightened and watched, unsmiling, as we passed.

"Gotta say, the locals don't seem pleased to see outsiders," said Maya. "Or is it just me?"

"The waitress was really nice. And the food was great."

"And it was *so* easy to park."

"So you keep saying," I teased.

"Maybe I've been driving in San Francisco too long?" Maya laughed. "Anyway, here we are: 182 11th Street."

"And just look at all the available parking!" I teased.

We gazed out the Mustang's windows at the home of the late Marcellus Tinley.

"A modest little abode," said Maya, with her characteristic understatement.

I had been expecting a house, nothing fancy, maybe just a small, postwar bungalow. The reality was a shipping container with rust and dents, a door and a window punched into one side, and a window box of dead flowers.

"This is it?" I asked, skeptically. "Are you sure?"

"According to my research, it is."

"I went to a restaurant in Dogpatch that was made out of a shipping container," I said. "People can get really creative."

"Based on what we're looking at, old Marcellus Tinley isn't striking me as especially creative, at least not in that way. But maybe the inside is more . . . tended to."

"Suppose anybody's home?" I asked, seeing no signs of life.

"Doesn't seem like it," Maya replied.

"I'm going to look in the window," I said, reaching for the door handle.

"Lily! You scofflaw!"

"Just a peek."

"Should I bother to suggest you leave this to the police?"

"I'm not going to break *in*. I just want to get a sense of who Marcellus Tinley was. Should there happen to be a clue lying out in plain sight as to why he was in Aidan's office, then all the better."

"Okay, but if we get arrested for trespassing, I'm going to blame you and throw myself on the mercy of the court. Consider yourself warned."

"Sounds fair to me."

Gravel crunched underfoot as we got out of the Mustang and walked across the weed-filled front yard. If not for the mailbox, the door, and the window, I would have assumed this was an abandoned shipping container like all the others we'd seen.

Seagulls squawked overhead, and the breeze off the ocean carried a familiar briny scent. And then came another sound: cooing.

"Do you hear that?" I asked.

Maya nodded. "Doves, maybe?"

I approached the front door and knocked. I had reconsidered peeking in the window without announcing myself. What if Marcellus Tinley was married or lived with someone? I didn't want to scare a grieving spouse coming out of the shower.

"Hello?" I called out. "Anyone home?"

No response.

So I went to the window and stood on tiptoe to peer inside. There was no curtain or shade, but the bright sunshine outside made it hard to see the dim interior. I cupped my hand to my face to block the sunlight and spotted a crystal ball, numerous stones and crystals, and candles strewn everywhere. And, on the floor, several books on witchcraft, and what appeared to be a salt circle.

"Baby witch," I murmured.

"A what, now?" said Maya, who was standing behind me and looking up and down the street to make sure we didn't get caught.

"I think Marcellus Tinley may have been a budding witch. There's a book on candle magic for beginners, but it doesn't look like he knew what he was doing. The jasper is set too near the dragon's blood resin, for instance. That'll never work."

"Oh, yeah, you never want to have the jasper too near the dragon's blood," Maya said wryly.

"I'm just saying . . ." I laid my palms on the glass. "I could be wrong, of course, but if he had been a powerful witch—one advanced enough to carry his familiar with him, for instance—I think I would be able to sense . . . *something*. When practitioners transition and leave this earthly realm, our sitting magic kind of . . . looks for a place to land, for a lack of a better phrase. I'm not feeling it here."

"You'd be able to feel it, even from the outside?"

"I think so. Where is that cooing *coming* from?"

We circled around the shipping container to the rear yard, which was as desolate as the front except for a well-worn path through the weeds that led to a large pigeon coop.

"How interesting," I said. "Seems Marcellus Tinley was a pigeon guy."

"Awww, they're cute," said Maya, then wrinkled her nose. "But they don't smell very good."

"Looks like the cage could do with a good cleaning. But that's hardly the birds' fault."

Hung on one side of the cage was a framed informational poster: "*Columba livia domestica*, or the common pigeon, is derived from the rock dove, the world's oldest domesticated bird. They have played important roles to humanity, especially in war, and have been awarded the Croix de Guerre and the Dickin Medal for their heroic service in saving human lives."

"Wait, Marcellus Tinley died night before last, right?" I said. "I wonder if the birds need food or water?"

"Poor things," Maya said, trying the latch on the main door of the cage. "It's locked."

"You see a key around here anywhere?" I asked, opening the lid of a nearby bin, which held a big sack of birdseed, but no key.

"Hey! What are you doing?"

Chapter 10

Maya and I jumped and flailed a bit, exhibiting our signature coolness under pressure.

Tall and strong-looking, a girl with box braids was standing with three other teenagers sporting athletic gear, two of whom had skateboards under their arms and tattoos.

"Sorry, we were just . . ." I trailed off.

"Marcellus isn't here," said another girl, this one petite, with long blond hair in a loose bun on her head.

"We know that," I said, pulling myself together. "I'm Lily, and this is Maya."

"I'm Shanda," said the girl with box braids.

"Y'all live here?" I asked.

"Yeah, we live nearby. Marcellus hasn't been around for a coupla days so we've been feeding the birds."

"Oh, good," I said. "I was trying to figure out how to open the cage."

"It's right here," said Shanda, opening up the frame

that held the informational poster and taking a key from the back. "Marcellus says to hide things in plain sight."

Shanda opened the cage. The birds fluttered and squawked but did not try to escape. She reached in and filled the birds' feeders, then changed their water.

"I'm Cece," said the blonde. "What do you want with Marcellus?"

"I just had a few questions," I said. "How well do you know him?"

"Well enough. He's all right, lets us hang out here," said another girl, with a short brown pixie cut. Shanda and Cece nodded.

"Hang out and do what?"

"Don't ask me," said the only boy in the crowd. I noticed a can of spray paint peeking out of his jacket pocket. "He likes the girls, not guys."

"C'mon, Antwan, he isn't that bad," said Cece.

There was some snickering and poking in the ribs.

"What kinds of things do you do with Marcellus?" Maya asked, an edge to her voice. "Or do I want to know?"

"Naw, it isn't like that," Shanda said. "Mostly we like, feed the pigeons and stuff. Did you know that during World War Two pigeons carried messages that couldn't be sent any other way?"

I nodded. "I've heard that."

"Plus, they're cute," said Cece. "Marcellus likes old stuff like that; he doesn't even carry a phone, can you believe that?"

"Are you serious?" said Maya, giving me a side-eyed look. "Who doesn't carry a phone in this day and age?"

"Right? Doesn't even have a landline," said Antwan. "Says the pigeons are all he needs, and phone calls are usually telemarketers anyway."

"Marcellus promised to take us to Burning Man," said the pixie cut girl.

"Aren't you a little young for Burning Man?" Maya asked.

"Age is just a number," she scoffed.

"Also, he's like into crystals and witchy-type stuff," Cece said. "So that's fun."

"Was he a witch?" I asked, inwardly cringing at my bluntness. *Way to be subtle, Lily.*

"He's like, searching, I guess?" said Shanda. "That's what he said. But why are you talking about him in the past tense?"

"I . . . I'm sorry to tell you this, but Marcellus Tinley passed away."

"*What?*" exclaimed Cece. "No way."

"Are you being serious right now?" demanded Shanda. "What happened?"

"A heart attack or something?" asked Antwan.

"He *was* pretty old," the pixie cut girl said.

According to Carlos, Marcellus Tinley's driver's license revealed he was fifty-five. Not old unless you're a teenager. *So much for age is just a number*, I thought wryly.

"We're not sure about the cause of death," I hedged. "It's still under investigation."

"You're police?"

Skeptical eyes ran over my sundress, sweater, and Keds. Maya was dressed in one of her mother's reproductions from the 1960s, a pair of patterned pedal pushers and a sleeveless button-up shirt, and her favorite walking sandals. We did not exactly look official.

"Like, undercover, or whatever?"

"It's sort of hard to explain," I said. "So, Marcellus kept pigeons? Did you ever see him with a bat?"

The group laughed.

"Marcellus wasn't exactly athletic," Cece said.

"Are you talking about a baseball bat or a flying mouse?" asked a newcomer, who seemed slightly older than the others. His head was shaved and he wore a T-shirt and jeans, but where the others sported a few small tattoos, this fellow had ink on every exposed inch of skin, with the exception of his face. His words were friendly enough but his tone was not, and he radiated something menacing, like a young man who had done time. The others had stopped talking, and I noticed Shanda rolling her eyes and looking away.

"Hi, I'm Lily," I said. "This is Maya."

"Zane. You're looking for a bat?"

"Not exactly. We—"

"Marcellus isn't here."

"Yeah, we were just—"

"So maybe you should leave."

We had a bit of a staring contest. The newcomer's pale eyes and shaved head reminded me of some of the young men from my hometown, highly unpleasant individuals who did not enjoy diversity of thought on their best days; on their worst, they believed in that Old Testament adage: "*Thou shalt not suffer a witch to live.*"

"Okay, we're just touring the island," I said. "And sorry about Marcellus."

"Whatever," said Zane, not sounding particularly broken up.

"Well, it was nice meeting all of you," I said, and Maya and I headed toward our car. I looked back to make sure Zane wasn't following and noticed the other teens were coming over to join us.

"Ignore Zane," said Shanda. "He's a jerk, likes to scare people. Can you tell us what happened with Marcellus? I mean . . . I can't even."

"I don't know much, I'm afraid. Like I said, the police

are looking into it. It's possible his death was an accident. I hate to ask this, but . . . did Marcellus use drugs?"

"Only natural stuff, like pot and maybe peyote or whatever," said Cece. "Nothing, like, hardcore."

"He said something about wanting to try licking those psychedelic frogs," said Pixie Cut. "But I think it was just talk. Like Cece said, nothing hardcore. Are you saying he OD'd?"

"I honestly can't say," I said. I had probably said too much already, and doubted Carlos would be pleased. I wondered whether the police had been here yet. There was no police tape up, but then since it wasn't a crime scene there wouldn't be. "What can you tell me about the 'witchy' stuff Marcellus was into?"

The girls looked at each other, then Shanda spoke. "The way he explained it to me was that he had been on a spiritual quest for a long time and was taking a course in paganism. You know, the power of nature and crystals and stuff. He thought he could speak to his pigeons and they like, understood him. I really . . ." She blew out a long breath, and I saw a sheen of tears in her dark eyes. "I really can't believe he's gone."

"I know," I said. "It's hard, especially when it's so sudden."

The others nodded.

"Did Marcellus cast spells?" I asked.

"Um, sort of? I mean, I guess he tried?" said Cece. "He had a book on candle magic and an encyclopedia of witch stuff, but from what we could tell he didn't seem to know what he was doing. I think he was just learning."

Sounded like a baby practitioner, all right. Not someone who would have a familiar.

"So, you never saw him with a bat?" Maya asked. "Not the baseball kind, the flying kind?"

They shook their heads.

"Why do you keep asking about bats?" Antwan asked.

"Just curious," Maya said.

"I think that's, like, a stereotype? About witches?" Cece's statements often sounded like questions. "Just 'cause he was into Wicca doesn't mean he had bats."

"So true. So, are you all islanders?" I asked, changing the subject.

They nodded.

"It's kinda weird, right?" said Shanda. "Like we're officially San Franciscans, but most people who live in the city have never set foot on the island."

"Everybody drives through the tunnel and just keeps on going," said Pixie Cut.

"And if they do get off the freeway, they treat us like it's a zombie island or something," Cece said.

"That's not nice," Maya said, looking a little guilty. "Though parts of the island do seem a little . . . abandoned."

"I know. There's not much to do here," Cece said. "But the Number 25 bus takes you into the city, ten minutes with no traffic. We have an elementary school here, but we go into the city for high school. Good views, though."

"Beautiful," I said, looking out across the wide expanse of bay.

"My grandma lives here, so I've been here my whole life," Antwan said with a shrug. "All I know is when we were kids we couldn't play in the dirt, like, and we're not allowed to plant things."

"Not at all?"

"If you do, you have to bring in clean dirt and plant in beds aboveground. When I was a kid I used to think it was so weird that my nana had to buy dirt. Like, it seems like something that should be free, you know?"

"And parts of the island are still off-limits because of the contamination," said Pixie Cut. "No one's allowed in there, even though some of us go anyway."

"Didn't the contamination happen a long time ago?" I asked. "It's still a problem?"

Maya nodded. "From what I read, these things linger. Half-lives, and all that. The residents have to bring in potable water, too, like they do for Alcatraz."

The teenagers nodded.

"Some of us think some of the signs have been tampered with lately," said Shanda.

"In what way?"

"Just the usual," she said. I noticed the can of paint in Antwan's pocket, the paint stains on clothes and fingers. Graffiti artists, I presumed.

"So, are any of these buildings from the original Golden Gate International Exposition?"

"Maybe the museum building? But most of the stuff you see in the old photos is gone," said Shanda. "It was mostly removed when the navy took over."

"I heard they dumped a bunch of it into the bay," said Antwan.

"Why would they have done that?" I asked.

"My mom says people didn't really think about the environment back then," said Pixie Cut. "Which means it must have been pretty bad, 'cause it's not that great today."

"That's whack," said Shanda. "Ever hear of John Muir, or Ansel Adams?"

The others shook their heads.

"I'm just saying, some people thought about it back then," said Shanda. "Maybe not as many, though. No Greenpeace, or Sierra Club or whatever."

"Hey, could I ask you guys a weird question?" Maya asked.

"Oh-*kay*," Shanda said slowly. "Depends on how weird."

"Were there synchronized swimmers at the World's Fair on Treasure Island? Maybe dressed in mermaid costumes?"

"Probably," said Cece. "There are mermaids on the posters, anyway."

"What posters?" I asked.

"The elementary school kids on the island used to go to the museum every year and learn about the World's Fair," Shanda explained. "They had a bunch of pictures and old posters and stuff."

I thought of the photos Maya had shown me. Surely there were more; now that I had a sense of the place, I wanted to see them, if only to imagine what the Golden Gate International Exposition was like, back in the day. It must have been something, though soon over-shadowed by the outbreak of World War II.

"You should talk to Nimue," Cece said. "She uses mermaids in her art and stuff."

"Who's Nimue?" I asked.

"She's married to Leo," said Shanda. "He's sort of like the unofficial mayor of Treasure Island."

"What do you mean by 'unofficial' mayor?"

"Like we said, Treasure Island is part of San Francisco, so our real mayor's the same as yours," said Pixie. "It's just that San Francisco kind of forgets about us."

"The 'redheaded stepchild,' huh?"

"The what?"

"Never mind," I said. "Something my mother used to say." Probably no one said that anymore, at least not here.

"Anyway, Leo's okay," said Cece. "He owns the motorcycle repair shop and has plans to develop the island. He's always going on about it. Says it'll improve things."

"My mom doesn't like the idea," said Shanda.

"My dad doesn't either," said Antwan. "But my nana says maybe we could make some money on the house and get out of here, go someplace better."

"Someplace you could grow vegetables right in the ground?" suggested Pixie.

"Like you've ever grown a cucumber in your life," Shanda teased with a smile.

"I'm just saying, if I want to grow vegetables, I should be able to," Antwan said. "Right?"

"Yeah," Cece agreed. "I mean, little kids should be able to play in the dirt and make mud pies. It's kind of creepy that we never could."

"What would development entail?" I asked, recalling what Bronwyn had said.

"I guess they've tried a few things, like building the towpath and planting the palm trees," Pixie said. "They renovated a couple of the old military housing units into condos, but there's a lot of opposition."

"I can't decide if I like the idea or not. But I don't think it really matters, 'cause I'll be long gone by then," said Shanda. "I want to go to college next year. I hope I get in."

"You'll get in," said Antwan, and they shared a smile.

"Anyway, it's really a shame there aren't many of the old buildings left," said Shanda. "Back in the day, they had a bowling alley and a skating rink and everything. The only one still standing is the big old pool building, but it's been empty as long as I've been alive."

"Now that would be interesting to check out," I murmured to Maya.

Maya gave me a Look.

Shanda overheard me. "It's right over there. We go in all the time. There's no alarm or anything. We can show you, if you want."

"Really?" I said. "Thanks."

"This doesn't sound exactly kosher," Maya frowned as we walked toward a large, hangar-like structure attached by a breezeway to a small office building that appeared to still be in use. In contrast, the actual natatorium looked abandoned. Several high windows had been broken, and the exterior walls were peeling and cracked. "You're seriously going in there?"

"It's not dangerous or anything," said Cece. "It's kind of fun to walk around and imagine how things were, once upon a time."

"But it's trespassing, right?" said Maya, gesturing toward a large NO TRESPASSING sign in neon orange against a black background beneath metal letters that spelled out NATATORIUM.

"I'll be quick," I said. "You can wait out here, if you want."

"Oh, sure, then *I'm* the one who gets eaten by zombies," said Maya. "I've seen the movies."

Antwan snickered. "It's not like there are *actual* zombies."

"I'm not taking any chances. Better an arrest for trespassing. Besides . . ." Maya cast a jaundiced eye at the broken windows in the warehouses, the newspapers wafting down the street, the general air of dereliction. "It doesn't look like there's a whole lot of law enforcement on patrol."

"We're, like, mostly left to our own devices out here. Kinda like the Wild West," said Pixie Cut. "That's what I like about it."

"That, and pretty low rents," said Shanda.

"And nice views," added Antwan.

"And easy parking," Maya added.

The four teenagers led us around to the back of the building, where a door was propped open by a brick.

"This was, like, the stage entrance," said Shanda. "The front door's kept locked, but the back door's been like this for a while, and nobody from the offices up front seems to have noticed. But you have to keep the door open, like this. If you shut it, it'll lock you in."

Antwan nodded. "My brother got locked in once. Said he had to go out a window on the second floor."

"How did he do that without getting hurt?" Pixie Cut asked.

"Said he made a rope with some curtains and rappelled down." At the skeptical looks on the girls' faces, Antwan added, "It could work."

The rear entrance opened onto a short corridor with a few doors on each side. The air was stagnant, almost sepulchral, and it was dim inside, the only source of light from the open door behind us.

"If you go through that next door, there's a light switch to your right," said Shanda, pointing. "It's connected to the offices in front, so the electricity still works. Anyway, we should be going. If I get caught in here again, my mom says she's gonna spend my college fund on a trip to Hawaii."

"Oh, okay . . ." I said, watching as Shanda headed out the back, the others trailing her. "Thanks for showing us."

"No problem," said Shanda. "Hey, wait, what are you—"

There was some shouting and what sounded like a scuffle.

"Zane, *don't*!"

The back door slammed shut, plunging us into darkness as black as obsidian.

Chapter 11

As we banged on the door from the inside, someone outside kicked it, hard.

"Serves you right!" the young man sneered. "Have fun!"

"Lily?" Maya said softly.

"Right here," I replied, reaching out. Our hands touched, and we held on to each other. "You okay?"

"I'm fine," Maya replied, her voice strained. "However, I should warn you of my very recent discovery that total darkness makes me extremely uncomfortable."

"I hear you," I said, then began to giggle nervously. "Get it? 'Hear' you, because I can't see you?"

"Now you sound like Oscar," Maya said, sounding calmer. "Know any good fart jokes?"

"I'll work on it," I said.

"I don't suppose you have a flashlight in that backpack of yours?"

"That would have been smart of me, wouldn't it?

For the moment, let's see if we can find that light switch Shanda mentioned."

Together we shuffled slowly down the corridor, feeling our way along.

"You okay?" I asked. "I don't think it's much farther."

"So far, so good. This would be easier if you had a cell phone, you know."

"Where's yours?"

"Left it in the car. It didn't occur to me we might get locked in. Clearly, I have a limited imagination."

"Well, nobody's perfect," I said, then stopped, groping at what felt like a switch plate on the wall. "I think I found it."

"Sure it's not a fire alarm?" Maya asked. "The only thing worse than being caught trespassing in the dark would be inadvertently summoning the fire department."

"Oh, I don't think we have to worry about that," I said. "Do you think Treasure Island even *has* a fire department?"

"I noticed a firefighter training center on the map, as a matter of fact."

"Oh. Well . . . if it does bring the fire department, they'll get us out of here. I'll take a ticket for trespassing over being trapped in total darkness, no question. Anyway, here goes." I held my breath and flipped the switch.

A few dusty lightbulbs overhead cast an anemic glow that broke through the darkness.

"I have never been so happy for forty-watt bulbs in my life," Maya said, banging on the closed rear door. "Hey! You guys! A little help?"

"They said it locked when closed, remember? And even if they wanted to help," I said, squatting and riffling through my backpack, "I'm guessing Zane has them intimidated."

"What are you looking for?"

"An amulet," I said, standing and slipping it over her head. "It's a pomegranate design, symbol of Persephone. Bringer of strength in the darkness."

"Is this literal darkness, or figurative?"

"Both. Darkness is often associated with evil but is also the place of creation: a seed grows in the dark, a baby in the womb, spells work best when performed in the middle of the night, the entire universe is dark beyond our star."

"Uh-huh. I'll stay with the light, if you don't mind. But anyway, thanks for this," Maya said, patting the amulet. "And what about you?"

"I've got my medicine bag."

"Is there anything else in that backpack that might be useful? Like a set of skeleton keys, or maybe a sledgehammer?"

"I really should start carrying such things around, shouldn't I?"

"In the meantime, what say we get gone? I'll check the rooms on this side of the hall, and you check the other side."

We tried the doors lining the corridor, but found only former supply closets and empty windowless offices. If Antwan's brother had indeed rappelled out of here, it wasn't from any of these offices.

"Lily, take a look at this," Maya said, standing in an office doorway.

"A phone?"

"Not so much, no."

Inside, tacked to a large corkboard on the wall, was a poster portraying the pool in its heyday. Beautiful young women in old-fashioned swimming costumes were perched on the edge of the pool and high diving boards. At the center of the pool, her arms raised as though in victory, a young woman with green hair was dressed like a mermaid, her tail splashing the water.

The poster declared: "Come revel in the magical display of swimming synchronicity, by Ingeborg 'Nixe' Nachtnebel and her Bathing Beauties, all the way from the Black Forest!"

"'Ingeborg Nachtnebel'?" asked Maya. "A nice Irish girl, I'm guessing."

"I had no idea the Black Forest was home to mermaids," I said. "Isn't it, like, a forest?"

"One would think."

"Anything else of interest in there?"

Maya shook her head as she rummaged through the drawers of an old metal desk. "No phone, and the drawers are empty. Well, at least we have a starting point; when we get back, I'll see what I can find out about Ingeborg Nachtnebel and the Black Forest Bathing Beauties."

"Nothing on my side of the hall," I said. "Time to leave."

Maya nodded. "It was awfully easy to get in through the back, surely there must be other ways out."

A wall sign engraved with POOL pointed toward a set of double doors.

"Seems the pool's that-a-way," I said. "I don't know about you, but I'm kind of curious now."

"Too bad it's not still in use," said Maya. "It could have offered these young people something to do, besides leading innocent visitors to the island into underground traps."

We pushed through the double doors, which opened onto a metal staircase that led down to a huge hangar-like room, at the center of which was a massive empty swimming pool.

"I guess . . . nowhere to go but down, right?" I said.

"Let's do this," Maya agreed, and we started down. "Figures we have Zane to thank for this little adventure. He looked like trouble."

"He did. I try not to judge by appearances, but . . ."

". . . but if you shave your head, cover yourself in ink, and act like an ass, people might think badly of you," Maya said. "Fashion choices aside, just acting like an ass will do it, as a matter of fact."

"When we were all back by the pigeon coop, did Zane give you the impression that he already knew Marcellus Tinley was dead?" I asked.

"I thought so, too," Maya said. "Maybe he overheard us talking about it. Or maybe there's a more sinister explanation."

"Just because he's an ass doesn't mean he killed Marcellus Tinley."

"True enough. But what about the swastika?"

"What swastika?" I asked.

"The one tattooed on his forearm," Maya said. "You didn't notice?"

"I noticed he was tattooed just about everywhere but his face, but I didn't pay attention to the actual designs," I said. "Maybe . . . could it have been part of an Asian design rather than a Nazi symbol? You know, a throwback to the Buddhist tradition of swastikas?"

"Does Zane strike you as a Buddhist scholar? Somehow I think the Nazi interpretation makes more sense."

"You're probably right," I said with a sigh. "He's clearly troubled—and trouble."

Our steps rang out on the metal treads as we descended to the pool deck. On one side were a pair of high diving platforms. Clerestory windows near the ceiling, though covered with grime, illuminated the pool area with natural light but did not offer an option for escape.

Despite the fact that we were, for the moment, trapped in an abandoned belowground pool, Maya and I toured the area with a sense of awe. The remnants of the old decorative tiles covering the walls hinted at what the space must have been like back in the day as sunlight splashed off the aqua and cobalt blue tiles, the metallic gold accents glittering. Dotting the walls were small alcoves that might have once held cloisonné vases or marble statuettes, the grandstands full of spectators thrilled by the divers performing their high-flying stunts and the costumed swimmers moving together in perfect harmony.

I could feel lingering spirits in this dim, almost ethereal hall. They sensed me, I supposed, and often reached out. But try as I might, I almost never understand what the ghosts want to communicate. Once or twice a spirit has been strong enough to appear to me, but in general I leave the necromancy to skilled mediums; it simply isn't in my wheelhouse. Oscar loves to tease me about it.

"This is really something," Maya whispered.

"It is," I whispered in reply. "I wish we could have seen 'the magical display of swimming synchronicity' with our own eyes, back in the day."

"You got that right."

"Why are we whispering?"

Maya chuckled. "I have no idea. It seems sort of . . . churchlike, or sacred or something, doesn't it? Or maybe I'm just feeling like a criminal. We really shouldn't be trespassing like this. Shanda's mom is right. Let's see if this door leads anywhere."

"There's an EXIT sign over it," I said. "That seems promising."

Maya tried the latch. "It's locked."

"Are you sure?" I asked. "Let's both try it."

We pushed, pulled, prodded, and kicked, but the heavy metal door didn't yield.

"Maybe we should look for some curtains to make a rope," Maya said. "That may be our best bet to get out of here."

"Not to cast aspersions on Antwan's brother, but I'm not sure I believe that story," I said. "Plus, I don't know about you but I haven't seen any curtains or even any windows to rappel from."

"People believe what they need to believe," Maya said. "And at the moment, I have a very deep need to believe that I can find some curtains, make a rope, rappel out a window, and walk down a building à la Wonder Woman."

"Well, let's go see what we can find, then." I looked around. "Look for something sharp or pointed, like a screwdriver. Or even a hammer."

"You have a plan in mind?" Maya asked.

"The hinges are on the inside of the door," I said, pointing. "See there?"

"Isn't that, like, a fire code violation?" Maya asked.

"Probably. But it's an old building," I said. "Nobody's used the pool in decades, so there would have been no reason to update it. If we can remove the hinge pins, we don't have to unlock the door, it will just fall off."

"Now, that's using the ol' noggin," Maya said. "Let's see if we can find anything to make that happen. I'll go this way, you go that way, and we'll meet in the middle."

In a deep alcove behind the high diving boards, I spied an interruption in the tile and realized it was another door, set flush with the wall and obscured by the tile work and shadows. I wondered if it might have led to a dressing area where the performers could quickly change their costumes between acts.

"Maya," I said. "I've found another door."

"Is it an exit door?"

"Probably not, but one never knows."

"I don't see a handle or knob," Maya said, coming over to join me. "Do you see a way to open it?"

"Let's try pushing the nearby tiles to see if there's a hidden spring lock," I said. For the next few minutes, Maya and I pushed every combination of tiles we could think of, high, low, and along each side of the door, without luck.

"Call me crazy, but now I am determined to open this thing," said Maya. "I just can't figure out how."

I felt around the seam in the wall made by the inset door. The opening was too narrow to get my fingers in, but maybe . . .

"Give me the car keys?" I said, and Maya tossed them to me. On my key ring was a large old-fashioned brass skeleton key that had opened the street-level gate to my apartment in Hong Kong, where I had lived before coming to San Francisco. I liked the key and had kept it as a souvenir. Now I slipped it into the seam at what I thought was probably the latch level.

"Latches are usually, what—about this far off the ground?"

"Usually."

Nothing happened. I moved the key up, then down. Still nothing.

"Maybe the door opens on the other side," Maya suggested.

I moved to the other side of the door and tried again, and this time I heard a *click*, and the door popped open half an inch.

Maya and I grinned at each other in triumph.

"I knew we could do it," she said. "There's no 'I' in team."

I took a step through the hidden doorway and felt

for a light switch. An overhead light illuminated the room, revealing a good-sized space. Whatever purpose this space had served originally, it now appeared to function as an informal lounge of some sort.

A sagging couch and a bench seat that had been removed from a car formed an informal seating area around an old crate, which served as a coffee table. On top of the crate sat several crumpled beer cans and an old beanbag ashtray piled high with cigarette butts. A few hard-to-read words were etched into the old wall plaster. A threadbare carpet of indeterminate color covered a portion of the room's concrete floor, and the walls were tagged with spray-painted graffiti here and there—several were illegible, but one read: WHITE POWER, another 14 WORDS, and another, BLUT UND EHRE. A half dozen or so folding chairs leaned against the back wall, next to an old metal music stand, and a small dorm fridge sat in one corner. The stench of tobacco smoke permeated the room. This space had been occupied, and recently.

"What was this used for?" Maya asked. "Band practice for racist chain smokers?"

I was struck by the low thrum of something malevolent. I could feel it in the soles of my feet, and the medicine bag at my waist issued a warning. I detected something salty, as I had with the mermaid costume. What *was* this place?

"Lily?" Maya said quietly, as she switched on a standing lamp to illuminate the far side of the room. It acted like a spotlight, highlighting an item hanging on the wall: a Nazi flag behind glass.

Unlike the rest of the room's ragtag furnishings, the shadow box was of high quality, the frame crafted from gleaming mahogany, with gold accents. The flag itself looked old; it was faded and frayed at the edges, and there was a burn mark on one corner as though someone had tried to set it on fire.

"What is this place? Some kind of Nazi clubhouse?" Maya whispered.

"It looks like it." I started walking around the room slowly, my hands open to vibrations. I felt the sensation of ants crawling up and down my spine, giving me goose bumps. A whisper of something pulling at my hair, and I sensed spirits reaching out to me. "Do you speak German? What does *Blut und Ehre* mean?"

"Since it's up there beside "White Power" and a Nazi flag, I'm going to guess nothing good," Maya said. "This place gives me the creeps."

"Me, too," I said. "But there's something about this flag . . ."

"It's a swastika."

"I get that. But there's something else, something more. . . . I want to take it out of the box and touch it to see if I can feel anything."

"I don't know if that's a good—"

The lights went off, plunging us into inky, absolute darkness.

"—idea," said Maya. "*Lily* . . ."

"Hold on. I saw a lighter on the crate, near the ashtray." I felt my way to the seating area, banging my shin on the heavy leg of the spavined couch.

My hands were shaking, and it took three tries to get it to light. Amazing what a tiny flame can illuminate in a room otherwise shrouded in black.

"Lily?" Maya asked. "Did you shut the door?"

"No."

"Neither did I. And yet, it's now shut."

I tried to ignore the hair standing up on the back of my neck. "So, we'll open it."

"How?"

There was no doorknob or handle on this side of the door, either.

"Well, that makes no dang sense at all." I kicked the door, my fear giving way to aggravation. "Who designs a door with no handle?"

"Is that really the question we should be asking?" Maya said. "Let's focus on how we're gonna get out of here. We don't know how long that lighter will last, and I don't want to be here when the Nazi Brownshirt Band shows up to practice. You sure you don't have anything of use in that backpack of yours?"

I shook my head. "Unfortunately, the brew and talismans won't help in this sort of situation. Next time I'll pack a hacksaw or something."

"Come on, let's try pushing."

Maya and I stood with our hands flat against the door and pushed. It didn't budge.

"You know, the strongest muscles in a woman's body are in her legs," Maya said. "What if we lean up against it and push off with our legs."

We leaned our backs against the door and planted our feet on the floor, knees bent. "Push with your quads, on three," Maya said. "One, two, three."

We strained and pushed and the door seemed to give a little but did not open.

"Let's try again. Third time's the charm," I said, and we lined up, backs against the door, feet planted firmly. "Ready?"

"Hey, what's this—"

The door flew open, and Maya and I tumbled to the rough tile on the pool deck.

"Ow," we said in unison, sitting up.

"What happened?" I asked, rubbing my scraped elbow.

"I felt a little doohickey sticking out of the wall near

the light switch," Maya said, her hands covered in scrapes. "So I pushed it. Probably should have mentioned that earlier."

"Well, at least we're out of the Nazi clubhouse," I said. "Let's take another look at the exit door. Maybe we'll find another little doohickey."

We got up and returned to the exit door that had defeated our attempts to open it.

"No doohickeys," Maya said.

"I am *so* over being locked in," I said. "Let's try it again."

Maya and I grabbed the door handle, planted our feet again, and pulled hard. The door was flung open and we fell backward, blinking as the bright sunlight poured in.

Someone was standing there.

Chapter 12

It was a nice-looking woman in her late forties or early fifties, her long salt-and-pepper hair wound in a messy bun. Dressed in a loose-fitting black tunic over pink polka-dotted leggings, with lots of chunky stone jewelry and a choker made of shells, she looked like an Earth Mother type, someone who might well have been a member of Bronwyn's Welcome Coven.

"The kids came to get me," she said. "Aren't you two a little old to be engaging in these kinds of shenanigans?"

"One would think," I said as we got to our feet. "We were . . . well, the truth is we were trespassing. We apologize. I'm Lily Ivory."

"Maya Jackson," said Maya, holding out her hand. "Nice to meet you. We really appreciate your rescuing us."

"I'm Nimue, resident Treasure Island artist and, apparently, den mother to a pack of teenaged miscreants," she said. "I'm sure you would have found a way

out, eventually. This place is full of tunnels and whatnot. But what were you doing here?"

"Following an ill-advised path, obviously," I said.

"I was just scared of zombies," Maya muttered.

"Maya and I have been doing some research into the
Golden Gate International Expo, and in particular the
synchronized swimmers," I explained. "The museum
is closed, so when the kids mentioned the pool, we
thought we'd check it out and, well . . ."

"A tattooed punk slammed the door on us," said Maya.

"Zane," Nimue said. It was a statement, not a question.

"You know him?" I asked.

"I do," she sighed. "He's my—he *was* my stepson.
My ex-husband's son."

Maya and I exchanged a glance.

"I hate to say this about any kid," said Nimue, "but
Zane might just be irredeemable." She shook her head
and blew out a long breath. "That's not right, of course
not. No one is irredeemable. Zane's still young, still
finding his way. And his father's choices have made it
hard for him, I know."

I didn't know what to say, so remained mute. My
father was in thrall to a *demon*, but somehow I had
managed not to follow in his footsteps. Then it occurred to me to wonder if the same could be said for
my half brother . . .

"Did Zane hurt you?" Nimue asked, her clear brown
eyes running over our disheveled outfits and scraped
hands.

"No, we sort of . . . fell." I wondered whether to con-
fide in our rescuer that we had found a creepy Nazi
headquarters in the pool house, but hesitated. There
was something very specific about that room, something I was going to have to think about . . . perhaps
over my cauldron. "We were trying to get a door open,

and then it did, and, well . . . it was a bit of a Keystone Kops routine, now that I think of it."

She chuckled. "Why don't you come to my studio? It's just down the street. Get you cleaned up, and I'll fix you a cup of coffee. Or maybe a stiff drink."

"That's very kind of you, thank you," I said. We started down the street, the expo buildings to the right, abandoned-looking warehouses on the left.

"Are you named after the Lady of the Lake?" asked Maya.

"I am!" she said, a delighted smile on her face. "Very few people get the reference."

"Arthurian legend," Maya said for my benefit. "Nimue was the Lady of the Lake who gave Arthur his sword, which then led to his reign."

"I'm not sure I live up to the name," said Nimue, "but I can always try."

"The kids mentioned you and said you know a lot about mermaids," I said.

"Ha, that's true!" She laughed aloud. "They call me 'the mermaid lady,' which I take as a compliment. You'll see why when we go in."

"I'm excited to see your studio," said Maya. "I go to the Academy of Art."

"Oh, I love that school!" said Nimue. "Have you met the ghost?"

"Um . . . sort of, as a matter of fact," said Maya, meeting my eyes.

I shivered, remembering my encounter with the ghost that haunted the bell tower of that old school. Me and ghosts. Not the best pairing.

Nimue paused in front of yet another vacant-looking metal building with numerous high windows, several of which were broken. As I looked up, a pigeon flew in through an empty windowpane.

Nimue followed my gaze. "Bored kids can get destructive. There's not a whole lot for them to do around here. They can't go to the winery because they're too young, and the café is too expensive and not really their style anyway." She hesitated, and a set of keys jangled as she unlocked a heavy padlock on the door. "I have no proof of who did what. But Zane's what my mother would call 'a bad influence.'"

The young people we'd met seemed more afraid of Zane than influenced by him, I thought, but refrained from saying.

"And voilà, my studio."

The old warehouse looked uninspired from the outside, but inside it was a different world. The industrial workspace was dusty and smelled of paint thinner, but it was enthralling. The mermaid motif was prominent: in a mural on the wall, and in the carvings and paintings everywhere we looked. A few mobiles, made of small drawings of mermaids, drifted on invisible air currents. Some were done in a primitive style; others were more fluid and highly refined. Some appeared sweet, others sexy, and still others were fierce and frightening.

"Please feel free to wash up in the utility sinks there, and I'll get the first aid kit."

"I'd love to wash up, but I don't think we're in need of first aid," I said of my scraped hands and arms. That pool deck had done a number on us, but I preferred to use my own mugwort salve at home.

"Nonsense," Nimue said, coming over to us with a well-stocked box of Band-Aids and antibiotic ointment. "Before turning to the life of an artist—my life of crime, as I like to say—I trained as a nurse. I wasn't really suited to it, but this much has stuck, at least. I can clean up the occasional boo-boo."

She knelt in front of Maya and dabbed carefully at

her scraped knee with a cotton ball wetted with hydrogen peroxide, then applied cream.

"This is really sweet of you," said Maya. "But I can do it myself."

"It's not a problem." A yapping sound alerted us to the presence of a little mop of a dog. "This is Gideon, but he goes by Giddy. Don't you, my little Giddy?"

"How do you do, Gideon," said Maya. When Maya first met Oscar, she had referred to him as "the other white meat." But he soon won her over, and she had since become quite the animal lover, even talking her parents into adopting an old hound dog named Loretta. "Your studio is amazing, Nimue. Truly. I'm impressed."

"As am I," I said, taking in the rich colors and textures.

"Thank you," she said, applying a large bandage to Maya's knee, then crumpling up the packaging to toss it in the trash. "Feel free to poke around. We don't get many visitors, even for Open Studios. It's hard to get people to come here from the city, even though we're so close as the crow flies—or as the mermaid swims! That's another reason I feel sorry for these kids. They may act like hooligans at times, but in large part it's because they feel isolated. My neighbor Marcellus and I tried to secure funding to start an arts program to get them into something productive, but . . ." She looked at me, and then at Maya. "What did I say?"

"I assume this is Marcellus Tinley, with the pigeons?" I asked.

She nodded, and looked up into the rafters, where a bird was cooing. "They've gotten a little out of hand."

"I'm sorry to tell you this, Nimue, but Marcellus has passed away."

She froze. After a beat, she whispered: "*What?*"

"He was found . . . actually, *I* found him, dead."

"I don't understand . . . I can't believe it. What *happened*?"

"I'm not sure and probably shouldn't speculate," I said, not wanting to stoke any island rumors.

Her face was sketched with worry. "Was it . . . drugs?"

"Did he have a drug problem?"

"I wouldn't want to cast aspersions. I just—I," she stammered, then shook her head. "He had a problem in the past, but he's been sober for quite a while now. For the last couple of years, he's been on a kind of spiritual quest, I suppose is the best word for it. I happened upon him once at the Purpose Church, here on the island, and then later spotted him at Yoga on the Labyrinth at Grace Cathedral on Nob Hill. I think he was searching for a faith, for something to believe in. But lately he's been under a lot of pressure, and sometimes old habits can pull us down when we're most vulnerable, if you know what I mean."

I knew exactly what she meant.

A long moment passed. I noticed Maya studying a series of photographs on a bulletin board.

"What's that a photo of?" I asked, more to cover the awkwardness than anything else.

"A massive statue of the goddess Pacifica," said Nimue. "She was the unofficial mascot of the expo."

"I've never heard of a goddess Pacifica," I said. I glanced at Maya, who knew more about the classical world than I. "Have you?"

Maya shook her head.

"I'm sure she was entirely made up," said Nimue. "It was an eighty-foot statue sculpted by Ralph Stackpole. The World's Fair employed scads of artists: John Wallace was a master carver of totems from the Haida people, and he carved right in front of an audience. It was really quite an ambitious event, but then again it *was* a

World's Fair, meant to introduce to the world the twin engineering feats of the 1930s: the Golden Gate Bridge and the Bay Bridge, which were completed just a year or two before the fair."

"What happened to all the art?" Maya asked.

"Tossed in the bay."

"The kids mentioned something about that," I said, "but I didn't know whether to believe them. Why would anyone do such a thing?"

"A lot of it was built out of temporary materials, just for the fair exhibits. Maybe some of it would have been incorporated into the airport that was supposed to be built afterward, but World War Two came along and the navy took over the site. A few murals and other items were saved—several are on display at City College—but a lot was thrown into the bay, to become the shoals of the new Treasure Island."

I thought of what Bronwyn had said, how attitudes toward building and destroying, toward environmentalism as a whole, had changed over the generations.

Next to the photograph of the goddess Pacifica was one labeled THE CAVALCADE OF FLAGS, which included the distinctive red, white, and black Nazi swastika banner.

"We saw a flag hanging in a room in the natatorium," I said. "A Nazi flag. I was shocked to see it there."

"Really? In the natatorium? I can't imagine how it ended up there," she said with a frown. "I remember hearing that some union members tried to burn the Nazi flag at the fair, but I can't recall the details. You know, long before the Nazis appropriated the swastika, it was considered a symbol of divinity and spirituality in ancient Eurasia."

"We were just talking about that."

"The Nazis developed a brutally efficient war machine, but were also into spirituality and the supernatural, oddly enough," said Nimue as she picked up a soft-looking paintbrush and ran the bristles along the top of her hand.

"I noticed Zane had a swastika tattoo," Maya said in a quiet voice.

Nimue grimaced. "I know. I try to convince myself it was an act of youthful folly. Anyway, like I say, I blame his father."

"How long were you married?"

"Not long, but too long, if you know what I mean. And then my ex screwed me in the divorce, which, I now realize, was entirely in character for him. I don't know what I was thinking, marrying that guy. Nothing will bring a woman down faster than love."

"Does he take an interest in his son?" asked Maya.

"Only when he has to bail him out of jail. Zane has never really been held accountable for his actions, so it's little wonder he thinks he can get away with anything. He's never cared for me, I can tell you that much."

"Where is his father now?"

"Don't know and don't want to know." She smiled and leaned in conspiratorially. "But I hear he's not doing well at all, and suffers from gout. Anyway, it's water under the bridge, and all that. I've remarried and we are infinitely better suited. If only we didn't argue about this ridiculous Treasure Island development project."

"What project is that?" I asked.

"Whether or not—and if so, how—to develop the island," she said. "I'm very much of two minds about it. My husband, Leo, sees only the positives, but I love our quirky little oasis. Maybe it's the artist in me. I hate to see the island overrun by high-tech folks with their expensive cars and huge paychecks, pricing the locals out. But we *are* cut off, and isolation has its own problems— just look at the kids. So in some ways it would be good to be better integrated into the life of the city, but in other ways . . ." She trailed off with a shrug and a rueful grin. "As you can see, I'm on the fence. I'm a Libra, have a hard time making decisions."

"You need a push, give me a call," Maya said. "I'm an Aries. We're decisive."

"I'll keep that in mind," Nimue said with a laugh. "You know, I didn't think to ask: What brought you out here to the island? Was it Marcellus's death?"

"Partly. But I have a vintage clothing store in the Haight-Ashbury," I said, handing her one of my business cards. "We found an old mermaid costume among some recently acquired garments. Maya was researching when and where such a costume might have been used, and came across a reference to a mermaid synchronized swimming event at the World's Fair—"

"In 1939," Nimue said, nodding. "That's so interesting! That's what started my fascination with mermaids. When I first moved here from LA, I found that poster." She gestured to a poster similar to the one we had seen, featuring Ingeborg Nachtnebel and the Bathing Beauties. "The images worked their way into my art, as such things are wont to do."

"A young friend of mine made me a beautiful drawing of a mermaid floating, dead," I said.

"Well, that's a disturbing thought," Nimue said, her forehead wrinkling. "I've never thought about mermaids *dying*. In the stories it's always the sailors who die, right? Except in *The Little Mermaid*—she died and became foam upon the shore. Anyway, listen to me go on about one of my favorite subjects! But tell me more about this mermaid costume: You think it's genuine?"

"We think so, yes," I said. "I've authenticated it as best I can, though I'm a vintage clothes dealer, not an expert in textile history."

"You know, when selkies lose their skin they leave them on the shore, and occasionally a human might happen upon it. . . ."

I smiled. "I meant 'genuine' as in true vintage rather than a reproduction. It's very much made of material, silk and cotton and wool and beads."

"But that's what mermaid skins look like here in our human world. They transform into things we can understand."

I couldn't tell whether she was being serious or not.

"There was a story about a mermaid at the fair," Nimue said. "A little girl who fell into the water claimed she was rescued by a mermaid and thus imbued with the power to heal."

"I read about that," said Maya. "Shirley-something. I remember because I thought of little Shirley Temple. Do you have any idea what became of her?"

"No idea," Nimue said with a shake of her head. "According to what I've read, she was quite the local sensation for a little while, but when the war began in Europe all eyes turned to Germany and Poland. So, you truly found a mermaid skin? I would love to see it."

"It's only a costume, Nimue. For one thing, it's Schiaparelli hot pink."

"Mermaids appear that way when they're out of the water," Nimue said. "Beneath the surface they are iridescent, and whatever color they were flashing when they leave the water stays with them on land."

Maya glanced at me, eyebrows raised, as if to say, *Can you believe this?*

I gave her a subtle shrug. I've seen a lot of strange things in my life, so I supposed it was possible mermaids were real. Still . . .

Nimue chuckled. "I see you're now wondering about

the state of my mental health. I truly do understand that mermaids aren't real, but it's *such* fun lore, isn't it? And according to the museum curator, there were rumors about the synchronized swimmers at the fair. It was said one or two real mermaids joined the group and afterward were sent back to Germany, never to be heard from again."

"Okay, setting aside the question of whether or not mermaids are real," said Maya with her patented skepticism. "*Why* would they emerge from their underwater paradise to join a synchronized swimming group?"

Nimue laughed. "It's said the merfolk, the females especially, are curious about humans. And some say that if a human falls in love with a mermaid, she has the choice to shed her skin for good and walk about on land when she so chooses."

"The fairy tales also say the mermaids earn a soul if they make a human fall in love with them," said Maya.

"That seems like a rather human-centric way of looking at things," said Nimue, and gave her dog Gideon a squeeze. "My little Giddy here has a soul. Or don't you think so?"

"Oh, I do," Maya said, holding her hands up in surrender. "I was just quoting the literature."

"As you probably know," Nimue said, "Mermaids were romanticized in later years. Originally they inspired fear."

"Is that so?" Maya asked, interested now.

"Oh, sure. And there weren't just mermaids, there were mer*folk*. Sirens were part bird, and very fierce. In Irish there's the Lí Ban, the Slavs had the rusalkas, the Thai Suvannamaccha. Ningyo from Japan, and of course the stylized Melusine that became the Starbucks logo," Nimue held up a to-go cup, stained with lipstick and marked in black ink with the name: Jane. She smiled. "Jane's my coffee name. Nimue seems a bit much to ask of baristas."

"My coffee name's Stella," Maya said. "I like to hear the baristas yell it. *Stellaaaaaaa!*"

I laughed. "Clearly, I have no imagination. I just go by Lily. The most they can do to mangle it is add an extra L." I wondered how Dragomir fared at the coffee shop.

"Anyway, listen to me go on and on about mermaids, when you came here to ask about Marcellus. You should really stop and talk with my husband, Leo Airey. He runs the motorcycle repair shop down by the water. He knows everyone on the island, and a lot more about history than I do." Nimue paused and appeared to choose her words carefully. "The thing is, we're a bit of an island of misfit toys out here. But the islanders are good people, if a little . . . different. And so was Marcellus."

"I appreciate that," I said. I knew far too well how often difference was interpreted as suspicious, threatening, even evil. Too many people in this world understood "strange" as "wrong." Many in the Bay Area were more open-minded, but not all. Not by a long shot.

"Also, the kids seem to enjoy speaking to outsiders, I imagine because they feel rather stuck out here. But just so you know, others may be less welcoming," she said. "Don't take it personally. Islanders tend to value their privacy."

Chapter 13

The mechanic's shop was large, located in what looked like an old military building. It was hard to believe there were enough motorcycles on a place like Treasure Island to support a business, but I supposed a top-notch mechanic might draw motorcyclists from San Francisco or the East Bay in search of his services. Several shiny, pretty machines peppered Leo's shop. They looked old-fashioned to my eye, and I wondered if he might be a collector or dealer of antique motorcycles. Other than taking an occasional ride on the back of Sailor's bike, I didn't know much about motorcycles.

Leo Airey was short, stocky, and strong-looking. In his dirty sleeveless T-shirt and stained jeans, he did not exactly cut a romantic figure. I would have pictured Nimue with a tall, rather dashing-looking character, but gave her points for looking past a man's outer shell. And for the alleged "mayor" of Treasure Island, informal or otherwise, Leo had given us a pretty chilly reception when we drove by earlier.

But when he spoke, his voice was deep and full of warmth.

"The kids came by and told me about you. Said you told them Marcellus Tinley died," he said with a frown. "Is that true?"

"Yes, I'm sorry to say."

He nodded thoughtfully, wiping his hands on a rag. "I thought they must have been talking about you. We don't get all that many visitors from San Francisco."

"We were told in no uncertain terms that the island is part of San Francisco."

"Treasure Islanders know that. Not sure the people in the city proper do," he said. "We tend to be forgotten."

"Is that what the redevelopment plan hopes to address?"

"Well, of course we wouldn't mind making some money from the redevelopment. But it's also about pull and status, I guess. If we had some nice condo developments, the good folks in city government would be more likely to listen to us."

"I gather Marcellus Tinley didn't agree?"

"He . . ." Leo hesitated. "I don't want to speak ill of the dead, and he and I knew each other for a long time. But yeah, there are some die-hard folks around here who aren't in favor of change. They tend to focus on the environmental issues, but I think they just like things the way they are. My wife's one of them. She's one of my biggest critics."

"She mentioned that."

"You've met Nimue?"

"Yes, she, uh . . ." I wondered whether to come clean

to him about snooping around the old pool. They'd probably discuss it tonight over dinner, anyway, married-couple style. "She helped us out. We had a bit of a run-in with Zane, her ex-stepson."

He made a snorting sound and tossed the dirty rag atop a pile that reminded me of our laundry pile at Aunt Cora's Closet.

"Most of the island kids are okay," said Leo. "They might look like a motley crew, and there are some issues with skateboarding and spray-painting graffiti and that sort of thing, but there's no real harm in 'em. They're just bored and looking to keep themselves entertained. Zane, on the other hand . . ."

He trailed off, looking out at the water, the sea breezes ruffling his thick brown hair. *The views truly were spectacular*, I thought as I followed his gaze. It was easy to see why developers would lust after this island, and certainly the city's housing crunch made Treasure Island's location and gorgeous views even more enticing.

Still, I was enough of a curmudgeon that I could understand those who preferred to keep the island as their little secret. If only it weren't so . . . abandoned-feeling.

"Anyway," Leo said, seeming to bring his attention back to us. "There are environmental issues, as I'm sure you're aware. We're awaiting the reports from the latest soil and water tests, which will make a big difference in where we go from here."

"Did anyone have a grudge against Marcellus? Might want to see him dead?"

He shook his head. "He's . . . he *was* a bit of an odd duck. Even for Treasure Island," he said with a charming grin. "An artist, to be sure, but lately he'd gotten into some kind of pagan something-or-other, and during the full moon last month he was seen dancing around a bonfire, naked."

"Sky-clad," I said. "It isn't for the sake of being naked so much as . . . a lot of Wiccans believe that clothing can interfere during a ritual."

"Wiccan, that's the word," said Leo. "I knew it was something like that. Anyway, the neighbors weren't wild about *that*. But like I say, Marcellus may have been a bit of an oddball, but he meant no harm."

"Can't say as I agree with that," said a tall, middle-aged man as he joined us. His hands were thrust deep in the pockets of his faded jeans, and he had a large potbelly and a belligerent expression. His face was jowly, and his head had a sprinkling of blond hair and male-pattern baldness. I remember seeing him scowl at us earlier when we drove by, looking for the café. "You ask me, he's far too friendly with underage girls."

Leo looked pained. "Come on, Orson, we looked into those allegations, remember?"

Orson glanced at Maya and me. "What do you two ladies want with that degenerate?"

"He's—," I began.

"Dead," said Leo in a flat tone. "Yesterday, or the day before."

"Yeah? Good riddance."

"Orson—," began Leo.

"How'd it happen?" Orson interrupted.

"We don't have details," I said.

"All's I'm saying is, we don't want that type here on the island. My girl—only sixteen years old—spent way too much time with that sort, as far as I'm concerned."

"You thought there was something inappropriate going on?" I asked.

"Any time a man in his fifties 'hangs out' with teen-

agers," growled Orson, "there's something inappropriate going on."

I didn't know how to answer that. Part of me agreed
with him, but it seemed unfair to make such accusations against someone who wasn't here to defend himself. Besides, I didn't want to agree with the unpleasant
Orson on principle. He reminded me of a middle-aged
Zane.

"Anyway," Orson continued, speaking to Leo. "I'm
here for my Harley. All set?"

"Yep," said Leo. "Key's hanging over the desk. We
can settle up tomorrow."

Orson looked us over again as he left.

"Ladies."

We nodded in reply.

"What will happen to the pigeons now that Marcellus is gone?" Maya asked Leo.

"Good question," said Leo. "The kids know how to
feed them and all that, so I'll make sure they're on top
of it until we can figure out what to do with them. I
don't suppose you want them?"

"*No*, no no no," I said quickly as Maya tried not to
smile.

"She's already got too many pets for a city apartment," Maya clarified.

"Do you happen to know—did Marcellus have a
bat?" I asked.

"Like, the animal?" asked Leo.

"Yes."

He shook his head. "Not that I know of. Is that even
legal?"

I had no idea. I didn't even know if Oscar, in his pig
form, was legal within the city limits, and had been too
afraid to ask.

"I always think of bats as vermin," said Leo. "Sort

of like the pigeons—what are they called? Rats with wings? But Marcellus really loved those birds. I suppose we could just open the cage, set them free."

"Please don't do that," Maya said. "Animals bred in captivity usually don't have the skills to survive in the wild."

"What about the parrots in San Francisco? You hear about them? A coupla people let their pets go free, and before you know it there's a colorful block of birds gracing the Presidio and Potrero Hill. They even made a documentary about it—it's a tourist attraction. See, that's what I'm telling you: I want to bring a little of that San Francisco magic out here to our humble Treasure Island. Maybe a flock of pigeons is part of that."

"Do me a favor and wait before you release them, will you?" said Maya. "They'll probably just come right back, anyway, since that's what homing pigeons do. I'll look into rescue groups, or petting zoos, or some such thing."

Leo agreed, we exchanged information, and then Maya and I headed back to the Mustang with audible sighs of relief. Maya was limping slightly from our foray in the natatorium, so I offered to drive on the way home.

"I'm not sure I'm a convert to island living," I said as I adjusted the seat and the mirror. "First Alcatraz, now Treasure Island . . . I guess I'm more a mainland-type gal."

Maya gave her low chuckle.

A few minutes later, as we pulled onto the crowded Bay Bridge and immediately slowed to a crawl, Maya said, "Okay, boss, give it to me straight. What's the deal with mermaids?"

"In what sense?"

"Any possibility they're real? I mean . . . after what

you told me about fairies and the woods-folk, my world is sort of spinning off its axis. Next thing you know you'll be telling me to beware of vampires."

"Vampires and werewolves are purely figments of overactive human imaginations."

I was almost certain, but just in case made a mental note to check with Graciela and her coven sisters. It wouldn't do to be caught unprepared.

"How come fairies are real but vampires can't be?"

"Fairies and sprites and that sort are related to the spirits of the natural world. And *maybe* unicorns and mermaids existed, once upon a time. But werewolves and vampires are figments of the human imagination, from fiction."

"Uh-huh," Maya said, not sounding convinced.

To tell the truth, neither was I. There was so much more in the world than I ever would have imagined, and I learned more every day. The magic never stopped . . . but neither did the wickedness.

We arrived at Aunt Cora's Closet just as Bronwyn and the Con were tidying up for the day.

"Welcome back!" Bronwyn said. "I can't wait to hear *all* about it, but now that you're here, Lily, I'm going to rush home and get ready. Duke and I are taking the Hornblower dinner cruise on the bay!"

"I'm going to pack it in, too, Lily, if you don't mind," Maya said. "It's been quite a day."

I handed Maya a small jar of my mugwort salve. "Not that I don't appreciate Nimue's first aid, but this will act faster. Apply it tonight and in the morning, and you'll be good to go."

"Thanks."

"And, Conrad," I said. "You're free to leave as well, if you wish. I'll be closing up in just a few."

"Thanks," said Conrad. "I have one more load to fold, and then I'll take off."

The Con headed into the workroom to tend to the day's final load of laundry while I settled in behind the counter. As I was going over the day's receipts, a woman came into the shop to ask me, as Aidan's proxy, to help her resolve a possible copyright infringement; someone had taken pictures without her consent and put a curse on them. On her heels came two other women, squabbling over magical territory. I was able to smooth things over and negotiate solutions, though this reminder of the pettiness and sheer unpleasantness among some magical folk depressed me.

I swore under my breath when I heard the bell over the door tinkle again, but this time it was my mother, Maggie Ivory.

"Mom!" I said, crossing the shop to give her a hug. "What a nice surprise. What brought you into the city today?"

"I spent the afternoon shopping for presents for my friends back home. The stores here have such fascinating items compared to the dollar store in Jarod! I can't stay long; the old school bus is supposed to pick me up on the corner at six so we can treat Calypso to some sushi for dinner. Do you have *any* idea how much sushi that coven can consume?"

"I didn't know you liked sushi," I said with a smile.

"Not sure that I do. To tell you the truth, I'm a little scared. I have never in my life eaten raw fish, and never wanted to. But I suppose travel introduces us to new and strange things."

"*Dude*," said the Con, joining us. "Hello Mrs. I. Don't you look nice this evening in that pretty scarf."

"Oh, thank you, Conrad, dear," said my mother. "How have you been eating?"

"Very well, ma'am."

She nodded. "Good to hear it. Lily, I just wanted to let you know that I've bought my plane ticket and will be heading home soon."

"Oh . . ." I said, disappointed. My mother and I had made our peace, but our relationship was still awkward, which wasn't surprising considering we didn't yet know each other very well—and our past was difficult. Still, I now knew I had her love and support, which was more than I'd had for most of my life. For the time being, that would have to be enough. "I didn't realize you'd be leaving so soon. Are you sure you can't stay longer?"

"I was really just waiting until you got back from your honeymoon, Lily," Maggie said. "I need to get back home, to my real life. And frankly, as much as I've come to appreciate the Aunties, I'm not sure I could handle the bus ride back to Texas."

I didn't blame her. The circuitous route the Aunties had followed from West Texas to San Francisco had made the trip at least twice as long as it should have been.

"I've always wanted to see you settled and happy, and now I have," Maggie said, taking my hand. "With a handsome husband who adores you, a circle of good friends, and a thriving business. You have grown up and become a wonderful woman, Lily. I'm so very proud of you, and I am so very sorry for not appreciating you long before this."

I felt a lump rise in my throat and shook my head. "We've talked about this, Mom. It's all good. *We're* good. What's past is past, and I, for one, am happy to leave it there."

"And I, for two," Maggie agreed with a smile.

"So, when's your flight? I'll drive you to the airport."

"No need. I don't like goodbyes."

"Still, you don't want the Aunties to take you on the bus, do you? You'll either miss your flight entirely or arrive so early you'll have to help housekeeping clean the terminal for the day."

"I don't have the flight information with me," she said. "I'll send it along. And now I have to go meet the Aunties on the corner, else I shall quite literally miss the bus."

"Oh. Okay. Enjoy the sushi," I said.

"Guess it's time for me to pack it in, too," said Conrad. "Good night, Lily, and thanks again. See you tomorrow!" Conrad turned to my mother. "I'll walk you out, Mrs. I."

"Thank you, dear."

As he held the shop door open for her, the bell tinkled overhead.

"Did you know I'm working here now? Lily gave me a job."

"Why, that's wonderful, Conrad," Maggie said, patting him on the back. "I told you if you put your mind to it, and stayed on the righteous path, you would be granted that which you desire."

Once again, I felt a twinge of jealousy watching my mother's easy interaction with Conrad. Where our relationship had been fraught from an early age, the two of them had immediately hit it off. Jealousy came in many forms; it wasn't a feeling I was proud of, but it was there.

I felt down and out of sorts as I finished closing up Aunt Cora's Closet and locked the shop door. I cleansed the place with saltwater widdershins, then used a smudge bundle deosil, feeling as though I were doing so by rote.

Still, even those simple motions made me feel more balanced, and I realized I hadn't been tending to my magic as I should. Time to get back on track.

Upstairs, the apartment was quiet. Sailor hadn't come home yet, and I wasn't sure where Oscar was, but I was happy to take advantage of the solitude. I changed into a black dress with large pockets and spent a while on the terrace, cultivating my plants, collecting snips of herbs and roots, and taking in the cool evening air. Winston wasn't in his box, but I placed some fruit in his bowl and refreshed his water.

Next I went into the kitchen and "fed" my medicine bag by adding fresh herbs and massaging oil and myrrh into the leather to keep it strong. I put my cauldron on the stove and began brewing more sobriety tonic for Conrad, as well as a general protection concoction. The rich scent of ginger and herbs assembled on the kitchen counter filled the air, and my tea grew cold as I lost track of time. The tinkle of glass as I mixed ingredients, the gentle sound of the potion burbling on the stove, and the fog rolling in outside calmed and soothed me.

I took a seat in the kitchen chair and pondered what else the elixir might need. Glancing at my growing collection of books on the kitchen shelves, I got up, the wooden floor planks creaking underfoot, and scanned the ancient tomes until, at last, I settled on my massive Book of Shadows.

Bound in butter-soft red leather, the pages had been turned so many times by so many hands over so many years that they were soft and pliable as fabric. The book connected me to the ancestors; it had belonged to Graciela, and to a long line of practitioners before her. She had gifted it to me when I left Jarod as a teenager, fleeing from small-mindedness. I had spent years wandering the world, searching for I knew not what, and the Book of Shadows was one of the few items I always carried with me. It was full of recipes and history, of spells and memories; many I cherished, others I wished I could forget but knew I must remember.

And occasionally my Book of Shadows held a new entry or spell that helped me address whatever I was facing.

I sat at the kitchen table and consulted the pages, looking up "*torana*," and portals in general. The entries affirmed what the Aunties had said: Any such doorways were symbols of rebirth and re-creation. And, of course, a closed door symbolized a blockage of some sort.

As with any kind of gateway between the earthly realm and the astral realm, the two sides must always be in balance; if a being goes through one way, another must come in the other direction.

Again with the balance thing. What else? I sat back in my chair and closed my eyes, trying to think of anything I might have seen on Treasure Island that seemed odd or out of place. The primary object was that Nazi flag, of course, but there was more.

I let myself think in terms of symbols. The skull and crossbones needed no explanation. But there were those two big buildings with six spokes. I found the sun sign, the equilateral cross within the circle. A simple line across a circle was the alchemical sign for salt, the upright triangle for fire, and the upside-down triangle for water. But there was no reference to anything with six spokes.

The trefoil—the sign of radiation—was not listed alongside any magical meanings, either, though the trefoil knot was associated with the common three-leaf clover; I had some in my terrace planters that I used in protection and prosperity spells. Come to think of it, the plants had nearly doubled in size since I left for my honeymoon.

I read: Trifolium pratense. *Gender: Masculine. Planet: Mercury. Element: Air. Powers: Exorcism, fidelity, love, money, protection, success. Clover blossoms are a fairy flower. Trifoliate leaves symbolizing the trinity; lucky "four-leaf-clover" symbolizing the cross and the four directions. May enhance psychic powers and detection of spirits. Can aid in ability to see faeries. White clover used to break hexes; red clover repels negative spirits. Used for: Love spells, protection magic, spirit communication, faerie communication, prosperity spells.*

So what did that tell me that I didn't already know? I made a note to include plenty of clover in my next batch of protection brew.

I paused, cocking my head at a bumping sound overhead. *What was that?* It stopped. Must be a squirrel on the roof.

Turning back to my Book of Shadows, I searched for references to mermaids.

Merfolk are not fish, nor are they mammals. They are elementals, spirits from the astral plane, and protectors of earthly bodies of water as well as all forms of marine life found within. Their communication is primarily telepathic, along with clicks, whistles, and pulses.

Mermaids tend to be more curious and willing to speak to humans than mermen. They can be ferocious and merciless, especially to those who lack respect and cause harm to the waters and the sea creatures.

It is said that if a mermaid takes mercy upon a child fallen overboard and saves her, said child would gain the gift of healing. In one case, when a girl's doll fell in the water and was "stolen" by a young mermaid, the mermaid's mother gifted the human child with a set of perfect pearls.

I jumped at the sound of scraping overhead, followed by a jangling, like a chain. *What in the world?*

Chapter 14

Oscar came strolling in and found me staring at the ceiling.

"Evenin', mistress," he said. "Whatcha lookin' at?"

"Oscar, what do you think is causing that noise?"

"What noise?" Oscar asked, opening the refrigerator. "What's for dinner?"

A loud boom rang out, and a little dust rained down from the light fixture.

"*That* noise."

"I figgered it was ghosts," he said with a casual shrug of his scrawny shoulders. "Now, with regard to dinner, how 'bout—"

"It's not *ghosts*."

"No offense, mistress, but you don't know a lot about ghosts. You couldn't even understand the one in the haunted hotel in Limoux."

"That hotel wasn't haunted."

"That's what I'm saying! How would you even

know?" He started chuckling, eternally amused by the notion that a witch might not understand ghosts. "Anyhoo, *Sailor* felt the one in Limoux. Say what you will about the man's taste in food, he's good at the whole spiritual dimension. Speaking of food—"

A loud rattling sound interrupted what would no doubt be a plea for cheese and carbs. Oscar made a spinning gesture with his oversized hand, a gesture I had always associated with someone being crazy. Now that I thought about it, it fit.

"Hear those rattling chains?" Oscar said, nodding. "Classic ghost move, that."

"That's only in old movies," I said.

"Yeah, well, where do you think they got the inspiration from?"

"You mean the ghosts inspired the movies, or the other way around?" I asked, then realized this was a ridiculous argument. I knew ghosts existed, but I had no desire to communicate with them. I had enough on my hands trying to communicate with the living souls that inhabited the same plane as me. I'd leave the spirits to Sailor and his ilk.

Another bump overhead, and a low hum of voices.

"Do ghosts speak, too? I thought they just moaned."

Oscar shrugged. "*That* sounds like cowans to me."

"The attic! Of course," I said, remembering at last what Lucille had said about an attic spanning our two shops.

"Where are you going, mistress?" Oscar said. "What about dinner?"

"Back soon!" I called over my shoulder. Lucille had mentioned there was no access from my building, so I went downstairs, out to the sidewalk, and next door to Lucille's Loft.

Lucille and her employees, mostly former residents of the Haight Street Women's Center, were preparing to close for the day, tidying up the sewing machines and sweeping up the scraps of cloth and bits of thread that littered the floor and worktables. Lucille's cleverly designed and well-made garments sold so well in Aunt Cora's Closet that we both make a nice profit. I paused to greet Loretta, the big old lazy hound dog, who thumped her tail when she saw me.

"Hi, Lily!" said Lucille, closing out the register. "How's everything?"

"I'm doing . . . okay," I said. "Maya and I had an interesting outing to Treasure Island today. Be sure to ask her about it. But right now I'm wondering: Is someone in the attic?"

"Sure, our landlord's up there. With Sailor."

"*My* Sailor?"

She nodded. "I assumed you were here to join them."

"I suppose I will, thanks."

"Just follow the back stairs all the way to the top," she said.

"Oh, by the way, could I take more of the discarded threads and fabric scraps off your hands to make my spirit bottles?"

"Of course," said Lucille. "Far better they go into spirit bottles than the landfill, I always say. I'll make you a bag."

The apartment above Lucille's Loft was occupied by two perfectly nice but rather reclusive women in their thirties who worked from home on some sort of Internet startup, or so I gathered. They accessed the apartment from the alley behind our buildings, and I had caught sight of one of them only twice and had never actually seen the other. Needless to say, I had never been invited in for tea.

The stairs led up to a second-floor landing, turned, and kept going. At the top of the second flight of stairs a door stood open.

"Hello?" I called out. "Sailor?"

"Hey there, Lily," said Sailor, appearing in the doorway. "You found us."

"I did, indeed. Hello, Khalil," I said to my landlord as I stepped into the attic. The eaves made for an irregular ceiling height, and because of the crossbars we had to duck here and there, but the space was surprisingly roomy. Or it would have been had it not been filled with stuff: stacks of cardboard boxes, old paintings and mirrors and frames, small side tables and assorted housewares. There was even a dressmaker's dummy, like in every classic movie. I thought of what Oscar had said, and wondered if this Hollywood convention had begun because, indeed, a lot of old attics contained mannequins. And ghosts.

"Wow," I said. "This is amazing. I had no idea there was this much space up here."

"The family has stored things here for years." A tall, nice-looking man, Khalil Singh was middle-aged and well-padded and spoke with a lilting British-Indian accent. He was also the perfect landlord: Though Lucille and I each paid a healthy rent, Singh could easily charge more—a *lot* more, given the prime location. But he seemed content with tenants who paid the rent promptly, took care of the place, and didn't make a lot of demands. He lived in Napa and did not enjoy coming into the city very often, so most of the time we left each other alone, to everyone's satisfaction.

"I thought you were raised in England," I said.

"Oh, I was, but my aunt and uncle came here from India, many years ago, and lived in this building, over their shop. Saved their money, eventually bought the two buildings. At the time, this was not considered a posh neighborhood, you know. I remember visiting them here, as a boy. There was a real sense of community, and everybody on the street knew everybody else."

"Really? I had no idea."

He nodded, and I thought I noticed a glint of tears in his eyes. "When my parents retired, they came and lived here with my widowed aunt, my mother's sister. That's one reason I've never wanted to let this place go, even though I could get a lot of money for it."

"I'm glad to hear it. A sense of community is important," I said, hoping to appeal to his better nature. If he decided to sell, or to double or triple the rent like so many San Francisco landlords had, we would be out of luck.

He nodded. "My mother would have approved of your shop, and Lucille's. She loved beautiful clothing and was a seamstress herself for many years in London. Those scraps of fabric and threads everywhere, downstairs? They remind me of her, of my childhood coming home after school. That trunk over there is full of her old saris, and some Western-style dresses she made."

"I was just telling Khalil that you might be able to sell some of the garments in your shop," Sailor said. "Assuming, of course, that he's ready to part with them."

"Do you think you could?" Khalil asked. "I really don't know what to do with them. They're no good to anybody stored away in that trunk, and my daughters have no interest in them. It would be nice to think they are going to a good home. And what about the rest of the things up here? My aunt and uncle and cousins have left many items. No one in the family seems to want them."

"I'll gladly take the clothes," I said. "But the other things look like they might belong in an antique store. Would you like me to help you find a place for them?"

"Would you?"

"I'd be happy to."

"Perhaps we could consider it as a percentage of the new rent?"

"The what, now?" I asked, meeting Sailor's eyes.

"Lily and I haven't discussed all this yet," Sailor said to the landlord. "But here's the basic idea, Lily: We could expand the apartment and create a bedroom like this." He sketched an area with his hands. "And this corner here, conveniently enough, is located directly over the existing bathroom in your apartment—"

"*Our* apartment," I corrected him.

"*Our* current apartment. My point is, a bathroom here would line up with the downstairs bathroom, so the plumbing would cost less to install. Khalil says he is willing to pay for the materials if I do the work."

"That sounds like a great idea. But do you . . ." I didn't want to cast aspersions on Sailor's abilities, especially in front of our landlord. But did my new husband have sufficient construction experience to do the job properly? Building a bat box was one thing. Renovating an attic into a living space was quite another. "Do you know how to put in a bathroom?"

Sailor held his hands up, as if in surrender. "I can fix a leaky faucet and rewire a lamp, but I don't claim any expertise in plumbing or electrical. That work will have to be done by professionals."

"It must all be up to code," said Khalil. "This is very important."

"Absolutely," I said, nodding.

"It's doable," Sailor said, sounding confident. "How hard can it be?"

"Pretty hard, I'm thinking," I said.

"So. How do you wish to proceed?" Khalil asked.

"Why don't Lily and I talk it over, take some measurements and get some materials estimates, and get back to you?" Sailor said. "Thank you for being open to the idea."

"Of course. And Lily, you will let me know what you think of the clothes, and the antiques?"

"I'm still catching up on a few things after being gone for several weeks, but I'll get to it soon," I said. "Is it all right if I come here and go through things over the next few days?"

"Indeed, yes, at your convenience. There is no hurry. Thank you, Lily. This is a kindness," Khalil said, handing Sailor a key to the attic door. "Every time I see my mother's things, I cannot decide whether to keep them or to throw them away, and I usually wind up feeling sad."

"I understand. I'm very sorry for your loss."

"Thank you. It has been many years now, and I am a grown man, and yet . . ."

And yet. Indeed. Mother stuff was hard.

Sailor and I followed Khalil downstairs and said good night. I picked up the bag of scraps Lucille had left for me on a workbench, and we returned to the now-closed Aunt Cora's Closet, locking up behind us.

"Well, you're quite the mover and shaker," I said as we took a seat at the workroom table. It would be easier to have this discussion without Oscar nearby. "I know you said you wanted to find a new living arrangement, but I didn't think you'd be moving quite this quickly. As the folks in my hometown would say, you've been as busy as a stump-tailed bull in fly season."

Sailor laughed. "When Lucille mentioned the attic the other day, I started thinking about the possibilities, and when I saw her this morning, she said the landlord was coming by. It seemed fortuitous, so I figured I'd take a look. I was pleasantly surprised to see how spacious it is."

"It'll be a lot of work, but it *would* solve our problem, wouldn't it? We could have more room without having to move. And I wouldn't have to give up the terrace or my plants. I love living here, above Aunt Cora's Closet."

"Exactly," Sailor nodded. "Oscar could have our former bedroom if he wants more space. Even *I* feel bad seeing him in that tiny cubby over the fridge. Or we could make it into an office, or a guest room."

"Or a library."

"Or a library," he said with a nod. "You're acquiring as many books as Aidan."

"You know, when I heard you two up there, my first thought was there were ghosts in the attic. Did you feel anything?"

He shook his head. "No lingering spirits. It feels good. I can pick up some sensations from all the things stored up there, but they're overwhelmingly pleasant. The Singh family seems like one of the lucky ones, hardworking but happy."

"Ghosts and construction sites . . . that reminds me," I said. "I know someone in the home renovation business."

"I doubt Khalil would be willing to pay the going rate for a construction company in this town. I also doubt *we* would be willing to pay the going rate for a construction company in this town."

"I'm not suggesting we hire a contractor. I just want to ask a few questions," I said. "And I'll bet she could recommend a good plumber and electrician. Her name is Mel Turner, of Turner Construction. Maya introduced us. As luck would have it, we met in a haunted attic."

"Think she'd be willing to help?"

"She came by the store not too long ago to get my opinion on a vintage dress. I imagine she'd be happy to return the favor." I made a mental note to give Mel a call and see if she had time to drop by for a quick consultation.

"Sounds like a plan, then," Sailor said. "Dinner? I'm starved."

"Now you sound like Oscar," I teased. As we started for the stairs, I grabbed the mermaid costume and brought it with us.

"Working on Halloween costumes already?" asked Sailor. "Oh, I get it. You'll be a mermaid because I'm 'Sailor.' Makes sense. You've bewitched me, all right."

I smiled. "I *hope* I have bewitched you, but this isn't for Halloween. I was wondering if you could read it, see if it tells you anything."

"I'll try, but fabric isn't my strong suit," he said as we climbed the stairs. "You might have more luck than I."

"I'm starving," Oscar said, meeting us at the door and tapping his foot as though he'd been waiting awhile. "What's for dinner?"

"Salad," said Sailor. "Maybe some tofu, if you're good."

"Mistress!" cried Oscar.

"Enough, both of you," I said. "Oscar, we'll talk

about dinner in a little while. Sailor and I are in the middle of a conversation."

"*Hmpf*," he snorted, and went back into the living room, where he was watching a horror movie. The sounds of shrieking and screaming emanated from the television, and Oscar kept covering his eyes with a pillow. On the coffee table was a massive bowl of popcorn, the fluffy white kernels glistening with butter.

"Anyway, about the costume," I said to Sailor. "I feel *something*, but I'm not sure exactly what. Will you try?"

I was purposefully vague, not wanting to influence Sailor's visions. When I felt vibrations from clothing, they were associated with feelings, but my psychic husband saw things in symbols, usually floral or botanical, which he then had to interpret. The notion seemed wildly romantic to me, but I also imagined it could be frustrating. In the past, Sailor's abilities had been fed and enhanced by his relationship with Aidan, and when their association dissolved, Sailor lost some of his abilities. Since then, he had been training with Patience to build them back up, and Sailor and Aidan were on speaking terms again, but with Aidan currently out of commission, I was unsure how Sailor's talents might be affected.

"Of course I'll try," Sailor said. "And if I don't feel much, you might ask Patience. She's good at this sort of thing, you know."

"That reminds me, I was going to ask if she or your aunt Renna could give me a tarot reading."

"Really?" Sailor said, surprise evident on his face. "You don't usually like to have your fortune read by anybody, least of all those two."

"I know, but Graciela—her entire coven, actually— think I should have a good reading, and Kay's chakras

have been blocked since an incident at the Exploratorium."

"What happened at the Exploratorium?"

"I was afraid to ask."

"Oh!" said Oscar, bouncing up from the couch to
join us in the kitchen. "I know this one! Auntie Rosa
and Kay were at the *Sip or Squirt?* display. You know,
the one where you have to decide whether to let your
partner sip the water from the water fountain or squirt
'em with it? Well, Kay decided to let Auntie Rosa sip,
but Auntie Rosa decided to squirt Kay, and the water
went right up Kay's nose, and she started snorting and
honking, you know, trying to get the water out, and
Auntie Rosa was laughing because Kay's all wet, and
then Kay got all upset because she said she should have
been able to trust her coven sisters, and then Auntie
Pepper said, 'Tough beans, kid, that's life,' and then the
rest of the Aunties chose sides, and Kay's still snorting
and honking, and then the security guards came over
and said, 'What's going on here?' and then the Aunties
started all talking at once, so the guards made everybody leave, and ever since Kay says her chakras are
blocked. Blocked by *water.* Get it?"

"Good to know," Sailor said wryly.

Disappointed at our lack of response, Oscar shook
his head and cackled to himself, then went back to his
movie.

"*Anyway,*" I said, picking up the thread of our conversation. "The *point* is, I need someone really good to
do the tarot reading, and I know Renna doesn't like me
much, but I think she's pretty good."

"All the show biz flourishes aside, she's the best."
He nodded. "All right, let me take this costume into
the bedroom for a little privacy and see if I can pick up
anything. Just think: If we add an upper floor to the

apartment, we could have all sorts of privacy. Just you and me."

Screams from Oscar's movie filled the room: "*No, no, no, no, no, please! Help! Aaahhhhhhhh!*"

A little privacy was sounding better all the time.

Chapter 15

"What's for dinner?" Oscar asked for the third time in fifteen minutes.

"I'm not sure, but if Sailor's cooking tonight, I imagine he'll insist on a higher proportion of vegetables to carbs than you are comfortable with. Good thing you just ate that huge bowl of popcorn."

"Popcorn isn't *food*," Oscar said. "It's practically all air."

"And the butter?"

Oscar blinked. "Why would you eat popcorn without butter?"

This is a question I've asked all my life. "Why don't you go finish your movie, and I'll root around the kitchen and come up with a couple of options. And then, I dunno, maybe you and Sailor can have a knife fight or arm wrestle or something to see who gets to choose."

"I can't hardly hear the movie, what with all that racket."

"What racket?"

"Sailor makes a racket when he goes into a trance."

"No, he doesn't. He's completely silent."

"Well, sure, silent on *this* realm. You're saying you don't hear that screeching sound?"

"I thought that was your movie."

"Ha!" He waved his hand in a dismissive gesture. "Not *that* kind of screeching."

I shook my head. "Maybe it's like they say, some sounds are silent to human ears but the dogs can hear them."

"You're calling me a *dog* now? I'm a *dog* in this scenario?" My familiar had a penchant for quoting from whatever movie or book he had just seen or read. In an attempt to steer Oscar away from horror movies, recently I had suggested the old classic *When Harry Met Sally*.

"Don't be silly," I said. Oscar did not like to be compared to a domesticated animal, no matter how adorable. "But maybe the noise thing won't be much of a problem in the future. Sailor was talking to the landlord about renovating the attic. If it works out, it would double the size of our apartment because the attic extends clear to the next building."

"He find any ghosts up there?"

"Nary a one," I said.

"It would be nice to have more room," Oscar said, looking thoughtful. "I know Sailor's your husband, mistress, and he's all right most of the time, but I ain't gonna lie: He's been kinda underfoot around here."

"I appreciate your tolerance, Oscar," I said, keeping a straight face. "You are a true gentleman."

He nodded. "S'okay. But still, a rehab project could be worse than ghosts, if you ask me. It's no fun living on a construction site. Take it from me."

"At what point in your life did you live on a construction site?"

"You kiddin' me? Those old castles need constant maintenance, amiright? Hey, Sailor! What's for dinner?"

I turned to see Sailor standing in the hall. He always looked a little vague after emerging from a trance, as if he wasn't sure of the time and place.

"Anything?" I asked.

"Yes—flowering eel grass. Murkiness. And tragedy."

Later, after a dinner of salad and spaghetti and meatballs, which had been decided upon after a lengthy and spirited negotiation, Sailor tried to explain what he had seen, and felt, in his trance.

"At first I saw seaweed and a lei, which is a sign of welcome. And flowering eel grass is one of the only flowers that blooms in saltwater. But then . . . I can't explain it, exactly, but my impression was something along the lines of an underwater cavern but with sunken artwork: totems and statues and carvings and the like. It could be I was influenced by the fact that it's a mermaid costume, but it felt like more than that. Then I saw several mermaids, floating in the water. They were dead."

"Selena drew me a picture of a dead mermaid."

He nodded. "I know, and it's possible I was influenced by that image as well. But there's something enticing, and yet very frightening, about that costume. I would not sell it, if I were you. You might consider burning it. Where did it come from, did you find out?"

Oscar scurried into his cubby. "G'night, one and all!"

I let out a sigh. "A dragon man gave it to Oscar in a city starting with a *B*."

"Excuse me?"

"When we were in Europe, my alleged brother, Dragomir, gave it to Oscar with no explanation, no nothing."

"Has no one warned Oscar about taking packages from strangers?"

"Oscar says Dragomir didn't seem all that strange, given how we humans are. Gobgoyle logic."

We heard a harrumph emanating from the nest of blankets over the fridge.

"But here's the thing: Maya and I went to Treasure Island today. Apparently, there were synchronized swimmers dressed as mermaids at the World's Fair there, in 1939."

"You think this costume comes from the fair?"

"Possibly. Carlos told me the dead man in Aidan's office lived on Treasure Island as well."

"That is quite the coincidence. Hard to imagine what the connection could be, though."

"Maya and I looked around the old natatorium," I said. "It's one of the few original buildings left from the World's Fair, and it's where the water shows were held."

"It's still open?"

"Not exactly."

"How did you get in?"

"It's a massive place, without a lot of security."

He had a pained expression on his face.

"I was with Maya," I said by way of a defense.

"I swear you're corrupting that young woman. There was a time when she was far too sensible to take part in such things."

"A fear of zombies was involved. *Anyway* . . . we found a secret room behind the high dive, a sort of Nazi clubhouse with an old Nazi flag."

"Has this room been closed up since the 1930s?"

"No, there were signs it's still in use. There was graffiti on the walls, and cigarette butts, and a mini-fridge."

"I don't like the sound of that."

"You're telling me. Sailor, the vibrations were incredibly negative. And there was something about that flag . . ."

"The Nazi flag has been associated with so much evil that it's not surprising it brought up some bad juju."

"Yes, but it wasn't just that," I said. "There was something else about it. . . . Unfortunately, the electricity cut out and we had to get out of there, so I didn't get a chance to touch it."

"I'm glad you didn't. With something like that, that kind of negativity and evil? If you weren't properly protected, it could lead to infection."

"I had my backpack with me, and my medicine bag. I would have been okay."

"Lily, I'm not trying to be patronizing, or an overprotective husband. But while you are wildly skilled in the area of magical mayhem, you are sometimes less attuned to the more prosaic evil of humans. Something like this, something entirely human and yet *in*human, can lead—*has* led—to some of the worst crimes on earth. Far worse than your average demonic force."

I nodded. "I'm getting that feeling."

"And you also know, far more than anyone, how human emotion can linger in cloth, especially if that cloth has been imbued with symbolic meaning."

I thought of Khalil Singh, reluctant to even touch

the clothes his mother left behind. To anyone else they would simply be old saris and dresses, but to him they represented maternal love and loss. I thought about uniforms and costumes, how by changing our clothes we change ourselves and the way the world sees us. I thought about what it meant to have a Nazi emblem tattooed upon one's skin, the ink injected under the epidermis, meant to last forever.

"You know, the Aunties have been talking about a '*torana.*' Have you heard that term?" I said.

"It's a kind of gateway, or portal, isn't it?"

I nodded. "Around here, of course, the natural gateway is the Golden Gate, where the bay and the Pacific Ocean meet." The coming together of bodies of water had a special significance in the natural world, just as the estuaries and deltas of rivers poured their fresh waters into the seas. "When we were on Treasure Island, I kept thinking it must be amazing to watch the sun go down between the Marin hills and the hills of San Francisco."

"You're thinking it's more than a spectacular view?"

"I'm wondering . . . could it be a portal of greater significance than the average mouth of the average bay? There's so much going on here in San Francisco, so much supernatural mayhem. And the World's Fair on Treasure Island was meant to celebrate and introduce to the world the Golden Gate Bridge, which had just been completed."

"As had the Oakland Bay Bridge."

"Could energies have been trapped here, somehow? Or the portal opened to something nasty? According to my Book of Shadows, when humans close off portals, the effects can be disastrous."

"That's true," Sailor confirmed. "It throws everything out of balance and allows evil to intrude on the human world."

"Such as?"

"Well, think about it: What happened right on the heels of the World's Fair?"

"World War Two."

Chapter 16

The next day, I fed Winston in his box on the terrace.

Marcellus Tinley seemed to be a baby witch at best, so had he simply kept the bat as a pet, perhaps believing he could communicate with it, like his pigeons?

I brought the mermaid costume and sobriety brew downstairs to Aunt Cora's Closet, stashed the costume in the back room atop the ironing board, and found Conrad sitting on the curb in front of the shop.

It reminded me of how, even before he got sober, he would sit there, a self-appointed "gutter punk" guardian of the store. My heart hurt for him, and I felt guilty for feeling even the tiniest bit jealous of his easy relationship with my mother. I still didn't know Conrad's full story, but I knew his parents had kicked him out of the house at a young age, and that the last time he tried calling his mother she refused to talk to him.

I was glad that Aunt Cora's Closet could offer a haven to him, at least.

I was about to run back upstairs to whip up breakfast for the chronically underfed young man when Maya arrived holding a steaming chai soy latte, and handed a bagel and a fruit smoothie to Conrad.

"I'm sorry, I didn't bring you anything, Lily," she said, entering the store. "I assumed you'd eat breakfast at home."

"I did, thank you," I said.

Oscar, lounging on his new chartreuse silk pillow, glared at me with huge piggy eyes, outraged at the idea of anyone passing on the offer of food.

Maya put her things away, took a seat behind the counter, and opened the store laptop. "I was looking for a mug shot of Zane," she explained. "But I haven't had any luck. We didn't catch his last name, plus he might well be a legal minor, in which case the records would be sealed. Not sure about that."

"Why are you looking for a photograph?" I asked.

"I thought you could show it to the ticket taker at the wax museum, see if Zane was there the night Marcellus died. Or better yet give it to Carlos, have him do it."

"That's really smart. Carlos said something about security footage so you're right, if we can tell him what Zane looks like, he might be able to determine if Zane was at the wax museum that night." I wrote myself a note to call Carlos.

"And the slogans we saw on the wall? *Blut und Ehre* means 'blood and pride'—it's a white supremacist slogan from the Nazis. The phrase '14 words,' believe it or not, refers to 'we must secure the existence of our people and a future for white children.'"

"I suppose since they were scrawled next to 'White Power,' I'm not too surprised. Plus the flag, of course." I let out a long sigh, saddened by this reminder that hatred and small-mindedness were alive and well, and that there were people carrying on this tradition even now, and in my beloved Bay Area.

"Hey, while you've got the search engine open, I was wondering," I said. "You know how those strange buildings on Treasure Island are shaped like a star-burst with six spokes? Any chance that could mean something?"

Just then Selena walked in. I had plumb forgotten it was Saturday, time for our weekly training session. I had arrived from Europe several days ago so could no longer blame my forgetfulness on jet lag; I would have to put my lack of focus down to working my way through that overly long to-do list that still rustled in my pocket.

"Hi, Selena!"

She did not respond.

"And you say, 'Hi, Lily and Maya and Conrad,'" I urged.

Ignoring me, Selena knelt by Oscar and whispered something to him.

"And hi to Oscar, too," I said, unwilling to cede the point.

Maya chuckled, shook her head, and tapped the keys of the computer. "Hey there, Selena. Um . . . how many spokes are there on the buildings?"

"Six," I said.

She read the screen. "Hmm, the sun cross, or wheel cross, is a solar symbol made up of a cross within a circle and is found in many prehistoric cultures. And, oddly enough, the same symbol is used as a modern astronomical symbol to represent Earth."

"But that's a simple cross, right?"

"Right. So it doesn't apply. Still looking. Let's see . . . the Sacred Hoop, also known as the Medicine Wheel, was used by the Plains Indians and other Indigenous peoples."

"Good morning, everyone!" said Bronwyn as she arrived at the store and went to her herbal stand to stow her bag. "Conrad, Maya, Lily, Selena . . . and Oscaroo! How is everyone? The Hornblower cruise was such fun last night! What are we talking about?"

"The symbolism of a cross within a circle," said Maya.

"How interesting," said Bronwyn. "In Wicca we call that the solar cross, and it represents not only the Sun but the four quadrants of the Wheel of the Year, corresponding to the four seasons."

"Okay, but Lily was actually asking about a spoked wheel," said Conrad, peering at the screen over Maya's shoulder. "It says here eight spokes makes the symbol of chaos. How many were there again?"

"Six," I said.

"*Dude*, the Imperial Crest was the six-spoked symbol of Palpatine's Galactic Empire."

"Was that in ancient Rome?" I asked.

"It's from *Star Wars*," Maya said with a roll of her eyes.

"Lily, you mean that despite watching all those movies on your transatlantic flights," said Bronwyn, "you *still* haven't seen *Star Wars*?"

I shook my head guiltily. Sailor was right: I knew a thing or two about the magical world, but the everyday human world was often beyond my ken.

"Care to explain it to Lily, Con?"

"*Dude*," said Conrad. "Under Palpatine's rule, Imperial domination resulted in the deaths and enslavement of millions of countless species throughout the galaxies. The Empire came to represent all that was evil in the galaxy, so the crest which used to be a symbol of unity and peace became a symbol of tyranny and evil."

"The man knows his *Star Wars*," muttered Maya. "I'll give him that."

"Interesting—I'll have to make a note to watch it."

"Which one?" asked Conrad.

"How many are there?" I asked.

"There are nine so far in the Skywalker saga, plus a coupla standalones and a TV movie."

"*Nine*? Um, could I start with the first one and whittle down the list?"

"Sure, but just so you know, the real first one isn't the first one, chronologically speaking."

"Clearly this will require some time and research to do it properly, which means back-burnering it for the time being," I said. "Maybe we should have a *Star Wars* Film Festival at some point."

"That'd be cool," mumbled Selena, who had taken a tray of jewelry from the display cabinet and started to shine the silver. Selena loved to polish things. She had a rare metal magic, and the pieces she worked on always sold well. Selena's touch imbued each item with a tiny bit of her energy, which people felt though most did not recognize.

Selena rarely displayed a preference or enthusiasm for much of anything, so I made a mental note to schedule a *Star Wars* festival, for real. Maybe it could be a shop event. I wondered what the licensing issues might be for something like that. . . . *Focus, Lily*, I reminded myself.

"But back to the buildings on Treasure Island," I said to Maya and Conrad. "I think the symbology is too general. And anyway, it was just a hunch. No worries."

"Hold on. Now, this is interesting," said Maya. "I noticed this before: When they started dredging to build Treasure Island in the 1930s, they desalinated the land. Aren't salts sort of important in your world, Lily?"

"I was thinking about that just recently," said Bronwyn. "How salts and crystals keep things balanced. Too much and you kill everything, too little and you're off-balance. Like electrolytes in the body."

"And like radiation," said Maya. "It gives us cancer but can also be used to *cure* cancer."

The Aunties said it was all about balance, Sailor had repeated that last night, and of course I knew that was true for witchcraft in general. Nothing happened in a void; there was always a price to pay, whether monetary, energetic, or spiritual.

It was high time I stopped dragging my feet and got my tarot read.

Time to call Patience Blix.

"*What*," Patience said flatly, when she answered the phone.

"Sorry. Did I interrupt something?"

"No, just in a bad mood. One of my clients this morning was being difficult. The only thing I don't like about making my living dealing with the public is dealing with the public."

"I hear you," I said. By and large I liked the customers at Aunt Cora's Closet, but there were always a few . . .

"Anyway, what's up?"

"I was wondering if you would do a tarot reading for me."

"Sure. Just give me their name and send 'em on over."

"No, I mean, it's for *me*."

"You?"

"Yes, me."

"I thought you didn't like anyone reading your cards."

"I don't. But Kay's chakras are blocked, and apparently it's necessary."

"How did Kay's chakras get blocked?"

"Trust me, you don't want to know."

"Let me guess: the Aunties in action?"

"Got it in one. Anyway, in one of their saner moments the Aunties recommended I get a tarot reading."

"Why? You planning on playing the lottery?"

"No, they think it might reveal something about the prophecy. How much do you know about that?"

I could almost hear Patience shrugging her elegant shoulders. "I know what everyone knows: that you're supposedly the Witch Princess of the Bay Area magical community, destined to save us all, or some such."

"I'm not entirely sure what it involves, either," I said. "I thought the showdown on Alcatraz was going to resolve everything for a while, but apparently that was just the appetizer. Thing is, my grandmother's coven has to go back home soon, and with Aidan gone, I'm feeling a bit at sea."

"Hmm. Listen, if it's that important—as in the future of San Francisco is involved, and all that—then you need a really straightforward, specific reading." She blew out a breath. "Our personal relationship will make it harder for me to read for you."

"Why is that?"

"I don't read for friends or family. Too much room for emotions clouding things."

"You mean it could cause bad feelings between us?"

"No, I mean personal feelings get in the way of clear readings."

"Oh." I was surprised to hear Patience talk this way. Though we had grown out of our early animosity, I always thought of her as a "sort of" friend.

"I should think Your Witchy Highness would know that already."

And that was why.

Patience continued, "I think Renna needs to do it."

Renna was Sailor's, and Patience's, aunt. Renna scared the stuffing out of me, but it went without saying there was no friendship between us to screw up a reading.

"Why? Now that we're family she shouldn't read for me, either, should she?"

"Oh, that's no problem," Patience said airily. "Renna doesn't like you. When it comes to readings, negative feelings don't cause complications."

I knew Renna didn't like me much, but it kind of hurt to have it confirmed. "Renna is a little . . . spooky."

Patience gave her husky chuckle. "She'd be pleased to hear that. A lot of what she does is *meant* to scare you. Not only does it enhance her mystique, but it keeps you off-balance, which makes it easier for her to get past your guard."

"I don't know. . . . Maybe I should think about it a little more." Allowing a powerful seer who didn't much like me to do a reading was starting to sound like a really bad idea.

"Oh, pishposh."

"Why are you channeling Mary Poppins? I'm all grown up, you know."

"Then stop being childish. You're part of the family now, Lily. Renna wouldn't hurt you, even if she wanted to. Which she probably doesn't, not really. She's just pissed because you captured the heart of her precious Sailor. Want me to talk to her, make an appointment for you?"

"'Want' is such a strong word."

Another chuckle. "Tell you what: I'll make an appointment, and we'll go together. In all seriousness, Lily, if the Aunties say you need a reading, then you need a reading. Isn't that what you would tell me?"

Dangitall. "Thank you, Patience."

I hung up and dialed Carlos Romero. I got his voice mail, so I left a message about a suspicious fellow named Zane and asked him to call me back.

Finally, I called Mel Turner, contractor and reluctant ghost whisperer. Mel sounded pleased to hear from me and agreed to take a look at the attic and give us a realistic idea of what the renovation would entail.

"I'm having dinner with a bunch of architects in Chinatown tomorrow night," Mel said. "Which, believe it or not, is more fun than it sounds. How about if I come by after? Eight thirty, nine at the latest?"

"That's perfect. Thank you, I appreciate it."

After lunch, Maya and Conrad tended to a steady stream of customers while I showed Selena how to create spirit bottles in the back room.

"Spirit bottles are meant to keep negative spirits or bad influences away from your house," I said. "Sometimes they're filled with sharp metal objects, such as needles."

"Cool. I like metal."

"I know you do, sugar-pie," I said. "And any needles you polish will have an extra-strong influence. In the old days, the bottles were sometimes filled with urine."

"Ew!"

"I know, right? But people used what they had back then. Now they're sometimes filled with vinegar. But the one we're making today is packed with short pieces of thread." I brought out the bag of scraps Lucille had given me. "The idea is to create a dense maze to confuse the spirits so they can't get past the bottle."

"You could stick some needles in there, too," said Selena.

"You certainly could," I said, sensing a theme.

"These threads and bits of fabric and fluff are from Lucille's shop next door. Because they come from a positive place of creativity, they'll exude a little of that magical energy as well."

She nodded. Selena had a hard time focusing on her lessons in school, and was severely lacking in social skills, but when it came to magic, she had a true thirst for knowledge.

"As always, with any kind of magic . . ."

"I know, I know," she waggled her head. "The most important thing is to focus my intent."

"Exactly. Why don't you try creating a spirit bottle while I tend to more paperwork."

We worked side by side for a while, accompanied by the occasional tinkle of the bell over the front door as customers came in to browse, Oscar's hooves tapping on the broad-planked floor as he sought their attention, and music from the 1920s and 1930s emanating softly from the sound system. Maya rang up purchases, Bronwyn mixed herbal teas, and Conrad steadily worked his way through the piles of laundry.

I sighed in contentment. If it weren't for an unexplained death, a Nazi clubhouse and its flag, and slogging through paperwork, all would be well. Oh, then there was my alleged half brother to think about, and the prophecy, and the fact that I was going to get my tarot read by Renna . . .

Selena announced: "I'm finished."

I inspected the bottle. It was neatly done: packed with threads, at least one needle, and a couple of silver charms. I held it in my hands and felt her intent: a little sloppy, a little all over the place, but it was there.

"Very good. Now, come help me with a few things in the attic?"

"'Kay."

As we walked next door to Lucille's Loft, I said: "I've been wondering whether your drawing might be a mode of divination for you, Selena."

"What's that mean?"

"You draw what's on your mind, right? You drew lilies before we even met, you drew islands when we were dealing with Alcatraz, and then you drew a mermaid."

"A *dead* mermaid. I've done more drawings like that."

"I'm not sure how to interpret them, Selena, much less how to put your sensitivity to its best use, but we should think about it. Maybe ask the Aunties, or Aidan, when he's feeling better."

We walked through Lucille's busy shop, saying hello to everyone, and then proceeded up the back stairs to the attic.

"When's Aidan coming back?" Selena asked.

"I'm not sure. Soon, I hope. But he was badly injured, and healing can't be rushed. It takes its own time."

"Aidan has a *vila* chasing him, you know," Selena said.

"Who told you that?"

She shrugged. "What's that like? To have a *vila* chasing you?"

"I don't really know. But I imagine it's harrowing. Sort of like being pursued by the Furies, which follow people around after they've committed a crime, never letting them forget."

"Like, nightmares and stuff?"

I nodded. "Other people might call it a 'guilty conscience.' There are a lot of hard choices to make in life, and sometimes we make the wrong ones. Sometimes it's out of greed or anger, but other times it's because we're humans and humans make mistakes."

"But we're not regular humans, are we? We're witches."

"Witches are just as fallible as anyone else, I'm afraid. More so, in some ways, because we have to navigate the magical world as well as the human world and learn how to mesh the two. It's not easy."

"I've been training with the Aunties," Selena said, her eyes lighting up. "They're really cool, and funny."

"And powerful. You've had quite the immersive training during your slumber parties at Calypso's house."

"Calypso's pretty cool, too. She's sad, though."

"Well, some people have reason to be sad. And others are melancholy by nature. The important thing, as their friend, is to be supportive and never, ever, try to talk them out of what they're feeling."

"'Kay," she said, apparently done with this discussion. "How about these old dresses? You want them for the shop, too?"

"Yes. Let's bring the boxes down to the store so we can go through them there."

We navigated the stairs with a box in each hand, and Conrad joined us to bring down the rest. It took three trips, and each time I entered the attic I grew more certain: Sailor's plan was sound. The space felt good. Solid, a little quirky under the eaves, but calm, with a pleasant hum of the happy family that had once lived in this building.

Back in Aunt Cora's Closet we opened the boxes and spread out the clothing. Soon the shop looked like the inside of a stereotypical gypsy caravan, with all the bright colors and textures. We admired the bright pinks, greens, and oranges of the silk saris, and the swirling patterns of the complex paisley designs. The late Mrs. Singh's "Western" dresses were equally beautiful; they appeared to date from the 1960s and 1970s, and blended London chic with a traditional Indian aesthetic. Clearly Khalil's mother had been not only a seamstress but a talented designer as well.

Absorbed in the beautiful clothing, I glanced up and was shocked at the sight of a tall, potbellied man glowering at us through the shop's front display window.

Orson. From Treasure Island.

Chapter 17

"Check out this one, Lily," Maya said, holding up a mod, multicolored Twiggy-style dress. Noticing my stare, she followed my gaze and grimaced.

We stood, wary, our hands dangling loose by our sides, as if preparing for an old-fashioned shoot-out.

Orson made no attempt to come into the shop, but Leo Airey did.

"Wow, some place you have here," he said, looking around. Dressed in a fine-quality suit and tie, with his hair slicked back, he looked like a different man. "Am I interrupting something?"

"No, not at all," I said, relaxing. "I got some new things in and we were looking through them."

"What's with the pig?" he asked.

"Dude, Oscar's a Vietnamese potbellied pig," said Conrad. "He doesn't bite or anything."

"I'll just put this stuff away," volunteered Maya. "Conrad, give me a hand?"

"Thanks," I said, as she and Conrad gathered up the

richly colored fabrics. I glanced at Orson, still peering into the shop and looking as malevolent as ever.

Leo shook his head ruefully. "The ever-charming Orson refused to enter such a 'girly establishment,' I believe he called it. Ignore him. We came to town to meet with the owner of a motorcycle shop in South San Francisco, and Nimue asked me to drop her off in the Haight to do some shopping. When we saw your store, I thought I'd stop by. Do you have a minute to talk? In private?"

"Of course." I led the way into the back room, and we sat at the jade-colored linoleum table. "I'm surprised to see you here."

"I did some snooping around," Leo said, leaning back and looking relaxed. "And learned you've been working with Aidan Rhodes. In fact, standing in for him while he's on sabbatical."

"I, um . . ."

"You should know that I'm in the Satchel."

"You are," I said, more as a statement than a question. *Dangitall*, when was Carlos going to allow me access to Aidan's things, such as the Satchel?

"I would so appreciate it if he, or you I suppose, could help us with the governmental agencies investigating the environmental issues out on Treasure Island. This can't wait until Aidan returns. You have the mayor's ear, don't you?"

"I'm sorry to say that, because of Marcellus Tinley's untimely death, I haven't had access to Aidan's office, or his things there."

"Why not?"

"It's a possible crime scene."

"Crime scene?" He cocked his head in surprise. "I assumed it was an accident of some kind. Marcellus died in Aidan's office?"

I nodded. Although Leo had been polite to me and

Maya, the fact that he was hanging out with Orson put me on edge. I did not want to discuss the circumstances surrounding Marcellus's death, and I was fairly certain Carlos would not want me to, either.

"Do you have a prospectus of some sort?" I asked. "A report pointing out the pros and cons of development on Treasure Island, the investment opportunities, community impact, that sort of thing?"

"I gave it to Aidan."

"Then it will have to wait until I get back into his office and can go over everything."

"I can send copies if that will speed the process."

"Thank you, that would be helpful." I handed him my business card with the shop's e-mail on it.

"And you'll help?" Leo's gaze was steady, his manner open but pushy. A salesman.

I wasn't sure I *wanted* to help. Was magic meant to be transactional, a service people paid for? That's how Renna and Patience made their living, and I tried not to judge them for it. Many people used their natural talents to support themselves. But I had never felt comfortable doing so, which was one reason I opened my vintage clothing shop. Besides, I had no intention of facilitating a condo development on possibly contaminated soil. Also, there was the whole out-of-balance thing, and the portals to worry about.

But neither did I want to flat-out reject Leo until I knew if Marcellus had been murdered and by whom. So I said, "I'll look into it."

"I honestly think Aidan Rhodes would be pleased to help," said Leo. "He said as much before he left town."

"Send me the documents, and I'll look into it," I repeated.

He gazed at me for a long moment, as if confident

he could convince me to do as he asked. Never mind
that we were both small-business owners: I was a
younger woman in a vintage sundress, and he was an
older man in a suit. In my experience, men such as he
were accustomed to women like me deferring to them.
But in this case the advantage was all mine. Leo just
didn't know it yet.

"Really, Lily—"

"I'm *so* sorry to cut you off, Leo," I said, standing to
signal this meeting was over. "But I'll have to show you
out, unless you'd like to peruse the merchandise. I'm
tutoring a young friend today."

"Now you sound like my wife."

"Your wife and I are fond of young people."

He grunted, but followed me out to the shop floor,
said goodbye, and left. I watched through the window
as Nimue met him on the sidewalk. They spoke briefly,
exchanged a quick kiss, and Nimue came into the shop.

"I think I may owe you an apology," said Nimue.
"Was Leo being an ass? He gets single-minded when
he's talking about that damned development plan. He
and Orson have a lot of money invested in the idea."

"It's fine," I said with a diplomatic smile. "I told him
I'd see what I can do. So, Nimue, let me introduce you
to my friends and coworkers: You know Maya, of
course, and this is Bronwyn and Conrad. Everyone, this
is Nimue, whom Maya and I met on Treasure Island."

"You were holding out on me," said Nimue, looking
around the shop. "You said you sold vintage clothes,
but I had no idea it would be such a wonderful shop! I
should bring the girls here with me next time—and why
am I being sexist? Antwan, too. I see you carry men's
clothes as well."

"We like to say there's no strict division," I said.
"People can wear whatever they like."

"Brava! I like that way of thinking." Glancing around as if nervous to be overheard, she dropped her voice. "Leo mentioned you work with Aidan Rhodes."

"I do, sometimes. I'm currently filling in for him while he's out of town."

She cleared her throat. "Does that mean . . . that is to say, it probably sounds silly, but . . ."

"She's a witch," said Selena, suddenly materializing next to me.

I frowned. I had been trying to impress upon my young charge that one simply did not go around announcing that one was a witch. I respected Selena's directness but feared for her. My traumatic experiences as a young witch haunted me, and so my default was discretion, if not out-and-out secrecy.

"*What?*" Selena demanded. "You *are* one. A *good* one. Probably the best in the city now that Aidan's—"

"*Out of town*," I insisted.

"Whatever." Selena shrugged. "Why don't grown-ups say what they mean?"

"Selena, let me introduce you to Nimue. Nimue, this is Selena."

"That's a weird name," said Selena.

"It refers to the Lady of the Lake from the legend of King Arthur," said Nimue. "And your name refers to the moon."

"It does?"

Nimue nodded, not at all put off by my charge's abrupt manner.

"Selena's an artist," I said. "Selena, why don't you get some of your drawings? Nimue's also an artist and is fascinated by mermaids."

"I've been drawing those lately, too," Selena said, darting off and returning with a stack of drawings. Usually she was shy about sharing her art with strangers.

"Oh, well, now," said Nimue. "These are fine, just fine."

"Just 'fine'?" Selena asked, looking insulted.

"As in 'fine' art," said Nimue. "You have real talent here, Selena."

"I've never taken lessons."

"You don't need to. A true artist will sit in a corner and draw on a rock with a chunk of charcoal if that's all she has to create her art. But if you are ever interested in lessons and are willing to come out to Treasure Island—the Number 25 bus goes out there—let me know. I would love to work with you."

Selena's eyes shone, her flat affect softening. "Thanks."

"You're welcome. Lily knows how to get in touch with me. Now, I'd like to speak to Lily in private for a moment, if you don't mind."

Selena nodded. "I have to go anyway. I have to help my *abuela* in her shop."

"Tell her hi from me," I said. "And could you ask her for some *epazote* and more *milagros*? Maybe you could bring them with you next time?"

Selena's grandmother ran a *botánica* in the Mission. She was an accomplished apothecary, but her granddaughter's strange talents were too much for her to handle, which was why she had asked me and Aidan to help with Selena's magical training. In exchange, she was a wonderful source for certain herbs and magical items.

"'Kay." Selena gathered up her drawings and left.

"I wanted to ask a favor," said Nimue slowly, as though choosing her words carefully. "It's a long story, but . . . I'm feeling a bit . . . harassed. I'd like to keep someone away. I've heard you're able to help with that sort of thing."

"There are protection and banishing spells that can help with that."

"Could I hire you to do one for me?"

"Selena's right, I am a witch. But my business is vintage clothes. I sell amulets and witch's jars, but I don't sell my services. However, I can refer you to a number of excellent practitioners. My friend Hervé Le Mansec, for example . . ."

I trailed off as I watched Nimue's face fall. "No, that's all right. I enjoyed meeting you the other day, and when Leo discovered your reputation, I thought maybe I would ask. Don't worry about it."

I thought about how nice Nimue was to Selena and to the other island kids. Anyone who could deal with sullen teenagers—indeed, appeared to *enjoy* dealing with sullen teenagers—got an A in my book.

"You know," I said. "A personal protective spell is usually most effective if you do it yourself."

"Oh, I don't know about that. . . ." She looked wary. "I wouldn't have to kill an animal or anything, would I?"

"Land sakes alive, no!" I said with a laugh. "I was thinking of a freezer spell, which helps to freeze someone's negative speech or actions against you."

"That sounds . . . interesting."

"It will also freeze someone out of your life, so don't use it if there's any chance of reconciling. It's serious defensive magic."

"Gotcha. Do you have time to tell me about it?"

"Of course. Maya, I'm going to consult with Nimue in the back for a moment."

"No problem."

I led the way through the brocade curtain, and we sat at the table. Nimue placed her phone on the table in front of us.

"Mind if I record you?"

"Actually, I do. I'm not wild about electronic devices. It's a quirk of mine."

"Whatever you say," Nimue said agreeably. "Do you have a pen and paper? I'll take notes."

I grabbed a pad of paper and handed her a pen. She sat across the table, upright and attentive, like a stenographer ready for action.

I had to laugh. "I promise you, Nimue, it's not that complicated. In fact, you could probably look up the directions on the Internet."

"I prefer the personal approach."

"Me, too. Okay, so freezer spells are a kind of container spell, so first you need to choose the container. A simple jar or box would be fine, but if you'd like to use something more symbolic, you could find something that feels linked to that person. For example, a fruit or flower that makes you think of them, or a square of cloth from a garment that once belonged to them. Or if you're dealing with cruel gossip, you might use a cow's tongue."

"I thought there would be no ritual animal slaughter."

I smiled. "I was thinking you could buy one from a butcher. But it is a bit gruesome, isn't it? Magic can get real, no doubt about that."

"And once I've chosen a container?"

"You'll need to prepare a totem of your target. A photograph of the person is perfect, but you could also write their name on a card or, in your case, draw a sketch of their likeness. For the most power, a strand of hair or something they've worn would work nicely. When we speak about magic, it's about focusing our intent."

"And then you place that in the container, like a jar or a zucchini?"

"If you're using a vegetable, or something made of fabric, you have to sew or pin it shut. The container needs to be closed tight. Then add a wetting agent, such as vinegar or saltwater. Add red or black pepper if you want their lies to burn them."

"What about plain water?"

"Not tap water. It usually contains chlorine or other elements that lack a magical charge. River or creek water would do, or bay water. The best way to seal the container is to drip black candle wax on the lid or opening. And this is very important: While the wax is dripping, focus your intent on the flame and visualize the spell coming to fruition. Imagine the person being gone from your life, the sense of freedom when the connection is severed. Picture the person's words turning bitter in their mouth."

"Okay. Then what?"

"You can put the whole thing in a baggy, fill it with water, and place the container in a freezer. Then you wait and watch your magic work."

"That's it? Just like that?"

"Magic is . . ." I pondered how to explain it. "It's not a simple equation: Do this and add a pinch of that, and all will be granted to you. Rather, it's a way of concentrating one's intent in order to manifest. That's why baby witches need to stick to protection spells, so things don't get out of hand."

Nimue still looked worried and had a little line between her eyebrows. "And once the spell is complete?"

"If your enemy has been cut out of your life and you have no reason to fear them again, then you can toss the spell out with the trash, since they don't deserve more of your energy. If it's a bigger deal, you could ritually dispose of the spell by leaving it out at a crossroads at midnight—but if you used pins, make sure to remove them so animals who might eat the fruit or vegetable don't get hurt. Another option would be to let the spell thaw, pour the liquid into a running body of water, and bury the container.

"Finally, your last option is to leave the spell frozen forever. If you need to recharge the spell, remove it from the freezer, let it thaw for a few days, and then place it back in the freezer. You can repeatedly freeze and thaw the spell every few days to intensify its power."

"This is fascinating."

"Remember that a freezer spell will completely ice someone out of your life, so don't use it on a lover or anyone else you might want back one day, or you may regret it."

"And that's it?" asked Nimue.

"Pretty much," I said with a nod. "Like I said, it really is about focusing your intent to get what you want. Most of us have enormous capacity, truly limitless depths, and yet we don't know it, much less how to handle it."

She smiled. "You sound like me, talking to the teenagers. Having faith in oneself and one's own actions is the toughest thing, isn't it?"

"It gets easier with experience," I said. "But no, it's never simple."

Her eyes fell on the mermaid costume. "Is that the one you've been talking about?"

"It is, yes," I said.

"Could I— Is it weird if I ask to look at it?"

"Of course not," I said with a smile. "This is a vintage clothing store, after all."

"Is it for sale?" she asked, moving toward it, her attitude almost reverent.

"No, I don't think I'll sell it. It's special, though, isn't it?"

She ducked her head as she laid her hands upon it, reminding me of myself when I'm trying to pick up vibrations. When she straightened and dropped her hands, I could have sworn she looked disappointed.

Nimue didn't really think this was the skin of an actual mermaid, did she?

"It's pretty, isn't it?" I asked.

"Oh, yes. Lovely," she said, and turned to leave. "Well, I've taken up far too much of your time already. Thank you, Lily."

"Of course."

As we returned to the shop floor, Nimue said: "Oh, I meant to tell you that the police were out at Marcellus's place this morning."

"Is that right?" I said. I hadn't broken into his house or anything, but Carlos would not be pleased to learn I had been there.

"No worries, I didn't mention your little foray into the natatorium, by the way."

"Ah, well, I appreciate that."

"The authorities really need to fix up that building or get rid of the whole thing. Just leaving it to rot does not seem like the best plan, does it? I've asked Leo to push the city to act, but that's never an easy prospect," said Nimue. "But then, the same could be said for Treasure Island as a whole, I suppose. I love it, but sometimes I agree with Leo: Fix it up or get rid of the whole thing."

But how, I wondered, did one get rid of an entire island?

Chapter 18

Just after Nimue left the shop, the phone rang.

"Aunt Cora's Closet," I answered, adding our tagline: "It's not old, it's vintage!"

"What were you doing on Treasure Island?" Carlos Romero demanded.

"I, uh . . . well, hello Inspector, how are you?" I said, wondering if I had somehow conjured this call by talking about Carlos with Nimue.

"I'm hungry and sleepy and wondering what you were doing out on Treasure Island."

"It's sort of complicated."

"See if you can uncomplicate it for me."

"It has to do with that mermaid costume I was asking about the night I came home. Remember, at the party?"

"Go on."

"Maya did some research and thought it might have been from the World's Fair, which had synchronized swimmers dressed like mermaids."

"Uh-huh. Was Marcellus Tinley a synchronized swimmer?"

"I can't imagine he was, but—"

"So why were you at his house, looking in his window?"

Busted. "I didn't go in or anything. Just took a peek. It's not like he was home."

"And?" he asked.

"And that's it."

"Nice try. By 'and' I meant 'and what did you see?'"

"Not a lot. It looks like he was experimenting with paganism and witchcraft, but nothing serious."

"How could you tell?"

"You wouldn't understand if I explained it, but trust me."

"All right. What about the bat?"

"I haven't been able to communicate with it. I think it's possible it's just a regular old bat. Maybe somebody's exotic pet. Some people are weird like that."

"Tell me about it."

"And how about you?" I asked, hoping the answers might go both ways. "Have you concluded that Tinley's death was an accident or suicide?"

"Ask the medical examiner, it was an accident. Ask me, it was murder. But I still don't have any proof. According to what I've learned, Marcellus Tinley was making a nuisance of himself by standing in the way of some development plans for the island. There were also some suspicions about him because he liked to hang around with underage girls. But there's nothing concrete to indicate murder. And he may have lived in a rusty shipping container, but he was worth a decent chunk of change—owned some property in New York State, where he's from, which means somebody's going to profit from his death. So there are a few possible motives, but not enough facts to add up to murder. On the other hand, as I always say—"

"It doesn't take much," I finished his thought. I had this revelation, time and again: Something one person might shrug off could inspire another to kill. It was a depressing thought. "Who stands to inherit?"

"Let's see . . ." I heard the pages of his notebook being flipped. "His assets are to be liquidated and invested in a college fund for the benefit of two teenagers from Treasure Island, one Shanda Monroe and one Cece Goff."

"Shanda and Cece? I met them when I was there. They're nice kids, Carlos. I can't believe—"

"It's fine, Lily, I'm not looking for a character reference. I've already spoken with them. Shanda and her mother were either genuinely shocked to learn of her good fortune, or they're excellent actresses. Cece also seemed like a decent kid. A little naive, maybe, and clearly stunned to learn Marcellus Tinley had any money. Her father's another story. Piece of work, that guy. He didn't have anything nice to say about Tinley until I mentioned the terms of the will. Then he changed his tune, though only slightly."

"Sounds like that's a dead end, then."

Carlos blew out a loud breath. "This whole case is a series of dead ends."

"Did you happen to meet a young guy named Zane? He seems hinky to me."

"In what way?" Carlos asked.

I didn't want to tell the inspector about trespassing in the natatorium, so I remained vague: "He's just sort of bad news, seems that was a consensus among the Treasure Islanders we talked to. And it appears there was no love lost between him and Marcellus Tinley. I have absolutely no proof, but if he happened to be in the wax museum the day Marcellus was killed . . ."

"Yeah, okay, thanks. No last name on him?"

"No. Sorry."

"Gotcha. Late teens, skinhead, tats."

"The tattoo on his forearm is a swastika."

"Sounds like a charmer."

"He really is. Not to change the subject, but: Do you know when I can have access to Aidan's appointment book and the Satchel?"

"Yes, as a matter of fact. We've released Aidan's office, if you'd like to get back in there. No luck getting you something Marcellus was wearing at the time, though."

"It's okay, probably a moot point by now, anyway. By the way, Carlos, while I have you on the phone: What do you know about right-wing extremists in the area? Nazis, for example?"

"You mean like actual Nazis? Or your garden variety white supremacists?"

"I'm not sure. We happened upon an old Nazi flag on Treasure Island, and apparently since the German government was Nazi at the time of the World's Fair, the flag was flown in the international cavalcade of flags."

"A flag like that might be symbolic of evil now," said Carlos. "But it's also a part of history. If it's on display there, that's probably why. It doesn't mean anyone's actually spouting Nazi ideology."

"True," I said. No sense bringing up our little escapade in the Nazi clubhouse, especially since I had no idea what any of it might mean.

"There are plenty of whack jobs running around," said Carlos, "and as a general rule it's best to stay out of their way. Especially if you happen to be a witch. Promise me you'll be careful, Lily."

"Thanks, Carlos. I will. You, too."

We hung up. I checked my antique Tinkerbell wristwatch: It was nearly four.

"Conrad, can you stay until closing?" I asked. "Bronwyn's leaving soon to visit with her grandkids, and I don't want Maya in the store alone."

"Dude," Conrad said, nodding. "No problem."

"Is something going on?" asked Maya.

I shook my head. "Just the normal level of crazy."

"That was Carlos, wasn't it?" Maya said. "What did he say?"

"He's released Aidan's office," I said. "I should get over there."

Before I'd completed the sentence, Oscar got up from his silk pillow, shook himself, and trotted over to stand next to me.

"Looks like the little dude wants to go with you," said Conrad.

"So it does," I said.

"Lily, please do be careful," said Bronwyn. "Remember what you found there last time."

Not much chance I could forget. The visual of the man slumped over Aidan's desk was going to take some serious time to fade. Before leaving, I gathered a few supplies: a smudge stick made of white sage, palo santo, cayenne pepper, comfrey root, frankincense resin, and three different types of crystals. Aidan's office needed a thorough cleansing, not only from the spirit of the man who died but also from the jangly vibrations left by the police and investigators. I added a couple of rags and my vinegar and orange oil spray to my bag for a more prosaic kind of cleaning: fingerprint dust.

No doubt about it, the forensics team did important

but dirty work. And in my experience, they rarely cleaned up after themselves.

And then I grabbed a bag of Cheez Doodles. Because: Oscar.

At the wax museum, I stopped at the ticket booth to talk to the sullen young woman with her nose buried in a romance novel.

"Book any good?" I asked, hoping to make conversation.

"You need a ticket," Clarinda said, for the thousandth time.

"I really don't."

"$24.99. Cash works fine. And double for livestock." She cast a jaundiced eye at Oscar, who snorted loudly in reply.

"Clarinda, can you think back to the night of the . . . incident?" I kept wanting to refer to the death of Marcellus Tinley as a murder, as did Carlos, but the medical examiner did not agree, and that was the only vote that counted. "Do you remember selling a ticket to a young man, around eighteen, with a shaved head and lots of tattoos?"

"You know how many people are walking around this town with a shaved head and lots of tattoos? Of *any* gender?"

"One of the tattoos was a swastika."

She grimaced. "Ugh. I hate Nazis."

"A lot of people feel that way. And, to be fair, it's possible he's not really a *Nazi* Nazi. I mean, the design actually harkens back to an ancient symbol of . . ." I trailed off when she raised her book in front of her face. "Never mind. Anyway, Inspector Romero tells me he's released Aidan's office, so we'll just run along upstairs. Unless you remember anything else about that evening?"

"I went over all this with the police *ad nauseum*," she said, still hiding behind the pages of a book titled *Love's Lust and Found*.

"Okay, I'll just go on up, then. Let me know if you think of anything?"

"You'll be my very first call," she lied.

Oscar's hooves clicked loudly on the treads as we ascended the floating staircase and continued past the Chamber of Horrors and through the Hollywood Legends exhibit, me ignoring the waxed figures as best I could.

The problem with the medical examiner's accidental death ruling was that I knew it could not have happened that way. Aidan had placed a glamour over his office door. The glamour didn't make the office invisible, but it did mean most people would not even notice the heavy wood door at the back of the Local Celebrities exhibit. Aidan had also placed a protection spell on his office that was much stronger than the one I cast on Aunt Cora's Closet. Even if someone did detect the door through the glamour, it would be very difficult to open it. And these were the kinds of spells that endured even in the spellcaster's absence.

I remembered feeling the power of the spells on the night I arrived to find the door ajar. The night of the . . . *murder*. The fact that Marcellus Tinley had been able to find the door and enter the office despite the protection spells meant his death *had* to be more than a random accident. I was almost positive.

According to Carlos, the possible motives for murder included Marcellus standing in the way of development projects, his running afoul of someone by harming underage girls, or money in the form of an inheritance. But could there be something else, something he had been looking into—something dangerous? Or had he arrived in Aidan's office for something entirely unrelated, found it empty, took a seat behind the desk . . . and someone, mistaking him for Aidan Rhodes, killed him?

First things first: magical housekeeping. I unloaded my supplies on Aidan's big desk as Oscar watched. He remained in his piggy guise in case anyone noticed the open door but nonetheless lent me his magical assistance. In this way, if in no other, Oscar functioned as a true familiar: his mere presence allowed me to more easily access my own magical pathways, opening the portals between me and my ancestors, and even to the astral plane. This put me in mind, once again, of the possibility that the erection of the Golden Gate Bridge might have somehow knocked things out of balance. And if so, what was I supposed to do about it?

First I helped smash Alcatraz, and now I was supposed to, what, take down one of California's most beautiful, iconic engineering wonders? Maybe that was why I kept thinking about my hometown, Jarod. If I didn't find another solution, I might soon be run out of San Francisco by an angry mob, old-timey witch hunt style.

I cleansed the office, taking my time and leaving the door open to allow the energies to vacate as I used the ritual broom propped in one corner, which Calypso had made for Aidan long ago. I swept the chamber with long, smooth strokes, starting in the farthest corners. And then I smudged with the sage bundle, and burnt the palo santo incense, dissipating the smoke with a fan made of crow feathers.

Next I checked the octagonal room. All seemed untouched. My lachrymatory was still in its tiny alcove, kept safe by an Etruscan binding spell. Seeing the lachrymatory reminded me of times Aidan and I had worked together. We did not always see eye to eye, in fact we butted heads a lot, but Aidan had a way of putting things in perspective. He also had helped me to remember my time in Germany long ago, when I was searching for my father. I wished he were here now to consult with me about my alleged brother, and the prophecy, and whether the odd and strangely enchanted Treasure Island had anything to do with either of those. But then I wondered about the *vila* Selena had mentioned, and what that would mean for the future. Were the witches taking care of Aidan able to deal with the *vila*?

After smudging the octagonal room, I set out the crystals and the frankincense resin, and closed and locked the door.

I recalled poor Marcellus's amateur attempts at entering the world of magic, his candles, his pigeons, and could not bear the thought of sitting in the chair where he had died. So I dragged Aidan's expensive leather desk chair into the far corner of the office and replaced it with one of the wing chairs used by clients.

Cleansing finished and office straightened up to my satisfaction, I sat at Aidan's desk and handed Oscar the bag of Cheez Doodles, which he munched on enthusiastically.

I rummaged through the Satchel, where I found Leo's signature on a document. Aidan was the witchy godfather to the Bay Area magical community, but he also dealt with cowans, or non-witchy people, who believed in magical powers—or, at the very least, believed in Aidan's ability to make things happen. Leo had signed the document in blood, which meant he was in debt to Aidan. Why?

I felt a squeezing on my arm, exactly where Graciela

had put her hand the first night I returned from my honeymoon.

A man stood in the open doorway.

"You again?" I said.

Dragomir grinned.

"I suppose you're going to tell me you made another appointment?"

"Not at all. I was hoping to find you here, as a matter of fact." His gaze shifted to the floor by the desk. "Cute pig."

Oscar snorted but remained in his porcine form, his pink snout covered in orange dust from the Cheez Doodles.

"Thank you. I thought you two had met." In a city beginning with a *B*.

He tilted his head. "Not in this form, I didn't."

When he failed to elaborate, I asked: "What made you think I would be here?"

He shrugged. "You were here last time. Why not this time, too?"

"The SFPD have been looking for you."

"Have they, indeed?"

"You have to speak with them, you know," I said. "They'll track you down eventually."

"Maybe they will. Maybe they won't. I can't wait to find out."

I was starting to think we just might be related, because Dragomir was really starting to annoy me.

And then it hit me: If Dragomir *was* my half brother, he was family. Blood. For most of my life the people I felt closest to were my chosen family. Even Graciela, whom I loved fiercely and thought of as my grandmother, wasn't my blood. Why, then, should it matter that this man might be? And yet, it felt . . . different. Special. I had been an only child my whole life. I was forever the weird one, the strange one, the outcast. Dragomir and I had no history together, but we had *something* in common. Something important.

And I also realized that I had never looked like anyone. I took after my father, and growing up, my dark features were often compared, unfavorably, with my mother's blond good looks. This fellow, though, looked a lot like me. Enough to be my brother.

"You have to . . ." I began again, and then reconsidered. "Take a seat."

"I 'have to' take a seat?" he said, still smiling.

One of my weaknesses, as a witch, is in accurately sensing auras, especially when people had their guard up. But in this case I did not have to strain to see: Dragomir's aura was bright and sparkly, glowing red for energy and power, but also danger. Black auras spoke of drama and protection, but also of death and evil. Purple was for ambition and mystery, green for prosperity, growth . . . and envy, jealousy, and guilt. As usual, the devil was in the details.

"*Please* take a seat," I said. "We should talk."

"Indeed, we should." He sat in the chair across the desk from me, still smiling, confident to the point of cocky.

I stroked my medicine bag, reaching for calm. Long ago, I had learned from my old pal in the SFPD homicide department that the best way to get someone to talk was to remain silent.

I stared at him. He stared at me.

Dragomir was either immune to that trick or had learned it from his own encounters with the police. Somehow, I wouldn't be surprised to learn that this man had dealt with a few authorities in his time.

After another minute, I cracked. Clearing my throat, I began: "So."

"So," he repeated.

"What brings you to town?" I leaned back in my chair, trying—and failing—to channel Aidan's nonchalant confidence.

"You," he said, then smiled. "Also, a conference on higher education."

"I see. First things first: Your name is Dragomir Ivory?"

He nodded. "You sussed it out, huh?"

"We have the same last name."

"We do! Suppose that's a coincidence?"

"No."

"Of course not. We have the same father."

I swallowed. I had sort of known it, but the confirmation took a moment to wrap my head around.

"I don't trust your father," I said.

"And I don't trust yours," he replied.

Chapter 19

"I guess this means you're my brother," I said.

"So it seems. Dragomir and Lily. I must say, you got the better deal when it came to names. Must have been your mother's influence. Far as I can tell, dear old Dad contributed mostly the last name. But that's a conversation for another day. Did you receive my gift, dear sister?"

"What gift?"

"The mermaid costume." He cocked his head. "Didn't you get it? I explained it all in the note."

I heard a thud, then the clacking of hooves on the wooden floor as Oscar jumped down from the chair and fled the office.

"Was it something I said?" Dragomir said.

"What note?" I asked.

"The note I gave to your familiar."

I let out an exasperated breath. "Oscar's not exactly a detail guy. I'm afraid the note must have been lost."

He frowned slightly. "I thought he was your familiar."

"Yeah. He is, sort of. He's just not typical of the ilk."

"Ah. Well, now, that explains a lot."

"Such as?"

"Such as why you weren't sure who I was. I thought perhaps you were playing with me."

"Why would I do that?"

"How should I know?" Dragomir shrugged, then grinned. "I don't even know you."

I was struck again by how attractive he was. He wasn't movie star handsome; his features were nice enough but nothing special. The appeal was in the way he held himself, his swagger, the sparkle and ambition of his aura, the deep intelligence flashing in those dark eyes.

"What did the note say?" I asked.

"It was an introduction. How's that for old-fashioned manners? It said that I, Dragomir Ivory, had only recently learned that I had a sister, one Lily Ivory. And that, given your profession, I thought you might enjoy a vintage mermaid costume handed down to me by my great-aunt, who was a synchronized swimmer at the 1939 World's Fair, right here in glorious San Francisco."

"Sounds like quite a note," I said. It would have saved me a great deal of time and worry. "Sorry I missed it."

"I'm sure there'll be other occasions to exchange familial belles lettres filled with bons mots."

"Uh-huh. Anyway, speaking of the World's Fair," I said. "Did you know a man named Marcellus Tinley?"

He shook his head. "Should I?"

"He's the man who died here a few days ago. He was from Treasure Island."

"Now that's what I call a coincidence."

"The older I get, the less I believe in coincidence."

"You and me both. The costume was handed down through the family, on my mother's side, along with a certain amount of lore. It has always felt powerful to me, used to call to me when I was a boy."

"And why did you want me to have it?"

He paused and seemed to assess me. "Some months ago my mother told me about a prophecy regarding the child of my—*our*—father. I had been planning to attend a conference here in San Francisco, so I made an appointment with Aidan for a consultation. Later, when I found out I had a sister here in town, I assumed, with relief, that the prophecy referred to you rather than me. And since the mermaid costume was last worn here in San Francisco, I thought you might be able to use it."

"Use it how?"

"I have no idea."

"Why didn't you bring it to me yourself?"

"I wasn't entirely sure I would be able to come to the US. There was a visa issue. And I certainly didn't want to put such a valuable heirloom in the mail. I happened upon your familiar in a bar in Budapest, and I thought to entrust it to him. My mother consulted her black mirror and assured me it would be safe."

"Your mother is a practitioner, then?"

"Of course. Isn't yours?"

"Not really, no," I said, feeling a twinge of jealousy. What would it have been like to grow up with a mother who understood my out-of-control magic and had been able to help me? "Actually, not at all."

"That's a shame," he said, his gaze sympathetic. "That must have been difficult."

I shrugged.

"But look at you now, queen of the Bay Area witchy community. That's quite a rags-to-riches story, magic-wise."

"First of all, I certainly am *not* queen of the Bay

Area witchy community. I'm filling in for Aidan for a few days, that's all."

"What about the prophecy?" he asked in a low voice.

"You tell me. My sources say it might refer to you, rather than to me."

He nodded and blew out a breath. "It's possible. But I doubt it. Among other things, this is my first time in your charming City by the Bay. I can't imagine why I would have been named in a prophecy that takes place here."

"I'm a relative newcomer to the area myself," I said. "But there appears to be some sort of imbalance, something to do with a portal, or *torana*—"

"Or *vandanamalikas*," he said with a nod. "My demon told me that as well."

"I'm sorry, your what, now?"

"My demon, Dantalion. Don't tell me you don't have a demon under your control. I would have thought with your abilities, you would command several."

I stared at him. "You are familiar with what happened with our mutual father, are you not?"

"Only too familiar," Dragomir said, a pall cast over his face. "But unlike dear old papa, I have no intention of losing control and becoming in thrall. In the old days it was common for humans to call on the aid of demons. My mother passed those ways down to me, through the maternal line. I'm the first magical boy in my family for seven generations."

"And what kind of aid does your demon give you?" I wouldn't even say the name of a demon for fear of accidentally summoning one.

"Dantalion is the seventy-first demon to be named in the demonological grimoire—"

"The *Lesser Key of Solomon*." I nodded. A fat,

nineteenth-century version of that tome sat on Aidan's bookshelf.

Dragomir gave me a smile. "Then you're familiar with it. Good. He is a duke who rules thirty-six legions and is prolific at teaching any art or science. He's really quite handy, especially on a college campus."

"Hence the interest in higher education."

"Precisely. I can channel his power and use it to help people. Students, mostly, but also professors. Anyone seeking higher knowledge, as a matter of fact. For the average cowan, is there anything more truly transformational, more 'magical,' if you will, than education?"

"Oh, I'm a big fan of education. Got my GED a little while back, as a matter of fact."

He looked a little shocked, but said, "Good for you."

"But I hate to keep coming back to this: The reason people don't tend to call on demons for help anymore is that they can easily get out of control."

"Indeed they can! Which is why my mother trained me in the old ways. I'm quite skilled, you know. As are you, I can only imagine."

"Still," I shuddered slightly. "Demons give me the creeps."

"It is good to respect their strength, but no need to be overly fearful. Dantalion himself once said that demons might help *inspire* chaos and horror—apparently they find it very funny to bring out the worst in us—but it takes a human to be inhumane. Think about it: Demons don't commit genocide, people do. The Holocaust was orchestrated and carried out by those who were only too human."

"Why would you bring up the Nazis?"

"Hard to talk about genocide without mentioning the Holocaust."

I jumped at the sound of a knock on the door. I had

been so intent on my discussion with Dragomir that I plumb forgot the door was left open.

A worried-looking young woman stuck her head in, glanced at me, then gazed at Dragomir, sighed, and smiled, her rigid posture becoming languid. This sort of thing happened a lot when I hung around Aidan, too.

"What is it?" As a witch, I avoided saying "Can I help you?" or "What can I do for you?" which could imply that I was beholden in some way. Witch stuff. I felt a headache coming on.

She tore her eyes away from Dragomir long enough to explain that she wanted to check on the progress on a border dispute that Calypso had told me about, so I was able to fill her in on the new developments in the negotiations.

"Anything else?" I asked, as she lingered near the door, gazing at Dragomir.

"Um, no, that's about it. Oh! Now that I'm here, a friend of mine needs to get licensed as a professional seer."

"Tell her to go down to city hall and fill out the paperwork. She should only come to me if there's a problem of some kind. But she can't have been convicted of a felony."

"She was . . . oh wait. She wasn't *convicted*."

"Well, then. Here's to evading the law. She should be fine. Run along now, and please close the door behind you. Dragomir and I are in a meeting."

"Your name's Dragomir?" she addressed my half brother, sparing nary a glance for me. "Seriously? That's totally *awesome*."

He gave her a warm smile.

"Okay, then," I said, urging her to leave. "Buh-bye, now."

"Perhaps our paths will cross later," said Dragomir

as he stood and ushered the woman out of the room, "but for now I fear Lily and I need to talk in private."

He closed the door and returned to his seat.

"This sort of thing happen to you a lot?" I asked.

"At times too often, at times not often enough," he said with another grin. "Not my fault. Born this way."

"Uh-huh. Anyway, let's shelve your own personal demon for the moment and circle back to Treasure Island and your great-aunt."

Just like that, Dragomir's easy grin fell and his charm ceded to a serious tone. "She was Jewish and begged for asylum in the US. But her appeal was denied, and she was sent back to Nazi Germany, where she was promptly arrested. She perished at Auschwitz."

"I'm so sorry," I said.

"I never knew her," he said. "But of course it's a family trauma. And there's no denying family history, is there?"

"No. No, there's not." The desk phone rang, and I picked it up.

"Hey there, princess," said Patience. "Renna says she'll read for you if we go right now. Pick me up in twenty?"

I gazed at Dragomir. There was so much more to discuss, but the Aunties had urged me to have my cards read, and it was seeming more urgent than ever.

So I said: "I'll be right there."

"Sounds like you're busy. I'll get out of your hair," said Dragomir as he swanned out of the office.

"*Wait*—," I called out, but he kept walking. I slumped back in the seat with a sigh.

"Sounds like you're too busy to cook," said Oscar, who suddenly appeared by the desk in his natural gobgoyle guise.

"Where'd you go?" I asked.

"When?"

"You vamoosed when Dragomir arrived. I thought you were supposed to help protect me."

"He didn't do nothin' to you, did he? He's funny-looking, but you can't hold that against the guy. Besides, I thought you two might want to catch up, after all these years."

"It had nothing to do with the fact that you lost his note?"

"Like I was saying," he said, blatantly ignoring my question, "sounds like dinner might be late tonight?"

"I'm afraid so. I have to go to Oakland first."

"Guess I'll get dinner out, then."

"Out? Where?"

"There's lotsa options in this neighborhood. Maybe clam chowder in a sourdough bread bowl. You ever have that? It's delish."

"But . . ." I trailed off. I wasn't sure how Oscar managed on his own, since a restaurant was unlikely to serve him as a pig or a gobgoyle, but as Sailor liked to point out, he appeared to do just fine. "Okay. Just . . . be careful."

He cackled at the thought that he might be at risk in some way, transformed into his piggy guise, and trotted out of the office. I called Sailor to let him know I would be late, then pondered whether to take the Satchel and Aidan's appointment book, which I hadn't taken the time to study yet. There had been a lot of car break-ins lately. I could cast a glamour, but that would consume part of my psychic energy, and I needed all I could get if I was going to get my tarot read by Renna.

I could just imagine trying to explain to Aidan how I had lost the *Satchel*, of all things. I still didn't understand quite why it was so important and inspired so much awe in the hearts of practitioners everywhere, but it did. So I decided that it and the appointment book would be safer in Aidan's office. I would come back tomorrow when I had more time.

I gathered up my things and ran to the car.

Chapter 20

Sailor's aunt Renna was not my biggest fan. I was surprised when she came to the handfasting and hadn't seen her since. Sailor, though, had assured me that once Renna ate the food at the wedding she would have to support our marriage, or be appeased, or something along those lines. Also, I had once helped save her from a fire, and had recently relieved her of being semi-possessed, so one might have thought she'd warm up a little. But no such luck.

I picked Patience Blix up at her house, an old Victorian in Noe Valley that stood tall and straight, rubbing shoulders with the neighboring houses on the block.

"I heard some gossip about you," I said when Patience climbed into the Mustang. She was, as always, drop-dead gorgeous, and was wearing her usual colorful ensemble: a full, multicolored skirt; a pure white peasant blouse that showed off her lovely neck and collarbones; yards of gold chains and beads; gold anklets with tiny gold bells; long gold earrings; and a scarf in her luxurious, near-black hair. Edith Head herself could not have done a better job of designing an outfit for the stereotypical Rom fortune-teller.

"I can't wait to hear this," she murmured as she put on her seatbelt.

"Bronwyn tells me you went to dinner with Carlos? *My* Carlos."

"If you wanted him to be your Carlos, you should have laid your claim. Too late. Not to mention you just married Sailor."

"I didn't mean 'mine' that way, as you very well know. So, how was it?"

"How was what? The dinner, the dancing, or the sexual chemistry?"

"All of the above. Or at least as much as you're comfortable sharing."

"Oooh, we're sharing. Aren't we just the BFFs?"

"Or not," I said, with a twinge of annoyance.

"Hey, now, don't be offended. You know me, I never take anything seriously."

That was true.

"Well, let's see," Patience said as we waited at a red light on Guerrero. As usual, the sidewalks of the Mission neighborhood were crowded with locals and out-of-towners looking for great tacos. "The food was great."

"Where'd you go?"

"A new French place downtown, off an alley near Belden Place. Want to hear about my entrée?"

I ignored that. "And the dancing?"

"Surprisingly fun. I mean, we Rom are born dancing, but I didn't really expect a homicide inspector to have the moves. And he didn't, but he did all right."

"Sounds good," I said, glancing at Mission Dolores, home to Misión San Francisco de Asís, an ornate,

Spanish-style church from the late eighteenth century. In Europe a building of that age would not have gotten much attention, but in San Francisco it was one of the oldest in town.

"So that leaves chemistry."

"It does, doesn't it?" Patience was uncharacteristically quiet for a moment. "I like Carlos, and no doubt about it, he's a hottie, dance moves or no dance moves. But overall it was . . . kind of awkward, to tell the truth. I had a hard time feeling comfortable around him."

"Was there something in particular that bothered you?"

"He's a homicide inspector. He's got that whole badge-and-penal-code thing going on."

"On the other hand, those handcuffs could be fun."

"Lily! You made a risqué joke! I'm proud of you."

I laughed. "Anyway, I get what you're saying, but Carlos is pretty open-minded—"

"For a cop, maybe," she interrupted, then gave a shrug. "And as you know, I'm not a big one for following the rules. There's no denying the chemistry, but I'm thinking it might be a case of opposites attracting. Not sure it has much potential for the long haul."

"Is the long haul important to you?" I asked. Patience had never indicated any interest in settling down, though I suppose most of the time we'd spent together had not really lent itself to having those kinds of conversations. Maybe now that we were BFFs, we would.

"Haven't decided. Maybe, if it's the right guy."

"The right guy makes all the difference," I said, thinking of my husband.

"You do realize you get a really sappy look on your face when you think of Sailor," she said. "The bliss of the newly married is so annoying."

"Sorry," I said. "Maybe you need to give it more time. You and Carlos don't really know each other yet. I didn't like Sailor at first, you know."

"I'm not surprised to hear it," Patience said. "I love my cousin, but he's a real pill a good portion of the time. He takes after Renna, I think."

"Now that's a troubling thought," I said.

"Anyway, thing is, I have a new admirer. I was going to come by the shop to find a new dress for our date."

"Really? Who is it?"

She gave a cat-who-ate-the-canary smile. "Wouldn't *you* like to know."

"Yes, I would. That's why I asked."

She laughed. "I'll see if he's worth a second date, and then maybe we'll talk."

"Fair enough," I said, as I guided the car onto the Bay Bridge. "Hey, what's up with the new venture with Sailor?"

"Hasn't he told you? I don't want to step on any newly married toes."

I gave her a Look. I used to be jealous of the time Sailor and Patience spent together, though now, when I look back, I realize how absurd that was. They were completely unsuitable, romantically. And even if they weren't, I had no cause for concern. A lot of things about Sailor gave me pause, but the thought that he would be unfaithful was not one of them.

"If this is something Sailor wants to do, of course I'll be supportive."

"Good for you," she said, with a genuine smile. "You have changed."

"Hey, it's not where you start out, it's where you end up."

"I do so love fortune cookie wisdom. Anyway, it's a little hard to put into words, but essentially I've been approached by some Silicon Valley types who are interested in my services."

"Your psychic services?"

"No, my *call* girl services," she said waspishly, reverting to form. "Sailor's gonna be my pimp."

I held my tongue and counted to ten. This BFF business wasn't going to be easy.

"*Of course* my psychic services. A guy came to me for a reading a while ago, and my advice with regard to his IPO was spot-on. He made a bundle of money and now some of his colleagues have approached me, so I'm thinking of making it into a regular thing. It's all on the down low, though. These high-tech folks pride themselves on being supremely logical, which emphatically does not include consulting a psychic."

As we crossed the western span of the Bay Bridge and entered the tunnel through Yerba Buena Island, my thoughts naturally turned to Treasure Island.

"What do you know about portals?" I asked.

"You mean like this tunnel?"

"More broadly. Psychically, I suppose."

"Any sort of gate or door or portal is symbolic of passing from one state to another," she said. "It can be as simple as an opportunity, a new adventure, or a relationship. Conversely, it can be a sign of fencing yourself in if it's closed or locked."

I nodded. I knew all of this, but I kept going over it in my head, hoping all the pieces might fall into place.

"Thresholds also refer to the line between life and death, allowing the connection between the living and the dead, the underwater and the land-based. In any case, a portal usually implies an action that happens quickly. You either step through or not, so it's a point of decision. One mustn't linger on the threshold. Why are you asking?"

"I'm afraid I might have to blow up the Golden Gate Bridge."

"You *what*?" She whipped around to look at me.

"No, not really." At least I *hoped* not. "But it's possible that when it was built, it closed off a *torana* of some sort, which led to a crucial imbalance and ultimately to World War Two."

There was a long pause. "Well, damn. I love that bridge."

"Me, too," I said quietly.

We exited the freeway and wound our way up the narrow residential streets that snaked through the Oakland hills. I pulled up to heavy iron gates, behind which sat a large bubblegum-pink house belonging to Renna and Eric, Sailor's aunt and uncle.

"*Bon courage*," said Patience as the gates slowly opened. "We who are about to sit and drink coffee while you deal with Renna salute you."

I took a deep breath and went up the drive.

Eric opened the door. He was wearing old jeans, boots, and a plaid shirt, which he filled out nicely. He reminded me of a fifty-something Rom cowboy.

"Nice to see you, Lily," he said, giving me a big hug before doing the same with Patience. "Come on in; Renna's in the kitchen. She's expecting you."

Sailor's aunt Renna was a full-figured woman with an abundance of wavy salt-and-pepper hair I imagined had once been much like Patience's. And, like her niece, she wore a lot of gold jewelry and scarves, like a stereotypical fortune-teller at the carnival. A good ten years older than her husband, Renna emanated power in waves.

Eric had always been friendly to me, Renna not so much. When she saw me, her lips pressed together and she nodded. "Lily."

I returned the nod. "Renna."

"Come along," she said, leading the way down the hallway.

I cast a last "help me" look at Patience, who smiled, took a seat at the large kitchen table, and asked Eric to play his accordion. Soon the soothing, lilting tones floated down the hall to the master bedroom, where Renna did her readings.

It always seemed strange to me that Renna allowed her clients, some of whom were on the sketchy side, into her bedchamber. But ours were very different kinds of power, rooted in very different kinds of talents. For Renna, the intimacy of the setting allowed her to more easily connect with the spirit of the tarot and improved the divination.

The last time I was here Renna had been suffering from a kind of magical illness, and the room had been a wreck. But now all was put to rights: the bed was neatly made with a royal blue silk coverlet; a corner cabinet held her private altar, with several lit candles and mementos of loved ones, both living and deceased. Also on the altar was the *auribus teneo lupum* amulet I had placed around her neck the last time I was here to overcome the partial possession that afflicted her. There was also a human skull, a live toad, and a shallow bowl of water with floating rose petals. Herbs were scattered here and there, and the room's mirrors were adorned with colorful scarves.

All in all, it was a carefully orchestrated, stagelike setting meant to enhance the seer's power. Not for the first time, I wondered how Eric felt sleeping in here.

In the center of the room was a table covered in a brocade cloth, upon which sat a dog-eared oversized deck of tarot cards.

"Have a seat," Renna said. "I'll spare you the little

ditty I usually sing to my customers, since you know it so well by now."

"'The art of the Romani,'" I said with a nod. "I remember."

"Tell me why you are here. Patience said it is not about your personal life this time."

"According to Graciela, it might well have to do with the fate of the entire Bay Area."

"Graciela sent you?"

"Her whole coven suggested I needed to have a reading."

"The Aunties are wise women. Powerful, too."

"Indeed."

"And this is because of the prophecy?"

I nodded. "My half brother is in town."

Renna stared at me for several minutes. At last, she said, "You remember what to do?"

I picked up the tarot deck and shuffled the cards, mixing them well, and then made a fist, then a chop, then a fist, repeating three times. Renna reached out and splayed the cards across the table in an arc.

"These are all gate cards," she mumbled. "The Three of Wands, the Eight of Cups, the Six of Swords, the Ace of Pentacles . . ."

"By 'gate cards' do you mean literally, or . . . ?"

"*Shush*." She placed her hands flat on the cards, her head hanging down. Then she leaned back and tilted her head up until she was staring at the ceiling, as though receiving messages from the heavens. Her eyes closed, and she twitched.

I watched in silence, wondering how much of this was for show and how much was part of the ritual that allowed her to enter into a trance. My friend Hervé put on a big show, too, when he went into a trance. I tried not to judge. My own magic did not require this kind of performance, but then I brewed alone while they had to impress paying clients. Not everyone was lucky enough to have a thriving vintage clothing business to pay the bills.

Renna mumbled, her head rolling from side to side. Then she said, "Astral twins."

"What's an astral twin?"

"You and your brother were born at the same exact moment but in different parts of the world."

"I was born at midnight." I'd always liked that fact.

She nodded. "And he was born at the same moment, in Germany."

Chapter 21

Renna closed her eyes and started mumbling again. "The child of the innocent, the child of the damned . . . the sins of the father and the blessings of the mothers . . . the girl, the boy, the twin, the namesake . . ."

I had no idea what any of it meant, or even if Renna was making it all up.

As if reading my mind, Renna's eyes flew open and she frowned. "I can tell you one thing with certainty: There is magic afoot, yes. But the immediate threat you are facing is human, not supernatural. Your grandmother's coven will not be much help and might indeed be in danger themselves if you involve them."

"What kind of threat? From whom?"

"A human threat. I just said that. Aren't you listening?"

"Of course I'm listening, but it would be helpful if you could be more specific. Can you tell me anything else?"

"You see here, the fire in the foreground, the water

at the back? The creativity of fire yearns for the fluidity of water. Water is vast and deep and mysterious, unexplored, its depths are as a concave mirror to the astral world."

"And that means?"

"There is an island here. Surrounded by crystals. You see the isolation?"

"I've been out on Treasure Island, which feels isolated, but it's actually connected by a bridge to—"

"The cards speak metaphorically," Renna interrupted, sounding annoyed. "An island speaks of isolation, whether actual or figurative. Islands may be more vulnerable than the mainland to certain spiritual influences, Lily. Also, that's not your first name."

"Excuse me? Lily isn't my name? What are you talking about?"

"What do you want from me? Says right here in the cards: You were known by another name, a different name. Not a flower. I see war. I'm seeing *D*."

"I . . . okay. Anything else? Something specific about the prophecy, maybe?"

"First, you must return to the place where you were the most frightened."

"You mean, in my whole life?" That would be a pretty long list.

"No, in the last day or two."

That was easy: The Nazi clubhouse behind the pool on Treasure Island.

"And then what?" I asked.

"One of the problems with clients who want to rush me is that they do not understand the dynamic, energetic relationship between the cards and my visions," Renna said, sounding peeved.

She was right. Renna made me nervous and having my cards read made me anxious, and as a result I was giving in to frustration. I knew, as a brewing witch, that there was no rushing magic—not without making a lot of mistakes, anyway. I took a deep breath and tried to relax.

"That is better," Renna said. "I see here the *torana*, the gateway was opened and then spanned by humans, rather than by the spirits. The alchemical sign for water is an upside-down triangle, like this, you see? And salt is a circle with a line through it—the salts are out of balance. There are moments in time when the threats are magnified, when the solar winds enter our universe, and the water spirits have not been respected.

"This island you speak of, Treasure Island, I've never been there," she continued. "It is unnatural, there are no spirits there, no astral presence, no fairies or woods-folk. The water spirits are very angry, and must be appeased. You see this card here? The Tower?"

I nodded. The sixteenth Major Arcana, or Trump card, showed a tower being struck by lightning, flames pouring out of high windows, and people falling to their deaths. It was not what one would call a positive card.

"Most people who don't understand tarot are afraid of the death card, but it is the Tower Card to be feared. This card speaks of disaster, crisis, destruction, catastrophe."

I swallowed, hard.

"But it also speaks of transformation," Renna continued. "Painful and sudden change may lead to liberation, if it is handled properly. But remember, there is an immediate threat and an overarching threat. You must use your own wits and power to overcome the immediate, human challenge—if you can."

"And the overarching threat?"

"Again, I'm seeing the water spirits. The human

danger involving the island is a clue, a pointer, if you will, to the larger threat. I see the letter *D*, several *D*s, as a matter of fact. Things must be put aright with the merfolk through the *coincidentia oppositorum*."

The *coincidentia oppositorum*, as Aidan Rhodes had explained to me, was a kind of magical partnership that drew strength from the female-male duality. It was the only alliance considered powerful enough to keep San Francisco safe from the coming paranormal challenge.

"Aidan is not available. Which means . . ."

"It might be him."

"Who 'him'? Sailor?" I asked, a hopeful note in my voice.

She rolled her eyes. "I swear, it's as if you aren't even listening."

"Then who is the 'him'?"

Renna smiled and held up a card with a dragon and then another with an upright triangle. "The sign for a dragon and the sign for fire, combined with the Eight of Cups, which refers to intellectual precision, higher learning . . ."

Dragomir Ivory.

"Renna said you and your alleged brother were born at exactly the same time? Sounds like your father really got around," said Patience as we left Renna's house. "He wasn't a seaman, was he?"

"Why would he be a seaman?"

"You know that old saw about sailors having a girl in every port?"

"Very funny. I don't know about Dragomir's home-town, but there isn't a body of water within a hundred miles of Jarod, Texas," I said, concentrating on navigating the twisty hill roads of Oakland.

"So how did your parents meet?"

"I don't know." It dawned on me that I had never asked. "I know my father trained with Graciela when he was young, before going rogue. How did your parents meet?" I pictured some kind of Rom reunion, an encampment, maybe in Spain or Hungary, the elders gathering the far-flung clans to introduce the rising generation to potential partners.

"High school sweethearts," Patience said.

"Really?" I asked.

"Sometimes life really is that simple."

Something else dawned on me. "You have a cell phone, right?"

"Everyone has a cell phone," said Patience.

"*I* don't have a cell phone."

"Everyone *normal* has a cell phone."

"Could you call . . . there's a folded piece of paper in my backpack, should be right on top . . ."

She grabbed the backpack and started rooting through it.

"It should be right on top," I repeated.

"Oh, I already found it," she said. "I just want to see what else you carry around in this big bag. What *is* all this?"

"I had to cleanse Aidan's office."

"You're doing janitorial work now? Because if you're free, my place could use a good scrubbing."

"No, a magical cleansing."

She gazed at me.

"Dead body, remember?"

"*Another* one?"

"I assumed Sailor had mentioned it."

"No. No, he didn't. Okay, that accounts for the sage and the salts." She held up a mason jar filled with a murky liquid. "What the hell is this? It's not— I mean, you know how to find a public restroom, right?"

"Don't be ridiculous. It's a general protection brew. Just in case."

"Well, now, isn't this the cutest thing." She held up an ugly little poppet made of crude rags and bopped it in my direction. "Personally, I never leave home without my voodoo doll."

"It's not a voodoo doll," I said. "It's a generalized poppet. Again, just in case."

She raised an eyebrow. "In case of what?"

"You never know," I said, feeling defensive. "Best to be prepared. There's a Swiss Army knife and a flashlight in there, too. Mustn't get caught in the dark." Again.

"Aren't you a good little Scout," Patience said. "Oooh, a PAYDAY bar."

I laughed. "Help yourself. But first, do me a favor and call that number for Eugene Leimert, see if he's available? He lives in Berkeley, and since we're already in the East Bay, I thought we might stop in and speak to him about Treasure Island."

"What about it?"

"He used to live out there and became concerned about the level of toxicity from when the naval yard used to clean ships that carried atomic bombs, or something like that."

"And?"

"And I'd like to talk to him. Look, a dead man was found in Aidan's office, and I'm trying to figure out why the poor sod was killed. This is my process."

"What is your 'process'?"

"Bumbling around and asking a lot of people a lot of questions until I finally trip over the truth."

"I don't know. . . ." She trailed off with a shrug. "My time is precious. What's in it for me?"

"You'd be doing me a favor."

"Yeah, I got that part. I say again, what's in it for me?"

"Hey, I thought we were BFFs."

"We are. I'm just not a very *good* BFF. You could probably do better."

I already have, I thought smugly, thinking of Bronwyn and Maya. Still, I wanted to talk to Eugene Leimert, and we were already here. . . . "Tell you what: You do this for me, and you can have your pick of dresses from my store for your upcoming date."

"Now we're talking. You got yourself a deal," Patience said and placed the call. There was a brief exchange, and Eugene Leimert agreed to meet with us. She jotted his Berkeley address down on the note with his phone number.

"Got it," she said, and told me the address.

"Which way do I go?"

"How should I know? I live in San Francisco. Find a freeway and head north, get off at University."

"There should be a map of the East Bay in the glove compartment."

"What century do you live in?" Patience said. She typed something into her phone and a mechanical voice said, "Continue straight onto Mandana, make a left turn onto Lakeshore."

I don't care for mechanical voices and especially don't enjoy being told what to do by a computer. But I couldn't deny it was handy. No folding and refolding of paper maps involved.

It was early evening, and the streets of Berkeley were busy, as always. Students, professors, researchers, and staff from the massive flagship campus of the University of California abounded, as did the businesses that catered to them: cafés and fast food and fine restaurants, bookstores and boutiques, computer shops and sidewalk vendors hawking everything from exquisite blown-glass bongs to cheerful Indian jewelry to tie-dyed onesies for very hip infants. Businesses tended to stay open late in a college town.

Berkeley was no longer the progressive hippie haven it became famous for in the sixties and seventies, but the spirit of that long-ago era was still evident, and a number of people trailed wildly colored scarves and ringing bells and wore bangles and long jangly earrings. Patience stood out in most neighborhoods of San Francisco but fit right in here in Berkeley. Still, she was so brashly beautiful, with her long flowing hair and haughty demeanor, that she earned more than a few second glances.

I smoothed today's plaid sundress and red Keds, feeling plain and gremlin-like. *Good thing I'm no longer jealous of her*, I thought wryly.

"How well do you know Berkeley?" Patience asked.

"Not well," I admitted.

"This area's called the 'gourmet ghetto,'" she said. "Because of Chez Panisse, mostly."

"Oh, really?" I said, though I hadn't a clue what she was referring to.

"Alice Waters, Chez Panisse, a pioneer in California cuisine? Doesn't ring any bells?"

"I'm not much of a foodie. I'm more a hush puppy and collard greens type."

"I'll bet you ate well in Europe."

"That, we did," I said, my hand going to my rounded belly. I had to rein myself in soon or I would no longer fit into my own vintage garments.

"This neighborhood is also home to the original Peet's Coffee, which, if you ask me, was a real gift to humankind."

"Now, Peet's I've heard of," I smiled. "How do you know so much about Berkeley?"

"Took some extension courses a while back. *What?* You're surprised I'm a college gal? I'm not just about the fortune-telling, you know. I enjoy a life of the mind."

"I think that's great, Patience. Honestly. I just never thought about you going to school, somehow." I like to think of myself as reasonably imaginative, but Patience had always seemed to me to have emerged like Venus: fully formed and sui generis.

The phone announced we had arrived, and I found a parking spot not far away, even without using my parking charm.

"This is it," I said as we stood in front of a wood-shingled, three-story structure with exterior walkways leading to several different offices. We consulted a directory and located Eugene Leimert, Climate Change Specialist, up an exterior stairway and around the back, near a small but well-tended garden with benches and a Zen fountain.

"Mr. Leimert?" I asked as I opened the door and poked my head in. I had been expecting a waiting room or a foyer of some sort and was surprised when the door opened directly onto his small office, with a single desk and three chairs for guests. The walls were covered with photographs of the ocean and mountains, and a large poster featured hazard symbols: a skull and crossbones, and several different signs warning of radiation.

"Call me Eugene, please," he said, standing. Eugene was a portly, red-faced man, the kind of big person who seemed unfamiliar with his own size. His blazer was too small and clearly strained at the shoulders. "Come on in. You must be Patience."

"I'm Lily," I said, and gestured to Patience. "This is Patience."

His eyes lit up with appreciation. "A pleasure," he

sighed. "Please, have a seat." He dropped into his desk chair with a pronounced "*oof.*"

"Thank you for meeting us. I hope we're not interrupting your dinner."

"No problem. Any friend of Bronwyn's, as they say. How's she doing?"

"She's doing well," I said. "She's a joy to work with."

"Yeah, she mentioned you're a vintage clothes type gal. So what are you doing on Treasure Island? Probably not the best venue for a resale shop."

"I'm not scouting for store locations," I said. "In fact, it's sort of odd, I guess, but I wanted to ask you about a suspicious death."

"Is this about Marcellus Tinley?"

"I take it you've heard."

He nodded. "Still plugged into the island gossip network. Poor guy. Have they figured out what happened?"

I shook my head. "Do you know anyone who might have wanted to harm Marcellus?"

He stuck his chin out and looked thoughtful. "Marcellus was quirky, but if you ask me, he wasn't the type to inspire a homicidal rage. Still, I haven't seen him in a long time, so maybe he'd changed. The one *I'd* like to kill is Leo Airey."

"Leo? The motorcycle repair shop guy?"

"Stands to make a fortune on a bunch of condos he wants to develop. If, that is, he can get the plans approved. Right now, that's a big 'if,' and rightly so."

"You don't favor the development plans?"

"Look, it's an artificial island, I get that. Mother Nature didn't put it there, a bunch of engineers did. So if some developer's going to plant a bunch of condos on an island, it's the logical choice because there's nothing natural there to be despoiled. That being said, there are a slew of other environmental problems that have to be addressed and resolved first." He shook his head. "Leo and I have had several run-ins over the years, personal as well as professional, so I'm probably not an unbiased source of information about his character. Suffice it to say, I trust Leo about as far as I can throw him."

"I've heard there are some rumors about Marcellus and underage girls," I said.

He grimaced. "Sounds like you've been listening to Orson Goff. He's another one on the list, as far as I'm concerned."

"'Goff' is Orson's last name? As in Cece Goff?"

He nodded. "He's her father. He had a bug up his ass—pardon my French—because Marcellus let the kids hang out at his house and help him with the pigeons and all. Those kids don't have a lot to do out there on the island. You ask me, I think it's sad that a man can't do that sort of thing without being thought of as having an ulterior motive."

"What's *really* too bad is that some men do have ulterior motives," said Patience.

"True enough," said Eugene. "So, speaking of having designs on beautiful women: Is Bronwyn seeing anybody?"

"Um," I responded, surprised by his question. "Yes, she is. A very nice fellow named Duke. They've been together for a while now and are going strong."

"Oh, well. Good for her. She's a lovely lady and deserves to be happy. Personally, I'm a three-time loser," he said with a long sigh, and ticked off the numbers with three fingers: "Denise, Sandra, and Jane. Finally figured out that marriage isn't a good fit for me. Now it's just me and the cause. Climate change."

"The cause needs you," said Patience.

"That it does. More than any of my wives ever did, I guess."

I couldn't stop looking at the hazard symbols. It seemed so odd to see them sprinkled all over the island.

Eugene noticed my gaze. "The trefoil design for the radiation warning was developed right here, at the UC Berkeley Radiation Laboratory, in 1946. It was originally magenta against a bright blue background. I don't know why I like that fact, that a bunch of scientists favored magenta."

"I noticed it out on Treasure Island," I said. "Bronwyn said you thought the island was making you sick? Was it the radiation?"

"No way to know, really," he gave a wry chuckle. "Part of me thought it might be my wife at the time, tryin' to kill me—and let's face it, she probably had cause—but then I realized it was the island. And I'm not the only one."

"Are you feeling better, now that you've left the island?" asked Patience.

"I am, yes, thanks for asking."

"You're a Treasure Island native, right?" I asked. "Would you happen to know of any elders who had attended, or heard stories about, the World's Fair?"

"That was . . . 1939 to '40? That's an awfully long time ago."

"I know. But I was thinking perhaps someone who had attended as a child? Apparently millions of people went."

He nodded. "It was a world's fair, so a lot of those came from elsewhere, even abroad. I heard about the fair my whole life, of course. Going to school on the island, it's always a topic in our local history. Too bad the museum's closed."

"Yes, it really is too bad. I've read a lot about it online and seen a lot of photos, but it would be nice to speak to someone directly."

"The only person I can think of, offhand, is Shirley Faderin. She used to come speak to our classes in school, and later I got in touch with her about the environmental situation out there."

"Does she still live on the island?"

He shook his head. "Oh, no. She never lived on the island. I think she was originally from San Francisco, but last I heard she was in Emeryville, not far from here. Her maiden name was Mangicaro."

"She's the little girl in the articles—," I began.

"Yup," he said with a nod. "The little girl allegedly saved by a mermaid."

Chapter 22

"Kudos to him for taking on any aspect of climate change," said Patience after we left Eugene's office. "But I gotta say, he's a bit of a sad sack, sitting alone in that little office at this hour. Hard to imagine what-all he could be getting done. On the other hand, I'm one to talk, right? I should probably get more involved."

Patience surprised me for the second time that day.

"I suppose we all should," I said.

"Or I could make a few million off those Internet startups and throw some real money at the problem," she said. "But for now, I need coffee. Quick, before they close."

We stopped at the original Peet's, on Walnut. We hadn't eaten dinner yet, so I ordered a muffin in addition to a regular coffee, plus a pound of French roast for home.

Patience ordered two muffins and a "coffee" that turned out to be essentially an espresso-based smoothie topped with a mountain of whipped cream.

"Back home they'd call that a milkshake and charge you a buck, tops," I teased.

"This 'back home' is the godforsaken town you're always going on about?"

"It wasn't all bad. There's a Frosty Freeze, with dip cones and soft-serve."

"Be still my heart," she said, sipping her drink through a thick paper straw.

As we walked toward my car, I choked on my coffee when I saw someone I recognized.

"What's *he* doing here?" I asked, stepping into a closed storefront alcove to avoid being spotted.

"He who?" asked Patience.

I yanked her into the alcove with me.

"Hey!" she said. "What's gotten into you? I nearly dropped my muffins."

"See that guy?"

"The skinhead with all the tattoos?"

"Yeah. He's from Treasure Island. He locked Maya and me in an abandoned pool building."

"Maybe you shouldn't have been there in the first place."

"That's not relevant at the moment."

She frowned, took a big bite of a muffin, and slurped more of her coffee drink. "You think he followed you here?"

"I have no idea, but I'd like to find out. There's something about him that puts me on edge."

"Probably because he locked you in an abandoned pool building."

"Even before that."

"Not all skinheads are political, you know," she said with a shrug. "Some are far right, some far left, and sometimes it's just a fashion choice."

"He has a swastika tattoo."

"Okay, definitely off-putting, then."

We watched as Zane went into a shop that sported a pastel pink and lilac sign declaring: LAVENDER FIELDS SKIN CARE AND SALON DE BEAUTÉ.

"Huh," Patience said. "I guess a skinhead would need good skin care."

"He doesn't look like a guy who gets facials," I said.

"What does a guy who gets facials look like?"

"Not sure, but not him."

We stood there for another moment.

"Are you going to *do* something, or are we just going to wait here until his botanical mask treatment is finished?" Patience demanded.

"What would you suggest?"

"You're the Witchy Princess of the Bay Area, aren't you? Can't you throw your jar of brew at him, or something?"

"And then what? Hope he steps on the broken glass and cuts his foot so he can't run away? I've told you before, Patience. I can't just whip out a magic wand and turn him into a frog. That's not how magic works. At least, not for me."

"Some Witchy Princess you are," she said, checking a slim gold watch on her wrist. Her bangles clanked pleasantly. "Can we hurry this up? I don't have all night."

"Look! He's coming out. Let's follow him."

"Why?"

"To see where he goes, of course."

"Why?"

"Come *on*, Patience, he's getting into his car."

She sighed and tossed her empty drink cup into a nearby trash receptacle. "Lucky for you, I'm now fully caffeinated and ready to make all kinds of bad decisions. Let's hurry, then."

We jumped in the Mustang and I pulled an illegal U-turn on busy Shattuck Avenue, earning myself several honks and a raised fist or two. Patience rolled down her window and made a rude hand gesture in return.

"Stop that, Patience. I was the one in the wrong. And we're trying to be discreet, remember?"

"The honking and the bright red classic Mustang might well have foiled that plan."

"You think he spotted us?" I asked as Zane's car sped up before coming to a sudden halt as a gaggle of UC Berkeley students crossed the street. I stopped quite a ways behind him, to the consternation of the driver behind me.

"Here's a piece of career advice for you: Stick with vintage clothing. You have no future as a private investigator," said Patience. "Why don't you pull over and let me take the wheel?"

The students finally cleared the street and traffic started moving again. Unfortunately, downtown Berkeley is crowded with pedestrians and full of stoplights, so it was hard to be inconspicuous. Still, I figured as long as Zane didn't pay attention to his rearview mirror, I was okay.

"Remind me: Why are we following him?" asked Patience. "I mean, what are we going to do if and when we catch him? Are you carrying?"

"Carrying what?" I asked, watching the car ahead of me closely.

"A gun, of course."

"A—? Of *course* not."

"So, what's your plan? Steal something from his car and hex it?"

"I don't *hex* people," I claimed. "That's an ugly witch stereotype."

She raised one eyebrow.

"I *rarely* hex people," I conceded. "And it's still an ugly stereotype."

By now we had left Berkeley and were driving along the narrow streets clinging to the sides of the Oakland hills.

"Where is he going?" I asked.

"How should I know?"

"It was a rhetorical question," I said as I careened around a hairpin turn, narrowly avoiding nicking a parked car that sat half in the roadway. Night had fallen, the soft light of early evening fading rapidly as we drove through the thick redwood forest. "But come to think of it, why don't you know? You're a psychic, aren't you?"

"It takes tools and concentration. I can't just figure out where some random skinhead is going."

"Some psychic you are."

"I think we lost him," said Patience. "Do you see him? I don't see him."

"No, I don't, either," I said, discouraged.

"Where are we, anyway?"

"On Skyline, near Sibley Regional Park. I came here a long time ago, with Oscar. It's pretty interesting—there are labyrinths of stone set into a deep canyon, and the volcanic rock of the area is considered by many to be imbued with power."

"*And?* I don't care how many vintage dresses you promise me, I am not tripping around volcanic canyons in the dark looking for a swastika-covered skinhead."

"I have a flashlight in my backpack."

"Not enough dresses in the world," said Patience with finality.

"You're right," I sighed. "So, what now?"

"We could head home for cocktail hour, like sane people," said Patience, switching on the overhead light to check her lipstick in the vanity mirror.

"What if I throw in a darling little cashmere shrug and a Hermès scarf I picked up at a flea market in Paris?" I offered.

"I suppose we could retrace our steps and go back to Berkeley," Patience said, accepting my bribe. "Skinhead was coming out of a beauty salon, the kind of place that gives Botox injections and does electrolysis, right? We could ask what he was doing there and see if they have a last name for him, or something along those lines."

"Good idea!" I said, shifting the Mustang into gear, then drove back down the hill to Berkeley, again aided by the GPS on Patience's phone.

We found a parking spot around the corner from the salon, but as we turned onto Shattuck, I noticed someone getting off a Harley-Davidson motorcycle. He pulled off his half helmet. It was Orson Goff.

I pulled Patience into the same alcove as last time.

"Again?" She asked. "Why is it that every time we're together we end up running and hiding? Have you ever thought about that? Because I gotta say, I'm starting to think you're not ideal BFF material, cool vintage store or not."

"See that unpleasant-looking guy over there, the one with the big belly? He's from Treasure Island, too. Maybe . . . I don't know. Maybe he's here to meet Zane at a secret Nazi get-together?"

"At the Lavender Fields Skin Care and Salon de Beauté?"

"It would be the last place *I'd* look for Nazis."

"True enough."

Patience tapped her foot and grumbled about dresses

and cashmere shrugs while I tried to decide my next move, then Orson came out of the salon, threw his leg over his Harley, pulled on his half helmet—leaving it unfastened—and roared off down Shattuck Ave.

"What say we see what the Lavender Fields aestheticians have to say for themselves," I said.

The sleek front counter was staffed by a perfectly coiffed and made-up young woman. She gave us a brilliant smile that could have been featured on a toothpaste ad.

"May I help you?"

"I hope so," I said. "I have a question about the man who just left. Tall, thinning blond hair . . ."

"Yes?" She didn't volunteer anything, but she also didn't seem spooked, as if he had been in here threatening anything, or anyone.

"Was he . . . looking for something?"

"As a matter of fact, he was asking about a potential client. Why?"

"Who might that be?" I wished I could think faster on my feet. Why hadn't I thought this through while lurking in the alcove? I stroked my medicine bag and cast a quick comforting spell, hoping she would trust me enough to spill the beans.

"Oh, I don't think I'm supposed to give out that sort of information. I didn't tell him anything, either. Client privacy, and all that. I hope you understand."

"I see. What about the young man who left about twenty minutes ago, the fellow in the Raiders sweatshirt? His name is Zane . . . something . . ." I trailed off and mumbled a quick charm.

She nodded but remained mute.

"Was he here because of his . . . ?" I trailed off, hoping she'd fill in the blank.

"Tattoo?" She grimaced. "It's the main reason guys

come in here. We do laser tattoo removal. He made an appointment for next week."

"Oh. He has a lot of tattoos."

"No one wants to see a swastika though, right? I mean, if you're trying to apply for a job, or going to school, or really just anywhere decent. A thing like that has to be pretty awkward. Swastikas give me the creeps."

"That seems to be the consensus opinion. Could you tell me his last name?"

"Oh, I'm not supposed to give out that kind of information."

"Okay . . ." I tried to think of another way to get it, but nothing occurred to me. Maybe Patience had picked up on something. "Thank you so much for your time."

"No problem! Oh, here," she said, handing me a brochure on Botox. "Those tiny wrinkles? Gone, just like that. We do lip injections as well." She leaned toward me and lowered her voice. "We don't want to neglect our skin and lose the plump lips of our youth, now do we?"

Without intending to, my hand went up to my lips. Patience looked amused. I dropped my hand, feeling self-conscious.

"What did you pick up from the receptionist?" I asked as we walked around the corner to the car.

"She was telling the truth."

"That's it?"

"Wait. . . . Hold on. . . ." Patience held her fingertips to her temples as though sensing something otherworldly. "Eeny meeny jelly beany, I'm feeling the spirit of déjà vu. . . . I wonder, why would that be? Oh, *right*," she said as she dropped her hands. "Because we've already been over this. I tell people's fortunes with the aid of a crystal ball and/or tarot cards and/or a pendulum and/or scrying in a black mirror. I don't go around reading people's minds. It doesn't work that way."

"Too bad," I said. "It would make life a lot easier."

"You're telling me."

We climbed into the car.

"Any more hoodlums you'd like to chase through the East Bay?" asked Patience. "Want to try to track down the Harley?"

"No," I said as I pulled out into traffic. "I need to get back to the shop. I have a contractor coming by to look at the possibility of expanding into the attic."

She raised one eyebrow. "Sailor mentioned that. He sounded as excited as a child with his first bike. Gotta hand it to you, Lily. You have certainly domesticated that man."

"I haven't! I mean, it was all his idea."

She gave a husky chuckle. "I'm just saying, princess, Sailor was always a wild child, but he's changed since he's met you. In a good way, if you want to know the truth. He used to hang out at dive bars, smoking and drinking. But of course we can never really change anyone unless they're looking to change themselves, right?"

I was going to have to ponder that one. After all, I loved Sailor just as he was and certainly didn't want him to change for *me*. I hoped we both brought out the best in each other. So maybe I brought out his domestic side? Was there any problem with that?

I couldn't wrap my mind around that at the moment, so I changed the subject.

"You know what's weird?" I said as we headed down University, toward the freeway.

"That you're even contemplating Botox injections."

"I'm *not*," I said, though I could feel myself blush.

"No, it's that Zane lives on Treasure Island. Good for him for getting his tattoo removed, but wouldn't there be options closer to home?"

"You think Treasure Island has a lot of tattoo-removal options?"

"No, probably not. You're right."

"It makes sense that there would be more choices in Berkeley, given the number of tattoos I saw on the people walking the streets," said Patience. "Doesn't seem like much of a stretch to me. Same reason people from Burlingame come to the Haight to look for great vintage clothing at places like Aunt Cora's Closet."

That was about the closest thing I'd ever heard to a compliment coming from those beautiful lips. *Patience* was in no need of Botox, I noticed with a pang.

As we passed through the toll booth and started on the Oakland span of the Bay Bridge, toward the tunnel at Yerba Buena, I thought about the inhabitants I had met on Treasure Island and what Renna had told me. I guess I was destined to go back not only to the island but to the pool building and the Nazi clubhouse.

And what had Orson Goff been doing in Berkeley? Had he been following me? Or Zane? Or might he have needed a swastika tattoo removed himself?

Chapter 23

After dropping Patience at her place, I let myself into a silent Aunt Cora's Closet, which was already closed for the evening. As usual, simply walking into my shop helped to soothe my nerves. I breathed deeply of the subtle aroma of the rosemary, clove, and dried orange peel of this week's fresh herbal sachets, and the ever-present scent of fresh laundry. The sensations here were peaceful, mellow, not only from the hum of the clothing but also from the lingering energy of all my friends and family. Good vibrations.

I picked up the phone and called Maya.

"Guess what? I have a phone number for you," I said. "Shirley Faderin, née Mangicaro."

"She's still alive?"

"Last Eugene Leimert heard, she was. Want to give her a call, see if she's willing to speak with us? We could go tomorrow afternoon, if she's available. Conrad and Bronwyn are both scheduled to be at the shop."

"Will do," said Maya. "See you in the morning."

Just as I was hanging up, Mel Turner walked in.

"You're not still open, are you?" she asked.

"Only for the likes of you. Thank you so much for coming by! I know how busy you are."

Mel ran a highly sought-after renovation company, Turner Construction, that had been founded by her father. She had been raised on construction sites and seemed able to fix just about anything, from a malfunctioning toilet to a crooked stairway to a building permit bogged down at city hall. And she did almost all of it in wildly flamboyant, sparkly outfits, typically paired with steel-toed boots. She told me she carried around a pair of coveralls in case she needed to crawl around muddy basements and dusty attics, but the sight of her in her usual party garb always made me smile. She was a curvy, strong-looking woman who didn't seem to care what anyone thought of her style choices. She fit in just fine in the Haight in general, and in Aunt Cora's Closet in particular.

"Oh, I've been looking forward to it," she said, waving off my concerns. "Like I said, I was in Chinatown for dinner, so it was no problem. Besides, it's always a hoot to check out your new merchandise."

"Would you like to take some time to look around?" I asked. "I have a nice new sparkly sheath, just came in. If you don't snatch it up, I guarantee my grandmother will."

Mel laughed. "You're saying your grandmother and I have similar tastes in clothes?"

"You haven't met my grandmother," I said. "She's pretty special."

"Sure, I'd love to check out the sparkly dress, but then I should take a quick look at your proposed project. It's movie night at my dad's place. Wouldn't want to be late, or I'll miss out on the ice cream."

The sheath looked beautiful on her, but I refused to let her pay for it. "You're the one doing me the favor, after all," I said, wrapping it up.

"But you assessed a dress for me, not so long ago. And I'm going to ask you to check out the rest of the contents of the closet very soon."

"It would be my pleasure. Anyway, keep the dress, Mel. It looks great on you. Consider it an early wedding present."

"Thank you," said Mel. "I hear congratulations are in order for you as well."

"Yes, we had a handfasting in a redwood circle. It was very small," I added hurriedly, feeling rude that I hadn't thought to invite her.

"Sounds perfect, actually. We're still not sure what's happening with ours, but Landon would like to invite the entire city of Oakland and most of San Francisco, while I just want to get it over with. We're still in negotiations."

I called Sailor down from the apartment, made the introductions, and we went next door to Lucille's shop, where we made more introductions, and then climbed the two flights of stairs to the attic.

Sailor sketched out his ideas, referencing the current floor plan of our apartment, and after listening carefully Mel clicked on her flashlight and looked behind things, knocked on walls, assessed window frames, measured with an electronic measuring device, and nodded and hmmed a lot.

While she was thus engaged, I started going through some of the non-clothing items Khalil Singh had asked me to take care of, deciding how to best find them good homes.

Finally, Mel switched off her flashlight, returned to the center of the attic, and nodded.

"Great idea," she said. "With space at such a pre-mium in the city, I'm surprised it hasn't been attempted before. You're thinking of spiral stairs?"

Sailor nodded and pointed. "There, in an inner cor-ner of the downstairs living room. Given space con-straints, it seemed like the best option."

"I agree. As long as your knees are okay, spiral stairs not only save on space but also on headaches. Stairwells can be a real pain to retrofit."

"You don't think it'll cost too much?" I asked.

"Oh, well, if *we* at Turner Construction did it, it would cost you a fortune," she said with a grin. "But seriously, you don't need us. As long as these walls are in as good a shape on the inside as they appear—and they do look good but no promises; sometimes you find unexpected damage in old buildings—the work should be fairly straightforward. I'll give you the names of a licensed plumber and electrician, but if you're handy," she said, with an assessing eye running over Sailor's muscles, "putting up walls isn't rocket science."

"That's what I thought," said Sailor.

"They just always seem so . . . permanent," I said.

"I know," said Mel. "Psychologically, we think of our homes as fortresses, or wombs, or something like that. Like magical shells. But they're just plaster and wood, easy enough to tear down and rebuild with a little hard work and skill. Don't want to put myself out of business, but there are some helpful videos on the Internet. But once again, I'll warn you away from the plumbing and electrical. There's a reason those profes-sions require years of apprenticeships."

"I have nothing but respect for that kind of skill," said Sailor as we headed to the door to the attic stairs. "I will leave plumbing and electrical in the hands of professionals."

"By the way," said Mel, rapping on the door. "This should be rehung to open inward, just to be safe."

Sailor nodded. "I'll put that on the list."

"That reminds me," I said. "The other day I was in an old building where the doors opened inward, but someone mentioned they should have opened out."

"Was this a public building?"

"Yes, it was."

Mel nodded. "In private homes the code usually specifies that doors open inward, so that if debris falls in front of the door you're not trapped inside. Also, you can take the pins out and remove the door altogether from the inside, if need be. But public buildings are different. In the 1940s there was a fire at the Cocoanut Grove nightclub in Boston. The surge of people trying to escape prevented the door from opening inward and hundreds died who might have been saved if the door had only opened outward. After that, the codes for public buildings were changed."

"What a tragedy," I said as we started down the stairs.

"Unfortunately, it sometimes takes tragedies for changes to be made. People love to complain about building codes, and I get it, but there are often very good reasons for them."

"Hey, Mel, did you feel anything *eerie* in the attic?"

Mel smiled and shook her head. "Not at all. I'm sure you would have noticed my glassy stare before now."

Mel always struck me as unflappable, but she had told me herself she had a hard time, at first, when spirits reached out to her.

We passed through the after-hours quiet of Lucille's shop and out to the bustling nightlife of Haight Street. Sailor thanked Mel profusely and returned to the apartment, while I walked Mel to her car.

"One more thing," I said, as Mel unlocked a battered, dusty Scion. "I've been . . . pursuing something out on Treasure Island."

"The place in the bay?"

"Yes. And of course, it's possible there may be some lingering spirits . . ."

"There probably are," Mel said. "But in my experience, they're seldom out to do harm."

"I guess what I'm wondering is, if I do find someone, or something, or . . ."

"Some*one*."

"If I *do* make contact with someone, I mean . . . what do I do then?"

"I wish I had an easy answer for you, Lily. The only thing I know to do is to listen. Really listen, and if there's some way you can help, then do that. There's usually a reason they're still hanging around, so bear that in mind. Most are harmless, but don't be surprised if one is unpleasant. Rather like the living, I suppose, the ghosts you least want to meet up with sometimes show up in your face." She stopped and studied my face. "Do you want me to go with you?"

Slowly, I shook my head. "I certainly do appreciate the offer, but I've got backup."

Upstairs I found an essential member of my "backup" playing with Winston-the-bat.

"Mistress! Check this out!"

Winston was hanging upside down from Oscar's finger, and Oscar flipped him around.

"Careful not to hurt him, Oscar."

"I won't. He's a cute little guy, isn't he? Can we keep him?"

"We'll see."

Oscar's face fell. "That means no."

"What do you mean?"

"When you say 'we'll see' that means no. I'm real good at languages, you know."

"I'm sorry, Oscar, I'm just exhausted. It's been a heck of a day. Why don't we give it a few more days and see if Winston makes up his own mind? He's welcome to stay if he wants, but if he needs to be free, well, you know what they say."

"Set it free and if it doesn't come back, then hunt it down and kill it, right?"

"No, you let it come back if it wants to. As you very well know."

"Are you grumpy 'cause you learned something about the prophecy from Renna?" he said, now cuddling Winston in the crook of his arm and poking him in the belly with his fingertip.

"How did you know I went to speak with Renna?" I asked, though I assumed he wouldn't answer me. Oscar almost never answered a question he didn't like. Also, Oscar knew things. How, I had never figured out. But he knew.

The bedroom door opened and Sailor emerged, his hair damp from a shower. After a long kiss, which prompted Oscar to snort with derision, Sailor poured us both glasses of wine as I went over what Renna had seen concerning the "immediate" threat that involved returning to the natatorium, and the "overarching" threat, which was still vague.

"She indicated that whatever human threat we're facing on Treasure Island is like a warning, or a clue, to the overarching threat looming over San Francisco. In fact, it might have something to do with the water spirits, or merfolk," I said.

"What is it with you and islands lately?" asked Sailor.

"I was wondering the same thing. According to

Renna, it has to do with the perceived isolation, psychological if not real. If the Golden Gate Bridge somehow created, or blocked, a natural portal, then the individual islands in the bay might be vulnerable, and act as beacons to . . . things that are not good."

"And being ringed by saltwater doesn't hurt," said Oscar, munching on Goldfish crackers.

"That, too," I said with a nod. "There was a whole lot about the salts being out of whack, because they desalinated the land when they built Treasure Island—"

"And proceeded to replace the salts with radiation?" asked Sailor.

"I'm sure no one set out to do so, but maybe that's part of the problem, yes."

"The spirits don't like things like that," said Oscar, shaking his head. "Ain't natural."

Winston-the-bat still clung to him, and I decided it might not be the worst thing in the world for my ersatz familiar to have a little critter of his own.

"Renna says you have to go back to this pool building? I'll go with you."

"She indicated I should go alone."

"I'll go with you," said Oscar. "I ain't afraid of no Nazis."

"No, *I'll* go with you," Sailor repeated.

"I haven't even decided yet if I'm going, but thank you both for offering." I decided to set that aside for the moment. "What's bothering me is that Renna said the overarching threat can only be confronted with the *coincidentia oppositorum*."

Sailor understood. "That's not me."

"I wish it were. It would make things so much simpler."

"Then who *is* your counterpart?"

"Aidan," said Oscar.

"I think it might have been," I said. "If he were here, and healthy. But Renna mentioned the possibility . . . what if it's Dragomir?"

"Your brother," said Sailor.

"She says we're astral twins."

Sailor reared back. "*Really.* Huh. That actually makes a lot of sense."

"Does it? I've never heard of it before; I was going to look in my Book of Shadows."

"The astral plane, as I understand it, is a dimension much larger, and very like, our earthly plane, teeming with astral beings and spirits. It's where I go when I'm in a psychic trance and able to intuit symbols. If you and Dragomir are united in the astral plane, it means you knew each other before."

"Yup," Oscar confirmed.

"That would explain why he felt so familiar to me," I said.

Sailor nodded. "It also means you are fated to travel at least part of this life together. In tandem. Looks like I'd better check this guy out. You have a phone number for him?"

"I imagine he'll be in touch."

"Guess we'll have to wait, then. I don't like how mysterious he's been about the whole thing. Why not just call you up and introduce himself?"

"There was a lost note. Don't ask. Anyway, he's as wary of me as I am of him," I said. "We have a scary father, you know."

"Darn tootin'," said Oscar. "A demon's minion is like that."

Chapter 24

The next morning, Maya came into Aunt Cora's Closet and announced: "Guess what? There's a pigeon rescue group right here in San Francisco. It's part of a national group, called Palomacy, rhymes with 'diplomacy.' They do pigeon and dove rescue—it turns out pigeons bred in captivity do need to be taken care of. I'll call Leo and let him know."

"Oh, that's great," I said. "What a relief."

"And then I looked up Ingeborg Nachtnebel, and her Black Forest Bathing Beauties."

"What did you find out?"

"Well, first off, there are plenty of rivers and ponds in the Black Forest, so maybe that explains the mermaid thing. But Nachtnebel's story is really tragic. She was Jewish, and with everything going on in Germany in 1939, she asked to remain after her gig at the fair came to an end. But the government would not grant her refugee status."

That matched what Dragomir told me about his great aunt.

"And she was sent back," I said.

Maya nodded. "According to what I could find out, she was deported and died in Auschwitz. Along with millions of others."

That afternoon, Maya and I went to speak with a woman about a mermaid. But as we climbed into the car, Maya seemed unusually subdued.

"How are you doing, Maya? Is everything okay?"

"Nothing serious. I get migraines occasionally, as you know. That tincture you gave me really helps head off the worst parts, but it's still there. Threatening. Vulture-like."

"Oh, you poor thing," I said as we drove down Haight Street. "Are you sure you're up for this today? We can reschedule."

"Are you kidding me? Miss out on a talk with little Shirley Mangicaro? My recorder is primed."

"Oh, good." I kept driving, heading down Oak and skirting the Golden Gate Park panhandle. "I was thinking . . . maybe there's something else on your mind?"

"Like what?"

"It's really none of my business. But as Bronwyn would say, maybe there's romance in the air?"

"What are you talking about?"

I wished I hadn't started this. "Is there something between you and Conrad?"

"*Conrad?*" She let out a little chuckle. "No, of course not. Why would you think that?"

"You two seem to have grown close, much closer than you used to be."

"We *are* close. We've gotten to be really good friends. . . . I don't think I've ever had a close guy friend. It's really nice."

"I'm glad to hear it."

It was early Sunday afternoon but there was still a decent amount of traffic, and we slowed down at the approach to the freeway leading to the Bay Bridge.

"Besides," said Maya. "I mean, the Con is great and all, but I'm not into men."

"They can try one's patience, that's for sure," I said, thinking of the little boy excitement in Sailor's eyes as he was sketching out the floor plan for the apartment. I found it simultaneously adorable and annoying, even occasionally alarming.

"I don't mean in that way. I'm actually . . . into women."

"*Wait*—what?"

"I'm gay."

"You *are*?"

"You seem shocked," she chuckled. "Is that . . . you don't have a problem with it, do you?"

"Oh, of course not! I just didn't realize."

"I don't talk about it much. And for a long time, I didn't admit it to myself, totally."

"I get that. But I'm a witch, after all. You'd think I might have picked up on . . . something."

"Like what? Are there gay auras or something?"

"Not at all," I said with a chuckle. "And you know me, I'm not that great at reading auras, anyway. But now that I think of it, I've never seen you with . . . anyone, romantically. I guess I've always thought you were solitary, and okay with that. Sort of like I was, before Sailor."

She shrugged. "I've seen myself that way, too. Anyway, to tell you the truth, it's been kind of hard coming out, with my mom."

I was surprised to hear that. Lucille and Maya always seemed so close, and while I knew Lucille was active in her church, I had a hard time believing she would reject her daughter for *any* reason. I thought, again, of my mother rejecting me, and my magic, when I was a girl. How could we deny the essence of who we are, our power, our very selves?

"Is she . . . having a hard time with it?" I asked gently.

She nodded. "But you're okay?"

"Of course! You're exactly the same person you were yesterday," I said, "and the day before that. An extraordinary person."

"Mom is mostly upset that I didn't trust her enough to tell her earlier," Maya said, gazing out the window. "I guess she's suspected for some time. No, the real problem is with some of her friends, and the rest of our family. My dad is a little freaked out, trying to wrap his head around it, but Mom says he'll come around." She shrugged, as if to shake it off. "Anyway, Conrad and I have become good friends, really good friends. I have an old friend from high school who's been struggling with addiction, and Conrad has sort of taken him under his wing. They've been going to meetings together. And he helped me find the courage to finally come out to my parents."

"That's great, Maya. I'm glad you were able to tell them. And me. Not that your love life is any of my business, but I want you to be happy."

"And extraordinary?" she said with a smile.

"Extraordinary, indeed."

Once we finally got on the Bay Bridge the traffic moved at a good clip, and twenty minutes later Maya and I stood outside a tall condo building perched on a small thumb of a peninsula in Emeryville, at the foot of the Oakland span of the Bay Bridge.

"Somehow, I pictured her living in the woods somewhere," said Maya. "Somewhere like Calypso's house."

I knew exactly what she meant. Calypso's house was the perfect setting for a magical woman: a beautiful old farmhouse nestled in a glade, surrounded by redwoods and ferns, cats lolling on the deep porch.

Shirley Mangicaro Faderin, on the other hand, lived in a modern, sleek high-rise.

"I'm not certain she self-identifies as a witch," I said.

"You get to choose?" asked Maya. "How does that work, anyway?"

"Like a lot of things in life, I suppose: Some people aspire to it, and some who are born this way spend a lot of time denying it." I thought of how different my upbringing was from that of my half brother: Dragomir was born to a mother who accepted him for what he was and taught him how to refine his talents, while I had spent most of my childhood denying who I was and trying, and failing, to be someone my peers and my mother would accept. Had it not been for Graciela, I might have wound up hating myself and become a very angry witch. "But it's a personal choice. I don't like to assume."

Maya nodded, and typed a number into the phone pad outside the main entrance. A quavering voice answered: "Yes?"

"Ms. Faderin?" Maya asked. "I'm Maya Jackson. We spoke on the phone?"

"I've been expecting you," she said. "Would you be a doll and bring up my mail? The code on the box is the same as my apartment number: 421."

"Of course," said Maya. The buzzer made a rude

sound, and we pushed through the glass door. The neat but nondescript lobby boasted two crushed velvet wing chairs and a credenza, over which hung a large gilt-framed mirror. To the right was a long bank of brass mailboxes, and on the back wall were two sets of elevators.

Maya gathered the mail—a few bills, a greeting card, a couple of large manila envelopes, and an assortment of advertising fliers—and we headed up in the elevator to the fourth floor. Halfway down a long, narrow hallway, we knocked on #421.

An elderly woman opened the door. Her smooth white hair was cut in a chic bob, and she wore an emerald green cashmere cardigan over a silk shirt, a pair of cream-colored wool slacks, and a string of perfectly matched pearls. In her understated elegance, Mrs. Faderin would not have been out of place in one of the Bay Area's many upscale suburbs: Alamo or Hillsborough or even Belvedere.

"Thank you for bringing up my mail," she said. "Sometimes even just getting downstairs can be a bit much. I don't like to use my walker in public, but it's essential for my safety."

"My pleasure," said Maya as she handed the stack to the older woman, who flipped through the items briefly before setting them aside.

"It's nice to meet you face-to-face, Mrs. Faderin," said Maya. "This is my friend Lily Ivory. She's also my boss, so be sure to make me look good."

"How do you do? But please, call me Shirley. Mrs. Faderin was my mother-in-law, and we never really got along." Shirley chuckled and ushered us into a large living room. Now I understood the appeal of the otherwise soulless building. A long wall of windows looked out across the San Francisco Bay: at the Bay Bridge immediately to the left, Treasure Island, all of downtown San Francisco, the Golden Gate Bridge, and part of Marin to the north. A picturesque thick blanket of fog lingered over the hills, but the bay, the city, and the bridges sparkled in the afternoon sunlight.

"What a stunning view," said Maya.

"It really is," I seconded.

"I count myself fortunate to have found this place. When my husband was alive we had a beautiful house in the hills, but after he passed I needed a change. And, well, I don't care for old things," she said. "And that includes me."

I wasn't sure what to say to that.

Like many of Graciela's coven sisters, I couldn't quite tell Shirley's age. She certainly wasn't ancient, at least not compared to a lot of the witches I've known. Her hands were thin and lined with ropes of blue veins, her eyes were rheumy and her face wrinkled. But if I hadn't known she was a child at the Golden Gate Exposition, I might have assumed she was a hard-fought seventy.

"Shirley," said Maya as we sat on the dove-gray living room couch. "Would you mind if I record our conversation, so I don't forget anything?"

"I don't mind at all," she said. "Where shall I begin?"

"Wherever you like," Maya said, and Shirley launched into her story. She grew up in San Francisco's Washington Square neighborhood, in the Italian area—"It wasn't nearly so fancy back then, we were all Italians, going to the Catholic school there"—until she married and moved to Oakland with her husband. He fought in the Korean War, she worked briefly as a secretary while he was in the service but mostly was a homemaker. And there was her true calling: her healing.

"Could you tell us more about that?" Maya asked.

"I thought that was why you contacted me, because of my healing work. I don't do much of that anymore; I seem to be a forgotten old lady now. But back in the day, I was quite well known."

"I read that you healed an injured man at the World's Fair," said Maya.

"Yes, that's where it started." She looked out at the view, toward Treasure Island. "It's funny, I thought no one was interested in the World's Fair anymore. But you're the second person to ask me about it in so many weeks!"

Maya met my gaze, but before I had a chance to ask who she might be referring to, Shirley went on with her story. "Oh, it was so exciting! I'm a child of the Great Depression, you know, and those were grim years. And then the Bay Bridge connected Oakland and the East Bay to San Francisco, and the Golden Gate Bridge connected the city to Marin, and it felt like such *progress*! The flags of all nations flew on the streets of San Francisco, and the fair was billed as a grand Pan-Pacific celebration of world peace and neighborliness. Walking through those elephant gates felt like entering another world! It was just lovely."

Maya smiled warmly at the old woman. "I've seen photographs, but I'm not sure they do it justice."

"They *don't*, I assure you," she said with a nod. "No photograph can. There was a vibrancy in the air, you see, the feeling of excitement when stepping foot on that new island. They created it, out of nothing, right there on the shoals of Yerba Buena Island. Can you imagine? Lily, will you bring that big green album over here? There are some photographs I'd like to show you."

"Of course," I said as I went to a large bookshelf on the far wall and picked up the album. The other books on the shelf had a maritime theme: sailor lore, mermaids, dragons, chimeras, and other fantastical sea creatures. Another shelf held tomes about natural health and healing.

"It seems like quite the feat of engineering," Maya said. "To build an island for a fair."

"Oh, my, yes, it was. But then, that was when men *built* things: grand bridges and even islands! Not like today, when a person is drowned in paperwork and environmental reports just to remodel a simple bathroom!"

I bit my tongue, remembering what Mel Turner had said last night. Building whatever one wanted without concern for the environment or safety codes might have been easier, but it could cause other, sometimes disastrous, problems. But I pushed those thoughts aside to focus on what we were here to find out.

"So, Shirley," I said as I handed her the album. "You mentioned someone else had asked you about the fair recently?"

Shirley was flipping through the pages of the album, pointing to this photo and that, identifying the different areas of the Exposition: the Tower of the Sun, the statue of Pacifica. I couldn't be sure whether she was ignoring my question or simply wrapped up in her memories.

"During the fair they lit up the entire island so that at night, from San Francisco or here in the East Bay, Treasure Island looked like a floating 'city of lights.'" She sighed happily. "Can you imagine? It was something to see."

I recalled the lights I had seen in the bay from our airplane window. But that made no sense. Treasure Island was no longer lit in that fashion, was it? And besides, it wasn't attached to the Bay Bridge; I would have noticed that.

"And this part was called the 'Gayway,'" Shirley

continued. "It was a huge area featuring many naughty shows, along with Sally Rand's Nude Ranch. It was quite shocking at the time, let me tell you. Quite titillating. No pun intended." A pretty blush stained her cheeks.

We smiled.

"Of course, we children weren't allowed in that part of the fair," continued Shirley. "I remember my mother had gone to see the Liberty Bell exhibition and left me with my father. He wanted to see Sally Rand's girls, so he bought me a doll to keep me amused and told me to run along and play for a little while. It was different back then; kids were given more freedom to roam. And that's when I nearly drowned."

"What happened?" asked Maya.

"I was playing on the rocks at the edge of the bay and dropped my doll in the water. It was the prettiest doll I'd ever had, a Japanese lady dressed in a red silk kimono, and I didn't want to lose it. I tried to reach it and fell in the water. It was quite deep because the land dropped off suddenly."

"Because it was a manufactured island?" Maya asked.

She nodded. "I was in trouble, I don't mind telling you. I didn't know how to swim, you see. Still don't."

"And then?" said Maya.

"And then I was saved."

"By whom?"

She looked up, a twinkle in her eye. "Why, by a mermaid, of course."

Chapter 25

"When I dropped my doll in the water, a little mermaid girl took it. But her mother brought it back, and it was she who saved me. She didn't say a word, but I knew what she was thinking. I was scared, and to cheer me up she gave me these." Shirley touched the lustrous strand of pearls she was wearing. "Next thing I remember, I woke up on the rocks by the shore, with these around my neck."

Maya met my eyes, as if trying to decide whether or not to believe Shirley's story.

"It is said that a child saved by the merfolk returns with the gift of healing," said Shirley. "I don't know if that's true for everyone, and I've never met anyone with a similar story, so I don't think it happens often. But that's what happened to me. And when that man fell from the scaffolding, I didn't hesitate, didn't stop to think. I went to him and laid my hands upon him, and he was healed. I was only eight years old, but I knew I had the ability to heal him.

"You know," Shirley continued, in a thoughtful tone. "I wasn't the only one who saw a mermaid during the fair. There was another story, a few of the men with the German delegation claimed to have actually captured one."

"I read something about that," said Maya. "But I assumed it was just a gambit to increase interest in the synchronized swimming show."

"The rumors were much worse than that, I'm afraid. They said that the mermaid was killed for her pelt. Mermaid scales are said to be magical, you know."

"That's . . . horrible," I said. "What happened to the so-called mermaid pelt?"

She shook her head. "I imagine they took it back to Germany. The Nazis were very attuned to the power of the mystical, you know. More's the pity. Anyway, I don't mean to be maudlin." She gazed out at the bay. "I've never seen another mermaid, but I bought this place so I could watch for them. I keep hoping they'll speak to me."

Maya checked her recorder and rubbed her temples.

"Come here, child," Shirley said, patting the cushion next to her.

Maya got up and sat by her.

"May I?"

"May you . . . what?" asked Maya.

"Place my hands upon you, of course," said Shirley. "Your head is hurting you."

"How did you know that?" asked Maya.

Shirley smiled. "I'm a healer. May I?"

Maya nodded. Shirley placed one hand on either side of Maya's head, closed her eyes, let out a long breath, then drew in ten quick breaths.

Maya looked shocked, and pleased. "My headache is *gone*. Just like that. That's amazing, Shirley. Thank you."

Shirley smiled. "I guess I still got it. Now, Lily, would you pass me the stack of mail? I'd like to go through it quickly so you can take the recycling down with you, if you don't mind."

"Of course," I said, handing her the stack. Only then did I notice the return address on the top manila envelope.

"This is from Marcellus Tinley," I said. "From Treasure Island."

"You know him?" Shirley asked.

"I . . . sort of. I know *of* him," I said. "How do you know him, Shirley?"

"He's the one who came to see me, just last week. Rather an odd man, if I do say so. He said he was trying to have the island declared a historical monument, in honor of the World's Fair and what all went on there. He seemed to think my experiences might be part of the application package and said he would send me some paperwork. I told him to speak to a fellow named Aidan Rhodes."

"Aidan Rhodes is a good friend of mine."

"Is he, now?" She fixed me with a look, and I saw in her steely expression the strength that must have carried her through a long and eventful life. "Of course. I see it now. The magic. I'm not as keen to auras as I used to be, but I see it now. Plenty of turquoise and orange, with a few rays of purple and pink, and all a-sparkle." She fluttered her fingers.

Maya stared at me, as if trying to see the aura herself.

"That's where I met Aidan, you know," Shirley continued.

"What, at the Exposition?" asked Maya. "That was a long time ago."

"It certainly was! And oh, he cut quite the dashing

figure, I must say! I had such the little-girl crush on him. He was too old for me then, of course. And alas, now I'm too old for him!"

Maya looked confused. I wasn't sure how old Aidan was, though I knew the face he presented to the world was the result of a glamour. I had always assumed it was to hide the burns he had suffered at one point in the not-too-distant past, but perhaps it was also to present the youthful, virile version of himself. But if he had been an adult at the World's Fair . . .

"Anyway, Marcellus said his goal was to save the island from being developed. He mentioned a man named Orson something, as in Orson Welles, though I suppose the two don't have much in common. This Orson sounded like a dreadful sort."

I heard a cooing sound from the balcony. "And speak of the devil—I do believe that's his pigeon," she said. "Marcellus brought one with him when he visited and sent a message home, just for fun. Do you suppose this bird has a message?"

There was nothing attached to the bird's little legs, though he did seem tame and accustomed to being handled by a human. I considered taking him back to the coop on Treasure Island, then realized he knew his way home. He was a homing pigeon, after all.

We thanked Shirley for her time and collected her recycling to take with us. I paused for a moment.

"I was wondering . . ." I said. "Would you mind if we borrowed the photo album for a few days?"

"Not at all. I trust you."

"Are you sure you should?" Maya asked. "We're pretty much total strangers."

"Don't be silly, dear. I'm a very good judge of character," Shirley said. "Please keep the album safe, and when you return it, we'll have another nice visit."

"I'll look forward to it," I said.

"Me, too," said Maya. "I'll write up your story and show it to you before I finish it, in case there's anything you'd like to add or edit."

"That will be lovely. But please don't call me a healer. I'm not really one anymore."

"You cured my headache."

"Yes, but that was nothing. When I needed the healing power most, it let me down. I couldn't save my dear husband." Waves of sadness radiated from her.

"Not everyone can be saved," I said softly, casting a quick comforting spell. "Sometimes it's simply our time."

"But what good is the ability to heal if one can't help those whom we love the most?" Shirley said, tears glinting in her eyes. She shook her head, as though trying to rid herself of the memory. "And now . . . I can't save myself, either. Such is life, I suppose . . . and such is death."

Maya and I walked in silence to the car. When we climbed in, Maya spoke. "So, boss, what do you make of all that? You believe her, about the mermaid giving her the miraculous power to heal?"

"I don't know," I said, blowing out a long breath. "Sometimes a traumatic event can stir a latent talent, or even a magical ability. Or an encounter with a mermaid might have been a child's way to explain a frightening experience, like nearly drowning. Did you check out the books on her bookshelf?"

Maya nodded. "The thing is, Lily, when she placed her hands on me, my headache really did disappear. Just like that, just that fast. How is that possible?"

"There are individuals who have the gift. It's rare, but it's real. Graciela has healing power, though in her case, it is magical. But Shirley's ability might be explained differently. You know the energy you feel when you're hugged by someone you love? The warmth, the encouragement, the feeling of peace a simple hug can bring? Like when you hugged Conrad the other day."

"I remember," Maya said.

"All of us give off energy, like our auras. Some are deeply comforting, while others feel menacing."

"So you think that's Shirley's story? She has a really comforting aura?"

"Nope. I think she was rescued by a mermaid."

After dropping Maya at her apartment, I headed over to the wax museum.

I've always liked tourists. To me their vibrations are open and happy, filled with the desire to see and learn new things. A lot of San Francisco locals, weary of drivers unable to cope with the city's steep hills and pedestrians blocking the sidewalks as they try to figure out where they are and where they're going, do not agree.

One would be hard pressed to find an area of San Francisco more chock-full of tourists on a weekend than Fisherman's Wharf, unless one looked at nearby Pier 39, or Ghirardelli Square on a Saturday night. Visitors flocked here, which meant I had to stand in line at the wax museum in order to speak with Clarinda.

When I finally reached the head of the line, Clarinda glanced at me and declared: "Price of admission is $32."

"It was $24.99 the other day."

She shrugged.

"Anyway," I said, "I want to talk with you about Aidan's appointment book."

"What about it?" She avoided my gaze.

A large family jostled behind me, excitedly anticipating the waxen wonders of the exhibits.

"Would you come up to the office so we can talk in private?" I asked.

"I have a job, ya know. It's busy today."

"This is important. Could you get someone to sit in for you for twenty minutes?"

She hesitated.

I leaned in and lowered my voice. "Look, Clarinda, I know you don't like me and I'm sure you have your reasons. But Aidan asked me to look after things while he was gone, and then a man *died* here the other day, and I'd like to figure out what happened before someone else ends up dead. Now, you can either oblige me by giving me twenty minutes of your precious time, as you know Aidan would want you to do, or I can repeat what I just said in a *very* loud voice to the good people waiting in line behind me."

Clarinda backed down. "I have a break coming up. I'll meet you in the office in ten."

"Great. Thank you." I turned to the others still in line and said: "Y'all be sure to check out the award-winning Chamber of Horrors! It's worth every dime!"

Aidan's office still held the smoky scent of the sage and palo santo I had burned. Reviewing the appointment book, I noted Marcellus Tinley's appointment had been scheduled for three o'clock. I found him here, dead, after nine o'clock. So did that tell me anything? There were lots of other names on the schedule, written in Clarinda's loopy handwriting: Jonathan Primo, Maria Velasquez, Jane Parnell, Cody Jones, Jed Skinner. Carlos said they had followed up with everyone on the docket, but that all had received word their appointments were canceled. So why had Marcellus shown up anyway? And Dragomir, later that evening?

I was just starting to root through the Satchel, grumbling to myself that Mr. I'm-So-Organized Aidan Rhodes should really have some kind of sensible filing system, when Clarinda appeared at the door.

"Thanks for coming."

"Oh, it's my pleasure, I'm sure," she said in a sarcastic tone. As she entered the office, I sensed the slight sparkle of her magic and realized why Aidan kept this cranky young woman in his employ: She was a practitioner of some sort. Either she was skilled enough to cast a glamour to make her aura hard to detect or Aidan, not she, had cast the glamour to protect her. Interesting.

"So, the day Marcellus Tinley died—," I began.

She rolled her eyes. "I've gone over this with the police, like, a thousand times."

"I know you have, but now you're talking with me. And I hold the Satchel."

Her eyes widened, and she settled into a chair. *What is it with this Satchel?* I wondered.

"What do you want to know?" she asked, sullen but cooperative.

"Why wasn't his appointment canceled like all the others that day?"

"Calypso called in the morning to say she couldn't come in and asked me to cancel her appointments. So I did. But that Marcellus guy didn't have a phone. How'm I supposed to get in touch with someone who doesn't have a phone? I mean, who doesn't carry a phone these days?"

I recalled Shanda and the others on Treasure Island saying Marcellus didn't even have a landline.

"What about Dragomir?"

"Dragomir didn't have a phone, either," Clarinda said, sounding remarkably more indulgent of Dragomir. I could only imagine what she would say about *me*. "Or, at least not a cell phone. I tried his European number, but I guess he was already en route. He's such a hottie."

"Think so?" I asked. "He's my brother."

"You're kidding, right?" Her eyes raked me over and did not appear to be pleased by what they saw.

"Nope. He's an Ivory, through and through."

"*Huh*. Is he single?"

"To tell you the truth, I don't know."

"You don't know if your brother's single?"

"Long story, complicated family."

She nodded. "I get that."

"Tell me: Aidan has a glamour on his office door, right? So, how do his clients pierce the glamour?"

"When they pay his fee, I give them a code."

"They just show up at the ticket office and you give them the code to his office?" I asked, thinking that sounded risky.

"'Course not. It's all done over the phone or e-mail. That way, I don't know who they are. Aidan says his clients like discretion."

"What kind of code is it?"

She rolled her eyes. "It's like a charm. Changes every day."

"And you get that charm, how . . . ?"

"*Duh*, through, like, magic?"

"I see. I must say, Clarinda, I never realized how integral you are to Aidan's operation."

"You better believe it," she said, sounding mollified by my flattery. "That's why I should get paid more."

"I have no trouble believing that. Do clients pay Aidan by phone or online?"

"Online, usually. But sometimes clients bring tribute."

"What kind of tribute?"

She shrugged. "Could be lots of things. Esoteric texts, hard-to-find spellcasting ingredients, even exotic animals. It's like a zoo in here sometimes. And then you with that pig . . ." She shook her head. "What *is* it with you animal people?"

"Did Marcellus Tinley pay cash or a tribute?"

She snorted. "Get this: First he offered a pigeon, and I was like, 'Seriously? Those are all over the city, pal.' And then he offered a bat. So I gave him a thumbs-up."

"A bat."

"Yup, said he rescued it, or something? Anyway. You never know, but bats are tight. So, the point is, he asked if he could bring a bat and I said yes."

Chapter 26

Later that evening I was home alone, standing in front of the well-lit mirror in my bathroom, thinking about bats, murder, a little girl saved by a mermaid, and Botox.

The bright lights above the mirror revealed my many imperfections in all their imperfect glory. I had never been particularly focused on my looks, since I had always been preoccupied by things like casting spells and containing demons. But now that the woman in the salon had pointed them out . . . I leaned in closer to inspect "those fine lines" she talked about, and wondered whether my lips were less plump than they used to be . . .

"Whatcha lookin' at?"

I jumped and turned to see Oscar in the open bathroom door, a flowered plastic shower cap perched on his hairless head.

"*Nothing*," I said.

We stared at each other for a long moment.

"Was there something you wanted?" I asked.

"I was gonna take a bath before dinner. How long you plan on starin' at yourself in the mirror?"

I ignored that. "Since when did you start taking baths, Oscar?"

"A while ago. I read about it in a book, and it sounded nice. Don't sell yourself short, mistress. You mortals have some nice things going: movies, detective novels, donuts, baths . . . anyway, what's for dinner? And what did you decide about Winston? Also, didja find anything out about my mom? And what time's dinner?"

I sighed. Sailor was right. We needed another bathroom, and more space all around. Luckily for me, my new husband was on it: He had already made appointments with the plumber and the electrician Mel had recommended.

"Sailor said he was bringing home takeout for dinner."

"Cool! Should I call him and give him my order?"

"I imagine he'll buy enough for us all. To your other questions: No luck finding your mom, yet, Oscar, I'm sorry. With everything else going on right now, I haven't had the time or energy to track her down. And about Winston—I told you, he has to make up his own mind."

"I'm not sure bats have minds," he said in a thoughtful tone.

"Of course they do. Little bat minds, and little bat souls." I thought of the discussion Maya and I had with Nimue, what seemed like ages ago now, and her insistence that her "little Giddy" had a soul. How could anyone who has ever had a pet *not* believe they had a soul? As a witch I had always understood that every living thing, the trees in the forest and the wild creatures, had a soul. "Anyway, apparently it's not a good idea to try to keep bats as pets. They prefer to live in the wild, so I think a bat box on the terrace is for the best."

"If he was a familiar, he could stay with us."

"Don't get any ideas." I wasn't sure a regular animal could become a familiar, much less what that process might entail, but I wouldn't put it past my own peculiar familiar to take a shot.

I was enveloped with the scent of roses and heard the thump of heavy boots on the stairs. *Sailor.*

"Dinner!" said Oscar, abandoning his plans for a bath.

Early the next morning I drove out to Bolinas, a small coastal community about thirteen miles north of San Francisco. I wanted to meet with Calypso in person and to consult with Graciela's coven. I brought Shirley's album from the fair with me. When Oscar overheard me offering to bring breakfast pizza from Arizmendi, a local bakery cooperative, he insisted on coming along.

He may be a dubious familiar, but he's no fool.

Calypso's house was hidden from the road by a very tall and dense hedge. The lush branches encroached upon the long gravel drive so much that at times it seemed the Mustang wouldn't make it through. I cringed when I heard them scraping the car's finish, but they never left a mark, and at last they parted to reveal a big old farmhouse in a forest clearing, surrounded by redwoods and ferns and Calypso's verdant garden. There was a huge greenhouse out back, and a couple of cats snoozing on the cheerful wicker furniture on the deep porch. Calypso's garden was always in bloom, no matter the season. The scene was as tranquil and pastoral as a painting.

On this foggy morning, I spied several of the coven members working in the garden, a few others in the greenhouse, and Viv reading on the porch with a blanket over her knees and a black cat in her lap. Our arrival caused a stir as several elderly witches came to greet us and to help carry the pizzas into Calypso's big farmhouse kitchen, which was replete with bundles of herbs hanging from rafters, and hanging plants in every corner. A mandragora I had made for Aidan sat on one shelf like a lifeless doll, though it was anything but.

Calypso Cafaro was a lot like her home: an aged, graceful beauty. She had a special affinity for plants, and as we stood chatting, one length of a vine lovingly wound its way around her arm. She wore her long salt-and-pepper hair in a thick braid and had the kind of silent warmth common to wise women who had seen too much. I thought about what Selena said: Calypso carried a heavy burden of sorrow, which in her case led to an even deeper well of compassion.

Kay and Pepper and MariaGracia fawned over Oscar, who remained in his piggy form around the coven, though they would not have batted an eye at his natural form. The Aunties were not women with faint hearts.

We gathered around the kitchen's big butcher-block table and opened the pizza boxes. Calypso offered to reheat the pies, but most of us couldn't wait. Arizmendi's crust is deservedly renowned in the Bay Area, and their version of pizza is more akin to a delicious, freshly made flatbread, topped with locally sourced cheese and vegetables. The breakfast version features a fried egg on top. Conversations bubbled and swirled as the women chatted about the margaritas they'd enjoyed last night at a restaurant in the Mission, various plants in Calypso's lush greenhouse, and the funny thing the mandragora had done the other day.

"Where's my mom?" I asked, setting a plate with a

big slice of pizza on the floor for Oscar, and helping myself to a piece. "She's not still sleeping, is she?"

The Aunties fell quiet and looked at Graciela. My grandmother, who wasn't one to mince words, shook her head and said: "Maggie doesn't like goodbyes."

"She *left*?" I demanded. "Without telling me?"

"She said she called the apartment, but you didn't answer."

"It's been a busy couple of days," I said, feeling guilty. Maybe I should just get a cell phone, already. Disturbing vibrations be damned.

"She said she told you she was flying home soon," said Graciela.

"Yes, but she didn't say when," I said, disappointed. "I was hoping to drive her to the airport."

"We dropped her off last night, just before half-price margaritas at Pancho's." Graciela patted my hand, and I could feel her casting a comforting spell in my direction. "Don't fret, *m'ija*. She did what she came here to do, which was to reconcile and support you in your wedding."

I set my piece of pizza on a napkin on the counter. I had lost my appetite.

"It is because of you, Lily, that she opened her heart," said Nan, laying a hand on my shoulder.

"That's exactly right," said Winona, laying a hand on my arm.

"Hers was a long journey to understanding," said Iris, and I felt another soft hand land on my back.

Soon I was encircled, each woman laying a hand upon me. They were old, and their hands were covered in crepe paper skin that exposed ropy blue veins, knuckles swollen from arthritis. These were precious, powerful, potent hands, and they enveloped me in their comforting energy.

"Remember, *m'ija*," said Graciela. "Naming your

grief is like naming a demon: It takes away some of its power."

"But naming a demon can also summon it," I pointed out.

"It can. But if you've done your preparations and confront the demon from a position of protection and strength," said Graciela, "you need not fear."

I nodded and let out a long breath. Thirteen gray heads nodded, I felt several squeezes, and the hands fell away as the witches returned to their pizza and conversation.

"I have a question," I said. Appetite restored, I took a big bite of the delicious pizza. "I know my father was born in Texas, which is how he trained with Graciela, but he left before finishing his training, right?"

"A little like you," said Darlene with a nod.

"So how did he wind up back in Jarod?"

"He was exiled," said Betty.

"Exiled? To Jarod?" I asked. "I know I talk trash about my hometown, but it isn't all *that* bad. There is a Frosty Freeze, and some nice people. I mean, it wasn't right for me, but it's not exactly a prison."

"To your father it was," said Graciela, examining the pizzas to select just the right slice. "As you say, he did not fit in, or so he liked to think of himself. He went to Europe to reinvent himself but ran afoul of some powerful people and was sent back."

"What did he do to be exiled?" I asked. "Or . . . do I want to know?"

Graciela shook her head. "It is best that he tell you himself. I imagine you'll be seeing him soon, now that your brother is here."

Yay, I thought. That should be one hell of a family reunion.

"Another question," I said. "He and my mother

seem like such a mismatch. How did they ever get together?"

"He was bored," said MariaGracia with a shrug.

"And she was the prettiest girl in town," said Iris with a shrug.

"And they were young," said Kay.

"And it was spring," said Pepper.

"*Es verdad*," said Graciela. "This is true."

"That's all?"

"What did you expect?" Agatha asked.

"I'm not sure. Poor Mom. She needed him in her life like a tomcat needs a trousseau," I muttered.

"Speaking of trousseaus," said Darlene, "your mother's working on a new one for you, with the knot magic we taught her!"

"She is?" I asked, surprised by the news. My mother had sewn me an old-fashioned trousseau in honor of my handfasting with Sailor, but I had been forced to destroy it to bring a spell to fruition.

"It was *supposed* to be a secret," hissed Caroline in a loud whisper.

"Oops, sorry," said Darlene, giving an apologetic shrug. "But truthfully, her trefoil knot is just lovely."

"Oh, that reminds me," said Rosa. "Lily, guess what came up, just this morning, to herald your arrival? Trifolium."

"It's part of the legume or pea family, Fabaceae," said Calypso.

"Three-leafed clover?" I asked. "That's come up in my garden as well."

"Lots and lots of lush clover," said Rosa with a nod. "Anyone going to eat that last piece? Oscar's looking awfully thin."

As Rosa slipped the last piece of pizza to a grateful pig, I thought about what the appearance of the clover might mean. It wasn't the first time plants had grown overnight in response to something I was involved in. Three-leaf clovers, or trifolium, called to mind the trefoil symbol of radiation, which appeared to confirm Renna's tarot reading. That reading also said I must return to the place I was most frightened recently, which was the Nazi clubhouse on Treasure Island. Seems I would have to go back there, like it or not.

After pizza, Calypso brewed tea and we sat around the kitchen table, flipping through Shirley's album, looking at photographs from the fair, and discussing the existence of mermaids. The consensus opinion was that water spirits were real, but whether they took the form of what was commonly called a mermaid was still up for discussion.

"Aidan's such a handsome fellow," said Agatha, with a sigh.

"Yup, he's a hottie," said Rosa.

Calypso looked away. She and Aidan had once been partners in romance as well as in magic.

"Any update on his health?" I asked.

"He is not fully recovered," said Graciela. "But he is intuiting what is happening here and is growing restless."

"How is it," I asked, "that Aidan looks exactly the same today as he did in these photos, taken many decades ago?"

The coven sisters, to a woman, shrugged and continued turning the pages of the album. Looked like I wouldn't be getting an answer to that question anytime soon.

When I finished my tea, Rosa grabbed the cup to read the leaves.

"I see two wheels and an emblem of some sort," she said. "Wings? With flames coming out? And the letter *H*, and perhaps a *D*?"

"That sounds like the Harley-Davidson logo," I said, thinking of Orson's motorcycle. "What else do you see?"

"Violence," said Rosa. "The images are ringed by violence."

"And I'm sensing an imbalance, again," said Iris. "I asked the pendulum, and it confirmed the salts are wrong."

"Maya said that when the engineers dredged the bay to build Treasure Island, they took the salt out of the land," I said.

Iris looked shocked, then nodded. "That explains it."

"What do you mean?" I asked.

"Building that island disturbed the balance of the bay," she explained. "The Golden Gate Bridge was constructed about the same time, wasn't it?"

"Both were completed in the late 1930s."

"Well, there you go," she said. "The bridge blocked the bay's natural opening to the sea, creating a kind of portal that allowed evil to enter. The water spirits were enraged, and for good reason."

"There are no fairies or other creatures on Treasure Island because it was not made by nature," MariaGracia said, confirming what Renna had seen in the cards.

"But the Golden Gate Bridge is so beautiful—," I said.

"It is! And it created the perfect *torana*, this is a good thing," said Graciela. "But they did not consult the water spirits."

MariaGracia nodded. "The humans showed no respect to the water spirits, and threw the salts out of balance, inviting the negative forces. What did they expect would happen?"

"The hieroglyph for 'horizon' depicts two hills between which the sun sets," said Caroline. "It plays a critical role in the symbolic architecture of re-creation and rebirth."

"Every dawn begins with darkness, *m'ija*," said Graciela.

"So, you're saying the creation of Treasure Island and the construction of the Golden Gate Bridge—"

"*And* the Bay Bridge," Winona added.

"And the Bay Bridge, created a kind of supernatural hotspot in the Bay Area?"

"Don't forget the magnetic field," said Pepper. "Especially considering the salts were replaced by radiation."

"Oh, yes, the magnetic field," said Rosa. "It gets even more complicated if you know about the solar winds."

"Let's assume I don't," I said.

"There's a crack in the magnetic field at equinox," said Agatha. "It allows the solar winds to pour in."

"I thought that happened in the north—in Alaska, or Norway, or somewhere?"

"You think it's restricted to Norway?" asked Maria-Gracia. "When this happened in 1939, the impact on the autumn equinox was . . . well, you know what happened next."

"Let me get this straight: you're saying that the imbalance of salts in the San Francisco Bay, and the building of the Golden Gate and Bay Bridges, contributed to World War Two?"

"She hasn't read the Popol Vuh," said Iris, shaking her head.

"You haven't read the Popol Vuh?" asked Darlene. "It's the sacred text of the K'iche' people."

"I know what it is," I said. "But I haven't read it."

"You really should," said Caroline.

"And I'll be sure to do so soon," I said. "But I feel a sense of urgency given everything that's going on at the moment."

"We'll come with you to the island," said Nan.

"Road trip!" said Viv.

"*No*," I said.

They were taken aback, blinking at the ferocity of my response.

"*Porque, m'ija*?" Graciela asked. "We are here for you, after all."

"I know, and I can't tell you how much I appreciate it. But the thing is . . ." I trailed off, thinking of the Nazi clubroom and what Renna had seen in her cards, and worried that the coven's presence on the island might well put them in peril. "Renna said the immediate danger is human, not supernatural."

There was a long silence as Graciela and the Aunties looked at one another. Finally, Graciela gave a firm nod, and one by one each of the Aunties nodded her gray head in turn. "In this matter, *m'ija*, you know best."

The thought that I, the former student, might know better how to proceed than this coven of wise women, my former teachers, was profoundly unsettling. "You will draw down the moon while intoning my name, though, won't you?" I asked. "And support me from afar?"

"Of course," said Kay. The others nodded and murmured their agreement.

"But afterward, you must reset the balance," said Graciela. "Or this might well happen again. That will require the power of the *coincidentia oppositorum*."

And that meant Dragomir. Too bad I didn't know how to get in touch with him; not even the SFPD had been able to track him down. I wondered whether he had a familiar that might act as a go-between. Maybe Oscar would be willing to figure that out. He'd do just about anything for Tater Tots.

"Dragomir told me he controls a demon," I said, still loathe to speak the demon's name.

"He was trained in the old ways?" Viv asked.

"That could be useful," Nan said. "But not in this case."

"No, never in this case," Iris agreed.

"Why?" I asked. "I mean, personally, I think it's always a terrible idea, but y'all seem to disagree. So why not in this case?"

"Because of Deliverance Corydon," said Betty.

"That could be bad if they got together," said Caroline.

"Oh, my, yes, very bad," murmured Darlene.

"How bad?" I asked.

"Sink-Alcatraz bad," said Viv.

"You'll need your lachrymatory salts, for sure," said MariaGracia.

"Can you describe what might happen?"

"Hmm. . . . You know the pneumatic tubes some drive-up banks use to send deposits and whatnot between the customers in their cars and the tellers in the bank?" asked Nan.

I nodded.

"Brilliant pieces of engineering, actually. Suck things right through the tube!" said Iris. "It'll be sort of like that. Once the portal is open, the spirits are sort of fast-tracked."

"So I need to . . . stop the suction?"

Graciela nodded. "In a manner of speaking."

"Nature abhors a vacuum," said Caroline.

"But demons love it," said Graciela.

Before leaving, I used Calypso's phone to call Carlos.

"Let me start by saying that I don't have any real proof," I began.

"A lot of our conversations begin that way, you ever noticed?" Carlos said. "Just tell me what you got."

"I think Orson Goff might be our culprit. Not only did his daughter stand to inherit money to pay for college, but he's set to make a *lot* of money from a development deal he and Leo are planning. Marcellus was in the way of both and was trying to get the island designated as a historical zone of some sort. Also, I'd bet my cauldron that Orson is involved in a weird underground Nazi group that meets on the island."

"What's a Nazi group got to do with anything?" asked Carlos.

"I don't know, exactly," I admitted. "But: Nazis. Anyway, you should take another look at him."

Carlos sighed. "I'm fairly sure it wasn't Orson Goff. Or, if it was, it doesn't matter."

"Why not?"

"His body was found floating in the bay, on the shoals of Treasure Island."

Chapter 27

So much for my number one suspect.

Carlos asked me to meet him on Treasure Island, so I packed up my familiar and Shirley's photo album, kissed everyone goodbye, and headed to San Francisco.

"*Dangitall*," I said, blowing out a frustrated breath as I drove south on Highway 1.

"What's wrong, mistress?" asked Oscar. The highway from Bolinas was devoid of cars at the moment and was bordered by thick redwood forests, so Oscar shifted into his natural form and sat in the passenger seat, snacking on leftover pizza crusts.

"I don't like it when I'm wrong," I said.

"That's a shame," Oscar said. "Especially since you're wrong a lot."

"Yes. I am. Thanks for that."

"I'm just sayin', it's your process. Am I the only one who noticed?"

"What do you mean?"

"You're usually wrong a few times before you're right, so you just have to keep going. It's all about persistence even though you fail, and fail again."

I glanced at him. "You know what? You're right. Thank you, Oscar. For real, this time."

"And fail again."

"Got it. Thanks."

"No problem." Finished with the pizza crusts, he pulled the heavy photo album onto his lap and started flipping through the pages. "*Heh*, Sally Rand's *Nude* Ranch, instead of *Dude* Ranch. Get it?"

I nodded, distracted by thoughts of what the coven had said. "Hey, if Dragomir has a familiar, would you have any way of finding it?"

"Don't think so. Not like there's a registry or anything, if you know what I'm sayin'. Why?"

"Just trying to track down my wayward brother."

"The dragon guy?"

"Yeah."

"I got his address."

"You do?"

"Sure. From the note."

"I thought you *lost* the note."

"Well, I did, but I remember the address. I got a real head for numbers, you know. That's something not a lot of people know about me. I got me all kinds of untold abilities."

Once again, I was reminded that if I didn't ask Oscar a direct question, he was unlikely to volunteer the information.

"So where is he?"

"At Aidan's."

"At *Aidan's*? You don't mean his office."

"'Course not. His house."

"Where does Aidan live?"

Oscar's eyes grew huge. "I can't go around telling every Tom, Dick, and Harry where Aidan lives. Wouldn't be prudent."

"I'm not 'every Tom, Dick, and Harry,' Oscar, I'm me."

Oscar remained unmoved by this argument.

"*And* I'm filling in for Aidan while he's gone. Doesn't that suggest that he trusts me?"

Oscar shrugged. "Dunno."

I tried a different approach. "You said Dragomir wrote Aidan's address on the original note," I pointed out. "The note you were supposed to give to me. So it can't have been much of a secret."

He gazed out the car window and did not answer.

"Oscar, did you lose that note on purpose?"

He shrugged and would not look at me.

I tamped down my frustration. Oscar had his reasons for doing what he did, and as inscrutable as those reasons often were, he always came through for me in the end. I would just have to trust him.

"How about this: Would you get a message to Dragomir for me?"

"Oh, sure, no problem."

"Thank you. Tell him we need to talk, and soon. It's important."

"How important?"

"We have to work together to ward off World War Three and the destruction of the Golden Gate Bridge, or something along those lines."

"Okey dokey." Oscar turned another page in the album and gasped. "Mistress!"

"I know," I said. "It's the spitting image of Aidan, right? Even though it was from a very long time ago."

He shook his head. "That's not it."

He sounded so shocked that I grew worried. We had just reached Stinson Beach, so I pulled into the parking lot to give him my full attention.

"Oscar? What is it?"

His bottle glass green eyes were even larger than normal. "I think . . . it's my *mother*."

"What? Show me."

Oscar pointed to a photo of a stone gargoyle. It had horns that curved like a ram's, an exaggerated underbite from which protruded fangs, heavy eyebrows, and a fierce expression. Oscar had tried to describe his mother to me in the past, but his description had left a lot to be desired.

"Are you sure?" I asked, peering at the grainy black-and-white photo. "It's kind of hard to see clearly, and I have to say, there's not a lot of family resemblance."

"Yeah, I take after my dad. But see those hands? That's where I got 'em from. I can't *believe* it! Mistress, where are these gargoyles now?"

I hesitated. I couldn't bring myself to say that, if it were his mother, she was most likely at the bottom of the bay, tossed away like garbage with the rest of the decorations when the fair closed. And what did I know, maybe she had ended up somewhere else.

"Why don't I do some research into what happened to the gargoyles at the Golden Gate International Exposition, and we'll see what we can find."

"Promise?"

"I promise. But it may not be her, Oscar," I warned as we got back onto the highway.

"It's her. I feel it in my bones, mistress."

I felt bad leaving Oscar after this stunning revelation, but I was expected at the scene of a homicide. So I left my gobgoyle and Shirley's photo album in the loving arms of Maya and Bronwyn at Aunt Cora's Closet, and hurried to Treasure Island.

The streets leading to the old dock were jammed with police vehicles, their red and blue lights flashing. Uniformed officers swarmed the area, taking photographs and placing evidence tags.

I parked a block away and joined the crowd of locals waiting behind the police barricade. I spied the waitress who had tended to me and Maya at the café, and the group of teenagers we had met the other day. Shanda and Cece were crying, and it was only then that I remembered that Orson Goff was Cece's father. Poor baby. I was glad to see Nimue approach them, enveloping them in hugs.

Carlos spotted me and nodded to a policeman, who moved a barricade to allow me to slip past. "Took you long enough," Carlos said, glancing at his watch.

"I was in Bolinas."

"At this hour?"

"Had to consult with my grandmother's coven. They're at Calypso's place."

He nodded. "Speaking of whom: When are they leaving for Texas?"

"I'm not sure," I said, thinking it was going to be hard to say goodbye. "Why?"

"There was a little dustup at Pancho's, in the Mission. They didn't mention it?"

"They mentioned half-priced margaritas."

"Yeah, well, somehow they got their hands on my private number, and I had to go out late last night to smooth things over."

"I am sorry about that."

He shrugged. "I've got a few homicides to attend to,

is all I'm saying. Can't go around bailing out elderly covens in the wee hours of the morning."

"I'll talk to them. And thank you." I looked around at the scene and once again was struck by the spectacular views. It was sunny on Treasure Island and in the East Bay, but the fog still covered San Francisco and Marin like a heavy shroud. "So you're sure it's Orson Goff?"

He nodded.

"What happened?" I asked.

"That's why I called you," said Carlos. "You've been poking around, so I imagine you know some of the players. What led you to think Orson killed Marcellus? Walk me through it."

"He . . . mostly because he was so unpleasant, though I suppose that doesn't make a lot of sense," I said. "Also, he had a lot of animosity toward Marcellus Tinley, who he thought might have been fooling around with underage girls, including his daughter."

Carlos nodded. "Your reason for suspecting Orson Goff was that he was a jerk?"

"Guess it's not much to go on, now that I think of it. I saw him in Berkeley and thought he might be following me, or someone else . . . and one of the Aunties had a vision of the Harley-Davidson logo, the wings with flames, surrounded by violence. But now I'm thinking the vision meant he was in danger, not that he was the killer. I'm sorry, Carlos. Magic goes only so far in these situations."

He nodded. "What do you make of Leo Airey?"

"I know he's ambitious and has been wanting to develop the island, along with Orson Goff. But when I told him about Marcellus Tinley, he seemed genuinely shocked and saddened. Why?"

"He confessed to the murders."

"*Leo?*"

Carlos nodded. "Right before you arrived. Broke down, said Tinley and Goff were standing in the way of his development plans so they had to go."

"Simple as that?"

"Simple as that."

Chapter 28

"But . . . that doesn't seem right," I said. "Orson was investing *with* Leo in the development plans, not opposing them."

"Sure about that?"

"That's what Leo told me," I said, then realized how silly that sounded. "Obviously, he could have lied."

"Murderers often do."

"Fooled again," I sighed. "I've never been very good at understanding motives for murder."

"You and me both," said Carlos. "But here's the thing: I don't think Leo did it, either."

"Why not?"

"Seems a bit . . . too convenient, I guess. Doesn't feel right. Leo insists he killed Tinley at the wax museum and tried to make it look like an accidental OD, right? But there's no evidence to support that. I spent hours looking through the museum's security footage for the day Tinley died. *Hours.* Leo Airey wasn't there."

A police officer walked up and said something to

Carlos, who said, "Excuse me," and went to speak to a knot of uniformed officers. I heard the crowd murmur as an officer led Leo, his head hanging down and his hands handcuffed behind his back, to a squad car.

I blew out a long breath and gazed at the Golden Gate Bridge. Could something so beautiful really have been a trigger for something so ugly? Was the imbalance the Aunties kept talking about related to the murders, or was that purely a human phenomenon?

I heard a ruckus and saw Cece yelling at Nimue, Shanda trying to calm her down. Had Cece just realized Nimue's husband, Leo, had confessed to murdering her father?

There were a few more words exchanged before the teens turned and stalked off, leaving Nimue standing by herself, looking stunned and devastated.

I felt a chill as I approached her, like ice water pouring over me.

"*Lily*," she said in a broken voice. "I didn't expect to see you here."

"Are you . . . ?" I was about to ask if she was all right but realized she couldn't possibly be. Her husband had just been arrested for murder. "How are you holding up? Is there anything I can do?"

"It occurs to me that I've got really bad—make that *terrible*—taste in men. First my ex-husband, and now . . ." She blew out a long breath, shook her head, and I thought I saw the glint of tears in her eyes. "The girls blame me, you know. I just can't believe Leo would . . . but I guess he must have, right? He confessed."

I didn't know what to say, so I remained silent, hoping to offer support simply by listening.

"*Why?*" she continued. "For money? I've never understood why men care so very much about money."

Had Orson's death been a crime of passion? I wondered. Orson was certainly pugnacious enough; it was easy to see how he and Leo might have gotten into a fight. Maybe Leo shoved Orson, and the big man slipped on the shoals, as little Shirley Mangicaro had so many years ago. Maybe he hit his head, and there was no mermaid to save him.

That scenario seemed possible. But what about the murder of Marcellus Tinley? That was no crime of passion, that was cold-blooded, premeditated murder. Tinley was killed by a syringe full of lethal drugs. But if Leo had done it, where had he gotten the drugs and the syringe? Of course, maybe Leo had contacts among some of the less savory elements of society, like a biker gang with illicit connections. . . .

"Lily," Nimue said, interrupting my thoughts. "I appreciate your being here, and the offer of help to someone you barely know. But I'm going to go to my studio, call a lawyer, and see whether my losing myself in my art might help calm me."

"That sounds like a good idea," I said.

"What a day," she said. "I really thought you might have had your fill of our island of misfit toys."

As she left, I realized one "misfit toy" was not among the crowd: Zane.

Renna had told me to return to the place that had recently scared me. Hands down, that was the secret Nazi clubhouse. Since I was here . . .

I hesitated. On the one hand, Carlos had advised me not to go back to the abandoned natatorium. Maybe I should listen to the inspector investigating not one but two island-related homicides. I glanced at Carlos, who was listening intently to Shanda, perhaps taking her statement. On the other hand, Renna had told me I *had* to go.

Besides, I wanted to figure out why that secret room

had felt so odd. It would be easier to concentrate without Maya by my side and without the fear of being trapped.

The magical world was going to win out this time. I even had a flashlight.

As I walked to the natatorium, I thought about the two deaths. For Leo to have killed Marcellus Tinley by lethal injection, he had to have accessed Aidan's office. Carlos said there was no sign of Leo on the security footage, nor had I seen his name in Aidan's appointment book. Could he have made the appointment under a different name?

I reached the natatorium and circled around to where the stage door was once again propped open. Making sure no one was watching, I piled extra bricks and a heavy rock in front of the door, just in case, and slipped into the building.

I switched on my flashlight, went down the empty hall, and descended the stairs to the pool, thinking it was a crying shame to allow this once-magnificent building to decline into decrepitude. Maya was right: It felt almost cathedral-like, a sacred place.

Those feelings passed as soon as I reached the pool deck, opened the door to the secret room in the alcove behind the diving platforms, and flicked on the lights.

I was again immediately struck by disturbing sensations, overlaid by the stench of stale cigarette smoke and sweat. This time I saw something I hadn't noticed before: a cardboard box about twice the size of a shoebox. I opened it and found a foul sludge of bat guano at the bottom. This was not a bat house like Sailor had built, but a cage. Was this where Marcellus had found Winston? And what had the bat been doing here, of all places?

I turned my attention to the framed Nazi flag, trying

to identify the source of my unease. Was it simply the associations of this flag with the crimes committed against so many: Jewish people, gay people, Rom, political dissenters, anyone deemed "antisocial," shot by the roaming death squads or sent to their deaths in the camps and gas chambers?

Or was there more to this particular flag?

I laid my hands on the shadow box but couldn't tease out the vibrations through the thick protective glass. I took the heavy box off the wall, set it facedown on the crate "coffee table," and crouched down next to it. If I could undo the fasteners at the back, it should open up and I could touch the actual fabric—

Footsteps rang out on the pool deck outside.

I looked around but there was nowhere to hide. My backpack was across the room, by the door. The medicine bag at my waist was vibrating like mad, and my arm was being squeezed at the spot where Graciela had held me.

A figure appeared in the doorway, and I sighed in relief.

"Nimue! You about scared me half to death!"

"*Lily?* I'm so sorry! I noticed the back door had been propped open and thought maybe one of the kids was upset and looking for a place to hide, or maybe something worse," Nimue said, looking around the room. "What are you doing in here?"

As she stepped toward me, she banged her shin on the couch and swore a blue streak worthy of a very profane sailor.

"I did that, last time I was here," I said. "Let me see if there's some ice in the fridge."

"Oh, no, no need—," she said, but I already had the door open.

The lower shelves held cans of beer, but inside the

small freezer compartment was a white lily encased in ice and sealed in a plastic baggy, along with my Aunt Cora's Closet business card and a stylized drawing of a woman in a vintage dress. The image looked like me. Frozen.

"You lied," said Nimue. "You said the spell would freeze you out of our lives, but you didn't go away."

"I'm a witch," I said, recalling the icy feeling when I saw Nimue earlier, which I had assumed reflected her feelings of devastation. "Spells don't work the same on me."

Oscar was right, I thought, *this was my process*. My mind raced and the pieces suddenly fell into place: Nimue was a former nurse who might well have access to a syringe, and heroin and fentanyl weren't hard to get if one was determined. I remembered Nimue saying her Starbucks name was Jane, and a Jane was listed in Aidan's appointment book on the day Marcellus Tinley died. Eugene Leimert said his last wife's name was Jane, and that he suspected her of poisoning him. Could Eugene be the "awful" ex-husband Nimue spoke of—which would mean he was Zane's father? And if so, what did that mean?

Slowly, I stood and turned to face her, trying to formulate the words in my head, words that would somehow convince her to allow me to leave this cursed space.

Nimue balled up a fist and punched me, hard, in the belly.

I doubled over, unable to breathe. Nausea engulfed me and before I could react, Nimue picked up the heavy shadow box and struck me on the side of the head. The glass did not break, but I went down, falling to the dirty carpet, tasting blood. She kicked me in the temple, and my head felt as if it had split open, and I saw a kaleidoscope of colors.

Gasping, unable to focus, I retched, dizzy and disoriented. My medicine bag vibrated fiercely, and I focused on that. I drew upon the taste of the blood in my mouth and the pain in my body and started murmuring a charm.

"You went down awfully easy," Nimue sneered. "Some witch you are. Gotta say, I expected more of a fight."

She wasn't wrong. I had been caught off guard, assuming the warning buzz of my medicine bag, the squeeze of my arm, was a response to my surroundings rather to an imminent threat. I had been duped by Nimue's apparent kindness to young people, and once again had been reminded, in a very painful way, that I wasn't a particularly good judge of character.

"Nimue?" said a man's voice.

Yes. Hope rose in me at the thought that someone was here to help.

Through the haze of pain and fear, I realized it was Zane. *No.*

I was done for. Even if I could regroup, call upon my guiding spirit, summon my magical abilities, it would be two against one. Witches are humans, not superheroes. This is why so many of us died in the burning times. My mind called out for Oscar, on the slim chance he would sense that I needed him and could somehow get here in time. *Stay conscious, just stay conscious*, I told myself, and continued to murmur the charm.

"What the hell are you doing?" Zane said. Through the fog of pain, I realized he had placed himself between Nimue and me. "Nimue, stop! Enough!"

I felt myself slowly slipping into unconsciousness, but just before I blacked out I sensed Deliverance Corydon emerge within me. I felt a rush of energy, the pain faded, and I surged to my feet. With a roar that was not of this world, I launched myself at a startled Nimue. We crashed to the floor and I felt myself tearing at her hair and landing blow after blow with my fists. She screamed in shock and pain, and tried to crawl away, but I followed her and didn't let up.

Zane leaned over to grab her but Nimue lashed out, punching him in the eye. He fell to the floor, and now it was the three of us rolling and hitting and kicking until finally Zane pinned Nimue to the floor. "Stop it, Nimue!"

She relaxed for a moment and I leapt upon her again.

"And you, too!" I heard Zane's shout, but Deliverance heard nothing, saw nothing, responded only to the rage and the desire for revenge, to maim, to destroy, to *kill*.

Deliverance got Nimue in a chokehold from behind and squeezed, hard.

"*Stop* it, lady!" Zane cried, trying to pry my arm from Nimue's neck. "You're gonna kill her!"

For a moment, control of my body hung in the balance. Then Deliverance Corydon slithered back to wherever she had come from and I came back to the present.

I released my hold and Nimue collapsed, choking and moaning.

Chapter 29

No one spoke for a long moment. Then Zane got up, rummaged around in a box in the corner, and returned with a rope. He squatted next to Nimue and bound her hands and ankles.

"She's probably not much of a threat at this point," said Zane softly. "But just in case."

I sank onto the lumpy couch and watched him with a sense of unreality, ashamed of my rage and bloodlust. There wasn't a doubt in my mind that I—or Deliverance Corydon, in control of my body—would have killed Nimue had Zane not intervened.

"I'm sorry," I said.

"What for? She had it coming," Zane said with a shrug. "She would have killed you if you hadn't fought back, you know. Look what she did to Marcellus and Orson."

Nimue groaned.

"Don't start fights if you don't want your ass kicked," Zane said to his former stepmother.

"But Leo confessed to Orson's killing," I said.

"Leo's no murderer," Zane scoffed. "He's just scared of her. She's tougher than she looks. She has, like, this way about her . . . she gets people to do what she wants."

Zane had a cut above his eyebrow that dripped blood, and his eye was swelling and would be black by morning. My hands were throbbing and swollen, and I was covered in cuts and bruises. My cheekbone ached, and so did my ear. Suddenly everything hurt, a lot.

"Do you have a cell phone?" I asked. "We need to call the cops, and all of us probably need medical attention."

"I don't . . . I mean, I don't have a great track record around cops."

"Zane, you saved my life. Carlos Romero, the inspector investigating Orson's death, is a friend of mine. I'll tell him what happened. You haven't done anything wrong, have you? I mean, right now?"

"Not recently, anyway," he said, looking around the room. "But once you get involved in something like this, it's hard to get out."

"You mean being a neo-Nazi?"

He nodded.

"How did you get into it in the first place?"

"Jane. Nimue, I guess she'd rather we call her. She was married to my dad."

"Is your dad Eugene Leimert?"

He nodded. "I guess . . . I dunno, things were hard after my mom left. And maybe it's weird, I mean, I know Jane's old enough to be my mother, but I sort of fell for her. She's really smart, you know, and she taught me a lot of things and was, like, the only person who seemed interested in what I was thinking and feeling. I was really unhappy, dropped out of school, felt like a total loser. And when she let me in on her secret, and her group invited me to join, I felt, like, special, I guess."

"I know the feeling."

"Were you a Nazi, too?"

"No. But I know what it feels like to be a pariah."

"A what?"

"An outcast. To feel like you don't fit in. It can make us vulnerable to bad influences."

Nimue stirred and mumbled a string of profanities. Zane stared at her, his young eyes looking old with pain and disillusionment.

"What happened to change your mind?" I asked.

"I don't know, the rituals and everything were kind of fun at first, but when I started thinking about what I was saying—you know, like 'White Power' and the 14 words and all the rest—it started to bother me. I look at Antwan and Shanda and everything, and they're all right. And I knew this kid? Back in middle school. He was Jewish and invited me to a Hanukkah party, and it was okay. You ever had potato latkes?"

"I have, yes."

"They're really good."

I nodded, trying not to smile because an aspiring Nazi had been saved by the memory of really good potato pancakes.

"Anyway." He kicked at the dust with his heel. "I've been trying to pull back for a while, but the last straw was when she was gonna enact some kind of weird ritual by sacrificing a bat she'd captured and kept in that box over here," he said, gesturing to the dirty cardboard box I'd seen earlier. "That's sick. So I kidnapped the bat and brought it to Marcellus, you know, because he had all those pigeons? I thought maybe he knew how to take care of it. That's why I feel like I was sort of responsible for what happened to Marcellus."

"What do you mean?"

"When I told him where I'd found the bat, Marcellus was really pissed off. He was a weird guy and everything, but he was a real animal lover. He confronted Nimue, told her he knew what she was up to—which wasn't true; I hadn't told him much, really, but I guess he must've figured part of it out—and said he was going to talk to somebody about it. Somebody with more power than she had."

That "somebody" was Aidan Rhodes, I presumed.

"Why did you lock my friend and me in this building, that first time?" I asked.

"Sorry about that," Zane said, looking sheepish. "I thought you were a coupla stupid tourists from San Francisco. I don't like how they come here, with their big cars, and act all holier than thou. Here's a question for *you*: Why'd you tail me through the Oakland hills?"

"You knew it was me?"

"Cherry red Mustang? Not exactly a stealth car. Yeah, I knew it was you."

"I was wondering what you were up to. I thought maybe *you* followed *me*."

"Nah, my dad lives in Berkeley. He found this place where they might be able to remove this stupid swastika tattoo. Even said he'd pay for it."

"I'm glad to hear it," I said. "Why do you think Nimue killed Orson?"

"Same reason she went after Marcellus, I guess. As a warning to others. And Orson was part of our group, but he didn't agree with what she was planning."

"Which was . . . ?"

"She's been looking for something. Something

'powerful,' she kept saying. She'd heard somewhere that some officials of the Nazi party came to the island for the World's Fair, caught a mermaid, and scraped off some of her scales. They killed her."

"That's horrific."

"They claimed mermaid scales had magical powers and would make their army unstoppable. But they hid them somewhere, wound up getting sent back to Germany without them, and got killed in the war. Nimue thought if she could find the scales, it would make us powerful when we take on the enemy."

"And who is the 'enemy'?"

"Anybody who doesn't think like us, I guess. She was kind of vague on that part. She said it had something to do with bringing back the Nazi mission, from World War Two. She thought, like, there was going to be a race war and we would prevail. I dunno. Sounds pretty stupid now."

I stared at the Nazi flag in the shadow box, now lying on the floor. Flags are symbols and therefore do convey a certain kind of power. But I had sensed something more, much more, with this particular flag.

"And here I thought the murders had something to do with the plans to develop the island," I said.

"Well, they did. That was how she was going to finance the whole thing."

"How many of you are there on the island?"

"Nazis? Here on the island it was just us, but lots of others came from all over for our meetings."

I blew out a long breath. Every fiber of my body seemed to be throbbing and aching, and the adrenaline that had fueled my muscles during the fight had dissipated, leaving me bone-weary. "I have to call the police, Zane."

I saw fear in his pale eyes.

I put my hand on his arm and tried to sway him. "Zane, please listen to me. The authorities need to hear all of this from you, directly. It's the right thing to do."

"My dad's gonna blow a gasket if I get arrested again."

"Why would you be arrested? You didn't have anything to do with the deaths of Marcellus and Orson, did you?"

He shook his head vehemently. "That was all Nimue. She always called Marcellus a degenerate and an addict, and after he died she said we could use his death to scare our enemies. I don't know what happened with Orson, but he was trying to pull away from the group, too. He was trying to get in touch with me, said he wanted to talk, but I didn't call him back because he kind of gave me the creeps. I feel bad now."

"I'll tell Carlos how you saved my life," I said. "I'll be on your side. And Nimue really does need medical attention, Zane."

He shrugged, not particularly concerned for Nimue's well-being, but handed me his cell phone. Carlos sounded equal parts angry and stunned when I tried to explain where we were and what had happened and said he would be right over.

"You know what," I said, getting to my feet. My muscles screamed, my head throbbed, and I couldn't make a fist with my left hand. *Ow.* "I have to go."

"*Wait*, you said we were supposed to talk to the police."

"I know, but there's something important I have to do, and it can't wait. You'll be fine, Zane. The inspector's name is Carlos Romero. Just tell him what happened, and don't lie."

"Okay," Zane said, slumping a bit. "I hope you're right. Want me not to mention you were here?"

"No, tell him everything, the whole truth. I'll call him and tell him what you did to help me. And again, thanks, Zane. I think you saved my life." Or Nimue's life.

I grabbed the shadow box with the Nazi flag and ran.

Chapter 30

"I got distracted by the talk of the prophecy and demons and whatnot. Turns out the murders were all about money and power," I said, wincing as Rosa cleaned the abrasion on my forehead. "Seems so petty, somehow, doesn't it?"

"The lust for money and power is more than enough to invite evil," said Graciela, mixing a little comfrey root and myrrh resin into a salve. "But, *m'ija*, I am sorry to tell you this, but it is not yet over. There is still the prophecy to worry about."

We were crowded into the back room of Aunt Cora's Closet, the Aunties tending to my wounds while an enraged Sailor simmered silently in the corner. Oscar was beside him, in his natural guise for the first time in front of Graciela's coven, none of whom blinked an eye at his appearance.

After I limped home, Oscar took one look at me, shook his head, and said: "I should have been with you, mistress, but I was distracted by my mom. I let you down. I'm sorry. I don't blame you if you want to trade me in, maybe when Aidan gets back. . . ."

"Don't be ridiculous," I said, pain and exhaustion shortening my temper. "I need you more now than ever."

I've dealt with a lot in my day. I've seen true evil and have fought with demons. But being attacked and beaten by another human was a new one for me. It wasn't the stitches or the bruises that most disturbed me. It was the memory of my own rage, the desire to maim and to kill, that was so frightening. I had pulled back at the last moment, with help from Zane, but the yearning lingered. A hunger for blood. A thirst for vengeance.

Deliverance Corydon.

Would I be able to stop her the next time I found myself in a similar situation? Given the trajectory of my life in San Francisco, I had to assume there would be similar situations in the future. Murder and mayhem seemed to follow me about, and the Bay Area was a hot spot, a portal, a rip in the veil. I wondered: Should I leave town? Maybe join Aidan in the salt mines of Michoacán for a while? Try to alter my core and rid myself of Deliverance Corydon once and for all?

The coven had insisted that I needed her rage to survive. But how did I balance her out?

Balance. Magic was all about balance. Nothing came without sacrifice; nothing went unpaid for.

And speaking of paying my dues, I placed a call to Carlos to tell him what had happened and what Zane had done for me.

"Do I have to tell you what I think of you leaving the scene of a crime?" Carlos demanded, irate.

"It was unavoidable, Carlos. I'm sorry. I promise I'll explain the whole thing to you, and you can grill me for just as long as you want, but I have to do a thing first. An important thing. A magical thing."

He grunted in displeasure, but short of sending officers to arrest me, he had no choice but to trust me. Luckily we'd been through a lot together. He agreed to wait twenty-four hours.

"Hey," I asked Graciela. "Renna told me Lily isn't my original name. That my name starts with a *D*."

"That's true."

"Mistress's name is *Dily*?" Oscar asked.

"No, Oscar," Graciela said. "Your mistress had another name before Lily."

"Why am I only learning this now?" I asked.

"Because you did not need to know. Your father named you Duellona. It is the ancient form of Bellana, the Roman war goddess."

"But your mother liked lilies," said Rosa. "And the nurses asked her, so that's the name on your birth certificate."

Renna kept seeing *D*s in the cards—as in Dragomir, Dantalion, Deliverance, and Duellona? It made a weird kind of sense.

"Because the Golden Gate is a magical gateway, a membrane if you will, the threats will keep coming. This is the prophecy," said Graciela. "This is why you, and now your brother, were called here, to face the challenges. I have summoned Aidan back from Mexico to help."

"But why?" I asked. "You said yourself he's not fully healed, and Renna suggested Dragomir and I would form the *coincidentia oppositorum*, not Aidan and I."

"Aidan has a special relationship with the water spirits," Graciela said. "He met them long ago."

"At the fair on Treasure Island," I said, and wondered if Aidan might have been involved, somehow, with the rescue of little Shirley Mangicaro. Stranger things had happened when Aidan was around. He and I had a lot to talk about. "Just how old *is* Aidan?"

The old women tittered and exchanged glances.

"One never tells one's age," said Caroline primly. "Much less that of another."

"Indeed," said Nan.

"Old enough," Iris said.

"*M'ija*, I fear for you and Dragomir coming together in that way," Graciela said, frowning and jutting out her chin. "If you are very sure this is necessary, you must do everything you can to protect your heart—and your skull. Remember, they are both as fragile as egg-shells."

Dragomir insisted he had Dantalion under his control, which I hoped was true. I had Deliverance within me, and she wasn't a demon, exactly, but a demon-like elemental who was a part of me. The Aunties had warned me that if Dantalion and Deliverance got together, that would be . . . bad. Like, sink-Alcatraz bad.

But if Dragomir and I managed to maintain control of Dantalion and Deliverance, could our combined power be enough to save the Bay?

Graciela and her coven sisters offered to remain by my side to support and sustain me while I studied the contents of the shadow box, but I wanted only Oscar with me to more easily access the magical plane. The thirteen elderly women tut-tutted, but I had been a solo witch my entire life. I needed the psychic space to concentrate.

Hardest of all was leaving Sailor behind. He wasn't very happy about it, but after a wordless hug and tender kiss, he stepped aside. He understood.

Upstairs in the apartment I took my time, harvesting fresh herbs from my garden, chopping dried leaves and roots, and assembling the myriad ingredients on the kitchen counter beside my cauldron. I mixed the dried ingredients in the ancient stone mortar and pestle Graciela had given me years ago when I first left Jarod; it had been handed down to her through the generations, woman to woman, from a powerful Aztec shaman.

The grinding of stone-on-stone helped me to center myself, to feel calm and sure.

As I dropped various bits and pieces into my cauldron, I felt my determination strengthen. This is who I was, this is what I did. I brewed. I brought the water from the bay to boil, then added eye of newt and toe of frog—which were more familiarly known as mustard seed and buttercup. I stirred in spider silk, and mud dredged from the shore of the bay, then tossed in a sprig of belladonna and a dram of goat's milk . . . the list went on and on, my confidence and power growing with every burble of the cauldron. And finally, the most important ingredient for whatever it was we were facing on Treasure Island: three-leafed clover. Lots of it.

I stirred, slowly and carefully, as the steam rose and the brew came together until at last the draught began to stir itself. Then I flipped over the old-fashioned hourglass on the kitchen counter. The concoction needed time to mature, the heat transforming and melding the ingredients, solidifying my intent. While the sands silently fell through the hourglass, grain by grain, I went into the living room to investigate the Nazi flag. It hummed with malice.

The glass had a large starburst crack on the front, no doubt caused by Nimue hitting me over the head with it. A close inspection of the flag behind the glass revealed nothing that I didn't already know: there were burn marks along one edge, and the wear and tear and detailed needlework suggested the banner was genuinely vintage. I turned the shadow box facedown on the table, encircled it with salt, and murmured a charm as I set out my favorite stones for protection and strength: tiger's eye and jasper, obsidian and moonstone.

A pungent smell signaled the brew was nearing completion. I returned to the kitchen just as the last grains of sand passed through the tiny waist of the hourglass.

"Time, mistress?" Oscar asked.

I nodded. Clutching my ceremonial athame in my right hand, I held my left hand over the cauldron, cut a small X, and allowed three drops of blood to fall into the brew.

In a burst of steam, a grayish-yellow cloud rose to the ceiling. I looked up, searching the mist for the gentle features of my guiding spirit, the Ashen Witch, as I had my whole life. This time, instead, I saw the fearsome, awful countenance of Deliverance Corydon.

"Um, mistress?" Normally, Oscar loved watching me brew. Now, he sounded wary. "Is everything . . . okay?"

"It's fine," I assured him. And it was. Deliverance Corydon was fierce, she was vicious, and she was a part of me. This was the way of it. *So mote it be.*

I filled a number of small glass vials with the noxious brew, stoppered them carefully, and slipped them into my pocket, then poured the rest into a wide-mouthed mason jar.

I returned to the living room, breathed deeply and chanted a protection charm to center myself, and used a small blade to pry the rear wooden panel off the shadow box.

Something was hidden beneath the Nazi flag. I felt magical power coming off it in waves: tragic, terrible, salty. This was what Nimue had been searching for, and it had been right under her nose the whole time, hidden in plain sight.

"*Ew*," said Oscar, peering over my shoulder. "Is that a *fish* skin?"

"No," I said. "They're mermaid scales."

"*No.*"

Oscar and I stared at the scales in silent horror.

"But that's wrong!" Oscar said.

"It certainly is. Oscar, would you do me a favor?"

"Yes, mistress?" Oscar said.

"I need Dragomir. It can't wait. Bring him here, please. Now."

"Yes, mistress."

Chapter 31

It was nearly three in the morning—the witching hour—when Oscar returned to Aunt Cora's Closet with Dragomir. At long last, we had the talk we should have had when we first met. A clear, honest talk about the threats San Francisco was facing, about his powers compared to mine, about Dantalion and Deliverance and what their melding, *our* melding as the *coincidentia oppositorum*, might mean. We spoke of Dragomir's far-ranging knowledge of languages and lore, and my equally extensive knowledge of brewing. With Sailor at my side, I invited Dragomir into my apartment, allowing him into my private realm, my sanctum.

I even showed him my cauldron.

We went back downstairs to the shop floor to go over our strategy when, shortly before dawn, the bell over the front door tinkled and Aidan Rhodes walked in. He was every bit as gorgeous and vibrant as he had been the first time I met him, long ago, when I had just arrived in the Haight-Ashbury and was still not "out" as a witch. The periwinkle blue eyes I knew so well gazed at me for a long moment.

Now I understood the timeless nature of his aura, for Aidan Rhodes had been around a very, very long time.

"Lily," he said.

"Aidan."

Then, throwing caution to the wind, I flung myself at him. His arms enveloped me, returning my embrace.

"Don't tell me you missed me," Aidan said, his voice gruff but betraying his surprise.

"Never," I said, pulling back and studying his face. He looked as fresh and rested as though he had spent the last several months lolling about a European spa rather than in a salt cave, desperately trying to heal deep physical as well as psychic wounds. "And I didn't cast healing spells for you from afar, and I didn't worry about you at all."

He smiled and his gaze shifted to my half brother.

"You must be Dragomir," said Aidan.

Dragomir nodded, but neither man made a move to shake hands. Among magical folk, the pressing together of palms can create a conduit. We do it purposefully, not in casual greeting.

"Good to meet you face-to-face," said Dragomir. "I've heard a great deal about you."

"Same," said Aidan. "And Sailor, I hear congratulations are in order."

My new husband remained with his arms crossed over his chest, glowering. Sailor was not happy about any of what we were proposing, but he would support me, nonetheless. I needed these three men, and the strength of their alliance.

"We need your help, Aidan," I said. "And we don't have much time. I've brewed, and we need to be on Treasure Island before the sun comes up."

"Yes, your grandmother filled me in on what's going on. And she's right, I have a relationship with the water spirits. It's been a long time, but with Sailor's help I should be able to communicate with them."

Sailor gave a curt nod.

"Thank you," I said.

"And in return, I ask only that Oscar and Sailor come back to work for me."

"Say *what*, now?" I asked, casting a glance at Sailor that said, *Leave this to me.* Oscar, for his part, was nowhere to be seen; he had run to hide when Aidan walked in. The powerful practitioner made him nervous, for good reason.

"I believe you heard me," said Aidan smoothly. "Nothing in this world comes without sacrifice, Lily."

This was the thing about Aidan: I liked him despite myself . . . so I sometimes forgot why I didn't like him.

"That's the deal," he said with a confident smile.

"Yeah, well, it's a crap deal," I said, and suddenly an idea occurred to me. "And the answer is no."

"No?" Aidan looked surprised. "Best think it over carefully, Lily."

"I have a counteroffer: You agree to leave Oscar and Sailor alone, once and for all, and I'll help you get rid of the *vila*."

Aidan clenched his jaw at the mention of the *vila*.

"You know about that, do you?" he asked in a quiet voice.

"I know a lot of things, Aidan," I said. "Everyone has their secrets."

We stared at each other for several long moments, then Aidan inclined his head slightly. "All right, you'll come to work for me."

"Nope," Sailor interjected. "Lily will never work *for*

you. But she will work *with* you. We both will, and maybe even Oscar, too, *if* you do this for us."

Aidan sighed. "You drive a tough bargain. But I can see I have little choice. We have a deal."

At the break of dawn, Treasure Island's breathtaking views were obscured by a thick veil of hovering fog and a low-hanging mist that clung to the surface of the bay.

Dragomir and I stood by the shoals within a protective circle of the salts from my lachrymatory that I had reinforced with my brew. I had wrapped the mermaid scales in black silk and tied the package with brightly colored silk strings—pink, orange, and blue—which I had braided and knotted while chanting an ancient spell to comfort the grieving. The bundle hummed at our feet.

Dragomir and I turned to face each other, and I saw my father in my brother's eyes and he saw the same reflected in mine.

We raised our hands and pressed them together, palm to palm.

"*Coincidentia oppositorum*," Dragomir and I intoned in harmony.

Our palms tingled with energy as we entered the trance. I felt a surge of energy as Dantalion and Deliverance met, their combined intensity so fierce it was almost overwhelming. I fought the instinct to break off, to pull away, lest we lose control of these two so unnatural creatures. Dragomir and I would keep them in line . . . we *had* to keep them in line.

And, in this, we had help. Graciela's coven had invited Selena to join them to form a circle behind us, drawing down the moon. Oscar was perched on the nearby rocks, watching and boosting our energy. And Aidan and Sailor stood to the side, poised to play their part.

Together, Dragomir and I searched for the portals, sensing the imbalance of the *torana* formed by the Golden Gate, the mouth of the bay, and the bridge that spanned the gap. The wind picked up and we could hear the bridge "singing" to us, the mournful tones reverberating through the bay waters. The salts of my lachrymatory echoed the salinity of the seawater, and I called on their power to help keep Deliverance in check. The circle of brew vibrated around us, glowing a reddish-orange, rising from the earth and gently falling back down, helping to protect us and piggybacking on the force of Dragomir's control over his demon, Dantalion. I could feel Dantalion's power of language— of deep, scientific understanding—as Dragomir and I used our combined powers to call on the injured and angry water spirits.

Just as the orangey rays of dawn began to appear over the mountains to the east, the merfolk arrived, glimmering, gleaming, casting tiny rainbows everywhere as they broke the surface of the salty waters. Their movements were sinuous and graceful, swimming in formation, peeling off and diving, then circling back and reuniting, reminding me of what the Black Forest Beauties must have looked like at the World's Fair. But as the merfolk left the water and pulled themselves onto the shoals, their movements were clumsy, like seals navigating the rocks, and their skin glowed in dazzling colors, neon green and brilliant blue and Schiaparelli pink.

They weren't conventionally beautiful, as they were commonly portrayed in old European paintings and book illustrations. Their eyes were overly large, flat, and unblinking, rather fishlike. And yet they were enticing, entrancing, their seductive magic palpable even from a distance.

Dragomir and I remained palm to palm within the protective circle as Aidan and Sailor slowly approached the shore to communicate with the merfolk.

The men stood still and intense, engaging with the merfolk in a wordless exchange.

At long last, the merfolk nodded.

Together Dragomir and I picked up the black silk bundle and handed it to Aidan, who brought it to the shoals. He untied the strings to reveal the mermaid scales.

The merfolk cried out, their piercing shrieks assailing not only my ears but my soul. I felt their anguish, their anger, their misery, their grief. As the screaming grew in intensity, the coven and Selena covered their ears and started to cry. Sailor and Aidan cringed but did not flinch, stoic and solid and silent, bearing witness to the merfolk's tragic loss.

Suddenly Marcellus's pigeons appeared, swarming and flying in a murmuration over the bay, reminding me of the white butterflies whose presence signaled the arrival of the wood spirits and the fairies. As we watched the beautiful sight, I recalled that sirens were often portrayed with feathered wings and claws, more bird than fish.

At long last the wailing stopped and the merfolk took the scales of their lost mermaid and disappeared back into the bay, with only a final flick of their bright tails splashing the gray waters in farewell.

Chapter 32

"And what about that space over there, under the eaves?" I asked. We were standing in the attic space, where Sailor had started sketching out where the new walls would go. "What's that for?"

"I was thinking that might be the nursery," said Sailor.

I gaped at him.

"We agreed we wanted children," he said. "Right?"

"We do, but not *immediately*."

He grinned. "Best to be prepared, though, right? And now that Aidan's back, you'll have nothing but time on your hands."

To my great relief, Aidan was back in his office at the wax museum and once again in charge of corralling the magic folk and handling the Satchel. He was more subdued than he used to be, but still had that impish grin and brash self-confidence. We had a meeting scheduled to go over, in detail, what had happened in his absence as well as to strategize about the *vila* that haunted him.

I was pleased when Dragomir announced that he was planning to extend his visit for a while. We had a lot more to discuss and to plan, not the least of which was how our united efforts would continue to keep San Francisco safe from supernatural terrors. The *torana* still provided a thin membrane through which spirits—and demons—could too easily pass.

Dragomir had a more personal reason for sticking around the City by the Bay, which I probably should have seen coming. He was the "mystery date" Patience had been so interested in. She was supposed to drop by Aunt Cora's Closet tomorrow to find the perfect frock for their night out—plus that cashmere shrug I had promised her.

Having helped us out on Treasure Island, Graciela and her coven sisters had decided it was high time to return to Texas. As the bus once again blocked traffic in the street in front of Aunt Cora's Closet, Graciela took my hands in hers and said: "You have a warrior's heart, a healer's hands, and an ancient spirit. Never doubt that you are the magic, *m'ija*. You will grow to be a powerful crone, like us." Then, with a decided cackle, she climbed onto the ancient school bus and the coven roared down Haight Street in a cloud of diesel exhaust, the Aunties waving vigorously out the windows.

Carlos Romero, true to his word, called me down to the station for a very long interrogation. He reported that he had tied up the loose ends in his murder investigations, thanks to Zane's cooperation. Zane was doing all right, and had reached a new understanding with his father, Eugene. Shanda told me Cece was sad and grieving, but she had been seeing a counselor and the girls were making plans to attend college at UC Santa Cruz. Cece's mother had known of Orson's involvement in the Nazi group, but no one had fully understood how far Nimue's extremist ideology had gone.

Sailor and I went back down through Lucille's Loft and to Aunt Cora's Closet. It was after hours, so the shop was quiet as we crossed the fragrant space, passed through the back room, and climbed the stairs to our apartment, where we found Oscar playing with Winston-the-bat, who was hanging from his oversized finger. Winston was free to come and go as he pleased, but appeared to have made the little bat box on the terrace his home.

"Where have y'all *been*?" demanded Oscar. "A critter could faint from hunger around here."

"Is your arm broken?" growled Sailor. "You could have started dinner."

"Oscar!" I said. "I'm glad you're here. I have some news."

"I know, I know, 'Be careful with the bat,'" he said in a singsong voice.

"Well, that's true, but that's not what I was going to say. Eugene Leimert put me in touch with the curator from the island museum, who had some information about the fate of the gargoyles from the World's Fair."

Oscar gulped, set Winston down, and gazed at me with his huge bottle glass green eyes.

"You think we could find her?" he asked, his voice small.

"I think so, yes. The only problem is, she's probably underwater."

"What do you mean?"

"I'm afraid a lot of the art and even whole buildings were dumped into the bay when they were constructing the naval station."

"They *dumped* my mother in the bay? Who would do such a thing?"

"It was wartime," Sailor said, his voice gentle. "A lot of terrible things happen in wartime."

"So how are we gonna get to her?" Oscar asked. "Gobgoyles don't swim. We sink."

"Even if you could swim, this isn't going to be easy." I wrapped an arm around his shoulders and gave him a squeeze. "But you're not alone. We'll figure this out."

Sailor came to stand on Oscar's other side and wrapped his arm around Oscar's shoulders, too.

"You bet we will. I happen to be an excellent swimmer, and Aidan introduced me to the merfolk, so I'm known to them now. Perhaps we could make a deal with them, see if they'll find her for you."

"The merfolk can find her!" Oscar said, then paused. "But mistress, there'll be a price to pay."

"There's always a price to pay," I said. "But we'll figure it out."

"Really?" asked Oscar.

"Really," I said. "After all, look at the three of us. We pack quite the magical punch, and what is all that power good for if we don't put it to use?"

"*Hey*, you know what?" said Oscar, his tone upbeat.

"What?" I asked.

"With Sailor on one side, and you on the other, we're making an Oscar sandwich! And speaking of sandwiches . . . anyone hungry?"

Continue reading for an excerpt from
another thrilling book in Juliet Blackwell's
bestselling Witchcraft Mystery series

BEWITCHED AND BETROTHED

Available now from Berkley!

Chapter 1

A salty, heavy shroud of fog obscures the night.

Frigid waters close over my head. Sparks of silvery moonlight dance on the surface of the bay, calling to me. I flail and kick, struggling to lift myself, to breathe sweet air, my arms and legs numb with cold and exhaustion. The cheerful lights of San Francisco peek through the fog, tantalizingly far away; the island behind me is closer, but gleams and pulsates in the light of the full moon like a living, malevolent thing. The Golden Gate is the third point on the triangle, and I am in the center.

A foghorn sounds in a mournful cry.

Strong currents wrap around my legs, tugging at my feet, pulling me toward the Golden Gate and out to the vast Pacific Ocean. Lost at sea. Lost forever.

I can't go on.

I fear drowning, but remind myself: *Witches don't sink*.

At least *I* don't. I had been in the bay once before and popped up like a cork. But . . . what about now?

Icy fingers grip my ankles, drawing me down. The water closes over my head again, and I try to scream.

"Mistress!"

I struggle toward the surface. Fighting, flailing. I have to.

I *have* to.

"Mistress!" a gravelly voice called again. "Are you all right? Why are you all wet?"

I opened my eyes. I was in my own home, in my own bed. Safe.

Oscar, my ersatz witch's familiar—a shape-shifting cross between a gargoyle and a goblin—perched on my brass bedstead, leaning over to peer at me. His fearsome face was upside down and his breath smelled vaguely of cheese.

Soaked and shivering, I let out a shaky sigh. I wasn't sweaty from fear, but *dripping* wet—and smelling of brine—as though I had, indeed, just emerged from the San Francisco Bay.

"I had a nightmare," I said.

"Yeah, no kiddin'. That's one heck of a nightmare if you're manifesting in your sleep. Were you swimming or something?" Oscar waved a handful of travel brochures under my nose. "Hey, check these out. I think we should go to Barcelona first, maybe."

"Oscar, I can*not* discuss my honeymoon plans with you at the moment." My brain felt fuzzy. I sat up and glanced at my antique clock on the bedside table. Its hands glowed a mellow, comforting green that cut through the darkness. City lights sifted through my lace curtains, but even raucous Haight Street was hushed at three o'clock in the morning.

"But it's the witching hour," Oscar whined.

"Ideal for spellcasting, not for making travel plans."

Oscar cocked his head. "What better time is there?"

"In the morning. After coffee. When normal people are awake."

"But we're not 'normal people'—like we'd even *want* to be, *heh*!" He chuckled, a raspy sound reminiscent of a rusty saw.

I'm Lily Ivory, a natural-born witch from West Texas who wandered the globe for years, searching for a safe place to settle down. On the advice of a parrot named Barnabas, whom I had met in a bar in Hong Kong, I had come to San Francisco—specifically, to Haight Street— where a witch like me could fit in.

I love it here. For the first time in my life I have friends, a community, a *home*.

If only the beautiful City by the Bay weren't so chock-full of murder and mayhem.

Oscar was right, I thought, plucking the soggy night-gown away from my skin. It was unusual to manifest during a dream, to bring a physical object—in this case, water from the bay—from the realm of slumber into the waking world.

I shivered again.

"Just saying, we're both awake right now," Oscar continued. "And not for nothing, but you might want to dry off and maybe put a towel down before you ruin your mattress."

Throwing back the covers, I hopped out of bed and headed to the bathroom to take a shower. Washing away the waters of the bay with lemon verbena soap, I lingered under the hot spray until warmth settled down deep in my core.

I emerged from the bathroom to find that Oscar had gone. He had left the travel brochures fanned out in a semicircle atop my comforter, and on the nightstand was a steaming mug of chamomile tea. He had also managed to dry the bed, somehow, and to make it up with fresh sheets.

Oscar might not be a typical (read: obedient) witch's familiar, but he definitely had his moments. Not to mention he had saved my life on more than one occasion.

I sat on the side of the bed, sipped the tea, and picked up a brochure with a glossy photo of Barcelona's famous Sagrada Família. The next brochure featured the Eiffel Tower, and the last the Voto Nacional de Quito, in Ecuador.

I had promised Oscar he could tag along on my honeymoon so that we could search for his mother, a creature suffering under a curse that transformed her into a gargoyle. The problem was he had no idea where she might be, only that "gargoyles live a *long* time." I reminded myself to discuss this with my fiancé, Sailor, so that we could come up with a targeted approach before Oscar whipped up an entire world tour for us. Recently it had been difficult for Sailor and me to find the time—and the peace of mind—to talk about much of anything, much less gargoyle-guided tours.

I yawned. Speaking of honeymoons, I had a bucket-load of decisions to make before the wedding, and more than a few wrinkles to iron out. My grandmother's eccentric coven had recently arrived in town; I was about to be married to a beautiful but secretive man—an attachment to whom, I had been warned, might weaken my powers. Oscar kept disappearing to search for his mother even though he was supposed to be helping secure the perfect venue for my upcoming wedding, and recently I had come to realize that instead of one guiding spirit, I had *two*, and they weren't getting along, which was messing with my magic. And finally, my beloved adopted city of San Francisco was facing a frustratingly nonspecific existential threat that primarily involved a cupcake lady named Renee.

I took another sip of tea. I also still needed to find just the right vintage bridesmaid dresses for my friends Bronwyn and Maya. Under any other circumstance I would have said "Wear what you like!" but the style editor for the *San Francisco Chronicle* was planning to do a feature on our antique bridal wardrobe, which would be great publicity for my vintage clothing store, Aunt Cora's Closet.

I may be a witch and a soon-to-be bride, but I'm also a small-business owner vying for customers on increasingly competitive Haight Street. I needed the exposure.

I also needed some rest.

Grabbing an *in fidem venire praesidii* amulet off the dresser mirror, I held it in my right hand and walked the perimeter of the bedroom in a clockwise direction, chanting:

I have done my day's work,
I am entitled to sweet sleep.
I am drawing a line on this carpet,
over which you cannot pass.
Powers of protection, powers who clear,
remove all those who don't belong here.

As I lay back down and switched off the light, waiting for sleep to take me, I couldn't shake the sensation of the waters closing over my head.

It wasn't like me to have a nightmare. Much less a *manifesting* nightmare.

It was enough to worry a weary witch like me.

Ready to find
your next great read?

Let us help.

Visit prh.com/nextread

Penguin
Random
House

Other Books by
Faye Kellerman

THE RITUAL BATH
SACRED AND PROFANE
THE QUALITY OF MERCY
MILK AND HONEY
DAY OF ATONEMENT
FALSE PROPHET
GRIEVOUS SIN
SANCTUARY
JUSTICE
PRAYERS FOR THE DEAD

Coming Soon in Hardcover

MOON MUSIC

FAYE
KELLERMAN

Serpent's
Tooth

A PETER DECKER/RINA LAZARUS NOVEL

AVON BOOKS ◆ NEW YORK

AVON BOOKS, INC.
1350 Avenue of the Americas
New York, New York 10019

Published in hardcover by William Morrow and Company, Inc.; for information address Permissions Department, William Morrow and Company,
Inc., 1350 Avenue of the Americas, New York, New York 10019.

First Avon Books Printing: June 1998
First Avon Books International Printing: February 1998

To Jonathan after having reached
the twenty-five-year mark.
There may be silver at your temples,
but there's only gold in your heart.
Thanks a heap, Colonel.

Now the serpent was more cunning than any other beast of the field.

—Genesis 3:1

Because you did this, you are cursed from among all the animals and beasts of the field.

—Genesis 3:14

From this we learn that we do not give one who seduces people [to do evil] the opportunity to justify his actions.

—Rashi
Sanhedrin 29a

1

Nobody noticed him.

Not Wendy Culligan, who was too busy pitching million-dollar condos to a half-dozen Japanese businessmen more interested in her rear than in residences. Still, she patiently went about her spiel, talking about in-house services, drop-dead views, revolving mortgages, and great resale values.

Leaning over the table, showing a touch of cleavage while spearing a jumbo shrimp off the seafood appetizer plate. Along with the prawns were oysters, abalone, gravlax, and raw sea-urchin sashimi, the last item a big hit with the Asians—something about making them potent.

Men—regardless of race, creed, or color—thought only about sex. And here she was, trying to earn an honest buck while they popped squiggly things into their mouths, washing the tidbits down with sake as they licked their lips suggestively.

What's a poor working girl to do?

Inwardly, Wendy acknowledged that Brenda, her boss, had been generous in arranging the dinner at Estelle's. The restaurant was exquisite—all silver and crystal and candlelight. Antique mahogany buffets and chests rested against walls lined with elegant sky-blue Oriental silk screens. Exotic flower arrangements adorned every table—giant lilies, imported orchids, and twotone roses. A hint of perfume, but never overwhelming. The chairs were not only upholstered in silky fabric but *comfortable* as well. Even the bar

1

area was posh—plush stools, smoked mirrors, and rich walnut panels, all tastefully illuminated with Tivoli lights.

She felt as if she were dining in a palace, wondered why the rich ever had any problems. So what if they came with baggage—their scheming mistresses and lovers, their tawdry secrets and perverted kinks, their whining children and mooching relatives. Wendy could have withstood the pain, just so long as those big bucks kept rolling in.

Transfixed by the splendid surroundings, so intent on doing her job—getting a fat and much-needed commission—Wendy didn't blink an eye when the young man with the green sport coat walked through the door, eyeing the room with coldness and calculation.

Neither did Linda or Ray Garrison.

At last, Ray was enjoying a little solitude with his wife of thirty-five years. Recalling the anniversary party that their daughter, Jeanine, had thrown for them even if she had thrown it with *his* money. At least it had gone well. Jeanine was one hell of an organizer. The guests had remarked what a wonderful party it was, what magnificent parents he and Linda must have been to have raised two such devoted children . . . politely including David in the same category as Jeanine. No one had dared to hint at his son's recent jail term.

An elegant affair. But Ray knew it had been just as much for Jeanine as it had been for Linda and him. Lots of her ''club'' friends—people Ray barely knew—had come along for the ride.

Still, it had been fun. And David had behaved himself. At last, the boy finally seemed to be moving in the right direction, was using his God-given talents. Ray would have disinherited him years ago, but it had been Linda's soft heart that had kept the avenues of communication open.

Linda. Soft, beautiful, generous, and solid, his backbone for three and a half decades. At times, he was aware of the age in her face, the webbing around the corners of her eyes and mouth, the gentle drop of her jaw and cheeks. But Linda's imperfections, completely absent in her youth, only served to increase his desire for her.

He loved her with all his heart. And he knew that she returned the sentiment. At times, their closeness seemed to exclude everyone else, including their children. Maybe that was why David had grown up so resentful. But more than likely, their love for one another had nothing to do with their son's problems. Weak-willed and cursed with talent and charm, Dave had drifted into a Bohemian life at an early age.

But why think about that now? Ray reprimanded himself. Why think about Jeanine—her spending habits, her high-strung hysteria, and her fits of temper when she didn't get what she wanted? Why think about David's repeated stabs at rehab? Concentrate on the moment . . . on your lovely wife.

Ray took his own advice and reserved his remaining attention for Linda. Although his eyes did sweep over the young, grave-faced man in the green jacket, holding a drink, they failed to take him in.

Even if Walter Skinner had noticed the odd man, he wouldn't give the punk the time of day. At this stage in his life, Walter had no patience for youngsters, no patience for anyone. He had worked in Hollywood for over fifty years, had earned himself a fat bank account and a modicum of recognition and respect. He wanted what he wanted when he wanted it with no questions asked. If you didn't like it, you could take a long walk to China.

And what Walter wanted now was the young lady sitting across from him. A lovely lass with big, red hair, and long shapely legs that melded into a firm, round ass that sent his juices flowing.

Not *here,* Walter scolded himself. To calm himself down, he thought about Adelaide.

A good woman, a *tolerant* woman. Once she had been a beautiful woman, a Vegas dancer right after Bugsy had turned the desert sands into dunes of gold. Walter had chased her, pursued her relentlessly. Finally, she gave in. For her, it had paid off. As a minimally talented show girl, Adelaide had been destined for obscurity. Instead, she became a Hollywood wife. He gave her status, money, and a role she could have for life. *If* she was willing to indulge him from time to time. Which she did gracefully.

Good old Addie. As steady as the old gray mare.

Walter looked across the table, through the diamond-cut stemware. Good grade Waterford. Estelle had done it up nicely. Elegant without being pompous. And *good* food. No wonder the place was always jammed.

He'd had doubts about bringing Big Hair here. She had dolled up for the occasion, and much to Walter's surprise, she had pulled it off without looking cheap.

A gray-haired old lady smiled at him, nodded.

Walter nodded back.

Ah, recognition. It was sweet.

However, it was not quite as sweet as Big Hair's ass. Walter looked deeply into his table companion's baby blues, his eyes shifting downward to her superb surgically designed chest. He felt a tug in his pants and that was wonderful. At seventy-eight, no hard-on was ever taken for granted.

Face it, Walter said to himself. At seventy-eight, waking up in the morning was a cause for celebration.

So enamored of his sexual response and his beating heart, Walter didn't think about the serious young man leaning against the bar, his eyes as chilled as the drink he was nursing.

Carol Anger *did* glance at the thin young man in the green coat, thinking he looked familiar. She couldn't quite place him. A face that had changed and had changed again. But she couldn't dwell on it because she was too busy. Gretchen had called in sick and Carol was running double shift.

On her slate was a nice group of tables. Carol especially liked the party of sweet-sixteeners in the corner. Eight giggly girls trying to pretend they were grown-ups, decked out in sophisticated suits and too much makeup.

Like she had been at sixteen—sans the suits and jewelry of course. She had grown up in a home where money had always been tight. But down deep, all sixteen-year-old girls were the same.

Where had the time gone?

At first, right after her divorce, her life had been a blur of tears. Tears of fury at her ex, tears of gratitude at her parents for their love and understanding.

And their *help*.

Mom had come through. Always there when Carol needed her. Saying she'd take care of Billy so Carol could go back to nursing school. Carol had insisted on doing her fair share. Hence the job . . . this job. And it was a doozy.

She had Olaf to thank for that.

She had met him at a bar, had laughed when he had told her his name.

OLAF!

OLAF, THE VIKING MAN!

He had blushed when she laughed. Which of course had made her feel terrible. Olaf had come to America to be a cook. When he told her he worked at Estelle's, she had nearly fainted.

You're not a cook, she had chided. *You're a* chef!

Within a month, Olaf had convinced Estelle to give Carol a job interview. A week later, she was dressed in a tux and ready to work.

How she loved Olaf, with his half smile, his stoic manner, and his thick upper lip that was often dotted with sweat from the heat of the kitchen. She had often wondered how she could have been so upset over her failed marriage, since from it came all this good fortune.

So occupied by her fate and work, Carol failed to see the thin young man's mouth turn into a twisted smile, his eyes as blank as snowdrifts.

Ken Wetzel didn't think twice about him. He was too busy slurping up oysters while giving his wife the bad news. He was trying to be as gentle as possible but it wasn't coming out right.

It wasn't that he didn't love Tess. He guessed he still did. She had been there for him, was still a decent wife, a good mother, and a passable lover. Unfortunately, she just didn't fit into his world anymore.

Especially since he had been promoted to *assistant vice president*.

He needed a partner who was more dynamic, not some ordinary woman whose sole occupation was raising children. Granted, the kids were good kids . . . Tess's doing. But that wasn't enough anymore. A woman had to know things—how to dress, how to smile, how to make conversation about the vagaries of the market. A woman like that could help him get *ahead*. Trouble was, Tess was holding him *back*.

A great gal, but a high-school dropout. And with the last kid, she had gotten heavy. Those awful tents she wore. Why did the prints always have to be so garish? Why didn't she realize she would have looked more sophisticated and sleek in a plain black suit?

That was Tess.

Ken sighed inwardly, wishing she'd wipe the tears off her cheeks. Because she was embarrassing him. He closed his eyes for a moment, allowing himself a brief fantasy of Sherrie. Sherrie, with her milky eyes, her sensuous mouth, her wonderful hips, her full breasts, and her MBA from Stanford.

They had met on interoffice E-mail, she being in marketing, he being two floors up in stock research. He joked that it had been love at first byte. The affair was almost immediate, fueled by the thrill of their respective infidelities and what each one could do for the other's career.

Yes, Ken still loved Tess on some level. And yes, Ken still cared for the kids. But life was about reaching one's potential. The marriage just wouldn't work any longer.

Times change, he had told her.

Life changes.

You move on.

With each pronouncement, Tess had shed a new batch of tears.

Still, the drama of the evening did little to quell his appetite. As much as he hated himself, he had to admit that telling Tess it was over was a definite *high*. The exhilaration of liberation.

Flying high with freedom, Ken paid no attention to the thin young man. Not even when the young man's face fell flat, turning his physiognomy into something inanimate, his eyes as murky as pond water.

No one even noticed when he reached into the pocket of his green jacket.

Not until he pulled out a gun and the lead began to fly.

But by then, it was too late.

2

A microsecond flash of yesteryear as images too frighteningly clear burst from the hidden recesses of Decker's brain. A familiar scene with familiar sounds and smells. Charlie's discards. Twisted corpses. Moans of the wounded echoing through a gripping fog of panic. Medics worked frantically, hands and arms bathed in blood and flesh. The metallic odor of spilled blood mixed with the stink of emptied bowels. Surreal. The magnitude of death and destruction. It destroyed faith in a hand clap.

Decker swallowed, trying to lubricate a parched throat. Rationally, he knew Nam was over. So what was this? An instant replay? Except the surroundings were off. Confusion reigned. But only for a moment.

Because there was work to be done.

Instantly, he rolled up his jacket and shirt sleeves, gloved his hands. Saw a woman whose leg had been turned into Swiss cheese by dime-sized bullet holes. Lying in a pool of crimson. Her complexion pasty . . . clammy. Pushing aside debris with his foot, Decker made room for himself . . . knelt at her side.

Stop the bleeding, treat 'em for shock, get 'em to a chopper.

Scratch the chopper, make it an ambulance.

"You're going to be all right," Decker spoke soothingly as he worked. Perspiration had soaked through his jacket from his armpits. His crotch was as hot and humid as an

8

Orlando summer. Sweat was dripping off his hair, off his face and brow. He turned away from his patient, shook off the water like a drooling mastiff. He said, "Just hang in there."

Lots of bleeding, some of it arterial. Rhythmic squirts of bright red blood. Decker put pressure on the leaking area as the woman screamed, tears rolling down her cheeks.

He bit his upper lip, nibbling on his ginger mustache, trying to keep his own breathing slow and steady. He examined her torn tissue, working through bits of bone. Femoral artery appeared to be intact . . . the other major arteries as well. Arter*iole* bleeding, probably from one of their branches. She didn't realize it, but she had been a very lucky pup. Much better than her male companion, who'd never again see the light of day.

"I need a blanket, STAT!" Decker shouted.

"We're out!" someone shouted back.

"Then get me a tablecloth, napkins . . . something!" Decker screamed back. "I got shock settling in!"

"You and half the room! Get it yourself!"

"For Chrissakes—"

"Here!" A tiny female paramedic with green eyes threw Decker a tablecloth. She was bent over a bearded man, wrapping a bandage around his neck. Instantly, the starched white linen turned tomato-colored. Her eyes glanced at Decker, at his shoulder holster peeking out from under his jacket. "What ambulance company are *you* from?"

"LAPD. Lieutenant Peter Decker."

The paramedic raised her brows. "Celia Brown. Need anything, just ask."

"Thanks." Spreading out the tablecloth as best he could, Decker raised the woman's good leg, dabbing her forehead and face as she sobbed and spoke. She told him her name was Tess. She had heard popping noises. Then everyone had started screaming, running for cover. Her leg exploded as she dived under her table.

Taking mental notes.

The victim wore a thick gold chain around her neck; her purse was still at her side. A horrific crime but robbery didn't appear to be a motive. Or maybe the gunman just didn't bother with her. She wasn't decked in diamonds and pearls, not like some of the other patrons. She wore a loud print dress that appeared to be a couple of sizes too big for her body. She asked Decker if her leg was still there. She couldn't wiggle her toes. All she felt were throbs of agony.

"Your leg is there." Again Decker checked for bleeding. "You're doing great."

"My husband . . ."

Decker was quiet.

"He's dead?"

Again there was silence.

"I want to know," Tess whispered.

Decker took a deep breath. "The dark-haired man wearing a blue serge suit?"

"Yes."

"I'm sorry, ma'am. He's gone."

Tess said nothing, looked away with tears in her eyes.

"Just keep as still as you can." To the paramedic, Decker said, "Got any spare wound gel, topical, and bandage?"

Celia gave him some equipment. "You need a shot of coagulant?"

"Bleeding's subsided. Besides, I'd prefer if one of you administered the meds."

"Fine." Celia thought a moment, then said, "You're a lieutenant . . . as in a cop?"

"Yes."

"Calling in the big shots for this one."

Muted by the enormity of destruction, Decker couldn't make chitchat.

Celia said, "They must be training you guys pretty well in ER services."

"I was a medic in the army."

"Ah, now it makes sense. Vietnam?"

"Yes."

"Betcha had lots of experience."

Too much, Decker thought. He applied the salves, unfurled a roll of gauze. "She's going to need a neck brace and a hip and leg splint. Can you finish her up for me when you're done?''

"No problem. Thanks for helping. We need it.''

They both worked quickly and quietly. When she was done with her man and his bloodied neck, she yelled out. ''Gurney and transport.''

Within seconds, she ungloved and regloved. Walked on her knees over to Decker's patient. ''Unbelievable.''

"Truly."

"I'll finish her up now.''

"Thanks. Her name is Tess. She's doing great.''

"Hey, Tess,'' the paramedic said. ''We're taking good care of you.''

Decker stood. A dozen doctors charged through the door, scattering themselves about where needed.

Trampling on evidence.

As if that were important at the moment. But down the line it would make his job harder. As yet, no one was in charge. Since there seemed to be enough medical staff, he figured he might as well take control. He called over some officers, flashed his badge.

"We need to secure the area. I want a fifty-yard radius around the place, two officers stationed at every entrance. No one will be allowed *in,* no one will be allowed *out* unless it's medical personel or Homicide detectives. And I mean *no one*. Not even survivors of this mayhem may leave until it's cleared with me. As hard as it will be, don't let in any family members. Be polite and sympathetic, but firm. Tell them I'll come out, speak to them, tell them what's going on. I'll inform them of . . . of their loved ones' conditions just as soon as we make identifications. Certainly no one from the press corps will be permitted on the premises. If they start asking questions—which they will— tell them someone from the department will hold a conference later. Reporters who break the rules get arrested. Go.''

From the middle of the restaurant, Decker surveyed the room—the disheveled tables, the knocked-over chairs, the pocked walls, and shattered window glass. Graceful wall-paper had been turned into Rorschachs of blood and food,

gleaming parquet-wood floors were now deadly seas of
spilled fluids, broken crystal, and pottery shards. His eyes
scanned across the bar, the kitchen doors, the hallway leading to the rest rooms, the windows, and the front entrance.
He took out a notebook, began dividing the area into grids.
He heard someone call his name—or rather, his rank. He
turned around, waved Oliver over.

"I think I'm going to throw up," the detective said.

Decker regarded him. Scott Oliver's naturally dark complexion had paled even through his six o'clock shadow; his
normally wiseass eyes were filled with dread.

"We've got to ID the dead." Decker ran a hand through
sweat-soaked, pumpkin-colored hair. "Let's start a purse
and pocket search." He showed Oliver his sketch. "I'll
take the left side, you do the right. When the rest of the
team comes in, we'll divide up the room accordingly."

"There's Marge." Oliver beckoned her near with frantic
hand gestures. She arrived ashen and shaking, her shoulders
hunched, taking a good inch off her five-foot-eight frame.

"This is horrible." She touched her mouth with trembling fingers, then pushed thin blond hair off her face.
"What happened? Someone just started shooting?"

Oliver shrugged ignorance. "We're doing a pocket and
purse search for ID of the dead. Loo, what about interviewing the survivors?"

Decker said, "Scott, you do the search. Marge, you start
interviewing on Scott's side—Bert, over here!"

Martinez pivoted, jogged over to his team. "Mary
Mother of God, I think I'm gonna be sick."

"Take a deep breath," Decker said. "Bathrooms are in
the back."

Martinez covered his face with his hands, inhaled, then
let it out slowly. "It's just the putrid smell. Actually, it's
. . . everything. God, I'm . . ."

No one spoke.

Then Decker said, "Scott and Marge are working the
right side. You work with me on the left."

"Doing what?" Martinez picked at the hairs of his thick
black mustache.

"Interviewing the survivors or IDing the dead. Take your pick."

"I'll do the survivors," Martinez said. "Tom's on his way. You heard from Farrell?"

"Got hold of his wife. He's coming down."

"Think that's a good idea, Loo? Man's got a heart condition."

"Gaynor's survived close to thirty years on the force, he'll survive this. Besides, he's a wonder at detail work . . . which is what we're going to need . . . lots of detail work."

"And the captain?"

"He was at a meeting in Van Nuys when this went down. Should be here momentarily."

Decker started in the far left corner of the room, at a large round table for twelve. Two Asian men lay crumpled and unattended on the floor, spangled with bits of china and slivers of crystal. Loose flowers had fallen upon their torsos as if marking the grave site.

Decker did a once-over of the area. About fifty feet away sat a huddle of business-suited Asian males. Nearby were two Caucasians—one female and one male wrapped in blankets and bandages. He nodded to the woman, she nodded back. Her hands and face appeared cat-scratched, probably scored by flying glass. Decker shook off anxiety, gloved, and carefully kneeled down. He checked the bodies' pulses.

Nothing.

He went through one of the men's pants pockets. A portly man shot several times in the face and chest. He pulled out a wallet. Carefully, he wrote down the deceased's vitals from his driver's license.

Hidai Takamine from Encino. Black hair, brown eyes, married, and forty-six years old.

Decker winced. His own age.

He glanced up. Martinez hadn't moved, was looking down, staring at the bodies with vacant eyes.

Gently, Decker prodded him. "Get to work, Bert."

Martinez blinked rapidly. He said, "You in Nam, Loo?"

"Yep."

"So was I. Sixty-eight to seventy."

Decker said, "Sixty-nine to seventy-one."

Silence.

Martinez took a swipe at his eyes, then got to work.

By the time Strapp showed up, Decker had finished identifying the bodies on his side of the restaurant. The captain had given up the pretense of maintaining a calm demeanor. His thin features were screwed up in anger, his complexion wan. Decker brought him up to date as Strapp tapped his toes, his right hand balled into a fist that continuously pounded his left palm.

"Seven dead on my side." Decker rolled his massive shoulders, stretched his oversized legs as his kneecaps made popping sounds. The bending was doing wonders for his floating patellas. "I've identified the victims from driver's licenses. I'll go out and inform the next of kin just as soon as I get a body count and names from the other side."

He looked around, saw that Tom Webster and Farrell Gaynor had arrived. Tom was interviewing survivors along with Bert. Farrell was going through the pockets of the corpses on the right side as Marge and Scott attempted to calm the distraught.

Strapp shook his head, mumbled something.

"Sir?" Decker asked.

"Nothing," Strapp said. "Just cursing to myself. At last count, there's something like twenty-eight over at Valley Memorial's ER. This is just . . . I've got a slew of shrinks outside for support groups . . . some ER docs as well . . . in case someone has a heart attack or faints when the news hits."

"Shall I do it now, Captain?"

Strapp was still hitting his palm with his fist. "We'll do the dirty work together."

"What about the press?"

"Okay, okay." Strapp started bouncing on his toes. "You handle the press, I stay with the family members. Keep the vultures behind the ropes. No announcements until I've finished dealing with the next of kin.''

Decker said, ''Here's a partial list of the dead. I'll bring you the completed list as soon as I can.''

Both of them stalled for a moment; then they went their separate ways.

3

Though bandaged tightly, the arm was still leaking blood. But the waitress refused to budge, watching over her brood of eight teenage girls with hawkish eyes. Her face was damp with blood, dirt, sweat, and fury. "I am not leaving them until they're safe and sound with their parents."

Marge said, "That may take a while, Ms. Anger. You really need to take care of that arm."

The man sitting with them was the kitchen's assistant chef—Olaf Anderson. He was pale, but his eyes were steady and his manner stoic. "You don't do any good if you make yourself sick, Carol."

"I am *fine,* Olaf!"

One of the girls—dressed up in a pink mock-Chanel suit—spoke up. She had long permed hair and red-rimmed blue eyes. Her mascara had streaked down her cheeks. "We'll be okay, ma'am. You should get fixed up."

Immediately, the girl collapsed into tears.

The waitress hugged her with her good arm, looked up at Marge. "When can they leave? It's inhuman to keep them here. Right now, everyone's too hysterical to help you out."

"It's true," said the Chanel girl. "No one was paying attention, we were just like . . . ducking, you know. And screaming. Everyone was screaming."

"And praying," added another.

16

"You're . . ." Marge looked at the pink-suited girl, then down at the list. "Amy Silver?"

The girl nodded.

"You just ducked under the table when the shooting started."

Again, she nodded. "And screamed. I must have screamed a lot. My throat hurts."

"Everything hurts," added another teen.

This one wore a navy suit. Marge consulted her list. Navy suit was named Courtney. "Do you need medical attention, honey?"

Courtney shook her head, her eyes filling with tears. "We just heard like these pops. Then everybody like started to scream. Then we like ducked under the table and like hugged each other. And cried . . . but like quietly. We were real scared."

"Too scared to look at anything," Amy said. "Except that awful green jacket . . . moving like a blip on a radar."

"I didn't see a *thing*," Courtney said. "I had like my eyes squeezed shut and was praying real hard—Please, please, just let this be over." Her eyes overflowed with water. "I'd like to call my mom if I could."

"When can we see our parents?" Amy asked.

"Soon—"

"*How* soon?" Carol demanded. "At least let her *call* her mother?"

"I'm sure she's outside."

"So tell her that her daughter's okay, for godsakes! And when can I call *my* mother? She must be worried sick about me. She's not in the best of health."

"Please, Carol," Olaf said. "The woman is just trying to do her job—"

"I know that, Olaf. We are all trying to do our *job*!"

"You must have patience—"

"I've been plenty patient," Carol shot back. "Now I want some action!"

Marge said, "Let me consult with my boss. You all stay put—"

"Well, we can't exactly go anywhere with the Nazis blocking the doors."

Marge kept her expression neutral. "I'm so, so sorry. Believe me, the last thing I want to do is cause anyone additional pain. I'll be right back."

Carol's face was still irate, but she held her tongue.

Marge tried out a smile, but Carol responded by rolling her eyes. Before Marge made it to the door, Oliver flagged her down. "You're going to see Decker?"

"Yeah, we've got to start letting some of the people out of here. It's not fair—"

"I'll go with you," Oliver said.

They both stepped into the cool night air, shielding their eyes from the blinding glare of the headlights. Marge quickly counted fifteen vehicles—police cars, press vans, ambulances, and several meat wagons. Her eyes quickly adjusted to the shadows as she made out a group of people inside the tape barrier, off to the left. They'd been sidelined. She could hear their anger stabbing through the mist.

The family members.

The gawkers, along with the press, had been penned outside the yellow tape perimeter, at least fifty yards away.

Marge spotted Decker. His complexion had turned pasty, his big hands had been tightened into white-knuckled fists. She shouted his name. He stopped walking, turned, and came toward them.

Decker said, "You have the finalized list of the dead?"

Oliver showed him the ominous white sheet. "Give it to the captain?"

"Please. I've already delivered my allotment of bad news."

Marge said, "I've got a group of teenage girls—"

Decker said, "Go tell their parents. See some tears of joy instead of tears of agony."

Marge felt her throat tighten. "You all right? What a stupid question."

"I'm lousy," Decker said. "Not a fraction as shitty as the group I just left."

He took a deep breath, let it out slowly, and looked upward. A starless foggy night, a crescent of moon floating in an endless gray sea. "I've got to deal with the press." He turned to his detectives. "Anyone tell you anything useful?"

Oliver said. "Everyone ducked as soon as the shooting and screaming started."

Marge added, "Lots of screaming, lots of praying."

"Bullets flying around the room from all directions."

"From *all* directions?" Decker asked.

"I think they were using hyperbole," Marge said.

"Most of them were too busy ducking," Oliver said.

"Shooter say anything?"

Marge shook her head. "People I spoke to said someone just opened fire. No warning, no nothing."

"Ditto."

"So that seems to eliminate robbery as a motive." Decker rubbed his eyes, told them to go and bring some good cheer.

As he watched them approach the anxious relatives, he tried to collect his thoughts . . . rid himself of the shrieking and sobbing he had just heard from the unlucky family members. Slowly, he let his fingers uncurl, realized his hands were shaking. He wiped wet palms on his pants, tucked them into his pockets.

He needed something.

He needed a smoke.

As he neared the press corps, he bummed a pack of cigarettes and some matches off one of the uniformed cops. He tried to steady his hands as he lit up, sucking hot, dry smog into his lungs.

It felt acrid, but it did the trick. As nicotine coursed through his body, Decker felt his hands settle down, his brain beginning to clear.

He polished off the cigarette in four inhalations, immediately went for number two. Only after he had smoked it down to the butt was he ready to face the cameras. He ducked under the crime tape ribbon, was charged upon by a cavalry of multimedia representatives. He held up his palms, keeping them at arm's length, then shouted as best he could. His voice traveled well in the night air. "I'm only going to do this once, so let's give everyone a fair shot. Anyone out there need a little extra time to set up?"

"Five minutes to set up my camera?" a male voice yelled out.

"Make it ten," replied a female.

Decker said, "Ten minutes. I'll read from a prepared statement. Please, please, be respectful, ladies and gentlemen. I will take questions afterward for about fifteen, twenty minutes. Then I'm going to have to get back to work."

With his announcement, Decker turned inward, lit up a third cigarette, and spoke to no one, ignoring the questions that were thrown at him. He smoked two more cigarettes until the requisite time had passed. After checking his watch, he threw down his fifth butt of the evening, crushed it harder than necessary with his heel. He smoothed his hair and spoke to a wire wheel of microphones. Flashbulbs and video lights attacked his eyes.

"Our first concerns are with the people who need immediate medical attention. All the hospitals and medical institutions in the area have been notified and are giving those inside the benefit of their expertise as well as their staff, facilities, and supplies. We've received an abundance of community help from local physicians. The help is needed and appreciated. To everyone out there viewing this broadcast, please, *please:* If you are not involved in the primary medical care of those injured, stay away from the area so that doctors, nurses, medics, ambulances, and police personnel can move in and out of the area freely."

The questions started.

What happened?

How many killed?

How many wounded?

Do they have a suspect?

Do they have a reason for the shooting?

What's it like in there?

Decker turned to the last questioner. A Latina. Sylvia Lopez from the local news station. One of the few broadcasters who gave LAPD a fair shake during its bad times. He took her question.

"What's it like in there?" Abruptly, he broke into a cold sweat, shuddered involuntarily. "It's your worst nightmare."

He wiped his face, was about to field another series of questions, but over an ocean of scalps, he saw Martinez waving at him. One of the many benefits of being six four.

"I've got to go," Decker said. "Excuse me."

He extricated himself from the lights, cameras, and actions, ducking under the yellow tape and meeting Martinez halfway across the parking lot. Decker threw his arm around Bert's wide shoulders. "What?"

"There are a lot of people unaccounted for, Loo." Martinez pushed strands of black, wet hair from his forehead. His face had been bathed in sticky sweat. "We're directing the families to Valley Memorial, but some of the wounded may have gone to Northridge Pres. We're trying to get names, but everything's such a mess—"

"One step at a time."

"Speaking of which, we may have found the perp. He could have been one of the victims, but it looks like a suicide. Close-range single shot to the head around the temple region. You can see the powder burns—"

"Got a weapon?"

"Smith and Wesson double-action, nine-millimeter automatic—"

"Jesus!"

"Yeah, lots of spraying ability. Pistol's about five feet away from the body. Forensics is waiting for you or Captain Strapp before they move in. Farrell's guarding the corpse. No ID on the body, but we got a name from a couple of Estelle's employees: Harlan Manz."

"Disgruntled postal worker?"

"Disgruntled bartender."

4

"*Harlan worked here* for around three, four months—"

"Closer to six months—"

"Yeah, well, maybe it was closer to six months." Marissa, the waitress, sneaked a sideways glance at Benedict, the waiter. "God, I can't believe it." Sitting on a barstool, she shivered under her blanket, blond hair falling over her shoulders. "I knew he was angry when he left, but who would have expected . . ."

Decker stood between the two food servers, his back against the smooth oak bar top. Ten minutes earlier, he had gone through Harlan's empty pockets, observed the man's twisted body and blood-soaked head. A close-range shot and a clean one. A 9mm automatic lay a few feet away.

As a corpse, Harlan evoked pity rather than fury. Once he had been a good-looking man. Dark, brooding features now covered with sticky serum. He had died wearing dark slacks, a white shirt, and a green jacket that was splattered with blood, turning him Christmas-colored. The whole evening defied logic.

He returned his attention to the witnesses. "Was Harlan fired from his job?"

"Rather unceremoniously." Benedict shifted his weight on the stool, scratched a nest of black curls. He was sipping hot water, shaking as he talked.

"What happened?"

22

"Some asshole at the bar got plastered, started giving Harlan a real hard time. He just blew it, told the guy to get the hell out."

"A big no-no," Marissa interjected. "You have trouble with a patron, you're supposed to report it to the manager and let her deal with it."

"Any idea why Harlan decided to handle the matter?"

"He probably just had it up to here with rich dicks." Benedict looked upward. "You get tired of being pushed around."

Marissa said, "Robin must have heard all the commotion. She came charging in . . . it was real intense."

"Is Robin the restaurant's manager?"

"Yeah," Benedict said. "She just . . . started in on Harlan, told him to pack his bags and leave. That was that."

Decker was skeptical. "Harlan left without a fight?"

"Nothing physical," Marissa said. "But Harlan and Robin exchanged a few choice words. He was really mad. But she didn't have to call the cops or anything like that."

"Was this the only time either of you had ever seen Harlan explode?"

"Harlan was impulsive," Marissa said. "Did what suited him."

The servers exchanged brief glances. Decker's eyes darted between Marissa and Benedict. "What's going on?"

Marissa looked down. "I went out with him a couple of times. Nothing big. Just a drink after work."

Silence.

Marissa's eyes watered. "I had no idea he was . . ."

"Of course not," Decker soothed. "Tell me about him, Marissa."

"Nothing to tell. I thought he was kind of cute."

Decker looked at Harlan's corpse, now being worked on by Forensics. It lay some ten feet from the entrance to the bar, resting faceup, eyes open, mouth agape, arms splayed outward, legs bent at the knees. The complexion had taken on a grayish hue, but once it had probably been mocha-colored. Skin that showed wear and tear. Not craggy, but wrinkles about the eyes and mouth. Dark eyes, black hair, a broad nose and strong chin. Latino mixed with a hint of Native American. Looked to be around six feet. Well-proportioned.

"He seems like he could have been a very sexy guy." He homed in on Marissa's red cheeks. "Maybe we should talk in private?"

Marissa averted her gaze. "It was nothing serious. Does it really matter?"

"I was just wondering if maybe you were the intended target?"

The girl turned pale.

"No way," Benedict said. "If he was after anyone here, it would have been Robin." His voice dropped to a shadow. "And she's dead, isn't she?"

Decker nodded. The young man just shook his head. Marissa had tears in her eyes.

"We were never serious, Lieutenant. Honest. He was just studdin' around. Harlan did a lot of that."

"A lot of what?"

"Messin' around. I wasn't even his *real* girlfriend."

Decker sat up. "Who was his *real* girlfriend?"

"Rhonda Klegg," Benedict said. "Used to come in here sometimes. Harlan would comp her drinks. Tequila. She could down shooters as fast as any guy I know."

"Was she an alcoholic?"

Again they exchanged glances. Benedict said, "Well, she could get a little intense. But she kept it under control. I never saw them going at it in public."

"Going at it?" Decker asked.

Marissa said, "Harlan would come in with a black eye every once in a while. I asked him about it, he laughed it off." She studied her hands. "God only knows what she looked like."

Decker said, "Did you ever see them fighting?"

"Not personally, no."

"Is she also a wait . . . an actress?"

Benedict said, "Artist. She actually makes money in her chosen field. Got a great gig going. Paints pictures on the walls of rich people's houses."

"Murals?" Decker asked.

"No," Marissa said. "She'll paint a make-believe garden scene on a wall. There's a word for it."

"Trompe l'oeil," Decker said.

"That's it," Marissa said. "Her apartment is full of her stuff. It's real weird. She's got the statue of David on the wall of her john."

"You've been to her apartment?" Decker said. "With Harlan?"

Marissa turned bright red. "Well . . . just once."

"Did she and Harlan live together?"

"No, Harlan has . . . had his own place. But he liked being bad . . . God, I feel like an *idiot.*" Marissa rubbed her face. "It seemed so harmless at the time."

Rule number one. Fooling around is *never* harmless. Decker asked, "Did Harlan have a key to her place?"

Marissa nodded.

Decker became aware of his heartbeat. "Where does Rhonda live, Marissa?"

"The apartment was called the Caribbean. Third floor. It's near Rinaldi. I could get you the address."

"I'll get it." Decker looked at Benedict. "Anything else you want to add . . . something that might give us a clue to what went on?"

"Sorry, but I didn't see a thing," Benedict said. "When the shooting started, I ran for cover."

"Where?"

"Made a beeline for the coat closet. I hid there the entire time, too scared to even breathe."

"I couldn't tell you anything, either," Marissa added. "Everyone just started screaming. I dropped under a table."

"Where were you?"

"Carol Anger and I were working the left rear portion of the room. I had the odd tables, she had the even."

"Do you recall where the shooting originated?"

"God, no. It seemed like bullets were flying from all directions. I was too petrified to look up."

Decker looked over his notes, showed them a page.

"These are your current names, addresses, and phone numbers?"

Both servers nodded.

"Okay, you can leave." He handed them each a business card. "If you think of something important about what happened here . . . or anything important about Harlan Manz, give me a call."

"Why bother with Harlan?" Benedict said. "He's dead."

"Yes, he is," Decker said. "But by studying men like him . . . just maybe we can avert . . . another tragedy. Workplace violence is on the upswing. Least we can do is publicize warning signs."

Marissa said, "So where do you go from here?"

Decker said, "Right now, I'm going to call Rhonda Klegg. If I have any luck at all, she'll be alive and pick up the phone."

"Oh my God!" Marissa said. "You think that maybe Harlan . . . before this . . ."

No one spoke for a moment.

Marissa said, "If she's alive . . . are you going to tell her . . . you know . . . about Harlan and I?"

Harlan and me, Decker thought. He regarded the waitress, looked at her straggly hair falling over a war-ravaged face. "I don't think it will come up."

Tears streaming down her cheeks, Marissa thanked him profusely. Decker patted her shoulder, then left to search out a private phone.

There were two offices upstairs, each fitted with phones attached to answering machines that winked red in the dark. Decker flipped on the light switch in the larger of the two rooms. This one was Estelle Bernstein's personal salon, done in wood paneling with plush hunter-green carpets. Expensively furnished—antiques or good replicas. The abstract artwork wasn't his style, but it didn't look cheap. Decker closed the office door from the outside, chose to use the phone in manager Robin Patterson's hole in the wall.

Small. Utilitarian. A metal desk with a secretary's chair parked inside the kneehole. A scarred leather couch. The back wall was lined with file cabinets. A swinging door was tucked into one of the corners. Decker pushed it open. An old white toilet, a scratched sink, and a fan that made a racket when the light was turned on. Robin had tried to dress it up by adding a mirror to the wall and a crocheted toilet-paper cover. On top of the john's tank was a bowl of potpourri. Staring at the dried leaves, flowers, and spices, Decker felt a wash of sadness.

He called the station house, got the number he wanted. Within moments, Rhonda Klegg's phone was ringing. Her machine picked up. Decker waited until the beep.

"This is Detective Lieutenant Peter Decker of the Los Angeles Police Department. I need to talk to Rhonda Klegg. I don't know if you're home or not, Rhonda, but if you are, please pick up the phone. If you don't do that, I'm going to come over and have your apartment opened up. I have concerns for your safety. So if you don't want—"

"I'm fine! Go away!"

The phone slammed down.

Obviously, she had seen the news. Decker called back. This time she picked up.

"Look . . ." Her voice was slightly slurred. "I meant what I said. I don't wanna talk to the police or anybody else."

Decker said, "I'm at Estelle's. Been here since eight-thirty. Thirteen people are dead, Rhonda. At least thirty-one are wounded—"

"It's not my *fault*!"

She erupted into sobs. Decker waited until he could be heard. Calmly, he said, "Of course it's not your fault. You are completely blameless—"

"Then *why* are you calling me?"

"I wanted to make sure you were okay."

"I'm okay. Just . . . leave me alone."

"Be nice if I could talk to you, Rhonda."

"Do I *gotta* talk to you?"

"No."

Silence.

Her voice got very heavy. "What time is it?"

Decker checked his watch. "One-thirty."

A heavy sigh. "Can this wait till morning?"

"Yes, it can wait. Is anyone staying with you, Rhonda?"

"No."

"Can I call someone for you?"

She began to sob. "No. No one. Just . . . let me sleep."

"Did you take anything to help you sleep?"

"Coupla Valiums."

"And that's it?"

"Yeah, course that's it. Whaddaya think? What did you say your name was?"

"Lieutenant Decker. LAPD. Devonshire Substation."

"LAPD?"

"LAPD."

"If you're a reporter, I'm gonna sue you."

"I'm not a reporter."

"I'm not talkin' to reporters."

"A very good idea. Can I drop by your apartment around . . ." Decker checked his watch again. Yes, it was still one-thirty in the morning. There were still witnesses to interview, bodies to transport to the morgue, and he hadn't even touched his paperwork. Definitely an all-nighter. "How about eight in the morning?"

"Fine." She paused. "If you're a reporter—"

"Peter Decker, detective lieutenant one. LAPD, Devonshire Substation." He gave her his badge number. "Give them a call."

"I will, ya know."

"You should. So I'll see you at eight, Rhonda?"

"Fine. Good-bye."

Once again the phone slammed down.

At least she hadn't added "Good riddance."

5

Decker expected to talk to the machine. Instead, Rina picked up after a half ring. He said, "You should be asleep."

"I was worried about you. I'm glad you called."

"Nothing to worry about. I'm fine. I'm just not going to make it home tonight. You probably figured as much."

"Can I do anything for you?"

"Kiss my kids. Say a prayer. I don't know."

He sounded drained . . . lifeless. She said, "I love you, Peter."

"Love you, too."

"Don't hang up."

No one spoke.

Rina said, "I guess you have to get back to work."

Decker could picture his wife fidgeting with her hair, wrapping a long, black strand around her index finger or nibbling on the ends with her luscious mouth . . . her long pink tongue. Gave him a nice buzz between his legs. Obscene to think about sex after witnessing such atrocity. But he wasn't shocked by his response. After clearing the trail of Charlie's carnage . . . after doing the body count . . . Decker had often made a trip to the whorehouses the first item on his agenda. An old man housed in a nineteen-year-old body. Sex had been the thing that had made him feel alive.

29

He said, "I have a couple of minutes. Tell me about my kids."

"They send their love."

"Did they see the broadcast?"

"The boys did, sure."

"Are they upset?"

"Honestly, yes, they were upset. You looked so . . . pained. Are you sure I can't do anything for you, Peter?"

"Feeling helpless?"

"Exactly."

"Join the crowd. No, I'll be all right. The shock's starting to wear off . . . that old wartime numbness—"

"Oh, my God! This must evoke such terrible memories for you."

Decker waited a beat. "I used to get nightmares, Rina. Didn't remember too much in the morning, but Jan said they were pretty bad. She never admitted it, but I think I scared her. Maybe we should use separate bedrooms for a couple of weeks—"

"I wouldn't hear of it." Rina paused. "I love you. Just . . . know that."

"I know you want me to be okay. Honestly, I am okay. It just has to run its course. You want to help me, just take care of the kids and yourself. Did Sammy pass his driver's test, by the way?"

"He is now officially licensed for solo expeditions."

Something else to worry about, Decker thought. "Tell him congratulations. I'm really proud of him."

"He wants to take the Porsche out for a spin."

"Uh, that will have to wait."

"He thought that might be the case."

"Your voice is wonderful. I'd love talking, but you need your sleep. And I still have a mound of paperwork facing me."

"You're not going to sleep at all?"

"Oh, I'll probably catch a few fitful hours at the station house. I promise I'll be home tonight. Did I tell you I love you?"

"Never tire of hearing it," Rina answered. She kissed

the receiver. "Can I call you up in an hour or so?"

"I may not be available. I'm going out for a little bit."

"Catch some air?"

"I wish." Decker let out a tired laugh. "I'm planning to break into the apartment of a mass murderer. Not part of the job description when I joined the force. But sometimes you've just got to wing it."

Using a Thomas map and dimly lit street signs, Decker managed to find Harlan Manz's apartment. It was located on a deserted side road, shaded with oversized eucalyptus that loomed spectral in the gauzy night. No sidewalks. Pedestrians trod upon a dirt path that hugged the street. The block owned about a half dozen old multiplexed residences, all of them two-story stucco squares with small balconies. An occasional weed-choked vacant lot was interspersed between the buildings. Probably the land had once held structures that didn't make it through the '94 quake.

The former bartender had lived on a top floor, access to his unit provided by a rusted, wrought-iron outdoor staircase. The night was as still as stone. Not a soul in sight and that was good. Decker gloved, took out a penlight, and examined the door lock—a snap. Keeping his picks in his pocket, he removed a credit card from his wallet, snapped the latch bolt, and turned the knob. Closed the door and flipped the light switch.

He was standing in the living room. A beige couch, a couple of chairs, and a coffee table that held a remote control, a mug with a brown-stained bottom, and yesterday's local newspaper. A TV rested against the wall opposite the couch, a twenty-six-inch Sony sitting inside a particle-board bookcase. A half dozen paperbacks rested on the shelves alongside numerous videotapes. Most of them seemed to be action/adventure films but there were the requisite adult films as well. Harlan liked blondes. A stereo/cassette/CD player complete with speakers. Decker flipped through a few CDs; Harlan's taste leaned toward thrash bands and rap.

Decker's eyes scanned the walls. A few framed movie

posters hung from single nailheads on white walls. Cable
TV films that Decker had never seen, had never heard of.
The carpet was brown and worn—a few scattered crumbs,
but relatively clean.

The kitchenette was an outpouching off the living room.
The compact fridge contained a quart of juice, a quart of
milk, three six-packs, and a tub of margarine. Decker
opened the fruit bin—two apples dotted with soft spots, and
an orange. Cabinets stocked with salsa, chips, a half loaf
of moldless bread, a yellow plastic bottle of French's mustard, Heinz's ketchup, a box of raisin bran, mismatched
dishes and cookware, and a dead fly. Built-ins included a
two-burner cooktop and a microwave-oven combo. No
dishwasher, but the sink was cleared of plates and cutlery.

Completely unremarkable.

The bedroom was the same story. Queen-sized bed
topped with an older but clean spread. One nightstand containing packets of gum, a bottle of aspirin, and a pack of
cigarettes. A small desk was tucked into the corner.

Decker rummaged through its contents. Piquing his interest were several black-and-white head shots. Eight-by-
tens of Harlan peering into the camera lens with intense
eyes, his full lips slightly agape, and a well-trimmed—ergo
calculated—five o'clock shadow. He'd been posed to make
the most of his exotic sensuality. Dark and brooding.
Heathcliffian.

Portfolio pictures. Like everyone in Hollywood, Manz
had been touched by the industry, had taken a shot at the
tarnished screen.

The closet was another insight into Harlan's personality.
Lots of clothes. Not expensive threads but the duds had a
flair. Well-designed knockoffs. Decker counted seven pairs
of shoes, including an expensive pair of Nikes.

The bathroom was a tiny thing which squeezed in a tub
with a shower curtain, a toilet, and a sink with a medicine
cabinet. The shelves were chock-full of analgesics, nasal
sprays, and decongestant capsules. Harlan also stocked dis-
posable razors, several sticks of antiperspirant, and a sandwich bag dusted with white powder.

Decker dipped his pinkie into the bag and touched it to the tip of his tongue.

The real stuff.

He'd bag the rest and submit it for evidence.

Evidence of *what*, he wasn't sure. But he wasn't about to leave cocaine sitting around.

Cologne and aftershave sat on the rim of the tub. Cheap stuff. Decker organized his thoughts as he walked back into the living room. This time he examined the movie posters with a keen eye. As plain as daylight, Harlan's name had been listed in the cast.

The man had met with some limited success. Of course, that meant nothing.

Decker sat on the couch, rubbed his tired eyes, a puzzling picture emerging in his sleep-deprived brain.

Movie posters on the wall.

Portfolio pictures in the desk.

Stylish clothes and lots of shoes.

Bottles of cologne.

Someone who took pride in his appearance.

Someone with an *ego*.

Yet the place was completely devoid of personal effects. No scrapbooks, no picture albums, no reminder notes or scratch pads, no would-be scripts, no appointment book for the *big* auditions, no Filofax, no little black book of phone numbers, no desk calendar . . . no calendar, *period*.

There was beer in the fridge, cigarettes in the drawer, cocaine in the medicine cabinet. Which told Decker that the guy was a user. Then there was the coffee table on which lay a dirty coffee mug, yesterday's newspaper, and the remote control. Forming an image of a lived-in room . . . untampered with . . . untouched.

But something was off.

As if someone had carefully emptied the place of Harlan's true personality, leaving just enough items to form a sketchy impression—like his taste in drugs. The home of a disturbed man, a vicious mass murderer. Yet Decker didn't find a single threatening note, any written psychotic ramblings, nothing that even hinted of a desperate man driven to murder and suicide.

Decker exhaled, his brain buzzing.

Not all psychos leave behind their history—a blow-by-blow schemata, explaining what had led them to their atrocities. Some just explode, spontaneously combust, letting their bloody legacies talk for themselves.

Maybe Harlan had been one of those.

Maybe he woke up one morning . . . and simply popped.

❧6

The girl reeked of mint—hiding her booze breath with Scope or Certs—leaving Decker to wonder if the orange juice glass Rhonda Klegg held in a white-knuckled grip had been laced with vodka. He presented his badge. She examined it carefully, then allowed him inside. The place pulsated with color, throwing Decker's equilibrium off balance. The slamming door brought him back into focus.

"Sorry about being so paranoid," Rhonda stated. "Thought you might be the press."

Decker blinked. "Have people been bothering you?"

"Not since I took my phone off the hook."

She offered him coffee; Decker nodded yes. Cream and sugar? Straight black was fine.

With trembling hands, Rhonda sipped her orange juice, stared at him. He stared back at a ravaged, ashen face, lifeless blue eyes and thin pale lips. She probably hadn't gotten much sleep. She looked to be in her mid-twenties. Her hair had been bleached candy-apple red and was tied back into a ponytail. She had a nose-pierce, the helices of her outer ears completely covered with tiny hoops and studs. Lots of chains dangled from the many holes in her earlobes. She was garbed in jeans and a white T-shirt, wore a denim work shirt as a jacket. Her feet were stuffed in lace-up ankle boots.

She finished her juice and said, "I really don't have any-

35

thing to say.'' She held aloft her empty glass. ''Get you one of these along with your Colombian?''

''No, thank you. Just a cup of coffee would be fine.''

''Mind if I take another?''

''Of course not.''

''S'cuse.''

She disappeared behind a swinging door painted to simulate a wooden lattice intertwined with blooming pink rose vines. Indeed, Rhonda had used her entire apartment as her canvas, living art done up in the style of classical Mediterranean gardens. Painted boxwood hedges replaced baseboard molding. Behind the hedges—on the wall itself—were trellises of ivy and flowering vines, citrus orchards, classical marble statuary, and fountains—all of it serving as a foreground for distant, rolling green hills. Her perspective was outstanding. Decker felt dizzy from the three-dimensional effect. The molding and ceiling had been bathed in light blue hues, tufted with clouds, and populated with gliding blackbirds and a circling hawk.

So distracting was the scene, Decker hadn't noticed the furniture. But it was there and it made a statement. An old carved English park bench sided by two upside-down garbage cans doubling as end tables. The room also had an Adirondack lounge upon which rested a duffel bag, and two bentwood rockers. Old-fashioned streetlamps had been placed in the corners, and the hardwood floor had become a windblown field of grass—green swaying blades laced with yellow dandelions and clumps of white clover.

Rhonda returned with Decker's coffee, more orange juice for herself.

Decker thanked her. ''Interesting place you've got here. You're very talented.''

She sipped her juice. ''Ain't gonna make *Architectural Digest,* but it suits me.'' Her eyes hardened. ''Although this town is sure filled with star-fuckers. Think the ex-girlfriend of a homicidal maniac counts?''

Decker was quiet.

''Hollyweird. A penchant for the bizarre. Sure I can't get you some OJ as in orange juice?''

"I'm fine, Rhonda." Decker's eyes fell on the duffel bag. "Impromptu vacation?"

"I'm getting outta here. At least until this thing blows over. Who the hell wants this kind of notoriety?"

A savvy point. Decker placed his mug on an upside-down trash container. "Is that okay?"

Rhonda laughed. "It's a garbage can. I'm not exactly worried about coffee rings." She looked him up and down. "You're cute. Wanna fuck?"

"No, thank you."

"I look like shit, huh?"

"You look fine, Rhonda." Decker took out his notepad. "You know, the sooner we get started, the sooner I'm out of your hair."

"You're gonna ask me questions about Harlan?"

"Yep."

"Why do you care? He's dead." Her eyes watered. "They're all dead. I thought the only things that the pigs cared about were looking good on the witness stand and beating up minorities. You're real big. I bet you've punched around more than your fair share of niggers."

Decker said, "Me? I shuffle paper."

"Bullshit," Rhonda shot out. "You look defensive, cop. Betcha I hit a nerve. See, we all have pasts. So don't you go judging me like I'm some freak because I hooked up with a nutcase."

"I don't think you're a freak, Rhonda. Right now, I see you as a very vulnerable woman."

"Where'd they teach you that? Cop Psych 101? You should stick to pounding the shit outta motorists."

Decker was quiet.

She gave him a long hard stare. "You were there last night, weren't you? At Estelle's?"

"I was there the entire night."

"I saw you on TV. You're the one who said it looked like your worst nightmare."

"Glad to be remembered as a sound byte."

"You're also in today's paper—picture, quote, and all." She glared at him. "You had tears in your eyes."

"Did I?"

"Yeah, you did. Did they also teach you how to cry in Cop Psych 101? Or was it Cop Compassion 101?"

Decker offered a sad smile. "Wish I conformed to your hard-ass image. I'd sleep better at night."

Again, her eyes moistened. She rubbed her cheeks, wiped away tears. "I'm real attracted to you. Sure you don't want to fuck? Might put me in a gabby mood."

"I'm going to have to pass."

"You're married?"

"Yes."

"I don't care."

"But I do. Can we get started?"

"Why do you need to ask any questions if the case is solved?"

"Because there are still lots of unanswered questions—"

"Like *why* he did it?" She gulped her juice. "Hell if I know." She cocked her hip. "I knew I had bad taste in men. But this . . ."

"You called yourself an ex-girlfriend."

"This is true."

"When did you two break up?"

"You mean, when did I kick him out? 'Bout four months ago."

"Why?"

"*Why?*" Rhonda let out a bitter laugh. " 'Cause I got sick of his running around. More than that, I just got sick of Harlan Manz. The man with the plans that never panned out."

"He was an actor?"

"He was a jerk."

Decker waited.

Rhonda sighed. "Harlan was a professional *wannabe*. Wannabe actor, wannabe model, wannabe tennis pro, wannabe stud, wannabe this, wannabe that. What he was . . . was a nothing."

Decker said, "In his apartment, I saw film posters with his name on them."

"Yeah, he was a card-carrying member of SAG. Showed it to you at every opportunity. Those films were shelved, never even made it to *video* . . . what is your rank again?"

"Lieutenant."

"A big shot."

"A legend in my own mind."

Rhonda smiled briefly. "Harlan was . . ." She sighed. "He was a slacker . . . a loser with a good backhand. And that's about it, bub."

"A wannabe tennis pro." Decker waited a beat. "So he had tennis ambitions?"

"Maybe. Guy had some talent but not good enough to be pro. He used to teach tennis at a country club—"

"What?"

"No joke. The big one about two miles up the road."

"Greenvale?"

"That's the one. Greenvale Country Club."

"This wasn't one of Harlan's delusions? You know this for a *fact*?"

"Check it out yourself." She grinned. "Bet they'll welcome your inquiries with open arms."

Decker wrote furiously. "How long did he teach at Greenvale?"

"Off and on for about three years."

"Off and on?"

"Yeah, Harlan couldn't hold anything steady. Greenvale took him in for summer work. He taught tennis in the day, tended bar at night. Harlan could maintain in short spurts. I mean the guy was good-looking, had a certain amount of charm. And he was well endowed. Used it, too. He made more than a few lonely women very happy."

"Married women?"

"I said *lonely* women. 'Course they were married."

"Lucky he didn't wind up with a gun to his head."

"Nah, he wouldn't do anything dangerous. Greenvale has lots of married women whose husbands are fuckin' sweet young things. I know because I've *been* there. Not the old, lonely, married woman, but the sweet young thing. Lots of rich geezers in this city. Am I shocking you?"

"Not at all."

"Yeah, you look pretty worldly. You mess around on your wife?"

"No. So Harlan taught tennis to lonely women?"

"No, he taught tennis to anyone who was assigned to him. Women, girls, men, boys." Rhonda paused. "Occasionally, he'd give a lesson to some hot shit producer or director. Harlan was big on name-dropping. He'd brag to me that *this time,* he really made an impression. Jerk . . . he just didn't *get* it. What that poor schmuck wouldn't have given for the life of a big shot . . . partying . . . tennis . . . doing beautiful, rich women . . ."

She stared at her empty glass.

"Will you excuse me?"

She left, then came back with a fresh glass. The liquid looked pale, lots of vodka, not too much juice. This time, she nursed her drink.

"I tried to tell him that just because you teach some jack how to ace a serve doesn't mean he's going to star you in his next movie. But Harlan . . ."

"But he must have been a good tennis player to teach."

"Good enough to teach those yahoos."

"Good enough to make the circuit?"

"He told me he was actually seeded in the top two hundred or something like that. Maybe it was true. But probably not. Harlan lived in fantasies."

"But he was a member of SAG."

"Sure, he got a few parts . . . just enough to feed his delusional brain. Lieutenant, Harlan was a hanger-on. A walking-around guy."

"Pardon?"

"A walking-around guy. There's lots of egomaniacal people out there. No offense to Barbra, but people who need people are *not* the luckiest people. In fact, they're cursed. They need people to create their identity, to feel important, to look busy, and to be wanted. And they're rich enough to buy these little trained spider monkeys like Kato and his ilk to walk around with. So the hot dogs never look unattended. *That's* what Harlan was. He was a walking-around guy.''

Tears ran down her cheek. She turned her head, fiercely swiped her eyes.

''I still have feelings for him. That shock you?''

''Not at all.'' Decker waited a beat. ''Can we talk a minute about Harlan's termination at Estelle's?''

''Nothing to say. He broke their cardinal rule. Customer is always right.''

''But he was upset—''

''Of course he was upset. He was furious. Some drunken A-hole gets abusive and Harlan's canned. I was so angry, I almost came down and made a scene.''

She seemed to wilt.

''Then . . . I don't know. I guess I thought it was par for the course. Harlan getting axed.''

''Did Harlan continue to talk about it?''

''At first, he talked about getting even. I thought it was just talk . . . venting.'' With watery eyes, she looked at Decker, pointedly. ''God, I need to fuck.''

''Why'd you kick him out of your life, Rhonda?''

She sighed. ''I found someone else. Also a loser, but at least he's *gainfully* employed. A porno actor. Ernie Beldheim aka King Whopper. Can you believe that name?''

''It shows a certain amount of creativity. How did Harlan take the breakup?''

Rhonda sat on a bentwood rocker, legs pushing against the floor, her body moving back and forth. She gazed upward, eyes on her sky ceiling. ''I wasn't real tactful. I told him I was dumping him because he wasn't big enough.''

Tears streamed down her face.

''I wanted to *hurt* him. Because he'd been messing around on me for so damn long. If I had known he was so unstable, I wouldn't have . . .''

''You couldn't have known, Rhonda.''

She looked down into her orange juice glass as if reading tea leaves. ''After we broke up, he did things. Weird things. I guess I knew he was flipping out. But I didn't know it would lead to this.''

"Of course not. What did he do?"

Rhonda returned her eyes to Decker. "Tried to scare me. Made calls in the middle of the night, ranted on about how he was going to get me. But I never took him seriously." She looked up. "Thinking it over, I have a feeling I was one of the lucky ones."

True enough. Decker pointed to her duffel bag. "Where are you planning to go?"

Rhonda stopped rocking, blew out air. "I got an offer to do a gig in Hawaii. Some honcho wants me to paint *Playboy* playmates on his walls. No accounting for tastes."

"Vacation might do you good."

"Hope so."

Decker said, "Do you have some old pictures of him?"

"Maybe one or two. Why?"

"I didn't find any recent pictures of Harlan in his apartment."

Rhonda was taken aback. "That's odd. I know he has a portfolio—"

"No, I found that. I'm talking about things like photo albums."

She shrugged. "Weird. Because we took quite a few . . ." She smiled. "Quite a few *compromising* ones. After we broke up, he told me he was going to send them to my mother. I told him to go ahead . . . ain't nothing she's never seen before."

"Did he?"

"If he did, Mom never said a word."

Decker said, "Rhonda, if Harlan was a member of SAG, he must have had an agent."

"He had a couple light-years ago. Fired them all."

Decker's beeper went off. Rhonda stood up from the rocker. "Phone's on the wall."

Decker's eyes scanned the mural, rested on a painted phone kiosk. Mounted on the wall, inside the painted booth, was a real, three-dimensional pay phone. "Do I need money to make the call?"

"Credit card's fine."

Decker said, "I'm slow on the uptake, didn't get much sleep. I can't tell if you're putting me on."

Rhonda smiled tightly. "It was a joke."

"Sorry to be so dense."

"Mr. Dumb Lug." Rhonda rolled her eyes. "About as slow as a roadrunner. Sly, too. So why do I find myself trusting you? Is that how you extract confessions? You get people to trust you, then you slam them?"

"I don't slam anyone, least of all someone like you." Decker looked at the pager's number. Strapp's office.

Rhonda said, "I'll be back in a minute. Help yourself to the phone."

"Thanks." Decker punched in numbers; the captain picked up on the fifth ring.

"Get over to the station house. Community is planning a major memorial for Estelle's victims this afternoon. You're expected to be there. Show some community support and help me field the press."

"I'll be at my office in ten minutes."

Strapp said, "Good quote yesterday, Decker. About the scene being your worst nightmare. If you can think up a few more like that . . . something that shows compassion . . . that would be good for us . . . for LAPD."

Decker was silent.

Strapp said, "Look, I know it sounds politico, but tough. This is our chance to make a *good* impression. Our asses have been fried in print for so long, it would be real nice if we could be represented as the public servants we really are."

"I understand, sir."

"Good, then. Get down here. We'll strategize together."

❧7

After a full day of hospital visits, bereavement calls, and heart-wrenching services for the dead, Decker made it back to the station house, his energy depleted, his brain crashing against his skull like a tidal wave. Advil wouldn't cut it. Dry-mouthed, he swallowed a couple of Darvocets, but knew even that wouldn't be enough. Rooting in his shirt pocket, he pulled out a pack of cigarettes. Lit up a smoke and rubbed his aching temples. Marge came in a few moments later, holding a half-dozen manila envelopes which she used to fan away smoke.

"You must feel like shit warmed over."

Decker stubbed out the cigarette. "Trying to compose myself before I go home. I don't want Rina to see me like this. How'd the interviews go? Learn anything?"

"Depressingly unremarkable. Can I sit?"

"Of course." Decker pointed to a chair, eyed his smoke.

"Go ahead, Pete. I remember well your smoking days."

"Just a temporary lapse." Again, Decker lit up. "Tell me about the interviews."

"Nothing to tell. Bullets started flying, people started screaming, running for cover. Truly terrifying." Marge paused, collected her thoughts. "From what I could gather, it seems that Harlan wasn't deliberate in his shooting. Didn't shoot at any one person specifically, or even aim at people for that matter. He just opened fire. A lot of it. The

44

boys and I have been comparing notes. They agree with that assessment.''

Marge paused.

"Since this kind of thing is rare, I don't really know what's considered the typical behavior for mass murderers.''

"Off the top of my head, the compatibles that come to mind are Tasmania, the Long Island Railroad, the San Ysidro McDonald's, and Dunblane—''

"The elementary school in Scotland.'' Marge paled. "God, what a world!''

Decker inhaled his smoke, tried to keep his mind focused. "I remember that in Tasmania and in San Ysidro, the murderer aimed at people. Picked them off like prey. But you're saying that *wasn't* what happened. Harlan just sprayed the place.''

"Appears that way. We've been working a time frame . . . how many minutes did the actual shooting last? Time elongates during these catastrophic events. What seems like hours could have been minutes. At the moment, we're guesstimating.''

She held up the manila envelopes.

"I picked these up for you. Just came in from the Coroner's Office. Probably some prelim autopsy reports. Want me to go over them? You look tired.''

Decker sat back in his chair, closed his eyes, breathed in wisps of nicotined air. "Who's still out there?''

"All of us—Scott, Tom, Bert. We're still writing up reports. Oh, Gaynor left about an hour ago. He said you told him to work on the case at home.''

"I've got him doing some computer work. His home equipment is better technologically than what we've got here.'' Decker stubbed it out. "Give me the reports. Call the others in.''

"Right away.'' Marge handed him the envelopes and left.

Decker broke open a seal, pulled out some slice-and-dice autopsy photos. Hitting him like a mace in the gut. He sifted through them with deliberation . . . concentration.

Marge soon returned with the others. They pulled up chairs, sat in front of Decker's desk, all of them uncharacteristically quiet.

Decker said, "I've got some prelim autopsy reports. Finals won't be ready for days, so we'll go over these—"

Oliver interrupted, "Like they're going to tell us something we don't know?"

"Never know." Decker placed the photos back in the envelope. "We've got to re-create the shooting. Where Harlan first stood when he opened fire, who appeared to be his first victim, who was his next, and so on and so forth."

"How do we do that?" Martinez asked.

"We'll start with the floor plan. Draw each table and who sat where, using the reservations book. Who checked the book into evidence?"

"Yo." Marge held up her hand.

Decker said, "Okay. We draw each table and label them. Next comes the brain work and the tedium. For this part, we'll need basic geometry and gunshot angles. Since we couldn't rod the victims, we'll have to rely on Forensics."

Decker leaned forward.

"Harlan was found dead at the bar. Don't know if he started his shooting at the bar, but assume that he did. The bar area is off the entrance, correct?"

Nods all around.

"So assume he entered there and just started shooting. Here's what we're going to do. We ask ourselves . . . *if* Harlan started shooting from the bar area and was facing left, where would the first bullets have landed? Say they would have landed on table three. We look in the reservations book, find out who was at table three, and determine the nature of their wounds, if any. If it seems consistent with Harlan's position, we go on to our next assumption. If it's not consistent, we change our first assumption—"

"I'm lost," Martinez said.

Decker said, "We're trying to trace bullet paths using geometry. Go down the friggin' list. If Harlan shot from the bar, where would his first bullets have landed? If that matches, we move on.

"If Harlan had turned to the left and shot, who would have been his next hit?

"If Harlan had turned to the right and shot, who would have been his next hit?

"If Harlan had taken a couple of steps forward, who would have been his next hit?

"If Harlan had taken a couple of steps forward and *then* turned to the right, who would have been his next hit?

"If Harlan had taken a couple of steps forward and then turned to the *left,* who would have been his next—"

"This could take months!" Oliver blurted out.

"Yes, it probably will take months," Decker said.

"Loo, pardon mah ignorance," Webster drawled, "but just what do you reckon to accomplish?"

"Let's talk politics for a moment. There are bound to be lawsuits—against Estelle's, maybe even against the city. Our police reports are going to be scrutinized with a microscope. And we're going to be judged, folks. Every single one of us. You, me, and this entire beleaguered department."

Decker rubbed his temples.

"I want every single bullet accounted for. Make sure that all the slugs came from Harlan's gun and not some other outside source that we overlooked because we were too lazy—"

"Outside source?" Marge grimaced. "You think there was more than one shooter?"

"Who knows? Last count we've got thirteen dead, thirty-two wounded. Lots of damage for one guy, Margie."

Martinez said, "Harlan was packing a nine-millimeter automatic double action, Loo. Fourteen rounds per magazine—"

"How many rounds did he fire, Bert?"

Martinez was quiet. "Don't know."

"Anyone?"

No one spoke.

Decker said, "Thirteen dead people, thirty-two wounded, and we can't answer a simple question like how many rounds the fucker fired."

Oliver said, "So we'll do a bullet count."

"We'll do a lot more than a bullet count. I want this crime scene *nailed*. Every step and every shot that Harlan took must be checkbook-balanced."

Decker leaned back in his chair.

"We'll start tomorrow with the bullet count. Dunn and Oliver, you two take the corpses in the morgue as well as the shells and bullets left behind at Estelle's. Check the walls, check the furniture, check the potted plants, turn the place upside down if you have to. I want every bullet, every shell, every empty magazine cited and bagged."

"Talk about tedium," Oliver muttered.

Decker looked at his detective—worn, disheveled, spent. "I don't envy your assignment, Scott. The place gives me the creeps. But someone has to do it."

Oliver ran his hands through his oily black hair. "I'm not complaining, Loo. I'm just tired."

"I know." Decker looked at Webster and Martinez. "You two go over to the hospitals, talk to the victims' doctors. Have them help you get a bullet count from their patients' medical charts or surgery dictation or even from the X rays. And if any of the victims feels like talking, you can start conducting interviews. Once we get the bullets accounted for, we'll start analyzing the angles—"

"Y'ever think of using a computer, Loo?" Webster asked.

"Forensic reenactment." Decker said. "Farrell's working on a program for this as we speak. It's a very useful tool, but first we've got to have data to plug into the computer. Then it'll probably take months before he comes up with something. But that's all right. We have time. If we're meticulous in our calculations, maybe the computer will spit us back a step-by-step simulation of Harlan's movements at Estelle's."

Webster said, "Welcome to Cybermurder."

"Except the victims were flesh and blood." Decker stood. "We start tomorrow. For now, *all* of you. Go home."

*   *   *

As Decker pulled into the driveway of the ranch, he noticed the living-room light shining through the bay window. Immediately, his heart took off. Not that it was late—quarter after ten. Still, when Rina waited up for him, she always kept vigil in the kitchen or their bedroom.

He shut off the Volare's motor, jogged to the front door, and opened it. His wife was asleep on the living-room couch. On the floor was his dog, Ginger, nestled among piles of loose papers. Next to the sheets were a calculator, pens, pencils, and a couple of ledgers.

Instant relief. Everything was all right.

Then came the curiosity. What was Rina working on? He considered rifling through the pages, but discarded the thought. All in due time. For now, let her sleep.

He regarded the room. In dim light, it seemed worn, his furniture over a decade old, purchased during his divorced days. The buckskin couch had been rubbed shiny in spots, the coffee table was scratched, the two wing chairs had faded. Keeping guard at the bay window was Rina's pine rocker purchased after Hannah was born—the only new thing standing.

Yet Rina never said a word about replacing his shopworn pieces. Guess she was waiting for him to relinquish the last vestiges of his bachelor years. Not that his wife hadn't added her own feminine touches. The silk-screened floral couch pillows, two hand-crocheted throw blankets, fresh flowers, and lots of framed family photos. Observing her sleeping form . . . he really needed to do better for her.

She stirred. Even without makeup, her face was striking, though her creamy skin was a shade paler than usual. Her lips—lush and red and always alluring. Eyes moving behind translucent lids. She was dressed in a black angora sweater and black knit skirt. Her outfit matched her raven hair, which fell over her shoulders like a sable shawl.

He shut off the light, put Ginger outside, debated checking the horses' stables but nixed the idea. Too damn tired.

He headed into the bedroom, stripped in seconds, then beelined into the shower. Turning the water up to full pressure, he stood under the faucet, allowing the blast to run over his stubbled face while razor-hot needles rained down on his aching back, cooking his freckled skin bright red. He continued his baptism by fire until the water grew cold. By the time he was done, Rina had tucked herself into bed. She was half awake, her lids still hooded. But she spoke. "S'right?"

"I'm just fine." Decker toweled himself off as he spoke. "Go back to sleep."

"Boys send their regards."

"Regards back." He ran his hands several times through red shocks of wet hair, then went over and kissed his wife. A short one, then a long one. She purred. "That was wonderful."

He slipped under the sheets. "That's because you're half asleep."

She opened her eyes fully. "How are you holding up?"

"Been better, but I'll survive." Immediately, he switched the topic. "What were you doing out there in the living room with all those loose papers? Building a nest?"

Rina thought a moment. "Oh. That. Rav Schulman called—"

"Why? What's wrong?"

"Nothing. He had some bookkeeping questions. They turned out to be a bit complicated, so I stopped by the yeshiva and picked up some of the ledgers."

"The yeshiva doesn't have a bookkeeper?"

"Peter, I didn't question him. He asked me to do him a favor, I said yes."

"You have that much spare time, go ahead."

Rina was quiet. Decker forced himself not to push it. But he knew there was more. Lately Rina had been using the learned Rabbi for therapy . . . just as Decker had done many times in the past. His wife had been very depressed since an old friend of hers—and her late husband's—had died. Abram Sparks had also been a friend of Rabbi Schulman. Decker was sure that Bram's name had come up in the course of their conversations. Holding that thought, Decker rolled over, buried his head in the pillow.

Rina turned off the light. "Your father called today."

Decker pivoted to face her. "And?"

"The shooting must have made the news over there. He was concerned about you."

"What'd you tell him?"

"I lied. I said you were fine."

"That's not lying, I am fine."

Rina didn't answer.

Decker hesitated. "Did he mention my mother at all?"

"No . . . why?"

"No particular reason. Let's go to sleep."

Rina knew he was fibbing, that tight catch in his throat. He was worried about his mother, leaving Rina to wonder if her mother-in-law was ill. Eyes closed, Rina waited and waited, then gave up. She was just about asleep when he finally decided to talk.

"She called me about two weeks ago. She'd been clean-ing out the garage . . . had some of my childhood junk and wanted to know what to do with it. I told her to send it here . . . or throw it away . . . whichever was easier. Then . . ."

He paused.

"Then I asked her why . . . at this moment in time . . . was she cleaning out the garage . . . which has been a stor-age house of our family junk for God only knows how many years. She just said, 'If not now, when?' "

Rina touched his arm. "Did you ask her if something was wrong?"

"Yes, of course. As I expected, she denied any prob-lems."

"Did you press her?"

"I can't press my mother, Rina. This is as big a hint as I'm going to get."

He waited a beat.

"I can't approach my father. Because she could be keep-ing something from him, too. I did call Randy. He doesn't seem to know anything, so I guess they've kept him in the dark."

"Or maybe nothing's wrong."

"Maybe. Either that or my brother hasn't picked up on

Mom's nuances. He's not a font of sensitivity.''

"Peter, why didn't you tell me this earlier?''

"I don't know. You have your own parents to deal with . . . your own problems as well.''

Rina was silent, guilt coursing through her body. "I know I've been very upset since—''

"It's not important.''

Again neither spoke.

"Do you want to go out for a visit, Peter?''

"She wouldn't like that . . . me, just popping in. She needs her privacy, I've got to respect it.''

"Darling, can you try talking to her? Hiding behind a wall of stoicism isn't good for either of you.''

"Rina, I respect your culture. You respect mine.''

She counted to ten, told herself to breathe calmly. "How about if I called her up—''

"No—''

"Can you let me finish?''

Decker waited a moment. "Sorry. Go on.''

"I'd like to invite them out here for Thanksgiving.''

"A nice thought, honey, but I'm afraid it would rob her of her dignity. You *know* what Thanksgiving means to her.''

"Yes, I do. But hear me out, okay?''

"Sure.''

"Peter, *I* don't like making Thanksgiving. It's no charge for me to make yet another big feast a month after our major holidays are over. And yes, I *do* know what that holiday means to her. Peter, we've gone down to Gainesville twice for Thanksgiving. It's lovely, but it isn't the kind of holiday she wants. It hurts her tremendously that we can't eat her beautifully cooked food in *her* house on her *special* china.''

"Why? She says things to you?''

"No, of course not. But that doesn't mean I don't notice her wincing when we sit there at her table with fruit and raw vegetables on our paper plates.''

Decker was quiet.

Rina said, "I can't change the fact that we're observant,

kosher Jews and they're Baptist. That's just life. I can't take over her kitchen. But she can take over mine. Let me invite her out here to make *her* Thanksgiving with my pots and pans. Cook everything in *my* house in *my* kosher kitchen—''

"Rina—''

"I'll buy the meat and all the trimmings, but she can have free rein. I'll even go shopping with her to pick out a set of china of her choice. I have so many sets of dishes, one more won't hurt. She can cook to her heart's content. Do all her favorite recipes including her pumpkin pie. Only accommodations she'll have to *kashrut* is using nondairy margarine and Mocha Mix instead of butter and milk. And, of course, no honey-glazed ham.''

"She won't do it.''

"She doesn't even like ham—''

"It's not the *ham*, Rina, it's the whole thing. She'll feel displaced.''

"At least let me try. I think she'll come out. I think she'd love to cook up a storm, actually have us *eat* her meals. And then there're the grandchildren—Cindy as well as our Hannalah—''

"That means Randy's left alone.''

"So I'll invite Randy and the kids and wife number . . .''

"It's still three.''

"Your nieces and nephews will love it here. Disneyland—''

"They've got Disney World, Epcot Center, and Universal Studios. Theme parks are no big deal to them.''

"Yes, but we've got Las Vegas—''

"Oh, my sister-in-law will love that.''

Rina sighed. "Just *think* about it, okay?''

Decker was quiet. "You'd put up my brother's family?''

"Absolutely. I find Randy . . . interesting—''

"I love my brother.''

"I know that.'' Rina smiled. Even though Randy worked two jobs—he was a vice cop and moonlighted as a security guard—he was always flat broke. Peter had been sending him cash for years.

Silence. Then Decker said, "I'll call Mom tomorrow."

Rina said, "*I'll* call her tomorrow. She'll say no to you, but yes to me."

Decker knew that was all too true. He turned toward his wife, draped an arm around her shoulders, and drew her to his chest. He kissed her mouth, licked her lips. "I love you."

"I love you, too." She kissed him again. "Want to make more out of this?"

"Wish I could." He laughed. "I'm afraid I'd be arrested on charges of Assault with a Dead Weapon—"

Rina laughed, slapped his shoulder. She kissed him gently, licked his mustache. Her hands snaked around his body, stroked his long muscular back with tender fingertips.

He let out a soft rumble. "Feels good."

"I think I detect signs of life—"

"That's not life, that's just a reflex."

"Whatever it is, it's good enough for me."

8

Waking up before the sun, Decker showered, shaved, and said his morning prayers alfresco, bathed in the golden light of dawn. Afterward, he let the dog out, pitched fresh hay to his stable of four horses, changed the animals' water, went through yesterday's mail, and had coffee brewing by the time Rina roused the crew for school.

Although anxious to get his professional life going, Decker forced himself to make a little time for breakfast and family affairs. The day's topics included his stepson's driver's license, buying a newer car for Rina, and giving Sam his own set of wheels in the form of Rina's old Volvo. Decker promised they'd hit the car lots on Sunday. And if Rina had the inclination, maybe they'd look at new living-room furniture as well. His wife was surprised, delighted. Immediately bright with ideas. Decker felt good. It had been a long time since he'd seen Rina's smile.

After the boys left for school on the bus, Decker played zoo with Hannah, her stuffed animals being nefarious creatures of prey, and Ginger, the Irish setter, doubling as Simba the Lion. Then Decker carted his daughter off to school. Hannah threw her pipe stem arms around his neck, kissed him on the cheek with soft little lips. Decker felt an overwhelming desire to cling to her, to lug her into work in a papoose. Instead, he lowered her to the ground and watched her scamper off. The experts talk about separation anxiety. Were they referring to the child or the parent?

Cloaked in wistfulness, Decker left the neon-painted schoolhouse, arriving at the station by half past eight.

All business, he made phone calls, signed papers, went over reports, checked in with his detectives, then buried himself in pathology reports and bullet trajectories for the next four hours. Head buzzing, he finally broke for lunch at one-thirty. At his desk, he opened his brown bag—two chicken sandwiches, two pieces of fruit, two bottles of Martinelli's sparkling apple juice, and a half dozen cookies. Food that could be easily eaten in a car.

He took his lunch and his briefcase and headed for the Volare. Within minutes, he was on the road, felt his shoulders relax, his face go slack with freedom.

Devonshire division patrolled a varied geographical area—some residential, some small business, some factories, and lots of rolling foothills and fallow acreage waiting for a land boom that was always "just around the corner." Developers ran scared out here and not without reason. The district had been the center of two major earthquakes, was Saharan hot in the summer, and was situated far from city action. Still, it was God's green acres in the late autumn— glorious blue skies with long stretches of wildflower fields and oak-dotted hills ribboned with miles of hiking and horse trails. Giant sycamores and menthol-laden eucalyptus swayed in the winds.

The division also contained several million-dollar housing developments—big mama, multiroomed mansions floating in seas of green lawn. The gated communities ran complete with pools, spas, tennis courts, recreation rooms, and banquet facilities. When Greenvale Country Club opened its doors fifteen years ago, Decker wondered why the rich would join a club, paying hefty premiums for amenities available on their own premises.

Yet Greenvale had made itself a known quantity. Though it wasn't as prestigious as some of the older, established L.A. clubs, it had its own cachet, boasting an elitist membership and hosting its fair share of society weddings and black-tie-only charity events. It seemed that human beings had an infinite capacity to rate—to separate and segregate into in-or-out crowds.

The club sat on twenty-five acres, the buildings obscured by umbrellas of specimen trees. As the Volare chugged up the long, shaded drive, Decker noticed several gardeners tending the lawns and numerous flower beds. Going into the fall, they were planting jewel-colored pansies. Within moments, the buildings came into view, Tudor in style, but with L.A. modifications: thin brick facing over stucco because solid brick crumbled in earthquakes. There were several structures loosely connected to one another, probably built at different times. Lots of stained glass, lots of crossbeams and peaked roofs. A theme park re-creation of the Tower of London.

By the time Decker reached the gatehouse, he had finished his lunch. Displaying his badge, he told uniformed guards that he was there to speak to the manager. And no, he did not have an appointment. His sudden appearance was disruptive to their sleepy flow. The guards conferred, scratched their heads, made phone calls, until one of them decided to lift the booth's restraining arm, told Decker to handle it at the front desk.

Instead of parking in the ample lot, Decker used the circular entrance driveway and instructed the valets to keep the car in front. With reticence, a red-coated attendant settled the ten-year-old algae-green Volare between a sleek black Jag and a dowager brown Mercedes.

Through the double doors and into a two-story white-marble-floor rotunda. The walls were wainscoted—walnut panels on the bottom, cream-colored paint on top. A circular band of white rococo molding marked the division between the walls and the ceiling. A giant canopy of crystal lights dangled from an ornate plaster medallion. The rest of the dome was painted with angels and cherubs floating on cotton clouds in a turquoise sky. A winding staircase carpeted with plush peach pile led to a second-floor landing. In front was a short hallway that bled into a paneled library/reading room. Decker strolled to the front desk which was tucked away on the right-hand side. A bespectacled thirtysomething blonde sat behind a glass window; she slid it open and smiled.

"Can I help you?"

"Probably." Decker held up his badge. "Lieutenant Peter Decker, LAPD. Who's in charge at the moment?"

The blonde's smile faded, wary brown eyes looking him over. "Let me make a phone call, sir."

With that, the woman shut the glass window and dialed. Her face was expressive—the wrinkled brow, the downturned lips. It was clear she was getting bawled out by the person on the other end of the line. She hung up, reopened the window.

"Can I take your name and number and have someone call you back this afternoon?"

Decker smiled. "Why don't you get back on the phone and tell your boss that I'm getting pushy."

She closed the window a second time. Reopened it, told him that someone would be coming and he should take a seat. Decker glanced at the satin-covered French-style benches. Looked way too small and very uncomfortable. He elected to stand.

Within minutes, a man jogged through the hallway. Short, stocky, a head of curls and a shadowed face even though he'd recently shaved. He was built like a tank— barrel chest, thick legs creasing his gray slacks, muscle-packed forearms. The sleeves of his white shirt were rolled to his elbows. He stuck out a meaty hand but kept walking.

"Barry Fine. Follow me."

Fine never broke step. Decker kept pace with him through the hallway, into the club's library/reading room— as big as an arena. More leather here than at a rodeo. Hard to notice any people in the soft lighting. Perhaps it was because they were hidden in the corners or behind the backs of wing chairs. But Decker could ascertain signs of life— the clearing of a throat, the rustle of a newspaper, a hushed conversation between a man and his cellular phone. A uniformed waiter traversed the furniture maze, a tray of drinks balanced on the palm of his hand.

"This way," Fine said.

Steering him away from the room. The message being: no fraternizing with the elite.

Fine unlocked a piece of paneling which turned out to be a door. He held it open for Decker, who crossed the threshold.

The business offices. No luxury here. Just working space and cramped at that. As Decker's eyes adjusted to the glare of bright, fluorescent lighting, he noticed stark-white walls, linoleum flooring. A phone was ringing, lots of clicking computer keys. Fine led Decker into his cubicle, shut the glass door. He sat back in his desk chair, thick sausage fingers folded together, resting in his lap.

"Mind if I have a look at your identification?"

Decker showed him his badge, flipped the cover back, and pocketed the billfold after Fine had nodded.

"Please." Fine pointed to a folding chair and Decker sat. "Must be important to send out a lieutenant."

"Thanks for seeing me. I have a few questions. Thought that you might be able to help me."

"Questions about . . ."

"Harlan Manz."

Fine's face remained stoic. "The monster who shot up Estelle's."

Decker said, "I understand he worked here for a while."

Fine said, "You've been misinformed."

Decker rolled his tongue in his mouth. "How long have you worked here, Mr. Fine?"

"Seven years."

"And you're saying that Harlan Manz never worked here?"

"To the best of my recollection, that is correct."

"To the best of your recollection?" Decker waited a beat. "Sir, this isn't a grand jury."

Fine didn't flinch. "I always try to be as specific as possible."

"Perhaps you knew him under a different name—"

"Don't think so." Fine stood. "I'll walk you out."

Decker remained seated. "Mr. Fine, are you honestly

telling me that Harlan Manz never worked in this country club?''

''Never heard of the man until he hit the news,'' Fine said. ''Not that I'm about to do it, but if push came to shove, I'd open my books and show you. Never had a Harlan Manz on the payroll.''

''Ah . . .'' Decker licked his lips. ''You paid him in cash.''

Fine's smile turned hard. ''Lieutenant, I don't have to talk to you. You get pushy, I call the owners. The owners get upset and they call their lawyers. The lawyers get upset, they call your captain. Gets you a black mark on your record.''

Decker stared him down. ''Are you threatening me, sir?''

The tip of Fine's nose turned red. He stammered, ''No, I'm just pointing out a logical chain of events.''

Decker lied straight-faced. ''Harlan Manz had listed income from Greenvale Country Club on his 1040 federal tax forms—''

''You're bluffing,'' Fine busted in.

''As well as state—''

''What is this? A shakedown?''

''No, Mr. Fine, this is a simple fact-finding mission. Quiet, discreet, friendly. Be a shame if damaging information was leaked to the press, that an insane mass murderer once worked here as staff.''

Fine raised his voice. ''He was never on staff!''

''You explain that distinction to the press.''

''Now who's threatening whom?''

''I'm not threatening you, I'm *telling* you. Press wants information about Harlan, I'm more than happy to oblige. You want to sue me for false allegations, go right ahead. Only in court, you can't bluff. Because if you do, that's perjury.''

Fine started to protest, but turned quiet. He buried his head in his hands. ''The stupid *idiot*! I told him it was strictly off the record. He promised me . . .'' He looked up at Decker. ''I can't read your face. Ever play poker?''

Decker took out a notebook and pen. "Tell me about Harlan."

Fine let out a gush of air. "Worked here about two years ago. Used the name Hart Mansfield . . . supposedly his *stage* name, though I've never seen him on any sort of a screen. A summer fill-in. All cash. Nothing on the books. That's it."

"What were his assignments?"

"Not much. Which was why he wasn't on staff. He taught tennis when we were short-staffed. In the summertime, our regular instructors go on vacation."

"I was told he tended bar as well."

"He was an extra pair of hands when we had a big event."

"And you paid him in cash for bartending as well?"

"Yep." Fine bit his lip, ran a hand through his curly hair. "Not that I was doing funny business with the books. The cash-out was listed under miscellaneous expenses. I just never bothered to put him on the payroll."

"Owners know he worked here?"

Fine rubbed his face. "Hasn't come up . . . yet."

"You haven't received phone calls from some of the membership?"

"Sure I got a few phone calls. People asking 'Was that asshole at Estelle's the guy who used to work here?' kind of thing. Names were different. I told them no."

"You lied?"

"If it should come back to haunt me, I simply made a mistake because the names were different."

Fine grimaced.

"You want to know something, Lieutenant? The people who called me . . . far from being squeamish . . . they hung up from the conversation *disappointed*. It was an exciting notion to them . . . a safe brush with the dark side. Personally, I think it's sick. But then again, I just cater to the rich. I don't really understand them."

"They accepted your denials?"

"I tell them it's not the same guy, they don't have the conviction of character to debate me."

"And the owners don't know about Harlan working here?"

"No. Owners know a great deal about the membership, but not too much about staff. They don't want to be bothered with business details. That's what they pay me for. And like I said before, I've accounted for Harlan's expenses. Just not on the payroll—"

"Avoiding taxes and Social Security—"

"Hired him as freelance. Club's only responsible for the taxes and Social Security of its full-time employees. And Harlan never worked enough hours to warrant putting him on the payroll. Our books are clean. You find cause to subpoena our books, you won't find a hint of an irregularity."

"Owners won't be happy if Harlan's alias is publicized."

"No, they won't be. I'll probably be blamed. And I'll probably lose my job."

"That's not my goal, sir."

"But it still may be an end result." Fine blew out air. "Hell with it. What else do you want to know, Lieutenant?"

"Harlan taught tennis?"

"Yes."

"Groups? Individuals?"

"Mostly private lessons."

"How was Harlan with his tennis students?"

"Never had a complaint. If I had, Harlan would have been out on his ass." Fine smiled, but it lacked warmth. "I wish someone had complained. It would play a lot better with the bosses if I had *fired* the guy."

"Why didn't you hire him on as a regular?"

" 'Cause he was a jerk. Sure, he was okay for an occasional lesson, but that's about all. All these wannabes." He shook his head. "If I hired tennis instructors and bartenders on the basis of stability, I wouldn't have much of a roster. Harlan was also chronically late and drank a lot. *But . . .*"

The manager paused, held a finger in the air.

"He usually showed up when called. And that's about

as much as you can hope for in a temp. You have no idea how flaky a summer staff can be.''

"I've heard that Harlan had some potential as a tennis player.''

"Actually, he wasn't bad. Wasn't pro quality, of course, but he had some power serves. Good speed. A natural athlete. But that isn't enough. You want to make it big, you've got to work . . . train. We've got a couple of members on the circuits. They train here every single day, usually start at something like six in the morning. They're talented, but even more, they're dedicated. Harlan? Sure, he had *some* talent, but he lacked drive. Takes a heap of both to make it in the pros.''

"Did Harlan have any regular students when he worked here?''

"Strictly fill-in. His schedule changed daily depending on who was on vacation or who called in sick.''

"Did he ever get chummy with any of his students?''

"If he did, I never heard about it.''

But Decker wasn't so sure that Fine was being up front. "If you didn't get complaints about him, did you ever get *compliments* about him?''

A fire lit in Fine's eye, smoldered quickly. "No.''

"None of your ladies ever say to you what a fine teacher he was?''

"Are you implying something?''

"Asking a question, sir.''

Fine said, "It was a long time ago, Lieutenant. I don't remember so well.''

"I don't suppose you'd be willing to give me names?''

"You're right about that. Anything else?''

"Just one more question. Were any of the people tragically murdered at Estelle's also members of the club?''

Fine turned red. "You know I'm not going to answer that. I think I've been very patient.''

Decker smiled. "You've been helpful. Thank you.''

Fine said, "Explain something to me, Lieutenant.''

"If I can, sure.''

"What do you possibly . . . *hope* to accomplish by digging up Harlan aka Hart's past? He's dead. I thought analyzing nutcases was the bailiwick of shrinks, not cops.''

Man had a point. Decker's job was cleaning up the crime scene, not doing psychiatric Monday morning quarterbacking. Truth be told, he wasn't sure why he was there . . . trying to make sense out of the incomprehensible.

Decker said, ''This was a horrible event. A very big case with lots of publicity, lots of questions and finger-pointing. LAPD has a vested interest in tying up loose ends.''

Fine was incredulous. ''That's it? You take time away from my business to grill me . . . just to tie up loose ends?''

''Yes, sir, that's exactly right. I'm tying up loose ends. You know *why,* Mr. Fine? Because you leave a loose end hanging around, the sucker has an annoying tendency to unravel.''

9

Marge knocked on Decker's doorjamb, walked through the open door to his office. "A one eighty-seven came in while you were gone—a domestic turned nasty. Wife took the bullet between her eyes. I was in court, so Oliver and Martinez caught the call. If you want, I can go join them."

Decker frowned, took off his reading glasses. "Why didn't someone page me?"

"We did," Marge said. "You didn't answer."

"What?" Decker checked his pager. "What the . . ." He stared at the blank window, flicked his middle finger against the instrument. When nothing happened, he tossed it on his desk. "Remind me to pick up a new one from Bessie. Tell me the details."

"Husband and wife were slugging down shooters when the altercation broke out. A neighbor heard them arguing, didn't think too much of it."

"Frequent occurrence."

"Yeah, except *this* time the husband . . . his name is Meryl Tobias . . . went psycho. Showed up at the neighbor's door—gun in his hand—bawling like a baby. He didn't mean it, he didn't mean it. The neighbor called nine one one. The rest is . . ." She threw up her hands. "His blood alcohol was over point-two-o. Hers wasn't much lower. What a waste!"

Decker glanced at the clock. "It's almost four. We've

all been working overtime. Pack it in, Detective.''

Marge sat down, dropped her head in her hands. ''Honestly, Pete, I'm all right. Just give me an assignment that doesn't involve counting bullets.''

Decker smiled. ''How's it coming?''

''I wouldn't have made a good accountant.''

''Why?'' Decker's interest suddenly perked up. ''You've got discrepancies?''

''I don't know yet.'' Marge lifted her head. ''Because we're not through. So far we've recovered an awful lot of shells for one shooter . . . even if the shooter was using a double automatic.''

''Interesting.'' Decker started making notes. ''Tell me.''

Marge was thoughtful. ''We picked up lots of strays, Pete. In the walls, in the floor, in the furniture. Which puzzled Scott. He mentioned the same point that you did yesterday. That mass murderers often hunt their victims. Part of the thrill.''

''But that wasn't what happened,'' Decker said.

''No, not according to witnesses. The killer just sprayed the place.''

No one spoke. Then Marge said, ''You know, it's a miracle that more people didn't die.''

''How many bullets did you recover?''

''So far enough to account for around . . . ten, maybe twelve magazines. We've found eight empty cartridges.''

''About a hundred and fifty rounds upward. And Harlan's shooting time was what . . . three to six minutes?''

''It's possible to peel off twelve rounds in a double automatic in six minutes if you're not aiming at anything. But you'd have to work quickly. Go in and blast the place and hope the sucker doesn't jam.''

Marge studied Decker, reading his face not as her boss but as her ex-partner.

''You've got something on your mind, big guy?''

''Just speculation.'' Decker began to doodle. ''Doesn't amount to much.'' Marge pushed hair out of her eyes, stared at him with purpose. ''Out with it.''

''I've been going over some of the prelim autopsy re-

ports on the victims." Decker paused. "I'm . . . disconcerted by them."

"What in particular?"

"The bullet trajectories. People at the same table being
hit with shots at different angles."

"They were probably facing in different directions."

"I took that into consideration. Still, there are things that
don't make sense." Decker spread out several police photographs. "For instance, look at this couple. Victims numbers nine and ten—Linda and Ray Garrison."

Marge's eyes swept over the snapshots. She winced.

"The couple was seated . . . here." Decker showed
Marge a floor plan of Estelle's. "Right here. At table number fifteen. I figure they must have been among the first to
be hit because they died in their seats. Didn't even have
enough time to duck under the table."

Marge studied the prints. "They weren't really close to
the entrance to the restaurant."

"About a hundred feet away. If the shooting took place
as soon as Harlan entered the place, they should have realized what was going on . . . had enough time to duck or
run for cover."

"Which may mean that the shooting broke out closer to
them."

"Or possibly they both just froze," Decker added.
"Anyway, look at the photograph. They died in their
chairs, sitting opposite each other, slumped over the table.
Both of them . . . riddled with holes. On the surface, no difference. Except Forensics tells us an alternate story. The
bullets entered Linda Garrison's back and exited through
her chest. Mr. Garrison was *also* shot from back to front."

Decker paused.

"Think about it, Margie. If Harlan was shooting from
one position—say he stood in back of Mr. Garrison—the
bullets would have entered Garrison's back and exited Garrison's chest. Agreed?"

"Yes. Go on."

"Those same bullets . . . flying in the *same* direction . . .
should have entered Mrs. Garrison through her chest and

exited her back. Instead, it's just the opposite. What'd Harlan do? Shoot in one position, then move to the opposite side and shoot in the other?"

Marge was silent. "Weird."

"Perhaps a bit suspicious," Decker said.

"Maybe Harlan immediately picked off one of them, walked around and shot a little bit more, then changed his direction and picked the other one off."

"But that contradicts what you just reported . . . that the shooter wasn't picking people off." Decker sat back in his chair. "Taken out of the context of Estelle's . . . even forgetting about all the eyewitness accounts . . . just looking at the forensics . . . it looks deliberate. It warrants further investigation."

"I concur."

"So this is what I want you to do. I want you to go over the list of the victims and find out if any of them belonged to Greenvale Country Club."

Marge stared at him. "Now there's a non sequitur. Why?"

"Because Harlan once worked there."

"So?"

"Well, it's like this. I see lots of stray bullets and unexplained bullet trajectories. Suggestive of maybe more than one shooter—"

"Possibly."

"Possibly. I told you this is speculation."

"Go on," Marge urged.

"I'm just wondering if this isn't a botched hit masked as a mass murder. Looking at the case from that perspective, I'd like to see if maybe we can find a connection between Harlan and a specific victim."

"Harlan Manz committed suicide, Pete. Most hit men don't whack themselves."

"Maybe he didn't whack himself. If it was a botched hit, maybe the second shooter whacked him by accident—"

Marge made a face.

"I know I'm stretching. Ballistics confirms that the bullet in Harlan's head matches the gun." Decker paused. "I'm

trying to make sense out of it . . . looking for a catalyst that
drove him over the edge. Even if I'm completely off base,
it wouldn't hurt us or LAPD to be thorough. Get all the
possible connections so we don't get caught with our pants
down."

Marge nodded. "No big deal to cross-check the victims
against Greenvale's membership list. How do I get hold of
the names?"

"Uh . . . that might be a bit of a problem."

Marge stared at him. "You've asked them for a list?"

"Yes."

"And they've refused."

"That sums it up."

"So now what?"

"Harlan's employment at the club was kept secret . . .
off the record. Now you could go down and be intimidating
. . . threaten you'll leak the information to the press unless
they help you out. Or you could be quiet and discreet. There
are thirteen victims. You could try to contact their surviving
relatives and friends. Casually ask them if the victims belonged to Greenvale."

"And if they did?"

Decker twirled his thumbs. "Ask them if the victims
took tennis lessons at the club. If they did, maybe they've
met an instructor named Hart Mansfield, known to us as
Harlan Manz."

Decker recapped his conversation with Barry Fine. "Or
maybe they might have met Harlan/Hart at a party."

"And?"

"I don't know, Marge," Decker said. "Just go out and
seek and maybe we'll find something. Or if you're tired,
you can call it a day. All of this can wait."

"No, it's all right." She smiled bitterly. "Lucky for you,
I canceled my heavy date."

Decker looked at her. "You need some time off, hon?"

Her smiled turned warm. "You care. That's so sweet."

Decker laughed softly. "Why don't you and Scott come
over on Sunday for a barbecue."

"Why do you always invite me *and* Scott?"

"Margie, I invite you, he finds out, calls you up. Then you wind up inviting him along out of pity. I'm just saving you the agenting."

He was right. Marge said, "Sure, I'll come. I'm tired and lonely and ain't about to play hard to get. Your family's the only thing that gives me a sense of normalcy. It's really pathetic."

"Honey, my family's the only thing that gives *me* a sense of normalcy."

"Then we're both pathetic."

"I call it dedicated." Decker grinned. "But I'm big on euphemisms."

Pulling the Volare into the driveway, shutting off the motor, Decker sat for a few moments, enjoying the dark and the silence. It was restful. It was peaceful. For a few blissful seconds, he was utterly alone and without obligation and it felt wonderful. He took a deep breath, let his body go slack, allowed his eyes to adjust to the shadows and starlight. He might have sat even longer except he suddenly realized there was a red Camaro parked curbside.

Cindy's car.

His heart started to flutter. His daughter was supposed to be in school three thousand miles away. What did this mean? After he had asked the question, he wasn't sure if he wanted to hear the answer.

He bolted out of the Volare, unlocked his front door. She stood when he crossed the threshold, gave him a timid wave and a "Hi, Daddy."

A beautiful girl in a big, strong way. She was around five ten, built with muscle and bone. Her face was sculpted with high cheekbones; her complexion was overrun with freckles but as smooth as marble. Wide-set, deep-brown eyes, long, flaming red hair, a white, wide smile. She photographed well, had done some small-time modeling to make some pocket change a few years back. But it wasn't for her. Her career goals focused on jobs involving her mind equally with her heart. Cynthia was a girl of extreme generosity and blessed intellect.

She was dressed in jeans and a white T-shirt, some kind of army boot as shoes. She looked troubled. No doubt why she was here instead of in New York.

"My goodness!" Decker gave his daughter a bear hug. "To what do I owe the pleasure? Aren't you supposed to be in school?"

"Something like that."

Before he could question her, Rina came into the room, smiled, and said, "She just showed up on the doorstep. I let her in. I take it that's okay with you."

"More than okay."

"Are you hungry?"

"Starved."

"Go wash up and sit down."

"Baby asleep?"

"For about an hour, *Baruch Hashem*. She is getting so feisty. But sharp as a whip. Takes after her daddy . . . and her sister."

"In the feistiness or sharpness?"

"Both."

Cindy laughed.

Decker said, "Maybe I'll say hi to the boys first."

"They're not home. Sammy and Jake went with some friends for pizza."

Perversely, Decker felt relieved. One less human element to deal with. Then he felt guilty. They were his sons, for godsakes. But then again, they were doing what they wanted to do. Why should he feel negligent if they were out having a good time? He realized that within the span of a few moments, his emotions had gone the gamut. Which meant he was unstable. Not the best time to deal with his daughter, who obviously had a thing or two on her mind.

After he had washed, Cindy led him to the table. "Sit. Rina made a delicious stew. One of those dishes that gets better the longer you cook it."

"With my hours, she cooks a lot of those," Decker said wryly. "Are you going to join me? Tell me what's going on?"

"It can wait until after dinner."

"That bad?"

"It isn't bad at all."

Rina came back in, set up dinner for her husband. "I told them to be home by eleven. Do you think I gave them too much freedom?"

"No, not at all."

"It's just that Sammy's so excited."

"It's a big event in a boy's life."

"A girl's too," Cindy said. "I remember when I got my license. The feeling of freedom . . . it was . . . exhilarating."

"Never knew you felt that oppressed." Decker smiled.

"It wasn't that—"

"Cindy, he's teasing you," Rina broke in. "It doesn't deserve an answer." She gently slugged her husband's good shoulder. "I know you're tired and cranky, but be nice."

"I am cranky." Decker ate a few heaping tablespoons. "This is wonderful. Did you eat, Cin?"

Cindy nodded, smiled. But she seemed anxious. Decker felt a protest in his stomach. He wasn't sure if it was his daughter's nervousness or hunger pangs. After two bowls of stew, two helpings of salad, and a couple of cups of decaf, he felt ready to take on his daughter.

Take on.

As if there were an impending battle.

Rina excused herself, went into the kitchen to clean up. Cindy suggested they talk in the living room. Decker took a seat on the suede couch, patted the space next to him. Cindy sat, but her spine was ramrod straight. She was all tics and fidgets. Finally, she said, "I quit the program."

Decker absorbed her words. "You quit the program. Meaning you're no longer in school."

"Yes. I have my master's, I'm tired of all the bullsh . . . of all the academic hurdles. I don't need a Ph.D. It does me no good other than to teach the same material to other Ph.D. candidates."

Decker rolled his tongue inside his cheek. "After six years of tuition and room and board, when you're finally self-supporting with scholarships and fellowships, you now decide to *quit*?"

Cindy glared at him. "You *are* kidding, aren't you?"

"Of course I'm kidding." *Sort of.* Decker leaned back. "So . . ."

"So . . ."

Decker said, "I guess I should be a parent. Maybe ask about your plans. Like . . . do you have any?"

"I think I need to get a job."

"Good start." Decker bit his mustache. "Want me to ask around the department . . . see if I can get you on as a part-time consultant?"

"Won't be necessary."

"You've found a job."

"Yes, I have." She closed her eyes, then opened them. "Daddy, I joined the Police Academy. Actually, I signed up a while ago. But you know how it works. There's the exam, then the personal checks, then I had to wait until they started hiring again. Anyway, it's a done deal. I'm starting in three months, right after the first."

Decker stared at his daughter. "This is a joke, right?"

"No joke." She opened her purse, pulled out a few sheets of paper. "Here's a copy of their letter of acceptance. Here's my letter of commitment—"

"So you haven't mailed anything in."

"Yes, I have. See, these are just copies. The originals are at home or with the Academy." She held the paper up for her father to see. "See, right here—"

Angrily, Decker batted them away. He stood up and began to pace. "Cynthia, what on earth could have possibly possessed you—"

"Dad, before our emotions get the better of us, can we be reasonable?"

"No, we *can't* be reasonable! Because you did something *unreasonable*. How could you act so . . . so damn impulsively?"

"It wasn't an impulsive decision. I told you I signed up a while ago."

"So you've thought about this? For a long time?"

"Yes."

"And it never even *dawned* on you to talk this over with me?"

"Of course it *dawned* on me, Daddy. I thought about telling you for quite some time. But I knew you couldn't possibly be objective—"

"Cindy, that's a truckload of bull."

"Can we keep this civil?"

"Are you trying to get even with me for not being around when you were growing up?"

"What are you talking about?"

"You're obviously trying to rile me—"

"Dad, believe it or not, I really want to be a cop, actually a detective." She smiled sweetly. "Just like you."

"Oh, cut the *crap*!"

"Peter!" Rina said.

Decker whirled around, focused on his wife. "Rina, this isn't your affair. Would you kindly leave, please?"

"Last I checked this was my house, too."

"I'm not telling you to leave the house, just the room."

"She can stay," Cindy said. "I don't mind."

"You stay out of this!" Decker directed a pointed index finger at his daughter. "This is between me and my wife."

"No, Daddy, it's between you and me and you're taking it out on her."

"You've got a lot of nerve, talking to me like that—"

"I'll leave," Rina said.

"Good idea," Decker said.

Rina went into the bedroom without slamming the door. Which surprised Cindy. If that had been her, she would have made her displeasure known very loudly. Dad was talking, more like ranting . . . as *usual*.

". . . even *bother* to come and talk to me about it?"

"I knew what you'd say," Cindy retorted.

"So you're a mind reader."

"No, just a dad reader. And I'm right. You're not objective."

"It's not a matter of objectivity," Decker shot back.

"Not only would I discourage you from joining, I'd discourage *anyone* from joining."

"Good thing you don't write ad copy for LAPD."

Decker honed in on her. "Cindy, there are *some* cop types. And even most of them don't make good officers. But if you're of a certain ilk and *if* you have a little bit of brainpower and *if* you have untold patience and *if* you can keep your mouth shut and *if* you have a good intuition and *if* you think before you react, then maybe you'll make a good cop. And yes, political correctness notwithstanding, it helps to be big and strong. Which you are not!"

"I'm not a ninety-pound weakling—"

"Any man your size with normal musculature could take you down in a minute."

"So that's where my superior brain will come in."

"You do have a superior brain. You just aren't choosing to use it. Cynthia, you don't have patience, you don't like orders, you're not detail-oriented, you're way *too* emotional, and you're impulsive . . . like just . . . dropping out of school—"

"I thought about it for a long time—"

"Then you didn't think it through. And I don't care *how* much you work out, you're no match for most men. Someone my size could squeeze you like a tomato."

"We're going around in circles, Daddy."

"You've neither the temperament nor the inclination. You'd make a lousy cop and a lousy cop is a dead cop—"

"Gee, Dad, thanks for the encouragement—"

"Better for you to be furious than for me to accept a flag at your funeral." He turned to her, his eyes burning with anger. "Do yourself a favor. Find a better way to get even with me."

"So you think I'm doing this from some sort of Freudian revenge motive?"

"Frankly, I don't know why you're doing this. This isn't the first time in your life that you've done something outrageous. But it *is* the most dangerous stunt you've ever pulled."

Cindy's eyes filled with water. "You're not being reasonable *or* fair."

"And you, Cynthia Rachel, are *crying*. You think I'm talking tough, just wait. You think your drill sergeant's going to be impressed with your tears? Or worse, how 'bout your perp. 'Better stop shitting around or I'll charge you with ten to fifteen for felonious tear-jerking.' "

Angrily, Cindy dried her eyes. "Touché."

Decker suddenly stopped pacing. He closed his eyes, tried to vent some of the rage. This was his daughter he was talking to. Gently, he put his hands on Cindy's shoulders. Angrily, she wiggled out of his touch. What did he expect?

"Cindy, I'm not trying to win points. But I am being brutally honest. This is one area I know."

Her voice was a whisper. "And I respect that. But with all due respect to your knowledge, I'm twenty-four. I'll make my own decisions. And suffer the consequences if they're bad ones. Dad, I think we've both said enough—"

"No, we haven't said *nearly* enough—"

"Telephone, Peter," Rina said.

Decker whipped his head around, asked her a testy "*Who* is it!"

"Marge."

Decker barked. "Is it an emergency?"

"I don't know," Rina answered quietly. "Would you like me to ask her?"

Decker made fists with his hands, released his fingers. "You stay here, young lady. I'm not through yet."

Decker charged into the bedroom and slammed the door, which made Cindy startle.

As soon as he was gone, she leaped from her chair and started to pace.

"What a supreme jerk! No wonder Mom had an affair." Then Cindy gasped, suddenly remembering that Rina was in the room. She felt herself go hot and cold at the same time. Sheepishly, she looked at her stepmother's face. "Oh, my God! Did you . . . did he . . . did . . ."

"It's all right, Cindy. I knew."

Cindy covered her mouth. "Oh, my God! I can't believe I said that! God, I'm such a *moron*!"

"You're riled. Would you like some coffee? Maybe tea?"

"How about a half dozen Advils."

"How about one?"

"He's right, you know!" Cindy flopped into one of the buckskin chairs and dried her eyes. "I've got an incredibly big mouth. Things just . . . slip out!"

Rina said nothing.

Cindy looked at Rina. "So he told you?"

Rina nodded.

"He must feel real close to you."

Rina stifled a smile. "Guess so."

"It's not as idiotic as it sounds. Dad never ever talked about it. And it didn't come up in any of the divorce proceedings. Even during their worst arguments, Dad never brought it up or threw it in Mom's face. There were times I actually wondered if he even knew. But then I figured how could he *not* know. Mom wasn't exactly subtle . . . all those hang-ups every time I picked up the phone."

Rina nodded.

"It wasn't all Mom's fault, you know. He was never home. Even when he was home, he wasn't home. He was a decent father. Did the right things. Showed up at all the school events and conferences. But there was this distance. He was dreadfully unhappy. So was Mom. They had to get married, you know. Because of me."

"They both love you very much."

"I know that. They dragged it out as long as they could. Though I never asked them to do that. They're so different. You know how they met?"

Rina nodded. "Your dad arrested your mother."

"Some stupid antiwar rally. The pregnancy meant Mom had to drop out of college. At twenty, she was stuck at home with a whining baby and no help at all, while all her friends were out partying. I don't know why she didn't get an abortion."

The room was quiet.

"Actually, I do know why. Dad wouldn't have let her. Anyway, I know she was very resentful. To this day, she still talks about her lost youth."

"Your mom and Alan have made a nice life for themselves. I think you're feeling worse about it than either of your parents."

"I suppose." She sighed. "Dad seems happy now . . . happi*er*."

Rina smiled. "Yes, your father isn't exactly a jolly fellow."

Cindy smiled.

"You comported yourself very well," Rina said.

"Yeah, felons should be a snap in comparison." She paused. "You heard us then? We were screaming that loud?"

"It's a small house."

"God, I have a headache."

"I'll get you the Advil."

"Thanks."

Rina left, came back a few moments later. "Did you tell your mother yet?"

"No. Believe it or not, Dad's the lesser of the two evils. Mom will not only go hysterical—just like Dad—but she'll start blaming Dad. I hate it when she does that. Those two are incredible. They really hate each other."

"I'm sure they don't."

"Oh, I'm sure they do."

Rina said, "What made you decide to join the Academy?"

"Oh, my goodness, someone really wants to hear *my* side of the equation."

Rina nodded encouragement.

Cindy cleared her throat. "I thought I wanted to study criminal behavior. I found that what I really wanted to do was solve crimes. Analyzing the deviant mind is useful, but it's too academic. It doesn't make neighborhoods safer places to live. It doesn't give victims a sense of justice. It doesn't do anything to enhance the quality of life. Criminal Sciences is about publishing papers, not about community service. And that's what I want to do. Use the knowledge I've learned and *apply* it. To *help* people. Pretty corny. But as I speak, it is the truth.''

''I think that's wonderful.''

''In theory, yes. Unfortunately, Dad has a point. I am impulsive, I am emotional, and I don't take orders well.''

She leaned forward.

''But I'm also *very* adaptable. Had to be to get along with my parents. I can learn, Rina. Because I really want to do this. I'll make it. I'd like his help and blessing. But if not, I'll make it anyway. If he can't deal with it, too bad.''

She sat back.

''I love my father, but there are times he is just impossible. So domineering! So *bossy*! How do you deal with him?''

''He's a good man.''

''I didn't say he wasn't. I just said he was a control freak. You know, I'm not excusing Mom. But my dad is just . . . such an imposing man. I guess she felt just so . . . swallowed up. I don't know how you put up with him.''

Rina shrugged. ''I'm not much of a fighter.''

''I wish I were like that. I just refuse to be stepped on.''

''I didn't say I get stepped on.''

Cindy blushed. ''I'm sorry. I didn't mean . . . God, I've got a big mouth. I guess I'm more like Mom than I'd like to believe.''

''I do express myself, Cindy. I'll stick up for what's important. Which I've learned isn't too much. This baby boomer generation on down . . . all of us . . . we've become so . . . confrontive. Stand up for yourself! Speak your mind! Tell it like it is! All this righteous anger . . . I find it very loud.''

''Better that than being walked on.''

''No one wants to be a *shmatta* . . . a dishrag. But sometimes it's a good idea to keep your mouth shut. Think if it's worth the effort. And yes, I freely admit to being occasionally two-faced. There have been times when I had agreed with your dad to do things his way, then turned around and did it the way *I* wanted. Most of the time, he forgot what he had been so insistent on. And the couple of times he was cogent enough to call me on it, I played *dumb*. I'm sure some psychologist would call me sneaky or tell me I have low self-esteem. Or tell me I was paralyzed by my domineering mother and an unapproachable father or something or other. *I* call it being practical. Because in the end, I get what I want and he saves face.''

"I don't think Gloria Steinem would approve of your methods.''

"Oh, forget about Gloria Steinem! She never nursed a husband through cancer, only to watch him die. She never labored in childbirth. She was never a widow with two small children. She's never been married to a police lieutenant. She never had a hysterectomy at thirty. And she's *not* an Orthodox Jew. So she has no concept of *shalom bais*—peace in the house. Which, in my humble opinion, is to her detriment!''

Cindy looked at her. "You're tough.''

"Tough enough to handle your dad.'' Rina sat down next to Cindy. "And so are you.'' She gave her a kiss on the cheek. "You'll work this out. You'll be okay.''

"If I ever learn to keep my mouth shut.''

"Cindy, youth is impulsive, thank God. Like you said, it was the reason you were conceived. It's what made me run off and get married at seventeen, then go have a baby a year later, then have yet another before my first son was out of diapers. It's what made me enter into a heartbreaking relationship after my husband died, knowing it was doomed from the start. And it's what made me ignore raised eyebrows in my community when I started dating your father. Within days of meeting him, I was head over heels in love. Impulsive yes. But it worked out.''

Cindy said. "Yes, I *am* impulsive. But this wasn't an *impulsive* decision. It's really what I want.''

"How could you know?'' Decker retorted. "You haven't the slightest notion what it is to be a cop.''

Both women turned around as if he had intruded in their conversation. Fine with him! Let Rina handle it! Tempted to escape and go burn the Porsche out at 120. Instead, he sat back down on the couch, rubbed his temples.

"How about this? We talk this over calmly. I tell you what being a cop is all about. You ask me questions. If you're still gung-ho . . . after I get done with you . . . then you can go ahead and join."

"What happened to *you* in ten minutes?" Cindy asked.

Rina said, "He overheard me talking about how much I loved him and it made him feel guilty for his outbursts."

Decker grumped, "Got it all figured out."

"True or false."

Decker ignored her, turned to Cindy. "Well?"

Cindy said, "Daddy, nothing would give me greater pleasure than to talk to you about my decision. I'd love to hear about your experiences and your insights. But I'm in the Academy regardless."

"That's being very pigheaded."

Rina interjected, "Peter—"

"She's acting like a mule."

"There's no reason to name-call—"

"Why is she afraid of hearing the truth?" Decker said.

Cindy said, "Listen, guys, I'm really tired. I want to go home."

"You tell your mom about this?"

Cindy sighed.

"You haven't *told* her?" Decker began to pace. "Great. I don't have enough garbage in my life dealing with friggin' mass murderers—"

"Dad, I'm really sorry about that. It must be terrible. And I certainly don't mean to add to your stress—"

"But you'll do it anyway."

No one spoke. Cindy sighed. "I'm going. We'll talk later. When everyone's calmer." She smiled at her father. "Good night."

Abruptly, Decker stopped walking, plunked himself down in a chair, and stared out the window, his eyes a thousand miles away.

"She said good night, Peter."

"Good night, good night," he muttered.

"Give her a hug, for godsakes."

Cindy waited a beat. When Decker didn't move, Rina said, "Peter, did you hear—"

"Yes, I heard you."

Cindy felt her eyes start to moisten, but quickly she held back the tears. "That's okay, Rina. Everyone needs their space. Even parents."

Again, she waited a moment. When Decker didn't move, she bade Rina good night and left quietly. Soon the car's engine faded to nothingness. Rina broke the silence.

"You should have given her a hug, Peter," Rina rebuked him. "Your intransigence was nasty. God forbid, suppose she has an accident or something. How would you feel?"

"Horrible. I'd never forgive myself."

"So how could you let her leave like that!"

He turned to her, his own eyes moist. "Because . . . I was afraid if I hugged her, I would have never let her go."

🌿10

The temperature in the office was arctic. Why did the city feel it necessary to keep the station house in a deep freeze? Or maybe it was just Decker's mood. Because things weren't going well. He sat at his desk, looking out at a wall of eyes. His Homicide team arcing around him. Protective. Like a moat. His brain pounded. With any luck, ibuprofin would work its magic. He nodded for Oliver to begin.

Scott scanned his notes, hand raking through his black hair. "Loo, we've gone through Estelle's room to room, wall to wall, floor to floor, ceiling to ceiling. Neither Dunn nor I could find enough empty magazines at the scene to account for all the bullets and casings."

Decker's eyes glanced at the newspaper on his desk. A couple of days had passed, but Estelle's was still front-page news. He spoke quietly. "Would it help if you looked again?"

"We were very thorough." Marge smoothed out the leg of her beige pants. She wore lightweight fabrics today— white cotton shirt, viscose pants. But if the weather continued its cooling trend, it would be time for the wools. "I'll show you our grid maps if you want. Right now it doesn't look like much . . . a mass of dots."

"We marked every place where we extracted a bullet or found an empty casing," Oliver explained.

Bert Martinez twirled the ends of his bushy mustache,

his stocky frame bowing the seat of the folding chair. "Whole damn case is starting to smell fishy. Anyone show the Loo Harlan's autopsy report?"

Decker sat up. "When did that come in?"

"You were in a meeting with the mayor, city council, and Strapp," Marge said. "We tried paging you . . ."

Decker grimaced. He'd forgotten to pick up a new pager.

"How'd that go?" Oliver was concerned. "Are our asses on the line?"

"Why should our asses be on the line?" Martinez asked. "We've got the perp . . . of sorts."

"Lawsuits, right?" Oliver said. "Police should have showed up sooner, right? If they had, more lives would have been saved, right? What was time of arrival on that one? Something like two minutes?"

"First cruiser arrived in two-twenty-eight," Webster said.

Oliver said. "Am I right, Deck?"

"Close."

"No matter what happens, we'll get blamed. Earthquake could drop the city into the center of the earth, it would be our fault."

"For the time being, the Detective division isn't a point of concern." Decker paused. "But if this turns out to be . . . how should I say this? If this is something more than a straightforward mass murder, the focus will shift to us. Who has that autopsy report?"

"That would be me." Webster handed the folder to Decker, his blue eyes focused, alert. Today, Tom was dressed in a black suit, sunglasses dangling from his jacket pocket. Looked more FBI than LAPD with his perma-pressed Anglo good looks. Suave manner. But Decker didn't hold it against him. Webster was a damn good cop.

Decker thumbed through the pages, eyes working like strobes. "What should I be looking for?"

Webster drawled, "The bullet that killed Harlan Manz. It was fired at a range consistent with a distance of around two to two and a half feet—"

"*What!*" Decker raced through the report. "Where?"

"Page eleven or twelve. I marked it with a pencil."

Decker fast-forwarded to the paragraph. Read it once, then read it again. He sat back in his chair, ran a hand down his face.

Martinez said, "I called up the morgue . . . asked if they were sure about that distance."

"And?"

"They were sure. Said that if the gun had been fired at a closer range, more damage would have been done to the brain."

Webster said, "Bigger entry and exit holes, more tearing and ripping, more extensive powder burns on the hands and temple."

"So when Harlan fired, he looked something like this?" Oliver made a gun with his fingers, extended his arm from his shoulder, then flexed his wrist so that his fingers were pointing back to his temple. "What's this, guys? About three feet?"

"Anyone have a measuring tape?" Marge asked.

Decker pulled one from his desk, gave it to Marge.

Marge measured. "Thirty-seven inches. Bend your elbow a little bit, Scotty."

Oliver complied, his elbow making a hundred-and-fifty-degree angle. "Now I'm pointing over my head."

"So lower your arm." Martinez got up, positioned Oliver as if he were a Gumby. "There. About like this. That looks like two and a half feet."

Marge measured. "Thirty-one inches to be exact."

Webster said, "Now point to your head."

Oliver did so, maintained the pose. They stared at him.

Marge said, "Might be me, but I think he looks awkward."

Martinez said, "He looks ridiculous. You want to pop yourself, you put the gun to your temple. You don't hold it two feet away."

Marge said, "You know, I could understand someone holding the gun away from his head if he had doubts or wasn't used to a firearm. Almost like an avoidance thing."

"Maybe at a little distance," Martinez said. "But not in

the position Scotty's in. Unless you like contorting.''

"Maybe he had short arms," Marge suggested.

"Not that short," Martinez answered.

"Could it have been a misfire?" Oliver asked.

Martinez made a face. "You mean he was aiming for someone and caught himself in the *head*?"

"No. I mean the gun just accidentally went off."

"Catching him square in the temple?" Marge was dubious.

"Excuses, excuses." Webster shook his head. "Why aren't we saying what we're all thinkin'?"

"Two shooters," Oliver said.

"Just what you said yesterday, Loo," Marge said.

Oliver said, "You did?"

Decker replied, "I was looking over some of the victims' autopsy reports. Some of the bullet trajectories were inconsistent with a one-killer theory."

"And you didn't like the number of bullets we recovered."

"A lot for one shooter," Webster said. "Even for someone using a double automatic. What did we recover? Something like two hundred bullets?"

Martinez said, "Two killers means Estelle's was planned."

Oliver said, "What do you mean by planned, Bert?"

"Harlan went into Estelle's with the intention of killing someone specific. He and his cohort masked it by popping others. Like putting a bomb in an airplane to collect insurance."

"A hit gone bad," Marge said. "If so, next step is to figure out who the intended target was."

Webster said, "So y'all take a look at the victims."

Decker said, "We need to look at the victims who might have crossed paths with Harlan in other capacities."

Marge reached into her oversized purse and pulled out a sheet of paper. "Which brings us up to date with my current assignment. Discovering which victims—if any—belonged to Greenvale Country Club."

"What's this?" Webster asked.

Decker filled them in on Harlan's job at the country club, on his conversation with Barry Fine, and on yesterday's brainstorming with Marge. "Harlan Manz worked at Greenvale about two years ago. You know how snobs can be. Treating the hired help as nonentities. I was trying to determine if Harlan had a long-standing grudge against one of the restaurant's victims."

Oliver said, "Deck, if a grudge from Greenvale was the motive behind Estelle's shooting, why didn't Harlan shoot up the club?"

"Maybe security was too tight. Look, I don't know any more than you do. But something's hinky here."

Oliver asked, "So you're thinking that one of Estelle's victims offended Harlan at the club *and* at the restaurant. And that's why he went batshit?"

Decker said, "Just trying to find a connection."

Marge asked, "Maybe you'd like to hear if there *are* any connections?"

Decker laughed. "We're going on with these flights of fancy and we don't even have facts. What do you have?"

Marge settled herself. "Okay. Table number twenty-two: People there were from Ashman/Reynard. A Realtor named Wendy Culligan was pitching to a bunch of Japanese businessmen. Some of the businessmen were murdered, but she survived . . . which made my job of asking questions a lot easier. The firm is a corporate member of Greenvale. Has been for the fifteen years since the club opened."

"Is she a member?" Oliver asked.

"Through her business. Wendy's been at the club maybe six times . . . goes there for power lunches. Theoretically, she could have crossed paths with Harlan."

Oliver said, "But she's still alive, Margie. She obviously wasn't the target of a hit."

Webster said, "Or maybe Harlan missed."

"So what does Greenvale have to do with a bunch of Japanese businessmen who probably never set foot inside its doors?" Martinez asked.

Marge shrugged. "Well, they were making deals with Ashman/Reynard, Bert. Maybe Harlan was resentful of some of the realtors. So maybe he was trying to screw up the agency or block the deal.''

Decker wrote as he spoke. "What else do we have?"

Marge said, "Then we have Walter Skinner, the actor. He was also a member of Greenvale."

Martinez said, "Now that was a real shame. I used to love him in *High Mountain*. Anybody remember that show?"

"Yo," Oliver said. "Saturday morning, ten o'clock."

"You coulda set your watch by me, I was that loyal a viewer," Martinez said. "Remember the stampedes? Each episode had at least one stampede. All that sand and dirt and stomping hooves. Scared the shit outta me when I was a little boy."

"Y'all see *The Lion King*?" Webster asked. "Took my son to see it. They had a cartoon stampede. Scared the shit outta him. Had nightmares for weeks."

Oliver said, "Yeah, *High Mountain* always had a stampede or a twister. Couple times it was both."

"Yeah, I remember that show!" Martinez said.

"The one where the wagon train stopped in Laredo, Texas," Decker added.

"That's the one!" Oliver said, bringing his hands to a clap. "God, that brings back memories. Man, wind was whooshing all over the place. And there was Walter—aka Cattle Foreman Kirk Brown—riding high in the saddle, barking orders, doing a jig with his horse, trying to bring in all those raging dogies while a tornado was blowing everything to shit."

Marge said, "Maybe we could get back to the business at hand?"

The men stared miserably at her. Decker held back a smile. "So Walter was also a member of Greenvale?"

"Yes. A founding member," Marge said. "Both he and his companion were murdered in their seats." She looked at Decker. "Their table was right next to the Garrisons'."

"Ah, interesting." Decker took notes. "I haven't gone over their entrance and exit wounds. Be interesting to see if it matches the patterns of the Garrisons."

"Skinner and his companion . . ." Webster paused. "As opposed to a wife. By any chance, is there a wife?"

Marge said. "Yes, there is. Adelaide Skinner. I haven't talked to her yet."

The room went quiet.

Oliver grinned. "So the old goat was stepping out on her."

"It doesn't mean he deserved to die," Marge said.

"Certainly *I* don't think so. But his wife may have had other ideas."

"So she hired someone to whack him by shooting up a restaurant?" Webster made a face. "How old is she anyway?"

"Seventy-seven," Marge answered.

"Y'all picture a little seventy-seven-year-old lady telling someone to massacre thirteen innocent people just to get to her old man?"

"Maybe she hired out without knowing what the killers were going to do," Oliver said.

Martinez said, "So they decided to execute the hit by attacking an entire restaurant? Pretty clumsy."

"Worked in the past for the Mafia," Oliver said.

Martinez added, "Then, for a topper, one of them decides to whack the other?"

"More money for himself," Oliver said. "Plus someone to pin the blame on."

Webster said, "Is Walter's wife a member of Greenvale?"

"Yes, of course," Marge said.

"Let's slow it down," Decker said. "We're getting wild with our speculations. Any other connection, Marge?"

"Linda and Ray Garrison. From the people I've talked to, it's clear that the couple was worth beaucoup bucks."

"So who inherits the estate?"

"Don't know for sure, but they have two adult children, a son and a daughter. David Garrison is twenty-six. And guess what? He has a record. Drug arrests. First time was probation. Second time, he served two years. He's now out on parole. I've got a call in to his officer."

"Good going, Dunn," Webster said.

"Daughter Jeanine is completely different. Twenty-eight. A patron of the arts and theater and ballet. Very big in society events . . . raising money for charities. Now get this, guys! She specifically raises charity money with *tennis* matches."

Oliver said, "Didn't you say that Harlan taught tennis at Greenvale?"

"Yes, I did." Decker's intercom rang. He excused himself, took the call. A rape. Everyone from Sex Crimes was busy in the field. Did he want to send down someone from CAPs? Decker turned to Marge. The woman had been a top-notch Sex Crimes detective for six years. He had almost felt guilty when he pulled her away from the detail to follow him into Homicide. After the call was completed, he looked at Marge. "I need someone with experience, Detective Dunn."

Marge checked her watch. "Sure, I can catch it."

"Thanks."

"Are we done here?"

"For the most part," Decker answered. "Just let me get a couple of assignments out. Bert, you remember Walter Skinner as Walter Skinner the actor. Why don't you go out to his house and feel out the wife?"

"Feel her up?" Oliver said. "Feel *who* up?"

"*Out,*" Decker said. "Feel her *out*. What are you doing now, Scotty?"

"I got a court case in a half hour. Meryl Tobias."

Martinez groaned. "Mr. 'I'm sorry, I'm sorry.' What a stupid shit!"

"At least he was sorry," Marge said.

"Don't help Mrs. Tobias."

Decker said, "What's the DA going for?"

"Man one."

"Cut-and-dried case?"

"Should be."

"So when you're finished, go over to Ashman/Reynard. Find out what business they were conducting at Estelle's. While you're there, check out the other agents, see if any of them had had prior contact with Harlan.'' He turned to Webster. ''You're the youngest of the bunch, Tommy. You take on David Garrison.''

Oliver grinned. ''Two young, good-looking white boys mentally duking it out.''

Marge said, ''How do you know David Garrison's good-looking?''

''I don't know that he is,'' Oliver said. ''He just *sounds* good-looking. Aristocratic. Like he should have a 'the third' after his name.''

Webster said, ''What about Jeanine Garrison, Loo?''

''You want to take her, Marge?''

''You mean after I catch the rape call?''

''That's right. I'm going senile.'' Decker glanced at the clock. ''No, catch the call, then meet up with Scotty at Ashman/Reynard. I've got an open lunch hour. I'll take Jeanine myself.''

❧11

The house was small, disappointingly so. Martinez hadn't been expecting anything ritzy, but at least "Cattle Foreman Kirk Brown" should have been living in something *western*. A ranch house set on acres replete with tumbleweeds and cacti. Maybe a couple of horse stables. Instead, Walter Skinner, the man, had lived out his last years in a three-bedroom one-story bungalow in an anonymous residential block in the heart of the Valley. A simple house plopped onto a patch of recently fertilized lawn. A lifetime of nostalgia washed away by the stench of manure.

Badge in hand, Martinez trod up a red-painted cement walkway, hopped the two steps up to the porch. Knocked on the door, and when no one answered, he knocked again. This time he heard someone telling him just a minute. An elderly voice—not feeble, just old. A minute later, she opened the door a crack. Just enough room for Martinez to show her his ID. Then the door opened all the way.

She must have been under five feet, hunched over, hands resting on a cane. Her face was as round as the moon, lined but not overly wrinkled. Her cheeks had a dash of blush, her lips were painted pink. Her eyes were clear blue; her hair, thick and silver, was tied neatly into a bun. She wore a red turtleneck top over black pants, mules on her feet. Her hands were spotted, the fingers bony and bent. Though she had lived almost eight decades, she still struck a nice pose—all seventy-seven years and about eighty pounds of her.

One palm remained on the knob of her cane, the other extended itself to Martinez. "Adelaide Skinner. Pleased to meet you, Detective."

Martinez took the birdlike hand. "Likewise. Thank you for letting me in."

"I was afraid you'd arrest me if I didn't." A brief smile. "Come in, come in before you catch a chill."

Martinez stepped inside. Adelaide closed the door. "Is this a condolence call from the police? Someone named Strapp already did that."

"My captain."

"A nice man. Sharp. A good politician."

Martinez went inside the house. "Actually, I came to talk to you, Mrs. Skinner."

"Me?"

"If you wouldn't mind."

"No, I don't mind."

She stood for a moment, caught her breath. "Fine. We'll talk. First let me give you a tour. Which shouldn't take very long. Because it's a small house. My idea, not his. If it had been up to Walter, we would have been living on a grand-scale *Ponderosa*."

Martinez smiled to himself. Her admission made him feel better.

"Not that Walter was the ranch type." She walked in tiny steps, directing him toward the left. "But when you're Kirk Brown you have an image to keep up."

She stopped, regarded Martinez.

"Or maybe you're too young to remember—"

"Oh no, ma'am. I grew up on *High Mountain*."

She smiled. "Anyway, this . . . was Walter's living room. It shows his personality, I think."

Martinez looked around, his heart beating like a little boy's. The personification of his western hero, the room's couches and chairs all done in brown suede and horn. The tables were fashioned from old driftwood. A handmade Navajo rug sat on a floor of knotty pine. A tremendous

stone fireplace. And the walls. Loaded with pictures of
Skinner as Cattle Foreman Kirk Brown, dressed in western
gear, posing with past cowboy luminaries. The daytime
ropers—Hopalong Cassidy, Roy Rogers, the Lone Ranger,
Wild Bill Hickock, and Sky King. Then there were pictures
of Skinner and the *nighttime* biggies, on the set of *Wagon
Train, Death Valley Days,* and *Paladin.* Kirk with Bat Mas-
terson and Sugarfoot and Mr. Favor. And *Gunsmoke.* Lots
of pictures of Skinner on *that* set. With Matt Dillon and
Chester and with the beautiful and alluring Miss Kitty. As
a boy, Martinez dreamed of Kitty's boobs, dreamed about
them for many years. Then the series got old and so did
Amanda Blake. . . .

The snapshots weren't the only things on the walls. Sharing the space was a display of stuffed and mounted sports
fish—a huge mother salmon, barracudas baring teeth,
swordfish and marlins flashing weapons on their snouts.
The bookshelves had been turned into showcases for more
snapshots, also for Skinner's fishing awards and trophies.
Adelaide saw Martinez eyeing the shiny gold cups. She
picked one up, hefted it in her hand.

"Yeah, Walt was quite the Ishmael in his prime. When
he got too old to fish for barracudas, he started netting in
the Barbies."

She raised a gray eyebrow.

"Which are practically the same thing as barracudas. I'm
sure if it was up to Walt, he would have gladly pegged
some of his tarts to the wall. 'Cause that's what he was
doing. Sports fishing of a different type. Much cheaper, I'll
say that much."

"Cheaper?" Martinez asked.

"I see you never chartered a fishing boat."

"No, ma'am."

"Money for the boat, money for the captain, money for
the trip, money for the supplies, money for this, money for
that. The tarts are bargain-basement prices in comparison."

A deep sigh.

"You had enough, Detective? I know I have."

"Anything you want, ma'am."

"I'll show you the back bedrooms if you want. But it's a bit of a walk for me and there isn't much to see."

"You don't have to bother—"

"Just my bedroom, Walter's bedroom, a spare room for our daughter and son-in-law or whichever grandchild happens to be in town. There're three of them." Her face lit up. "And of course, the newest. The first great-grandchild. A girl. Ashley."

"That's wonderful."

"Oh, she is such a love." Her face turned wistful, a tear rolled down her cheek. "Walter adored her. He was a doting grandfather. A good father, too. And a decent husband. I think . . ."

She looked up at the ceiling.

"I think he just didn't want to be an old man. Come, I'll show you my living room."

They did an about-face, headed to the right. Once the space might have been used as a dining room. Now it functioned as separate entertaining quarters. *Her* quarters. Chintz wallpaper decorated with old-fashioned oil landscapes. Velvet couches with lace throws and satin pillows. Overstuffed chairs. Little tea tables covered with doilies. Pleated lampshades rimmed with fringes, silver picture frames, knickknacks and bowls of potpourri permeated with cinnamon. Probably drowned out the stink of the fertilizer.

"Mind if we talk in here?" Adelaide lowered herself into a chair. "I'd prefer it."

"Not at all." Martinez paused, wondering where to sit.

"Just sit on the couch." Adelaide pointed a twiglike finger in its direction. "It's quite sturdy. Actually it's lasted through twenty years of grandchildren jumping on it, so let's amend that to *very* sturdy."

Martinez sank into down cushions. Had to right himself quickly to sit up. "Real soft."

"No support whatsoever. What the kids didn't accomplish, gravity finished off. How rude of me. Can I get you some tea?"

She took a bell from one of the doilied tables, rang it hard and furiously. A minute later, a thin young woman came into the room. She was wearing a white uniform and a nurse's cap. Probably an LVN. "Yes, Mrs. Skinner?"

"Two teas, Nicky. And bring in the cookies, too. The good ones. The butter cookies."

Nicky turned, disappeared.

Adelaide grinned. "Isn't this fun? Just like *Arsenic and Old Lace.*"

Martinez smiled nervously. "Not *too* much like it, I hope."

Adelaide was puzzled, then she laughed. "No, no, no. That would be carrying things a little too far."

The room fell silent.

Martinez said, "Truly, I am sorry for your loss."

"So am I." Again, her eyes moistened. "I loved Walter. My bitterness is a hollow shell. If I remember the bad times, maybe I won't miss the good so much." Her lip trembled. "Faults and all, I did love him."

Martinez cleared his throat. "The monster who did this to your husband . . . to all the victims—"

"Harlan Manz." Adelaide's face went hard. "Who is this . . . this . . ."

"That's what we're trying to figure out." Martinez took out a photograph. "I know this might be hard for you. But can you look at a snapshot of him for me?"

"Why?"

"I'd like you to tell me if he looks familiar."

Martinez held out the picture. Slowly, she secured it, brought it into her line of vision.

"Should he look familiar to me?" She looked up, saw her nurse carrying a tray of goodies. "Ah, Nicky's back. What kind of tea did we make, love?"

"Chamomile. It's still brewing in the pot. And it's very *hot.* Don't burn your lip like you did last time."

"Scold, scold, scold." She frowned. "Where are the butter cookies?"

"They're not on your diet. I brought tea biscuits—"

"Oh, bosh!" She picked up a hard biscuit, nibbled it. "These taste like cardboard. I can't serve these."

"I'm not hungry anyway," Martinez said. "Tea's just fine."

"It's hot," Nicky reiterated as she poured. "She likes it very hot."

"Only way to drink tea," Adelaide insisted.

Martinez cooled his heels as he drank hot tea. They made genteel chitchat—about the tea, about the biscuits, about butter cookies, and the weather. Then he reopened the conversation. "So, what do you think of the snapshot? Could you have seen Harlan Manz before?"

Adelaide picked up the photograph again. "He might look *slightly* familiar. Now I know I'm old. But I'm not brain-dead yet. I don't think I ever met anyone named Harlan Manz."

"How about Hart Mansfield?"

The old woman furrowed her brow. "Now, why does *that* name sound familiar?"

"He taught tennis at Greenvale Country Club."

A slow smile formed on her lips. "Detective, do I look like a tennis player?"

Martinez felt his face go hot. "He also tended bar there. For parties and charity occasions."

Adelaide continued to think, then she turned pale. "Yes . . . yes, he did. Oh my! Oh my, oh my—"

"What, Mrs. Skinner?"

She brought her hand to her chest. "Oh my goodness!"

Martinez stood up. "Are you okay, ma'am?"

"Oh yes . . . I'm okay . . . this is the bartender Walter had words with at the Hausner party."

Martinez felt his heart hammer. He picked up his notebook, scribbled furiously. "Words? What kind of words?"

"Nothing earth-shattering. Just that I remember him . . . because I talked to him . . . for a minute or so after Walter lost his temper."

"What happened?"

"Oh, the usual. The line at the bar was moving too slowly. Walter was in a bad mood and made a fuss. Something like 'Stop making time with the girls and gimme my Scotch!' "

She looked down.

"Walter called the boy a nitwit. He was half drunk and half joking. But he said it in a loud voice, and I think it embarrassed the poor child—"

She stopped herself, her face angry, her hands shaking, her eyes far away.

"Anyway, I told this . . . this whoever he is . . . that Walter was just a little grumpy. He seemed to take my explanation with equanimity and went about his business. I went about mine."

She focused her attention back to Martinez. "You couldn't possibly think that . . . he *remembered*!"

Martinez played with his mustache. "It doesn't seem real important. Did they ever have any other dealings with each other?"

"Not that I know of." She thought a moment. "But I do know that . . ." She closed her eyes, then opened them. "That Walter went to the club with other women at times."

"I see."

"So it's possible that Walter could have had other run-ins with this . . . this . . . this . . ."

"Did Walter ever mention Harlan/Hart again to you?"

"No, he didn't. Still, it's eerie. A random crime that cuts off Walter's life. And here I live, having met my husband's murderer face-to-face."

Martinez nodded.

Adelaide said, "You don't think it's random, do you?"

"We're investigating all aspects of the case—"

"A two-year-old insult? It doesn't seem like a decent reason for murder!"

"No, it doesn't."

"Still . . ." She picked up her teacup, sipped quietly. "You never know what motivates people to do such vile deeds."

"You're saying that this whole bloody mess was a conspiracy?"

Marge looked out the window. She was on the tenth floor of a fifteen-story building, had a view of other tall buildings and a peek at the distant mountains. Ashman/Reynard was located in an industrial park in Woodland Hills, one of the older parks in the Valley, old in these parts defined as built twenty years ago. Her eyes returned to Brenda Miller, executive veep. She was dressed in a red power suit, wore black stockings and pumps that could have been lethal weapons. A petite woman in her thirties with short dark hair, active brown eyes, and good skin.

Oliver said, "No, we're not saying that. We were just wondering if you or anyone else at Ashman/Reynard had ever had dealings with Harlan Manz prior to this incident?"

"Dealings where? At Estelle's?"

"Anywhere," Marge said.

"What kind of dealings? Or are you really asking me if I remember Harlan? The answer is yes, I remember him. Cocky kid. He worked the bar there."

"At Estelle's?" Oliver said, writing as he spoke.

"Yeah, at Estelle's." Brenda frowned, rested her elbows on her desk. "Isn't that what we're talking about?"

"He also tended bar for Greenvale Country Club. Your company's a corporate member at Greenvale," Marge said.

"I know that." Brenda was irritated.

"Do you remember Harlan Manz from Greenvale?" Marge asked. "He might have been using the name Hart Mansfield."

Brenda took a breath, then let it out slowly. "I knew him . . . took a couple of tennis lessons from him."

Marge tried to hide her surprise. This might prove to be more productive than she had originally thought. She slowed it down. "Tell me about Harlan."

"What's to tell?" She laughed but it lacked mirth. "Good ole Hart. Mr. Charmer. He was there for maybe . . . one summer. Then, poof, he was gone. Like most of Greenvale's employees. All of them . . . pretty people without brains."

She became quiet.

"About . . . oh, I don't know . . . a year later, I took some clients out to Estelle's. And there was Harlan tending bar. I gave him a hug." She shuddered involuntarily. "Gives me the creeps thinking about it. Anyway, I saw him at Estelle's maybe half a dozen times. Then he was gone. You know these hangers-on. They're always moving . . . moving.''

''Ever have any words with him?'' Oliver asked.

Brenda thought a moment. ''Not that I can remember.''

''So you don't recall ever offending him?''

''I offend lots of people. Him, specifically?'' She shrugged.

''Did he ever ask you for a handout?'' Oliver said. ''Could be you refused?''

She hesitated. ''You know, I do remember him talking about needing temporary work . . . until he got his *big* break.'' She smiled sarcastically. ''I told him to come by the office. We can always use temp workers. He never took me up on it. I knew he wouldn't. Must have made that offer to twenty people and not one of them has ever been sincere.''

Brenda got up, walked over to the window, her gaze focused outward.

''All of them. Male and female bimbos. Always with the big break just around the corner. Meanwhile, they ain't getting any smarter. But they are getting older. New studs and starlets come in. See it all the time. Competition's fierce out there.''

The room was quiet.

Marge said, ''So you took tennis lessons from him.''

''A couple of times. Hart was strictly fill-in. Good player, though. Strong legs. Who would have thought . . .''

Marge said, ''Did he ever try to pick you up?''

''Me?'' She shook her head. ''No. As I recall, he went in for the older set—fifty-plus with big bucks. And he also went for the cuties. I don't fit into either category. Besides, I'm way too threatening for him. Too independent and successful.''

Marge said, ''Did he ever try to pick up Wendy Culligan?''

''I don't know. Ask Wendy.''

''I did,'' Marge said. ''She said no. But I don't know if

I believe her. I didn't press her because she's still in bad shape. No sense adding insult to injury. But I'm asking you, Ms. Miller. Did Harlan ever try to pick up Wendy Culligan?''

Oliver looked at Dunn questioningly. First he had heard about a connection between Wendy and Harlan. When Marge gave him a quick wink, he realized she was winging it.

Brenda appeared uncomfortable. "If Wendy said no, it's no."

Marge hesitated. "Are *you* being straight with me, Ms. Miller?"

Brenda turned to Marge, her face tense and hard. "Listen, Detective. The poor kid has gone through major trauma . . . lost four pounds in three days. She doesn't eat, can't sleep or work. I've begged her to see a specialist. The company would pay for it. Wendy's a real asset here, one of our top sellers. But she refuses. Right now, the woman can barely function. Let's not make things worse for her."

"That's why I'm asking you these questions and not her."

Oliver said, "If there's a connection, it's going to come out. Why don't you tell us the story before some other jerk gets wind of it and leaks it to the tabloids for money—"

"What?" Brenda spat out. "*Who'd* do that?"

"I'm just talking theoretically—"

"Are you talking about yourself?" Miller's eyes were fire. "You got ambitions, Detective?"

"If I did, think I'd be talking to you about them?" Oliver laughed. "Believe it or not, Ms. Miller, I have integrity." Under his breath, he added, "It's about all I *do* have."

Brenda softened, looked at Marge. "Is he married?"

"Divorced."

"Is he seeing anyone?"

"Not that I know."

Oliver said, "I'm in the room, ladies. You can talk to me directly."

Brenda waved him off. "I never ask the men these questions. They always lie." She looked at Oliver. "You promise me dinner, you might break through my ball-breaking exterior.''

Oliver broke into a big grin. ''I'd be happy to buy you dinner, Ms. Miller. But it won't be at Estelle's.''

Brenda said, ''How about Crab and Barrel?''

''A little rich for my wallet . . .'' Oliver looked dubious. ''Maybe you could make it work.''

Brenda said, ''When?''

''Pick a night.''

''Friday?''

''You're on.''

Marge said, ''Tell us about Wendy Culligan and Harlan Manz.''

Brenda turned serious. ''They went out for drinks a couple of times. Nothing serious because he had a girlfriend, she had a boyfriend. I told her she was crazy. Yeah, Harlan was good-looking, better-looking than her boyfriend, that was for sure. But Ken—that's her boyfriend—he's got a job, he's got his own car, he's got his own condo . . . he's got a *future*. Harlan was a *loser*. I guess Wendy caught on because they stopped seeing each other . . . remained on good terms according to her—''

''She spoke to you about this?'' Marge said.

''Yes. When I came to visit her, she immediately pulled me aside and begged me not to tell anyone. First off, she didn't want her boyfriend finding out. Second, she didn't want to be associated with him. Can you blame her?''

''No,'' Marge said. ''But she should have been truthful with the police—''

''Are you going to call her up?'' Brenda was nervous. ''Ask her about it?''

''Yes,'' Marge said. ''But I don't have to say it came from you.''

''I'd appreciate it.'' Brenda sighed. ''I didn't tell you to be a fink. I told you because I didn't want anyone else to make more of it than it was.''

''You have anyone specifically in mind?'' Marge asked.

''No, and that's the God's honest truth. But you know people talk. After something like Estelle's, they feel nervous . . . helpless. Sometimes they make up stuff. Poor Wendy doesn't need shit like this after what she's been through.''

"You did the right thing," Oliver said soothingly.

"Honestly, Detective. Wendy's a straight arrow. She says it was only a couple of times, it was only a couple of times. If she says it was no big deal, it was no big deal.''

"Maybe to her it was no big deal," Marge said. "But to Harlan it could have been a very big deal!''

Oliver dropped a fistful of pumpkin seeds into his mouth, smirked. He was very proud of himself. Marge rolled her eyes, opened the passenger door to the unmarked. Oliver slid in, leaned over and opened the driver's door from the inside. When she got in, he made a point of going through his wallet.

"Well, I got three dollars to my name. Maybe it'll buy Brenda a glass of house wine.''

"I know what I make, I know what you make." Marge started the engine. "I'm not falling for that, Scotty.''

Oliver laughed, offered Marge pumpkin seeds. Marge shook her head no and backed the car out of the parking lot. She headed for the 405 Freeway, turned into the north on-ramp, revving up the motor until they were flying. She said, "We might be onto something. Harlan knew Wendy. *More* than knew her. They dated.''

"But Wendy isn't dead, Marge.''

"So Harlan aimed at her, but missed.''

"Meanwhile, he caught thirteen other people in the process, including two men at her own table?" Oliver was skeptical.

"Maybe he was showing off for her. 'Look what you drove me to.' ''

"Why would there be two shooters at the scene if Harlan just wanted to show off to Wendy? He could have done that without help.''

"We don't know that there were definitely two shooters.''

"But we're leaning in that direction.''

"Frankly, I don't know what we're leaning toward. Because we don't know what we're looking for.''

Oliver was quiet. Then he said, ''Before we came here, I talked to Bert about Walter Skinner's widow. She's fond of *Arsenic and Old Lace*.''

''The movie?''

''Yeah, the movie.''

''I can see why she'd like it. Central characters are two old ladies.''

''Two old ladies who *kill* people.''

''People at Estelle's were shot, Scott. Not poisoned.''

''Still, it gets you thinking. Her old man was stepping out on her.''

''Did Bert say she acted psycho about that point?''

''No, he didn't. He said she seemed to bounce back and forth between being pissed at Walter for messing around and feeling truly sad about his death.''

''Sounds normal to me,'' Marge said. ''Only thing about the case that does sound normal.''

''Yeah, it's getting complicated.'' Oliver ate more pumpkin seeds. ''You hungry, Marge? These morsels ain't cutting the pangs.''

''I could use a bite.''

''How about Oscar's Deli?''

''Where is that? Woodley and Ventura?''

''A block west.'' Oliver ate the last batch of pumpkin seeds. ''You can pay. I have to save up my dimes for Crab and Barrel.''

☙12

Jeanine Garrison was a hard person to reach. Decker was put on hold, talked to a series of secretaries and assistants, all of it puzzling to him because he was not sure exactly what Jeanine did that required a staff. Marge had mentioned something about her being a patron of the arts and being involved in charity work. But how she earned her keep was anyone's guess. When she finally did come on the phone, she sounded polite enough. They made an appointment to meet at her office, which was one of those retro-Victorian numbers with stained-glass and mullioned windows. Like Greenvale. Decker wondered if the same architect had designed them both.

Her office was the penthouse suite. The waiting room was small but posh, paneled in high-polished walnut; a burnished chesterfield, flanked by two tray tables, rested against the wall. One table held fresh-cut flowers; the other was topped with local weekly newspapers featuring Valley notables on the front pages, and several issues of *Architectural Digest*. A fortysomething secretary told Decker to have a seat, that Jeanine would be right there. "Right there" turned out to be a half hour later. But if Decker had been a single guy, he would have felt it was worth the wait.

Because the woman was very, very nice.

A lovely face with an excellent figure. Shoulder-length blond hair that shimmered and swayed as she walked. Wide-set aqua eyes—an unnatural shade, probably enhanced by contact lenses. An oval face, high-set cheekbones, and lips coated with something that made them look wet and sexy. Statuesque—around five eight with shapely legs. She might be—or have been—a dancer. Tapered ankles and slender feet. Pale, flawless skin, pale hands. She was dressed modestly in a black double-breasted skirt suit, a bright, almost garish, Versace scarf draped around her neck.

Her eyes hooked into his, hands delicately wrapping around his fingers. She sighed heavily. "Would you think I was too terrible if I asked you to come back in an hour?"

Decker broke physical contact. "Not at all. Something come up?"

"Something *always* comes up, doesn't it?" She looked away, her face troubled ever so slightly. "You're a love. I'll see you in an hour then."

A love? Decker thought.

"Certainly," Decker said.

Without another word, she turned and walked away . . . very slowly . . . hips sashaying with a beat.

Decker went back to the car, aware that he had become hot . . . confused.

Who was *that woman?*
What did that matter?

An hour to kill. Might as well go back to work.

Easier to sustain bodily injuries than to deal with ex-wives. Having done both, Decker knew this to be true.

Five messages from Jan.

He made himself comfortable at his desk, stared at the phone. Grimacing, he punched in the numbers, wincing at each ring. When he heard his daughter's voice, he breathed instant relief. She was cool to him. As to be expected. But he didn't care. Too steeped in gratitude.

"I was actually returning your mother's calls."

"She's not home."

"Tell her I called. Tell her I'm swamped and I'll try to get back to her tomorrow. So she can stop calling the station house—"

"How many times did she call?"

"Five."

"I'll speak to her—"

"Don't get in the middle, Cynthia. You don't need any more grief."

A pause over the line. "I started the whole thing."

"I appreciate your help, but please don't take sides. It will make both our lives more difficult." Decker turned quiet. "Are you mad at me?"

"I love you very much, Dad."

Her voice remained chilly, but on the verge of a thaw. He said, "Cin, I want to apologize. You were very civil last night. I wasn't."

"You were angry."

"Yes."

"And hurt that I didn't talk it over with you first."

"A bit."

"Frustrated?"

"Definitely. I haven't changed my mind. I'm still against your decision. But you *are* twenty-four. If I can't talk you out of it, maybe we could have lunch next week. Perhaps you wouldn't mind a few pointers from a veteran. Tell me again when you're scheduled to start?"

"Right after the first of the year."

"Too bad baseball season is over," Decker said. "You're a stone's throw away from the Dodgers box office."

Cindy laughed over the line. "Daddy, I have a request."

"Shoot."

"I'd love to hear what you have to say. I respect you not only as a father but very much as a cop. But don't run interference for me, all right? Don't call up the Academy. Don't talk to my supervisors or my sergeants or my teachers or whomever and ask about me. I really thought hard about using Mom's maiden name because I didn't want people to know we're related. I'll have enough problems as it is. Everyone comparing me to you—"

"Whoa, this sounds serious."

"You're patronizing me. That's all right. Patronize all

you want. Just as long as you actually *honor* my request. Then we'll both be fine.''

Decker paused, realizing his little girl was in fact a young woman who needed and deserved independence and respect. The transition was excruciating.

"I'll do my best, Cynthia."

There was silence over the phone. Even with all the pain, it was still infinitely better than talking to Jan.

She said, ''So we're squared away on this?''

"I wouldn't say squared away. I'm not actively fighting you anymore."

"I'll call you later, Daddy. Take care of yourself."

"I love you, princess."

"Love you, too. Bye."

Abruptly, she hung up the phone. For a moment, Decker sat, receiver in hand, dial tone humming in his ear. Finally, he disconnected and turned on his computer and modem, hooking into the L.A. public libraries' data banks. One of the splurges from last year's tight budget. It had saved the squad room infinite hours of tedium. After logging in, presenting the passwords, he was offered a menu. A few minutes of searching and he found what he was looking for—back issues of the local West Valley throwaways.

Punching up the name Jeanine Garrison. Searching for the information. Most of the data came from society columns and articles relating to charity events. Some of the older issues—ten years prior—showed pictures of the slain parents, Ray and Linda Garrison. A handsome couple. Linda had been blond and beautiful. Kindly eyes. A warm mouth. Young-looking. From the pictures, Decker could hardly believe she had been forty-three at that time. Looked more like twenty-three. Ray had shown his age even then. Salt-and-pepper hair, craggy complexion. Ruggedly handsome. Type of father a girl would have adored.

Decker continued to scan the columns.

Jeanine was first mentioned on her own at her "coming out" party. A debutante ball. Decker could hardly believe they still did things like that, especially in Los Angeles. But there she was in her full glory. A stunning eighteen-year-old in a gown that was anything but virginal. A long, form-fitting job with a seductive center slit to mid-thigh and a plunging neckline. It plunged into plenty of womanly pulchritude.

Decker took off his glasses, rubbed his eyes. For some reason, he found reading a monitor more taxing than a newspaper. Maybe it was the stiff position. He put on his glasses, continued to glean through the electronic print. Jeanine and her parents hosting a charity fete for Children's Services. Jeanine and her father organizing a dinner for a local old-age home.

Increasingly, the articles had more of Jeanine and less of her parents. Jeanine and her charity parties. Lots of them and all for good community causes. Celebrity-studded. Not A-list people, mostly retired character actors—has-beens hoping for a resurrection. But they had turned out. Not only stars, but Strapp and the mayor. Jeanine sandwiched between the two, giving the photographer a mouth full of ivories.

Again, Decker rubbed his eyes, checked his watch.

A full hour had passed. Now he was late for the appointment.

What the hey. He'd just tell her that something came up.

Because something always does come up.

David Garrison opened the door wearing a bathrobe, pajama bottoms, and slippers, leaving Webster to wonder if this was his normal dress or if he had actually woken the man up at three in the afternoon. The detective presented his badge, and a pair of anxious hazel eyes scanned the ID as well as the cop. Red-rimmed eyes. Garrison was pale and thin and sported a day's growth of beard. His head held a blond thicket of unkempt oily tresses and dark shadows sat under sunken orbs. Musta been one hell of a party last night.

"May I come in?" Webster asked. "Unless you'd prefer to talk out here."

The door opened and Webster went inside. Garrison had yet to speak.

An incredible view. Two walls of glass framing canyons as well as the Valley skyline. The place had been done up as sleek as a leopard, everything cold and unyielding and achromatic. A scheme of gray, white, and black. Marble floors. Stark white walls holding abstract art. Black leather sofas devoid of adornment. Glass tables. A stereo system resting in ebony bookshelves. Metal blinds instead of wooden shutters or cloth curtains. The only hint of color came from the outdoor vistas.

"Did I wake you, sir?" Webster asked, politely.

Garrison shook his head. "Wish it were so. And call me Dave. Sir is . . . was . . . exclusively reserved for my father."

"All right." Webster strolled over to the stereo, regarded the CDs. Classical works. Good pieces and good recording editions. His eyes swept over the titles. "This is interesting."

"My little hobby." Garrison's voice was bored.

Webster said, "I specifically meant this '62 Bernstein release of Sibelius's *The Oceanides.* I have the vinyl. When did they master it for CD?"

A pause. Garrison said, "It's a new edition."

"Obviously." Webster smiled. "Been doing a lot of overtime. I know where I'm going as soon as my working hours are up. Can I take a seat?"

Garrison pointed to the couch. "Get you something to drink?"

"No, thank you."

"Mind if I take something?"

Webster said, "It's your house, Mr. Garrison. You're doin' me the favor."

"Well put." Garrison walked over to a mirrored wet bar. He took out a cut-crystal tumbler. "Would you like to hear the CD?"

"You put it on, reckon I won't object."

"So I reckon I'll put it on." He poured himself a double shot of Johnnie Walker Blue straight up. "You work that Southern Boy shit very effectively. It must bring you an ample supply of pussy."

Webster grinned. "Ah suppose it did when ah was single."

The young man took a swig, then removed the cassette from the disc player and slipped in the Sibelius CD. "And now you're a faithful married man as well as a hard-working, dedicated cop."

"Correct."

Garrison turned on the receiver. Instantly, the room filled with pastoral beauty. What Webster wanted to do was close his eyes and be swept away. Instead, he took out his note-pad, waited for Garrison to finish his booze and sit down. After polishing off the Scotch, the young man refilled his glass and sat in a slouch leather chair. His bathrobe had fallen open, revealing a thin upper torso tufted with fine chest hair. He sat with his legs spread apart, revealing the partially opened fly of his pajama bottoms.

The man weren't wearin' underpants.

Webster said, "I'm sorry for your loss. Mr. Garrison."

David looked directly at him. "Don't feel too bad on my account."

Webster digested his response. "Mind if I ask you a couple of questions?"

"Phrasing it as if I have a choice." He smiled. "Do I?"

"Just a couple of questions, sir."

"Whatever is your wish, *suh*."

Webster smiled. "You're a toughie."

"Ply me with enough alcohol and I'm putty." Garrison winked, laughed. "Going through a little panic, suh? Don't worry. You're not my type." He leaned in close. "I've done lots of experimenting, but alas, I am a dull, dull boy. Much to my Bohemian nature's dismay, I really do prefer girls. Pity. Except for this one minor flaw, I might have made a most excellent queer."

He finished off his booze, got up, and poured himself another shot. "In reality, I'm just a boring, bisexual drunk-ard."

"Do you work?" Webster asked.

Garrison swallowed liquor. "Set design. I just finished

Tosca at the Dorothy Chandler. Berticelli's conducting if you're interested.''

"I don't know the man."

"A . . . limited man with a limited vision. I created a magnificent set—larger than life, full of pomp and special effects. Extremely garish and very Disney. Tailor-made for the vapid L.A. audience."

Another gulp.

"I also work for the movies. But less so each year since many of the sets are now done with computer graphics. Not to fret, though. I've just landed a very lucrative contract with a movie F/X computer company."

He gave Webster a loopy smile.

"Garrison is my name, graphics is my game."

"You do well for yourself, sir?"

"I do *exceedingly* well since my parents died."

A hesitation. Then Webster asked, "How much are you worth now?"

"Nosy little critter, aren't you?" Garrison allowed himself another finger's worth of booze. "I'm not worth nearly as much as my sister. But at least I wasn't disinherited. That came as a shock to me. I thought Dad had given me the boot. Mom must have talked him into something right before they . . .''

He looked down at his drink.

"I really don't know the exact amount. Something in the low seven-figure range, I suspect. Jeanine has all the details. She is to dole out my money to me at certain intervals marked by the passage of time. She's my . . . *trustee*. Which I suppose designates me as the *trustor*. Which would be comical if it wasn't so ludicrous."

"You don't trust your sister?"

"In a word, no." Garrison held a finger in the air. "But even if Jeanine embezzles everything, well then, I suppose I'm no worse off than I was two years ago. When I was in jail and disinherited. Ah! Here it is! My favorite passage of the work! Those harmonies!"

Webster listened to the music for a moment, trying des-

perately not to be distracted with the siren's call.
"Lovely."

"It's sublime, Detective."

"Yes, it is."

"But you have work to do."

"Yes, I do." Sourly, Webster returned to his case notes.
"Why did you think your father disinherited you?"

"My cocaine use. He really didn't like drugs." He held
up his glass. "This doesn't count, of course."

Garrison sipped Scotch.

"He must have been impressed with my rehab . . . with
my steady employment this last year. I guess it boils down
to the fact that I didn't need him anymore. Once his money
ceased to be a bargaining chip, I was allowed my piece of
the rock. Cheers!"

He finished off the fourth round. Then he sat down.

"My sister . . ."

His smile was wicked.

"My sister, on the other hand, was completely indulged,
utterly spoiled because (a) she was a beautiful, beautiful
little girl and (b) as a child, she was of mediocre mind and
wholly without talent. Jeanine is now twenty-eight years
old. She has never held a paying job, has never worked a
day in her life. She has lived neither with responsibility nor
with the consequences of her behavior. I, on the other hand,
was not permitted such luxury because I was precocious, I
was intelligent, I was *gifted*. There it is. My family saga in
its pure, unadulterated form. Have you any more questions
for me, suh?"

Webster waited a moment. "Were you on speaking terms
with your parents when they died?"

"Yes."

"Visit them often?"

"No. But we were on speaking terms. Occasionally, I
played the dutiful son and called my mother." He paused
a moment, swallowed hard. "I . . . liked my mother."

Garrison looked away, spoke softly.

"No one . . . including my old man whom I disliked . . .
deserves to *die* like that! Slaughtered like a trophy of some

demented man's hunt. It is an abomination! The man who did it should be destroyed ... completely ... thoroughly ... without remorse.''

Garrison marched back to his bar. With shaking hands, he poured himself another drink. And that's when Webster realized how much Garrison had been hurting. The drinking and the slovenliness, his way of dealing with grief. Gently, he said, "Been gettin' outta bed lately, David?"

"What?"

Webster said, "You've been showin' up to work at all?"

Garrison spun around, drink in hand. "I *told* you I just finished a set."

"Was that before or after what happened at Estelle's?"

Garrison looked down. "I've got a gig lined up in a week. Not to worry, Detective." He gulped down a shot. "I'll pull myself together."

"Your parents were founding members of Greenvale Country Club, correct?"

He stared at Webster. "This is leading somewhere, I hope."

"Am I correct? They were founding members?"

"You are correct, suh!"

"In your teenage years, you spent some time at the club?"

"I despised the club. And everyone in it."

Webster paused. "Didn't hang out there much then?"

"I believe I used the word *despised,* Detective."

"So you never visited the club as an adult ... maybe to meet your parents for dinner there or something like that?"

"Never." Garrison hesitated. "You're asking about Greenvale for a reason. Must have something to do with what ... what happened at Estelle's. Does it?"

"The murderer, Harlan Manz ..."

"Yes?"

"He worked at Greenvale before going to Estelle's."

There was a moment of silence. Garrison's face was unreadable. "What does that mean?"

"We're not sure it means anything," Webster said. "Just trying to get a fix on Manz, hoping to figure out why he busted loose. Thought maybe you might have spoken to him at Greenvale . . . could give us a clue about what made him tick.''

"When did he work at the club?"

" 'Bout two years ago.''

"No . . .'' Garrison shook his head. "No, suh, I wasn't around two years ago. I was working off a drug sentence at County. I assume you're aware of that?''

Webster nodded, hoping his embarrassment wasn't showing. Stupid of him not to commit the dates to memory.

Garrison sat down. "This murderer . . . Harlan Manz . . . he had worked at Estelle's, right?''

"Yes.''

"He had been at Greenvale, then he went to Estelle's. My parents were members of Greenvale and they often went to Estelle's.'' His face went white. "Was this monster *stalking* them?''

"I have no evidence—''

"Then *why* are you implying a connection?''

"If I am, I don't mean to do that. I told you, we're just trying to figure why Manz freaked. You seem like a real perceptive fellow. I was hoping that maybe you knew him from Greenvale . . . could lay a little insight on him.''

"I've never met the man in my life. You doubt me? Give me a lie detector test.''

Webster chuckled. "That won't be necessary. You're not a suspect.''

Not yet.

Because a sudden seven-figure inheritance really did sound like a right fine motivation for a hit.

Garrison said, "What did this Manz do at the club?''

"Tended bar—''

"Ah, so I can see why you thought . . .'' Garrison lifted his tumbler of booze and laughed. "No, in my past, I was a coke fiend. I assure you my friendship with Mr. Scotch is of a quite recent nature.'' He appeared pensive. "My father drank . . . he wasn't a drunk, but he drank. It is conceivable that he ran into this Manz at the club. You might want to ask my sister.''

"Has she spent some time at Greenvale in recent years?"

"She plays tennis there just about every afternoon. She's a fanatical player, though she isn't very good. She's clumsy actually. Although you'd never believe it to look at her. Because she truly is gorgeous."

"Harlan Manz also taught tennis at Greenvale."

Garrison's eyes widened. He gave off an overly loud laugh. "Perchance is someone asking questions of my sister?"

"Someone is talking to her, yes." Webster looked up from his notes. "Think she might have met Harlan?"

"Detective, if Manz taught at Greenvale, Jeanine not only knew him, but she slept with him."

Webster waited a beat. "You're pretty sure about that?"

Garrison raised his glass and grinned. "To paraphrase your boyhood Suthen lingo: Suh, ah gar-run-*tee*!"

❧13

With a wave of her hand, she invited Decker into her personal office. Fabulous view, art on the walls, handsome furniture, and a big desk. A state-of-the-art computer, but nothing on the screen other than the screen saver, a whirl of geometric shapes gliding across the monitor. She took a seat behind her desk, giving no explanation for her delay.

"Thank you for seeing me," Decker said.

She spoke in a moderated voice. "Why'd you come here? Out of courtesy? Or was it guilt?"

"Guilt?"

"Crime in the city has become rampant. The police have completely lost control. How else could you explain what went on in that place?"

Decker waited. Jeanine made a pair of fists, knuckles whitening. But her eyes remained steady. "How can I help you?"

Decker met her gaze. "I'm very sorry for your loss, Ms. Garrison. I hope my questions won't be too intrusive or too painful."

"But perhaps they'll be both."

Decker reasssessed the situation. Her demeanor had abruptly changed since their first encounter, leaving him to wonder if she had taken legal advice in his absence. Best to keep it brief. "Certain inconsistencies have come out during our investigation of the tragedy at Estelle's—"

"Inconsistencies?"

"Yes, ma'am."

Jeanine's gaze was still on him, eyes never wavering. "Go on."

Decker made a conscious effort not to squirm. "We're interviewing a number of people. Your parents belonged to Greenvale Country Club, correct?"

Jeanine waited a beat, lips slightly parted. "Why are you asking me this?"

"Pardon?"

"Why are you asking questions about my parents? Why are you dragging them into your investigation?"

A long pause. With a planned casual manner, Decker leaned back in the chair. "It's a simple question, ma'am. We both know the answer is yes."

"So why are you asking me the question if you know the answer?"

"Do you know how long they've been members?"

"I suppose you know the answer to that one as well."

"I was under the impression they were founding members . . . which means they've been there for fifteen years."

"You can count."

"You spend some time there growing up, ma'am?"

"How do you quantify time?"

"Did you spend weekends there, for example?"

"Sometimes."

"Doing what?"

"I don't see how that's your business, either."

Decker tapped his pen against his notebook, put on edge by her sexuality and sudden hostility. He had come for simple information. For some reason, she was perceiving it as an interrogation. "Do you spend time at the club now, Ms. Garrison? I know you have privileges through your father's lifetime membership."

Jeanine observed Decker with appraising eyes. "Are you hiding some kind of crucial information from me?"

Again, under her scrutiny, Decker found it was hard to appear relaxed. He realized he had tensed up, been sitting with erect posture. He relaxed his shoulders, loosened his spine. "I wish I were holding back. Unfortunately, I'm not."

"Then is there a point to all of this?"

Decker rolled his tongue in his cheek. "Is this a bad time for you to talk to me, Ms. Garrison? If it is, I could come back another day."

She stared at him. "I resent these questions. Actually, not the questions but the subterfuge."

"Pardon?"

"You're ostensibly here to ask questions. But in fact, you're shifting the blame from the LAPD to the victims. Like it was somehow their fault for being in the restaurant."

"Ms. Garrison, I'm confused—"

"Typical of LAPD philosophy," she said, dismissively. "My parents were mercilessly . . . *slaughtered* in a crime-riddled city . . . and somehow it's my fault. Or Greenvale Country Club's fault. You know what? Do me a favor. Stop attending funerals where you don't belong. Like I don't have enough grief in my life without the police harassing me."

Decker let her words hang in the air. Yes, her parents were slaughtered. But he was on *her* side. Why was she drawing lines in the sand? Could be she, like some of the others, had known Harlan and felt guilty about it.

Then he thought about the Garrisons. Marge had said they were worth beaucoup bucks. Inheritance—pause for thought.

He started to ad-lib. "I hear you're a tennis player. A pretty good one at that."

Jeanine was quiet. She closed her eyes and opened them, the blue jewels homing in on Decker's face. "Where'd you hear that?"

He stepped over her inquiry. "How long have you played?"

"A long time."

"Do you prefer sod or clay?"

"I only play on clay."

"Yeah, sod leaves too much to chance, not enough to skill."

"Are you trying to establish rapport with me, Lieutenant?"

Decker gave her a boyish grin. "Probably."

Jeanine looked downward, took out a tissue and dabbed tearless eyes. "Do you play tennis, Lieutenant?"

"Not too much anymore. I'm getting too old. You need to be in shape."

Jeanine gave him a once-over, let her aqua-blue eyes linger on his chest, then his face. "You're big . . . well-built. Of course, if you lost ten pounds, you'd probably be lighter on your feet."

"I'm sure you're right."

"Ah, well, we all battle the bulge."

An attempt to extract a compliment? Because the woman was as thin as lamination. Decker smiled. "Some more than others."

Jeanine smiled back. A sexy smile with healthy teeth . . . just like the newspaper photographs he had pulled up. It was getting hot in her office. Still looking at him, she said, "Do you ever play charity games?"

"Charity games?"

"Play sports to raise money for charity. Specifically, tennis."

"I'm not good enough."

"How about being on an LAPD team? Does the LAPD even have a *tennis* team?"

"I believe we do."

"We should set something up . . . for charity. How about police versus the fire department? Or West Valley LAPD versus West Valley LAFD? Proceeds can go to . . . to building a community center. Or revamping the one we have."

"Sounds great."

"I could get you good press coverage. Maybe even show it on cable TV. I've got pull. It's what I'm known for."

Decker said, "I'm a little dense today. What exactly do you do?"

Jeanine became impatient, but not hostile. "I organize and host charity events. It used to be parties. But now I concentrate on tennis matches. Brings in the right people."

"The right people?"

Jeanine smiled. "Rich people."

"Ah—"

"Those who can afford to give money. Tennis lovers seem to be of a higher socioeconomic bracket. Hence, more money. And rightly or wrongly, that's the bottom line."

Decker paused. "And you . . . take a percentage of the gross for your services?"

"Oh, no!" Jeanine was offended. "Every ounce of profit goes to the charity. I take nothing other than the costs of rental or catering or . . . whatever. It's called philanthropy—a lost art."

She sighed.

"My father was very philanthropic. But he lacked time to put his good thoughts into deeds. That's where I came in. I made it *happen!*"

"But your father finances—"

"Through his charitable foundation, which pays the bills, pays the payroll including my salary. Which is generous. My dad was a very generous . . ."

Again, she lowered her head, patted at her eyes with a tissue. "I'm sorry . . ."

"Ms. Garrison, I'm sorry to be opening up wounds—"

"I know. You're doing your job." She looked up. "You were the one on TV. The one who said the inside of Estelle's was your worst nightmare." She looked solemn. "That was so insightful."

"Thank you."

Still grave, Jeanine said, "So . . . maybe we should set something up? Show the world that we survivors of that terrible tragedy hold no animosity toward the LAPD?"

Decker paused. From the grieving daughter to the society hostess in five minutes. He said, "Let me talk to my captain."

"I'll call him if you'd like."

"Sure. I'll give you his number in a min—"

"Oh, I have his numbers." She pointed to her electronic Rolodex. "I've been doing this for a while. I have lots of contacts."

Decker took in her words, wondering how much of it was bravado. Then he remembered the newspaper picture with Jeanine standing between Strapp and the mayor. Casually, he asked, "How long did you take lessons at Greenvale?"

"Years," Jeanine answered. "I had some talent, but not enough. In the world of professional tennis, you learn your limitations quickly. Instead of moping, I directed my energies into fund-raising. And in that, my friend, I am a star. Do you know that just last month our culture committee's celebrity-studded party in our library raised over thirty thousand dollars for the new West Valley Art Museum?"

"Really?"

"Yes. I believe your captain was there. Because the mayor was there. And where there are mayors, there are police officials."

Decker made a mental note to watch his words. Because this one was not only sexy but *sly*. Seductive was the word. Ms. Femme Fatale wrapped in a cloak of charity.

"Have you been there yet? To the museum? We're strong on the California pleinairists. We've opened with two special exhibits right now. Grandville Redmond and Edgar Payne. Both painters are extraordinary."

"Have to get over there."

Jeanine glanced at Decker's hand, at his wedding ring. It didn't seem to deter her. "If you'd like, I'll be happy to give you a guided tour."

Decker smiled. "Thank you, but—"

"How about . . ." Jeanine pulled out her calendar. "I can do it tomorrow. Twelve or oneish?"

Again, Decker smiled. "I'm booked this week."

"I'm sure I can call your captain and tell him—"

"No, Ms. Garrison, that's quite all right. I'm old-fashioned. City pays me to work, I work."

"Very refreshing." Again the sexy smile. "How about after work? I could arrange a private tour after the museum's closed."

"Thank you, but my family likes me home for dinner."

"How about after dinner?" Jeanine's smile turned to a

grin. "You can bring your wife and kids if you'd like. I'm assuming you have children. Most married men do."

She was toying with him, *vamping* him. And getting the upper hand. He looked directly into her eyes. "Thank you for the invitation. I'll take you up on it sometime."

"Do that."

"Who'd you take tennis lessons from, Ms. Garrison? Someone at Greenvale?"

Jeanine stared at him, slowly put the calendar away. Her face had suddenly turned gelid and unforgiving. "You can call me Jeanine. Why are you so interested in my tennis years?"

Decker shrugged, still holding her eye. "Just wondering if anyone famous ever taught at the club."

"Famous?" Jeanine's tone was condescending. "Oh, yes, at one time, I learned with Martina and Jimmy and Chris and John and—"

"I get the point." Decker was quiet. She wasn't giving him an inch to work with. "I was just wondering . . . if anyone remotely known might have ever taught there . . . spurred your interest in the game." He stood. "Not important. Sorry to bother you. And I'll try to get to the museum. Thanks for the tip."

Jeanine's eyes turned distant. "You know who *used* to play at Greenvale?"

"Who?" asked Decker, still standing.

"Wade Anthony."

Decker sat back down, trying to conjure up an image of a face. Nothing. "Don't know him."

"I know," Jeanine said softly. "And that's too bad. Once, he was a rising star. He was . . . in his teens when he played at Greenvale. Sixteen to be exact. I was fourteen. I had a mad, mad crush on him."

She smiled sadly.

"Me and all the other teenyboppers. He was simply gorgeous. Outrageous as well. He had sex with at least two of my friends. Rumor had it that he had sex with some of their mothers as well."

"Sounds like a tennis player."

"Yes, he was strictly *bad boy*. My father ordered me to stay clear of him. Of course, I did the opposite. I watched him play almost every day. He was wonderful to watch."

She was quiet. Decker waited. When she didn't continue, he prodded further. "What happened to him?"

"Though he was a master tennis player, he was still a sixteen-year-old. He got drunk one night. Took out Daddy's Ferrari and smashed up the car with him inside. He's now confined to a wheelchair."

Decker paused. "That's very sad."

"It was more than sad, it was terrible. I was heartbroken. He stopped coming to the club. Just dropped out of sight."

She faced him.

"I hadn't thought about him in years. Then about a year ago, I saw an article on him in the sports pages of the *Times*. Not the front of course, page two or three."

"Really? What's he doing?"

"Apparently he's a top-seeded player in *wheelchair* tennis."

"Wheelchair tennis?"

Jeanine nodded. "Played on a regulation-size court. Only difference is the players in the chairs get two bounces instead of one. Fascinating to see how fast they can move."

Her mood had suddenly darkened. Decker knew he was treading dangerous ground. "What'd they say about him in the article?"

"It was a write-up on some charity games in New York—a major fund-raiser for the physically challenged. Five hundred fifty a ticket. Do you know who his partner was? *Ivan Lendl*."

"That's incredible!"

"It brought back a flood of memories, Lieutenant. I'm glad he's doing well."

Decker said, "I don't mean to sound thick-headed but . . . did Lendl play in a wheelchair?"

"No." Jeanine raised her eyes. "It was Wade and Lendl against John McEnroe and some other paraplegic. It drew a huge crowd." She stared into space. "Wade and Ivan won. They showed a picture of them . . . of him. He still looks good . . . great to be exact!''

Decker looked at her. ''Ever think of asking him to play for one of your charities?''

A wistful smile. Jeanine said, ''I think we're a little small-time for him. I had tried to convince Dad to go out for better, more major causes—things like AIDS—but Dad was *so* conservative.''

''A terrible tragedy that took your parents' lives,'' Decker said. ''Lots of victims including yourself. Maybe you could host a game for the victims of the shooting.''

Jeanine opened and closed her mouth. ''I . . . I don't know. I hadn't thought about it.'' Her sculptured face took on an animated glow. Again, she threw open her calendar. ''That is a *marvelous* idea. I could arrange something magnificent, something that would rival the Open.''

Dream on. He said, ''Maybe you could hold the event at Greenvale.''

''Another good idea.'' Jeanine's body language was suddenly exuberant. ''Listen, I'm so sorry I jumped down your throat. It's just this thing with my parents . . . it's thrown me for a loop.''

''Of course.''

''Did . . . did you have any other questions you needed to ask me?''

He had lots of questions to ask her. Originally, he had wanted to know if she or the family had known Harlan Manz, if she or the family had ever taken lessons from him, could have offended him in any way. But her odd behavior had sent his antennae quivering overtime.

Be honest, Deck. She quivered other things as well.

Brushing that aside . . . which took some effort . . . he knew, as a professional, that she was acting strange. Her hostility, her flip attitude, her vamping, her summing up the Estelle's tragedy by calling it a ''*thing* with her parents,'' her evasive answers when it came to her past teachers, her strong passion for tennis, her sudden enthusiasm at the thought of hosting a big event tied to the deaths of her parents. Bizarre. Left Decker wondering if she had perhaps known Harlan in an intimate way.

Yet, he sensed he had gained some kind of rapport with her. He knew that implying any kind of relationship between this eerie but beautiful woman and a mass murderer would blow the trust to smithereens. He was reminded of what a psychologist friend had once told him about his field.

Good therapy is an art. Timing is everything.

Decker kept his manner professional but warm. "I do have a few questions, but they can wait until later."

Until he found out more about her.

Until he could calm himself down.

"Really, it's all right."

Decker stood. "Some other time. We'll be in contact."

"I certainly hope so."

Jeanine's smile was brilliant. "Nice to have met you."

"Same."

She offered him her hand. Gently, Decker shook it.

❧14

Some would call him obsessive. Decker referred to himself as thorough.

More digging. Trying to find some *personal* information. After an hour he found it—columns in the locals entitled "Milestones." A small sentence about a failed marriage two years ago. Brent Delaney. No picture. Decker backtracked, tried to find a wedding announcement. Indeed it existed, but not in the local throwaways, in the *L.A. Times*. Brent had dark hair, thick brows . . . handsome features. Slick. Striking resemblance to Harlan. Brent's occupation was listed as actor. His hobbies were car racing and tennis. Their marriage had lasted a total of seven months.

Then nothing. Still, Decker continued to search and search. For any little telltale hook that could formally tie her to Harlan Manz. He never did find the mother lode. But his prospecting wasn't a total bust.

Farrell Gaynor let go with a congested cough. The elder statesman of the five-person Homicide team had the floor and was making the most of it.

"The kids stand to inherit . . ." Another spasm. "Inherit a lot of money . . ."

He was now hacking dry. Decker pounded his back, said to Oliver, "Get the man a drink of water."

Oliver made a face. "I'm his personal valet?"

"For godsakes, Scott!" Marge stomped out of the room.

127

Oliver said, "I was going to go . . ."

"You okay, Farrell?" Decker asked.

"It's the season." He brought up mucus, spit it into a handkerchief.

"Christ, Farrell!" Oliver said in disgust.

"Quiet, or next time I'll aim it at you."

Marge came back with the water. Gaynor drank it greedily. He was in good health other than his allergies. Overweight, yes. Old, yes. In need of a lube job in the morning, yes. But considering where some of his peers lay, he was in *very* good health. His wife had knitted him a new cardigan—the hunter-green one he had on today. He liked it. Went with his gray slacks. He thanked Marge for the water, cleared his throat.

"You were saying . . ." Martinez prompted.

"What was I saying?"

"Garrison kids are gonna inherit . . ."

"Money," Gaynor said. "Now, they don't get their inheritance all at once. David gets about a third of his share now and the rest at thirty. Jeanine also gets a third now and the rest at thirty-two."

"About four years from now," Oliver said.

Marge said, "Does Jeanine work?"

"Not according to her brother," Webster stated.

"So as of right now, she has no income?"

"She arranges charity events," Decker said. "Said her father's foundation gave her a salary and expenses came out of profits."

"What kind of expenses was she talking about?" Oliver asked.

"The catering, the hall, the setup—I don't know the details." Decker looked to Farrell. "Maybe you could help me out on that."

"I could try."

Marge said, "So what happens to her now that her father is gone?"

"Her inheritance should keep her well afloat," Gaynor said. "Ray Garrison was worth ten to twelve million—"

Marge said, "How do people amass that much *money*?"

Oliver held out his hands. "Don't look at me."

Decker said, "The age for dispersal in the trust. Can that be changed? Or is the trust irrevocable?"

"In theory, it is irrevocable," Gaynor said. "But that doesn't mean much if one chooses to contest it."

"Is anyone contesting it?"

"Not so far."

"Who's the executor?" Oliver asked.

"Executor of the will?"

"No, of the trust."

Gaynor said, "There's no executor for the trust, only a trustee."

Oliver held his temper. "So who is the trustee, Farrell?"

"Jeanine Garrison on behalf of herself and her brother, David. I don't know how the money is divided. I don't even know if they inherit the entire estate. I couldn't push my mole that far without skirting the bounds of legality."

Webster said, "David seems to think his inheritance is something in the lower seven-figure range."

Oliver said, "Which means Jeanine gets something in the higher seven-figure range?"

Gaynor said, "If the estate was divided . . . let's say . . . sixty/forty. That means Jeanine would get around two million now, David would get a cool mil."

Marge said, "I call that rich."

Decker said, "Millionaires, to be sure. All the same, there are estate taxes, lots of hidden costs. Did Ray and Linda Garrison have any insurance?"

"Like a *second to die* policy?"

"Exactly."

"Nothing I could find."

"So she's going to have to fork out some cash to the IRS for death taxes. What is it now? Around sixty percent?"

"Something like that."

"She'll live well," Decker said. "But she isn't going to live like a princess."

"I ain't crying for her," Oliver said.

Martinez said, "What'd this guy do to earn all that money?"

"He was a corporate lawyer—his own firm. Seven partners. Seems to have invested wisely—real estate, stocks, bonds. Some risky stuff—futures, derivatives, commodities. Obviously, he came out on top."

"And son David was a druggie." Oliver smiled. "Another American tragedy, yawn yawn."

"Stop being so smug," Marge said.

"And why not?" Oliver grinned. "I may not have millions but my kids are earning their own keep." His grin turned malicious. "Hey, how's Cindy doing, Loo? Still forking out those tuition bills for her schooling?"

Decker's face went dark.

Instantly, Oliver knew he had hit a nerve. Maybe the guy was broke. Decker *seemed* well heeled, but tuition could stretch any wallet. "Hey, I'm just kidding. You've got a terrific kid. Smart, too. I'm threatened by her . . . by your whole family . . . especially by—"

"Oliver, shut up," Marge said.

The room went quiet. Webster broke it. "David Garrison is troubled. But he's nobody's fool. He's talented and bright."

Oliver said, "Then why did he do eighteen months in County?"

" 'Cause people screw up," Decker said.

Webster said, "From David's perspective, he got the short end of the deal. Because Jeanine was beautiful but *ordinary* in the brain department, nobody ever made demands on her. David, on the other hand, had lots of demands made on him. Mostly from his father. Probably wasn't strong enough to stand up to Papa directly so he did it in other ways."

He turned to Decker.

"You ask Jeanine if she knew Harlan Manz, Loo?"

Decker said, "I kept trying but she kept changing the subject. Clearly didn't want to talk about her tennis instructors at Greenvale."

Webster said, "David was sure that Jeanine not only

knew Harlan Manz, but had probably slept with him.'' He related everything David had told him.

"But he has no proof that Jeanine and Harlan knew each other,'' Oliver said.

"Jeanine knew him.'' Decker pulled out a newspaper photograph, gave it to Oliver. A snapshot of a charity tennis match with the proceeds going to New Christian Hospital. For the infirmary's diagnostic radiation division. It was a couples game—Jeanine Garrison and Harlan Manz alias Hart Mansfield against Sonia Eaton and Terrance Howell. The four of them, smiling in a frozen capsule of time.

Oliver passed the picture around, each one taking their turn, studying the photo in silence.

Finally, Decker said, "Now we know that Jeanine knew Harlan. How well?'' He shrugged.

Again, the room was quiet.

Decker said, "We've got a mass murder that produced excessive bullets for the number of empty magazines found. We've got a man who committed suicide by shooting at his head, but the gun was held at least two feet away from his temple. We've got Ray and Linda Garrison, probably among the first victims to be gunned down, riddled with entrance and exit wounds that defy logic. We know that Garrison's son has or had a drug problem, and daughter Jeanine has an office and secretaries and no visible means of support other than Dad. Now Gaynor tells us that they stand to inherit around twelve million bucks. You want to tell me what this smells like?''

Oliver said, "A perfume called Menendez.''

Webster said, "Except brother don't like sister.''

Marge said, "That's what David told you. Maybe that's what he *wants* you to think.''

Martinez asked Decker, "Does sister like brother?''

"Never got that far. I told you, Jeanine's sly. Didn't talk about her instructors at the club, never mentioned Harlan Manz by name. The woman is also a roller coaster of emotions. First time I met her, she was all sweetness and light— overly touchy-feely. You know . . . holding my hand, looking me straight in the eye. Like some inspirational guru. She asked me if I'd return later in the day because something had come up. I said sure. I came back and suddenly she was cautious . . . wary. Gave me the feeling that she'd consulted an attorney in my absence. Asked what to say to a police lieutenant.''

"Maybe she did call up counsel," Marge said.

Oliver raised his brow. "You call your lawyer when you've got something to hide?"

"I'm not saying she did," Decker clarified. "Just that the shift in attitude was strange. *She's* strange. Referred to the murder as 'this thing with my parents.' "

"Can't arrest someone for filial indifference, Pete," Marge said.

Webster said, "Didn't one of the French existentialists write a book along those lines? The one where they had him arrested and tried for murder because he didn't cry at his mother's funeral?"

The group stared at him.

Gaynor said, "Maybe the character was in shock. You know people have different reactions to grief."

"That wasn't the point of the book, Farrell—"

"Can we get back to the case?" Oliver interrupted.

Martinez said, "Does this woman look as good in life as she does in the picture?"

Marge said, "You know we've completely ignored Wendy Culligan. Harlen actually went *out* with her."

"Who's Wendy Culligan?" Farrell asked.

"Real estate agent." Oliver went through his and Marge's interview with Brenda Miller, leaving out the dinner date he made with the veep. Marge had left it out as well.

"But Culligan isn't dead," Webster said.

"No," Marge said. "But maybe Harlan was trying to prove a point with her. 'This is what you drove me to!' That kind of thing."

"Was she seated near the Garrisons?" Decker asked.

"Other side of the room."

"The businessmen with her . . . were they shot in their seats?"

"Under the table."

"Garrisons were murdered in their seats. I'm assuming they didn't have time to duck."

"You're still leaning toward Jeanine and David?" Marge asked Decker.

"I'm not leaning toward anyone or anything because we still may have a random murder here. A simple case of a disgruntled employee looking for revenge."

Oliver said, "Don't know about you, but twelve million bucks makes me skeptical of the lone killer theory."

"Okay. Try out this hypothesis. Assume Estelle's was a hit gone bad. If we see Jeanine and David Garrison as setting up Estelle's as a murder for hire, then it would be nice to establish a *close* relationship between Jeanine Garrison and/or David Garrison and Harlan Manz."

Decker held up the newspaper photo.

"We need *concrete* evidence first. Something that ties Jeanine to Harlan in a personal way. I'll have a little talk with Sonia Eaton and Terrance Howell. See if they can tell me something."

"Say you establish a close relationship between Jeanine and Harlan," Marge said. "Then what?"

Decker smiled. "One step at a time."

Oliver waited until he was the only one left in Decker's office. Then he closed the door and sat down.

"I was out of line with the remark about college tuition. Cindy's a bright kid and I know you're proud of her. It's good that you're keeping her in school. More education, the better. My ex would have done anything to keep our boys in college. It just wasn't their thing."

"You've got good sons, Scott."

"Thanks." Oliver turned grave. "I did something dumb, Deck. I asked a woman out, someone I questioned in the case. Brenda Miller, the veep at Ashman/Reynard. Actually, she asked *me* out for dinner. Took me by surprise. But I did accept."

Decker looked at Oliver. "How'd you fall into that?"

Oliver sighed. "She was holding back information. She used dinner with me as an excuse to spill about Wendy Culligan dating Harlan. Once Brenda did talk, I guess I felt obligated to go through with my end of the bargain. Stupid. Anyway, you know how some women are. They don't get what they want, they can make trouble. I could cancel it.''

He paused.

''Or now that I told you, I could go ahead with it and pretend that I'm doing it for work. Maybe I'm better off just . . . going out—''

''Cancel it.''

Oliver was quiet. ''All right. Can I tell her I'll call her after the case is resolved?''

Decker exhaled. ''She seem like the vindictive type?''

''Who can predict?''

Decker exhaled again. ''Yeah, go ahead. Tell her you'll call her after . . . do you even want to call her up after everything's resolved?''

Oliver turned rosy. ''Yeah, I'd like to see her. She's not beautiful like Jeanine Garrison. But she's lively. Probably be an animal in bed.''

Decker said, ''Watch yourself, Scotty.''

''I'll be more careful.''

''Marge know what you did?''

''Yeah, she was right there when it happened.''

No one spoke.

Decker chuckled. ''She didn't say a word to me. She's a good partner.''

''Yes, she is.''

Decker stood and so did Oliver. He placed his hand on Scott's shoulder, then slapped his cheek. ''Keep it in your pants, guy.''

''Such simple advice. So hard to follow.'' Oliver smiled. ''Thanks.''

''Your shoe's untied,'' Decker said. ''Don't trip.''

As Oliver bent down to reknot the laces, pocket change tumbled from his pants pockets.

Decker retrieved the silver, handed the metal to Oliver. ''Your meter money, Scotty.''

''More like total worth.'' Oliver counted the coins. ''At least I know I'm safe. My sons ain't gonna pop me for a haul of seventy-three cents.''

ꙮ15

It was after ten, but Rina was still up. More than up. She was working, had spread junk all over the dining-room table—pens, pencils, ledgers, papers, receipts. Gnawing on the back of a pencil, staring down at columns and rows of numbers. She did look up when Decker kissed her, gave him a peck on the cheek. But then she returned her attention to her books.

"Dinner's in the oven."

Distant. Preoccupied.

Well, that was some hell of a greeting. Decker said, "We're doing self-service tonight?"

Rina stopped what she was doing, her expression surprised. She dropped the pencil on the tabletop. "Would you like me to serve you, Peter?"

"Not if you put it *that* way."

Neglected, Decker stormed into the kitchen, threw open the oven door, then pulled out the warming plate, burning his hands in the process. He dropped the plate on the floor. It crashed into bits, spewing around food and pieces of pottery.

"Shit!" he screamed. Ran to the tap and threw his hands under a blast of cold water. "Shit, shit, shit!"

Rina walked in. "I'll get you some ice—"

"I can *manage,* thank you."

Rina said nothing, got out the ice tray and tapped it on the counter. She wrapped the loose cubes in a towel, then

135

cleaned up the floor. Prepared another plate with leftovers from the refrigerator, and placed it in the microwave.

Decker turned off the tap. "I don't expect the red carpet treatment . . . which is good, because I don't get it. But you could actually seem glad to see me."

"I am glad to see you."

"If that was your being glad, I'd hate to see you when you're angry."

"Here's your ice."

Decker stared at his wife, then took the ice bag. "Thank you."

"You're welcome." Rina opened the cutlery drawer, retrieved a knife and fork. But Decker snatched the implements away. "Don't bother. I can do it—"

"Peter, if you want to make an issue of this, you can do it by yourself, all right?"

Rina left the kitchen, but Decker dogged her heels. "Is it too much to expect a little TLC?"

Rina studied her husband. "It looks like you've had a hard day."

"Don't be shrinky on me."

She stood on her tiptoes, brushed her lips against his. "Go back into the kitchen and we'll try it again, all right?" He didn't move. She gave his rear a pat. "Go on. I'll be there in a moment."

"Fine." He stomped off into the kitchen. Rina heard soft laughter and pivoted around. Sammy shaking his head. Rina placed her finger on her lips. "He'll hear you, Shmueli—"

"Is he being a butt—"

"Don't talk that way."

"Okay, is he being a jer—"

"I get the point, Shmuel. Please. You'll make it worse."

"Why don't you have that kind of patience with *me*?"

"Has this date been codified as 'pick on Rina day'?"

Shmuel went over to his mother and kissed her cheek. "I'll go in with you . . . deflect the whole situation."

Rina kissed him back. "Actually, that's a good idea." She looked at him sternly. "Just behave yourself."

They came into the kitchen together. Sammy appeared casual. "Hey, Dad. Nice to see you." He kissed his stepfather's forehead. "How was your day?"

Decker regarded his son, stared at his wife. "What'd you do? Bring in the reinforcements?"

Rina smiled brightly. "How's your hand, *dear*?"

"Hurts."

"What happened?" Sammy asked.

"I burned it . . . being a jerk."

The microwave beeped. Rina took Decker's dinner out and set it before him.

"Thank you," Decker muttered.

"You're welcome." She sat down. So did Sam. Both of them staring at Decker, watching him eat. He felt as if he were undergoing a taste test. Finally, he asked, "Where's Jake?"

"Over at a friend's," Sammy said. "I'll pick him up in a few minutes."

Rina said, "It's wonderful now that he can drive. So liberating not to have to schlepp the baby everywhere. To have backup—"

"Because I'm never home, right?" Decker said.

"Poor, poor, Peter. Overworked and underappreciated."

"You mock but it's true." Decker looked up from his dish. "What am I eating?"

"Lamb curry on basmati rice. Do you like it?"

"It is absolutely delicious!"

"Would you like more?"

"Definitely."

Sammy said, "I think he was just malnourished, Eema. His color looks better."

"I believe you're right."

"Stop talking about me in the third person," Decker grumped.

Sam said, "I think you can take it from here. The code red has been averted."

"Go ahead. Have fun at my expense."

Sammy kissed his parents. "I'm going now. Can we stop off at Berger's and get some dessert, Eema?"

"It's after ten, Shmueli."

"No school tomorrow morning. Teachers' curriculum conferences. We can sleep in. C'mon. Everyone's gonna be there. We'll be home before midnight, I promise."

"Don't you guys ever have school?" Decker asked. "I should be paying tuition per diem."

"Don't blame me," Sam turned to his mother. "Please?"

She turned to Decker "Eleven-thirty?"

"I think that's fair."

Sam grinned. "Thanks." A shake of his car keys and he was gone. The kitchen became silent. Decker continued to wolf down his dinner.

"You're quite the gourmet."

"Curry's wonderful. The more you cook it, the better it gets."

"I suppose you're wondering why I'm so testy."

"Actually, it's become quite the norm."

"Humorous, Rina. Just for that I won't tell you."

"Up to you." She stood up. "Would you like something to drink?"

"Beer would be great, thank you."

Rina brought out a bottle of Michelob, poured it into a glass . . . watching the head spill over the rim. Rina sat down, stared at her husband, smiling when he looked at her.

He said, "Am I keeping you from something?"

"Not at all."

Decker put down his fork. "Someone got the better of me today. Only person who's allowed to do that is you."

Rina said, "Who was the woman?"

Decker smiled tightly. "How do you know it's a woman?"

"A sixth sense."

Sixth sense? Decker wondered if she had smelled his pheromones.

"Who was she?"

"Not important." Decker pushed his food away. "This tragedy at Estelle's . . . horrible enough to think of it as some maniac's vision of going out with a bang. Unfortunately, I'm getting the feeling it's more complicated.''

Rina became attentive. "In what way?"

"Certain bullet angles contradict a lone killer theory. And certain individuals have a lot to gain from some of the untimely deaths. You know, murdering an individual for profit is vile enough. But to take out thirteen other innocent lives just to cover your tracks—it's truly monstrous . . . bestial.''

"You have evidence of this, Peter?"

Decker looked at his wife. She sounded upset. She *was* upset. Dunce that he was. Can't just lay the job on civilians. He tried to sound matter-of-fact. "Just a sixth sense. Kind of like yours, I suppose. I'm sorry I jumped on you. I'm feeling misogynistic today. First, I got an earful from Cindy last night. Then Jan's been calling me at the station house all day. Then, this woman . . . giving me a hard time . . . playing games—''

"Why would she do that?"

"Because she's probably *hiding* something." He picked up his fork and speared another piece of lamb, feeling his face turn red. Hopefully, Rina would assume it was from anger, not from embarrassing sexual feelings. "Anyway, none of this is your fault. Go back to work. What are you doing, by the way?"

"The yeshiva's books—"

"Oh, that's right. How's it going?"

"Frankly, it's a mess. Contributions from institutions I've never heard of. Stocks and limited partnerships in exchange for tuition. The yeshiva supposedly owns real estate holdings and has bank accounts in foreign countries. At least, on the books.''

"What's going on?"

"Well"—Rina scrunched up her brow—"I know the place went through quite a few in-house accountants, each one with a different agenda. Some of them obviously went in for creative bookkeeping . . . not that I found anything illegal.''

"But . . ."

Rina sighed. "The books were not as neatly kept as they should have been. Because the yeshiva used *kollel bochers* instead of professionals. You know, a man would do the books for the place in exchange for room and board for himself and his family. Then he'd leave after a few years and another one would take over. No consistency."

"Just like now."

"What do you mean?"

"Why is he asking *you* to do the books instead of a professional?"

"Yes, a professional is definitely going to have to be brought in. I think Rav Schulman knows the books are in terrible shape. He wants me to organize things *before* he hires a professional. Just to make sure everything's . . . kosher."

Rina stood up.

"Old-time Europeans are another ilk. Always bartering. In this case, stock instead of cash for tuition."

"Meanwhile, someone gets a free ride along with a nice write-off."

"My, *you're* feisty today. Why don't you give it a rest and go to bed?"

"Is that a nice thing to say?"

"Well, I'm grumpy now. *You* made me grumpy."

"So why don't *you* go to bed?" Decker brightened. "Better yet, I've got a great idea. Why don't we both go to bed?"

Rina eyed him. "The boys'll be home—"

"They'll be gone at least an hour." He raised his brow. "How about it?"

"We're both too cranky."

"So how about a little cranky love? 'Not so slow, not so fast, not this way, not that way, watch the back, my knees are locking, watch the hair—' "

Rina whacked him. "You're impossible!"

"I'm making fun of *myself*!" Decker laughed. "You don't have bad knees *or* a bad back."

Rina chided, "Listen, Lieutenant Geriatric, may I remind you that one of us is still a youthful thirty-four—"

"Low blow—"

"However, she is quickly aging from the stress of an overworked and very *moody* mate."

Decker said, "True. In spousal stress years, you've got me beaten by a mile. To bed? I promise I'll behave myself the rest of the night."

"Not good enough. You've put me in a bad mood."

"So I'll make it up to you."

"How? I don't see any flowers."

"How about if I tell you I love you?"

"Not good enough."

"Then how about if I do the dishes?"

"No dice—"

"And wake up for Hannah tomorrow—"

"Nope."

"I'll be home early tomorrow night."

"Don't feel like delaying gratification."

"Give you a back rub?"

"We've already established that I don't have a bad back."

"A foot rub?"

"My feet are fine."

"Run you a bubble bath?"

"I've already showered."

Decker was running out of options. "Hey!" He snapped his fingers. "I *got* it. The ultimate female aphrodisiac. How about if I tell you you're *right*!"

"Right about what?"

"About . . . everything. Anything you say, you'll be right. Unconditional rightness."

"For how long?"

"Twenty-four hours."

"Forty-eight hours."

"Deal—"

"Starting Friday night. I want it over a *weekend*. When you're *home*. And *around*."

"You drive a hard bargain."

Rina shrugged. "I'm worth it."

"Yes, you are." Decker scooped her up in his arms. "How's this for being romantic?"

"It's a start." Rina put her arms around his neck. "And a good one at that."

Abruptly, he awoke—eyes popping open, heart beating, head pounding, a ringing in his ears, and the dead bodies in his brain as clear as daylight.

A Nam dream.

Something he hadn't had in many moons. At least he roused himself before the thrashing, before he woke Rina up. He realized he must have had some kind of control over his reactions even in sleep. Otherwise, how could he have lived in hell so quietly?

The routine was second nature by now. Tiptoeing into the kitchen, turning on the light over the stove, putting the kettle on the fire. A minute later, he sat down at the table, sipping a hot mug of tea that steamed his face.

He glanced up at the kitchen clock.

It was only eleven-fifteen. Boys had fifteen minutes.

He was glad Rina hadn't heard him get up as she usually did. Sex had knocked her out. A good night. The juices had been flowing for both of them. Pure fireworks. Afterward, Rina seemed joyous . . . a word that hadn't been in her vocabulary for quite some time.

She needed escape more than he did. Though she tried valiantly to hide it, she'd become a different woman since Bram had died. Difficult because she had never confided to Decker the depths of her feelings for him. On some level, she had loved him. But it had to be more than that. He'd come to the conclusion that Bram had been Rina's last link to her late husband, Yitzchak. In Bram's untimely demise, she had relived both deaths at once. Been hell for her. For him and the boys as well.

Maybe this would signal good times.

If Decker could ever exorcise his own demons.

Eleven-twenty.

Late. But not too late for a night owl like Cindy. She

picked up immediately. He asked her how her day had gone.

"Nothing exciting." She paused. "I did speak to my ex-professor of Criminal Sciences. Told him about my decision to enlist with the LAPD. He said I should have signed up with the FBI—"

"You've *got* to be kidding!"

"He says LAPD are a bunch of clowns—"

"Oh, fu—for *this* kind of advice, I was forking out twenty grand a year?"

"He says that the FBI is a more professional outfit with a more highly educated crew—"

"A bunch of yahoos—"

"They've lifted their hiring freeze, Dad. I'm just the type of person they're looking for. Young, female, well educated, with a parent in law enforcement—"

"Congratulations. You've succeeded in really *aggravating* me."

"The thing is, Father, I really want to *solve* crimes, not wear sunglasses."

Decker laughed so loudly he was afraid he'd wake up Rina. "Now I know why I love you, Cin."

"Although there are some good agents out there."

"Maybe one or two."

"So why are you calling at eleven-thirty at night? No, I'll tell you. Like most men, you never use the phone for chitchat. You use it to make appointments or to do business. You want to do chitchat, you invite me over for dinner or out for breakfast. So what do you need to know?"

Decker was surprised by her perceptiveness. "Which French existentialist wrote the book about a guy getting arrested for not crying at his mother's funeral?"

"Camus. *The Stranger.* Why?"

"I take it you read the book, then."

"In French actually."

Decker broke into soft laughter.

"What?"

"A Columbia graduate who reads Camus in French becoming a cop. Maybe you *are* better suited for the FBI. Sit around all day musing about life while constructing serial-killer profiles. They certainly don't *solve* any serial killings—''

''You're being very insular and petty.''

''Your ex-Criminal Sciences professor is a jerk. What is existentialism anyway?''

''Everything is random . . . purposeless. Each person for himself.''

''Sounds like the FBI—''

''Daddy—''

''Kinda like a dog-eat-dog philosophy?''

''Not exactly. Since the world is purposeless and meaningless, it's up to humankind to impart humanism into it through *free will*. Ultimately, our job is to civilize our societies.''

''*Human*kind?''

''Columbia was very PC. Why are you asking about Camus?''

''Just wondering if I got my money's worth from Columbia.''

Cindy laughed. ''There's more to it than that. But I won't press. However, if you'd like to tell me . . . take me out for breakfast—''

''You're on.''

''Great. When and where?''

''Gotta be somewhere kosher. How about Noah's bagels? I'll meet you halfway in Sherman Oaks. Six-thirty on the dot.''

''Six-thirty? You mean A.M.?''

''Some of us have jobs. Six-thirty at Noah's. Are we on?''

''Yes, *if* you promise to tell me about your case.''

''No dice. This isn't business, just chitchat.''

''But maybe you'll accidentally let a few things slip?''

''At six-thirty A.M., this is a real possibility.''

She laughed, hung up, and so did he.

But his thoughts weren't on Cindy. They were glued to a mental video camera that was in rewind. Back to Jeanine Garrison's office. The moment he first saw her. Again, he felt a jolt of lightning in his groin. In his head, he went through the interview, slowly . . . deliberately. Her initial anger, her sudden display of inappropriate sexuality, her animation when she talked about tennis.

A stunning, erotic woman in black. Dabbing her eyes with a tissue.

Another jolt hit him. But this one came straight to the brain.

Jeanine patting her eyes. Then she had looked up. Decker had seen her face, had seen those eyes.

They had been totally clear—bright blue and shining like diamonds.

Completely dry.

❧16

A pleasant breakfast with Cindy followed by a morning of meetings, paperwork, and crime. Decker took his lunch break at two-thirty, eating his sandwiches, going over the articles from yesterday's computer search on Jeanine Garrison. A half hour later, he heard a knock on the door. Scott Oliver entered the office, noticed the clippings on Decker's desk.

"You're kinda fixated on this—"

"They knew each other," Decker sat up, stretched. "Something she didn't admit in the interview."

"Why should she? Who'd want to be associated with a mass murderer?"

"That's the point, Scott. If she didn't know him well, she would have admitted it openly . . . *wondered* about it. At least, she might have brought it up. Because it's weird not to."

"Wendy Culligan didn't bring up knowing Harlan."

"But she brought it up to Brenda Miller. Besides, Wendy had nothing to gain by anyone's death . . . as opposed to the Garrison offspring. Harlan Manz takes out thirteen people and suddenly Jeanine Garrison's a millionaire."

"Along with her brother." Oliver paused. "Why do you think it's *her* and not David Garrison?"

"Picture shows Manz with Jeanine, not Manz and David."

"Can I play devil's advocate for a moment?"

146

"Shoot."

"Deck, why would she do it? And don't just say for the money. Obviously, Daddy took *good* care of her. Even her brother admitted that. Besides, a piece of ass like Jeanine . . . she could marry money in a snap."

"But in both cases, she'd still be dependent on someone else's goodwill."

Oliver said, "All I'm saying is, her addict brother has as much to gain as she does."

"Absolutely." Decker stretched. "And according to Webster, David had lots of animosity toward his parents . . . his father. But . . ." He organized his ideas. "Webster saw David as a talented but troubled individual. David's a *successful* artist. You see him hanging out with a loser like Manz?"

"Not hanging out with him, Pete. *Using* him."

Decker thought about that. Oliver had a good point. "So give me something that links David Garrison with Harlan Manz, and I'm all over his ass, too." He stacked the printouts, laid them neatly on his desk. Focused his attention on Oliver. "How'd that call to Brenda Miller go?"

Oliver smiled—a white crescent of teeth. "She was great! Understood completely. Even said she *admired* my integrity." He rubbed his hands together. "Can't wait until this case is over. At this point, I don't care *how* it's resolved, just as long as it *is* resolved." He paused, eyed his boss. "Jeanine got to you, didn't she, Rabbi?"

Decker felt his face get hot. "She's dangerous, Scott. A knockout bitch with an ice-queen smile that gets you rock hard. Not too many of those around."

He paused.

"Men'll do incredibly dumb things to get laid by a gorgeous piece of ass. Something tells me she knows how to use that fact for her own purposes."

Oliver's eyes fell on the pile of articles. "So if you can't fuck her in the flesh, you'll fuck her over instead."

Decker smiled. "Believe me, I'm *not* interested in fucking her. And even though I think she's hinky, I am *not* out to get her. But then I examine what we have. So far, things are . . . well, they're not pointing *to* Jeanine. More like . . . revolving *around* her.''

''You want to revolve around her, Deck?''

''No, Scott, I'd like to keep my marriage intact.''

''But she did get to you.''

''Yep. She's got a Svengalian quality to her . . . the voice, her manner. Very rhythmic, very intoxicating. She's the type of woman who could get even honest men to do hinky things . . . let alone slackers like Harlan Manz.''

''Things like pop her parents? Then pop himself?''

''Who said he popped himself?''

''Ballistics.''

''Not exactly. Ballistics says that the bullet in Harlan's head came from the gun at Harlan's side. It never said that Harlan actually fired that *specific* gun.''

''You're stretching.''

''Yes, I am.'' Decker laughed. ''Aw, well. Maybe I'm doing this because it's better than attending a lunch meeting with some brass from Parker Center.''

''Now that I can believe.'' Oliver paused. ''An ice queen, huh? I gotta meet this woman.'' He produced a sickly smile. ''Then again, my track record with the opposite sex ain't too hot.''

''You're showing some unusual insight.''

Oliver squirmed. ''Loo, you're so straight, at times I think you've got a rod up your ass. She makes *you* poke your zipper . . . man, that scares the shit out of me.''

Before Decker signed out, he made two quick calls. First one was to Terrance Howell, who wasn't in or wasn't answering. Decker left a message on his machine. As luck would have it, he caught Sonia Eaton right as she was leaving. She couldn't talk now. Perhaps they could talk tomorrow evening. Could she ask what it was about?

Decker hedged, then said something about Harlan Manz aka Hart Mansfield. As he understood it, Sonia had played tennis with him a couple of times. Just wanted to ask her a few questions about him and the matches. The police were trying to get a lock on the mass murderer. Maybe insights could prevent tragedies like this in the future.

Sonia's voice turned cold. "Lofty ambitions. I didn't know the LAPD cared."

Decker was silent.

"Look, I barely knew Hart. Maybe I spoke a dozen words to the guy."

"You played a doubles match with him for the New Christian Hospital charity games. About two years ago?"

A long pause. "Where'd you dig up that? *Why'd* you dig up that? You aren't going to publicize it, are you?"

She sounded horrified. Decker was soothing. "Not at all."

An impatient sigh. "I swear I barely remember him."

"But you did play tennis with him."

"Just that once. And that was at the behest of one of my friends."

"Maybe I could talk to your friend, then?"

Sonia snorted. "I'm not about to give out names and numbers over the phone. I don't even know if you're for real."

"I can give you the number here at the station house—"

"I'm a busy woman. I don't have time for this nonsense! What's your name again?"

"Lieutenant Peter Decker."

Sonia said, "Look, Lieutenant, *if* you know about that tennis match, *and* you know about me, you probably know about my friend. So what's this all about?"

Decker weighed his options. He decided to be truthful— at least partially truthful. "I found a photograph of you with Harlan from the local newspaper—*The Valley Voice.* There were two other people in that match. Your partner, Terrance Howell, and Manz's partner, Jeanine Garrison. And yes, I'm going to phone both of them. You could help me out by telling me which one of them asked you to play with Manz."

A long pause. She said, "I suppose you'll find out soon enough. It was Jeanine."

"Thanks. Were they an item, ma'am?"

"That's all I'm going to tell you, Lieutenant Peter Decker from the LAPD."

Decker laughed. "Thank you for your time. I really do appreciate it." He tried one more time, doing the sympathy ploy. He sighed deeply into the phone. "This terrible ordeal at Estelle's . . . I don't know . . . we were all affected by it."

The line was quiet.

Decker continued, "I would really like to prevent things like that in the future."

"How *can* you?" Sonia sounded upset. "How can anyone *prevent* monsters from going crazy?"

"Well . . . we talk to people." Decker was really winging it now. "We try to get profiles, ma'am. On who may be likely to do this kind of thing."

"I hope you conclude that it's not *too* many people."

"No, no, no," Decker reassured her. "No need to be alarmed. But if we, as law enforcement providers and protectors, get . . . even a tiny, tiny insight into what makes these guys tick . . . what can I say? I think it's worth the intrusion."

"Maybe."

Sonia sounded wary. But she continued to talk anyway.

"Look, I wish I could tell you more. But I'm not going to talk behind Jeanine's back. She's not a close friend, but she is a . . . an acquaintance. A very formidable person. You'll know what I mean once you meet her."

"I'm sure you're right." Decker paused. "Formidable, huh?"

"You don't want her as your enemy."

"Ah! Can you tell me if she and Hart dated?"

"Jeanine doesn't date." Sonia's voice had turned flat. "She has . . . admirers. Shuffles them around like cards in a gin game."

"She likes tennis players, doesn't she?"

"She likes . . ." Sonia paused. "I've really talked too much. I've got to go."

"Ms. Eaton, let's do us both a favor. I won't say anything about this conversation, if you won't say anything. Strictly confidential?''

"Fine with me."

"Can you do me another favor?"

"What?"

"Since this is just between the two of us, can you just complete your sentence?" Decker asked. "Jeanine likes . . . what?''

Faint laugh. Sonia said, "Jeanine likes anything that doesn't stand in her way."

It was only six-thirty. Surely some florist would still be open.

Decker got off the freeway, started cruising the boulevard for an open shop. If he didn't find one, he could always go to the market. Smiles carried flowers. Not very nice ones. Dyed mums in a terra-cotta pot. Emergency flowers. Like if you forgot the secretary's birthday. Not for the wife. Rina would see through it. Besides, he really did want something extra special . . . something that conveyed what years of being a man had taught him to repress.

Lord, he was tired. Weary and disappointed in himself. He used to think he was impervious to women's wiles. After his divorce, he had developed a hard shell, a seasoned air, and a wizened attitude. No bitch was ever gonna fuck with his brain again, thank you very much.

When he met Rina, he had known immediately that she was a jewel—a rare, precious diamond. Still, he had taken his time. Hadn't stopped dating other women until it had become clear *she* was committed. That she wanted him as much as he wanted her. And even when she wanted to go to New York to think things over . . . well, that had been cool with him. Though when she had returned, he had been glad to see her.

Glad, but cautious.

He doubted his blood pressure rose beyond a notch.

Everything on an even keel.

The courtship had proceeded nicely. She placed no demands on him—other than religion.

Religion.

Yeah, that had been a biggie. But once that was resolved, things ran smoothly. Of course, he had to become the type of Jew she wanted. An Orthodox Jew. Keeping kosher, keeping the Sabbath, keeping family purity. Had to do it. Otherwise, marriage would have been out of the question. And he had wanted to get married . . . very, very badly.

But he never felt compromised. Because Rina was a traditional woman herself. She took care of the house and children, he took care of *everything* else.

An old-fashioned family and that was fine with him.

And he was in *charge* . . . the illustrious *paterfamilias*.

Man, had he been fooling himself. Meeting Jeanine, being bowled over by her sexuality, realizing what a sensual woman could have done to him. If Jeanine carried the moniker seductive kitten, Rina would have been tagged a full-fledged man-eating tigress. There had been times when Decker had thought about her . . . times late at night. His lust had been so overwhelming, so damn powerful, he had needed no physical contact to achieve orgasm. Only had to close his eyes . . . picture her face . . .

He would have done anything to *get* her. Anything at all. And had another man entered the picture, he would have done anything to *keep* her. Lie, cheat, steal . . .

Maybe even murder.

He broke out in a sweat.

All of his macho posturing . . . a facade maintained by Rina's indulgence. After Jan, he hadn't become any smarter. He had just been lucky. Really, really lucky. He had met a femme fatale, but thank God she turned out to be as beautiful on the inside as she was on the outside.

Thank you, God. Thank you, thank you, thank you!

✒17

The message was on his desk when Decker walked into his office.

See me immediately.

Not a good omen. What could Strapp want with him at seven-thirty in the morning? He went around the corner to the captain's office.

Strapp waved him inside. "Shut the door."

Decker complied, regarded the man. In his thin face sat intense, angry eyes and a hard mouth. But his hands... fingers kneading one another. He was anxious.

"Sit down."

Decker sat without speaking, eyes scanning the room. Walls filled with diplomas and certificates as well as pictures of the captain with VIPs—the mayor, the governor, the president. Still, the furniture was strictly departmental issue. A serviceable desk and standard chairs. Metal file cabinets. The man had an ego, but he wasn't peacock vain.

Decker directed his eyes to his superior. "What is it, sir?"

"Do you have hard evidence against Jeanine Garrison?"

Decker continued to stare, said nothing.

Strapp met his gaze. "I got a wake-up call this morning. You've been implying an involvement between her and Harlan Manz—"

"So much for keeping confidences," Decker muttered.

"You toss Jeanine Garrison's picture around with Harlan

Manz to Garrison's friends, you think it's *not* going to come back on you? Are you out of your mind? She's furious, screaming police harassment. Threatening a lawsuit.''

"I didn't toss anyone's picture around. I mentioned the picture to a mutual friend, trying to get a fix on Garrison's relationship to Manz. I'm running an investigation, Captain—"

"That's right. You're running an investigation, not a witch-hunt.''

Decker looked at the ceiling. "Get a call from the mayor, Cap?"

"You're fucking outta line, Decker!"

Decker was quiet and so was Strapp. The captain was breathing audibly, cheeks and the tip of his nose bright red. But there was more than that. Decker knew that someone had tied Strapp's hands. It didn't sit well with him.

Quietly, the captain said, "We've got a society woman, Pete. She's hosted umpteen charity events for some very good causes. A philanthropic woman with a lot of contacts. And she just lost her parents in a horrible, devastating tragedy—"

"Ah, yes, the *thing*.''

"What?"

"Never mind."

Strapp glared at him. "You go around talking about a newspaper article that's over two years old, implying that she played a part in her own parents' murder—"

"Not at all. You want to hear the truth?"

"Not particularly. I want you to stop whatever the hell you're doing until you get evidence. Good, solid, concrete, carved-in-stone *evidence*."

"If I stop what I'm doing, I won't get evidence—"

"You don't have evidence, you quit pestering her. You can go now."

Silence.

Decker said, "At least Jeanine's not a liar. She does have her connections—"

"Decker—"

"An O. J. and Menendez rolled into an eye-pleasing package."

"Are you done with the sarcasm?"

"Yes, I suppose I am."

"Then get back to work."

Decker took a deep breath, let it out slowly. "Cap, you tell me how I'm supposed to get evidence against *anyone* if I can't conduct an investigation."

Strapp said, "Harlan Manz came into Estelle's and mowed down thirteen people, maimed thirty-two others, then shot himself. We got forensics, we got witnesses, we got a cut-and-dried case. Why are you turning this into a conspiracy?"

Decker was about to speak.

Strapp blurted out, "She said you came on to her. She refused you and now you're seeking revenge."

Decker kept his face flat, his heart suddenly pounding in his chest.

Strapp said, "You want to tell me about it?"

Decker said, "She's a very sexy woman."

"And?"

"And that is it."

Strapp rubbed his temples. "You didn't come on to her?"

"No."

"Let anything slip out?"

Decker was about to respond, then laughed at the unintentional double entendre. They both did. "No. I was completely professional. I was aware of her attraction. So I was especially conscientious."

"Maybe you're going at her because of your strong attraction to her?"

"I didn't say *strong* attraction—"

"Don't argue semantics with me, Decker. Are you out to get her?"

"No, I am not, sir. I am out to explain some gross inconsistencies in a very puzzling case."

Strapp eyed his man. Quietly he asked, "She come on to you, Pete?"

"Looked straight at my wedding band, then invited me to a private tour of the new museum."

"What'd you say?"

"I told her thanks but no thanks. My family likes me home at night. Would you like me to reconstruct the conversation verbatim?"

"Don't get smart-assed with me."

Decker blinked a couple of times. "Is she slapping me and/or the LAPD with a formal suit?"

"Not yet. But I got a call from her lawyer . . . among other people. He made noises, Pete. Told me to control my men."

"Christ!" Decker reminded himself to unclench his jaw. "Okay. *What* do you want me to do?"

Strapp said, "If it was anyone else . . . anyone else . . ."

No one spoke.

"The fact that I believe you doesn't mean squat. If she presses charges, I'm hogtied. You go through the whole routine."

"I know."

"Do you think she's doing this to keep you from doing your job? Or is she a spurned woman who's getting even? *Or* is she just a nutcase?"

"Maybe all three."

"What do you have?"

Decker paused, then pulled out his notebook and began to recount the case, item by item. He told Strapp about the suicide position, about the inconsistent bullet trajectories, about the number of bullets per number of empty magazines. Then he discussed Jeanine: how she had put him off the first time. Later, when he returned, her friendly attitude had turned hostile. He spoke about how she stood to inherit millions, her interest in tennis, and her acquaintance with Harlan Manz. How close, no one knew. At the moment, that's what Decker was trying to figure out.

"What you have isn't conclusive of anything."

"Of course not. That's why I'm running an investigation. If I had *conclusive* evidence, my job would be over."

"What you have doesn't give you the right to accuse victims of murder."

"I don't point fingers, I gather evidence. Accusations are for the District Attorney's Office. Would you like to hear what I have so far?"

Strapp was quiet. "Go ahead."

"I've got witnesses claiming that gunshots were coming from every direction—"

"Because they were hysterical."

"Granted. They were all hysterical. And if that's all we had, I would have dropped it. But then Forensics comes back . . . we got bullet trajectories inconsistent with the position of the shooter *and* a suspicious suicide."

For the first time, Strapp's interest was piqued. "In what way?"

"Harlan apparently held the gun about two and a half feet from his head."

"Some people have problems putting a gun to their temple."

"Six inches, maybe . . . but thirty? I got long arms . . . but even I would have problems bringing my arm out two and a half feet, then precisely aiming the gun at my temple."

"How long is Harlan's arm?"

"About three feet from the shoulder to the tip of his fingers. But you've got to remember that to shoot himself, he would've had to flex his wrist backward to aim the gun at his head. Which takes away his hand as part of the distance. I'm not saying it's impossible. But it *is* an unusual angle."

"What else?"

"I've got more shell casings than magazines—"

"In all the hullaballoo, we lost magazines."

"Sir, everything you're saying is possible. But all these glitches . . . they have a cumulative effect, Captain. So I took it a step further. I asked myself the logical question. What could explain the inconsistencies?"

"A second gunman."

"Exactly." Decker tried to hide the excitement in his

voice. "First thing I zeroed in on was Harlan Manz. Estelle's wasn't a robbery, we know that. So if it wasn't a robbery, and if it wasn't the work of a lone madman who committed suicide, what was it? To me, it was beginning to shape out as a hit."

"Keep going."

Decker paused. "Here's the speculation part. I'm thinking that the person who hired Harlan to do the hit also hired a second gunman. Two people to do the job. And then the *second* gunman did a double-cross—either on his own or as part of the plan."

The captain spoke in a flat voice. "A conspiracy worthy of Oliver Stone."

Decker went on, ignoring the skepticism. "If we assume a hit, then someone who died in that restaurant was set up."

Strapp said, "So you went through a list of the victims, looked up their loved ones and friends and enemies. Figured out who had the most to gain by the victim's death."

"You got it."

"Narrowed it down to those who had a lot to gain *and* those who might have known Harlan Manz."

"Right on the nailhead—"

"Came up with Jeanine Garrison."

"Actually I narrowed it down to three parties because all the victims belonged to Greenvale Country Club, where Harlan had also worked." Decker began ticking off the list on his fingers. "A real estate broker and her entourage, Walter Skinner and his date, and Ray and Linda Garrison. Marge and Oliver took the real estate group, Martinez took Walter's widow, Webster took David Garrison, I took Jeanine. I went into the interview expecting nothing. *Nothing.* Then, out of *nowhere,* she started going hinky on me."

"You hit a nerve—"

"The whole damn spinal column."

"So she wasn't the only one being looked into?"

"No, she wasn't the only one. Captain, I didn't know this woman from Adam. There was no hidden agenda."

"Webster questioned the brother?"

"Of course."

"That's good . . . strengthens your case . . . our case."
Strapp made a tepee with his hands. "Still, you have nothing on her. And even if there was a connection between
her and Manz, it doesn't mean she ordered anything."

"You know, sir, we're talking thirteen homicides. The
woman lost her parents. I think she'd be thrilled to hear
about an investigation—if she were innocent."

"Not an investigation that implicated her. Even innocent
people don't want to be *associated* with a mass murderer.
Use your brain, Deck."

Oliver had said the same thing. Decker said, "She's *lying*
about the harassment. So you've got to ask what else she's
lying about. And why does she want me out of the picture?"

"Because you're implying nasty things about her. She
claimed she rolled out the red carpet for you, took time out
of her busy day, was civil and answered all your questions.
Afterward, you were slow to leave. She didn't know what
to do, offered you something to drink—a soft drink, a glass
of wine—"

"I don't drink while I'm working."

"You took the glass of wine, had a couple of drinks,
then asked her out. She was shocked, tried to be nice, but
you were insistent. Finally, she flatly refused your advances
and you became angry. Next thing she knows, you're
spreading rumors about her."

"Her allegations are patently *ridiculous*! I didn't come
on to her, I wasn't slow to leave, and I didn't have a glass
of anything, let alone wine. I don't drink on the job. It's
grounds for dismissal. Why would I do something so stupid?"

"Because we think with our cocks."

"Sir, I'm not impervious to sexual feelings. Still, I keep
my mouth shut, my hands to myself, and my zipper closed
at all times. Because I love my wife, I love my children, I
love my marriage. Bottom line, sir. What do you want me
to do? You want me to back off, I'll back off."

"Until we work things out with her lawyers, stay away
from Jeanine Garrison."

Decker made a fist. "Crazy bitch—"

"I didn't hear that," Strapp said. "These are direct orders. Stop showing that picture you have of her and Harlan Manz together. Makes us look like the tabloid press. And stay away from Garrison's friends."

"What about her enemies?"

"Decker—"

"*Who* can I talk to?"

"You talk to anyone you'd like about Harlan Manz. And if Jeanine Garrison's name happens to come up in the conversation . . . someone wants to talk about her . . . I suppose you can listen."

Quietly, he walked through the door, heard Rina's distant hum. The gentle soothing song of a mother to her baby. She was putting Hannah down for a noontime nap. He could picture them mentally . . . his wife's smile, Hannah's little head peeking out from the covers of her bed, carrot-colored curls over her forehead, Rina brushing them aside. Such pure love. It almost brought tears to his eyes.

He swallowed dryly, sat down at the dining-room table. Waiting. Waiting some more. Head in hand, his stomach in a knot. His brain played the bongos against his cranium. Finally Rina came into the room, surprised and delighted to see him.

"First roses, then this . . ." Suddenly, she became alarmed. "You're ashen, Peter. What's wrong?"

Decker paused before speaking. "Remember that woman I interviewed a couple of days ago? The one who got the better of me?"

Rina turned pale, sat down herself. She exhaled deeply. "Yes, I remember."

"Well . . . there's a possibility that I might get slapped with a sexual harassment suit."

She brought her hand to her chest, whispered, "Thank God."

Decker stared at her. "Thank God?"

"No, I mean . . . that's terrible. What happened?"

Decker was quiet. Then he said, "Am I misreading you

. . . or did you just think I was about to confess something
. . . like an affair?''

"Well, I don't know." Rina took a deep breath, let it
out slowly. "I mean, first the roses out of the clear blue
sky. Then you come in all white and hangdog."

"Thank you for the trust." He got up and walked into
the kitchen.

Rina followed. "I'm sorry, Peter," she said softly. "I'm
really sorry. But I can't help my feelings."

"Do you trust me?"

"Of course I do."

"Then how could you *think* a thing like that?"

"Peter, I love you so much . . . and things have been
kind of tense around here. I guess I just got . . . scared."
She wiped tears from her eyes. "Also, you blushed when
you talked about her."

"I did not."

"Yes, you did."

He paused. "Okay, I did."

"She's beautiful?"

"Yes."

"Sexy?"

"Maybe to the unsuspecting." Decker felt his mouth go
tight. "Right now, I'd like to kill the crazy loon."

"So you found another woman attractive—"

"*Found* is right. *Found*. As in the *past* tense."

"You don't have to sugarcoat it. It's okay. Because I
know you, Peter. Her mind must have been inventing
things. You're much too professional to let an attractive
woman get in the way of your work."

Decker stared at her.

Rina shrugged. "The whole allegation's frivolous. Don't
worry about it. How about some coffee? You want regular
or decaf?"

"Decaf." Decker eyed her suspiciously. "You're taking
this very well. Much better than me."

"Than I." Rina fetched a bag of coffee. "If this
woman's crazy, is it your fault? As a matter of fact, I bet
she came on to you. Just like Lilah Brecht, right?"

"God, I forgot about her." Decker raised his brow. "Obviously, you didn't."

"Obviously. Did she make a pass at you?"

"Sort of."

"So you rejected her in a very professional manner. Which probably made her mad. Who is she anyway?"

"Jeanine Garrison."

Rina scrunched up her forehead. "Why does that name sound familiar."

Decker gave her some background information.

Rina scooped out coffee and put it in the drip machine. "Then I've probably seen her picture on some society page."

"I can't believe how calm you're acting. I was a nervous wreck driving over here."

"Well, you needn't have been worried just for being a healthy man."

Decker couldn't get over her attitude. So dispassionate! It was worrisome. Was she keeping her anxiety inside for his sake? Or was there more? He stared at her. "Rina, are you keeping something from me?"

Her cheeks took on a rosy hue. "Now, what would I be keeping from you?"

Decker studied her, said nothing for a long time. Then he said, "It was Bram, wasn't it?"

Rina was quiet. "He's dead, Peter. Can we change the subject?"

"When you two were alone together here . . ." Decker rolled his tongue in his cheek. "Nothing happened, right?"

Rina turned to him, her face angry. "Thank you for the trust." She stalked out of the room.

Decker followed, his heart thundering in his chest, his head pounding. "Well, you have to admit there was a little history behind my question. I saw the way he looked at you. I saw the way you looked at *him*."

Rina picked up a magazine, sat down at the dining-room table and began to scan it angrily, turning the pages with force.

"Don't ignore me!"

"Why not?"

"Because I'm your husband, for Chrissakes."

Rina said nothing.

Decker ripped the magazine from his wife's grasp.

Rina looked up in shock. "Excuse me. Where I come from we don't bully people into having conversations."

Decker felt his emotional thermostat going haywire. He looked at his hands, realized they were shaking. He took a deep breath, closed his eyes. "Look, I'm sorry, all right? Here." He offered her the magazine. "Take it back . . . please."

Rina saw her husband's trembling hands. Something was terribly wrong. She didn't move; tears rolled down her cheeks.

Decker put the magazine on the table. Clasped his hands together. "I'm sorry, Rina. I'm sorry for the accusation. I know nothing happened. We're going through a rough period. It's been sticky around here since Bram's death. We'll weather it. Let's just work together, all right?"

Rina nodded, her face crumbling. Decker raised her up, swept her into his arms, and rocked her as they stood. "It's okay, honey. It's okay. I know you loved him. He was a very good man. You have good taste in men."

Rina talked through tears, hugged Peter tightly. "Very."

"I didn't mean to extract a compliment, but I'll take it anyway."

Rina broke away, dried her eyes. "You want that coffee now?"

"Fine." Decker followed her into the kitchen, sat down at the table. "Man, what a week."

Rina retrieved mugs from the cupboard. "What a year."

"That, too."

Rina said, "I haven't been easy to be around."

Decker was quiet.

"His death hit me hard, Peter."

"I know. I'm sorry."

"I feel so . . . *guilty*. Like it was divine retribution or something."

Decker was taken aback. "That's ridiculous!"

Rina was quiet.

"That didn't come out right," Decker said. "I don't mean to minimize your feelings—"

"It's all right," Rina wiped her eyes again.

Decker said, "Neither one of you did anything wrong, Rina. There's no reason to feel guilty."

"Except that my husband was barely cold, not much more than three months in the ground, I was a religious woman. And Bram was a *goy*. Not just any goy, mind you. A seminary student studying to be a priest *and* my late husband's best friend. I felt like I *violated* everything that I held dear. Such betrayal—"

"Yitzchak had died, Rina. Betrayal is for the living, not the dead."

"You can betray a memory." Rina poured coffee into the mugs. "Bram didn't feel too good about it, either. It was horrible—the mixture of love and guilt. We shouldn't even have started." She plunked a mug in front of Decker. "So now you know. Are you any richer because of it?"

"Maybe I am. Because maybe now I understand why you've been so upset. Rina, God didn't strike Bram dead. A very disturbed person lashed out and he happened to be in the way."

"Maybe she was just an instrument in God's plan."

"And maybe we're just protozoa under a microscope."

"What does *that* mean?"

"They're both equally absurd thoughts."

"Not that you're minimizing my feelings."

Decker felt his jaw tighten. He willed it slack, weighed his words. "Darlin', I'm just trying to ground you. Keep you from going further into your blue funk. Bram was a *wonderful* man, Rina. A brilliant scholar and a caring individual and good-looking to boot. He was also very complex and troubled coming from that dysfunctional family."

"Yes, he was."

"Take my word for it, honey. You were the *best* thing that ever happened to him. Man, he would have jumped bridges for you, he loved you that much. And there you were, a young, young widow who had just lost her husband to a monstrous, lingering illness. You had two small children and not much in the way of support.''

''My parents were around.''

''I *know* your parents, Rina. They're wonderful people, but they're also camp survivors and very emotional. I know you didn't unload on them like you did on Bram.''

Rina was quiet.

''You were lost and lonely and so was Bram. You took each other through transitional periods in both your lives. And that wasn't a bad thing. It paved the way for me.''

Rina sat down with her coffee, leaned over, and kissed her husband tenderly. *Poor Peter. Dealing with my past upheavals while your own dam of troubles is cracking.* ''Don't worry about this Garrison woman, okay? You're a very attractive man who's in a very attractive profession—''

''I thought the LAPD ranked behind a leper colony in attractiveness.''

''Despite the press, cops still carry cachet. And a detective . . . well, he has even more clout. If she tries to make these fatuous allegations actually stick, you'll fight it. And you'll win because the truth will prevail.''

''If it were only that simple.'' Decker ran his hand over his face. ''Thanks for not being angry—''

''Why should I be angry? You may have had thoughts, but you didn't *do* anything.''

''No, I didn't. Still, it's a load off my mind.'' Decker gave her a sheepish look. ''So you'll support me?''

''All the way.''

''The little woman standing behind me?''

''You mean standing in *front* of you, chump. They want to talk to *you,* first they go through *me.*''

❧18

Marge said, "I can't believe they *did* this to you."

Decker said, "It's not that bad. Jeanine's screwy reaction shows we may be onto something."

Oliver said, "Fucking bitch—"

"We'll just have to find another way," Marge said. "You can't stay on her ass, *I'll* do it. Like to see her slap *me* with a sexual harassment suit."

Webster said, "Reckon I could tote a few pictures around of Jeanine and Manz, ask her friends and ex-husband a few questions—"

"No, no, no!" Decker said. "No pictures of Jeanine Garrison with Harlan Manz. Strapp made that clear."

Martinez said, "So how are we going to make a connection between them if we can't talk about them in the same breath?"

Decker said, "I'll tell you what we're going to do. We're going to take a connection between Harlan Manz and Jeanine Garrison as a *given,* okay? *We* are going after a phantom: the second shooter—who may or may not exist."

"What's the game plan?" Oliver asked.

"Find out who Jeanine might have been dealing with *prior* to the shooting." Decker turned to Farrell Gaynor. "This is your specialty. I want a complete paper trail on Jeanine—every phone call, every credit card slip, every bank account, every withdrawal slip, every will or legal document—"

"I'm foaming at the mouth."

"But we also have to work on the sly," Decker said. "Quietly. No slipups. Because Jeanine is a liar . . . and a connected one. It's just a small step from slapping me with charges to slapping all of you with police harassment. Ergo, I want an equal investigation of her brother. Not only because it will play well for the lawyers, but also because he's a suspect—a former drug user with a record, who hated his father. Harlan Manz turned him into a millionaire, too."

Webster said, "Want me to lean on him, Loo?"

"Not just yet. First, let's get paper on him." He turned to Marge. "Dunn, you're on target with Jeanine. She can't claim sexual harassment against you. If we need to question her, you'll be the one."

"Agreed."

Webster said, "Since y'all're trying to figure out this unknown second hit man, reckon it might be a good idea to try to profile him?"

Decker said, "What do you have in mind, Tom?"

"Examine what we've got and come up with a composite of this phantom."

"Don't like profiles," Oliver said, "They're misleading."

Webster said, "I'm talkin' generalities. For instance, this phantom killer . . . if he were one of *Jeanine*'s beaux, I reckon he'd be young and impressionable, rather than an old experienced hit man."

Martinez said, "Why do you say that?"

"Because this woman uses her sexuality to get things. Younger the guy, the faster the boner."

"Experienced hit men don't get hard-ons?" Martinez asked.

"She's into *power*, Bert," Webster said. "Easier to have power over a young untested stud than an experienced race-horse."

Marge said, "He's got a point. Look at the kind of woman Jeanine is. She sets things up, takes charge of events, and *coordinates* everything."

Webster went on. "Then just look at what she did to the Loo here. Using her sexuality to mess with his brain. When that didn't work out, she went straight for the jugular. She's into power . . . power over men."

"Manipulating men," Marge said. "Couldn't do it to Daddy, so she offed him?"

Martinez said, "That's a leap. But I like it."

Oliver turned to Webster. "So you're thinking she roped some young stooge into doing her dirty work by fucking him?"

"Or by promising to fuck him," Webster said. "It don't even have to be the real thing. I know lots of women like that. Southern belles who are steel magnolias. They love to dangle things and I don't mean worms on a reel."

Oliver said, "So Jeanine was working on Manz and some other jerk at the *same time*?"

Marge said, "Why not? She's good at organizing things."

"Men aren't things."

"True. They're easier to manipulate. All you got to do is *moan*."

Oliver threw her a dirty look. Marge gave him the peace sign.

Webster regarded Decker. "You're awfully quiet."

"Just thinking about what Sonia Eaton said about Jeanine. That the woman has admirers . . . shuffles them around like cards in a gin game . . ."

Martinez said, "Look, I don't want to lose her. Let me *tail* her. Even if she should notice me, I'm completely harmless-looking. Blend into crowds."

Decker said, "I'd love for you to tail her, Bert. Problem is, you've got a heavy current caseload that can't be neglected for a 'what if.' "

Martinez rubbed his stomach. "You know I'm not feeling so hot, Loo. I really wouldn't mind taking the day off."

"No dice," Decker said.

"It's already two o'clock, Loo," Martinez said. "Let me go take a peek. Especially now that you've made her nervous. She might do something stupid."

Decker sat back in his chair. "I take any of you off your cases and put you on Garrison without some very strong indications of guilt, we all become vulnerable to lawyers."

"Who's running the investigation here?" Oliver asked. "Some slick Beverly Hills eagle or Strapp?"

Marge looked at Webster. In unison they said, "The slick eagle—"

"That's not entirely fair," Decker said. "Strapp's getting squeezed. If he really wanted his ass protected, he would have pulled me off the case entirely."

Martinez said, "Loo, I got a light day tomorrow. I can do my paperwork and phone calls from the car. It's my idea, not yours, okay?"

"How about if we all take rotating code sevens tomorrow," Marge said. "I'll do a couple hours, Bert'll do a couple hours, Oliver'll do a couple hours—"

"I'll go first round." Webster sat back in his seat. "Reckon I'll be in the mood for a long lunch break."

"At eight in the morning?" Decker smiled.

"A breakfast break then," Webster said. "Y'all know it's unhealthy to work without proper nutrition. Besides, stakeout is pleasant for me. Put a couple of Bach cantatas in my CD player, I'm not only happy but very *alert*."

Martinez said, "Hey, it's our problem, Loo. Not yours."

"I may regret this, but . . ." Decker nodded.

Martinez gave his hands a clap. "Great. I got a couple of court reports to finish up. I can knock off around . . . maybe three, three-thirty."

"Y'got a video camera, Bert?" Webster said.

"I'll check one out from supplies."

Oliver said, "Overtime work without overtime pay! What the hell! Can't let the bitch push us around." He looked up and grinned. "Only wives get to do that."

"You ain't bitter, are you, Scotty?" Marge said.

"Me?" A finger in his chest. "Never!"

This time, it was Marge who was the last to leave. Stalling until she was alone with him. She closed the door, tried to smile supportively. "How's Rina taking the bad news?"

"Well. Thanks for asking."

She waited for more. When nothing came, she smiled again and said good-bye.

Decker said, "Margie, I really appreciate your support. Thanks."

"Of course. The bitch is out of her mind."

"Yes, she is. And that makes her . . . formidable." He stood. "I'll walk you out."

"Where are you going?"

"A couple of errands to take care of. And no, I'm not going anywhere near Jeanine Garrison."

Marge studied him. Decker knew she was leery, but she remained quiet. A smart lady. He left the station house, drove the unmarked about a half mile, then stopped at a pay phone. The phone rang twice, then Cindy picked up. He said, "I need your expertise."

"My *expertise*?"

"Can you come over to the house? If you can't, I'll meet you."

"No, I can come over. Can you give me a hint?"

"Later. Come over for supper. Afterward, I'll fill you in on the details."

They had been going at it for over an hour without interruption. Quietly so as not to disturb Rina or the baby. The boys were out as usual. Decker studied his daughter, feeling a mixture of love, admiration, and curiosity. Slowly, he was making his way over that interminable hump . . . viewing his daughter as an independent adult rather than his charge.

Cindy perused her notes, her father's notes as well. Piles of them. Brow wrinkled in concentration, she said, "To prevent any misunderstandings, maybe we should review at this point."

"A good idea."

"You've got this guy—Harlan Manz—who by newspaper and witness accounts went postal at Estelle's."

"Right."

"But *you* think he was just some hired gun."

"Maybe."

"Daddy, I've read your own case notes, the *original* assessment you took at the time of the shooting."

"You can read my handwriting, that's pretty good."

"I can not only read your handwriting, I can forge your signature."

Decker's eyes widened. "What?"

"That's a separate issue." Cindy grimaced. "Using your own notes as a backdrop, Harlan Manz does fit the standard profile for a mass murderer . . . whatever that means."

"Which is?"

Cindy began to count on her fingers. "He was male, he was under thirty, he used a firearm, he worked and was terminated from his employment at the location of the shooting, he talked about revenge to some of the co-workers—"

"Only right after he was fired, Cin. Subsequently, no one remembered his belaboring the point."

"That's not unusual. Many times, these things are premeditated. So if he had been planning the shooting, he would have kept it quiet."

"Cynthia, I combed Manz's pad. Didn't find anything there to suggest he was out to get Estelle's. No letters, no notes, no pictures of his ex-bosses on which he was doing target practice, nothing to imply a man on the edge."

"Dad, you didn't find much of anything in his apartment period. You wrote that down right in your notes."

"Where?"

Cindy showed him the pages. "See? Right here. A loner's apartment. Also consistent with mass murderers."

"Or consistent with the fact that someone got to his apartment first and removed all his personal effects." Decker clenched his jaw. "Harlan was no loner. A slacker, yes, but no hermit. He was good-looking, a sharp dresser, had girlfriends, made the social scene, taught tennis, tended bar, went to auditions—"

"More like the Ted Bundy type," Cindy answered. "Used his wiles to get his victims. Except he wasn't a serial killer. But there might be some similarities here. I bet you he used drugs or alcohol before his final act. Something that lowered his inhibitions, calmed his nerves. Did you do a gas chromatography on his blood?''

''I'll call Pathology in the morning and find out if one was done. If not, I'll order it. They still have his blood, so it shouldn't be hard to get a complete analysis.''

''Daddy, it's not that I completely disagree with you. Manz was not your typical schizoid. It does appear that he was able to maintain an outward social facade.''

She paused.

''He was also an actor of sorts. He could have been better than average at emotional deception.''

A very good point. Decker told her so.

Cindy smiled. ''So let me get this straight. You think that Manz was hired by Jeanine Garrison to kill her parents and he covered his tracks by committing mass murder at Estelle's. And then, someone else—also hired by Jeanine Garrison—was chosen to shoot up Estelle's as well as kill Harlan Manz with the same type of double automatic?''

''Maybe. Ballistics lab can't do a weapons match on each and every shell. Just too many bullets. They don't have the time or the manpower.''

''But the gun at Harlan's side was the gun that killed him.''

''Appears that way, yes.''

''So if it wasn't suicide, how'd that gun get there?''

''Someone exchanged weapons at the scene.''

''O-kay.'' Cindy was dubious. ''And then this mystery killer fled the scene, leaving a dead Harlan—the disgruntled employee—to take responsibility for all the killings.''

''Yes.''

''Pretty darn artful.''

''And pretty darn cold.''

''I'll say.'' Cindy thought a moment. ''A perfect crime.''

''Except forensics doesn't lie.'' Decker briefly explained the inconsistencies of the weapon angles.

''Ah . . .'' Cindy nodded. ''So, obviously, Harlan Manz didn't know about this other mystery killer.''

''Or maybe he did, Cin. Maybe Harlan thought they were in it together. And the other person double-crossed him.''

"So then they both would have gone into the restaurant and opened fire at the same time."

Decker thought a moment. "No . . . that's not how the witnesses described it. They only noticed Harlan. No one mentioned a mystery killer."

"But you did write that people claimed that the bullets were flying all around them . . . indicative of more than one gun going off. Maybe it makes more sense to assume that Manz didn't know about a second shooter."

"Maybe."

"Then Jeanine was working with them both independently."

Decker said, "Possibly."

Cindy looked at her father. "I don't quite understand how that would work."

Decker said, "Suppose Jeanine was doing a number on Manz, getting him worked up over the loss of his job and the need for offing her parents. When Jeanine finally convinced Manz to do it, they set up a date. Then she hired another guy to murder Manz and mop up her parents' killings—in case Harlan screwed up."

"At the same time, Harlan was murdering everyone else?" Cindy shook her head. "Wow."

Decker smiled. "Pretty far-fetched. Then again, Jeanine Garrison is one hell of an organizer."

"By your definition, she'd have to be."

"What I'm looking for is a profile on the *mystery* killer. Any ideas, hon?"

Cindy shrugged. "If she indeed did use Manz to kill her parents, she probably would have used someone similiar to Manz for the second kill. Because most killers are pretty unoriginal. They use roughly the same methods unless they're serial murderers out to play games. But you're assuming Jeanine is not a serial murderer."

Decker said, "No, I think she's just a greedy woman out to get an inheritance."

"I agree with Detective Webster's assessment. That the phantom killer would be a young guy, someone she could psychologically and sexually manipulate. Maybe even a teenage boy in her sexual thrall. Teenagers are very high on the impulse scale.'' Cindy made a face. "I wonder how she coordinated it all.''

Decker sipped coffee. "I'm probably over-psychologizing. Maybe she's actually . . . dare I say it? . . . innocent.''

Cindy thought a moment. "Except she did react very strongly . . . accusing you of sexual harassment. That's typical of people who kill for inheritance. They view themselves as victims, think everyone's out to get *them*, standing in the way of what *rightfully* belongs to them. *Or* she could just be a nutcase. Able to maintain on the outside, but fragile once you peel off that protective layer.''

"What else can you tell me about Mr. Phantom Murderer other than that he's likely to be young?''

"Well, like I said, most people aren't too original. If she recruited someone from her club first time out, she could have gone back to the club for number two. Maybe another tennis teacher or a bartender or the pool maintenance man or a waiter at the restaurant.''

She thought a moment.

"If you want me to probe further, I can call up my professor tomorrow. See if he'll let me use their computers.''

"Is this the professor who told you to join the FBI?''

"The very same one. Actually, he's a nice guy. We dated, you know.''

This time, Decker paused before he spoke. "No, I didn't. Then it's over?''

"Yes. But we're still friends. I'm sure he'll let me hook into his data banks with my modem. I'll input the information and see if it jibes with anything. I'll also try to pull up profiles of femme fatales who've convinced men to kill for them. There're lots of those around. I can work from a much bigger sample size . . . a bigger pool of people.''

She thought a moment.

"I don't recall a case where a woman used two men at the same time for the same murder. But there's always a first.''

"You've been very helpful Cindy. Thanks.''

"For you, I'd do anything."

Decker felt a warm glow in his heart. He kissed Cindy's forehead. "You look tired. You *are* going to sleep here tonight, correct?"

Cindy checked her watch. "Yeah, it is a little late. I'll bunk down in Hannah's room. Baby's rooms always smell so sweet."

Decker looked into his daughter's eyes. "You take care of yourself, okay?"

"I will." She studied her father. "Your color's better, Dad. You look happier. Must be my positive influence."

"That—and the fact that I'm finally getting something back from all that tuition."

Cindy whacked him. Just like Rina.

Why were women always hitting him?

Must say something about their own helplessness. Or maybe something about dominance needs.

Even Jeanine. She had hit him, too. Only in her case, she had hit him where it hurt.

❧19

All dressed up with nowhere to go. But it didn't matter much. With stakeouts, image was everything. Dark suit, striped silk tie, white shirt, and a bulging briefcase with a gold clasp. The ensemble stated that Webster *belonged*. Because even without looking at the directory, he instinctively knew that Jeanine Garrison's building had to contain law offices.

He rode the elevators, a portable CD player stowed in his pocket, earphones indiscernibly tucked into his outer canal. Chopin. Piano études. They didn't get in the way. In his breast pocket was a Dictaphone, which he used instead of a notepad. Less conspicuous. Because lawyers did lots of dictation. He kept watch over who punched Jeanine's floor, who entered her office.

She didn't have many visitors. The mailman, the Federal Express guy, the UPS lady. Someone brought up coffee—cappuccino from a local coffee bar. When he wasn't riding in elevators, he loitered in the bathroom, listening to the rolls and frills of keyboard exercises. Time passed. Ten-thirty. He went back to the unmarked; Marge was already waiting for him. Within a minute, he had reviewed his two hours for her: Jeanine had come in around nine. She wore a red jacket with black trim over a black skirt and high heels. Great-looking legs. Great-looking ass.

"Her face wasn't too bad, either," Webster said. "The kind of woman who'd produce some interesting fantasies.

If she wasn't so crazy." He shook his head. "I reckon therein lies the rub."

Marge said, "Were you in the building?"

"Whole time."

"How'd you go unnoticed?"

"Just the anynomous West Valley lawyer."

Marge studied her clothing—black rayon pants, white blouse, black bomber jacket. She tapped her foot. "I'll stand out if I go in like I am."

"Agreed."

"Any ideas?"

"Uh, I hate to say this but . . ."

"What?"

"There's a weight-loss clinic up there—"

Marge hit him.

"Lots of ladies going in and out."

"And I'll just blend in perfectly, huh?"

"There's also a gym." He winked. "You can go for the burn, babe."

"What got into you?"

"Just cutting loose." He clicked off his CD, threw his tissue paper–stuffed briefcase in the back of his unmarked. "Glad to get rid of that thing."

Marge frowned. "You wouldn't happen to have a pair of sweats on you?"

"In the trunk of my car. Might bag on you a bit, but now's not the time for vanity." He retrieved the gym clothes, smelled the fabric. "It's livable."

She took the sweats. "Thanks. Watch the car door while I change?"

"Be glad to, sugar."

"And don't get so familiar with me."

Webster grinned. "Anything you say. I never argue with a lady. 'Specially if she's toting a gun."

Martinez was waiting in the parking lot, a smirk on his face. "How many calories a day did they put you on?"

"Yuck, yuck, yuck." She wiped her sweat-soaked forehead. "First, they weighed me in, then I got counseled by some yahoo thin person. Then they sent me over to the gym for a free introductory workout. Step aerobics on this stool thing. On, off, on, off, on, off. Talk about going nowhere. And all I'm gonna show for it is a monster-size charley horse tomorrow."

"Get a chance to work at all?"

"For your information, I took a stool near the window, could see the office the entire time. Very quiet place. Nobody in, nobody out. I wonder what she does all day? Probably preens in the mirror."

"Or tortures men." Martinez shrugged. "Well, I brought a good costume." He reached into a bag, pulled out a janitor's uniform. "No spee . . . inglaze."

"Except what are you going to clean, Bert? You don't have keys to the office."

Martinez held up a finger, opened the trunk of the car. Out came a vacuum cleaner. "Tommy said the halls were carpeted."

Marge laughed. "But what are you going to do if she suddenly takes off in her car? You can't follow her unnoticed, lugging a vacuum cleaner."

"Yeah, I thought of that. See, that's why I put a locator under the chassis of her car."

"That's illegal."

"I suppose it is."

Marge covered her face. "Are we breaking every rule in the book?"

"Nah, we got a few left."

"Good luck." Marge gave him a wave. "Off to testify."

"Which case?"

"*Tobias* versus *State*."

"Mr. 'I'm sorry, I'm sorry.' "

"Wait till the judge gets through with him." Marge grinned. "He'll give Tobias something to *really* be sorry about."

"So Jeanine has total control over David's trust money?" Decker asked.

Gaynor said, "Well, she can't commit fraud or embezzle.

Things like that would jump out if she were ever sued. But there are subtle things she can do to siphon off David's portion into hers.''

"Like?''

"As trustee of the fund and executrix of the will, she can take modest up-front fees for managing the cash. And she's allowed to invest the remaining portion of his inheritance in whatever she wants.''

"That's a lot of leeway. There have to be some restrictions, Farrell.''

"Anything she wants, Loo. As long as she's not reckless. She is liable if she goes beyond what's considered standard investment practices. But that's still miles of rope. She can get to him in a number of ways.''

"Such as?''

"Something simple . . . like tying up his money. Ironically, all the safe and sound investments are *long-term*. Things like munis and T-bonds.''

"There's a secondary market for them.''

"Yeah, but historically bonds drop over the long run. They're terrible for quick cash. And in the trust, there is a proviso for that.''

"Quick cash proviso?''

"It's called a one-time emergency dispersal. Works like this. If David needs instant money, he can go to his sister. At her discretion, she can grant him his request if it is determined that it is a true emergency.''

"Who determines that?''

"There's room for debate here.''

"He could say it's an emergency, but she could say no?''

"Exactly.''

"And then they'd take it to court?''

"Yes.'' Farrell coughed. "Anyway, if she were so inclined, she could give David a one-time payout of a percentage of his own money based on the fund's assets at the time. Now here's where a borderline ripoff could occur.''

"Okay.''

"Jeanine could claim that his assets are tied up with no liquid money. But . . .''

Gaynor held up a finger.

"Being a kind, caring sister, she could do him a favor. She could buy out a portion of his investment at current market value. Now if David's bonds happen to be lower than face value . . . which is usually the case with long-term bonds . . . then Jeanine gets a break."

"Still she's stuck with discounted bonds."

"Thing is, she can afford to do market timing. Either wait it out or sell if there's a sudden drop in interest rates. Because she controls her inheritance. She doesn't tie up *her* assets in long-term bonds."

"So she buys his money at a fraction of its worth."

"Exactly."

"And if David protests?"

"If Jeanine used standard prudent care when investing, he wouldn't have a case. Municipal bonds and T-bonds are definitely standard prudent care." Gaynor frowned. "If I were David, I wouldn't feel too secure. If Jeanine murdered her parents, I don't think she'd hesitate at murdering her brother if he got in her way."

"Except that it would start to look mighty suspicious." Decker thought a moment. "Of course, David could always meet with an accident in the form of a drug OD."

Gaynor said, "Carry that one step further . . . if Jeanine worked quickly, before the initial cash dispersal from the trust, his cash inheritance would probably go to her."

They were quiet.

Gaynor said, "We could tell him our thoughts."

Decker said, "But then if he goes ahead and tells Jeanine . . . that makes us liable for slander."

Gaynor said, "Not to mention setting us up for an invasion of privacy. I sort of skirted some legality here."

Decker thought a moment. "Still, we should talk to David again. Send Webster over there and see if he can slip it in subtly. Better yet, I'll send Scott to talk to him."

Gaynor laughed. "Scott? I thought I used the word subtle."

Decker laughed, too. "Oliver's interview could give us a different perspective, Farrell. Besides, maybe a second interview would jog his memory about other things.''

"I suppose Scott couldn't hurt too much." Gaynor gave out a friendly chuckle. "And just maybe, he'll even help."

So much smoke that the window view sat behind a jaundiced cloud of nicotine. The guy had downed enough cigarettes to put R. J. Reynolds in the black. Even so, Oliver liked David Garrison, his matter-of-fact manner when it came to his inheritance. He expected nothing. Anything he got out of it would constitute gravy.

"Generous brother," Oliver said.

"Practical brother," Garrison retorted.

Today he was dressed in a black silk tee and baggy black chinos. On his feet were suede loafers without socks. He sat on his sofa, legs crossed, arms crossed, puffing away. On the coffee table was an empty highball glass.

"Sure I can't get you anything?" Garrison asked Oliver.

"Nothing, thanks."

"Murine for your red eyes?" Garrison smiled, smashed out the cigarette in a mountain of butts. "Terrible vice."

"I know," Oliver said. "Pisses people off like you wouldn't believe." He grinned. "Don't you love it?"

David broke into unrestrained laughter. "One of my true pleasures. Irritating people." He regarded Oliver. "Obviously one of your pleasures as well. Is that why you became a cop?"

"One of the reasons."

"And another?"

"I do like putting scum in jail."

"Ah! So you *are* noble."

"Tarnished nobility . . . impoverished as well."

Garrison smiled, then turned contemplative. "One interview with the cops . . . now I would assess that as police standard practice. But *two* interviews?"

"We're thorough."

"No, you're redundant. I have two questions. Why are the police so interested in my inheritance? And . . . are you asking Jeanine these same questions?"

Oliver played with the knot in his tie. Today, he chose

to wear a brown glen-plaid sport jacket over a white shirt and khakis. "I take it you haven't had much contact with your sister since the funeral?"

"My contact with her has been through her lawyers."

"You don't get along with your sister?"

"No, although we're not openly at war. We each just pretend the other doesn't exist. Now that my parents are . . . gone . . ." He sighed. "It just makes everything that much easier."

Oliver said, "No reason to have contact with her."

"Exactly." Garrison lit another cigarette. "You know, the fact that I'm smoking is a very good sign. It means I'm waxing productive."

"Congratulations."

Garrison sat back, inhaled, then exhaled a billowing cloud of tar. "Yes, a very good sign. I've actually taken a job. F/X for an upcoming Van Grek movie. Sort of a re-make of *The Blob*. I saw the original just to get a feel for what had been done." He laughed. "It's ludicrous from a technical standpoint, but it has its moments. When that shit suddenly pours from the projection room into the movie theater . . . well, it took me aback."

Oliver smiled. "Scared the bejesus out of me when I was little."

"Yes, I can completely understand that." Garrison smoked in silence, his thoughts far away. "All these computer graphics . . ." He shook his head. "The guy next to me has been working on one story-board frame for *three* months. Van Grek's upper torso melting into a flaming sea of lava-crusted furniture." He looked at Oliver. "I wonder if the end result won't be so dazzling that it will cease to be scary."

Oliver was quiet.

Garrison smiled. "Ah, well. Silly musings. You never answered my first question. Why are you interested in my inheritance?"

His attitude was so nonchalant, Oliver couldn't help but wonder if Jeanine had gotten to him . . . offered him immediate bucks to keep a low profile.

"Insurance companies," Oliver lied.

"Pardon?"

"It's really absurd to waste police time with it," Oliver said. "But LAPD has been on the hot seat for so long. Anyway, seems insurance companies have had lots of requests for payouts."

"Of course," Garrison said. "People *died* at Estelle's."

"Well, they're doing lots of probing." Oliver sat up, talked to Garrison as if he were confiding in him. "They just want to make sure that Estelle's is what it is. You know—a crazy murderer gone berserk. That it wasn't a planned thing for someone to collect money."

"But the guy committed suicide."

"It's nutty to me, too. But I'm just doing my job, making sure that the police don't overlook anything."

"Did my parents even have life insurance?"

"I thought maybe you'd know."

"I don't. I was shocked when I heard I stood to inherit money . . . a lot of money."

"Do you know how much?"

"Something around a million dollars. I tell you I was *floored.*" Garrison thought a moment. "Actually, I think I ceased being the scapegoat once Dad saw that Jeanine was less than perfect."

Oliver paused. "In what way?"

Garrison laughed. "Well, the girl was completely overindulged. Always had to be center stage. I do believe even Dad was growing weary of her tantrums, her incessant demands for him to fund her charities."

"He told you this?"

"No. But Mom . . . hinted all was not perfect between Dad and Jeanine." He sighed. "Still, he set Jeanine up as Queen Bee. You want to know about our finances, talk to her."

"She's kind of difficult to reach."

"Yes, she does surround herself with worker bees . . . drones, as well."

"Lots of boyfriends?"

"Pu-leeze."

"Tennis players?"

"Are you asking a rhetorical question?"

Oliver shrugged.

"Yes, tennis players. Mainly because tennis attracts wannabes and hangers-on. And that's what she likes. Men who hang on to her ... admire her ... think she's something *special*. Because growing up, though she was the pretty one, I was the *special* one. Little did she know I would have loved to change places with her, to have nothing expected of me except to smile. Ah, well, seems as if nobody is ever happy with his or her lot in life."

"So you two have never been close?"

"Never. Our father did an excellent job of programming us to hate each other." Garrison lit another cigarette. "He boxed us into categories."

He started ticking off on his fingers.

"Jeanine's pretty, I'm average-looking. Jeanine's smart, I'm brilliant. Jeanine's social, I'm shy and snobbish. Jeanine's caring, I'm distant and cold. Jeanine's organized, I'm in constant disarray."

He laughed.

"At least I was always my own person. Jeanine was always dependent on my father's good graces for her fun. Of course now, with my parents gone, she's independent. Maybe now she'll finally do something with her life besides leech off others' talents."

He smiled wickedly.

"But probably not."

❦20

Sipping coffee, Decker flipped through the morning papers at four in the afternoon. *The Valley Voice* still had Estelle's as one of its hot items—a side column analysis on Harlan Manz. But the *Times* had relegated it to the back: a Hollywood tribute to Walter Skinner.

The one article that did grab his interest was found on page three of the sports section. More specifically, a photograph of Jeanine Garrison standing at the side of a handsome man dressed in tennis whites. A handsomely carved face. High forehead, a prominent chin. Clipped, curly hair, penetrating eyes, and a neatly trimmed five o'clock shadow.

He was also confined to a wheelchair.

Jeanine's hand resting on his shoulder.

Wade Anthony.

Both of them looking like models. Gorgeous but grave. A small caption underneath the snapshot. Their names. Their purpose. A wheelchair tennis tournament for victims' rights. A round-robin affair with stars promising to attend or lend support. But it was Wade Anthony who was the true star—a top ten seeded player in wheelchair tennis. He promised a big draw for a very important cause.

Decker stared at the photo, then broke into laughter.

At least it was for charity.

The knock distracted his attention. Decker looked up, told Gaynor to come in. He showed Farrell the photograph.

"This ditty was *my* idea."

185

"And then she slams you. A real sweetheart."

Gaynor sat down.

"Jeanine for victims' rights. Kinda like O. J. hosting a charity for domestic violence." He paused. "Come to think of it, O. J. *did* host a charity for domestic violence. What's this world coming to?"

At that moment, Marge and Oliver walked into his office. Decker looked up. "Someone call a meeting?"

Gaynor said, "I took the liberty."

Oliver pulled up a chair. "Figured it's a good time to recap, right before the weekend."

"Recap what? Jeanine's harassment?" Decker showed Oliver the newspaper.

"Ah shit!" He threw up his hands. "Now we'll *never* get to her!"

Marge read the caption. "So *this* is why the mayor put the vise on Strapp's balls."

Webster and Martinez came in. Oliver tossed Bert the newspaper. "Take a look at that."

"Ker-rist!" Martinez said.

Webster read over Bert's shoulder. "Fuck it. We'll find a way."

"She's makin' it harder and harder," Oliver said. "And I ain't talking about my shlong."

Webster turned to Oliver. "Whaddaya think 'bout David Garrison?"

"He smokes a lot."

"Talk about his sister?" Marge asked.

"Yeah. He hates her."

"You think it's genuine?" Webster asked.

"I'd say it was the real article," Oliver answered. "What about you?"

"My take as well."

"So you don't see brother in cahoots with sister?" Marge asked.

"Unless the guy's doing a right fine job of playacting," Webster said. "I think he really despises her."

"I agree," Oliver said. "Resents her Queen Bee status

as Daddy's favorite.'' He hesitated. ''He said something
that was kinda telling.''

''What?'' Webster asked.

''He said once he stopped being the family scapegoat,
his father began to see Jeanine in a different light. Said Dad
was growing tired of Jeanine's tantrums, getting sick of
paying for her parties.'' Oliver turned to Decker. ''Remember we were talking about a motivation for Jeanine popping
her parents. That she wasn't independently wealthy. I'm
beginning to like that theory.''

''Why?'' Decker asked.

''The mother . . . Linda Garrison . . . she had hinted to
David that all was not well between Pop and Daughter.
Maybe Jeanine became homicidally resentful.''

''Yeah, it sounds pretty,'' Decker said. ''Too pretty. Remember that David's a former druggie and ex-convict. A
notoriously dishonest combination. He could be setting her
up.''

Marge said, ''How do we get to either one of them?''

''Forget about them,'' Decker said. ''We're going after
the phantom killer. I've spoken to some people, come up
with a crude profile of who this ghost might be.''

Decker summarized Cindy's findings. If Harlan was recruited from Greenvale, someone like him might also have
been recruited from Greenvale as the number two killer.
The guy might be similar to Harlan but possibly younger—
angry, impressionable, unstable, grandiose in his thinking,
a big one for blaming life, and in a one-down position from
Jeanine.

Martinez said, ''So this is all we have to go on?''

Gaynor raised his hand. ''I think I might be able to help
you out here.''

All eyes turned to him.

''I just happened to get hold of some reservations books
from Greenvale—''

Decker exploded. ''Farrell, why didn't you *say* something when we began?''

''I didn't want to interrupt you.'' Gaynor shrugged.

"When my boss talks, I listen. Maybe this old dog can learn something new."

Oliver glared at him. "Can I ask you something?"

"What?"

"How do you come up with these tidbits?" In a mocking voice, Oliver said, " 'I just happened to get hold—' "

"The seniors grapevine. Good place to make connections. Old people love to talk. And to help out. And there are quite a few old people at Greenvale—"

"How'd you get through the door?" Marge asked.

"My wife's sister's brother-in-law is a member. Elwood Halstead. Nice guy. Made his money in plastics, has this big mart—"

"Farrell, we don't need the details," Marge said.

Gaynor smiled benignly. "Suit yourself. Anyway, I asked El for an invitation; he took me out to lunch. I try to maintain good relationships with the family."

Oliver hit his forehead with disbelief. "Bully for you."

"It got me somewhere, didn't it?" Gaynor retorted.

Oliver said, "I don't know that yet because I haven't *heard* where it got—"

Decker said, "Stop squabbling." He looked pointedly at Gaynor. "Farrell, I've got to get out of here in an hour."

"No problem, Loo." Gaynor said. "Anyway, while I was there, I took a massage. Good for the old muscles. The masseur was my age, had been working at Greenvale from the beginning." He paused. "But he didn't remember Hart Mansfield."

The room was quiet.

"And . . ." Decker prodded.

"Oh . . . sorry, lost my train of thought." Gaynor cleared his throat. "Anyway, he was . . . cooperative. And I sort of helped myself to the older reservations books. Some of them went years back. Anyway, Jeanine takes a weekly massage with a woman named Jane. Has been taking it for at least four years."

Martinez said, "Did this Jane act suspicious or anything?"

"Anyone can point a gun. But no, there's nothing suspicious about her."

A pause.

"So?" Webster asked.

"So nothing," Gaynor said. "I crossed Jane off the list. Jeanine had also made other appointments—with the restaurant, with the beauty shop, hair salon, aromatherapy, makeovers and nails . . . Jeanine's really into her nails."

Again, there was silence.

Gaynor said, "All of it looks perfectly normal—"

"Will you please speed it—" Oliver interrupted.

"I'm getting to it, all right?" Once again, Farrell cleared his throat. "Well, like I said, the bad news is that nothing looks suspicious. Because most of her cosmetic and therapeutic appointments were with women—"

Webster said, "Like you said, anyone can point a gun."

"That would be interesting," Marge said. "Jeanine working on a woman and a man at the same time."

"I think we're really *jumping* the gun," Martinez said. "Not only are we assuming she's involved—which is still an if—we have her sexual proclivities mapped out."

"No, her massage appointments really didn't pique my interest," Farrell said. "Not like her court appointments."

"Court appointments?" Webster asked. "Is she being sued?"

"No, not legal court appointments. I couldn't find any of those—"

"Farrell, spit it *out*!" Decker said.

"Her reservations for the tennis court. She's been playing with the same partner for the last six months."

Again, all eyes drifted to Gaynor's face. Farrell was quiet.

"And . . ." Decker waved him to continue.

"A gentleman by the name of Sean Amos."

Decker clenched his teeth. "Who is . . ."

"A very rich boy."

"Boy?" Marge said. "How old?"

"Sixteen . . . oh, wait." Farrell scanned his notes. "Just turned seventeen."

Oliver clapped his hands with joy. "Statutory rape here we come."

"Won't wash," Marge said. "Kid's too old."

"But this isn't peer sex," Martinez said. "Jeanine's twenty-eight."

"How do we know they were even having sex?" Martinez said.

"You have eyes, Bert," Oliver said. "You've seen Jeanine."

"Yeah, you're right."

"What does the kid look like?" Oliver asked.

Farrell said, "The reservations books didn't have pictures, Scott. But I did ask a couple of discreet questions about the family." Again he faced Oliver. "Through the seniors grapevine."

Decker opened his pad. "Go."

"The father's name is Lamar Amos. He's sixty-two. From Texas oil. Owns a chemical processing plant in Long Beach."

"And he lives in the West Valley?" Martinez made a face. "That's almost fifty miles away."

"No, he doesn't live in the West Valley. He lives in Palos Verdes Peninsula with his twenty-two-year-old fourth wife, Amber."

"Then who is Sean's mother?" Decker asked.

"Lily Amos. She's forty, lives in West Valley Estates. She's the one who's a member."

Decker thought about Cindy's profile . . . a club member, maybe even a teenager not big on impulse control. "You find out where he goes to school?"

"Of course. Westbridge Prep—"

"Love those spiffy blue blazers," Oliver said. "Should I have a chat with the lad?"

"On what basis?" Marge said. "That he plays tennis with Jeanine Garrison? She files something ridiculous on the Loo, she's going to file police harassment if we start questioning her underage tennis partner."

Decker said, "Farrell, how long has Mrs. Amos been living in her current house?"

Gaynor rummaged through his notes. "Six years. Member of the club for five."

"Good. So she has established a routine. Kid's not going anywhere over the weekend. We start fresh on Monday." Decker turned to Webster. "I'll need someone who talks in Ivy League language. Can you pull it off?"

Webster answered, "Tell me your approach, Loo."

"Sean's a tennis player, right?" Decker said. "His mom was a member when Harlan was an instructor there two years ago. So let's assume Sean has been taking lessons for a while. Let's also assume that maybe . . . just *maybe* . . . he remembers a summer tennis teacher named Hart Mansfield."

Oliver said, "So we ask Sean about *Harlan,* not about Garrison."

"Exactly," Decker said. "Ask Sean about Harlan Manz/ Hart Mansfield. You know teenagers. Love to be the center of attention. Even if Sean has only had a glimpse of Harlan, he'll play it to the hilt."

Webster said, "What kind of questions, Loo?"

"Does he remember Manz, remember anything weird about him, ever remember him being angry . . . any kind of bullshit? Let's just get the kid *talking*."

"And if he brings up Jeanine on his own?" Webster asked.

Decker waited a beat. "If Sean happens to mention Jeanine casually. Says something like . . . 'You know you should be asking my tennis partner these questions. Because she's played longer than I have.' Then maybe his tennis games with Jeanine are just that. Simple tennis games with a partner."

"And if he doesn't say that, Loo?" Marge asked.

Decker shrugged.

Webster said, "Can I ask him about his tennis partners without mentioning names?"

"Too pointed," Martinez said.

"I agree," Decker said. "First priority is to protect you people. Last thing I want is for Jeanine to slap Tom with a police harassment suit."

Oliver said, "Then what's the purpose of interviewing Sean in the first place?"

Decker said, "Jeanine didn't pull the trigger, Scotty. I told you we're going after the phantom, number two shooter—if he exists."

Martinez said, "Loo, even if Sean was screwing her, it doesn't mean he was involved in Estelle's."

Decker grinned. "No. But if they *are* having sex, it does show Jeanine's character. And that's good news for me in case she presses charges."

Before Decker could make it out the door, Strapp called him into his chambers, closed the door to his office. No preamble. Just straight talk. "We heard from Jeanine's lawyer again. She says you're harassing her brother—"

"That's ridiculous. They hate each other. According to David, they're not even in contact."

"That's what *he's* telling *you* to your face. Behind your back may be another story."

"Captain, is David Garrison complaining about harassment?"

Strapp shook his head no.

Decker spread out his arms as if to say, so there you have it.

Strapp said, "She thinks you're putting your men up to it. All part of your plan to get revenge."

Decker reminded himself to speak slowly. "Of course, I've assigned David to my people. We both agreed on that. I'm running an *investigation*."

"Yeah, but from her point of view—"

"Her point of view is bullshit. She's trying to stifle the investigation."

"Yes, it is beginning to seem that way."

Decker said nothing, feeling a little calmer. "You know, I had a team tail on her almost the entire day. I know that Jeanine didn't visit David. And she didn't call him—"

"How do you know that?"

"I'm thorough, sir. Just got off the horn with the phone company. No calls logged between them."

Strapp was silent.

"She must have had someone watching his apartment. Saw Oliver go inside . . ." Decker shook his head in awe. "She really is one hell of an organizer."

Strapp said, "Do you have anything concrete on David Garrison?"

"No."

"Any hot leads that might pan out?"

"Nothing."

"So I'm not creating any problems by telling you to keep away from him until we work out a plan with the lawyers."

"No, actually that's okay. At least for right now." Decker stood. "Can I go? I'd like to make it home for my Sabbath."

Strapp eyed his lieutenant. "You've got something up your sleeve, haven't you?"

"Come again, sir?"

"Don't play dumb, because you're not. I'm talking about Jeanine Garrison. If you're trying to get to her in a round-about fashion, you'd better fill me in."

Decker told him about Sean Amos.

Strapp started pacing. "Quash the plan. I don't like it. You see the paper today?"

"Sports section, yes."

"So you see what we're up against. Besides, what's your reasoning for going after this Sean Amos—other than the fact that he's Jeanine's tennis partner."

"That is the reason, sir."

"You've got to come up with something better than that."

"Sir, right now we're assuming that Harlan worked with an accomplice. I'm trying to find a candidate. Look, sir, I'm not going to question Sean Amos about his relationship with Jeanine Garrison. I'm going to question him about *Harlan Manz*. Simple point-of-information interview because Amos was a member of the club when Harlan taught."

"So you're questioning this boy about Harlan only?"

"Yes. No one's going to mention Jeanine." Decker

waited a beat. "Of course, if he brought her up, we weren't going to prevent him from talking."

Strapp didn't speak for a while. Finally, he said, "Okay. This is what we'll do. *I'll* order the interview. Take the heat off you."

Decker was stunned. "Thank you."

"But if *I'm* ordering the interview, you do it my way. If we question Sean Amos, we're going to have to question at least half a dozen other boys and girls his age who played tennis at the club when Harlan taught."

Decker grinned. "What a great idea. If Sean Amos is having an affair with Jeanine, he won't talk about it to us. But he might have bragged about it to one of his teenage friends. One of them might let it slip out to us."

"Okay, so Sean Amos is taken care of."

Strapp paused.

"Now here's the bad news. Jeanine is doing more than making noises. Our guys want to talk to you. I've set up a meeting at nine Monday morning."

"A Fact Sheet?"

"Yeah."

Decker nodded. Normally, when a complaint was filed, the presiding lieutenant took down the detective's story. Since he was a lieutenant, he'd probably be questioned by Myerhoff—the patrol lieutenant. Or by the Internal Affairs Department if Jeanine actually decided to file a 181 personal complaint. "Is Myerhoff doing the questioning?"

"IAD."

"Terrific." Decker rolled his eyes. "Why?"

Strapp shrugged. "Maybe Jeanine had her monkeys call them as well."

"Who's Jeanine's lawyer?"

"Guy by the name of Silverberg. Know him?"

"No."

"Neither do I. I'll have PPL look into him."

Decker asked, "Police Protection League going to send me someone good . . . as in competent?"

"You'll have a defense rep, of course."

"I repeat . . . a *competent* one?"

"We won't know until Monday. You want to think about hiring a private lawyer, that's up to you."

"Let's see how far it goes." Decker exhaled angrily. "This is a shitty deal."

"It's standard procedure, Peter."

"I don't have to like it."

"Do you have any other complaints against you on your record?"

"One. About ten years ago. A hype claimed I roughed him up."

"How'd the complaint resolve?"

"Unfounded."

"Good."

"That one was easy. He was a hype, lying was his native tongue. Jeanine isn't going to go down as easily."

"No chinks in her story?"

"Believe me, I've been racking my brains. So far, it's her word against mine. At this point, best I can hope for is an Unsustained. Unless we show her involvment in the murders at Estelle's."

"Wouldn't that be wonderful." Strapp paused. "You tell your wife?"

"First thing."

"How's she reacting?"

"Rina's been great. More than I deserve considering how testy I've been lately."

"So you've been completely honest with her about this?"

"Fortunately, there's nothing to be dishonest about. I didn't do anything."

"You told me you found Jeanine attractive, Decker. What if they offer you a polygraph?"

"I'll say go ahead."

"Then they hook you up to a machine, ask you lots of questions. Personal ones. About you and women. About your sex life. Ask you about Jeanine, if you found her sexy, if you wanted to fuck her. How are you going to answer that?"

"I'll tell the truth."

"What if this goes to a grand jury? They might ask the same questions. Your wife's going to hear things."

"It's not a problem."

"So you told Rina you found Jeanine a turn-on?"

Decker bristled. "Not in so many words, but yes, the gist came out that way."

Strapp raised his eyebrows. "And?"

"I'm not concerned." Decker sat back in his chair, pounding his fist to his forehead. "God, how can you find a woman so attractive one moment, then absolutely despise everything about her the next?"

"Don't let that attitude leave the office. It sounds vengeful."

"I know. Got to be stoic."

Strapp was quiet for a moment. "If you think Rina can handle it, it might be a good idea if she was with you at your questioning."

Decker was taken aback. "You're kidding."

"No, I'm not. She can't help you legally. But she can't hurt you, either. Because a wife can't testify against her husband."

"So why should I drag her into it?"

Strapp said, "I'll be blunt. Your wife is beautiful, Peter. And she's *young*. Quite a bit younger than you—"

"Twelve years."

"This kind of charge is a subjective thing. Like you said, it's Jeanine's word against yours. I know these jokers from IAD. Jeanine's a looker. They'll have no problem believing that you came on to her. You need to counteract that notion. Show them *your* side—your sterling record *and* your beautiful, charming wife who *isn't* at all concerned. It's going to influence the way IAD thinks. It isn't supposed to work that way. But it does. Think Rina could handle personal questions about your thoughts on Jeanine? Personal questions about your sex life?"

Again, Decker rubbed his face. "I'm not saying she'll view it as a cakewalk, but Rina's tough. She can handle it."

"She's got to play it right, Pete. Casual. No tears, of

course. But she can't present a defensive posture, either."

"Okay."

"No snit fits or hysteria."

Decker smiled wryly. "No, sir, that's my department."

✌21

No doubt Rina noticed how antsy he was. But she chose not to mention it. Instead, they ate and waxed festive, the kids monopolizing the dinner conversation. Which was as it should be. Dinner topics were the machinations of the school's student council and Sammy's rules of the road. As a week-old driver, the boy was now an expert. During the lectures, Rina served up a "modest" Shabbos meal—puree of carrot soup followed by chicken breasts stuffed with wild rice and broccoli Dijonnaise on the side. Dessert was a fresh apple cobbler. When Decker questioned her definition of the word "modest," she replied that she hadn't served a salad.

Decker sipped coffee. "The meal was wonderful."

"Top-notch," Sammy added.

Rina said, "Anything would taste wonderful after eating cafeteria food for a week."

"It's a compliment, Mom."

"I'm glad you liked it."

Jacob said, "Are we walking over to the yeshiva tomorrow?"

"Yes, of course."

"Are we walking back?"

"I'm sure I could wangle you a lunch invitation at Rav Schulman's if you don't feel like walking back."

The boy was quiet. He pushed black hair from piercing

blue eyes, looked at his parents. "We should move," he announced.

Rina and Decker exchanged glances.

"We're in the middle of nowhere," Jake said. "It's an hour's walk to the yeshiva and an hour and a half walk to visit anyone from our school. You know, Hannah's four. Eventually she's going to want to go to shul. We can't leave her with a baby-sitter forever. Either we should live closer to the yeshiva or move into the West Valley community."

No one spoke.

Decker closed his eyes and opened them. "You're right."

Jake grinned. "Really?"

"Really." Decker put down his coffee mug. "I'm sure it hasn't been easy for you being so isolated these past six years."

"It hasn't been bad." Sam took another piece of cobbler. "Actually, it's been okay. After Abba died, I didn't feel like being social on Shabbos. All those pitying looks. And then it was good to have some time alone with . . . you know . . . with Dad."

Decker felt his throat constrict. "Thank you. I felt the same way. But now it's different."

"What would you do with the horses?" Rina asked.

"We hardly ride at all anymore," Jake said. "Just sell them."

Rina said, "Slowly, Yonkie. It's not that easy."

Decker said, "Give your mother and me a few days to mull it over. We'll come up with something."

Jake tapped the table. "You know, we can fit into a smaller house. It doesn't have to be fancy. Whatever's convenient."

Decker smiled. "It would be very convenient if you two would clear the table and watch your sister for a bit. I need to talk to your mom."

Sammy said, "I'm still eating."

Everyone stopped talking, watched Sam eat. He pushed

the plate away and got up. "Talk about being center stage. I know when I'm not wanted."

"Hannah, help us clear." Jake gave his little sister an empty soda can. "Bring it into the kitchen."

The girl broke into a smile, ran into the kitchen holding the can. The boys gathered up the dirty dishes.

Decker turned to his wife. "How's tricks?"

"Nothing too much other than going blind from looking at numbers."

"Oh, yeah." Decker sat up. "The yeshiva's books. What's going on?"

"The yeshiva looks to be richer than I originally thought. Lots of paper profit. The yeshiva owns a ton of stock."

"Who's been investing for them?"

"No one. Most of the stock has been given to them. From what I can figure out, it seems that the donors probably bought the stock years ago."

"At cheap prices."

"Exactly." Rina handed Hannah another empty soda can. Again the little girl took flight into the kitchen.

Decker said, "Buying ten thou worth of stock and it's now worth twenty thou—"

"More like a hundred thou."

"What's worth a hundred thou?" Sammy asked.

Rina said, "Take the baby to her room, boys. I'll get the rest."

"Trying to get rid of us?"

"In a word, yes." Rina smiled brightly. "Good-bye."

Jacob scooped his sister into his arms. "What do you want to do, Han?"

Hannah said, "Well . . . how 'bout playing dinosaurs."

"Okay."

"And play Barney, too."

"Okay."

"Then read books!" Hannah kicked until Jacob lowered her to the ground. She took Jake's hand in her right and Sam's hand in her left. "Swing me."

The teenagers complied. Decker laughed. "Who really runs the house?"

"That's not even debatable."

"Unlike the yeshiva's books." Decker smiled. "Actually, donating stock is quite a common ploy in estate planning. You buy a stock, hold on to it. The shares increase in value. Then you donate the stock to a charity. Not only do you avoid capital gains tax, but also you get the deduction for the shares' increased value."

"The amounts are startling. Lots of blue-chip certificates just sitting in a drawer in Rabbi Schulman's office. They've been there for years."

"Does Rav Schulman know what he has?"

"I don't think he has a clue. I can't understand why he never put all these assets with a money manager." Rina shrugged. "Although maybe it's better. Somebody might have sold the stocks a long time ago. Instead, the shares have been splitting and growing and splitting and growing."

"Just going up and up . . ." Abruptly, Decker appeared pensive. "Has Jake ever mentioned moving before?"

Rina sighed. "He's hinted. He's a very social kid. You know how it is, especially in the teenage years. He really is away from the action on Shabbos."

Decker wrapped his hands around his coffee mug. "He's been a good sport."

Rina bit her nail. "How much do you think we can get for this place?"

"Not too much," Decker said. "I built it on spit and a promise. It's up to code, but it's sadly lacking in anything but basics. We'll take what we can get and buy what we can afford. Obviously, Jake doesn't care about luxuries."

Rina stroked her arms. "You know, I have money."

Decker felt his jaw tighten. "I don't need my wife's money to pay for my family's house."

"It's not *your* family, it's *our* family. You're being old-fashioned. What good is the money if we don't use it for things like this?"

Decker didn't say the obvious. Yes, he had life insurance, but it wasn't nearly enough to sustain a family and put three kids through college. Rina's trust from her parents was *emergency* money—in case something happened to him. And having been shot twice, he wasn't doing theoretical estate planning. He said, "We have savings. I make a good living. We'll work it out."

Rina looked away. "Why do you take everything on your shoulders, Peter? Why don't you let me help?"

"You do help. You run the house, take care of the family. You do *all* the finances. I haven't paid a bill since we married. You could be parking all of our money in a Swiss bank account, getting ready to leave me high and dry. And I wouldn't know the difference."

"That's an odd thing to say." She stared at him, placed her hand on his. "What's going on with you? It's that stupid harassment suit, isn't it? Is she charging you?"

Decker pulled his hand away, buried his head in his palms, then looked at his wife. "Strapp got a call from IAD. I've got to go through what they call a Fact Sheet on Monday."

"Which means?"

"IAD asks questions about the alleged incident."

"And?"

"They compare your answers with the charges brought against you . . . come up with a decision. Not right away . . . all this takes time. There are three decisions they can come up with. First, the charges are sustained. Which means they believe the charges against you are true. For that to happen, you have to have dates and witnesses—"

"Motel receipts."

"Even less than that. Just witnesses who confirm that they saw you two together outside the bounds of work. Like in a restaurant or at a movie. Corroborating evidence. I'm not worried about a Sustained verdict. It's the second conclusion they could reach. An Unsustained. Which is like a no-contest. There's not enough evidence to sustain *or* refute the charges. Third verdict is Unfounded, which says the charges are false. That would happen if we caught her lying, found a chink in her story."

"Such as?"

"Such as if she said . . . oh, I don't know. If she said I

had drinks with her at four o'clock and I have proof and witnesses that say I was in my office at four o'clock. Something like that.''

"And that's not likely to happen, either.''

Decker averted his gaze. "Correct. That is not likely to happen, either.''

Rina said, "So the best you can hope for is an Unsustained?''

Decker's fists were clenched. "Unless I can prove what I already know. That Jeanine had some involvment in Estelle's. You know, I don't even *care* about these ridiculous charges. I care about thirteen deaths and thirty-two wounded. I care about the trauma and mayhem that an evil, evil woman inflicted upon innocent people. I'm going to nail her, Rina. I swear, if it's the last thing I do, I'm going to *bury* that bitch where the sun don't shine.''

The room turned silent. Quietly, Rina said, "I admire your passion, Peter. Your unquestionable drive to do the right thing. But . . . but if you show emotion when you're questioned . . . it's going to look very bad.''

He bit his lip. "You're very perceptive. Strapp said the same thing.'' He looked her in the eye. "He wants you there for the questioning.''

"Me?''

"As an ornament. The charming, beautiful wife. To show IAD that I had absolutely no reason for wanting to stray.''

"The fact that you have an attractive wife would make a difference?''

"Strapp thinks so. I do too.''

"To have your unblemished twenty-five-year reputation hang on what I look like . . .'' She shook her head. "That's *nuts*!''

"Whole thing is nuts. But despite themselves, people are influenced by what they see. They see someone young and gorgeous and brilliant . . . Rina, they see you, they don't see a logical reason for me to cheat.''

"As if men were logical. You must know countless men

who have strayed with women much homelier than their wives.''

''Not countless—''

''Scott Oliver is a perfect example. You used to say his girlfriends were dogs. And his wife was very attractive.''

''Yes, she was.''

''Why did he do it then? Explain it to me, please.''

''Mid-life crisis, maybe.''

''Except he'd been doing it for a while.''

''I don't know, Rina. Some people have a hard time growing up.'' Decker unclenched his fists, laid his hands on the table. ''I'm sorry to drag you into this.''

''If you want me to be there, I'll be there.''

''I think it's a good idea.'' He smiled weakly. ''Besides, it'd be nice to see a friendly face.''

Rina's eyes started watering. She took his hand and kissed it. ''I love you.''

''I love you, too.'' Decker swallowed hard. ''They're going to ask lots of personal stuff. Maybe . . . it would be a good idea if I wrote down some of the possible questions. So we're both prepared. So I won't be embarrassed answering them in front of you.''

She held back tears. ''This is really a violation, isn't it?''

Decker smiled softly. ''Hey, like your mother says, as long as you got your health . . .''

Rina said, ''Let's go over the questions together. Then tell me what you want me to wear, tell me how I should act, tell me what I should say.''

''Just be yourself.'' He threw his head back, sighed. ''Ah well, instead of feeling sorry for myself, I should learn a little. Put my mind into something cosmic. Maybe I could even pick up a pointer or two from the holy books. Surely they must have something to say about a man being hunted down by an evil woman.''

Rina thought for a moment. ''Sort of like Elijah the prophet. Hiding out in the desert in a cave, depending on ravens for sustenance.''

''Who was he hiding from?''

''*Izevel* . . . Jezebel.''

"What happened?"

"To Elijah?" Rina said. "He went out with a bang. Taken to heaven alive in a chariot of fire—"

"Ah, yes . . . Sunday school's rearing its head. Elijah was a fanatic, wasn't he?"

Sammy entered the kitchen. "All the prophets were fanatics."

"Where's Hannah?" Rina asked.

"Fell asleep—"

"Shmuel—"

"Don't freak, Mom. I put her in a diaper and her pajamas."

Rina was shocked. "You actually had the foresight to dress her for bed?"

"No, he didn't," Jacob said. "But I did. Are we interrupting anything?"

Sammy said, "Just talking about fanatical prophets."

"They weren't fanatical," Rina countered. "They just said things that people didn't want to hear."

Decker squinted, trying to bring back ancient memories. "I remember Elijah. I don't remember reading about Jezebel . . . other than the fact that she's been immortalized as an evil temptress."

Rina said. "She was married to—" She stopped, looked at her sons. "Who was she married to?"

Sammy said, "It's 'know your prophets' time."

Jacob sang, "A-hab the A-rab—"

"He wasn't an Arab, he was a Jewish king," Rina clarified. "King of Israel to be specific. And who was the king of Judeah?"

Jacob and Sammy shrugged.

Rina looked disapprovingly. "You boys don't learn *Navi*—Prophets—in school?"

Sammy said, "*Navi*'s for wimps. Real men learn *gemora*—"

"Just answer the question."

"Students shouldn't show off in front of their teachers. You can answer the question, Eema."

Rina smiled. "Yehosophat was the king of Judeah."

"I don't know *what* you're talking about," Decker said.

Jacob said, "The Kingdom of Israel split into two after Solomon died. Rehovam was the King of Judeah, the legitimate king. The tribes of Levi, Judah, and one half the tribe of Benjamin remained loyal to him. The other ten tribes went with Jerovam—the king of Israel. Judeah was more righteous than Israel. Hence the other ten tribes were eventually lost in the Diaspora." He glared at his mother. "*Happy,* Eema?"

"Getting there."

"What happened to Jezebel?" Decker asked.

Sammy said. "She died. They all died. *Navi* are books about dead people—"

"Shmuel—"

"She was pushed out a high window," Sammy said. "Fell to her death, then was trampled by horses and finally eaten by dogs."

"Lovely," Decker said.

"It was a very fitting death," Rina said. "*Middah kenneged middah.* 'Measure by measure.' She bribed some men to bear false witness against a man in order to seize his vineyard. The poor guy was stoned and dogs lapped up his blood. Because of this, it was prophesied that in the end, dogs would do the same to her."

Jacob said, "They did more than lap her blood, Eema. They devoured her."

Decker asked, "They ate everything?"

"Except for her cranium, hands, and feet," Rina said. "Actually, just the palms of her hands and the soles of her feet remained intact." Again, she focused in on her sons. "Okay, guys. Now what's the logical question."

Decker said, "Why wasn't she eaten completely?"

"Exactly," Rina said. "The cranium you can understand."

"Too hard," Decker said. "But why the palms of the hands and soles of the feet? It's soft flesh. It's the first part dogs would have eaten—"

"This is real sick," Sammy said.

"That may be but your father is absolutely right." Rina

looked at her husband. "You've really got a scholar's head, Peter."

"What's the answer?" Decker asked.

Rina homed in on Sammy. "Why did Hashem spare her hands and feet? Because she did a mitzvah with them. A righteous deed from the heart. What deed could she have possibly done?"

No one answered.

Rina said. "What do you do with your palms?" She clapped her hands. "What do you do with your feet besides walking and running?"

Again no one spoke.

Rina said, "You dance."

"Kaitzad merakdim lifnai Hakallah?" Jacob said.

"I'm *impressed,* bro!" Sammy said.

"I win the prize, Eema?"

"You win the prize," Rina answered.

"What is . . . whatever you just said?" Decker asked.

"Kaitzad merakdim lifnai Hakallah?" Sammy said. "It means, 'How do you dance before a bride?' There are actually laws on what you should do before a bride . . . how you prepare her for her wedding, what to say to a groom."

Rina said, "The one and only nice thing Jezebel ever did was dance with a gladdened heart before a bride. Ergo, God spared her hands and feet."

Decker nodded, then abruptly burst out laughing, turning red in the process.

"What?" Rina said.

"Nothing."

"Uh-oh," Sammy said. "This must be good."

"No, it's really nothing," Decker said.

"Come on, Dad," Jacob piped in. "You usually don't laugh like that. What is it?"

Decker looked at Rina. "No, I think I'd better not push my luck."

"C'mon, Eema," Sammy said. "Give the man a break."

"I'm not his mother," Rina shot back. "He can say whatever he wants. And he often does."

Decker turned scarlet. "Well, I was just pondering what

would be left if the only good deed a man ever did was being fruitful and multiplying—''

The boys broke into unrestrained guffaws.

Rina stifled a smile. ''Is this Shabbos talk?''

Decker said, ''*You* set me up.''

''I was assuming you'd use good taste.''

Sammy chortled, ''That's where you went wrong.''

Jacob had tears running down his face. ''C'mon, Eema. You've gotta admit it's a funny image.''

She started to leave.

''C'mon, Rina,'' Decker said. ''Now where are *you* going?''

''To check on Hannah. I'll be right back.'' She left the boys to their infantile humor. When they were out of earshot, she exploded into unrestrained laughter. It soon turned into tears.

𝒮22

Choosing and discarding a number of outfits. Among the rejects: the brown "no-nonsense business" suit, the red "foxy lady" dress, and the "Bohemian" flowered ankle-length sarong skirt. In the end, Rina decided to be true to herself. A black long-sleeve sweater over a black A-line skirt, the hem falling below her kneecaps. She tucked her ebony waist-length hair into a large black net that stretched to the tips of her shoulders. Attached to the net was a black silk scarf adorned with gold trim. The scarf covered her scalp, the gold band running across the crown of her head like a tiara. Her makeup was light, her earlobes highlighted by pearl studs.

Walking into the station house, into the interview room. A conference table and lots of folding chairs. All eyes upon her. A nod to Peter. He nodded back. Three other men, all of them in dark suits. She recognized Strapp, nodded to him as well. There was one woman. She had short dark hair, focused brown eyes that scanned her intensely. Disapproving eyes, Rina thought. Her impulse was to look away. Instead, she met the stare and smiled. Habit made the woman smile back. Only half a smile actually, before she caught herself.

Strapp invited her to sit, introduced her. First to Jack Nickerson—a defense rep from the Police Protection League. Peter's lawyer, so to speak. He was in his forties, solidly built. Square face, big shoulders, and a gut. He wore his jacket open, displaying a tie too short for his stomach. A football player past his prime.

The younger suit as well as the woman were from the IAD: James Hayden and Catherine Bell. Both looked to be in their thirties and were more stylishly dressed. The man had on a double-vented, three-button wool crepe suit. The woman wore a double-breasted jacket and her pants had been tailored—straight leg and vented at the ankle.

Rina sat away from the others, at the far end of the conference table. She lowered her purse onto the ground, kept her hands loose but in her lap. Her posture was straight, but not stiff. Her eyes remained alert, taking in everything.

Peter, Nickerson, and Strapp were seated toward the middle of the table. But Hayden and Bell stood. Hayden was positioned behind Decker, Catherine in front of him, on the opposite side of the table. Strapp spoke first, telling the others that it had been his idea to invite Rina. Were there any objections?

There were none. So they went forward.

Turning on a video camera, the lens pointed at Peter's face. Preliminary identification statements akin to name, rank, and serial number. What this inquiry was all about. That all parties questioned were under oath. Then Hayden read from the "sheet." The charges made by Jeanine. He and the woman, Catherine, had some questions to ask Decker. At that point, Nickerson spoke up.

"My client claims the Fifth Amendment, reserves the right to refuse to speak on grounds that he may incriminate himself."

In a calm voice, Strapp said, "As the captain of the Devonshire Division of the Los Angeles Police Department and as Lieutenant Decker's immediate superior officer, I am ordering Lieutenant Decker to answer all questions regarding the charges made against him or risk immediate termination from his position."

Nickerson said, "Responding to a direct order from his captain, Lieutenant Decker will speak for the purpose of this inquiry only. It is therefore agreed upon by all parties involved that nothing said here can or will be used against

Lieutenant Decker in any court of law or at any future court proceedings should the charges advance to that level.''

"Agreed," Catherine stated.

"Agreed," Hayden said. "May I remind Lieutenant Decker that he is still under oath."

"He is duly reminded."

All standard procedure, Peter had told her. Rina remained calm. Nickerson turned to Peter, nodded. "You may answer their questions now, Lieutenant."

Catherine started first, leaned forward, trying to invade his sense of space. "How old are you, Lieutenant Decker?"

"Forty-six."

"How many years have you been a police officer?"

"Twenty-five years."

"How long have you been with the LAPD?"

"Seventeen years—"

"How many years as a detective?"

"Sixteen years as a detective."

"Have you ever had charges other than this one brought against you?"

"Yes."

"How many times?" Hayden asked over Decker's shoulder.

"Ever made the list of forty-four?" Catherine shot out. "You know about the list, don't you?"

"Yes—"

"Forty-four policemen with the worst track record," Catherine broke in.

"How's your track record, Lieutenant?" Hayden pushed.

"Can we *please* have one question at a time?" Nickerson asked.

Decker turned his head to look at Hayden. "As an LAPD officer, I've had one other charge brought against me. And *no,* I've never been on the list of forty-four."

"Positive?" Catherine said.

Decker looked at Catherine. Before he could speak, Hayden said, "What charges were brought against you?"

Decker craned, looked up at Hayden.

"*Alleged* charges," Nickerson broke in. "They were dismissed."

Hayden said, "Why don't you let the lieutenant tell the story."

Decker's eyes went to Nickerson. "Should I answer?"

Hayden was annoyed. "Yes, you should *answer*!"

Decker said, "Can you come around into my line of vision, Sergeant? I'm getting a kink in my neck."

Hayden moved slowly, exaggeratedly. He stood to Decker's side, leaning forward. "Better?"

"Much, thank you."

"What charges were brought against you, Lieutenant?"

Decker said, "Assault."

"Don't you mean police *brutality*?" Hayden asked.

"Yes, he did falsely claim police brutal—"

"Did the charges warrant an interdepartmental Fact Sheet? Were you questioned about the incident?"

"Yes."

Catherine said, "Did you go to court?"

"No, it never went that far—"

"But there were charges brought against you—"

"A Fact Sheet and an inquiry."

Nickerson said, "Why don't you ask him how the charges were resolved?"

Bristling, Hayden said, "I believe we ask the questions, sir."

Catherine said, "*Were* the charges resolved?"

"Yes."

"By who?" Hayden said.

"By whom," Decker corrected.

Strapp glared at him.

"By *whom*?" Hayden said, red-faced.

Decker said, "By the department."

"What was the resolution?"

"Unfounded."

Hayden said, "Are you sure you don't mean Unsustained?"

"No, not Unsustained. *Unfound*—"

"How long ago was the incident?" Catherine broke in.

"*Alleged* incident," Nickerson said.

"Answer the question, please, Lieutenant," Hayden said.

Decker said, "Ten years ago."

"Were any other charges ever brought against you?"

"No—"

"You said you worked for twenty-five years as a police officer," Catherine said.

"Yes."

"Seventeen years with LAPD?"

"Yes."

Hayden sat down, leaned into Decker. "*Whom* did you work for other than LAPD?"

"*Who* did I work for?"

"Decker . . ." Strapp warned.

Rina also shot him a "cool it" look. Still, she admired his spunk. The interrogators were jerks. But it didn't help his case to make them mad at him. Hayden leaned into Decker's face, waited for an answer.

Decker's expression remained flat. "I was employed by the Gainesville and Miami Police Departments in Florida. I worked three years as a uniformed officer, two years as an undercover agent in Narcotics, and three years as a detective in Sex Crimes."

Catherine faced him with intense eyes. "Were any charges ever brought against you while you were employed on the Gainesville force?"

Decker paused. "I have to think a moment—"

"It's a simple question, Lieutenant," sniped Catherine. "Yes or no."

"It was a while ago." Decker remained placid. "During my first year as a patrol officer, I think a complaint was filed but immediately drop—"

"What were the charges?" Hayden said.

"The complaint—in the singular—was police brutal—"

"So you've had two incidents of police brutality brought against you?"

Nickerson said, "Sergeant Hayden, may I remind you that the allegation against my client as a member of the

LAPD was resolved as being Unfounded, which means—"

"I know what it means—"

"Why was the Gainesville charge against you dropped?" Catherine asked Decker.

"It was a complaint." Decker smiled, then stifled it. "I don't know why it was made, I don't know why it was dropped."

Hayden touched his shoulder. "Something funny, Lieutenant? You were smiling. And may I remind you that you're still under oath?"

"I realize that."

"And you still contend that you don't know why the charge was made?"

"I *suspect* the complaint was registered by one of the *many* people I arrested during the *many* anti–Vietnam War demonstrations that took place during that period."

"Are you a vet?" Hayden asked.

"Yes."

"Made you mad to have those punks spit in your face, didn't it?"

Nickerson spoke before Decker could. "Can we go on with the immediate inquiry, please?"

"So you don't know who filed the complaint?" Hayden persisted.

Nickerson said, "Sergeant Hayden, Lieutenant Decker was not brought here today to answer questions about a twenty-five-year-old *resolved* incident—"

"He didn't say the incident was resolved—"

"He said the complaint was dropped."

"That doesn't mean it was resolved," Hayden went on. "For all I know he could have harassed the complainant just like he harassed Jeanine Garrison—"

"*Allegedly* harassed," Nickerson said. "Speaking of which, why don't you ask him about the Jeanine Garrison incident?" He turned to Decker. "They've read you the charges against you, Lieutenant. Would you like to respond?"

"Yes."

The room was quiet.

Catherine gave him the go-ahead. Unhurriedly, using his notes, Decker took them through his interview with Jeanine Garrison. Rina was impressed by Peter's organized mind, by his simple language. His recounting was followed by more questions. Specific questions about her charges. Procedural questions. Then, of course, came the personal questions.

"Jeanine Garrison is an attractive woman," Hayden said.

Decker said nothing.

"Did you hear me, Lieutenant?"

"Yes, Sergeant. You made a statement. I didn't think it required an answer."

"Do you agree with my statement?"

"Yes."

"Did you notice that she was an attractive woman when you met her?"

"Yes."

"Did you think she was beautiful?"

"I noticed she was good-looking—"

"Answer the question, sir."

Decker squirmed slightly. "Yes, I thought she was beautiful."

"Sexy."

"Yes."

"Very sexy—"

Nickerson interrupted, "Sergeant Hayden—"

Hayden shot him down. "Lieutenant Decker has agreed to answer questions for the purpose of this inquiry. Let him answer the questions."

Hayden waited.

Decker said, "What was the question?"

"Did you find Jeanine Garrison very sexy?"

"Yes."

"Were you sexually attracted to her? Remember you're under oath."

"And may I also remind you that you've offered to take a polygraph," Catherine added.

In other words, lying made no sense.

Hayden said, "Did you find Jeanine Garrison sexually attractive?"

Decker sighed. "At that time, yes."

"At that time, did you fantasize about having sex with her?" Hayden asked.

Rina winced at the directness. Decker glanced at her, at Hayden. "I don't remember—"

"Lieutenant, you're under oath," Hayden said. "Did you want to *fuck* her—"

"Sergeant Hayden," Strapp broke in, glanced at Rina. "Show a little courtesy, please."

Hayden said, "Did you want to have *sex* with her, Lieutenant?"

Rina nodded to her husband, telling him to answer the question.

Decker said, "Maybe."

"Maybe?"

"That's correct."

"Are you sure you don't mean *yes,* Lieutenant?"

"No, I mean maybe."

"You were attracted to her?"

"Yes—"

"Extremely attracted?"

"I wouldn't say extreme—"

"You're telling me—under oath—that no sexual thoughts about Jeanine Garrison entered your mind?"

"I had some sexual thoughts," Decker said.

"Such as?"

Decker said, "That she was attractive."

"I think my mother is attractive." Hayden laughed mockingly. "Doesn't mean I have sexual thoughts about her. You wanted her, didn't you, Lieutenant?"

"Sergeant . . ." Nickerson admonished.

Decker spoke calmly. "I don't remember my exact thoughts because they came and went very quickly. Then I was all business."

Catherine said, "During your interview with her, you never *once* entertained the thought of getting Jeanine Garrison into bed?"

"No."

"A moment ago, you said maybe," Hayden corrected.

Decker said, "I said *maybe* I had those thoughts when I first *met* her. During the actual *interview,* I had no thoughts other than my business."

"Amazing you can turn yourself on and off so quickly." Hayden's smile was mean. "You must be a man of considerable control."

He hadn't asked a question so Decker said nothing.

Hayden glanced at Rina, "How old is your wife, Lieutenant?"

"Thirty-four."

"And you're forty-six?"

"Yes."

Catherine said, "She's quite a bit younger than you."

"Yes."

Hayden said, "First wife?"

"No, she's—"

"Second, third, fourth—"

"Second."

"You're forty-six?" Hayden said.

"Yes."

"Mid-life crisis time, Lieutenant?"

Decker smiled. "No, I already went through that. Hence the age difference between my wife and me."

Again, Rina shot him a "behave yourself" look.

Hayden gave a sly smile. "You were married when you met your current wife?"

"Divorced."

"What was the reason for the divorce?" Catherine asked.

"Irreconcilable differences."

"Were you having an affair while you were married to your first wife, Lieutenant?" Hayden asked.

"No."

Catherine said, "You're under oath."

"I know that. No, I was not having an affair."

"Ever had an extramarital involvement?"

"No."

"Not even a one-nighter during your marriage to your irreconcilably different first wife?"

"Nothing until we were legally separated."

Hayden said, "Was your second wife married when you met her?"

"Widowed," Rina spoke up.

Abruptly, Hayden faced her with stern eyes. "I was asking a question to your *husband,* ma'am."

"My apologies." Rina's voice was sincere, her soft eyes upon Hayden. Immediately, he looked away. Her interruption seemed to throw his rhythm off. As he faltered, Catherine picked up the slack.

"How's your sex life, Lieutenant?"

"Fine."

"How would you rate it? Excellent, very good, good—"

"Excellent."

"How often do you have sex?"

"Meaning?"

"Once a week, twice a week—"

"Must be more than that if he rates it excellent," Hayden broke in. "How about it, Lieutenant? How many times a week do you have sex?"

Decker looked at Rina.

Hayden said, "Why are you looking at her, Lieutenant? Can't you answer the question for yourself?"

"It's complicated—"

"It's a simple question," Catherine said.

"With a complicated answer."

Rina broke in. "We're Orthodox Jews." She paused. "*I'm* an Orthodox Jew. The religion prohibits sexual encounters during a certain period of every month—during the woman's menses and for seven days afterward. Then she undergoes ritualistic purification by bathing in prescribed waters. When she is done, she is permitted to resume relations with her husb—"

"This is for real?" Hayden spoke derisively.

"Yes, sir, this is for real," Rina answered without malice. "If you'd like, I will bring you some beautifully written books explaining the sanctity of this ritual more clearly than I have done.''

Hayden averted his eyes, quieted his voice. ''Thank you, but that won't be necessary.''

Rina let his admission hang in the air. Then she said, ''Generally, it works out to two weeks of abstinence followed by two weeks of sexual activity. In our specific case, it's a little shorter—more like twelve days off and eighteen days on—''

''Why's that?'' Catherine asked.

''You get some kind of special dispensation?'' Hayden butted in.

''In a manner of speaking—''

''What was the reason?'' Hayden grew a sneer. ''He couldn't *wait*?''

Nickerson said, ''Sergeant Hayden—''

''She brought it all up!'' Hayden defended himself.

''Medical factors,'' Rina answered. ''Anyway, there was a reason I bothered to tell you all this. It explains why my husband couldn't answer your simple question about a *weekly* sexual allotment.''

Her eyes lowered, then rose to meet Hayden's head-on.

''A point of information. During the times of activity, *all* forms of play between husband and wife are permitted.'' She gave him a serene smile.

A blush coursed through Hayden's cheeks. Again, he looked away. *Son of a bitch,* Decker thought. Rina's modest dress notwithstanding, the jerk had the hots for her.

And why not?

Decker regarded his wife, studied her sculpted face, her open eyes shining like jewels, her red, moist lips. The band of gold fabric arcing across the top of her head, her hair tucked into a net, giving it the appearance of a Cleopatra cut. Just like the alluring Egyptian queen, Rina exuded confidence.

Hayden tried to regain his aggressive stance, stuttered out, ''So you consider yourself a religious woman, then?''

''Yes.''

"And you follow this . . ." He waved his hand in the air. "This . . ."

"Religious ritual?" Rina tried.

Nickerson broke in. "Sergeant Hayden, no charges have been brought against Mrs. Decker—"

Hayden said, "She's claiming religion to be an integral part of her husband's sex life."

"And . . ." Nickerson asked.

Hayden hesitated, eyes darting from Rina to Decker. Catherine glared at her partner, said, "Lieutenant, during the period when charges were brought against you by Jeanine Garrison . . . were you abstaining from sex with your wife?"

They say timing is everything. Decker smiled to himself. "No. We were involved during that period."

"So you were having sex with your wife?" Hayden said.

"Yes." Decker refrained from adding, "You wanna hear details, guy?"

"When was the last time you had sex?"

"Last night."

"With your wife?"

Strapp interrupted this time. "Sergeant Hayden, was that really necessary?"

"We have serious charges brought against your lieutenant," Hayden countered. "We'll do what's necessary—"

"That's what you think," Decker said.

Hayden zeroed in on Decker. "What did you say?"

Decker shrugged. "That's exactly what I was doing, Sergeant. Running an *investigation*. What started as a mass murder began to look like murder for hire. And no simple hit at that. Thirteen people dead, thirty-two wounded, many more traumatized for life. I'd say the stakes were pretty high."

Catherine said, "High stakes or not, no one in this department has a right to harass anyone else."

"I agree, Officer Bell. I assure you no one was harassed, sexually or otherwise. Jeanine Garrison is making noise because she's got something to hide."

Hayden said, "And you have proof of these allegations, Lieutenant?"

Rina asked, "Forgive a layman's ignorance, but why would Lieutenant Decker be investigating if he had proof? I thought that was the purpose of an investigation. To gather evidence."

Catherine said, "We've run far afield."

"No, we haven't," Strapp said. "As a matter of fact, Mrs. Decker is right smack in the center of the damn ballpark. We're trying to run an investigation and Jeanine Garrison's ludicrous charges are slowing everything down—"

Hayden said, "It's for us to determine whether or not the charges are ludicrous."

"Hook me up to a polygraph," Decker said. "Ask me the same questions. Draw your conclusions. You call the shots."

Hayden and Catherine exchanged glances.

Decker said, "Is there a formal one eight one complaint being pressed?"

Hayden said, "Yes."

Decker closed his eyes and opened them. "Then I can only help myself by taking a polygraph. How about this? If I pass, department rules it as an Unfounded. If I *don't* pass, I'll go along with the departmental ruling of a Sustained."

Catherine finally took a seat at the table. "We can't base our ruling on a polygraph. But you can take one."

"Set it up."

She pulled out a notebook from her jacket, flipped through some pages. "Possibly we can hook you up with a polygraph in two weeks."

"Why so long?" Strapp said.

"The examiner I use is on vacation."

"So get another examiner," Decker said.

"I like this one."

Strapp said, "My man has to cool his heels for a couple of weeks because your examiner is basking in the sun?"

"If he's innocent, it'll keep," Hayden said.

Decker said, "I can wait. Can I get back to work now?"

Catherine glanced at her partner. Hayden nodded, turned off the video camera, and removed the cassette. "I'll call you with the details."

Decker smiled. "I'll be waiting."

Strapp got up. "I want a copy of the cassette."

"Certainly," Catherine said. "Despite what you've been led to think, IAD is very up-front."

"A bastion of honesty," Strapp said. "Two weeks. You go longer than that, I make noise."

Hayden nodded deferentially. Even though he wasn't under Strapp's jurisdiction, the captain's rank still demanded respect. As soon as they were out the door, Strapp shoved it closed. "Bastards!" He turned to Nickerson. "What do you think?"

Nickerson yawned. "They're lightweights. All sound and fury signifying nothing. Brilliant stroke to bring the wife in. Kept it civil." He turned to Rina, smiled. "You were very good."

"Thank you." Rina paused. "Good at what?"

Nickerson laughed. "The way you explained your religious beliefs about sex. Open. Unembarrassed. Straight out. Even . . ." He smiled. "Excuse me, Lieutenant, for my candor, but your wife is very . . . appealing. At least Hayden thought so. See him blush?"

"Blush?" Rina asked.

"You'd better believe it," Decker said. "Frankly put, he had the hots for you."

"He did *not*!"

Nickerson said, "It was the sex talk combined with the dowdy dress. The quiet ones. Gets 'em every time. Good move, Mrs. Decker."

Rina said, "I always dress like this, Mr. Nickerson."

Nickerson stuttered, "Well, yes, of course . . ."

"Not always this somber," Decker remarked. "But she does always dress modestly. Can I have a few moments with my wife in private?"

Nickerson stood up. "I suppose you deserve that." He saluted. "We'll be in touch."

After the defense rep left, Strapp laid a strong hand on

Decker's shoulder. "Despite what they say, the polygraph means a lot to IAD. You beat that, we'll be fine."

"Thanks for your support, sir."

"Can't let the bastards get in our way."

Decker nodded.

Strapp looked at Rina. "Mrs. Decker."

"Captain."

Strapp went out of the room, closed the door. Immediately, Decker let out a gust of air, slid back in his seat.

"Are you okay?" Rina asked.

"Fine, fine." He pulled her onto his lap. "You were *wonderful*. People say they love one another. But you did more than words could ever convey. You came through for me. I'll never forget this, Rina. Never."

"It wasn't hard." Rina grew misty. "I love you."

"I love you, too." Decker grew tense. "Bastard! Probing like he did." He imitated Hayden. *"What was the reason? He couldn't wait?"*

Rina smiled. "For a moment, I considered telling him about my hysterectomy—"

"Don't you dare! None of the bastard's business!"

She shrugged. "I didn't because I thought it would work against you. Make me look . . . less desirable—"

"That would be *impossible*!" Decker said.

"Besides, then I'd have to explain why I got a period at all. And how a period is defined by Jewish law. In reality, I didn't think the sergeant was up to grasping the intricacies of remnant endometrial tissue sloughing from a subcervical hysterectomy. Hayden is just not very clever."

"He's an idiot!" Decker pulled her close, kissed the nape of her neck. "Know how I feel right now? Like the luckiest man alive. To be honest, it was harder than I thought it would be. I actually told a little fib."

Rina dried her eyes, turned around to face him. "What kind of fib?"

He pulled her back into his arms. Kissed her neck again. "Hmmm, you smell nice."

"What was the fib, Peter?"

"The complaint against me while I was on the Gaines-

ville force. It was justified.'' He kissed her again. ''Hayden
had my psyche nailed, darlin'. I *was* caught up in the whole
antiwar thing. But from the unpopular side. I had just come
back from Nam. Confused, scared, full of self-doubt . . . but
mostly angry. I had an ugly temper, Rina.''

''You?''

''You don't become this controlled a person unless
there's something to control. Most of the time, I could hold
it in check. Then . . . I don't know. There was this typical
college demonstration. Nothing unusual. Just wimpy, little
know-nothing jerks spouting off . . .''

He looked away.

''Something snapped. I lost it. I took the loudest, most
obnoxious one and dragged the kid, stomach down, over a
hundred feet of rocky, newly laid asphalt—''

''My God!''

''By the time I was done, the kid's stomach looked like
raw meat—''

Rina shook him off. ''That's terrible.''

''Yeah, it was bad. It's hard to understand unless you've
been there.''

Head pounding, Rina took in a deep breath, let it out
slowly. Obviously that had been a long time ago. Right
now, Peter didn't need a morality lesson. ''I suppose you're
right.''

Again, Decker kissed her neck, which he noticed had
visibly tensed. ''I acted out of anger and that was wrong.
But honestly . . . the release of such raw . . . fury . . . it felt
good.''

Again, Rina broke away, stared at her husband.

He met her gaze, thought for a moment. ''Don't worry.
It'll never happen again.''

''Why are you telling me this?''

''I trust you to know the truth.''

Rina tried to relax but failed. ''As long as it's true confessions, how'd you get him to drop the charges against
you?''

''It was a her,'' Decker said. ''I did a big no-no. After
the complaint was filed, unknown to my superior, I *con-*

tacted her. Went to her dorm. I remember putting on a T-shirt and jeans . . . sandals. Tried to look as uncoplike as I could. I apologized profusely. Just about went down on my knees. Offered to make amends any way she saw fit. Laid on the charm and hoped for the best. Much to my astonishment, the next day she dropped the complaint.''

''And?''

''And the rest, as they say, is history.''

Rina stared at him, openmouthed. ''Jan?''

Decker laughed. ''The one and only complaint against me that she's ever really *dropped*.''

⋙23

Tricky business, talking to teens. Authority figures left them frosty and distrustful. The "cool" grown-up approach was also out. They were suspicious of anyone who tried too hard.

How to manipulate them?

Webster figured he'd play into their overinflated sense of importance. Their opinions about Harlan Manz *really* mattered to the police.

He parked the unmarked about a block down, hit Westbridge Prep just as the four-thirty dismissal bell rang out. The campus sat on acres of lawn, a Federalist-style complex, complete with bell tower. Behind the main four-storied structure were wings and extensions. The buildings were herringboned in brick, unsuitable in L.A. earthquake country. No matter. To parents, New England architecture connoted New England universities. The physical image fueled the Harvard dream.

For the role, Webster had donned a black silk jacket, black T-shirt, and jeans. Professional but not off-putting. The school gates had opened, and adolescents swarmed out. Noise. Lots of it. Males letting off steam, shouting and cursing and posturing bravado. Estrogen-ladened girls, flailing their hands with exaggerated movement, while rattling off Valleyspeak between nervous giggles. The parking lots roared volleys of cars: four-wheelers and Jeeps as well as sports car convertibles—Mustangs, Camaros, Thunder-

226

birds, as well as older Jags, BMWs, a Mercedes, and a
Porsche Carrera. The driver of the Porsche was pitted with
acne. Who knew? Maybe the wheels helped him get laid.

Webster's eyes panned over the scenery, spied an average-looking group congregating on the sidewalk. Three
blue-blazered boys, and two white-shirted, plaid-skirted
girls. The boys were big and thick—football players or
wrestlers. One of the girls had blond hair; the other lass
had tresses of garnet red. Webster ambled over, presented
his badge, watched them grow wary. Then he spoke.

"Any of y'all happen to be members of Greenvale Country Club . . . through your parents, maybe?"

The tallest of the boys stepped forward, eyes focused on
Webster. Around six two with a refrigerator chest. Simian-
featured. Bushy hair, swarthy complexion, hooded eyes,
and the ever-present adolescent gaping mouth. "What's going on?"

Webster said. "We're doing a little follow-up on the
tragedy at Estelle's. On the shooter—"

"Harlan Manz," the redhead broke in. She had been
bronzed by the sun, her ruby mane tied back in a braid.

Webster took out his notebook. "And you are . . ."

"Kelly Putnam."

"Don't tell him your name," the blond girl scolded.

Long straight hair, blue eyes, creamy skin, and legs that
didn't quit. A nice young package. Then Webster thought
about the Loo's Fact Sheet earlier in the day, Decker being
raked over the coals . . .

Blondy said, "Can I see your badge again?"

"Sure." Webster showed it to her. "Detective Thomas
Webster, LAPD, Homicide Division."

The blond stared at the shield, wetting her lips with the
tip of her tongue. "How do I know that it's for real? You
could be a perv in cop's clothing."

"Good to be cautious," Webster said. "None of you
have to talk to me. I'm just trying to get a fix on Harlan
Manz."

"Why?" Simian asked. "He's dead."

"We're trying to understand the situation. Give some

closure to the victims of this terrible tragedy. Any of y'all happen to know him? Harlan?''

"Why would we know him?" Simian asked.

"That's why I asked if any of y'all happened to be members of Greenvale. He worked there . . . 'bout two years ago."

One of the boys spoke up. He was a tad shorter than Simian. Pug features, straight dark hair, and green eyes. He held out a meaty hand. "Rudy Wright." He pointed first to Simian. "Jack Goldsteen." Then he cocked a thumb at the last male friend. The smallest but only in relationship to the other two. He was fair and had the finest features but was far from delicate-looking. "He's Dylan Anderson."

"Pleased to meet you boys." Webster shook hands all around. "And thanks for talking to me. We're pretty upset 'bout Estelle's. Figured taking it to the public might help."

He turned to Blondy.

"I didn't catch your name, miss."

"It's ms. to you and that's because I didn't tell you."

Kelly the redhead let out an exasperated sigh. "It's Sarah Amos—"

"Kelly!"

"Stop being so nasty, Sarah."

"Screw you!" Sarah turned to Webster. "What do you want to know about Harlan?"

Webster looked into her eyes, hoping his excitement wouldn't show.

Sarah *Amos.*

In one school, how many Amoses could there possibly be?

"Did you know him, Ms. Amos?"

"Sure, I remember him."

"We all do," Kelly interrupted. "Hart Mansfield. I realized who he was right away. When I told my parents I thought it was the same guy, my dad didn't believe me. Said I was just being an . . ."

She sighed.

"An overly emotional, hormonally driven, hysterical female adolescent. Dad equates enthusiasm with hysteria. To Dad, excitement means an eagle on the eighteenth hole.''

Jack said, ''Yeah, your old man is pretty grave.'' To Webster, he said, ''He's a sports lawyer. Negotiates multimillion-dollar deals for free agents.'' He turned back to Kelly. ''Maybe it's me, but I think he's looking me over.''

Kelly said, ''Wouldn't doubt it, Lug. Despite your Neanderthal appearance, you do have solid raw talent.''

Webster said, ''Your dad belongs to Greenvale, Kelly?''

''But of *course*!'' She spoke in a French accent. ''He belongs to all the *right* places.''

''You know, I had a hard time believing it myself,'' Rudy said. ''About Harlan, I mean. What a shock! You don't expect a normal-looking guy with a good backhand to suddenly kill twelve people.''

''Thirteen,'' Webster corrected.

Rudy grimaced. ''God, that's awful!''

''You should be talking to Amy Silver,'' Jack said. ''She was there. At the restaurant.''

''She was one of the girls at the Sweet Sixteen,'' Webster said. ''She's been interviewed.''

''She hasn't come back to school,'' Kelly said. ''I'm not good friends with her, but I did visit her. She's really a basket case, poor thing.''

Webster said, ''So you remember Harlan Manz, Ms. Sarah Amos? Did you ever meet him?''

She shuddered. ''Couple of times.''

''Take lessons from him?'' Webster asked.

''Nope,'' Sarah said.

Kelly added, ''I don't think he taught teens. More like worked with women my mom's age.''

''He taught teens,'' Sarah said. ''He taught my brother.''

Webster counted one one thousand. ''And who might your brother be?''

''Sean Amos,'' Dylan said. ''Mr. Studmuffin—''

''Fuck off!'' Sarah whined.

''Don't tease her, Dyl,'' Kelly said. ''Ain't her fault that she has the bad luck to share progenitors with *him*.''

Sarah had become edgy. ''Sean doesn't like to talk about

Estelle's. I mean, he was really freaked when he found out about Harlan.''

Jack said, ''I was freaked, too.''

Rudy said, ''Speak of the studmuffin, that's him in the red Acura convertible.''

Webster's eyes went to a blond boy wearing a white shirt and sunglasses. His hair was down to his shoulders. Webster said, ''Nice wheels.''

Dylan said, ''Yeah, if you don't mind changing tires every five thousand miles.''

Jack added, ''Tread wears out faster than a virgin in an army barracks. Something screwy with the alignment and balance.''

Dylan said, ''Wasn't there a recall on the car, Sarah?''

''Beats me,'' Sarah said. ''I don't talk to Sean about his car.'' In an undertone, she added, ''If I can help it, I don't talk to Sean, period!''

''Would he mind if I spoke to him?'' Webster asked.

Sarah shrugged. ''Probably. Sean doesn't like anyone to invade his *personal* space.''

Sean honked, but Sarah waved him over. The boy frowned, blasted the horn. Sarah, God bless her, remained rooted, continued to motion to him. Finally, he killed the motor, double-parked, and got out. Jogged over to his sister. ''Whaddaya *doing*? I gotta go!''

Sarah said, ''Sean, this guy's from *Homicide*—''

''What?'' Sean took off his sunglasses. Glanced at Kelly, then at Webster with midnight-blue eyes. ''Who are you?''

Kid spoke with a very slight Texas drawl. Webster took out his shield, introduced himself. Sean's expression turned dark. ''Whaddaya doing talking to a cop, Sarah? You outta your *mind*?''

Sarah turned red. ''I didn't say any—''

''Just shut up and get in the car.''

''Sean, I—''

He grabbed her arm. ''Just *shut* up and get—''

''Drop her arm *now*!'' Webster ordered.

Immediately, Sean let go of his sister's biceps, raised both his palms in the air. ''No prob . . . *sir*.''

Webster glared at him. "You know the drill, son?"

"I don't know *what* you're talking about."

"How 'bout this? You keep your hands to yourself. Is that clear enough?"

"Fine. Can I go now . . . *sir*?"

To Sarah, Webster said. "You okay, Ms. Amos?"

"She's *fine*!" Sean sniped at his sister. "Now look what you've done. Get in the car."

Sarah hugged her books tightly, didn't move.

Webster said, "I'll take you home if you want, Sarah."

Red-faced, Sean silently mouthed, "Get! In! The! Car!"

Sarah blinked back tears and ran toward the Acura. Again Sean gave Kelly a sidelong glance, then turned his stormy eyes to Webster. "Is that what you do for kicks, Detective? Hassle *minors*? Your *superior* will hear about this!"

Webster said, "Uh-huh. In the meantime, quit grabbing girls, including your sister."

Sean bit his lip, spoke to the group. "You guys are stupid fucks. You're playing into their bullshit. You know how cops twist words. Go home." He slipped on his shades, muttered, "Bunch of retards!" and jogged off.

Webster let out a gush of air. "Whew! What's his problem?"

But the kids had turned silent. Sean had done his job. Finally, Rudy said, "Sorry. I've gotta go."

"We all do," Jack said. "Weight-training practice."

Rudy said, "That's not a problem, is it?"

"Not at all," Webster said. "Thanks for your help."

Dylan shrugged. "We really didn't do anything. You coming, Kelly?"

"In a minute."

Rudy paused, then said, "Sean's an asshole but he has a point, Kel. We shouldn't be sticking our noses where they don't belong." He turned to Webster. "No offense."

"None taken. Thanks again."

When the boys were out of earshot, Webster said, "You don't have to talk to me, either."

Kelly was silent.

Webster said, "You used to date Sean, didn't you?"

"Why do you ask that?"

"He kept looking at you."

"He dated my older sister, Tara."

"And?"

"Why do you think there's an 'and'?"

Webster looked around. "Kelly, it's not real private here. Can I meet you someplace public but more discreet? I'll call my female partner to come join us. Her name is Detective Marge Dunn. Phone the police station at Devonshire and ask for her and about me, too. We're both legitimate."

"It's okay. I believe you."

"Tell me a place."

"It's not necessary." Kelly fiddled with her plait. "I don't have anything to say."

"You don't like Sean much, do you?"

"Why is that relevant?"

"He seems . . . cautious around you."

"Why are you asking about Sean? I thought you wanted to know about Harlan Manz."

She's gotcha, Tom. "Well . . ." Webster's mind raced for a logical retort. "Sarah said he freaked when he found out about Manz. That he acted strange—"

"So?"

Webster stalled. "Maybe he knew something about Harlan. Something that made him feel guilty when the shootings at Estelle's went down."

Kelly played with her braid.

"Were they tight?" Webster asked. "He and Harlan?"

"How should I know?"

He was probing too deeply. "Yeah, that's true. Anyway, thanks a heap for your time—"

"I hate him," Kelly blurted out.

Webster paused. "Harlan?"

"No, Sean. I hate his fucking guts." Kelly's voice dropped to a whisper. "He knocked up my sister. Paid for the abortion, of course. Then dumped her. As if that wasn't bad enough, he spread rumors about her. Horrible lies. He said she was . . . she was *diseased.*"

"That's despicable."

"My sister hasn't been the same since. She was a straight-A student. Now she's lucky if she pulls C's. He ruined her. Just . . . buried her self-confidence."

Her eyes moistened. But she held the tears in check.

"Your parents know about the abortion?" Webster asked.

"Of course not."

"How old is Tara?"

"Seventeen."

"And you are?"

"Fifteen and a half." Kelly paused. "I saw him shove Tara once. After he dumped her. She just wanted to *talk* to him and he . . . he pushed her away like she was *rancid* or something! I became infuriated!"

"I don't blame you."

"Yeah, well, listen to this. Later that day, I caught him alone. I told him that if he ever, ever dissed my sister again, I'd go straight to his *mother*. He tried to scare me, grabbed my arm just like he did to Sarah. I took my other hand and slapped his face. Hard! I *stunned* him. He's been nervous around me ever since. He's all bluff and no bite."

"So his mother never knew about the abortion?"

"No."

"How'd he get the money?"

"Detective, obscenely rich boys like him *always* have money."

"And you think his mom would be upset about the abortion?"

"She'd have a fit and a half because she's a *real* right-to-lifer. Card-carrying protestor with pictures of aborted fetuses and all that crap. Never mind that she dresses like the whore of Bourbon Street. When it comes to politics, she's Madame Reactionary."

"Bourbon Street." Webster paused. "She's from Louisiana?"

Kelly nodded.

"But Sean's from Texas."

Kelly faced him. "How'd you know that?"

Shit, Webster thought. Sometimes a little learning is indeed a dangerous thing. Smoothly, he said, "I recognized the accent."

"You think Sean has an *accent*?"

"To my Southern ear, it screams Dallas, Texas."

"Ah." Kelly smiled. "Guess it takes one to know one. Accents, I mean. Are you *really* from the South?"

"Biloxi, Mississippi, if you please. Home of the Dixie Mafia."

"But you're college educated, aren't you."

"Tulane University." Webster smiled. "Ever thought of a career as a detective?"

Again Kelly smiled. Then she checked her watch. "I really gotta go."

"Out of curiosity," Webster said, "who's Sean dating now?"

Kelly shrugged. "Don't know. Why?"

Again, Webster was forced to ad-lib. "If she's young enough, might be helpful to warn her about Sean's temper."

"Oh." Kelly nodded. "That's nice of you." She thought a moment. "Could be he's seeing someone from Greenvale. He's there all the time practicing his backhand. He's on the school's varsity tennis team."

"Ever see him there with anyone specific?"

Kelly shook her head no. "Just his tennis partner, Ms. Garrison."

"Garrison . . ." Webster paused. "Why does that name . . ." He stared at Kelly. "Now that wouldn't be *Jeanine* Garrison, would it?"

Kelly nodded. "Her parents were murdered at Estelle's."

Webster said, "And she and Sean are *tennis* partners?"

Kelly nodded.

"Maybe that's why Sean's so freaked out about Harlan. That this monster killed his partner's parents."

Kelly looked at Webster. "Good observation."

"Thanks." Webster appeared to be thinking. "Jeanine Garrison. She's a bit older than Sean."

"She's in her late twenties, I think. Why?"

"Any chance that maybe she and Sean are . . ."

"*What?*"

Webster backtracked. "Just a thought."

Kelly laughed. "Sean may be hot stuff for high school. But Ms. Garrison is like . . . God, she's *beautiful*! And she always has like a ton of men hanging around her. Sean is *way* out of her league."

"I see. Thanks for talking to me, Kelly. Can I ask you a favor? Keep what we talked about confidential? It would make my life easier."

Kelly smiled sadly. "I've kept a zillion secrets in my life. One more ain't no big deal."

24

"Hassle minors," Decker repeated.

"Yes," Webster said.

"You're sure Sean used the word *minor*."

"I'm sure. And then he said that my superior would hear about it. 'It' meaning the conversation I was having with the kids."

"Hostile little bugger," Oliver said. "Probably thinks that a good defense is an offense."

"Reckon that about sums it up."

Decker sat back in his chair. "Jeanine prepped him."

"My take on the situation," Webster said.

Marge said, "You know, she might have messed herself up. By Sean making a case of his being a minor . . . if she and he are screwing . . . well, then she can't plead ignorance of his age."

Oliver said, "She can always claim he told her he was eighteen."

"But the onus is on her." Martinez turned to Webster. "You think he's spouting idle threats?"

"Maybe."

Decker sipped cold coffee. "My opinion? We're going to hear about it. Probably first thing Sean did when he got home was give Garrison a ring."

"She's calling the shots," Webster said.

Oliver said, "Probably told Seanny boy to call the police and make a stink."

"Not call the *police*," Decker said. "Call the *school*. Have them make the stink." He looked at Webster. "Where were you when you talked to the kids? I mean physically. Where were you standing?"

Webster thought a moment. " 'Bout fifty yards from the front entrance of Westbridge."

"On school property?"

"On the sidewalk."

"Public domain," Marge said.

Decker said. "But you were still standing in front of school buildings, correct?"

"Yes."

Without preamble, Strapp walked into Decker's office.

"We've been expecting you," Oliver said. "Get a call from a kid named Sean Amos, Captain?"

"Westbridge Prep." Strapp's eyes locked on to Webster's face. "You were out there today, Tom?"

"Yes, sir."

Decker said, "Captain, we agreed to interview the kids about Harlan Manz—"

"Not on school property, Pete."

Webster said, "I wasn't on school property. I was on the sidewalk."

"You didn't enter the school?" Strapp asked.

"No." Webster grew tense. "And last I heard interviewing kids politely didn't constitute police harassment."

Strapp said, "Tell me what happened."

Webster recapped his conversations with the teens for the second time in twenty minutes. Strapp listened carefully.

Afterward, Decker said, "When did the call from Westbridge come through, Captain?"

"About five minutes ago."

Decker said, "And when did you leave the school, Tom?"

"Around five-fifteen."

Decker's eyes swept over the wall clock. Six-thirty. "Okay. Sean waited before he called the school to register the complaint. First, he called Jeanine, asked her what to do—''

"Got their stories straight," Oliver said.

"So what do we do?" Marge asked. "Look for outgoing calls from Sean's number to Jeanine's. Or if he's involved, would Sean be stupid enough to use his own phone number?"

"People do stupid things when they panic," Oliver said.

"I say we look for incoming calls to Jeanine," Martinez said.

Decker looked at Strapp. "What would it hurt?"

"Go ahead."

Decker picked up the receiver, dialed the phone company, gave out his badge number, and waited.

Martinez said, "You know, it doesn't say much even if he did call her. They *are* tennis partners."

Marge said, "It's the timing, Bert. Sean hassles Tom, goes home, then *waits* to call the school. First, he calls Jeanine. You're telling me he's more interested in a tennis date than in registering a complaint?"

Strapp said, "It proves nothing, Dunn."

"Yes, I'm still here." Decker picked up a pen, wrote down the telephone number. "Thank you."

He hung up, held the slip in the air. "West Valley prefix."

Martinez said, "I'll look it up."

Decker said, "If it isn't in the backward directory, Bert, call up the phone company."

Martinez took the slip with the phone number and left to work at his desk.

"Even if Sean did call Jeanine," Strapp said, "just what exactly are you trying to establish?"

Oliver said, "That Sean's involved as the number two shooter—"

"If there even *is* a number two shooter," Strapp interrupted.

"If Sean was involved in Estelle's," Webster said, "I don't picture him as the number two shooter. Kelly Putnam summed him up as all bluff and no bite, and I agree. Sean's hotheaded, but a coward. Backed off immediately when I came on strong."

"He called the school on us," Oliver said.

"A phone call avoids direct confrontation."

"Tommy, if he's a red-blooded teenager, he'd do anything for pussy."

Webster said, "I don't think the little snot has the balls to pull a trigger."

Martinez came back into the office. "Phone call was made from a pay phone about a half mile from the Amos house."

Marge said, "We should send someone out right now. Dust it for prints."

Strapp said, "Since when is it against the law for Sean Amos to use a pay phone?"

"C'mon, Captain," Decker said. "A kid like that is bound to have either a cellular phone or a car phone or both. Why would he bother with a pay phone unless he's trying to hide something?"

Strapp said, "If Tom doesn't believe that Sean was involved in the shooting, why are we *hassling* him?"

"Sir, I think he was involved in the shooting," Webster said. "Just not as the triggerman."

"So how was he involved if he didn't shoot?" Martinez asked. "Orchestrated the thing? Brokered it out?"

"Maybe both."

Strapp threw up his hands. "I don't like this at all. You're chasing ghosts. Go back to standard investigating procedures."

Marge said, "So let me go out to the phone booth and dust for prints, Captain. That's standard detective procedure from the get-go."

"I'm putting myself on the line here," Strapp said, "allocating detective time without a decent reason. You know you're going to find Sean's prints on the phone. So what?"

"Sir, we connect Sean to Jeanine," Oliver said. "Then, twenty minutes later, the school calls us on a harassment charge—"

"That's reverse police harassment," Marge said. "You

know, we should check incoming calls to the school. Find out if any of them match Sean's number.''

Strapp said, ''This is really skirting the law.''

Oliver said, ''He's a suspect—''

''Suspect in *what*, Scott? You don't have an atom of proof of Sean's involvement.''

''That's what we're trying to establish, Captain,'' Webster said.

''But first you need reasonable cause, Tom! Right now, you don't have shit!''

''How about this, Captain?'' Decker spoke calmly. ''Sean roughed up his sister.''

''He grabbed her arm—''

''According to the law, it's assault,'' Decker said. ''True or false?''

''Go on.'' Strapp was irritated.

''According to Kelly, Sean has a history of roughing up girls. Now after Tom spoke to him, he was angry . . . hotheaded. Maybe we should put a tail on him. Just to *make sure* he doesn't do anything to his sister or Kelly or anybody else.''

Webster grinned. ''The Loo has a point, sir. Sean's a bully. I think he bears watching. What do you think?''

Strapp said, ''You're stretching longer than a hippo's condom.''

Decker said, ''Of course we're stretching. We're doing everything back door—''

''*Why* do you really want to tail him?'' Strapp was annoyed.

Decker said, ''Because Tom thinks he's immature and impulsive. And Bert made a good point. Maybe Sean is the broker for the hit. The middle man. The kid's already registered a complaint against us—''

''Westbridge never said it was Sean,'' Strapp said.

''Sir, we could check that out,'' Martinez said. ''All it would take is a quick call to the phone company.''

Marge said, ''Hate to be a broken record, but I'd still like to go dust the pay phone for prints.''

Strapp scowled.

Webster said, "What would it hurt to see where Sean'll take this?"

Marge said, "Scare him bad enough, maybe he'll lead us to a candidate for number two shooter."

"Or to Jeanine," Martinez said.

"And maybe he'll sit tight," Strapp said. "If Jeanine Garrison has half the cunning we think she has, that's exactly what she told him to do. Sit tight. Don't do anything because they have no proof. And she's right."

Marge said, "All the more reason to scare him."

"And how do you propose to do that without making contact with the boy, Detective Dunn?"

"I agree," Decker said. "No contact with Sean because he's a minor. But it's easy to shake him up, sir. Just make the tail obvious."

Oliver smiled widely. "Two-car tail. First for show. Second for real."

"What do you say, Captain?" Decker said. "Do we run an investigation or do we run?"

"That's not fair."

Decker was quiet.

Strapp swore under his breath. "All right. Go for it."

Gaynor threw up his hands. "Sorry, Loo. I checked through six months of receipts. I couldn't find any large sums of money debited from any of Jeanine's accounts."

Decker rubbed his eyes, looked at his wall clock. Seven-thirty. He had hoped to make it home a half hour ago ... take Rina out for dinner and a movie. If he hustled, they could still make a movie ... maybe have ice cream afterward. He said, "What are your criteria for large sums of money, Farrell?"

"Any lump sum over twenty-five hundred," Gaynor said. "During the past week, she has made several withdrawals of around a thousand each. But I've traced them to deposits—for a caterer and for the arena for her upcoming wheelchair tennis tournament."

"Don't talk to me about that!" Decker picked up an eraser, threw it across the room. "If she hired a hit man for Estelle's, she had to pay him somehow!''

"Hidden cash," Gaynor said. "Withdraw a couple of hundred one week, a couple of hundred the next . . . pretty soon she'd have a tidy sum."

"A couple of hundred a week?" Decker looked at Farrell. "Take her a while to save up enough to pay off two hit men."

"Two hit men?"

"I'm counting Harlan Manz as a hit man."

"So maybe she didn't pay out in money," Gaynor said. "Maybe she paid in sex."

"If Sean Amos hired a second shooter, she couldn't have paid *him* with sex. Money had to have been exchanged somehow."

"So maybe Sean paid and she paid Sean back." Gaynor frowned. "No, that wouldn't work. There'd still be cash out from her accounts." He paused. "She could have a secret account somewhere. I couldn't tap into everything."

Decker ran his hands through his hair. Marge walked into his office, her nose and cheeks blackened with print dust. "The good news is I have solid whorls. The bad news is Sean Amos doesn't have anything resembling a record. So I have nothing to match them against."

Decker said, "Label them and put them under Jeanine Garrison's file for the time being . . . until I figure out what to do with them."

Marge said, "Are both Scott and Tom watching Sean?"

"Just Oliver right now. Because the kid hasn't moved. Holed up in his manse." Decker blew out air. "Strapp's right. The kid's gonna sit. Whole thing's a bloody waste of time."

Suddenly, he stood and put on his jacket.

"It's been a long day for me. I'm packing it in."

Gaynor said, "Save my wife a trip if you took me home, sir."

"Be glad to."

"I'll take you home, Farrell," Marge offered. "If you don't mind waiting until I've finished some paperwork."

"Nah, I don't mind."

"Nonsense," Decker said. "I'll take you home now, Farrell."

"It won't take me long, Pete."

"It's not a problem for me, Marge."

"This is nice," Gaynor said.

Decker stopped talking. "What's nice, Farrell?"

"Being fought over." The old man smiled. "Been a long time since I've felt wanted."

❧25

Prayer in front of a mirror was forbidden.

Which was fine with Decker. At six in the morning, the last thing he wanted was to look at his haggard face. Of course, that wasn't the reason for the prohibition. The eyes were supposed to be focused inward to God, not outward, seduced by vanity. Yet every so often Decker caught his reflection in the living room's bay window. A large figure wrapped in a *tallith*—a long fringed religious shawl—and *tephillin*—known by the clumsy English word "phylacteries." They were small prayer-filled boxes which were secured to the body by leather straps. One set of long thin' strips of hide had been wound down the length of his right arm; another set encircled his skull, then dangled past his shoulders. A black leather box rested on his forehead; a second was perched on his biceps.

Weird.

Still, the primitive ritual worked. Every morning as he girded his arm and head, Decker thought about God even if only for a twinkle of time. Thinking about Rav Schulman's explanation . . . the beautiful allegories he had used. The box on the forehead representing God's gift of intellect to man, the other on the biceps connoting man's brute strength tethered to the spiritual.

But he looked strange. As he removed the paraphernalia, he wondered what his fellow professionals would think if they saw him bound in leather, as if embroiled in an S&M

244

sex game. He pondered this as he undid the straps, freeing himself of symbolic servitude.

The phone rang. The business line. Still partially tied, he picked up the receiver. "Decker."

Strapp spoke. "David Garrison was found dead in his apartment ten minutes ago. Looks like an OD."

Decker refrained from cursing. He still had God's name resting on his forehead. "Who found him?"

"Cleaning lady."

"She's sure he's dead?"

"As cold as Russian vodka."

"An OD. Okay. Let me guess. There was a needle conveniently gripped in Garrison's fingers."

"By his side."

"Jeanine's slipping—"

"There's no evidence that Jeanine was anywhere near the place."

"There's where you're wrong, sir. We've got concrete, carved-in-stone evidence that Jeanine *was* there."

"What are you talking about?"

"David Garrison's body. *There's* your evidence."

"Decker—"

"I'm coming down."

"I'll meet you there."

He ducked under the yellow crime-scene ribbon that had been stretched across the door.

The first detective at the scene, but not the first cop. Four officers, one of them talking to a young Hispanic woman in a white uniform, who was rubbing her arms. Beside her was a pail filled with bottles of cleaning solutions and brushes. The cleaning lady. She'd keep for a moment. He flashed his badge to the uniforms, went over to the body.

Stretched out on the floor, Garrison's arms and legs were bent at all angles. He had landed or had been positioned on his back, his head arched back, white lips apart. Clean blond hair framed a gray face, fell across open dead eyes, the pupils already fixed. A knocked-over chair was at his left side, the needle and tourniquet at his right. He wore

jeans and a short-sleeve T-shirt. Two puncture wounds in
the cubital fossa—the triangular depression below the elbow crease. The common plexus of veins where junkies
first shoot up—until those vessels collapse. Then they go
for the backs of the hands, the legs, the feet, the stomach,
finally settling on anywhere with a pulse.

Such ugly business.

He heard a grinding sound, looked up. Out of nowhere,
a wheelchair broke through the yellow ribbon, as if it had
just won a race. The machine's occupant was very muscular
from the waist up. Blond curly hair, manicured three days'
growth of beard.

Wade Anthony.

Behind him was Jeanine. Wide-eyed. Her mouth agape.
Dressed in loose sweats.

"I got a call from David's landlady!" she shrieked to
no one in particular. "What's going on?"

Decker stepped in front, blocking her view of the body.
"Ma'am, can you step outside for just a moment?"

Instant anger in her eyes. "What are *you* doing here?"
she snarled.

"Ms. Garrison—"

"Get out of my way! Now!"

Anthony spoke up. "Can someone tell us what's going
on?"

"Be glad to tell you, sir, once we're outside—"

"Get out of my way!" Jeanine charged him, bounced
off his chest. It was then that Decker noticed she was wearing makeup—including foundation. Because it had come
off on his shirt. She also wore earrings and had put on
perfume.

Two uniforms—a man and a woman—rushed over. Injected themselves between Jeanine and Decker. Stood their
ground, legs apart, arms folded across their chests.

"Back off, ma'am!" the woman ordered.

Arms flailing, Jeanine started screaming. "You goddamn
son of a bitch, bastard—"

"Back off!" the female officer insisted.

Jeanine screamed, "I want to see my brother and this bastard won't let me through!"

Decker shouted over her, "Ms. Garrison, can you let me talk?"

"You son of a bitch! Get *out* of here!"

Strapp chose that moment to make his entrance. Jeanine whirled to him. "Get this monster out of my way. He won't let me see my brother! He's trying to brainwash him against me! That's what David told me. The police were brainwashing him—"

Strapp said, "Ms. Garrison, the police are here because we received a call. I'm sorry to say that your brother has reportedly died of an overdose!"

Jeanine's hands gripped long blond hair. "Oh God! Oh no!" She yanked at her tresses. "My parents, then this! It can't be! It just can't be!"

Hate-filled eyes turned to Decker, advanced toward him. "You *killed* him, you bastard!" Abruptly, she drew back her hand, smacked him hard across the face.

Decker's fingers went to his stinging cheek as fury clouded his senses. The female officer—Heather Morgan—grabbed Jeanine's arm, turned her, and pushed her face against the wall. "Calm down this *minute*!"

"I'm going to *get* you, Decker!" Jeanine struggled against the officer's grip. "I'm going to get you *all*!"

Decker said, "Take her *out* of here!"

Anthony hoisted himself upward until his rear was off the seat. He yelled, "Let her go, man! She's just had a terrible shock!"

Strapp said, "Let her go, Officer Morgan!"

Decker's eyes grew in shock. *"What?"*

"I *said,* let her go, Officer!" Strapp reiterated. "That's an order." To Decker, he said, "Take a walk, Pete!"

A second slap across the face. Not a physical one but much deeper and harder. "I don't friggin' *believe*—"

"Now!" Strapp gripped Decker's arm, pushed him forward. "Take a *long walk*!"

Jeanine shook off Officer Morgan, smugness stamped across her face. She shrieked, "You'll hear from me in

court, Lieutenant. By the time I'm done with you, you'll
be begging on street corners!''

"Is that a *threat*?''

"It's a *promise*—''

Strapp pushed Decker forcefully. "*Out,* Lieutenant!''

Jeanine screamed, "I'll ruin you, you *bastard*!''

Decker stepped toward her. "The sentiment runs both
ways, lady!''

"*Out* now, Decker!'' Using an interlocking finger grip
and body leverage, Strapp was barely able to contain him.
He slowly managed to inch the big man away from the
scene, away from the apartment. Using maximum exertion!
Maximum effort!

And Decker wasn't even *fighting*. Just passively resisting. The guy must have the strength of a bull elephant.
Which gave Strapp pause for thought. Had Decker wanted
to lash out, there could have been real problems.

Onto the street. Decker was soaked in sweat . . . panting
. . . shaking . . . ready to strangle the next asshole who got
in his way. Seething at Jeanine, boiling over at Strapp. An-
grier at *him* than at *her*!

Goddamn son of a bitch!

As soon as Strapp had taken him to a secluded spot,
Decker shook off the captain's arm as if it were a gnat. He
spoke quickly and furiously. "You just cut off my balls in
front of that cunt—''

"Go back to basics, Decker!'' Strapp snapped back.
"First de-escalate the situation—''

"Bullshit!'' Decker spat out. "Bullshit, *bullshit*!''

"You're skirting the border of insubordination!'' Strapp
cut in. "Take a walk, Lieutenant, and cool off!''

Decker felt his head pounding, exploding fireworks of
white light. He closed his eyes, forced himself to count to
ten. Heard Strapp speaking softly.

". . . been through the mill, Pete. Why don't you take
the day off? Spend some time with that beautiful wife of
yours. We'll talk about this tomorrow.''

Again, Decker counted to ten. He opened his eyes. With
physical sight came the focus. Clarity of purpose. He

laughed bitterly. "This is unbelievable. You're shutting me down!"

Strapp blinked. "Pete, you're the best lieutenant I've ever had under my command. Incredibly hardworking, dedicated, not only book smart but street clever. Believe it or not, I'm trying to save you—"

"Thank you, Jesus—"

"—get you away from that bitch before she makes you react . . . giving her a *real* reason to sue you."

Decker's hand involuntarily went to his cheek. He didn't speak.

Strapp blew out air. "Go home, Pete!"

Decker waited a beat. Then he said, "I'm a good soldier, Captain. But I'm not a mindless one." He took his badge from his pocket, unharnessed his gun. Presented the package to his captain. "Here you go."

"Put it away, Peter."

"I mean it—"

"I know you do. Put it away."

Decker didn't move.

Strapp tightened his fingers into fists. "Don't draw lines in the sand, Pete. You have too much to lose."

"Fine. I lose. Take my job. I'll keep my pride."

"Don't be a schmuck, for godsakes. You've got kids to support."

"I quit now, I'll retire with half-time pension. My wife has skills. And a trust fund. A big one. Besides, I'm not exactly without resources. I've got twenty-five years of police experience behind me and I'm still licensed as a lawyer. So screw you—"

"Decker—"

"You want to cut off my balls, this is what you get. Take my damn badge. Either take it or stay the hell away from me!"

A standoff.

Strapp's jaw working overtime. "Just hear me out."

Decker didn't answer.

Strapp glanced around, over his shoulder. "Put your

badge and gun away. We have our differences. But we don't advertise them in public.''

"Yeah, I forgot. This is Hollywood. Image is every—''

"Fuck you!" Strapp blurted out.

Decker expected Strapp to stomp off. But he didn't. Decker stalled but eventually pocketed the equipment. "Make it quick, Strapp. My bullshit meter is about to blow.''

Strapp glared at him. "You asshole, don't you dare push me any further! I am still your *superior* officer. You talk to me, Decker, you call me *sir*.''

Decker held up his palms, took a step backward in mock retreat.

Strapp caught his breath. "Pete, I did what I just did for your sake. And I'm doing what I'm doing for your sake as well. I've *got* to take you off the case—''

"Fuck this noise—''

"I can't give the bitch any more fodder for her suit! And I can't have David Garrison's death ruling tainted by shouts of police conspiracy. The poor guy is dead! We owe him the truth—''

"What the *hell* do you think I've been looking for!"

"Jeanine's suit is a stumbling block to your involvement. You're off the case. *But*—''

"Ah, the *but*.''

Strapp continued. "Pete, it doesn't mean all your prior work on Estelle's has been shitcanned. It doesn't mean Jeanine's off the hook. It means we continue the investigation, it means you have input. But officially, I'll call the shots. Ergo, I take the heat. You have nothing to lose except aggravation. And maybe a little credit if we ever get to the bottom of this fucking mess!"

No one spoke.

Strapp sighed. "Can you live with that?''

"I don't give a flying fuck about credit.''

"Then you have nothing to lose. Lieutenant, you are a busy man. *You've* got a squad room to run. I refuse to allow that cunt to distract you any longer.''

Decker didn't answer, his head still buzzing like a jackhammer. He forced himself to breathe normally, to listen to ambient sounds—birds chirping, dogs barking, the faint rotors of a helicopter, the distant rush of morning traffic.

Strapp said, "We'll discuss the case daily. All you have to do is stay out of it *officially*. Let me direct."

"I have no problem with you directing. I don't give a rat's ass who directs as long as we get bottom-line results. I firmly believe that thirteen . . . *fourteen* people died because of that bitch. She's got to pay!"

"If that accusation turns out to be backed by solid evidence, she'll pay big time. Just let me handle it."

Whatever that was worth. Decker regarded his superior. Tense. Nervous. Angry. Upset. Was he telling the truth? Impossible to know.

Strapp took out a kerchief, wiped sweat from his forehead and face. "Call up Dunn and Oliver. You trust them, don't you?"

"Very much."

"So we'll let them secure the scene, gather evidence, and talk to the ME. Let David Garrison's death be their baby, okay?"

Decker paused. "Fine."

Again, Strapp wiped his brow. "You know, Decker, as much as you don't want to believe it, it could have been an OD. David had a history of drug abuse."

"How convenient for Jeanine."

Strapp didn't speak. Decker closed his eyes and opened them. "It's a good point . . . *sir*."

Strapp jerked his head up. "Go home."

"I'm going back to the station house."

"Fine with me. Go back to the station house, go run your division. We *both* have jobs to do."

With that, Strapp turned around and jogged back to the apartment.

☙26

Oliver said, "We ordered a full toxicology, including a blood-gas chromatography. See if David Garrison had any tranquilizers in his system—things like roofies or ludes—"

"Things that might have put him under," Marge said. "We'll also test to see if the junk was cut with cyanide, arsenic, thallium, or any other heavy metal or poison."

Oliver raked his hair with his hands. "I don't think we're going to find anything unusual though."

"Why's that?" Decker asked.

"First off, from our search, it appears the guy had his own private stash. Yeah, it could have been planted, but to my eye, it looked like it'd been dipped into before."

"Also Garrison reeked of booze," Marge added. "We did a quick blood analysis at the scene. BAL was point two five."

"Jesus!" Decker rotated his shoulders. "Guy was a pickled specimen."

Oliver nodded. "He probably did half the dirty work for her. Drinking himself comatose. Then all Jeanine would have to do is come in the house and pop him in the vein."

"No forced entry," Marge said. "But that doesn't mean anything. Jeanine has a key."

"She admitted it?"

"Right away."

Decker rubbed his forehead. "You have a point two five

BAL, you can't focus, let alone find a vein.''

"He had two pokes in the arm," Oliver said. "Maybe he didn't get it on his first try."

"He wouldn't have gotten it *period*!''

Marge said, "Maybe he shot up first. Then he started knocking off the shooters. Scott and I were going over this very thing. We both decided that Jeanine would have to have been really stupid to pop him at this moment—''

"Casting even more suspicion on herself—''

"And we know Jeanine's not stupid," Marge said, "so if she *did* do it, she must have had a pressing reason."

"Like what?" Decker asked.

"Maybe David stumbled onto something," Oliver said.

Decker perked up. "Such as?"

Marge said, "Maybe David found out that Jeanine was planning shenanigans with his trust."

Oliver paused. "Like what if Garrison wanted the money invested one way and Jeanine wanted to invest it another way?''

"Or what if she just wanted his money before he got a chance to spend it?" Marge said.

Decker said, "Farrell Gaynor and I talked about that. That's why I sent Scott out to see David Garrison in the first place."

"Talked about what?"

"That if Jeanine worked quickly—meaning if Jeanine offed David quickly—before the cash from the trust was distributed, she would probably inherit his cash as well as her own."

Webster walked into Decker's office, pulled up a chair next to Oliver. "Maybe she figured it like this. Her cash would go to her, his cash would pay her estate taxes."

"And the fact that she got away with Estelle's . . ." Marge paused. "That kind of lust for power . . . makes you arrogant."

"We all know about Jeanine's arrogance!" Oliver whispered. "And that bastard Strapp feeding right into it."

"Whole thing sucks!" Marge said.

"Sucks big time!" Oliver agreed. "Cunt may be able to

shut *you* down. But she can't shut down the entire Homicide Division.'' He paused. ''Though she's making a gallant effort.''

Webster said, ''Jeanine's getting pretty brazen . . . popping her brother like that.''

''Or maybe the OD was a lucky accident for her,'' Marge said. ''They do happen, even to evil people.''

Decker said, ''Neighbors see or hear anything suspicious?''

''Nothing.''

Decker turned to Webster. ''What's going on with Sean?''

Webster said, ''He went to school, he went home.''

''Did he pick up on your tail?'' Decker asked.

''If he did, I don't reckon he cared much. The boy just went about his business . . . buried in school most of the day. He could have been plotting murders, but I wasn't privy to his conversations.''

Decker sank into his chair. ''We're going nowhere fast.''

Martinez walked into the office. Webster was annoyed. ''Where've you been, Bert?''

Martinez stood against the wall. ''Checking out the license numbers. How're you doing, Loo?''

''All right,'' Decker said. ''Thanks for asking. What license numbers are you talking about, Bert?''

Webster said, ''Sean chatted with half a dozen kids after school . . . as he walked to the parking lot.''

Martinez said, ''At that point, we split assignments. Tom took Sean, I checked out some of the other kids.''

''And?'' Decker asked.

Martinez said, ''Tracked down three of them. First, the buxom blond girl who drives a Mercedes three hundred. She and Sean gabbed for a few minutes, he gave her something, she drove off. Then Sean talked to another girl for a minute or so. She was part Asian and maybe part black. Beautiful thing. She drives a Range Rover. He held the door open for her and she took off. The last person Sean talked to was a guy—a rangy Caucasian kid wearing jeans and a ski cap. He drives a ten-year-old Saab.''

Oliver said, "A ten-year-old Saab? I didn't think West-bridge allowed them."

Martinez said, "Ran all the plates through DMV. The Mercedes belongs to Barry and Susan Door. Range Rover is registered to a Jane Highsmith—"

"Jane Highsmith . . . why do I know that name?" Oliver snapped his fingers. "Got it! Family dispute ten years ago. Terence and Jane Highsmith. He's some kind of English lord, she's also from Brahmin background. Literally. Some upper-crust Indian family—"

"Upper caste," Webster punned.

The group groaned.

Oliver clucked his tongue. "Man, they were both skunk drunk . . . throwing things at each other—plates, dishes, flower vases, magazines. More things flying in that room than at O'Hare. And the kids." He shook his head. "Two little girls. Hiding in bed together, covers pulled up over their faces. Hugging each other. Scared shitless. Big blue eyes poking out of dusky skin. Beautiful girls."

"One of them still is."

"What about the Saab owner?" Marge asked.

"Doctors Kenneth and Elizabeth Rush," Martinez said. "But they're not MDs. Mr. Doctor is a professor of mathematics at Northridge, Mrs. Doctor is a professor of physics at UCLA. Their son, Joachim, is a senior at Westbridge. He's on scholarship."

Oliver said, "And you found this out from DMV?"

"Not quite." Martinez smiled. "Since Tom was on Sean, I figured I'd go for Joachim. Only I didn't know he was Joachim then. I followed the kid to Mycroft and Crane-pool—"

"The new bookstore on Devonshire," Marge said.

"The one with the café and espresso bar," Oliver added.

Marge stared at him. "You've actually been to a book-store, Scott?"

"Stick it in a dark place, lady," Oliver snapped back. "Yes, I've been to a bookstore."

"Singles night, Marge," Webster said.

"Fuck you, Uncle Tom," Oliver said. "And for your

information, lots of hot-looking babes were at the Jack Kerouac reading.''

Martinez went on, ''I followed Joachim to Mycroft and Cranepool. Kid got out of the car, carrying a bunch of papers. I didn't follow him into the store, but I could see what he was doing because the entire front is one big glass window. He didn't go there to browse. He left the papers on the store's counter, then came out again. I tailed him back to his house. Rather than just hang around there, I returned to the bookstore . . . picked up one of the leaflets.''

Martinez took a breath.

''An advertisment for a Scrabble tournament. I asked one of the clerks about it—a kid named James Goddard, who goes to public school. But he knows Joachim from the Scrabble matches. Once a month, they're held at Mycroft's. But games are hosted at other places as well. Seems that Joachim's a hot dog in the National Scrabble Association. A ranked player and an absolute fanatic. At the matches, he's known as Cyberword because he plays like a computer. Goddard was the one who told me about Joachim being on scholarship at Westbridge. He also told me that Joachim was accepted to Yale under an early admissions program. That's supposed to be impressive.''

''I'm impressed,'' Webster said. ''A formidable kid.''

Decker said, ''Is James Goddard a good friend of Joachim's?''

Martinez shook his head. ''Didn't get that impression. Just that they knew each other. Then again, I didn't want to pry too deep. Mostly we chatted. Talked about the store's special events.'' He looked at Oliver. ''Like singles night—''

''Fuck you!'' Oliver said.

''Stop being defensive, Scotty,'' Martinez answered. ''He told me that except for major author signings and children's bedtime story evening, the singles night is the store's biggest draw.''

Oliver didn't say anything, appeared to be mollified.

''Anyway, that's how I found out about Joachim's parents,'' Martinez said. ''They're not only regular customers but also faithful members of Mycroft and Cranepool's sci-fi book club. You join, you get discounts on sci-fi books and a monthly newsletter talking about upcoming sci-fi events, the whole nine yards.''

"Beam me up, Scotty." Immediately, Marge followed with "That's a trekkie saying, Oliver, not a come-on.''

Oliver looked crushed.

Webster asked, "Is Joachim a member of the sci-fi book group?''

"James didn't say, I didn't ask.''

Marge said, "Is Sean a Scrabble player?''

"I didn't ask that, either. Sounded too inquisitive.''

Webster loosened his tie. "You got Sean Amos. Mr. Hip Guy with the hip clothes and the hip convertible. Mr. Tennis Player who roughs up women . . . knocks up his girlfriend, then dumps her—''

"He paid for her abortion," Marge said.

"The kid's rolling in dough," Webster said. "Besides, betcha the boy's philosophy is God giveth, God taketh away. Because guess who he thinks *is* God.''

"Tommy, tell us how you really feel about Sean," Marge said.

"You should have seen the way he treated his sister. Like garbage.''

Decker said, "So you're thinking, why is a hip guy like Amos talking to Cyberword Joachim Rush? Mr. Poor Boy with the torn clothes and the old Saab.''

Webster said, "The two don't exactly seem like blood brothers.''

Martinez added, "Who says they're friends? I just saw them talking to each other.''

Decker said, "So why did you bother looking into him, Bert?''

"Good question." He gathered his thoughts. "I think it was the fact that Sean approached Joachim instead of the other way around.''

Decker pulled out his notebook. "And?''

"Nothing much. They walked to Joachim's car together.

Talked for maybe a minute with Sean doing most of the speaking—''

''Sean look nervous?'' Marge asked.

''More like animated,'' Martinez said. ''He talked with his hands, with his face. Joachim, on the other hand, appeared lost in thought except for the occasional nod. Apathetic. When the boys got to the Saab, Sean kept talking, even after Joachim was inside the car. But the driver's window was rolled down. Finally Sean reached into his pocket and pulled out an envelope, passed it through the open window—''

''A transaction?'' Marge was animated.

''Looked that way to me,'' Martinez said. ''Because afterward, Sean stuck his arm back into the car. I guess they shook hands. Then Joachim drove off.''

''A payoff,'' Webster said.

Oliver said, ''Okay. Here's what we got. We got Joachim, who's a nerd—''

''More like a weirdo,'' Webster interjected. ''A guy called Cyberword, who's a Scrabble fanatic—''

''My kids play Scrabble,'' Decker said. ''I play Scrabble. I'm not a nerd, I'm not weird, and I'm not a hit man. We don't know a friggin' thing about this kid. We've just made leaps that could traverse the Grand Canyon.''

No one said anything.

Decker gave a slight smile. ''Still, if I were TV typecasting for an outcast, theoretically Joachim Rush would fit the bill—a scholarship boy in a rich prep school. A loner because he's out of the social loop. Then both of his parents are not only math and science professors but also fanatic sci-fi readers. He's a fanatical Scrabble player. I'm always skeptical of fanatical anything—''

''Even religious fanaticals?'' Oliver said.

''Especially the fanatically religious,'' Decker countered. ''The Rushes don't sound like part of the typical Westbridge population. Neither the kid nor the parents.''

Oliver said, ''You add to your pot that a wad of money was exchanged between Sean and Joachim.''

"Who said it was money?" Martinez said. "I just said an envelope."

"What else could it be?" Webster said.

"Lots of things—"

"Including cash for a hit made to look like an OD that happened just last night—"

"Whoa," Decker said. "We're getting *way* out there with our theories. But it *is* an interesting postulation. Too bad we won't be able to check it out."

"Why not?" Martinez asked. "I can tail Joachim for a couple of days, Loo."

"It's okay by me except I'm off the case now." Decker felt his jaw tighten. "You've got to take it up with Strapp."

Oliver frowned. "You know what he'll say, Loo."

Martinez said, "Just let me tail him tomorrow."

"I'm not authorized to give you the go-ahead, Bert. Talk to Strapp."

"He'll bury it," Webster said.

"Probably."

Oliver said, "That means all our work—hell, all *your* work—it's all gonna be shitcanned. You know that."

"I know that," Decker said.

Marge said, "Aren't you frustrated?"

"I'm very frustrated."

"So what are you going to do?"

"At this moment, I'm grinning and bearing. But as for the future . . ." Decker shrugged. "I hear Montana's beautiful at this time of year."

Marge said, "If you don't mind militia men and Nazis."

"Margie, I've been a cop for twenty-five years," Decker said. "I'm used to nutcases with guns."

Freed by Strapp from the Estelle's shooting . . . the tragedy's persistent nagging . . . Decker polished off his paperwork by seven. He thought about his work, he thought about his life. What had happened to all the dreams? All the vacation fantasies? Hand and hand with Rina, running barefoot on empty beaches, toes tickled by the waves. Or hiking through pristine mountains, smelling clean air. Why had he allowed himself to become mired in the muck? His words to Strapp this morning crystalized his dissatisfaction. Openly admitting that the end might be near.

And maybe that was a good thing.

Because there was life beyond the LAPD.

Someone knocked on his doorjamb, jogging him out of his reverie. Marge said, "A woman named Tess Wetzel is waiting outside. She wants to talk to you."

"What's it about?"

"She wouldn't say."

Decker paused, the name pricking at his memory cells. "Tess Wetzel?"

"That's what she said." Marge looked at her watch. "It's kinda late. Tell her you left?"

"No, you can bring her in."

"You're the boss."

Decker laughed. "Right."

A moment later, a plain-looking woman of around thirty limped into the office. She walked with a cane, wincing at every step. Burdened beyond her years. She was on the heavy side, but still had curves. She wore baggy jeans under a loose cable-knit sweater. No makeup. No jewelry. A basic woman, yet there was something about her that connoted strength. Decker stood, held out the chair opposite his desk.

With effort, the woman lowered herself into the seat. Her voice was soft. "Thank you very much for seeing me."

"No problem." Decker sat, held out his hand. "It's Mrs. Wetzel, is it?"

"Tess." The woman laced her fingers around his, squeezed his hand, then quickly placed hers in her lap. Her eyes grew moist. "You don't remember me, do you?"

Decker stared at the face . . . the pained expression . . . the iron will. He blinked, then said, "That entire night was a blur, Tess, but I remember you clearly. Although I don't think we were ever properly introduced." Again he held out his hand. "Lieutenant Peter Decker. Pleased to meet you."

She smiled, then started crying. Buried her head in her hands. "I'm sorry."

Decker leaned over, about to place his hand on her shoulder. Thoughts of Jeanine's harassment suit flitted through his brain. Aw, *screw* that! He patted her arm gently, offered her a tissue. She took it and wiped her eyes.

He said, "It's wonderful to see you up and about."

"Of sorts."

"Can I get you something, Tess?"

"Nothing." She blew her nose. "I came to thank you."

"You're very welcome, although I didn't do anything more than my job."

"I didn't know cops were trained to splint legs."

"I had some medical training when I was in the army. Amazing. It came back to me in a second."

"You should have been a doctor," Tess said. "You have a great bedside manner."

Decker smiled. "Thank you. How are you coping?"

Tess looked away. "Not too awful. Been so busy thinking about myself I haven't been able to think much about . . . about Ken."

Decker nodded.

Tess blinked tears. "We weren't getting along so hot, you know."

Decker waited.

"That night . . ." Tess cleared her throat. "That night . . . Ken was telling me it was over . . . between us. That he was gonna leave me for some little . . . floozy he was messing around with . . . at the office."

"I'm sorry."

"I remember sittin' there, Lieutenant. Just sittin' there like a piece of wood. Not feelin' anything. Still, the tears wouldn't stop comin'."

Decker nodded.

"I remember thinkin' . . . thinkin' . . . I wish I was dead. I wish *he* was dead. Next thing I knew, he was."

Tears streamed down her cheeks as she cried silently, her gaze fixed on his wall.

Softly, Decker said, "You didn't mean it, Tess. Don't

you even give it a second thought because you didn't *mean* it. You think about yourself now—yourself and your kids. You have children, right?''

"Two."

"You had *nothing* to do with your husband's death. There's only one man to blame for what happened that night."

"Harlan Manz," Tess whispered.

"He's the only one responsible for your husband's death," Decker said. "Is that clear?"

Tess didn't respond right away. Then she said, "At the hospital . . . we formed a group . . . those of us who were hit but weren't on the critical list."

"A survivors' group?"

"Yes. We started talking among ourselves. Because only we knew what it was like."

"I think that was a great idea."

"I'm still in contact with a few of the women. The waitress there named Carol. We became friends. We have kids the same age and all. I was thinking like . . . maybe you could come talk to us one day."

"Anytime." Decker paused. "What do you have in mind?"

"Just talk about . . . what happened. And *why*."

"That's tough. Because we really don't know why. We have theories, we have suspicions, we have profiles and psychologists and criminal experts—all of them yakking about this kind of thing. But that's all we really have, Tess. Just talk. Still, I'd be happy to address your group and answer any questions you people might have."

Decker pulled out his calendar.

"Did you have a specific date in mind?"

She shook her head no. "I've got to call some of the others first. Can I get back to you?"

"Absolutely."

She started to rise. Decker bolted out of his chair to aid her, but she stopped him. "I can manage."

"Okay."

She stood, leaned on the ball of her cane. "This is gonna sound crazy . . . but . . ."

Decker nodded encouragement.

She started to talk, then stopped. She tried again. "The shooting . . . there was a lot of shooting."

"Yes, there was."

"Ken and me . . . it seems like we was hit right away." Her eyes moistened. "Right off the bat."

"I understand."

"There was all this shooting. Even after we was hit."

"Yes, there was lots of fire."

"I got this bad habit . . . of being curious . . . too curious. Even after I was hit . . . instead of just staying down like a normal person, I had to look."

Decker's heart started racing. "What'd you see, Tess?"

"Lots of very scared people. Somehow . . . seeing them so scared . . . it made me less scared. Does that sound crazy?"

"Not at all."

Tess grew silent. Decker tried to hide his disappointment. Well, what did he expect? "No, it doesn't sound the least bit crazy."

Tess dropped her voice to a whisper. "Suddenly it stopped . . . the shooting. After it was over . . . everyone moaning and crying . . . but nobody dared to move. Too afraid that it would . . . you know . . . start up again."

Decker nodded.

Tess said, "So no one moved . . . even after it was over . . . except that one guy."

One guy? Decker tried to keep calm. "What guy was that, Tess?"

"Some guy in a heavy green jacket . . . it was cold that night."

Decker sat up. A *green* jacket? Harlan was found dead, wearing a *green* jacket. "You saw a man in a green jacket walking around *after* the shooting stopped?"

Tess appeared confused. "He was more like standing around. But I'm not *positive*. Because the one time I mentioned him, no one knew what I was talking about. But like

I said, I have a bad habit of being curious. That's how I found out about Ken and his floozy.''

Decker forced himself to talk slowly. ''Tell me about this guy. What did he do?''

''He didn't do anything really. Just bent down, then stood up, put his hands in his pocket . . . he looked around, then walked out the door. Isn't that odd?''

Decker agreed. It was very odd. Casually, he told her that he'd look into it.

ᕈ27

Placing his hands on his desk, Strapp made a tepee with extended fingers. To Decker, he said, "And how many of Estelle's people did you interview?"

"All of them. But that doesn't—"

Strapp interrupted. "Tell me if I'm wrong about this, Lieutenant."

The captain's eyes went from Decker to his Homicide team minus the old guy, Farrell Gaynor. Dogs encircling him like prey. Well, fuck that. He'd run *his* investigation in *his* own way, at *his* own pace. Less chance of errors—procedurally as well as politically.

"Any of you in this room," Strapp addressed them. "I *welcome* the chance to stand corrected. Now you people interviewed every single patron and employee at Estelle's. Correct?"

The question was rhetorical so no one answered.

Strapp said, "How many were there, Lieutenant?"

Decker could see where this was leading. "One hundred forty-eight—"

"And not *one* of them mentioned a phantom man—"

"In a *green* jacket," Marge interrupted.

"Yes, Detective, I know the details. Can I finish?"

"Sorry, sir," Marge replied.

Strapp said, "So I'm right about this, am I not, Decker? That no one mentioned a *phantom* guy . . . in a *green* jacket?"

Oliver spoke up, "Sir, many of the witnesses mentioned that the shooter wore a green jacket."

"Harlan Manz wore a green jacket, Detective." Strapp grew irritated. "Forget about the jacket. I want to know *which* of your one hundred and forty-eight witnesses mentioned this phantom guy?"

Decker said, "Captain, it was right after—"

Strapp held up his hand, signaling quiet. "Yes, I know, I know. Everyone had been in shock. And it takes time for the shock to wear off . . . for the memories to come back. This is all true. And I'm willing . . . to entertain Mrs. Wetzel's . . . what was her first name, Pete?"

"Tess," Decker said.

Strapp clasped his hands together. "All right. Let's say Mrs. Wetzel's observation was more than a figment of her imagination. Before we proceed any further—with our outer-space conspiracy theories and teenage hit men postulations—we go back to *basics*. How about doing a little *police* work?"

Decker said, "I had every intention of having my team reinterview every single person at Estelle's that evening—"

"Good," Strapp said. "Because now it's an order! Just damn well make sure you don't *push* anyone. If they don't want to talk, we come back. Because it's only been what . . . about three weeks since the incident. We're still dealing with open wounds. So that's what we do. We concentrate on interviews."

The captain looked pointedly at Martinez.

"We forget about tailing a gawky teenager whose only crime is playing Scrabble." His eyes turned to Webster. "And we forget about Sean Amos, whose only crime is being a schmuck."

"He roughs up women," Webster said.

"He grabbed his sister's arm, Detective," Strapp said. "No, it's not *nice*. But if we arrested every older brother who manhandled his younger sibling, we'd have no civilian population."

"It's different when you do it in front of a cop," Webster said. "It makes a statement."

"It says nothing, Webster. More important, it means nothing with regard to the murders at Estelle's. Lay off Amos, is that *clear*?"

"Very."

"Good." Strapp faced the others. "We also forget about Jeanine Garrison—"

"What about David Garrison?" Marge interrupted. "Do we forget about him as well?"

Strapp's face turned red. His hands clenched into fists. "Detective Dunn, you're here by my good graces, not by *his*." He cocked a thumb in Decker's direction.

"It was a legitimate question, Captain," Decker retorted. "Do we view David Garrison as a plain suicide or do we hunt around?"

"For now, it's a suicide," Strapp said. "If Forensics tells us differently, we barrel ahead into a homicide investigation."

Strapp looked at his watch.

"It's eight-thirty. No sense bothering people at night. All the interviewing is to be done during work hours, but not at the expense of your other investigatory duties. Is that clear?"

"Couldn't be any clearer," Oliver said.

"Are you being snide, Detective Oliver?"

"I'm always snide, sir," Oliver answered. "It's part of my personality."

"It's a rotten part."

"I'm sure my ex-wife would agree with you, sir."

Decker smiled, looked down.

Strapp caught it, started to sneer, but smiled as well. He threw his head back, exhaled slowly, then looked at the group. "You should see yourselves. Like a bunch of hyenas ready to pounce. And for what reason? Because I'm telling you to do sound police work."

He turned to Decker.

"Lieutenant, given Tess Wetzel's revelation, what would you do?"

Decker ran a hand over his face. "I'd handle the investigation more or less the same way. Because at the moment, we have nothing on Jeanine Garrison other than a photo of her and Manz. And that's not indictable evidence. I do believe Tess Wetzel's disclosure. So maybe I'd make the interviewing more top priority. But basically, the captain and I are in agreement.''

Martinez said, "So then we don't have a problem.''

"I have a problem,'' Webster said. "We're sidestepping a killer because she's connected.''

"So get me evidence.'' Strapp became suddenly angry. "I can't *believe* you people. A bunch of asses. Finally, you get a big break . . . some outside confirmation that maybe there was a second shooter . . . and you're mired in shit. Stop blowing smoke through your butts and start asking the right *questions.* And maybe you'll even get the right *answers.*''

He turned to Decker.

"I don't want you questioning anyone, but you can draw up the list of people to be interviewed and divide them any way you see fit.''

Webster said, "Then I reckon you don't want us questioning Jeanine Garrison . . . 'cause she wasn't there.''

"That's right, Webster,'' Strapp said. "I reckon you don't do that. It's not only *pointless,* it's *stupid.*''

"Aren't pointless and stupid the same thing?'' Oliver asked.

Webster said, "You can be pointless without being stupid.''

"Well, your idea, Webster, was both.'' The captain turned to Decker. "Anything else you want to discuss?''

Decker shook his head.

"Meeting is over.'' Strapp turned back to Decker. "I need to talk to you alone. The rest of you . . . *out!*''

Slowly the group got up, left the captain's office feeling depressed and put down. Strapp found their resentment palpable. Too bad. You want to bolster the ego, get yourself a whore. Strapp waited until the last of them had filed out, then closed the door a little too hard. He took a deep breath, let it out slowly. "You want coffee, Pete?''

"You're offering me coffee?" Decker paused. "Gotta be bad."

Strapp sat down, buried his head in his hands. "God, what a mess." He looked up. "What a fucking mess!"

Decker waited. Strapp said, "I got an apology call from Jeanine's lawyer . . . her behavior this morning."

"Uh-huh."

"Quote, unquote. 'She was in shock at her brother's untimely demise, she was hysterical. She didn't know what came over her. She's extremely sorry for her unprecedented outburst.' "

Decker shifted in his seat. "Obviously someone told her that slapping constitutes legal assault. Her lawyer was feeling you out to see if I'm going to file an assault charge against her."

"They realize it's a possibility."

"A *strong* possibility."

"They want to deal. You be gentlemanly, she won't proceed with the harassment suit. Let bygones be bygones."

"And what about my hearing with the IAD?"

"What about it?"

"Does she call them up and tell them she was lying?"

"Decker, if she doesn't pursue the charges, you'll beat the in-house investigation."

"No, that's not true. If she doesn't pursue the charges, I'll get an Unsustained from IAD. Which is what I'd probably get in any case. I want my record to remain spotless. Which is what I deserve. I want her to call IAD and tell them she was lying. I want a decision of Unfounded."

"Decker—"

"You call up her legal eagle, tell him that *if* she admits she was lying, I won't bring her up on assault charges. Charges on which I—unlike her—have witnesses—"

Strapp broke in. "Pete, *listen* to me. Jeanine is not going to admit that she was lying. Yes, it's unfair. But look at the positive. This is a great chance to rid yourself of an albatross around your neck. Don't be an idiot."

"No dice."

Strapp flung himself against the back of his desk chair, looked up at the ceiling. "Would it help if I ordered you to do it?"

"You can't order away my civil rights."

The captain gazed intensely at Decker. "Don't you think you owe it to Rina to consult her before you make such a blanket decision?"

"Charges are against *me,* not her."

But even as Decker said it, he knew Strapp had him. No way he'd chance going to trial, making it public . . . becoming an embarrassment to Rina and the kids. Backed into a corner like a circus lion, seething with rage . . . lashing out in vain as the devil snapped the whip.

Quietly, Decker said, "Tell her lawyer I'll think about it."

Strapp cleared his throat. "Peter, we both know that Jeanine is unstable. She's giving you a bargain . . . now . . . at this moment. Tomorrow she may change her mind. If I call now, her lawyer will have the papers ready tomorrow morning. I'll have them reviewed by our legal staff, have them sitting on your desk before lunch. You sign them. And when you return from your break, you'll be rid of this whole fucking mess. What do you say?"

"I'll talk to Rina."

Strapp didn't push it. "I'll call the lawyer anyway. You can always change your mind. Be here in my office by eight tomorrow."

Decker forced himself to unclench his jaw. "Okay."

"For what it's worth, it stinks."

"Anything else?"

"Yes, there is something else." Strapp averted his gaze. "She wants to make amends . . . Jeanine."

"Oh, Christ—"

"Not with you necessarily . . . with the LAPD. You've been reading about this wheelchair tennis tournament?"

"Yes."

"I heard it was your idea."

"Go on."

"Anyway . . . if you've been following the articles—
which I'm sure you have—you know that the proceeds are
going to the Estelle's victims—"

"Robbing Peter to pay Paul—"

"Decker, the massacre made widows. Not all of them
were rich women."

"Unlike others who became millionaires overnight—"

"Didn't your friend Wetzel lose her husband?" Strapp
broke in. "And she has kids?"

"Yes, she did lose a husband, and yes, she does have
kids," Decker snapped back. "So what's the point? Jeanine
been elevated to hero status?"

"No. But the tournament is for a good cause."

The captain's voice turned soft.

"She hit upon a real winner, rabbi. A grand a ticket for
the courtside boxes. And they're selling like hotcakes because big names in the tennis world are going to be there.
And that attracts the press. Major publicity. The mayor's
ordered a box. So has the governor."

Strapp pointed to his chest.

"Me, I couldn't care less about that. But I do care about
the people I serve."

Once again, Decker felt anger race through his veins. He
knew too clearly what was happening.

Strapp said, "Jeanine has a box reserved for us—for the
police. Because she has rightly assumed that we'd want to
be there to show our support. As the captain at Devonshire,
it's my duty to be there as an agent of the community I
serve."

Heart and head pounding, Decker glared at him. Slowly
he said, "Jeanine whacks me across the face and you cut
off my balls in front of her—"

"Decker—"

"Out of respect for *your* authority, I say nothing. I *do*
nothing. You tell me to deal with her lawyer, I deal with
her lawyer. And you repay me by giving the bitch the honor
of your presence—"

"It's not for her, dammit!" Strapp pounded the table.
"If you'd get down off your self-righteous high horse for

one goddamn second, you'd realize the position I'm in. I've *got* to be there."

"No, you don't."

"Decker, what do I say when the victims' families question why their police captain was absent at their benefit?"

"You tell them the *truth*. That you think Jeanine Garrison is a lying scumbag—"

"That's called slander."

"It's called integrity."

Strapp started to speak, but stopped. He refused to meet Decker's eyes. "I've got nothing more to say. Be here tomorrow. Eight o'clock sharp. That's all. You can go."

Decker rose, stood in place for a moment. "Sir, I'm not as self-righteous as you believe . . . nor am I as righteous as I'd like to believe. I know how things work. So take my words as one political animal talking to another."

Strapp waited.

"Jeanine Garrison was involved in that massacre. And Jeanine Garrison *is* going to fall. Anyone associated with her and her causes—no matter how worthy they are—is going to wind up looking like a dupe."

"I'll take my chances, Lieutenant. Good night."

Decker walked over to the door, opened it, then turned around. "Do yourself a favor, Captain. On the day of the tournament, come down with the flu."

🌿28

And there was evening, and there was morning.

On the seventh day, God rested.

With any luck, so could Decker. It always took him a while to slip into Shabbos mode. Gourmet food and fine wine helped the process. As he sipped tea, he watched his wife shuffle papers.

She said, "The first contender's a four-bedroom, three-bath. Around thirty-five-hundred square feet. Center hall plan, living room, formal dining, a den. Central air and heat. Built-ins in the kitchen. And it's got a pool with a Jacuzzi."

"California living," Jacob added with a grin.

"Pools mean maintenance," Decker groused. "A Jacuzzi means lots of maintenance."

Sammy asked, "Can Ginger swim?"

At the mention of her name, the setter lifted her head. Decker told her to go back to sleep. "Yes, she can swim. That's all I need. Dog hairs clogging up the filter."

"I'll clean the pool, Dad," Jacob said. "Just show me what to do."

The boy's offer tugged at Decker's heart strings. So anxious to get out of here and into civilization. Decker picked up his teacup, eyes on the flickering Shabbos candles. Dinner had been scrumptious, and everyone, including the baby, had been in a good mood. Hannah had lasted until dessert, then announced she wanted to go to sleep. As Rina put her to bed, the boys cleared the dishes, restored a rose-filled vase to its rightful place at the center of the table. Decker stacked the plates, made the tea. For the first time in weeks, he felt at semi-peace.

Rina went on, "The house is a little bruised, but certainly something we could live with for a while. About six blocks from the shul—"

He returned his eyes to his wife. "How much?"

"They're asking three twenty five, but the realtor thinks there's flexibility."

"Should be at that price."

"Also the lot is small."

"How small?"

"Around sixty-five hundred square feet."

Decker winced. "Any yard at all?"

"Room for a swing set, a patio set." Rina showed her husband the tear sheet.

He scanned the vitals of the home. "At least Hannah'll be happy." He paused. "I've got acres here."

Rina sighed. "You must feel like Gulliver being thrown into Lilliput."

Jacob fidgeted, then said, "We don't need such a big house, Eema. Show him the other one. The three-bedroom. The lot's bigger, Dad. It's got room for a pool. Not that I expect a pool. I'm just saying it's got the room."

Jacob was trying so hard. Decker never realized how difficult the isolation had been on him. "We'll find something, Jake." He turned to his other son. "What do you think, Sammy?"

He shrugged. "I don't mind sharing a room if you want the bigger lot. I don't mind having my own room, if you want the bigger house. It's up to you."

Rina paused. "There is this one house—if you could call it that—on a good-size lot. Fourteen eight."

Decker considered the size. "Not bad."

"It's a little farther from the shul . . . about a mile, mile and a half away—"

"After what we've been walking, a mile and a half's *nothing*," Jacob said. "Besides, the house is inside the *eruv* so we can carry on Shabbos. And push a stroller. Which is good news for Hannah. The shul has a toddlers' play group. It's real cute. I'm sure she'd love it. She doesn't like being left behind when we go to shul, you know.''

Decker said, "Yes, Jacob, I know that."

Quickly, the teen said, "Not that I'm pushing you. Take your time, Dad."

Decker raised his brow. "What about the house?"

"It's tiny. A fixer-upper—"

"Yeah, like it should be rebuilt," Sammy said, laughing.

"It's salvageable," Rina replied. "But it *is* tiny. Two bedrooms—"

"We have three children," Decker said.

"There's a small den. We could convert it into a room for the boys until we add another bedroom . . . or two—"

"You mean until *I* add another bedroom or two—"

"And a couple of bathrooms, too," Sammy said. "It only has one bath."

"Five of us and one bathroom." Decker nodded. "Rich."

"We can always rent something portable," Rina said.

Decker looked at her. "You're kidding, right?"

She hit his good shoulder. "Of course I'm kidding."

"Actually, that wouldn't be a bad idea," Sammy said. "And while we're at it, we could pitch a couple of tents in the summer. Because the house doesn't have air-conditioning."

Decker groaned.

Rina said, "I thought you loved camping."

Jacob blurted out, "It's a great lot, Dad. Full of big trees. Lots of shade in the summer."

Rina said, "The boy is a hard sell."

Jacob blushed. "I'm just looking at the positive."

Rina kissed her son's forehead. "Good for you. You'll always be happy."

Sammy came to his brother's rescue. "The lot is awesome."

"It's a tenth the size of this place," Decker said.

"Yeah, but it's really well planted," Sammy answered. "This place is mostly dirt."

"I've got an orchard," Decker defended.

"Dad, the new lot's got like about three or four *huge* avocado trees—"

"And orange trees, too," Jacob said. "*Big* ones."

"Valencia oranges," Rina said. "Full-sized trees that they don't plant anymore because they're so tall. Must be thirty or forty years old. It's also got lemon, lime, and grapefruit trees. And giant eucalyptuses. Wonderful menthol smell."

"How much?"

"One hundred seventy-five."

"That's too cheap!"

"Actually, it's about plot price."

"Could we live in it?"

"For as much as you're home, yes," Rina said.

"Funny." Decker glared at her. "You have a tear sheet on this, Lucille Ball?"

"No. It's by owner. Another reason why the price is good."

"This doesn't sound like a house," Decker said. "It sounds like a project."

Rina shrugged. "It would give your father something to do if your parents come out for Thanksgiving. He loves to tinker and build."

"I have to live in a shack to give my father a life?"

Rina muttered, "To give yourself a life."

Decker snapped, "I heard that."

"You were *supposed* to hear that."

No one spoke for a moment.

Sammy cleared his throat, said, "Hey, Yonkie, wanna learn a little?"

"What?"

Sammy cocked his head at his parents, yanked his brother out of his seat. "Let's go."

"Oh," Jake said. "I get it."

Since the boys' bedroom was dark, they went into the kitchen. Decker kept his voice down, but he was peeved.

"I'm tired of your digs! I'm doing the best I can!"

Rina took Peter's hand. "I'm worried about you."

"I'm *fine*. I'd be a lot *finer* if I didn't have to think about you being mad at me for the hours I keep."

"I'm not mad at you—"

"Could have fooled me. Think I want to work this hard? Think I like coming home every night having missed dinner and the baby. We have thousands of ongoing cases, Rina—"

"I'm aware—"

"With new ones every day." Decker counted off on his fingers. "There're phone calls, there're meetings, there's paperwork, there's assignments, and lots of people with problems. Not to mention the dees and their problems. I must spend half my time doing counseling to keep them functional. I can't help my hours."

"I know that."

"I'm not stopping off at a bar with the guys. Although there'd be nothing wrong if I did. I'm not stopping off at the gym to play racquetball, either."

"I wish you did."

"What does *that* mean? You want me to spend *more* time away from you?"

"I want you to be happy."

"Then stop razzing me."

"Deal."

Neither of them spoke for a moment. Decker rotated his shoulders. "What are you really trying to tell me, darlin'?"

Rina said, "Even when you're here, you're not here. You're distracted. I talk to you and half the time you don't even hear it. You're thinking about your cases. You breathe and eat your job and that's not healthy."

Decker was quiet.

Rina said, "You used to spend hours with the horses. Now the poor things just languish in their stalls. The horses aren't the problem. We can sell them. It's the fact that you don't seem to enjoy life outside of work."

"It's been a miserable month." Decker rubbed his neck. "I'm very unhappy."

"Is it Estelle's?"

"For the most part, yes."

"It's only been about a month."

"It's getting colder by the day . . . damn near frigid."

Rina tried a cheerful smile. "At least the suit has been dropped."

"I'm very angry about that. I should have fought it. Instead I caved in."

Rina was quiet.

"Stupid to be angry." Decker looked away. "It's over."

Rina kissed his hand. "You didn't cave in. It's called being married." She waited a beat. "Maybe it's the same thing."

Decker's smile was genuine. Again, he moved his wounded shoulder, trying to relieve the dull throb of former battle. "I should move on. Because I'm sure not getting anywhere."

"Nothing productive from the interviews of the patrons?"

Decker rolled his eyes. "Sure there was a man. No, it was a woman. No, it wasn't a man at all. He was tall, he was short. He was blond, he was brunette, he was bald. He was fat, he was skinny. He was wearing a coat, he wasn't wearing a coat, he streaked naked through the restaurant. He had a gun. No, he didn't have a gun, he had an Uzi. No, he didn't have an Uzi, he had a cannon. No, he didn't have a cannon, he had a Sherman tank."

He looked at his wife.

"Garbage in, garbage out. People telling us what they think we want to hear. It doesn't amount to a hill of beans."

He drank cold tea.

"I'm starting to doubt my own instincts. Maybe Jeanine had nothing to do with it. Just a histrionic lady who had the bad luck to be in a picture with a mass murderer. And I had the bad luck to push her button."

"Peter, why don't you hire a private detective? PIs can do things you can't do. Why don't you see what kind of dirt they can dig up?"

Decker stared at his teacup. "Actually, I considered the

idea, then nixed it. I can't afford the fees myself. And with the evidence I have, there'd be no way to squeeze it out of the department.''

Rina hesitated. "How much do they cost?"

"About two hundred a day plus expenses—"

"Don't they give professional courtesy?"

Decker smiled. "No. Besides the expense, their use in these types of cases is not really effective. They're good for tracing missing persons or tracking down deadbeat dads—doing a paper trail. They're also good for photographing illicit encounters or stalkers or industrial espionage and theft. Things that happen on a regular basis. Things that can be caught in the act. Jeanine's basically a law-abiding citizen who happens to have murdered fourteen people. She's finished with her dirty work. Now all she has to do is hang tight. What's a PI going to tell me? She's hanging tight?"

Decker paused.

"What I really need is a stoolie. Someone who was involved in her plot to drop a dime on her. Or someone from the inside to whom she might have confessed."

"Inside of what?"

"Good question."

Decker got up, began to pace.

"Like this wheelchair tennis tournament she's hosting. Probably lots of handicapped around. Ideally, if money wasn't an object, I'd hire someone handicapped to work on the inside. Someone nondescript and nonthreatening who's a good listener. Someone who could get her trust *and* get her talking. Then I could wire him or her and catch Jeanine's slipups on tape."

"What about Wade Anthony?"

He stopped walking. "If I approached Anthony on this, it would be tantamount to cutting off my own head. First thing he'd do is tell Jeanine. Then she'd slap me with another suit—police harassment. And she'd have a legitimate case!"

No one spoke. Decker took his wife's hand, kissed it. "Rina, this shack . . . it's a good price. Something we can afford. Let me have an inspector out there. See what needs to be done. If it looks okay . . . like something I can handle, let's do it.''

She broke into a smile. "You've just made Yaakov's year.''

"In the meantime, since it *is* reasonable, we can afford to keep this place for a while. Maybe live *there* over the weekends and be here on weekdays, where it's more comfortable. At least until I can add an extra bathroom. Shouldn't take me more than a couple of months of Sundays if the sewer line's not a problem.''

"I was serious about your father, Peter,'' Rina said. "Buying it would give him motivation to come out. He loves anything that has to do with tools. So does your brother for that matter.''

"I'll get me my kinfolk,'' Decker drawled. "We'll have ourselves an ole barn raisin.' So, little lady, what are you and *your* hands going to contribute to this purchase?''

"I can sew, I can paint, and I can even hang wallpaper.''

"A real down-home family affair.'' Suddenly, he turned serious. "So my folks haven't made a decision about Thanksgiving?''

"Still thinking about it. But I'll get them out here. Especially now. I can work on your dad by dangling the new house in front of his face.''

"The new house . . .'' He laughed softly. "I love it. We're already talking like we own it.''

"All it takes is money.''

"Yeah, maybe we can ask Jeanine to float us a loan. She's rolling in it.''

Rina grew serious. "Peter, you'll get your resolution from Estelle's. It may take time, but you'll get it.''

"The woman's parents die a horrible death, her brother dies a horrible death . . . and she's out being Miss Social Butterfly . . . raising money for poor, poor victims like herself.''

Rina said nothing.

"I know,'' Decker said. "There were *real* victims. And why should they suffer?''

He pushed his chair from the table, threw his head back.

"I'm just . . . frustrated. Because the woman's smart. Suing me like she did . . . immediately deflecting the investigation. Then taking up the cause of the victims. Getting them as a support system. Placing herself behind a barrier of officials and hotshots."

He regarded his wife.

"Still, if we had evidence, she wouldn't be impenetrable. Trouble is, we have nothing. We can't even figure out the basics. Like how she could have bought a hit man. We've surreptitiously examined Jeanine's accounts. No big transfers of money either before or after Estelle's. She doesn't even show little transfers that could add up to big transfers. Of course, she could be hiding it."

Rina paused. "She will inherit a great deal of money from her parents' trust, correct?"

"Yes. We thought about that. We didn't spot any cash transfers from the trust, either."

"You know, Peter, I'm sure her parents didn't keep all their assets in cash. Vis-à-vis our discussion about the yeshiva's finances and its charity donations, people pay using all sorts of assets—"

Decker slapped his hands over his face. "How could I be so *dense*! She made the payoff with stock certificates—"

"Or maybe with bearer bonds inherited from her parents' trust—"

"Jesus! Of course!" He leaped to his feet. "The Garrisons had to have had coupon bonds. They fit the profile to a T. Middle-aged to elderly and *rich*. Furthermore, munis would be perfect contract money because they're untraceable."

"Not the new ones," Rina said. "They're all registered. To prevent capital gains tax evasion as well as state tax evasion. Instead of coupons, owners get the bond's interest in an annual or semi-annual check."

Decker said, "But there are still plenty of coupon bonds on the secondary market. The Garrisons have been rich for a while, probably purchased bearer bonds years ago. And *those* would be untraceable."

"At least very hard to trace."

Decker sat up. "You *can* trace them?"

"In theory, I suppose you could trace them via the coupon. You'd have to wangle a heap of private information from a broker or from the paying agency. I'm sure it's illegal." Rina looked at him. "Did you have something specific in mind?"

"Not really. We're sadly lacking in concrete evidence."

"What do you have?"

"Not much." Decker raised his brows. "We have Jeanine, who has been playing tennis with a seventeen-year-old male partner for the last six, seven months."

"And?"

"And that's about it."

"You think her tennis partner has something to do with the shootings at Estelle's?"

"Maybe."

"Why? Because he's Jeanine's tennis partner?"

"Yes."

Rina shrugged. "Thank God for due process."

Decker smiled.

"And you think Jeanine manipulated this boy into killing . . ." Rina squinted. "Who did he kill?"

"Harlan Manz."

"And how did Jeanine know that Harlan was about to shoot up an entire restaurant?"

"Two theories," Decker said. "Either she was manipulating Harlan as well, and knew he was about to explode. *Or.* The whole thing was a planned hit masked to look like . . . I don't know . . . a random act of violence. Ostensibly, Jeanine used two hit men. But then she did a double-cross. She got the second hit man to take out Harlan . . . and that made the whole thing look like a mass murder by one insane man."

"This is *very* far-fetched."

"No, I haven't gotten to the far-fetched part. At least *that* part of my theory is backed up by evidence that points to more than a lone gunman."

"Okay."

"The far-fetched part is the second hit man," Decker said. "We were looking at Jeanine's tennis partner. His name is Sean Amos—a snotty rich kid. Webster doesn't think he has the ba—the nerve to pull it off. So we were thinking that maybe Sean contracted the assignment out."

"With or without Jeanine's permission?"

"Don't know."

"And do you have any theories about whom he contracted with?"

"There's a kid in Westbridge Prep—"

"That's where Sean goes to school?"

"Yes. You know the place?"

"By reputation. It's a West Coast prep school. A pressure cooker for the kids of the country club."

"You got it." Decker sipped tea. "There's a senior there named Joaquim Rush. He's on scholarship . . . kind of a loner kid who keeps to himself. He's also a Scrabble fanatic."

"So what? I like Scrabble."

"No, Rina. A real fanatic. Like in tournaments."

"It's still harmless."

"The Scrabble isn't the interesting part," Decker stated. "This kid, Joachim Rush, he and Sean Amos had made some sort of deal together. Martinez saw an envelope exchange hands—"

"Ah, now *that* sounds interesting!"

"Indeed. We were looking into him as a candidate when Strapp pulled the rug out."

Rina sighed, said, "Stonewalled by the good captain. I'm sorry."

Decker laughed. "Maybe it's good he eighty-sixed it. Going undercover to Scrabble tournaments, tailing some cipher whose nickname is Cyberword. Not exactly a righteous allocation of department time."

"Maybe not." Rina smiled. "But heck, it could do wonders for the vocabulary."

*   *   *

In the darkened room, Sammy stared at the ceiling, listened
to the medley of the mockingbird. The critter wouldn't shut
up, just kept going from trill to tweet to cheep to caw. Yet
there was something comforting about it . . . like a lullaby
from nature.

Overhearing his parents talking . . . arguing . . . then talking again.

Because although the lot was acres, Peter's house was
real small.

Once the arguing had bothered him. Now he shrugged it
off and his indifference puzzled him. He thought about the
change. Probably had something to do with the fact that
now he could drive.

Joachim Rush.

A Scrabble fanatic.

Like Yermie Cohen.

He had once attended a Scrabble tournament with a
friend. Didn't place but he did okay. So what would it hurt
if he attended another?

And if he found this Joachim dude . . . then what?

And what if Peter was right? What if Cyberword was a
hit man?

Frustrating. To have ideas and not be able to use them.
Because he couldn't tell his mother. Not just yet. And he
didn't *dare* tell Dad. Because . . . well, you just didn't tell
Peter things like that. Things that he wouldn't approve of.
He loved Peter, but the man was sometimes too much for
him to handle.

So different from Abba.

Abba.

The memories kept getting dimmer and dimmer and dimmer . . . except for the few clear ones. The ones that had
been played out so many times that they'd taken on leg-
endary proportions.

Abba.

The move to the new house meant a final break from the
yeshiva, the padlock that would seal that childhood phase
of his life forever.

Time to move on.

Still, Sammy felt his throat clog.

Move on. To current things.

Like Joachim Rush. Simpler to think about him.

No harm in going to a tournament.

Still, he didn't want to do this alone. He felt he should tell someone first. Jacob came to mind. But he didn't want to get his brother involved.

Maybe he *should* tell Eema?

No, that wouldn't work. Sammy realized that he would be putting her on the spot by telling her and not Peter. Getting between them.

So Eema was out.

So who could he tell?

Who would understand?

Nestled in his bed, he thought a while, cooed into near slumber by avian songs and a comforter of night. Then his eyes suddenly snapped open.

As plain as the nose on his face.

He'd make the call as soon as Shabbos was over.

In the meantime, he closed his eyes and went to sleep.

✒29

Cindy picked up her latte, sipped foamy milk. "It's all interesting . . what you've told me. Still, I'm not sure what you have in mind."

"I don't know myself," Sam said. "That's why I'm talking to you." He took another bite of his bagel sandwich. "I was figuring you for a game plan."

Cindy picked at her cinnamon bagel baked on the premises of Harold's East. A retro New York dairy-only deli. One of the few places where Sam would eat because it was kosher.

She said, "I have no game plan, Sam. Because there's no game. If you have inside information, you should talk to Dad."

"I *can't* talk to Dad, Cindy." Sam grew frustrated. "First of all, I have nothing significant to tell him. Second, I don't want him to know I overheard my mom and him talking. Third, he knows about the Scabble tournaments and he's choosing not to go to them. Or rather Strapp's not letting him go. I thought that maybe we could have a look around—"

"I'll bring the wiretaps and you bring the hidden cameras?"

"Will you just hear me out?" Sam snapped.

"Sorry. Go on."

Sam thought a moment "I don't know. I thought . . . well, since no one under Dad's command can touch this

Joachim guy . . . that maybe you could follow him for a couple of days—''

"Well, I've always admired Nancy Drew—"

"Forget it!" Sammy's jaw tightened "It was a dumb idea. Sorry to bother you. You can go whenever you want. I'll pay."

Cindy sighed. "God, I sound just like him. Negative, sarcastic, sharp-tongued." She licked milk off her lips. "Terrible to be shut down. I'm sorry, Sam."

"You're just being honest." He adjusted his glasses. "You're right. It is ridiculous. But I'm not sorry I tried."

Cindy was quiet, observed her stepbrother. A quiet kid dressed neatly in jeans and a long-sleeved white shirt. He had a lean build, a head of sandy hair partially covered by a knitted yarmulke. Dark, intelligent eyes. He was turning into a very handsome kid.

Sam leaned on his elbows. "It's just that you don't know what's going on. You don't live with him every day. He's very frustrated."

Cindy grew annoyed. "I've seen him frustrated more times than you can count."

"Look, I'm not pulling filial rank or anything." Sam looked down. "I mean, biology is biology. I know you're the real kid—"

"Oh, *please*!" Again, Cindy caught harshness in her voice, reflective of her father's cynicism. Biology was biology and more insidious than she had thought. She softened her tone. "Sam, ranking my father's . . . *our* father's affections is silly. He loves *all* his kids. And yes, I know he's very frustrated. And I'm sure if he knew of our meeting, he'd appreciate the concern. But I don't see how we can help."

The boy blurted out, "What would it hurt if we showed up at one of the tournaments?"

Cindy said, "Say we show up. Say we see this Joachim guy. Say we even *talk* to him. Then what? Do you even know what Joachim Rush looks like?"

"Not a clue. But I'm sure we wouldn't have any trouble

identifying him. According to Dad, he's well known in Scrabble circles.''

"Yes, I suppose finding the sucker would classify as the easy part." Cindy's mind was racing. "Suppose we get a best case thing here, Sam. Suppose I go to the tournament and wind up talking to him. Suppose I can get him alone . . . invite him out for coffee. What then? I can't just drop names like Sean Amos or Jeanine Garrison into his lap. You just told me that this Joachim Rush was accepted on early admission to Yale. The guy isn't a moron.''

"This is all true.''

"Even if I could get him to talk to me . . . to get him into my confidence . . . Sam, that step could take weeks, *months*. I'm starting the Academy soon. I'm going to run out of time.''

"Move quickly.''

"Then what if I get him talking and find out he's completely innocent. Not only did I chance exposing confidential information crucial to Dad's case, but also I toyed with a kid whose sole crime is being a little nerdy.''

Sammy drank club soda from a bottle. "Hate to say it but you are making sense.''

Cindy finished her coffee. "I suppose I could tail him. See if he does anything weird. But let's face it. If he has anything to do with Sean, he's going to talk to him either over the phone or at school. Chances of me catching him doing something naughty are extremely remote.''

"That's why I wanted to show up at the tournament. At least that way, we'd get a chance to observe him in the flesh.''

"And . . .''

Sam smiled. "Never underestimate the powers of simple observation.''

Cindy shook her head. "This is against my better judgment.'' She sighed. "When is this shindig?''

"Next Thursday.''

It was Saturday night. Cindy had less than a week to hone her skills at the word game. She said, "We're also ignoring an essential fact. I'm not a good Scrabble player.''

"I know someone who could help you—"

"Nuh-uh. We're *not* bringing a third party into this mess. Really blow Dad's case to smithereens. You can't talk about this with anyone else but me. That's a given."

Sammy waited a beat. "I could show you a few tricks. Nothing fancy, but hey, you're smart. You should pick the game up pretty easily."

"I know how to play. I just don't play well."

"It's a matter of practice," Sam said. "And memory. You're gonna have to learn all these oddball two- and three-letter words. Plus all these screwy words that start with K and Q and X—"

"This really isn't my forte—"

"Plus, competitive tournaments are timed."

"Timed?"

"Usually like fifteen or twenty minutes per person per game. Both you and your opponent punch a clock. They're obviously connected to each other. You finish your word, you punch your clock, it starts *his* seconds ticking away—"

"I'm terrible at timed tests. I hate pressure."

Sammy looked at her. "Then why in the world are you becoming a cop?"

Cindy opened her mouth, then closed it. Quietly, she said, "Touché."

The boy said, "I'm not trying to score points. Just asking a question."

"I have my reasons."

Sam looked away. Her tone of voice told him not to pursue the topic. So he ate his sandwich and drank club soda.

Cindy nibbled on her food, her face hot with embarrassment and truth. The kid had scored very valid points. She might have furthered the conversation, but Sam seemed so oblivious to her mental anguish.

Sam finished his sandwich. "Cindy, you'll ace the game once you get the hang of it. Look, you're a Columbia grad—"

"That proves nothing."

"Well you took the SAT. That was timed."

"I had more than fifteen minutes."

"It's the same thing . . . only sped up. Trick is, do your thinking on your opponent's time. It's not hard once you get into the rhythm. You'll do great."

Cindy regarded the boy's earnest face. "Okay. I'll give it a whirl. Just to see if I can do it, if for no other reason."

"Besides, what could possibly happen at a Scrabble tournament? The contestants aren't the rowdy type." He checked his watch. "It's after eleven. I have to be home by midnight or else Eema will send out the National Guard. Worse, she'll send out *Dad*." A pause. "How about if I drop by your house tomorrow at ten?"

"Don't *drop* by the house. Don't go *near* my house. Don't even *call*. We've never been best friends—"

"We're not enemies, Cin—"

"No, of course not. But we haven't had much to do with each other except for the obligatory family affairs."

"True."

"If my mother sees us together for no visible reason, she's going to start asking me questions. That's all we'd need. For Dad to hear about this little escapade from my mother."

"Where then?"

Cindy said, "McGregor Park. Eleven o'clock. You, me, and all the old Russian people. Be there or be square. Call it a night, Sam?"

"Sure. You go on. I still have to *bench* . . . to say grace." Sammy's hand reached for the bill, but Cindy was too quick.

"A division of labor," she said. "You thank God for the meal; I'll pay for it."

❦30

It seemed to Rina that Hollywood got uglier and dirtier with each passing year, that the gentrification that was always being touted was just a word in the dictionary. And now with the Metro rail . . . all the construction and soot and dust and microorganisms being thrown into the air. Not to mention the bizarre parade of human flesh. Hard to believe this place was still a major tourist spot. But there they all were, all nationalities, wearing short-sleeved Hawaiian shirts even in the winter, toting cameras around their necks. And the local inhabitants. Unisexual sleaze with greasy hair, torn jeans, vests, and tattoos. What wasn't covered in ink was studded with pierces. They must never fly commercial airlines, Rina thought. Because they'd never make it through the metal detectors.

She found the address with no problem, parked her twelve-year-old Volvo in a pay parking lot. Sweaty hands. A pounding heartbeat. She hoped he wasn't home, but feared he was. He didn't get out much.

She had dressed simply. Black sweater over a denim skirt. Her hair was braided and covered with a kerchief. She knocked on the door, heard the uneven clomp of his compromised walk on the other side. It took a while for him to answer. His face registered instant surprise.

He leaned on his cane and grinned. "I b'lieve I know you."

"Believe you do." Rina smiled. "You were at my wedding."

"Ah . . . I remember the wedding . . . the food. Right fine Peking duck, ma'am. Think I ate enough to last me a year."

"Then we'll have to throw another wedding. Because it appears you haven't been eating much since then."

He patted his thin stomach. "I get by."

She glanced at him, then looked away. Abel Atwater. Peter's war buddy over in Vietnam. Hard to fathom that this man was ever fit for combat. Unbearably thin. A gaunt face given the illusion of fullness by a gray beard. His hair had turned silver, still fashioned in a long braid. His sweats hung on his emaciated body. Only giveaway of life was his eyes . . . clear . . . aware. She said, "Your clothes are literally falling off."

"You don't like the sagging look." He hiked up his pants. "Old person's move. The pants hike."

"Can I come in, Abel?"

"Absolutely." He swept his cane over the threshold, bidding her enter.

Rina walked into a room stuffy with heat. Small. The place overlooked the pay parking lot, had a kitchen the size of a closet. Thin gauzy curtains, a threadbare brown carpet. Furnished with junk. Faded, lumpy pieces. Formica table with two plastic orange chairs. But the place was clean. Spotless.

"Offer you a beer, Mrs. Decker?"

"It's Rina."

Abel smiled. "Rina . . . a pretty name. For a pretty lady. Would you like a beer, Rina?"

"No, thank you."

"I don't got much else beyond beer." Abel opened an ancient icebox, stuck his head inside. "Would you b'lieve I've got orange juice? Want some orange juice?"

"Nothing, thank you."

Abel straightened up, closed the door. "An easy customer." Again, the cane pointed, to the couch covered in something that might have originally been red and gold. Rina sat. Abel plunked down on the opposite side. "You

showin' up like this. I'd be a mite concerned about the big
man. But you're actin' too calm for there to be serious
trouble.''

"Peter's fine.''

"Glad to hear it. Should we continue with the chitchat?
Or do you want to tell me why you're here?''

"Actually, it has to do with the big man.''

"You throwin' a party for his birthday or somethin' like
that?''

"No. Peter hates surprises.''

"Don't we all,'' Abel said to himself. "What's up,
then?''

"I need help, Abel.''

The thin man smiled, then grinned, then laughed. A spin-
dly finger pointed into his sunken chest. "You want help
from *me*?''

Rina sighed. "Maybe it wasn't such a good idea coming.
When I first met you . . . I didn't treat you very nice. Perhaps I was jealous of your relationship with Peter. So it's
really hypocritical of me to ask you for help.''

"I put a gun to your head, Mrs. Decker,'' Abel said. "It
made you cautious around me.''

Rina lowered her eyes, remembering the incident. The
"big get-even'' Peter had called it. "I suppose I did have
my reasons for being reserved.''

Abel laughed, hobbled over to the window, and opened
it. "Sorry about the stuffiness. I wasn't expecting company.
Wanna tell me what's going on?''

Rina said, "It's about one of Peter's cases. The mass
murder at Estelle's—''

"I read about it, read his quote 'bout the shootup being
your worst nightmare.'' He looked upward. "Guess he
don't have any more Nam dreams.''

"Oh, he's had his fair share lately. All the carnage . . .
it evoked terrible memories for him.''

Abel nodded.

Rina said, "He's obsessed with the case, Abel. One of
the victims in the shooting . . . actually the daughter of two

of the victims . . . Peter feels she had something to do with it.''

''With the shooting?''

''Yes. He questioned her. The next day she charged Peter with sexual harassment—''

''Doc?'' Abel made a face. ''It's a lie, ma'am.''

''I know. The suit was frivolous and was eventually dropped. But the charges made it hard for him to do his job. He had to tiptoe around her. Eventually it got very complicated. His captain pulled him off the case entirely.''

Abel limped back to the couch, lowered himself slowly, using his walking stick for support. ''I thought the mass murderer committed suicide at the scene.''

''That's the official story.''

Then Rina told him all she knew. Abel listened, legs stretched out, crossed at the ankles, hands buried in the folds of his sweatshirt. When she was done, he sat up, drew his right leg upward so it folded at the knee. His left leg followed without help. He waited a moment before speaking.

Abel said, ''A woman manipulatin' two men to shoot up a restaurant. Gettin' one of 'em to blow the other's brains out—''

Rina said, ''That's the wild card. The second shooter. One of the victims remembers a man leaving Estelle's right after the shooting stopped. Just walked right out of the door. A very strange behavior unless he was involved, don't you think?''

''Don't matter what I think.'' He cocked his head. ''And Doc thinks this second shooter is a seventeen-year-old Scrabble player?''

''I know . . . it sounds ridiculous.''

Abel scratched his beard. ''The ice Pete's skating on is thinner than Saran Wrap.'' He hoisted himself up. Went over to the window. ''Still, Doc is an intuitive sort. I don't discount that. Woman gives him a hinky feelin', she's hinky.''

''I'm glad you feel that way.'' Rina fidgeted with her kerchief, then dropped her hands in her lap. ''He was stonewalled, Abel. She's been using her connections to obstruct him. He needs someone to get around her." A pause. "This is where you come in."

Abel waited a moment. "I'm not what you'd call 'high society.' Exactly what did you have in mind?"

Rina blushed, blurted out, "Peter seems to feel that if he had someone on the inside, he could maybe get information."

"Inside of what?"

"This wheelchair tennis tournament she's hosting." Again, Rina turned red. Her speech faltered. "It's filled with handicapped people. If Peter could place someone . . . you know . . . someone on the inside . . . someone Jeanine would never expect . . . he felt that maybe she'd let something slip up about the case . . . and Peter could learn something that way . . . about Jeanine . . . and about the case. Am I making sense?"

"Indeed you are. You're sayin' you need a gimp—"

"Abel—"

"Because you think that all us gimps have this Masonic brotherly bond with one another—"

"Abel, please don't make this even more nauseatingly hard on me."

No one spoke.

Abel said, "I'm sorry. That was rude."

Rina said, "I was thinking of people I knew who could maybe pull this off. You're the only one who could do it *and* the only one I could *trust*. Because you love Peter almost as much as I do."

Abel's eyes misted. "I take exception to the word almost, lady." He scratched his face, furrowed his brow. "Rina, these tournaments are ritzy things. You don't just walk in . . . or hobble in . . . and announce your availability for a job based on the fact that you're handicapped. I mean, even if I wanted to do it, they ain't gonna hire me . . . even for manual labor. They got their own crew."

Rina considered his words. "You're right."

"Besides, the paraplegics don't consider amputees among the real physically challenged. Because we can

walk. There's an unspoken hierarchy among us gimps. All
the quadraplegics want to be paras, the paras want to be
amputees, and we amps want to be able-bodied. And I'm
not even a bad amputee—only half of one of my legs. To
them, I'm barely crippled . . . the lowest gimp on the totem
pole.''

"Of course. Forget the whole thing." She got up. "Abel,
don't be a stranger, please.

"Invite me for dinner if it'll ease your conscience."

"How about Sunday night?"

"You don't think Doc'll find that a mite suspicious?"

"I can say I ran into you."

"I don't run into anything." Again, Abel scratched his
beard. "I'll take a rain check, Mrs. Decker." He started to
talk, then stopped, then said, "You're right 'bout one thing,
ma'am. I do love that son of a bitch." He sighed. "He's a
good man. I owe him big and I suppose it *is* payback time."

"Abel, it's not necessary—"

"Even so, give me a couple of days to think. I know a
few people in the network. Find out if any of them is working for this tournament. Ask them to throw some scut work
my way."

Rina bit her lip. "Thank you for hearing me out. It's
hard to see someone you love so frustrated. I'm trying to
help, which is probably a mistake—"

"Most likely a very big mistake. Your devotion, although overwrought, is touching."

Rina smiled. "Thank you for the backhanded compliment."

Abel looked her over. "You're a very pretty woman.
Doc's one lucky guy."

"You like pretty women, you'll love Jeanine."

"She's pretty?"

"A knockout."

"But a real Jezebel, huh?"

"Jezebel . . ." Rina waited a beat. "You went to Bible
school, Abel?"

"Kentucky Appalachian poor, ma'am. We lived on dust
and God. Bible was the only book in the house. That and

the Sears catalog. Learned how to read using the both of them. Then when I got hold of some *real* books, I couldn't figure out why people didn't use words like hast and doth and makest . . .''

Rina smiled softly.

Abel said, "Yes, I know who Jezebel was. She was a very evil woman."

"Yes, she was."

"So be it." Abel stroked his beard. "I've dealt with my fair share of evil women. Reckon one more cain't do me much harm."

❦31

The Scrabble tournament was set up on the second floor of the bookstore, all the way in the back, sandwiched between the video/audio section and the game department. Lots of board games. Old standards such as Monopoly, Life, Clue, Scrabble, chess, checkers, backgammon, and go. But there were also lots of the exotic and/or erotic adult games. Lots of "Host Your Owns." Host Your Own Murder Party, Host Your Own Stock Market Party, Host Your Own Baseball League Party, Host Your Own Strip Party. Host Your Own Sex *Party*?

Cindy wondered what *that* was all about.

Sam tapped her on the shoulder. She spun around. He said, "He's the one wearing the knitted cap and the orange jacket."

Cindy's eyes moved to the boy. Tall and thin. A pale but clear complexion with freckles thrown across the forehead and the nose. Patches of brown fuzz above his upper lip and under his chin. Dark eyes that skittered across the room, sizing up the crowd. Long, delicate fingers. Tapered nails. He wore an oversized white T under a tangerine cotton zip-up jacket, and old jeans. On his feet were Docs or facsimiles thereof.

"Doesn't look like a hit man to me," Cindy said.

"Yeah, he does seem pretty ordinary." Sam waited a beat. "Whole idea seems so stupid now."

"Nothing ventured, nothing gained."

"You sign up yet?"

"Nope."

"Come on. I'll show you where."

"You know, Sam, if we're gonna make headway, we can't be hanging around each other."

Sam didn't move. "I don't know about this. What if you talk to him afterward? What if he gets you alone and wham—"

"I'm not going anywhere," Cindy said. "Anyway, now's not the time for cold feet. I'll go sign up and you make yourself scarce. We'll meet up later."

Sam paused, then nodded. "Take care."

"Bye." Cindy walked away, studied the surroundings.

Folding chairs and card tables were scattered throughout the aisles, bordered by bookshelves on Games Strategy—Chess, Bridge, Whist, Go, Backgammon, Poker, Craps. Not to mention the tomes on Game Theory, Logic, and Probability. Math subjects that Cindy had assiduously avoided at Columbia.

About sixteen tables in all. Most held playing boards and timers. One table had been designated for snacks—bowls of pretzels, popcorn, potato chips, several water pitchers as well as paper cups and napkins. Another held the sign-up sheets for the tournament. Divided into three categories—two players, three players, and four players. Prizes and points were awarded to the highest score in each category. Ambitious ones signed up for all three. Joachim was ambitious.

Cindy did the same. That way she knew she'd get to meet him at least once during the one-on-one. With any luck, she'd be assigned a three- or four-person match with him, too.

She poured herself a cup of water, felt a tap on the shoulder, and turned around. Tried not to act surprised.

Face-to-face. Eyes that bored into her. She bit her lip, sipped water. She cocked her hip in his direction. "Yes?"

"Are you the Cindy on the sign-up sheet?"

"Yes. Is that a problem?"

"No, not at all." He spoke in a soft voice. "Just need to know if you have an ISN?"

"A *what*?"

"An International Scrabble Number."

Cindy said, "How about a Social Security number—"

He smiled. "Sorry—"

"Driver's license?"

Joachim said, "This is an ISN tournament. You have to have an ISN number to play."

Cindy said, "And where would I get one?"

"I can give you one. But it's five bucks—"

"*What!*"

"Sorry. Their rules, not mine."

"The man leaves me no choice." Slowly, Cindy locked eyes with him. His cheeks turned a shade of pale pink. She smiled pointedly, pulled out her wallet from her jeans, ruffled through its contents. "I've only got two . . . no, three dollars—"

"I'll give you the two bucks." Joachim held out his hand.

Cindy slapped three ones into his palm. "If you give me your address, I'll pay you back."

"Forget it." Joachim pocketed the money. "Wait here. I'll get you your number."

Cindy watched him, studied him. Nothing to suggest that he was anything other than a typical gawky teenager. He returned a moment later. "Here."

The slip was made out to Cynthia Cohen. As a precaution, Cindy had used her mother's maiden name. She said, "Four-seven-eight-two. My lucky number."

Again he smiled. "Have fun."

He walked away. Cindy turned, exaled forcefully. To herself, she said, "That was cool."

It took three uneventful matches before she hooked up with him. A two-person game. He smiled when he saw her, sat down across the table, and checked the timers.

"How're you doing?"

"Not too good."

"You play a lot?"

"I played in college," Cindy said. "But nothing like this. It's a no-brainer to bowl over a bunch of stoners bummed out on William Burroughs and weed grown from their windowsills."

"I like William Burroughs," Joachim said.

"That's because you're still young and impressionable."

"As opposed to you, Grandma?"

"Give me a rocker, I'm a happy woman."

He smiled. "You can go first."

Cindy looked at him. "That's not playing by official rules, bud."

"Yeah, I know. But I'll beat you anyway. Wind up with . . . oh, let's say, twice your score. For William Burroughs's sake."

"Arrogant little sucker, aren't you?"

"I just know my strong points. Go."

Cindy picked her letters. And suddenly the push of competition made her fierce. No way she could ever win him fairly. Go for the groin, she thought. She punched her clock, put down her first word, punched it again.

Punch, it was her turn again.

She let her shoe drop off. Made her word, punched the clock, then brushed her bare foot against his calf.

He looked up, looked back down. Said nothing and made his word.

Punch, it was her turn again.

Punch his.

Punch hers.

Punch his.

Again, she brushed his calf with her foot. Did it twice.

"You're kicking me," he said, red-faced.

Her voice was light. "Sorry."

Punch her turn.

Punch his turn.

Another brush. He turned red but said nothing, played his tiles, blinking back embarrassment.

The game was over in eighteen minutes. Cindy grinned. "You won. But not exactly twice my score, bud."

"That's because I played like an amateur." Joachim stood, his eyes shot with anger. "See you."

"You're mad," Cindy said.

Joachim said, "You *did* that on purpose."

"So?"

"So?" He glared at her. "It *distracted* me."

"It was *supposed* to distract you." Cindy grinned. "How else could I get a fair shot?"

Joachim continued to stare, then broke into laughter. "I don't believe . . ." He turned red. "Next round. Gotta go."

Cindy went through the rest of the evening without another chance to play him face-to-face. Joachim came in first in all three categories, graciously declined the gifts, which went to the next three highest scorers.

Trying to catch Joachim's attention. When she got it, she looked away. He waited a while. But eventually he walked up to her. He said, "You seem bored."

"This is true."

"You want to get a cup of coffee or something?"

"That's your answer to alleviating my boredom?"

He blushed, rocked on his feet, started to back away. Cindy took his arm. "I'm just funnin' with you, guy. Now the proper comeback would have been something like . . . 'So *this* is what I have to look forward to in college?' "

He let out a soft laugh. It matched his voice.

Still holding his arm, she said, "I'd love a cup of coffee except some gremlin took away my last three bucks—"

"I'll pay."

"If you pay, I'll come."

"I have to close up a few things first," Joachim said.

"That's okay. Meet you at the bookstore café in . . . ten minutes?"

"That would work."

"Good," Cindy said. "I'm glad it would work." She dropped his arm. "See you."

When she was downstairs, away from him, she made a fist and whispered, "Yes!"

Sammy appeared a minute later. "What'd he say?"

"He admitted he did the murders—"

"Cindy—"

"He didn't say anything!" Cindy said. "We're going to get some coffee in a few minutes. Go home. I'll call you later—"

"Nuh-uh, no way," Sam said. "This wasn't part of the deal."

"What wasn't?"

"You being alone with him."

"Sam, how can I find out information if I can't *talk* to him."

"The evening was supposed to be purely observational—"

"So it turned into something more—"

"This isn't what we talked about."

"I'm improvising. Now go home before he sees us talking to each other."

"I'm not leaving you alone—"

"Sam, did you get a good look at the kid? Could they make them any more harmless?" She patted her stepbrother's yarmulke. "Look, bro. No way we can ever prove Joachim's a hit man. But maybe I can prove his *innocence*. Find out where he was the night of the shootings. At least that way, if Strapp ever loosens the screws, Dad won't be spinning his wheels, wasting time on someone useless."

She was making sense. Still, Sam wasn't completely convinced. "I don't like it."

Cindy tried a different approach. "Didn't you tell your mom that you'd be home by eleven?"

"Oh sh—!" The boy stamped his foot in exasperation. "Look, Cin, you've got to call me. Let me know you're okay."

"You don't have your own line. What do I say when your mother picks up the phone?"

"You press two and then the pound sign. That makes the phone ring in my room and nowhere else. Deal?"

"Fine, fine. I'll call."

"When?"

"I'll call by . . . twelve," Cindy said. "Will you still be up? It's a school night."

"Yeah, I'm a night owl." Sammy rubbed his hands together. "So by twelve."

"Yeah. Twelve. And if I'm a little late, don't panic. I'm not going to turn into a pumpkin, all right?"

A pumpkin would be fine, he thought. Just so long as it wasn't a corpse. He kept his thoughts to himself. His hands had turned icy. He was spookin' himself. Stupid. Because Joachim did look harmless. Trying to calm himself down, Sam told himself to go home. Go home and pray. At least talk to Someone who could do some good.

"I went through like this voices of American literature phase. You know, Fitzgerald, Hemingway, Faulkner, Eudora Welty, Steinbeck . . ." Joachim dipped a chocolate-covered biscotti into a cup of espresso. "I was doing fine until I got to *Light in August*. Like I knew it was some kind of allegory for the expulsion from Eden and original sin. But man, it was so heavy with the prose—"

"That's his style," Cindy said.

"Yeah, but there's nothing wrong with making it readable. I mean I've waded through *The Magus* and *Clockwork Orange* and *Beowulf*. I'm not averse to experimenting with word origins and syntax. I'm talking about the actual phrases. I guess Faulkner's theory is why use one adjective when you can use twenty."

"He's a Southern writer, Joachim. They drip atmosphere. Something to do with all the humidity near the Gulf Coast."

"Could be." Again Joachim took a bite of his biscotti. "You ever read it?"

"Way back when."

"How old are you anyway?"

"Twenty-one," Cindy lied.

"So you're a senior then?"

"Just graduated."

"Ah. And now what?"

"Loose ends."

"Grad school isn't in the picture?"

"Nope."

Joachim said nothing.

Cindy said, "I'm sick of school. You'll understand when you get to where I'm at."

"You're too young to be patronizing," Joachim said.

"Four years of college puts us worlds apart," Cindy said. "Not in intellect, Joachim. I'm just saying you get tired of all the academic pettiness. All the profspeak and the braggadocio and the tired lines they use to get you horizontal—"

"Did they work?"

"Not on me."

Joachim blushed. "Sorry. That was rude."

"S'right." Cindy studied him. "You turn red a lot, you know that?"

Again he blushed. "I don't get around girls much. Or should I say women? What's the proper nomenclature anyway?"

"Females will always do in a pinch." Cindy sipped her caffe latte. "Yeah, you seem a little—"

"You can use the N word."

"Naive?"

"That was nice." He smiled. "You wanted to say nerdy, but didn't. It's true. I'm a little nerdy. But I'm not bothered by it." His face darkened. "Rather be nerdy than be like my snot-nosed, drugged-out, weak-willed, spineless, brainless, rich-kid classmates."

"So how do you really feel about your school?"

Joachim remained grave. "School's fine. Just the inhabitants whom I loathe."

"They give you a hard time?"

"I can handle them now. Brains do have their lucrative compensations. But there was a time . . ." He gobbled his biscotti, gnashed his teeth. "Not entirely their fault. I don't fit in . . . never did. You think I'm weird, you should meet my parents."

Cindy said, "I don't find you weird. You're just ill-suited for high school because you're bright."

The boy looked down, his face a primary color. And at that moment, Cindy saw how easy it was to manipulate teenage boys. And she wasn't exactly a femme fatale. Not like Jeanine Garrison. Man, she must have them dropping like flies.

The boy checked his watch. "It's getting late."

Cindy looked at her wrist. Eleven-fifteen. "Go ahead. I'm gonna stick around here for a while."

Joachim licked his lips. "You don't have to be home or anything?"

"I'm twenty-one, Joachim," Cindy said. "I don't *have* to be anything."

"You live by yourself?" he asked, shyly.

"With my mom. I'll find my own place as soon as I'm gainfully employed."

He drummed on the table. "You . . . want to come over my house? Watch a late movie or something?"

She stared at him. "Your parents wouldn't mind?"

"Actually, my parents are out of town." He squirmed in his seat. "I'll make some popcorn. Turn on the Monster Cable Station. It ain't much, but at least you won't have to worry about me feeding you sorry lines. I'm completely innocuous."

Cindy waited a moment. "You're gay?"

"Oh, no . . ." Again, he became scarlet. "No, that's not what I meant at all. It's just nice to talk to someone. That's all."

Cindy's brain went into overdrive. *What an opportunity. But what a dumb thing to do.* She shocked herself when she heard her lips utter, "Sure. Why not?"

The boy's face lit up. "Great. You can follow me home."

"Sure. But I've got to make a phone call first."

"Make it from my house. I live a couple of blocks away."

They both rose. Joachim left a twenty on the table. Cindy's eyes went to the bill. "That's a very generous tip."

"I've got a good racket going."

"Racket?"

"Uh . . . tutoring . . . thirty bucks an hour." He grinned. "Sometimes it actually pays to be smart."

❧32

She had a strange feeling. But the .22 in her purse made Cindy feel bold. Reflecting upon the situation: A poor boy who could suddenly afford to leave a twenty on a six-dollar tab. A boy with a good racket? He said it was tutoring. But where did he *really* get his money?

Asking herself more questions. What did she hope to discover?

Information, she guessed. Some event that would link Joachim to the nefarious Sean Amos. Either that or an alibi that would prove his innocence. She thought about this as she followed him home.

He drove a ten-year-old Saab, did a series of quick turns, pulled into the driveway of a one-story wood-sided ranch house. A scrub lawn, a few bushes in front. She pulled her Camaro in back of his car. They both got out at the same time. He fiddled with his keys, opened the front door, allowing her to enter first.

"Thanks."

She gave the room a quick once-over. Basic living-room furniture—a couch, a couple of easy chairs. Old gray carpeting. Wood shutters on the windows. Framed posters on the wall—Maxfield Parrish and Peter Maxx.

Joachim threw his jacket on the sofa. "Make yourself comfortable."

Cindy asked, "Were your parents hippies?"

"Hippies?"

"The artwork."

"Ah . . ." Joachim looked at the walls. "Actually, they're sci-fi buffs, although they're not averse to a good fantasy novel, either." He paused. "Better taste in novels than in artwork."

"Parrish is okay."

"If you like kitsch. You can take off your jacket, you know."

"I need to use the phone."

"Oh . . . right." Joachim pointed to the clear plastic phone on one of the sofa's end tables. "Help yourself."

Cindy picked up the phone. "Welcome to space age—"

"Actually, my father fitted it with this chip. You tell it the number and it'll dial automatically."

Cindy looked at him, at the phone. "I think I'll pass. Why don't you go nuke some popcorn? I suddenly have the munchies."

"Sure. Be right back."

She punched the numbers quickly, pressed two and pound. As soon as Sam picked up, she whispered, "I'm here, I'm fine, I'll call in later."

Sammy felt his heart go into his throat. "You can't be serious—"

"I gotta go—"

Sammy whispered, "You're insane. Get out of there *now*."

In the background, Cindy heard Rina's voice. "Sammy, get *off* the phone and go to bed now!"

Cindy said, "Looks like *you've* gotta go—"

"Cindy, get out of there—"

"Later." She hung up, heart doing the steeplechase. This *was* insane. All this intrigue, and for what purpose? What did she think she'd find? She felt her handbag, felt instantly relieved when her fingers pressed hard steel.

Calming herself. What could possibly happen?

She regained her composure, found the kitchen. Popping sounds were coming from the microwave. He said, "You want anything else?"

Keep him occupied.

"Got any veggies?" she said.

"I can cut some up if you want."

"If it's no problem."

"It's no problem."

Cindy stalled. "How about some nachos?"

Joachim turned around. "You want a banquet hall for this, King Henry?"

"Look, if it's too much work—"

"No." Joachim turned serious. "No, I'll rustle something up."

"That would be great."

"Anything else?"

"A Coke."

"You want some wine? You're over twenty-one."

"A Coke is sufficient, Mr. Innocuous."

He said, "I'm not trying to get you drunk. It was an earnest offer. My mom drinks wine all the time."

"A Coke is fine. You spike it with a roofie, I'll kill you—"

"Not a chance." He went to the refrigerator, took out a can of Coke. Opened it and guzzled. Then offered it to Cindy. "I'm a card-carrying member of drug-free America."

Cindy took the can. "You got a TV in your bedroom?"

He blushed instantly. "Yeah. Wanna watch in there?"

"Why not be comfortable?" Cindy said.

"Why not indeed?" Joachim whispered. But his tone was tight. "Go ahead. I'll be there in a few minutes."

Cindy hesitated. "Are you okay?"

"Uh, yeah." He saluted her with a carrot. "I'm fine."

Hesitating a moment. Then she left the room, hooking her purse over her shoulder. As soon as she shut the door to his room, she threw the purse on his bed and went to work.

His lair resembled her stepbrothers' bedroom. A huge desk upon which rested a computer, fax, phone, answering machine, something that looked like a digital sound board, other gadgets she couldn't identify. A couple of movie posters on the wall. Weird stuff . . . distorted images of faces and mouths.

She attacked the desk drawers first. Rummaging through them, looking for a gun, looking for phone bills, recent purchases, even a stash of heroin that could have been the junk used to murder David Garrison. *Anything* that might link him to Sean or Jeanine. She worked quickly and quietly.

And found nothing. Which was to be expected.

She opened the bedroom door, listened for a couple of seconds. He was still in the kitchen.

She tiptoed inside his closet, started going through the pockets of his jackets. A few receipts from bookstores, another from a computer store. She searched the upper shelf of the closet. Came up dry.

Next in line was the bedding—mattress and pillows. Looked under them, inside the covers. Gave them a few pushes. Nothing in there but foam. She dropped onto her stomach and looked under the bed. Nothing.

Then she heard his voice.

"What are you doing?"

On her knees, she peered over the mattress. He stared at her, holding a plate of veggies and another plate of nachos. She smiled benignly. "I dropped my earring—"

"You're not wearing earrings."

"Did I say earring?" Again, she smiled. "I meant my ring."

His face darkened. He placed the food on top of his bed, licked his lips. She got to her feet. "You look upset. What's wrong?"

"Nothing. Here's your food."

"Thanks."

Again, she felt her heart beat. Made a move for her purse, but he got there first. Lifted her handbag in the air out of her reach and stuck his hand inside.

Pulled out her gun.

Cindy froze.

Fingers around the trigger. A two-handed grip as he sighted down the wall. Showing her he knew how to use firearms. Then he lowered the barrel toward the ground, checked the safety clip. "Why are you carrying a twenty-two?"

"That's my business."

"With all due respect, I disagree." His voice had become gelid. "You carry a gun into my house, it's my business, too."

Think of something! Quietly Cindy said, "I went to school in New York. I got used to packing."

"You could get arrested for this, you know. Carrying without a license."

"Are you planning on calling the cops?"

He shrugged, hefted the firearm. "Not much weight to it."

"It can do damage—"

"That it can." He spoke more to himself than to her, examining the gun as he talked. "Bullets go in but don't always come out. Especially when you're talking about head shots, the ammo entering dense, solid bone like the cranium. Mostly . . . they bounce around, turning the brain to hamburger with each pass."

Cindy said, "You're making me nervous."

Joachim looked at her as if he had suddenly become aware of her presence. He lowered the gun, stuffed it back into her purse, and threw the purse on the bed.

It took all of Cindy's strength not to make a quick grab for her bag. But she managed to resist the urge.

Joachim said, "You like guns, let me show you some real weapons."

He removed a movie poster. Behind it was a safe. A few quick spins of the dial and the door popped open. He pulled out a revolver.

"You want real protection, you should be carrying something like this. Know what it is?"

"A Smith and Wesson thirty-two caliber Saturday night special. Snub-nosed front. Easy to pack, easy to carry—"

"I'm impressed—"

"Put it away, Joachim—"

"My parents . . ." He cleared his throat, stared at the

gun. "Like I said, they're *weird* people. They're not white supremacists, but they do subscribe to a certain . . . pioneer mentality. The each-man-for-himself kind of thing. Their idea of fun is playing survivalist. I spent many a summer in arid, isolated mountains, hundred-degree heat, munching on roadkill and squeezing water from cacti with cracked hands."

"That's awful."

"Yeah, it was pretty bad. Still, I preferred the summers to the freezing winters in the Great Divide. While my classmates went skiing, I pitched a tent on snowpacked ground in twenty below." He paused. "Oh, we had heat . . . little sterno things that prevented frostbite. But as far as being like . . . warm . . . or even just cold . . ."

His face was expressionless.

"I don't know. Made me strong, I guess. Sure as hell made me a crack shot." Joachim stared at the revolver. "One thing I like about these suckers . . . they never jam." He put it back in the safe, then pulled out another weapon.

"Unlike this. Bet you know what this is."

"A Beretta semi-automatic. Eleven rounds."

His eyes locked with hers. "Preferred weapon of policemen . . . people like Peter Decker."

Cindy felt her stomach drop. She said nothing.

"Suppose you're wondering why I brought that up."

"I'm a bit curious."

Joachim said, "Our phones are hooked up to a central computer. Any one of our ten terminals can give me an instant list of outgoing calls made from this number. When you made your phone call, I checked it against the computer's backward directory. I suppose you know what that is."

"How'd you get hold of one?"

"Survivalists have their ways." Joachim paused. "Of course, the directory only told me the name. Peter Decker. It didn't tell me he was a cop. But I read papers, Cindy. Mass murders in this area aren't everyday occurrences. Lieutenant Decker was quoted a lot. I'm a top-ranked

Scrabble player. Remembering words, even proper names, is something I do naturally.''

Cindy's eyes traveled to her bag. Joachim caught it. ''Go ahead. Pick up your purse. Pick up your gun. I won't stop you.''

''You have a Beretta in your hands. That stops me.''

Joachim put the gun back in storage. Eyes boring into her face. He said, ''You've been after me since the beginning of the tournament. From the moment you looked at me, I knew something was up. Because girls don't look at me that way. Especially older . . . attractive girls who are college graduates. You think you were being subtle, but you weren't. Still, I was willing to give you the benefit of the doubt. Because I enjoyed talking to you—''

''Joachim—''

''Just save it, okay?''

Cindy became quiet.

The teen said, ''You're using a floppy bag purse. You hook it over your shoulder. I can't quite make out the outline, but I can see it's weighted down by something heavy and inflexible. That, combined with the phone call to Lieutenant Decker . . . I just knew it was a gun.''

He sat down on the bed, averted his eyes.

''You're obviously a cop. What I can't figure out is why you're *spying* on me. This can't be a police matter 'cause I haven't done anything.'' He stared at her. ''Maybe you're moonlighting. Did Krieg send you? Is he *paying* you to do this to me?''

Cindy tapped her foot while stalling for time. Trying to come up with something. ''Paying me to do what, Joachim?''

''To *torture* me! Because I refused to take the SAT for him. Idiot doesn't realize they have *proctors* checking out things. I should screw up my entire future to get the asshole into the Ivies?''

Think of something quick, *you jerk!* She blurted out, ''But you've taken the SAT for other people—''

''That's an outright lie!'' Joachim's face had turned beet red. ''Who *told* you that? Where are you getting your information? I've never taken any standardized tests for anyone. Think I'm crazy?''

And then the lightbulb went on.

Sometimes it pays to be smart.

His *racket*! Sam had told her about an envelope passed through the open window of his car. Cindy said, ''How about for Sean Amos? You took the SAT for him—''

''Never—''

Cindy fired out, ''But you've been writing essays for him, haven't you? For him and Krieg and all the others. We know this for a fact, Joachim. So there's no sense denying it!''

The boy had turned ashen. He whispered, ''Who's . . . *we*?''

Cindy balled her hands in fists, eyes glued on the boy's face. She lied, ''Joachim, I've been hired by your school to root out cheaters—''

''Oh, God!'' Joachim moaned out.

''They've hired me to get to the bottom of all this deception. It's been a black mark on the school—''

''I'm gonna be sick!'' He beelined for the bathroom.

Cindy felt her own stomach rock. It was now obvious how Joachim had kept the rich boys off his back and earned bread. Money for tutoring, money for homework. And money for term papers and essays. The big question was . . . did he do other more heinous things for cash as well? Cindy wasn't ready to write him off as completely innocent. Not just yet.

The boy came out a moment later, his complexion gray, eyes and nose leaking water. ''Sorry about that.'' He smiled weakly. ''Not too good for a survivalist, huh?''

Cindy handed him a can of Coke. ''Drink.''

''I'm not—''

''Drink!''

Joachim took a tiny sip. ''Did the school hire you as part of a general crackdown? Or was this specifically against me—''

''Let me ask the questions.'' Cindy tried to appear official. "If you hope to get out of this, I'd better have some cooperation—"

"Whatever you want."

"Let's start at the beginning. Tell me about Sean Amos."

"What about him . . . specifically?"

"How long have you been doing his work?"

Joachim's voice was a whisper. "Maybe four years ago."

"Four years ago?"

"Yes. For him, for Krieg, for Denny, for all of them. How do you think I got the assholes to leave me alone?"

"And you charged them money to do . . . what?"

"Homework, essays, science projects, you name it." Joachim looked at her. "And yes, I charged them money."

Cindy asked, "How much?"

Joachim said, "Depends. Everything was negotiated."

"Is that why you were talking to Sean Amos in the parking lot of the school about a month ago? An envelope was given to you by Sean Amos. Were you negotiating a price for something?"

"A month ago?" Joachim sighed. "I haven't the faintest idea what I was doing a month ago."

"It was on a Tuesday. You talked to Sean . . . rather, Sean talked to you. Then you left, put notices in the local bookstore about the Scrabble tournament—"

"God, you people are thorough." He paused. "Who exactly do you work for?"

"Just answer the question, Joachim!" Cindy barked. "Why were you talking to Sean Amos?"

Joachim said, "A month ago . . . honestly, I don't remember. I could look up the date in my daily planner—"

"Go ahead. Do that!"

Joachim took a leather pouch from his desk drawer. From it he removed a small electronic device. Turned it on and began pushing keys. "A month ago, Tuesday . . ."

He paused.

"Here we go. Yeah, we had an English assignment. A three-page paper on comparing and contrasting the English versus the American Transcendentalists. Could be I was talking to Sean . . . about it . . . offering to help him out—''

''Cut the crap.''

Joachim stiffened. ''Look, Cynthia Cohen, or whatever your name *really* is, all I do is write a damn paper. And then I show it to him. If *he* chooses to put *his* name on it, is that my problem?''

''It's called plagiarism—''

''Is it any different from looking up the information in an encyclopedia?''

Cindy said, ''And when you talk to Yale's Office of Admissions, you can tell them just that—''

''What do you *want* from me!'' Joachim cried out. ''Please. I swear I'll never do it again. Please, please, please. My whole life depends on this. Just give me another chance—''

''What else do you do for Amos?''

Joachim's eyes darted in their sockets. ''What do you mean?''

Cindy picked up her bag. ''He ever hire you to help him out in other ways?''

''What other ways? What else would I do for him? I *hate* the son of a bitch! I hate them all. Fucker bastards. Fucking users.'' He laughed bitterly. ''Literally, as well as figuratively.''

Cindy's brain started racing. *Computer users? No, jerk, the other kind. Users as in drugs. David Garrison's OD.* ''They indulge, do they?''

''Boy, do they—''

''You ever buy Sean's drugs for him?''

Joachim's eyes got big. ''If he told you that, he's lying! Guy's a fucking liar!''

''Just answer the question—''

''No!'' Joachim said. ''No, no, no. I've never bought drugs for Sean or anyone. I don't do drugs. I have nothing to do with drugs or Sean or any of them. Especially *Mal*. I tutored him a couple of times. That guy is psycho! I avoid him like the plague.''

The mind sped into overdrive. She improvised. "You're referring to Mal Miller?"

"Who's Mal Miller?"

Cindy looked at him pointedly. "Which Mal are *you* talking about?"

"Malcolm Carey."

"Ah, yes . . ." Cindy nodded, knowingly. "Who does he sell to besides Sean and Krieg and the others?"

"Anyone who asks. But I don't really know. I told you, I don't go near him. Please. You've got to believe me."

Kid was pale, sweaty. Cindy's heart went out to him. She backed off. "You're willing to swear to that in a court of law?"

"Yes, of course!" The teen's face was a study in confusion. "Can you please, *please* tell me what's going on?"

"In a minute." Cindy steadied herself. Now or never. She took a calculated risk. "Let me see your planner."

Joachim's eyes went to his pocket computer. He handed it to her, but she didn't take it.

"Turn it on," she said.

The teenager did as told.

She said, "If I scanned through that planner, I wouldn't find any appointments between Malcolm Carey and you, would I?"

"Not a one. I swear—"

"So if I looked up some . . . random dates . . . I'd find nothing incriminating?"

Joachim looked ill. "Nothing I could go to jail for."

"But I might find something like . . . *essay for Sean is due*?"

The kid wiped perspiration off his brow, nodded.

She said, "You don't have to let me look at it, Joachim. Legally, I can't force you without a warrant—"

"It's okay." Again, he offered her the planner. His hands were shaking. "Just . . . I don't know. It's okay."

"I'm going to pick out some random dates," she said. "You look them up for me, show them to me. Got it?"

The teen nodded.

"Then show me your schedule for . . . a week ago Tuesday."

Quickly, he brought the date onto the small screen. "Here. Take a look."

She did. A couple of school tests, a doctor's appointment, nothing for the evening. And nothing of significance.

"How about two weeks ago Saturday?"

Joachim punched keys, offered her the monitor.

Nothing.

Heart drumming in her chest, Cindy gave him the date of the Estelle's executions. Without a pause, Joachim brought up the date on his planner and showed it to her. She looked at the demarcated hours, scanning the time until she hit eight P.M.

At the time Estelle's was being riddled with bullets from a madman, Joachim was at a Scrabble tournament at the local YMCA. Cindy pointed to the appointment. "Did you actually attend this event?"

Joachim looked at the tip of her finger. He thought a moment. "Uh . . . I've got to think. The YMCA match? Yeah . . . yeah, I was there, too. Why?"

"Let me ask the questions."

"Sure. Whatever you want."

"Your presence at this tournament . . . it can be verified by witnesses?"

"Of course. Why?"

Cindy waved her hand. "That's all for now."

Joachim stood frozen. "What do you mean, *that's all*? What are you going to do?"

Cindy said, "Nothing for the time being."

Joachim paused. *"Nothing?"*

"*If* you promise never to write another essay for anyone else but yourself . . . I suppose I could let the matter drop."

"I swear, I'll never do it again. Let the bastards drown for all I care."

"Okay. I won't report you. But you're not entirely off the hook. I've got a couple more questions."

Joachim slumped, looked visibly relieved. "Sure. What?"

"I want to talk about Malcolm Carey. Where does he operate from? Where does he peddle his merchandise?''

Questioning eyes went to Cindy's face. Joachim said, "Are you a narc—"

"Answer the question, Joachim."

"I don't know where Mal gets his shit. But I could find out if you want—"

"Joachim, I *don't* want you going around asking questions. Is that understood?''

"Sure—"

"Because Malcolm Carey is trouble. These questions are just between you and me.''

"Whatever you want, Cindy . . . can I call you Cindy?''

She held back a smile. "What does Sean buy from him?''

"I imagine everything. Uppers, downers, coke, roofies, scag—"

"Sean buys heroin from Malcolm?" Cindy interrupted.

"I suppose."

"But you're not sure."

"I know Sean occasionally smokes the shit. Where else would he get it from? I mean Malcolm *owns* Westbridge.''

"How do you know that Sean uses heroin?''

"Everybody knows. Sean brags about it, among other things. Guy has a big mouth.''

Cindy paused. "What else does he talk about?''

"What doesn't Sean talk about? What drugs he's taking, which girls he's screwing—''

"He talk about . . ." Cindy swallowed. "Sean talk about that *older* woman at all?''

"Jeanine Garrison?" Joachim nodded. "Yeah. All the time. He keeps telling people not to tell anybody. In the meantime, everyone knows they're screwing. At least that's what *he* says.''

Cindy nodded. "Tell me more about Sean and Jeanine.''

He paused. "You mean the rumors?''

Cindy felt her chest pound. She played along. "Yes, I mean the rumors. How valid are they?''

"Who knows?" Joachim paused. "God, you know *everything—*"

"I have my inside information," Cindy lied. "But right now I'm talking to you. So give me your take on the rumors."

Joachim said, "I think they got started because Sean's been acting so weird lately. Especially after Estelle's. You know about Jeanine Garrison's parents?"

"Shot dead at Estelle's. Go on."

"Okay . . . then . . . when Jeanine's brother OD'd . . . you know about that?"

"David Garrison. Found dead of an OD in his apartment. Continue."

Joachim looked grave. "I mean, the woman loses her parents . . . well, no one thought too much about that. Because we all thought it was just a lunatic doing target practice. But after her *brother* bought it . . ."

Joachim kneaded his hands.

"See, she came into lots of money after her parents were murdered. Sean was saying that Jeanine was resentful about sharing her inheritance, especially since her brother was a hype."

Cindy nodded. "Go on."

Joachim sighed. "Rumor was that Sean . . . paid Mal to stick a needle into David Garrison's vein. To make it look like an accident."

"Sean hired Malcolm to off David Garrison?"

"That was the scuttlebutt. And, you know, that Mal's psycho enough to do it." A pause. "It's probably just bullshit. But you know, once things get said out loud— they take on a larger-than-life scale. All of it . . . made Sean look like a real badass."

Cindy sat down on the bed. She said, "Joachim, it is of the utmost importance that you don't repeat this conversation to anyone. All of this, it's just between you and me. You can't breathe a word of it. For your own safety."

Joachim stared at her. "You're not really from the school. You're a narc, aren't you?"

Cindy didn't answer. Instead she said, "Now I want you

to repeat what you just told me about Sean Amos and Jeanine Garrison and Malcolm Carey. Talk about the rumors
and Sean being a user and Malcolm being a pusher and a
bad guy. I want you to repeat all of it.''

"Repeat it to you?''

"No. Repeat it to Lieutenant Decker.''

"When?''

"Now.''

"Now?''

"Now!''

Joachim looked at her. "He's your superior, isn't he?''

For once, Cindy didn't have to lie. "Yes, Joachim. Lieutenant Decker is my superior.''

❧33

Reading yesterday's paper at one in the morning. Decker wondered why he bothered. The news was never uplifting. Sitting in his pajamas and bathrobe at the dining table, sipping weak coffee, wishing the nightmares would vanish. Still, he couldn't complain. Only five weeks since Estelle's and he made it through the night about half the time.

He heard a bedroom door open, turned around. Sammy froze in his tracks, an odd smile on his face. "Hi."

"Hi." Decker put the paper down. "Trouble sleeping?"

Sammy shrugged. "I guess. Thought I'd get something to drink."

"Anything specific on your mind?"

"No, I'm fine." The teen rubbed his hands together. "Are you always up this late?"

"Sometimes. I like it when the house is quiet."

"So then . . . no one's called here in the last half hour?"

Decker's eyes bored into the boy. "What kind of phone call would come through at one in the morning?"

"Yeah, silly question, huh?" The teen looked away. "I'll be in the kitchen. Bye."

The boy scooted out.

Now what the hell was that all about?

Within minutes, Sam materialized. Again, that funny smile. "I'm going back to bed."

"Good night, Sam."

" 'Night.' '

Decker watched his stepson disappear behind his bedroom door, went back to his paper. A few minutes later, an engine purred, headlights shining into the house. Then silence and darkness. A door opening and closing. Again, he put the paper down, got up, and peered through the bay window.

What in the world?

A shadow resembling his daughter. He opened the front door and in walked Cindy. Decker's eyes shot down to his naked wrist where his watch usually sat.

"It's one-fifteen," Cindy informed him. "Glad you're up. I've got someone in the car you need to talk to as Lieutenant Decker. I'll give you a few minutes to get dressed."

Then she walked out. Decker was stunned. Resisted the urge to bolt after her. Instead, he went to get dressed. By the time he was back, Cindy had brought in a boy. Way too young to be a date. A gawky kid of around seventeen, garbed in baggy clothes. Peach fuzz sat on the face. But the eyes were alert and well focused . . . anxious as well.

Decker nodded. The boy nodded back. Unnoticed by his stepfather, Sam had tiptoed in, stopped, stared open-mouthed at Cindy and Joachim. Cindy's eyes drifted over her father's shoulder to Sammy, who was making gestures at her. Slitting his throat with his finger.

Still, she plowed ahead. "Lieutenant, this is Joachim Rush. I believe the name is familiar to you. Joachim, this is Lieutenant Decker."

Instantly, Decker's chest started pounding. That was all he needed—a heart attack at one in the morning. The boy extended his hand.

"Sir."

Decker shook it, managed to keep his expression neutral, hoped he could do the same for his voice. "Have a seat. I'll be with you in a moment."

Decker crooked a finger at his daughter. Cindy looked past him at Sammy, who was gesticulating frantically, swinging his arms out, mouthing the words: no, no, no.

"What are you looking—" Decker turned around.

Sammy gave him a little wave.

Cindy said, "Good night, Sam—"

"Hold on a minute," Decker said. "You're not going anywhere. Can someone tell me what's going on?"

Cindy spoke to the teen. "We'll get down to business in a moment. Sam, why don't you keep Joachim occupied for a little bit? Take out a Scrabble board."

Her stepbrother had the same sick grin on his face.

"Do it *now,* please," Cindy said.

Sam tightened his bathrobe. "Sure."

Before Decker could speak, Cindy took her father's arm, steered him into the kitchen, out of Joachim's earshot. Still, she whispered. "Dad, give me a chance and I'll explain everything."

He was a fraction of a second away from exploding. But his daughter's expression held him back. A look of intensity, of purpose. He spoke quietly. "You've got thirty seconds. Make it good."

"Joachim knows nothing about your suspicions regarding Jeanine Garrison, that she had planned Estelle's as a front for her parents' hits. My opinion? Joachim had nothing to do with Estelle's, period. He was at a Scrabble tournament when the shooting went down. I'll tell you how I found that out later. Actually, this isn't about Estelle's at all. It's about David Garrison. There have been rumors at Westbridge Prep that Sean Amos might have hired someone to ice David Garrison with a needle. Make it look like an accidental OD because everyone knew David was a hype. Prime candidate as hit man is a student/dealer named Malcolm Carey. I'd say more but my thirty seconds are up."

Decker stood speechless, then forced words from his throat. "Good Lord, what have you gotten into?"

"Me? Nothing. I'm just a conduit—"

"How'd you . . ." He glared at her. "Sammy drag you into this?"

She returned his fiery expression. "Does it matter, Dad?

The point is, you've finally got a way to get to Jeanine Garrison—"

"Estelle's isn't even my case anymore—"

"Oh *screw* that—"

"Shhh. Give me a moment to think. To absorb what you just threw at me." Decker's brain was awhirl. "What kind of rumors?"

"Might be better if you heard it from Joachim."

"Cindy, how do you know the kid's not onto you, snowing you with lies?"

"I have my reasons. But talk to him yourself. If you disagree, I'll defer to you."

"But you don't think he's involved in any crime?"

"Dad, far as I can tell, his only *crime* is dishonesty. He sells his brain, writes papers and essays for people like Sean Amos."

"For a price."

"Yes, for a price. Matter of fact, Joachim was negotiating a paper with Sean Amos when Martinez spied them in the school's parking lot. The envelope that he saw exchange hands . . . money for an English essay."

"You *asked* him about that meeting?"

"Of course not. Everything was done indirectly. Daddy, he didn't tell me about the plagiarism scheme. I guessed it. That's how I tripped him up. Joachim not only cribs for Sean, but for others. I told him I was Cindy Cohen, hired by the school to investigate a big homework deception scandal—"

"You figured out that cover by yourself?"

Cindy nodded.

"Just . . . made it up? On the spot?"

She smiled. "You're impressed?"

Decker was *very* impressed! But he didn't tell her. Instead, he said, "And he fell for it?"

"No, not completely. Now he thinks I'm a narc. He thinks I'm working under your command. Actually, I sense that he doesn't know *what* to believe. Except he knows that you really are a police lieutenant. So he's scared enough to talk. I suggest you take advantage."

Decker cocked his head over his shoulder. "What's Sammy's part in all of this?"

"He overheard you and Rina talking about the Garrison case, had some ideas of his own. He didn't know how to broach you, so he called me." Cindy waited a beat. "He did it because he cares about what matters to you. So do I."

No one spoke.

Cindy said, "Dad, Joachim might not be the break you need. He might not pan out. But he *is* an in to Westbridge. If you had hired your own private detective, you couldn't have done any better, correct?"

Decker didn't answer.

Cindy said, "Malcolm Carey's got a lock on Westbridge. You want chemicals, you go to him. Deals in pot, rock cocaine, powdered coke, roofies, ice, and heroin. He's a bad boy. Certainly Joachim is entitled to talk to the police about criminal activity at his school. Just hear him out. You know I'm making sense."

"Yes, I know. But I'm not objective right now." Decker spoke to himself. "I need a third party."

"How about Rina?"

"Better yet, I'll call Marge. Go take care of your charge and I'll be out in a few minutes."

Cindy said, "Thanks for keeping your cool, for not playing irate parent—"

"That'll come."

"No doubt." She kissed her father's cheek. "But nothing I can't handle."

Marge had brought Oliver. Martinez and Webster had wanted to come as well, but Decker had nixed the idea. Too many people. Might make the kid choke.

The burst of activity in the house had awakened Rina. She walked into the brightly lit living room, eyes squinting, a dazed look on her face. More than anything she wanted to know why Sammy was playing Scrabble at 1:45 in the morning. Cindy took her into the kitchen, tried to explain things. But it left Rina even more confused. Still, she didn't argue. Instead, she made a pot of decaf, deciding to sort it out later.

Sam finished his game with Joachim by two, put away the board and tiles, then retired. Rina went to sleep ten minutes later, leaving the group sitting around a table, coffee mugs in hand. Decker gave Joachim center stage. He told his story, speaking slowly and carefully.

Marge was the first one with a question. "Has Sean heard these rumors?"

"Yes, ma'am."

"What did he say about them?"

"Shrugged them off."

"Did they bother him?" Oliver wanted to know.

"No," Joachim said. "At least, that's my perception. I told Cindy . . . is that really your name?"

"Yes. Go on, Joachim."

"It seemed like Sean enjoyed the notoriety," the kid said. "Made him look like a hard case. Because up until then . . . he was just another whiny rich boy. No one took him seriously."

Cindy said, "He's popular. You told me that."

"You have that kind of money, you're superficially popular. But that doesn't prevent people from talking behind your back. Sean's a first-class slacker."

"He's on the tennis team," Cindy argued.

"Yeah, he does athletics," Joachim said. "But mostly he parties—gets drunk or stoned, then screws around. Also, he and his friends like to tag on the weekends. Mostly street or stop signs. Their big forays into criminal activities."

Joachim made a face as if to say Amos couldn't even cut it as a felon.

"Sean did get some brownie points when he started doing Jeanine. Impressive at first, but even then people started poking him behind his back."

"Could be they were jealous," Oliver said.

"Yeah, I'm sure they were," Joachim said. "Still, he was getting a rep of being pathetic, that she treated him like a trained dog—'Fetch, boy, roll over and play dead.' "

He paused.

"*I* never saw it. But you'd hear things."

The teen licked his lips.

"I've known Sean for a while. Seen him react to all kinds of situations. The talk about Jeanine . . . it got to him. He started acting weird. Especially after Estelle's. Because the dissing got worse."

"Why?" Oliver asked.

"Because everyone kept saying that Jeanine was going to dump him now that she'd inherited money. See, up until then . . . no one could figure it out . . . him and Jeanine. I mean, no one had any trouble understanding his attraction to her. But why would she be interested in Sean? They figured she had to be after his bread."

"Wasn't Jeanine rich in her own right?" Marge asked. "Even before her parents died?"

"I have no idea. But I do know that Sean's dad is really rich . . . Texas oil money. Sean has lots of toys."

"What kind of toys?" Oliver asked.

"Typical Westbridge stuff—the sports car, the skis, the wet suit and surf boards, the five-eight-five PC with CD-ROM, the winter vacations in Switzerland, the summers on the Riviera. Plus the private tennis lessons. Sean plays the local circuit. He's not very good. But I know professional instruction doesn't come cheap."

Marge asked, "Do most Westbridge boys belong to Greenvale, Joachim?"

The teen nodded.

"And most of them are rich?"

"Yes."

"Then Jeanine could have had her pick of boys."

"Probably."

"So why do you think Jeanine chose Sean?"

"I don't know."

Decker said, "After Jeanine's parents were killed, you said kids began to razz Sean."

"Yes, sir."

"And he began acting weird?"

"Yes."

"Define weird?"

Joachim thought a moment. "Short-tempered. Also physical. Apparently, he'd gone psycho at a couple of parties, got into a few shoving matches. Also . . ." He sighed. "He raped a girl. Sean claims it was a party thing . . . that everyone was drunk and the girl consented. But she claims it was rape. You know . . . rophynol . . . roofies."

"Any charges filed?"

"Not that I know of."

"So you have no way of knowing whether any of it is true or not."

"No. But when you hear the same story over and over . . ."

"What about Sean's drug use?" Decker asked.

"I tutored him," Joachim said. "I've seen him use."

"What does he use?" Decker pressed.

"Pot, coke . . . heroin. He used to smoke it. After he hooked up with Jeanine, he started chipping."

"Mainlines?"

"Don't know." He was quiet. "You know, you get a rep as a real badass if you use a needle. That and doing hookers without wearing skins. It means you don't give a shit. Viral Russian Roulette. They're all *crazy*. I mean, they've got *everything* and all they can think about is frying their brains. I don't *get* it."

The room went silent.

Joachim said, "That's when the rumors about Sean popping David Garrison got started. When Sean started using a needle."

Again, the boy paused.

"You know, it worked. The badass image, I mean. People stopped razzing Sean after David Garrison OD'd. I think they were . . . afraid of him."

Decker said, "Tell me about Sean and Malcolm Carey. Are they buddies?"

"Malcolm's kind of a loner. But he and Sean did start hanging out together after David Garrison died."

Decker said, "Malcolm is in charge of Westbridge's drug distribution?"

"Yeah."

"Does he have any competition?"

"Not that I know of."

"Who does he buy from?"

"Don't know," Joachim said. "But he speaks fluent Spanish. And he took French in school. I know this because I've tutored him."

"Is Malcolm a rich kid?" Marge asked.

"His father's an entertainment lawyer who became an agent. I'm sure he makes an obscene amount of money. Still, Mal is *not* in Sean's league."

Marge said, "You think Malcolm would do real nasty things for money?"

"Things like stick Garrison with pure heroin?" Joachim nodded. "Without question. Probably do it just for the kicks. But I don't know this for fact."

Oliver asked, "Did Malcolm suddenly start showing off any new toys after David Garrison died?"

"You mean like buy a new car or something?"

"Exactly."

Joachim thought a moment. "I don't know. But I don't pay attention to Malcolm. I could check it out—"

In unison, the detectives told him *No! Don't check anything out!*

Firmly, Decker said, "Joachim, it's imperative that you *don't* get involved. That you *stay away.*"

Marge added, "That way you don't get hurt and we can run our investigation."

Joachim looked at Cindy. "Your questions . . . they were just a front. This is really about David Garrison, isn't it? I mean . . . my doing papers for other people. You don't care about that, do you?"

"Nah, I don't care," Cindy answered.

"So I'm not in any trouble with my school or with Yale's Office of Admissions."

"Nope."

Joachim sat back in his chair. "God, you're a *sadist!*"

Cindy shrugged.

The boy said, "Don't be too remorseful."

Decker said, "Officer Cohen was just doing her job."

"So you *are* a cop!"

Decker tossed his daughter a surreptitious wink. "And a very good one at that."

Holding back a smile, Cindy said, "Sorry for the sub-terfuge. And I appreciate your help, even if it was co-erced." A pause. "You know, Joachim, being accepted to Yale . . . you might want to keep your nose clean for the next nine months."

"You're absolutely right." Joachim looked down. "It was never the money, you know. I don't care about money. I'm not saying I did it because I *had* to. I didn't have to. No one *made* me write the papers. But . . . sometimes you do things . . . because it makes your life easier."

Decker said, "That's valid. But I agree with Officer Co-hen. Keep your nose clean."

Joachim tapped his foot. His eyes grew big. "You know, if you want Malcolm Carey, I could help you—"

"No, Joachim," Decker said. "We don't want your help—"

Joachim blurted out, "Don't you use informants, Lieu-tenant?"

"Not minors," Marge said.

"I turned eighteen a week ago," Joachim said.

The room went quiet.

Joachim bounced his leg up and down. "I wouldn't even have to be involved in any transaction. Just keep my ears open. I blend into the crowd there. People talk around me—like I don't exist."

Marge said, "Joachim—"

The teen interrupted, "If you wanted to catch Sean doing a buy from Malcolm . . . that would be hard. Probably they deal at Sean's house. But if you want Malcolm . . ." He waved his hand in the air. "That's a snap. First off, he's got more shit in his car than the Medellín Cartel. Second, he deals openly at parties. All I have to do is keep my ears open. All you'll need is a couple of narcs and a warrant—"

Decker said, "I don't like it—"

Oliver said, "Uh, Loo. I think we need to talk—"

Decker said, "What if it got back that the information came from him?"

"How?" Oliver said. "All he has to do is make an anonymous phone call to me or you or Narcotics."

Joachim said, "Lieutenant, I have nothing to do with Malcolm—"

"Exactly," Decker said. "They suspect the one who has nothing to do with the dealer."

Joachim said, "Lieutenant, the entire school isn't on drugs. I'd say over fifty percent of the student body has nothing to do with Malcolm Carey."

Decker said, "Officer Cohen, don't you have to take Joachim home?"

Cindy frowned. Excluding her at this crucial time. Still, she understood her father's dilemma. "How about if we wait outside?"

"Good idea. Be with you two in a moment."

Oliver waited until the front door closed. Then he said, "Deck, you can't let an opportunity like this pass through your fingers—"

"Scott—"

Marge broke in, "Pete, he's right. Worse comes to worst, we arrest a felon, get a major dealer out of the school."

Oliver said, "Deck, we use Malcolm to get to Sean, we use Sean to get to Garrison. Yeah, there are a lot of holes along the way. So what? Marge is right. Even if we're *completely* off base, even if Sean and Malcolm had nothing to do with Garrison's OD. What's the worst that can happen? We jail a pusher."

"We'll bring Narc in on it," Marge said. "Really make it look legit."

"With the understanding that we get first crack at Malcolm," Oliver said. "It's *gold,* rabbi. The honest-to-goodness twenty-four-karat item. If the kid's willing to make a discreet phone call—"

"I'm worried about the kid going overboard," Decker said.

"So we'll talk to him," Marge said. "He's a legal adult, Pete. We can't get into trouble that way—"

"We're still using a kid," Decker said.

"We're not asking him to wear wires," Oliver protested. "Just to make a simple phone call if he hears something. Face it, Loo. We're not going to get Sean any other way. And if we don't get Sean, we won't get Jeanine Garrison. Think about those innocent victims from Estelle's—thirteen murdered, thirty-two wounded."

Decker said. "This whole thing has nothing to do with Estelle's."

"You don't know that," Oliver said. "Maybe Malcolm's the mysterious second shooter—"

"Or maybe he isn't—"

"Forget about Estelle's!" Marge blurted out. "Estelle's is irrelevant, okay? We're not *investigating* Estelle's. We're investigating David Garrison. His death is listed as an accidental OD, but homicide has *not* been ruled out. If we hear rumors that lead us to investigate his death as a homicide . . . well, then I'm gung-ho. Because that's what I do. I investigate homicides. And as far as I'm concerned, David Garrison is as good a homicide as any. And in the process of my investigation, if I get a rat's ass punk pusher out of a school, well, then . . . fine with me!"

No one spoke. Decker threw back his head. "God, what a night." With resolution, he gave his hands a clap. "We'll do it under two conditions. First, the reason we're going after Malcolm is to get to Sean and Jeanine, right?"

They both nodded.

Decker said, "We can't possibly expect Malcolm to admit to a *homicide* in exchange for a simple drug charge. Which means we've got to get *multiple* charges on him— pop him with so many drug felonies that he's *never* going to expect to see the light of day. To get that, we're going to have to arrest at least a dozen students who'll admit to buying from Malcolm. Which means we can't pop him for a simple buy. We're going to have to raid a dope party."

"Good point," Marge said.

"Agreed," Oliver said.

Decker said, "Once we have the kid convinced that we're his only hope, we bring up David Garrison—"

"You mean Sean Amos," Oliver said.

"No, David Garrison."

"But we don't have anything that connects Malcolm to Garrison."

"Then we'll just have to convince not only Malcolm but his lawyer that we have *compelling* evidence," Decker said. "We'll say we're going to run a gas chromatography on all Malcolm's heroin. Tell him the composition matched the shit found in David Garrison's apartment. Convince him that the odds of any one batch of heroin exactly matching another batch of heroin are extremely minuscule."

"Are the odds remote?" Marge asked.

Decker shrugged. "Who knows? But it sounds good. Let's bring Joachim back in here and explain the situation. Tell him not to call us unless he's sure that there's a big whopper going down. When he's *sure,* we move. And not a moment before. We move too early, we blow everything." He caught his breath. "Now for the second condition. In order to execute the operation, I'll need clearance from Strapp."

Marge frowned, "We can't circumvent him?"

"No, I've got to tell him what's going on." Decker rubbed his eyes. "I just have to figure out how to do it without bringing in Cindy."

Marge said, "I'll take the heat. We'll tell the exact same story except I'll be Cindy."

"I'll cover for you, Dunn," Oliver said. "I'll say I was backup while you were with the kid." He turned to Decker. "You know, your daughter was really clever to come up with that jive-ass cover on the spot."

"Yes, she was." Decker shook his head. "But she was completely out of line . . . taking a chance like that. I don't know whether to brain her or kiss her."

"Why'd she do it?" Oliver asked. "What was in it for her?"

"She was trying to help me out."

Marge said, "Then she accomplished her goal."

Words spilled from Decker's mouth. "She's entering the Academy after the first—"

"What?" Marge said.

"When did this happen?" Oliver asked.

"She told me about a month ago."

"Why didn't you *say* something?" Marge demanded.

"I kept hoping she'd change her mind." Decker sighed. "This bit of intrigue certainly dashes *that* hope. You notice that excitement-junkie look on her face? Like she took a vial of adrenaline and shot it through her vein."

"She did a good job," Oliver said.

Marge said, "For what it's worth, I think she'll make a good cop."

But Decker couldn't let go of the image—an hours-old infant nestling in his arms. Soft, red, and so very warm. He bit back mist that had clouded his eyes, said, "Let's go talk to Joachim."

❧34

Not much more than a shed. But it sat in the middle of an enchanted forest.

Decker said, "If you kiss it, will it turn into a palace?"

"Only works on frogs." Rina fiddled with the keys. "Shall we go inside?"

"Sure, let's live dangerously. You're positive this place has a sewer line?"

"Last I checked, it even had cable hookup." She placed the key inside the lock, turned the bolt. "Nice of the owner to give us the run of the place."

"He's probably hoping we'll burn it down so he can collect insurance."

As the door opened, they were spotlighted by dusty rays. Old lumpy furniture sat in an old house. Dirt-coated floors. Decker bounced on the planks. No squeaks. "Sturdy . . . solid wood."

"What kind?"

He bent down, regarded the grain. "Cherry."

"That's good?"

"Our dining-room table's cherry." He scratched the floor with his nail. "Yeah, this is all superficial gunk. It'll come right off." He knocked on the walls. A thud answered. "Lath and plaster."

"Is that good or bad?"

"Good." Decker rapped his knuckles against the walls several more times. "Here's the structural beam." More

336

knocking. "Several of them. Deceptively well built. Bet you could add a second story."

Rina gave off a soft smile. "You like it."

"Just trying to be positive."

Together, they explored the pint-sized den, two tiny bedrooms—between them a connecting water closet. The kitchen, though roomy, looked like it hadn't been touched in fifty years.

Decker stood, legs apart, arms folded across his chest. "A major undertaking."

"Up to you," Rina said. "If it involves too much, we'll keep looking."

"Could you live in this place?"

"As is?"

"As is with another bathroom."

She shrugged. "In Israel, this would be considered a luxury apartment."

"First of all, we're not in Israel," Decker said. "Second, I saw some of the apartments there, darlin'. They had granite and marble."

"I could manage," Rina said. "But eventually, we'd have to have another bedroom." She looked at the worn cupboards. "And a decent kitchen. Can you save any of the cabinetry?"

He examined the doors, gave them a gentle cuff. "I could save it all. This is solid stuff."

"What do you think?"

"With enough elbow grease, it could be something." Decker rolled his shoulders. "Now I could get another bathroom in within . . . oh, a month or so. But the rest . . . the kitchen, another bedroom, expanding the master bedroom if you could call it that." He exhaled. "It's going to take time. My Sundays'll be booked for the next year."

"Too much for you?"

"No, I don't mind," Decker said. "I was thinking about you—and Hannah. Cooped up with a little kid running around."

Rina said, "But, she's in school during the day. And

when she's not, there's the yard. It's smaller than you're used to . . . but isn't it beautiful?''

"Yes, it is nice."

Decker's beeper went off. Rina frowned. "Can't you disconnect that thing?"

"It would only come back to haunt me." He looked at the number. "It's Narc's extension." He took out the portable phone. "Niels, it's Decker. What's up?"

"You still looking for that kid, Malcolm Carey?"

"Absolutely."

"Call just came through. Westbridge is having a big party hearty scene at some kid's house. Parents are out of town. Starts around nine tonight. Call said Malcolm should be there with his pharmacy."

Decker felt a jolt. Joachim had actually come *through*. His beeper went off again—Marge. To Niels he said, "Start setting up operations. I'm sending over Bert Martinez and Tom Webster to coordinate with you. It's your baby, but I want Malcolm Carey."

"He's all yours."

"I'll clear it with the captain, then get back to you."

"Got it."

Decker hung up, called Marge. She said, "Guess what?"

"Joachim called. There's going to be a drug party." A pause. "He just called Narc. They got to me first."

"Joachim called Narc?" Marge was surprised. "Kid's real thorough."

"Apparently. Was Joachim invited to this shindig?"

"He said it was an open-invitation bash."

"So his presence shouldn't be missed."

"Probably not," Marge said. "Who's coordinating with Narc?"

"Bert Martinez and Tom Webster. That leaves you and Oliver to pull the warrant for the house and Malcolm's car if we're lucky enough to hit pay dirt. Who's on the bench?"

"Randall."

"Yeah, he's fine." Decker paused, trying to keep excitement out of his voice. "I just have to clear the whole thing with Strapp—"

"You haven't talked to Strapp yet?"

"Why would I have talked to him about it? I had no idea if Joachim would produce. It's only been two, three weeks since we talked to him."

"Something like that."

"I'll ring up Strapp right now."

A long pause. "Pete, I think he's at the tennis tournament."

A knife went through Decker's gut. "That's right. I'll catch him there."

"How about if I go—"

"No need."

"Pete, I think it would be—"

"Gotta go, Marge." He disconnected the line.

Rina said, "Joachim called?"

"Yes."

She smiled. "That's good news, isn't it?"

"Yes, very good."

She hesitated. "You don't look happy."

"I've got to okay the procedure with Strapp. Right now, he's probably gliding into his seat at Jeanine Garrison's wheelchair tennis tournament. Twenty bucks gets you into the place, a hundred lets you have a decent view, and a thousand puts you courtside. FYI, the arena is sold out."

Decker gave a bitter grin.

"But Strapp don't have to worry none. He's been comped."

A cloudless November day, the deep blue sky engulfing the L.A. basin with a gentle autumn kiss. Even though most of the deciduous trees had lost their leaves, the area still sparkled emerald from the perennial landscape and blades of freshly planted lawn. The West Hills Sports Center stood in the middle of parklike grounds.

Even with the official badge and placard, Decker stalled in the event's traffic. Though spacious, the center was not built to host major tennis tournaments. But Jeanine had done a fine job on short notice, setting up tiers of portable bleachers around a central court. He parked in a space marked LOADING ZONE, walked over to the gates, and showed the attendant his badge. She gave it a moment of her time, then allowed him to enter.

As people poured in, Decker's eyes swept across the scene. The space outside the arena's seating was filled with kiosks. Some were stacked with memorabilia—T-shirts, sweatshirts, visors, sunglasses, and wristbands, all of the items emblazoned with the title TENNIS FOR VICTIMS. Others hawked all types of ethnic comestibles. Diners munched their grub either standing up or sitting on folding chairs beside tables.

His eyes moved back outside, to the parking lot, to a roped-off and guarded area of trailers. Eight of them partnered two by two. The athletes' dressing rooms. Directly in front of the barrier was a crowd of reporters, photographers, and lookie-loos.

Decker thought a moment.

Extremely unlikely that Strapp was holed up inside a trailer. That whole business was really none of *his* business. But curiosity got the better of him. He left the arena through one of the makeshift gates, waded through the throng of fans, and presented his badge to one of the minimum-wage security guards who asked the usual question: What was this all about? Decker evaded with the stock reply of police business. Then he ducked behind the ropes.

Shingles posted on the vans. Names of well-known figures in the game, some of them seeded players. Jeanine had pulled out all the stops. Ramps instead of steps led up to the trailers' doors, which were also guarded. Some of the sentries stood, others were seated in wheelchairs. The paraplegic watchman stared at Decker, said nothing as Decker fast-walked past him. Turned the corner, squeezing between the backs of trailers. Took a step into the seam, then immediately retreated, his heart flying in his chest.

And there they were . . . Jeanine and Sean. Cautiously, Decker peeked around the corner, observing them with intense eyes, trying to interpret the body language.

It wasn't the tongue of love.

Jeanine looking away . . . peeved . . . bored. Hands on her hips, foot tapping. Sean talked with his hands . . . with his arms, the appendages flying as his face grew redder. His voice became louder, faster. Still Decker couldn't make out words. Only the sentiment. An argument.

Wishing he were a fly on the wall. He backed up, trying to find a way to get closer. A wheelchair-bound guard stopped him, asked for ID.

Decker took out his badge, which did little to erase suspicion from the watchman's face. The man adjusted his frame in his metal transportation and began the questions. Decker never got a chance to answer because Jeanine had suddenly appeared sans Sean. Frantically, Decker attempted to arrange his thoughts, tried not to stare.

She was as lovely as ever, dressed for the nip of fall in a long-sleeved white shirt that sat under a gray wool blazer and black slacks. The collar of her jacket had been turned up. Golden hair framing porcelain skin. Aqua eyes passed over his face. Quietly she said, "May I ask what you're doing here?"

Decker managed to hold her eyes. "I'm looking for my captain."

"Obviously he's not here."

The guard said, "Everything all right, Ms. Garrison?"

Jeanine's smile was benevolent. "Just fine, Brock. You can let us be."

Decker began to walk away. "I'm out of here."

Jeanine followed. "I'll be happy to escort you—"

"Not necessary." Decker picked up his pace. But Jeanine continued to dog his heels.

"Would you like a seat for the match, Lieutenant? I'd be happy to arrange it." She grabbed his arm, forcing him to stop. A teasing smile on her face. "After all, we're no longer enemies."

That's what you think, lady. Decker looked at her hand, gently but pointedly removed it from his forearm. Her touch made his skin crawl. "No thank you."

Jeanine grinned, showing teeth. "His seat is located off

aisle four, courtside. Are you sure I can't cajole you to change your mind?''

Decker said nothing, jogged off without looking back. Sweating from the interchange. Nobody had a right to affect him like that. Embarrassed. Angry.

He came back into the arena, now in the final frenetic moments before the event. The anticipation. Tennis talk. Celebrity talk. He made his way to the front rows as cameras flashed, blinding him with bits of light. Not for him, of course, but for the dozens of film and TV stars who had showed up wearing black solidarity ribbons.

Ostensibly for the victims of a very horrendous crime. Yet where were the survivors?

Not the biggest names in Hollywood. But not too shabby either. A couple of stars from a top-rated TV doctor drama, a sexy blonde who played a detective in a cop show, three of a sextet who starred as young but neurotic single/swingles in a weekly cast-driven comedy. Supporting actors and actresses. Drinking bubbly, laughing heartily. And smiling those famous smiles as adoring fans hounded them for autographs.

A tremendous affair for a quiet place like the Valley.

Decker's eyes continued to dust the crowd, falling on twenty or so elderly character actors—men in their seventies and eighties, as aged and weathered as the cowboys they once had portrayed. Sucking on unlit cigars, laughing and hacking about old-time mishaps.

Friends of Walter Skinner.

But Decker couldn't find the widow anywhere. He scanned the crowd, shaded his eyes with his hands until he saw another group sitting a couple of aisles away. They also wore solidarity ribbons, yet they sat unmolested by well-wishers and the press.

The survivors . . . friends and relatives of the victims. Far from being part of the gaiety, they looked out of place— tense, nervous, and angry. Yet they chose to make an appearance. Decker made his way to their seats. Tess instantly stood up to shake Decker's hand. She said, ''I was hoping you'd be here.'' She turned to another woman. ''Carol, this is Lieutenant Decker. He's the one who fixed up my leg.''

Carol was Carol Anger—the waitress who had suffered a gunshot wound to the arm. Though the limb was no longer confined to a sling, she still held it close to her body. She stood, shook Decker's hand, her face suffused with hostility. "Nice that the police made an appearance.''

Decker said, "My captain should be here.''

"Well, he's *not* here—''

"Carol, please!'' a big man interrupted. He introduced himself to Decker, extended his hand. "Olaf Anderson.''

Decker took the hand. "You were one of Estelle's chefs.''

"Yes, sir, I *am* one of them.''

"The place reopened, I hear.''

"Yes. Very busy ... busier than ever. Customers are ... curious.''

"You mean ghoulish!'' Carol shot out.

"Carol, don't be so cross.'' Tess sighed, looked around. "What a scene!''

Carol said, "Like one big party. As if these dingalings—including *her*—give a hoot.''

Tess said, "Carol, don't be so mad. She's doing good stuff and she's not taking a dime—''

"She doesn't need it,'' Carol broke in. "You might think she'd at least come over and say hello. After all, she lost her parents—''

"People mourn in different ways.'' Tess looked at Decker. "You must think we're awful. Being so mad and all.''

Carol said, "You're not mad. *I* am.''

Decker said, "An ordeal like Estelle's would turn anyone into a cynic.''

The waitress faced Decker. "Maybe your captain had something more important to do. Something like ... like a *budget* meeting?''

Decker said, "How's your arm, Ms. Anger?''

Immediately the woman loosened her grip on her limb. "It's fine.''

"You look like you're in lots of pain.''

"I'm *fine*!"

"Even if it feels like agony, you should try to move it. Keeping it tight against your body like you do . . . the muscles stiffen up. If you can remember, rotate your arm every hour or so. And don't forget the Advil or Aleve. If that doesn't cut it, ask your doc for something *stronger*. You don't seem like the addictive type, so don't be shy—"

"I'm not shy about anything!" Carol countered.

"This is the truth!" Olaf said.

The waitress studied Decker's face. "You've been shot?"

Decker nodded.

"In the line of duty?"

Again, Decker nodded. "Hardly the same circumstances."

"You bleed just the same."

Decker smiled. "Yes, you do."

A woman butted in. "What's going on down here?"

Carol said, "This is Lieutenant Decker. He was at . . . at the scene."

The brash woman stuck out her hand. Petite with short dark hair and penetrating eyes. "Brenda Miller. Nice to meet you."

Brenda was cute. No wonder Scott Oliver had liked her. Decker took the proffered hand. "You're from Ashman/Reynard Realty . . . Wendy Culligan's boss, correct?"

Brenda jerked her head back. "Someone prep you?"

Decker smiled. "I'm good with names. Is Wendy here?"

Brenda cocked her thumb upward a couple of rows. Decker's eyes climbed with her finger, rested upon a frail woman. "She lost a lot of weight."

Brenda said. "That's what happens when you don't eat."

"Who's next to her? Is that Adelaide Skinner?"

"Yeah."

"Maybe I'll go over and give them my regards."

"Better if you left Wendy alone. She's still . . ." Brenda extended her fingers, rocked her wrist back and forth.

"I'm sorry to hear that," Decker said.

"She should take lessons from the Garrison lady."

Brenda raised her brows. "Man, that woman knows how to party."

"Photo op, photo op," Carol mimicked.

Tess sighed, shook her head. "What a mob!" She smiled tearfully at Decker. "Wanna know the real sad part, Lieutenant? Kenny woulda loved this . . . just woulda ate it up. Anything that made him feel special."

Brenda said, "Have a seat, Lieutenant. Tell me something. How's Detective Oliver?"

"He's fine—"

"I said sit down," Brenda said. "That means you've got to bend the knees."

"I can't stay—"

"Doughnut break calling?" Carol said.

Tess chided, "Stop being so rude to him. He's the reason I'm walking today."

Carol became quiet, sullen. Decker said, "I'm very sorry I can't stay. But I'll be happy to meet with any of you— anytime, anyplace, anywhere. Just give me a little advance notice, that's all."

Olaf said, "We tank you for your offer very much."

No one spoke. Decker said, "Honestly, I don't know why Captain Strapp isn't here. You people were the *only* reason he had chosen to come."

"Obviously we just weren't that important!" Carol barked.

"On the contrary." Decker took out a portable phone and dialed Strapp's house. A few minutes later, he cut the line, paused, looking down at his feet. He said, "I just spoke to his wife. He's sick at home with the flu—"

"*Right!*" Carol said.

Decker said. "If she says he's sick, the man is bedridden. Trust me on this one."

Again, Carol studied him. "Why do I believe you? I don't *want* to believe you."

Decker said, "You're clenching your arm again."

Carol dropped her arm. "Why can't you stay?"

Decker said, "I have a very *pressing* matter. So pressing, I'm going to drag the captain from his sickbed." He shook hands all around. "I know money's not compensation for human life. But none of you should have to worry about paying the bills. I hope the games raise lots of cash."

"It would help." Tess paused. "I got the job, you know."

Carol said, "You did! When?"

Olaf said, "That's great, Tess! Congratulations."

"No big deal. Just answering phones. But it's better than nothing. And it's simple, too. So I can study for my real estate license when it's quiet." She looked at Brenda. "If the offer's still open."

Brenda said, "Of course. It's an open-ended offer." She stalled a moment. "So how is Detective Oliver anyway?"

"He's fine, Ms. Miller. I'll tell him you send regards."

"Do that." She sighed. "I've got to get back to Wendy."

"Give both Wendy and Adelaide Skinner my best."

Carol said, "I'll walk you out."

"Not necessary."

"I know that. I'll do it anyway."

The two of them left, walking silently as they steered through the stars, fans, and cameras on their way out. Then, as if conjured up by a demon, Jeanine appeared, the smile on her face widening when she saw Carol and Decker. Immediately, she wedged herself between them, linking her arms around theirs. She bubbled, "Photo op!"

A Nikon clicked and flashed.

Decker jerked away from Jeanine's hold, grabbed the camera, slapped open the back cover, and yanked out the roll of film, exposing it to the light.

The photographer was irate. "Da *fuck'er* you doing?"

Decker handed him back the camera, reached into his wallet. Four ones, two fives, and a hundred-dollar bill. He stuffed the Franklin into the photographer's hand.

To a shocked Jeanine, he said, "If you ever, *ever* touch me again, I'll sue you for assault. Like I should have done the first time. And notice that I'm talking in front of witnesses."

He stalked off, forgetting about Carol until she called out

to him. He stopped abruptly, took a deep breath, let it out slowly. She was panting by the time she reached him. She breathed out, "Are you okay?"

Decker counted to ten, said, "I'm sorry for stomping off like that. Are you all right?"

"Winded but fine."

Decker shook the waitress's hand. "Call me in a couple of weeks. Let me know how you're doing. Enjoy the matches."

Carol stared at him. "Lieutenant, what was that all about?"

"Not important."

The waitress smiled. For the first time today, it seemed genuine. "You hate her guts, don't you?"

Decker was quiet.

Carol said, "Seems we have more in common than just a bullet in the arm. C'mon, Lieutenant. You've got me curious. What's going on?"

"Talk to me in a couple of weeks."

"That's the *best* you can do?"

"For now, that's all I have to say."

"You sound like you're taking the Fifth."

"It's a good amendment." Decker started to walk off. "Not a bad commandment either."

Carol remained rooted as she yelled out to him. "What *is* the fifth commandment anyway?"

"To honor your parents," Decker shouted as he trotted off. "Go do God a favor. Call up your mom."

🍂 35

The woman stepped aside, let Decker in. He said, "How are you, Susan?"

She cocked her hip. A tall, shapely woman with auburn hair and bright green eyes. She wore a white blouse, denim capris, and flats. "He's got a hundred-and-three-degree fever. He says you cursed him."

Decker smiled. "I think the fever's gone to his brain. I do need to talk to him."

"He's dressing ... going to the tournament." Susan eyed him. "I don't suppose you could talk him out of it."

"Me?"

"He respects you."

Decker waited a beat. "How about if I drive him?"

Susan said, "He doesn't need a chauffeur, he needs rest."

Strapp walked into the room, his complexion ghostly, with a sweaty sheen. He had on a black jacket, a turtleneck sweater, and wool slacks. Boots on his feet. Still he shivered. He viewed Decker through sunken eyes. "Marge just called here. She was looking for you. Something about a kid named Joachim Rush who called her. What the hell is going on?"

"I'll tell you on the way over to the tournament, sir. How about a lift?"

Susan scolded, "No shop talk on Sunday."

"This better be important," the captain groused.

"Just ignore me," Susan muttered.

Decker said, "Yes, sir, it's very important." To Susan, he said, "I'll take care of him."

Susan shook her head, adjusted her husband's collar, and kissed his cheek. "Try to make it home in one piece, Strapp."

He kissed her back. To Decker, he said, "Let's go."

Strapp said, "Who's pulling the warrants?"

The light turned green. Decker depressed the accelerator. The Volare shot out. "Dunn and Oliver."

"For where? The party house?"

"The party house, Malcolm Carey's car—"

"How about Carey's house?"

"We don't have enough probable cause to justify a search. After we've pinned something on Malcolm, then I figure we can move to the house. I've got the papers written up, just waiting a signature."

Decker tapped the wheel nervously.

"If things go well, we shouldn't have a problem nailing them. I told Webster and Martinez to hold off with Narcotics until you'd okayed the operation. They're waiting to hear. Sir, I'd like to move on this as quickly as possible—"

Strapp interrupted, "Give me the damn mike."

"Thank you—"

Strapp cut him off with a wave of the hand. Phoned Narcotics and gave permission. Then he handed Decker the mike. "You're clear." He coughed into a tissue. "You got me in a weakened state, you son of a bitch. Otherwise, I'd really be pissed at you."

He paused.

"You'd better pray Joachim is legit. Which brings up another point. Last I heard the kid was a suspect."

"Not anymore. We've cleared him."

"How'd you get the info on him?"

"What do you think? I hired out."

"You spent from your *own* wallet?"

"With my own blood, sweat, and tears." Decker gripped

the wheel. "I hope it pans out. If not, we nail a pusher. Good PR if nothing else."

"Also makes us the target of some very rich parents," Strapp complained. "Fuck them. They start making noise, we tell them to keep their own houses in order first. Slow down. Your driving is making me nauseous. You put the whammy on me, you son of a bitch."

Decker said, "Me?"

"Telling me not to show up at the tournament. Telling me to get myself sick . . . to come down with the flu. You help it along with some voodoo dolls?"

Decker smiled, then grew serious. "For what it's worth, Captain, you were right. LAPD did have an obligation to the survivors to show up at the tournament." He sighed. "No matter who sponsored it."

"Swell," Strapp grumped. "In the meantime, I'm feeling like a truck ran over me and you're decking photographers—"

"I didn't deck anyone." He paused. "We'll ignore the pun—"

"Nor do I like your shit fit in front of Jeanine."

"Sir, the photographer isn't going to make noise. I slipped him a hundred . . . in front of witnesses."

"You hire out from your own pocket, you slip some jerk a C-spot in exchange for a roll of film. . . ."

Nobody talked for a moment. Then Strapp said, "Were you planning to interview Malcolm Carey? Because, technically, you're off this case."

"Look, sir, you want to keep me off Estelle's, do that. This isn't about Estelle's, it's about David Garrison."

Decker organized his thoughts. "I realize we have to keep the chain letter going to make this work. Using the busts to get something on Malcolm Carey. Then using Malcolm Carey to get to Sean Amos. Lastly, Sean to get to Jeanine. And then, if we're extremely lucky, maybe . . . just maybe, we'll be able to bring charges against her."

"For her brother's murder only," Strapp said. "Nothing about Estelle's."

"Right. We have nothing to tie her to that . . . so far."

"Maybe she didn't do it," Strapp said.

"Okay. Assume that Estelle's was the sole work of Harlan Manz. Could be that after her parents died, she got greedy. Fine. If that's the case, then we'll box her for the one murder—"

"Of which you have no proof other than rumors."

"Even if the rumors don't play out, we'll have busted a pusher. And if they do play out . . . if she took out her brother, using Malcolm to pump poison into David's veins . . . let her fry."

Strapp shook his head. "Greed. Gets 'em every time."

For a wild party, things seemed subdued. A couple of dozen cars outside, distant thrash metal music leaking from the windows, an occasional yelp and fit of laughter. No kids heaving on the lawn, no untamed screams of abandon, nothing to suggest a *scene*. Narcotics didn't like it. But something intuitive kept Decker calm, confident.

The hard part had been getting the vehicles inside the gated community without arousing suspicion. The cars had filtered in slowly to their prearranged spots. Staggered around the streets to make it look more natural. Clandestine meeting places for foot patrol. Waiting for the signal. Waiting to raid.

Quiet streets. Dim lights guarding sinews of private roadway. Lots of black patches amid gray forms. The target was a two-story Colonial sitting on a hill of grass. Magnolia trees cast gnarled shadows. Muted lights coming through the windows. They'd have to move fast. Narc would handle the entry, the initial busts. Decker's team would come in for arrests, evidence, and cleanup.

And Malcolm Carey belonged to him.

The countdown. The signal. The sudden spurt of activity. Officers running, pounding on the doors. Identification.

"Police! Open up!"

The ensuing shouts, the screams, the dull thuds of wood splintering as the hand-held ram butted against the locked door. The final shove. And then they were in.

Decker closed his eyes, prayed. Atavistic response. But at least it was proactive. He counted to one hundred, sprinted over, charged into the house.

Eyes skittering across the room. A dozen teens sprawled out on the floor, several boys attempting to bolt out windows and through back doors. Hauled in by agents, pinned against the walls.

The screaming.

The crying.

The smell of fresh piss.

A sofa table holding cellophane bags of powder, scattered loose pills, and brown clumps of rock crystal. A hookah oozing fumes. Used needles on the floor along with several handguns for good measure.

Thank you, Joachim.

Thank you, God!

Dashing through the house, Decker shouted, "Where's Malcolm Carey? I need Malcolm Carey!"

Two loud pops.

Gunfire.

Someone grabbed his arm.

Marge shouted, "Upstairs bathroom."

"Christ!"

They raced up the stairs, just as the bathroom door caved in. A body halfway through the second-story window, another figure desperately stuffing junk down the toilet. Narcs pulled him down first—to the ground, kicking open his legs, jerking his hands behind his back, intoning Miranda as they secured him for arrest. He wasn't the challenge. He melted like ice cream in the Sahara.

Decker's eyes went to the floor, to the white face. "Hello, Sean."

The kid retched, gagged. Decker said, "Turn his head to the side. Don't let him aspirate. And careful with his hands. I want them paraffin-tested. See if he fired the revolver—"

"I swear, I didn't shoot—"

His words were drowned out by screams.

The body out the window.

Officers trying to grab on to a set of kicking legs. Fighting with all their strength. The sounds emitted. Animal sounds. Grunts, growls, snarls. Agents sweating as they tried to pull his body back through the window and into the bathroom. As if reeling in the big one. Too bad no one had a gaff. Among the group was Niels Van Gelder, the detective who had called Decker earlier in the day. Big bull of a guy with big hands. All six of them talking at once.

Niels shouted, "Anyone find the gun?"

"Watch the hands! Watch the fucking hands!"

"No gun?"

"Watch the *fucking* hands—"

"Slow, slow . . . slow down!"

"Is he packing—"

"Does he have anything in his hands?" Niels asked.

"It's dark, man. Can't see a fucking thing—"

"Look at the hands!"

"Careful—"

"If you stick your hand out—"

"You wearing a vest, Condor?"

"Yeah, I'm covered."

Condor was Arnold Myerhoff. Five eight, one seventy, and bald. Five years with L.A. Narc, ten years prior with Miami Narc. He grunted, "Someone grab the fucker's arm while I hold the legs—"

"I can't see—"

"Watch your face. Pull back—"

"Go for the arms. The arms. You got the arm?"

Silence.

"Got it?"

"I . . . got it."

"Yank it inside—"

"It's in a bad position. Don't want to break the suck—"

"Just pull it inside, Marc."

Marc Kirby, a fifteen-year veteran Narcotics officer, pulled an empty fist into the room.

Niels said, "Now get the other hand so we can pull—"

"Check the pockets—"

"Hold this hand while I get the other—"

"Shit, bastard's trying to scratch me—"

"Wrap the hand up, Marc."

"In what?"

"Just push it up his back."

"Got the other arm?"

"No."

"Got it?"

"Yeaaaa . . . got it!"

"The hand, the hand—"

Finally, Marc brought up a second empty fist.

"All right!" Condor called out. "Pull the fucker up!"

First came the legs, then the torso, then the face.

A feral face. The mouth opened, a gaping hole, like a snake unhinging his jaws.

Decker screamed, "He's gonna bite!"

Marc jerked his face away, swore as he looped his arm around Malcolm's neck.

Coiled muscles popping from the teen's neck. Arms as stiff as wood. He continued to kick and flail, tried in vain to land punches using anything he had—including his head. Though he didn't have a chance against six grown adults, he fought as if he did. The ear-piercing screeches resonated throughout the room as the body was brought onto the floor.

And then it was over, the kid was down. Cuffed and shackled.

Decker recognized the boy. "Yo, Malcolm. What's up, dude?"

The kid's shriek seemed to emanate from his bowels.

Decker said, "Who's doing the booking?"

"Yo," Condor answered.

Decker said, "Arnie, before either one is washed down, paraffin-test the hands to see who fired."

"Where *is* the gun?"

"Fucker probably dropped it."

A sudden stench filled the small room. Decker looked down at Sean Amos's soiled pants. The kid had lost total control.

Niels said, "Who wants to play plumber in the john?"

"It's Gayola's turn," Marc stated.

Gayola Weyman was six one, one eighty, with a size-sixteen neck. Her specialty was hand-to-hand combat. She started gloving up. Malcolm screamed again.

"Will someone shut him up?"

Condor said, "Man, it *stinks* in here."

To Decker, Marge said, "I'll go look for the gun. Maybe he dropped it on the lawn while he was out there hanging."

Marc searched through Malcolm's pockets. "Got a nice packet of powder . . . two of them—"

Gayola moaned. "God, the toilet's backing up—"

"All the shit thrown inside. Might be needles there. You double-glove?"

"I double-gloved." Gayola stuck her hand down the plumbing, brought up the first load. Looked it over. A couple of packets of rock crystal, some packets of milky liquid—powder diluted by water. She went down for a second dip, brought up some melting pills and crinkled paper.

"What in the world is *this*?"

"What?" Decker asked.

Gayola handed Decker several crumpled, toilet-soaked glossy pictures, a sheet streaked with runny ink.

Decker smoothed out the snapshots. Neck-up portraits. Familiar face. It took a few moments to give it a name.

Wade Anthony.

"What the hell?" Decker looked at the paper, eyes scanning the writing. Appeared to be someone's schedule, the activities listed by the hours.

1. Eight o'clock: wakes up, dresses, eats breakfast, reads the paper.

2. Ten until two . . . tennis practice. Next to the line was an address. Four, seven . . . maybe a five or a two. With the runny ink it was hard to tell. The street name was clear.

3. Two to four P.M.. . . .in the spa, then physical therapy.

Gayola brought up another picture of Anthony. This one was a full body shot. He was sitting on a couch, looking quite content, smoking a big fat stogie. A nice picture except for the dart board bleeding ink over the snapshot. A big red heart drawn over the chest was the bull's-eye.

Suddenly the events of the day came into knife-edge focus. Decker grinned. Couldn't have planned it better had he tried.

Malcolm screamed once more.

Decker said, "Take them back in separate cars. Separate bookings, separate cells, and separate lawyers. No interchange between them. And don't forget about the hands."

To Condor, Marc said, "You want the screamer or the shitter?"

"I'll take the shitter."

Decker said, "Arnie, after you paraffin his hands, give him some jail rags and let the kid clean himself up before you book him. Let him have his shred of dignity."

✒36

Savvy kids.

They all immediately asked for lawyers.

No prob, man. Just need to take your picture first.

The station house had become a riot of activity. Twenty-one arrested as pounds of pharmaceuticals were bagged and checked into evidence. The firearms were entered separately. A mammothsized bust—children from some very high-powered families. Narcotics was elated. Parents were outraged. Throughout it all, Decker just did his job.

Not nearly enough cell space at Devonshire so the kids were transferred immediately to Van Nuys for booking and arraignment. Between the paperwork, cataloging, and carpooling, Decker didn't get to Malcolm Carey until hours later, about one in the morning. He brought Marge with him for backup.

Decker found the formerly out-of-control teen sitting comfortably, slouching in his chair, dressed in jail blues. He sipped water, smoked a cigarette. A square face, sporting patches of beard growth. A high forehead, strong jawline. Thin arched eyebrows. Pecan-colored hair clipped close to the scalp. Dull blue eyes. Still, they weren't completely expressionless—not like the eyes of hardened cons. That would come later on.

Since Malcolm was of age, his parents had been excluded from the interview. But Dad had sent along his best wishes in the form of Rupert Flame—a fifty-plus criminal defense attorney, whose haircut budget equaled a month of Decker's salary. He was of medium build, gray hair, brown eyes, ruddy face with the wet complexion of the recently shaved. He wore a superbly tailored double-breasted navy nailhead suit.

Decker took his seat, exchanged glances with Marge, both of them waiting for the lawyer to begin.

Flame said, "He's a kid—"

"Over eighteen," Marge corrected. "Birthday was two months ago."

"He isn't what you're after."

"What are we after?"

Flame said, "You want the big guys, offer me something. He doesn't talk until you lay something on the table."

Decker said, "You know what we have your client on, Mr. Flame?"

"I know what you have—"

"In order of severity, we've booked him on two counts of attempted murder of police officers—"

"Man, I thought you were robbers," Malcolm broke in.

"Mal, we *clearly* identified ourselves," Decker said.

"I didn't hear—"

"Malcolm, you mowed down the door with a semi-automatic," Marge said. "And you did fire the gun. Paraffin tests don't lie."

Flame said, "He was panic-stricken, Detective. His judgment was less than ideal."

Decker said, "Twenty counts of selling illegal substances. Five counts of possession—"

"I was framed, man. The Narcs put the envelopes in my pocket—"

"One count of resisting arrest. Two counts felony reckless discharge of a firearm, not to mention one felony possession of a firearm."

"Nobody likes a pusher," Marge turned to the kid. "Mal . . . can I call you Mal?"

The teen smirked, "You can call me sweetheart—"

"Lieutenant, listen to me. Malcolm *is* over eighteen. But

emotionally, he's still a *child*, a dumb kid—''

''A basic re*tard*,'' Carey broke in.

Flame snapped, ''Unless you want your asshole reamed, buddy boy, you shut your mouth!''

Surprisingly, the kid blushed, turned quiet.

Flame took a deep breath, said, ''He has a big mouth as you can see. Dumb and brash with a big mouth. But just bark, he turns into a lamb.'' The lawyer kept Malcolm silent with a stony look. ''Just rolls over and takes the beating. And that was what happened to him, Lieutenant. He started selling to be a big man on campus. Nothing heavy . . . maybe just a few joints of marijuana—''

''A regular saint—''

''We concede that the boy sold marijuana on his own. But within a few weeks, he was in *way* over his head, Lieutenant. He got involved with the *wrong* people. People you don't mess with if you want to breathe.''

''Uh-huh,'' Decker said. ''Meanwhile, he's racking up a grand or two a month.''

''The money wasn't the reason he pushed,'' Flame said. ''Yes, Malcolm continued to push. We concede that as well. But *not* because he wanted to play Mr. Big Shot. He sold only to prevent some foreign animal from cutting off his dick and stuffing it down his throat.''

Marge said, ''I see. He was *coerced* into making two thou a month. Slick defense, Counselor.''

''It's the *truth,* Detective,'' Flame insisted. ''When Malcolm tried to stop, he was threatened. Stalked. Even beaten. We have proof of that.''

''Uh-huh,'' Decker said.

Flame leaned in close. ''He's a pawn, not what you and Narc are after.''

Decker said, ''Actually, Malcolm is *exactly* what I'm after.''

''You're missing the big picture,'' Flame replied. ''We can give you names, Lieutenant. Make you and Narcotics very, *very* happy. Just give us something to work with.''

''I want to talk about Sean Amos,'' Marge stated.

Flame was taken aback. ''Sean Amos?''

"The kid who was with Malcolm when we took him down." Decker's eyes shifted to the teen. "He's sitting in a cell as we speak. I haven't talked to him yet. But that can be remedied—"

Flame broke in. "What are you talking about?"

Decker said, "Specifically? The pictures Amos tried to flush down the toilet. What was the deal, Mal? Things flew so well first time out, you decided to do a repeat?"

Flame's face was the picture of confusion. Malcolm turned pale, said nothing. But he was no longer smirking.

Flame stumbled, "Lieutenant, what are you *getting* at?"

Decker said, "Ask your client."

"Then give me a minute with my client."

"You take your minute now, you might as well make it an hour. Because you know what I'm going to do, Counselor? I'm going to talk to Sean Amos. He wants to go state's witness against your client—instead of the other way around—it's fine with me—"

"State's witness?" Flame stuttered out.

"He's bluffing," Carey blurted. "He's bullshitting—"

Decker lied, "I never bluff. I never bullshit. I want Sean Amos's head, Malcolm. Either his or yours. So either you talk or we'll talk to him."

Marge said, "You talk to us now, Mal, maybe we can cut you a deal with the DA. You play mute, then Sean'll do your talking for you—"

Flame cut in. "If you're planning to bring new charges against my client, you have to come clean. You can't conceal evidence."

"I'm not concealing anything," Decker said. "Counselor, we're not at the discovery phase of this case because as yet, I haven't charged him—"

"Lieutenant, you hold back, you're in procedural error. Which messes up your entire case."

"Now you got me quaking."

"What are you *talking* about?"

Decker said, "We're planning to charge your client and Sean Amos in a murder-for-hire scheme—"

"What!" Flame glared at Carey. "I thought you said you told me *everything*!"

The teen started to speak, instead looked down and stubbed out his cigarette.

Marge said, "The intended victim is a man named Wade Anthony. That's why there were pictures of Anthony stuffed down the toilet along with Anthony's daily schedule—"

Flame stuttered, "Who is Wade Anthony?"

"A paraplegic tennis player."

Flame said to Carey, "Do you know this Wade Anthony?"

Carey whispered, "He's talking shit."

"Actually, it was probably Sean Amos's idea," Decker went on. "He felt that Wade had stolen away his girlfriend. Looks like Sean got desparate, was in the process of hiring your client as a hit man when the bust went down."

"We hadn't agreed on anything yet," Malcolm said to Decker.

"Shut up!" Flame ordered.

Coolly, Carey said, "Can I just talk for a moment?"

"No, you may not!" Flame ordered.

Malcolm discounted his counsel. "Since when is it against the law to talk about things? Even things like murder? I mean, how many times have you said you'd like to kill someone?"

"It's isn't against the law to talk," Decker said, "but it is against the law to *contract*. More important, it's against the law to *act* on that contract. And you've climbed that mountain before, son. In the form of sticking dope into people's veins. And we both know what I'm talking about."

The teen blanched.

"What are you *talking* about, Lieutenant?" Flame asked.

Marge said, "If Sean drops first, you go home without a pot to piss in."

The boy stumbled, "You have no proof—"

"We have fingerprints," Decker lied.

"That's fucking *impossible*! I used glov—"

"Shut up!"

The room fell quiet.

Decker went on. "Not to mention the dragon we collected from you, Malcolm. It has the exact same gas chromatography spectrum as the heroin pumped into David Garrison's veins. Know what the odds are of that, son?"

"Evidence doesn't lie," Marge fibbed.

"Who's David Garrison?" Flame demanded.

The teen broke out in a sweat. "You're trying to freak me out—"

Marge interrupted, "Sean or you, Malcolm?"

Flame stood up. "Before you go two *any* further, I need to consult with my client. Obviously, we're in a different league now."

"We don't have all night," Decker said.

Marge said, "And Sean's awaiting—"

"No!" Carey protested.

"I insist that I converse with my client privately." Flame's voice had become as wound up as a catapult. "But, please, I am asking both of you to hold off talking to this other party. Just give me a few minutes."

"You know what? I'll give you five of them." Decker started for the door, turned around, looked at his watch. "Starting now."

Outrage was stamped across the defense lawyer's face. But he maintained an even voice. To counteract Flame, Decker had brought in Morton Weller—a man who had packed in over twenty years with the DA's office. Scrawny, with a narrow face, deep-set eyes, and a long neck bisected by the node of an Adam's apple. White downy fuzz sat atop his head. He had on a gray single-breasted suit, white shirt, and red tie. He shook hands with Flame, sat down.

Calmly, Flame said, "Give me a show of good faith."

Weller scratched his ear. "No death penalty—"

Carey screamed, "Fuck that! I didn't kill anybody!"

"Malcolm, calm down. He's trying to rile you."

"I assure you, Rup—"

Flame talked over him. "You want me to start, Mort,

I'll start. For turning witness, you drop everything except the murder two. Twenty-five with a minimum of five years—''

Carey screamed. "I'm not going to *jail* for five years!"

Decker said, "Penitentiary, Malcolm. Not jail."

Weller said, "Murder one, life—''

"No—''

"*With* possibility of parole—''

"I'll take my chances on a jury." Flame stood.

Weller said, "Rup, be reasonable. How can I deal effectively unless I hear what your client has to say?"

Flame said, "You take a chance here or take a chance with a jury."

Decker said, "Murder two, twenty-five to life, minimum fifteen years—''

"Seven," Flame said.

Weller said, "Counselor, he'd get a harsher sentence from the drug charges alone."

"Not after I finished with the jury."

Weller said, "Murder two, twenty-five to life, minimum twelve—''

"Seven."

Decker said, "Now he's bluffing. Morton, I *know* I can get the other kids to turn against him—''

Flame interrupted. "Murder two only, twenty-five to life, seven minimum before possibility of parole, no time off for good behavior. Do we have a deal or not?"

Morton and Decker traded glances. The assistant DA nodded.

Carey banged the table. "No way I'm spending *seven* years in jail!"

Decker said, "Penitentiary."

"Fuck you!"

"And it may even be longer than seven—''

Flame shot out, "Malcolm, you refuse, they talk to your friend and *he* takes the deal. Then look at what you have. The same evidence, the same charges against you . . . except now they have a witness to back up a first-degree murder charge. You want me to go to court with Sean

Amos as state's witness, I'll take the money. But you'd better believe in miracles, son, because that's what you're going to need.''

The room became silent. Flame broke it. "We'll take the offer.''

This time the teen didn't argue. All eyes went to him.

"Go on," Flame said. "The worst is over. You have nothing to lose. Tell them what happened.''

Carey spoke softly . . . deliberately.

"Sean came up to me one day . . . said he had a problem. There was this guy . . . a hype . . . who was harassing his girlfriend. He wanted the problem taken care of. Could I help him out?''

He scratched his fuzzy chin.

"I asked him what he had in mind. I figured maybe he wanted me to spook him or something like that. But as he kept going, I figured out he wanted something more permanent.''

Weller said, "What did he ask of you specifically?''

"Sean asked me to whack him." Carey looked up. "I was shocked, man. I wasn't in the business of murder. I told him he should watch who he talked to, man.''

He stopped, fidgeted.

"Go on," Decker said.

"Then . . . then Sean starts asking . . . 'Well . . . do you know anyone who'd want to do the pop?' So I'm like playing along. I ask him . . . how much? He told me ten grand. Then I asked him how he could produce that much cash.''

"And?" Marge prodded.

"He told me he had this trust fund with over two hundred and fifty grand coming to him in a couple of years. Now, I'm making, on my own, like one to two grand a month. So why would I risk my ass for only ten grand? But there are people out there . . . ten grand would be a lot of money.''

Marge arched her brows. "Hard to believe, but I suppose that's true.''

Weller passed her a look, then said, "Then what happened?''

"So then Sean . . . see, he knows that I know certain people." A small smile formed on Malcolm's lips. "He says
that if *I* don't want to do it, maybe I can ask around. I'm
still like playing along . . . I said sure. Then I forgot about
the whole thing."

A pause.

"Month later . . . Sean comes back to me, asks . . . did I
find someone to do the job? I say no. 'Cause I never asked
about it. I forgot the whole thing—"

"You already said that," Decker interjected. "Go on."

The boy seemed riled, took a few moments to find his
footing. "Sean got nasty. You wouldn't believe how pissed
he can get. Tell you the truth, he spooked me."

Right, Decker thought.

Malcolm became animated. "He started getting agitated.
Like . . . really aggressive. Said I gotta help him out."

He hesitated.

"Now this was where I fucked up. Like Mr. Flame said,
I got a big mouth. I talk without thinking sometimes. So I
told Sean this. I said, 'Look! If this guy's a hype, why are
you bothering to pop him? Why don't you play it natural?'
Sean looked at me, asked me what I had in mind. I told
him I don't have anything in mind *personally,* but if I was
going to do the pop, I might want to just . . . put him out
in a blaze of glory."

Carey stalled, went on.

"That's exactly how I said it. In a blaze of glory.
Sean . . ." The teen smiled. "Now he can be a little dense.
But I could see his brain working. He stuck out his arm
and made an injection into his vein with his finger. Looked
at me questioningly. I nodded. So he asked how. I told him,
'Man, you've stuck yourself. How do you think you do
it?' "

The boy took a sip of water.

"Sean thought a little bit. Then he told me that the hype
was also a drunk. I say, 'Man, what's the big deal? It's a
sure thing. You get the key from your bitch, wait until he
gets plastered, then stick him where it counts.' "

Malcolm tapped the table with his fingers.

"I could tell Sean liked the idea. But he didn't have the balls to do it alone. So he asked me to come along as backup."

Weller raised his eyebrows. "You went?"

"It was something to do." Malcolm shrugged. "I told him backup will cost. Ten grand. I never thought he'd go for it, but I was wrong. Sean was real serious about this thing—"

"You mean murder?" Decker clarified.

Carey looked away. "Sean told me the ten grand could be arranged. But for that price, I'd have to supply the dragon. He wanted pure scag. I told him it was stupid to use pure scag. Pure anything in a hype's vein looks suspicious. I told him I'd have to cut it. But I could deliver."

The teen licked his lips.

"Sean got a key . . . we waited for the right time. Garrison got drunk almost every weekend. We did a couple of practice runs . . . to see the layout. And we had to make sure the hype was under big time . . . sleeping off a real bender. Third time we checked, the guy was out cold. I put the scag in the medicine cabinet while Sean shot him up. I was out of the room when it happened. I never touched the guy."

Weller said, "Did you get the money, Malcolm?"

"Yeah, he paid me." The boy's lips turned upward. "Sucker wouldn't *dare* stiff me."

"Where's the money now?" Decker asked.

Malcolm sipped water. "Spent it."

"You went through ten thousand dollars in one month?" Weller said quietly.

A sly smile played upon his lips. "Fine wine and good women cost a bundle. I also bought things."

"Like what?" Decker asked.

"Coins, stamps . . . guns. Same kind of shit my dad buys. He'd be real proud."

"You're just a chip off the old block," Marge said in an undertone.

"Detective . . ." Flame warned.

"S'right," Carey said. "It's true. White-collar crime, blue-collar crime, violent crime . . . it's all the same. Dad and I *are* one of a kind. Only difference? I don't mind getting my hands a little dirty."

❧37

Strapp coughed. "Good news. Sean Amos is being held without bail." He checked his watch, let out a small shiver. "It's almost three. My head's about to explode. He'll keep until the morning. See you here at eight tomorrow. Now go home."

Decker hesitated. "All right."

Strapp studied his lieutenant. "Christ, Decker, what is it *this* time?"

Decker said, "Something was off with Carey."

"What are you talking about?" Strapp shot back. "I was behind the one-way. Saw and heard the whole thing. What was off?"

A long pause. "Didn't it sound . . . rehearsed?"

"No, it didn't sound *rehearsed*! It looked and sounded like a psycho kid getting a thrill out of telling us how bad he was."

Decker rubbed his eyes. "Maybe it's fatigue."

"I think so. Good night, Lieutenant."

"'Night, Captain."

Strapp muttered, "By the way . . . good job."

"Thanks." Decker left, feeling very unsatisfied.

A kid who had everything—money, looks, connections—and that *still* didn't stop him from screwing up.

What Martinez could have done with any *one* of those advantages. He smoothed his black mustache, his cheeks still stinging from an early-morning shave. He wanted to look good in front of the captain.

Pulling out his notes, he appraised the situation. Sean Amos in jail blues, head down, lips smashed together. No eye contact with his parents. Mom was a rail-thin bubble blond on his left. Sitting on the right was a big-boned, ultra-good-ole-boy Texas lawyer named Edgar Ray Trit, wearing a three-thousand-dollar Brioni suit and a string tie.

Dad was at the lawyer's right. Lamar Amos tried to hide his beer gut under a black suit and white shirt, but to no avail. Ruddy complexion, veiny nose, slicked gray hair like a silverback gorilla.

No ten-gallon hat.

With Martinez were Webster and Katherine Villard, a fortyplus, good-looking deputy DA. Black hair, black eyes, serious expression. A no-nonsense woman. Behind the one-way mirror were Strapp, Decker, Marge, and Oliver.

Webster got the ball rolling, made the preliminary statements. Identification of all the parties in the room. Then the current charges against Sean Amos starting with the murder one of David Garrison.

Trit interrupting, his voice booming, "Now, Kate, we're all friends here. So I'm going to open up the discussion with plain, old-fashioned honesty. I just don't understand where you got the gumption to take up on this murder one." He screwed up his face. "Now if you're relying on the word of that psychopath, Malcolm Carey . . . if you're planning to go to court with that, well, you're going to end up looking like a fool—"

"It's Katherine," the deputy DA answered curtly. "Has the bailiff forwarded you a copy of the statement?"

"Not yet."

The prosecutor opened her briefcase, took out several sheaves of papers. Handed them to him. "Here you go."

Again, Trit grimaced. "Reckon I could use a good laugh right now."

"Edgar, we're standing behind his statement. You want to go to court, we'll bring him to court on a murder one—"

Sean broke in. "I didn't *kill* anyone—"

"Hush up!" Trit snapped as he flipped through the pages, eyes racing over the document.

Katherine said, "I'm sorry you didn't get the statement sooner. You'll need time to look it over. We can reconvene at two—"

Sean said, "Malcolm Carey is a fucking liar—"

"Boy, close your mouth—"

"Oh, fuck you—"

An arm reached out and backhanded Sean across his face. Lamar Amos had turned beet red. "You just sit there and shut yo damn mouth and listen to yo lawyah, y'hear?"

Trit stuttered out, "Lamar, I'll handle—"

"Are you contradictin' me, Edgar Ray?" Lamar broke in. "I hope not lest y'foget who's payin' yo bills."

Sean held his cheek. Breathing hard, he said, "See what happens when you got a balloon inside your dick."

Veins bulging, Lamar charged. Mom screamed as Trit and Martinez held Daddy Lamar back, the Texan screaming obscenities until he was purple. The shrieks brought in a posse of backup. After a moment, Lamar stopped rushing, shook loose. He stalked out of the room. Mom's eyes went to her son, then to the open door. She rose, then raced out.

"Gee. Thanks for the support, Mom." Sean sighed. "Hasn't been married to him in ten years and she still licks his boot heels . . . goddamn bitch!"

Webster said, " 'How sharper than a serpent's tooth—' "

"Yeah, well, all the better to *bite* with, my dear," Sean retorted. "And I know that's from Shakespeare. I'm not as dumb as you think."

"Sean, we think you're very bright—"

"That's enough." Trit stood. "We'll reconvene at two—"

"I'm not going anywhere until this is hashed out. Malcolm Carey is a *crazy* fucker—"

Webster said, "Then why were you with him on the night David Garrison was murdered—"

"David Garrison wasn't *murdered*! He OD'd!"

Martinez said, "Sean, let me tell you so you know what

you're up against. We have witnesses that put you with Malcolm Carey on the night of David Garrison's death.''

Webster named the date. "First you went with Carey to shoot some pool, then you went back to your house to smoke some dope, then you went over to David Garrison's house—''

"I've *never,* ever been to David Garrison's house. If Malcolm told you that, he's lying!''

"Are you saying you didn't shoot pool with him?''

"Yes. I mean no. I mean yes, I shot pool, but—''

"And you smoked dope—''

"But—''

Trit said, "Sean—''

"I didn't *kill* anyone—''

"Why were you stuffing pictures of Wade Anthony down the toilet?'' Webster asked.

Sean broke into a cold sweat. "What are you talking about?''

"When we busted you,'' Webster said. "You were flushing pictures of Wade Anthony down the toilet.''

"Along with a daily schedule of Anthony's activities,'' Martinez added.

"I didn't know what I was doing,'' Sean said. "I just panicked—''

"What were you doing with those pictures of Wade Anthony in the first place?'' Martinez asked. "Starting a fan club?''

Trit said, "We're not talking anymore—''

"What does Wade Anthony have to do with this?'' Sean said.

Trit said, "He's a minor. Don't even *try* to use any of this.''

The DA broke in. "Edgar, he's been Miranda'd—''

"He's a minor—''

"He's seventeen. Old enough to understand—''

"Wade Anthon—'' Amos turned pale. "Oh, my God!''

"What?'' Martinez asked.

"Let's go, Sean,'' Trit insisted.

"The asshole set me up!'' the boy blurted out. *"Again."*

''What asshole are you talking about?'' Webster asked.

Sean slapped his cheeks with his palms. ''How could I be so *stupid*!''

''*Who* set you up?'' Martinez asked.

''Malcolm Carey! No wonder he asked me . . . he was gonna set me up. Just like he did the last time. God, am I stupid—''

Trit said, ''If you're going to talk, at least let me get you immunity.''

''Depends on who he implicates,'' Katherine stated.

''Who are you going to implicate, Sean?'' Martinez asked.

''Don't answer that!'' Trit said. ''I'll let him talk. But anything he says can't be entered in court unless we strike a deal—''

''No dice—''

''So you go to trial with Carey as your star witness?'' Trit muttered. ''Good luck to you.''

Martinez said, ''Can we just hear the kid out?''

Katherine said, ''No, we can't just hear the kid out. Unless we deal, the entire statement can't be entered as evidence.''

''So even if that happened, we'd be no worse off,'' Martinez plowed on. ''We'd just go to court with Carey.''

''Good point, Kate,'' Trit said.

''*Katherine!*''

''Deal?'' Trit asked.

Katherine threw up her hands.

''I'll take that as an affirmative response.''

Webster said, ''Tell us about David Garrison, Sean.''

''I don't know anything about *David* Garrison. That's what I'm *trying* to tell you.''

''He's your girlfriend's brother, isn't he?''

Sean became crimson, didn't answer.

''We're referring to Jeanine Garrison,'' Martinez said. ''Don't insult our intelligence and deny that you know her.''

''Of course I know her. She's my tennis partner.''

Webster said, "Sean, you've been blabbing 'bout her and you to just about everyone in your class."

"We're just friends."

"That's not what you've been telling people."

The boy was sweating. "Rumors get started. Maybe I went along with them. So what? That doesn't mean—"

"Sean, listen up," Martinez said. "You are seventeen, she is twenty-eight. If you two were in on some nasty thing . . . guess who's gonna wind up the baddie."

"We're not *in* on anything, let alone something nasty!" Still the boy continued to sweat.

Webster said, "And you expect us to b'lieve that?"

"Why would I lie?"

" 'Cause I reckon you got some kind of misguided notion that by protecting her, you're being noble. Well, you're not being noble. You're just being stupid. Might want to start thinkin' about savin' your own skin."

"He's not stupid," Martinez countered. "He loves her." He turned to the teen. "That's it, isn't it? You do love her, don't you?"

Silence. Sean swiped his eyes. Talked in a hush. "It wasn't supposed to happen like that. It's just that . . . David Garrison . . . he was really *bugging* her."

"Who is her?" Martinez asked. "Jeanine Garrison?"

Sean nodded.

"How was he bugging her?"

"Just asking her for money—all the time. Guy was a hype, shooting up dollars into his veins. Jeanine . . . like she helped him. But enough was enough, you know. Me? I just wanted to help."

Martinez commiserated. "Jeanine was so upset. You just couldn't turn her down."

"Turn her down?" Sean was confused.

"When she asked for your help," Martinez said.

"She never *asked* for my help." Sean was indignant. "She never asked anything from me."

Webster and Martinez exchanged glances. Webster said, "Sean, there's no sense protecting her—"

"I'm not protecting anyone. It was all *me*. Actually it was all Mal. *He* was the one—"

"Sean, *you're* the one in trouble," Martinez said. "You're looking at a long jail sentence . . . or maybe worse—"

"But I—"

"Sean, don't be an idiot," Webster said. "You can't mean to say you're going to let Jeanine get off scot-free—"

"But she didn't *do* anything."

"Sean, listen to me," Martinez said. "Your girlfriend's been two-timing you, making time with Wade Anthony—"

"No—"

"While you're holed up in jail, about to have your life flushed down the crapper."

"It doesn't have to be like this," Webster said, "Jeanine's the adult, you're the minor. She's the one responsible—"

"No—"

"Sean, she set you up!"

"No!" Sean shook his head vehemently. "No, *she* didn't do anything except *help* me—"

"Sean—"

"It was Malcolm who set me up." Sean's eyes bulged from their sockets. "Don't you *morons* get it?! It was Malcolm! IT WAS MALCOLM!"

The room was quiet. Trit broke it. "Y'all so anxious to hear him out, why don't you let him get through his story?"

Sean spat out, "You want facts, then listen to me, goddammit! *It . . . was . . . Malcolm!*" Suddenly, the boy slumped, shook his head, and rubbed his eyes. "I'm tired."

Trit said, "Go on, boy. You may never get this chance again. Tell them your story."

"I don't need lessons in talking. Problem is, I talk too *much*! Too much and to the wrong people. I musta been complaining to Mal. Just spouting shit. How hard things were on Jeanine. How much easier things would be on her if he croaked."

"He . . . being David Garrison," Webster said.

Sean nodded.

"Next thing I knew . . . he did croak. I remember thinking . . . what incredibly good luck!" He laughed bitterly. "Next day, Malcolm came over to me . . . asked me to pay up. Twenty-five grand in cash. I asked him what the hell he was *talking* about. He said 'David Garrison.' I almost dropped dead on the spot. I swear to holy Jesus, I never offered him a dime to kill anyone including David Garrison!"

A pause.

"Mal acted totally on his own. Totally. But to hear him talk . . . like I asked him to do it. But I didn't, I swear."

"And he asked you for twenty-five grand," Webster said.

Sean nodded. "Needless to say, I panicked. I didn't have that kind of bread at my fingertips. My dad holds the purse strings real tight. I can get around it, but I need time. I tried to explain that to Malcolm, but he got threatening. And when Mal threatens . . . he doesn't shit around. He gave me three days."

He wiped sweat off his brow.

"I didn't know what to do. So I went to Jeanine. Told her what happened."

Martinez said, "When you told Jeanine about your predicament, how'd she react?"

"She was *furious*! Really pissed! Ready to turn me in! I *deserved* to be turned in! 'Cause it was all my fault!"

The teen was breathing hard.

"*I* was in big trouble. With her, with everything."

Webster said, "Why did you feel you were in trouble if you didn't order the hit?"

"Because I made specific remarks."

"Like what?" Martinez prodded.

"Like how nice it would be if . . . someone stuffed something in his veins. Jeanine said that my joking could be misinterpreted. And since I was . . . connected to Jeanine in a personal way—and David had been bothering her—people might believe that I was actually capable of . . . planning it."

Moisture welled up in his eyes.

"She took pity on me when I was at my lowest. Even though she was real angry, she said she'd help me. Oh, God, when she told me that, I swear I fell down and kissed her feet. She *believed* me. You couldn't possibly realize what that meant."

"I b'lieve I'm getting the picture," Webster said.

Martinez said, "What'd she do for you, Sean?"

"She loaned me money to pay off Malcolm, that's what she did. Loaned me money from her own pocket."

"Twenty-five grand?"

"Actually ten."

"In cash?" Martinez asked.

Sean shook his head. "A bearer bond. Know what that is?"

"Yes," Webster answered. "Bearer bonds haven't been issued in years. Who'd she get the bond from?"

Sean shrugged. "I don't know."

"Jeanine Garrison gave you a bearer bond? And you gave it to Malcolm Carey?"

Sean nodded.

"And what did he say?" Martinez asked. "It wasn't the twenty-five grand he asked for."

"He said he'd accept it—this time. And that I should consider myself lucky."

He stopped talking.

"And?" Martinez asked.

"That was it," Sean said. "Jeanine never mentioned it again. And I never said anything."

"What about the rumors?" Martinez said. "Half the school thinks you popped David Garrison."

"Probably Mal started those. I played along. I was too scared not to. Mal wouldn't like it if the truth came out."

"You were never in David Garrison's apartment?" Webster asked.

"Never!"

"What were you doing with those pictures of Wade Anthony?" Martinez asked.

Sean sighed. "Earlier in the day . . . God, I'm such a

jerk . . .'' He sighed again. ''Jeanine and I got into this big fight over Wade. With the tournament . . . she had to spend time with him. All those pictures of them together. I know it's her profession but it pissed me off. His attitude. Like he *owned* her! Ordering her around. Mr. Fucking Roller-Legs! I guess I was complaining about him to Malcolm.''

''And?'' Martinez encouraged.

''What's to say?'' Sean said. ''Next thing I know, Mal's got pictures of Wade Anthony and this weird look on his face. *He* brought over those pictures. Not *me*. Then he starts telling me stuff . . . like how easy it would be to pop him. He was just starting to talk about it when the cops busted in—''

''So why did you flush the pictures down the toilet?'' Martinez persisted.

''I told you, I panicked. I just grabbed whatever shit I could reach and stuffed it in the toilet.''

''Now why don't I b'lieve that?'' Webster asked.

Sean said. ''Give me a lie detector test, if you don't believe me.''

Webster said, ''If you're lying, you won't beat the test, Sean.''

Sean smiled wryly. ''Sir, believe me. It'll be the *easiest* test I've ever passed.''

38

Closing the door to Decker's office, Marge said, "What is it with today's teenagers? Are all of them psycho?"

Oliver took a chair. "You know what? I believe Sean Amos—"

"He snowed you," Webster said.

"It's Carey who's doing the snowing. Kid's giving off more flakes than a bad case of dandruff."

Marge said, "Scott, we went into the interview charging Amos with a murder one. What was he supposed to say? I did it, yada yada yada?"

"Works in the prison movies—"

"Of course Sean's going to try to shift the blame," Marge went on. "The more he can pin on Carey, the better."

"Scott, you can't seriously believe Carey hit Garrison on his *own*." Webster frowned. "That don't make any sense."

"Carey thought he could squeeze a rich boy like Sean," Oliver said. "Plus he's a flaming psycho who likes hurting people."

Farrell Gaynor scanned through a thirty-page list of bearer bonds that had recently been called or redeemed. "This is going to take me a long time."

"Why are you even bothering?" Oliver said.

"The Loo says try to verify where the bond came from." Gaynor shrugged. "Have to start somewhere. At least we know it's state of California."

"Yeah, that narrows it to about thirty million—"

"Not quite that much."

Oliver said, "Decker *blew* it when he went with Carey. He should have gone with Sean Amos."

"Scotty, we needed Sean to get to Jeanine," Marge reminded him.

"Yeah, well, his strategy didn't work. We're not any closer to Jeanine Garrison than we were before."

"Not quite true," Martinez said. "If we go with Sean's story, we can hit Jeanine with aiding and abetting—accessory after the fact."

Webster said, "That's another thing I can't buy."

"What?" Martinez asked.

"That Jeanine's sole crime was aiding and abetting. By all accounts that woman is a manipulative bitch. Now you're telling me she's putting her own ass on the line to help some punk kid? C'mon . . . she had to be in on it. Sean is talking from his butt. Amos killed David and he did it for Jeanine."

Decker came into his office, glanced at the clock. One-thirty. "Anyone hungry? We can order in."

Oliver said, "How'd the polygraphs go?"

Decker said, "Elaine Reuter's still talking to Malcolm—"

"It's been over an hour!" Webster complained.

"To Elaine, that's a rush job," Decker said. "She likes to talk to her examinees at least a couple of hours before she does the test. So we'll just have to wait. Who's hungry?"

"Tuna on rye," Marge said.

"Times two," Martinez said. "Actually, give me two tunas. I'm hungry."

"Roast beef," Oliver said.

"Turkey," Webster said.

A pause.

Marge said, "Anything, Farrell?"

"Sounds good," Gaynor answered.

Oliver said, "*What* sounds good, Farrell?"

"Turkey. No mayo. Fruit instead of chips. Trying to watch my fat."

Marge picked up the phone to place the order. "Loo?"

"I'm fine." Decker showed her his brown bag, opened it. A barbecued-beef sandwich with pasta salad. The smell made his stomach growl, but, out of politeness, he waited for the others.

To Decker, Oliver said, "We were just discussing how you dealt with the wrong guy."

"No wrong guy in this case," Decker answered. "They're both psycho."

Oliver stated, "Question is which is the bigger psycho."

Decker said, "No, the question is who's more credible in front of a grand jury. Because Sean's going to tell his story and Carey'll tell his. Both tales have holes bigger than grottoes. And neither hands over Jeanine Garrison."

Martinez said, "Sean's story delivers Jeanine as an accessory after the fact. It's better than nothing."

"It's worse than nothing," Decker corrected. "Say we try her as an accessory. She gets on the stand, starts chucking up some sob story about not thinking it through because of the incredible stress she's been under since losing her parents, then her brother . . . blah, blah, blah."

Decker made fists.

"Let's say we even win. And she's convicted. Here's a woman without a record. If anything spells probation, this does. Then she goes merrily on her way." He paused. "Then, say six months later, we find out that she was involved in her brother's hit. Say we try to charge her. You know what's going to happen? Her lawyer'll raise hell, claim we can't retry her because of double jeopardy."

Marge said, "Pete, the hit's a new charge. That's not double jeopardy."

"It's still the same case. The law's not so clear-cut. It's like retrying O. J. for breaking and entering—"

"That's a damn good idea!" Oliver said.

Decker said, "All I'm saying is that a judge could easily rule that all the criminal charges against Jeanine should have been made at the onset of the first trial. Before we charge her with anything, I want to make sure she's completely innocent of David Garrison's death."

Martinez said, "Neither one's claiming she ordered the hit, Loo."

Decker frowned. "I know. Problem is, if we drop our deal with Carey, we won't be able to use *anything* he told us about David Garrison's hit. And Sean's confession isn't usable because we haven't struck an official deal with him. Besides, the idea *wasn't* to use Sean to get to Carey. We have plenty of narcotics charges on Carey. The idea was to use Sean to get to Jeanine. And he ain't playing that game."

"Maybe she wasn't involved, Loo," Martinez said.

Decker slumped down into his desk chair. "We're going to have to drop David Garrison until we get better evidence. Just bring the kids up on drug charges."

"We got lots on Carey, but not much happenin' against Sean Amos." Webster held his anger in check. "First-time drug conviction. . . . kid'll probably get probation. Not bad for a cold-blooded murderer—"

"Tom—"

"David Garrison's dead and now no one is gonna take the fall."

Decker scowled. "So what do you suggest, Thomas?"

"Run with Carey."

Gaynor said, "What about the gun recovered at the bust?"

"What about it?" Oliver said.

"I just think it's interesting that it was called in stolen about two months ago—"

Decker interrupted, "Farrell, *when* did this come in?"

"About a half hour ago." Gaynor shrugged. "Sorry. Must have slipped my mind."

Decker held his temper. "Who reported it stolen?"

"Lily Amos."

The room went quiet.

"So it was *Sean's* gun?" Marge said.

"No, it was Lily's gun," Farrell said.

"I knew that boy was evil," Webster gloated. "Now y'all gotta ask yourselves, why would Sean bring a gun to the party *unless* he was planning to do something with it?"

"Meaning?" Oliver probed.

"Meaning Sean was gonna give it to Malcolm to off Wade Anthony. Just like Malcolm said. Of *course* Sean has to claim that he didn't know anything about the pictures of Wade Anthony. Yet the Loo and Marge bust in, Amos has pictures of Anthony, his daily schedule, and a gun."

Martinez said, "We know that Amos was upset at Jeanine a few hours earlier. The Loo saw them arguing."

Webster said, "That argument was the final straw. Amos went berserk. He planned another hit . . . just like Carey said—"

Oliver said, "You're missing a crucial point, Tom. Paraffin test shows that Carey fired the gun."

"So what? He heard police coming, he just picked up whatever weapon was handy and let it rip. Loo, before you came in, I was saying that I just couldn't buy Sean's story. If Sean didn't hire Carey for the hit, why would Carey have gotten involved?"

"Money," Oliver said. "Sean's loaded. Mal was squeezing him."

Decker said, "And if Sean wasn't *hiring* Carey to pop Anthony, what was Sean doing with Anthony's pictures, the daily schedule, and a gun?"

Oliver said, "Maybe Mal was setting up Sean for a second squeeze."

The other detectives groaned.

Webster became frustrated. "You're being a broken record, Scott."

Suddenly, the light went on. Decker slapped his forehead. "Ker-rist! Scott's right!"

"I am?" Oliver grinned. "I mean, of course I'm right." He paused. "Why?"

Someone knocked at the door. Lunch had arrived. After five minutes of sorting out what belonged to whom, Decker spoke as everyone munched. Excitedly he said, "Who reported the gun stolen?"

"Lily Amos," Farrell said, between bites of turkey. "Didn't I just tell you that or is my memory that bad?"

Decker smiled. "It was a rhetorical question, Farrell. Look at this, people. Say Sean wants his mother's gun . . . why would he have to *steal* it?"

Decker dug into his sandwich. Chewed rapidly, then swallowed.

"Makes much more sense for Sean to borrow the weapon, then bring it back unnoticed. Which means—"

Marge broke in, "It means the gun was stolen by someone other than Sean."

"Malcolm Carey!" Oliver said. "Bastard stole the gun from Sean's house."

Decker said, "And that's why *Carey* fired at us. Because at that point, the gun didn't belong to Sean, it belonged to Carey."

Martinez gulped down tepid coffee. "I'm lost. Let's start with the basics. Wade Anthony. Who was planning his hit?"

Decker said, "Malcolm Carey—"

"C'mon, Loo!" Webster was dubious. "Why would Carey give a solitary shit about Wade Anthony?"

"He doesn't give a shit about Anthony, Tom," Decker said. "Carey was using him to set up Amos. Just like he did the first time with David Garrison—"

Webster broke in, "Loo, why would Carey take it upon himself to hit Garrison on his own? It just doesn't make sense!"

Decker said, "Malcolm Carey didn't hit Garrison on his *own*. He had a partner—"

"Jeanine!" Marge cried. "Carey was in on David Garrison's hit *with* Jeanine from the beginning!"

"Jackpot!"

Oliver said, "And that was why Jeanine loaned Sean the money. She wasn't helping Amos out. She was furthering the myth of being innocent. Because she had planned it with Carey from the beginning."

Ideas poured into Marge's brain like tumbling waves. "To save her butt, she made it seem as if the idea came from Sean's ramblings! So if the investigation ever turned up David's OD as a murder, she could pin it on Sean."

"And the ten-thousand-dollar bearer bond was the hit price from the beginning," Oliver said. "Instead of paying Malcolm directly, she acted like she was helping out Sean. Keeping him permanently in her debt." He grinned at Webster. "So whaddaya think, Tulane Tom?"

"Gotta admit. The scenario's starting to sound like Jeanine."

Decker said, "Manipulating men, Tom. You said it from the beginning. She loves to manipulate men. Just like with Harlan Manz. From the beginning, I'm sure she set Harlan up. She probably knew that Harlan had been fired from his job at Estelle's, had been bitter over his dismissal. You want to know how I think Estelle's went down?"

Everybody waited.

Decker said, "Jeanine's a primo manipulator. She wants her parents out of the way, but she wants it to look like a random murder. Better than a murder, how about a mass murder using Harlan Manz as a mass murderer? Bet she knew he fit the profile."

"That's absolutely malevolent," Marge said.

"It's absolutely Jeanine," Decker said. "So what does she do? She has an affair with Harlan Manz. We know from talking to Harlan's girlfriend that Harlan fooled around. And we also know from talking to everyone else that Harlan loved money and big shots."

Oliver stated, "Harlan musta thought he died and went to heaven when he met this dream girl."

Decker said, "Schmuck must have been made delirious by his good fortune. Only snag was that he had to keep it quiet. But even that was okay. Because Harlan had a girlfriend and it made it exciting."

Martinez said, "Okay. They have an affair. Then suddenly Harlan turns into a mass murderer?"

Decker said, "Check this out, Bert. Jeanine and Harlan have this affair. This way she can get Harlan to talk. Which is no big accomplishment. We know from our interviews that Harlan loved to talk."

"So they talk," Marge said. "Then what?"

"She gets him to open up about his unfair experience at Estelle's. She works him up. She works him up until people recall Harlan talking about how bitter he was at Estelle's for canning him so unjustly. She works him up until one day, she convinces him to go into the restaurant . . . man, it's all coming down."

Decker paused, gulped down water.

"She convinces him to go to the restaurant and confront the management. She even picks out his clothes. A noticeable *green* jacket. And the day Jeanine chose for him just happened to be a day her parents made reservations at Estelle's. Which I bet wasn't unusual. They probably ate at Estelle's often. Maybe they even had a standing reservation."

"A cold woman," Oliver said.

Decker said, "Meanwhile, Jeanine has contracted an unknown hit man to follow Harlan. She tells the second guy what Harlan's wearing—"

Marge said, "Remember what Tess Wetzel said about that odd man. *He* was wearing a green jacket."

Decker said, "Exactly. Any of you think that was just a coincidence?"

No one spoke.

Decker said, "At the agreed-on moment, Mr. Unknown Hit Man makes his move and starts popping people—"

"So you're saying we have only one shooter?" Marge asked. "So how do you explain the bullet-wound patterns on the Garrisons? The ones that led you to speculate on a second shooter in the first place?"

Decker thought a moment. "Could be the shooter had two guns. He used one to ice Harlan and left it at the scene. The other, he took with him. That's how he could do so much damage so fast. Also, he probably shot from all sides and angles. The shooter knew Harlan was going to be the fall guy. Betcha he popped Manz and the Garrisons early on. The Garrisons he wanted dead for Jeanine. Harlan . . . he wanted him dead and out in the open. To take the blame."

Martinez said, ''Deck, I think *someone* would have noticed this real hit man.''

''Someone did, Bert,'' Decker said. ''Tess Wetzel noticed a second man. And maybe a few others did as well. But no one was *sure*. Because they were dressed similarly. And once the bullets start flying, you duck, close your eyes, and pray.''

Marge said, ''So Harlan was a dupe.''

Decker said, ''Just like Sean Amos. It's Carey who's the real psycho. Leading us to believe that he was in cahoots with Sean. When in reality Carey was collaborating with *Jeanine*. Which is why he struck a deal with us. Because he really did pop David Garrison. So he saved his butt by turning state's witness against Sean, who didn't have anything to do with it. Worked us *perfectly*, the little fuck!''

''You're making logical leaps,'' Webster said.

'' 'Course I'm making some leaps,'' Decker answered. ''But I'm also making some sense. You know what we're going to do? Instead of going with Carey's story, we're going to *drop* the murder one charge against him. Try him on the drug charges alone. I'm going to find the nastiest antidrug judge in the court system. Someone who'll lock that bastard up and throw away the key.''

''What about Sean?'' Webster wanted to know.

''He'll be tried on his drug charges, resisting arrest . . . probably get off light.''

''Stinks,'' Webster said. ''Carey's deal gives the kid *seven* years in prison. If David Garrison was a contract hit with Jeanine as the brains behind the operation, Carey should have rolled over and given us Jeanine to save his own butt.''

Marge's eyes grew wide. ''He didn't do that because he was beholden to Jeanine in a *big* way. As in Estelle's—''

''Carey as Estelle's *hit* man?'' Webster shrugged. ''Marge, where is the evidence?''

Decker said, ''Lily Amos's gun was stolen about two weeks before Estelle's went down. We know we recovered more bullets than can be accounted for by the one gun we recovered. And Carey's weapon was a semi-automatic. Let's go back to Ballistics.''

Martinez said, ''Something is still bothering me. By all accounts, Jeanine got *along* with her parents. The woman had everything she wanted. Why would she whack her parents?''

Decker said, ''From the start, we knew that Jeanine was dependent on Dad's good graces to run her charities. David Garrison said that Daddy was getting tired of Jeanine's tantrums. Maybe she figured out she couldn't manipulate Daddy forever. Maybe Daddy actually stood up and told her *no*.''

❧39

"Even forgetting about the admissibility of polygraphs as evidence . . ."

Elaine Reuter scratched a nest of curls, licked her prominent teeth with a snakelike tongue. She had a long face and wide eyes. Today, she wore a zebra-striped shirt under a black suit, reinforcing her equine features.

"Tell you the truth, I wouldn't go to court on either one of these. Too murky."

Decker said, "*Both* of them were inconclusive?"

"Both had what I'd call unusual reactions—not clearly lying but nervous."

"How many questions did you ask?"

"Pertinent questions? Six. Which in this case is a lot. If I *had* to go with one, I'd pick Sean Amos. Talking to him . . . maybe he's redeemable. I think he might be lying, but could be he's very confused. Carey, on the other hand, is a hard case. I think he beat the test."

Decker nodded.

Elaine said, "Don't tell me. You dealt with Carey."

"Yes, I went with Carey. But it doesn't matter because we're not going to charge him with murder."

"You've got him on drugs, haven't you?"

"Yep."

"Then the kid'll serve *some* time." She smiled wanly. "Just probably turn him into a better psycho."

"Probably."

Elaine sighed. "I'm sorry. It's always hard when the big one gets away."

"The big one isn't even in the picture." Decker shrugged. "Damn shame. But life goes on."

The chill of fall tickled Decker's nose as he got out of the unmarked. The air smelled sweet—fresh, cool, and slightly mulchy from fallen flora. Evening mist blanketed his face. Though tired—having slept only three hours in the last two days—he nevertheless felt content. Life was good. He took a final whiff, then checked his watch. He had made it to his front door before six.

The house held the aroma of home cooking and love. The dining-room table had been set for dinner. Included was a place mat for him. That made him smile. He walked into the kitchen, expecting to find his wife. Instead, he found his daughter, his sons, and Joachim Rush sitting around the small kitchen table, playing Scrabble. Rush had brought along a girl. A pint-size thing who looked to be around fourteen. She had long blond hair and hazel eyes. Not a drop of makeup. She was also the first one who graced him with a smile. Decker smiled back.

Cindy stood, nodded, looking very policelike and official. "Hello, sir."

Decker nodded. "Officer Cohen . . ."

Sam looked up. "You need anything, Dad?"

"No, I'm fine. Where's your mom?"

"Out in the barn with Hannah."

The horses. Guilt pricking his skin. It had been a while since Decker had taken time to exercise and feed them. Rina had picked up the slack. He thought about joining her. In a minute. He said, "I thought the game was for four maximum."

"I'm just kibitzing," the girl answered. She introduced herself as Allison Berg.

Joachim said, "Have a seat, sir."

Decker regarded the teen. "You think it's a good idea for you to be here, Joachim?"

"Probably not."

"I invited him," Cindy said. "He was feeling a little antsy after the bust so I took him out for a ride. We wound up here. I hope that's not a problem."

"No, not at all."

"Did everything go okay?" Joachim asked. "I mean with the bust? No one at school could concentrate on anything else today. That's all anyone could talk about. Rumor has it that the haul was tremendous. And that Carey'll be gray before he sees the light of day. Any of that true?"

"It was a good tip," Decker said. "A very good tip and a good bust. But it's not in your best interests to be associated with the police. Let alone at my house. For your own sake."

The boy tried to hide his nervousness. "No one mentioned me, right?"

"No, Joachim. Your name never came up."

The teen looked relieved. Cindy said, "C'mon, Joachim. I'll take you home."

Decker turned to his daughter, "A word with you, Officer?" They stepped into the dining room. Decker said, "He call you or did you call him?"

"He called me. He was really nervous, Daddy. I was worried he'd do something stupid. Blurt out something. So I suggested we go for a ride to talk it out. To calm him down actually. I figured I owed him that much."

"You did the right thing. Is he okay?"

"Yeah, he seems to be fine now."

"I'll keep a watch on him. Thanks."

"No one mentioned his name?"

"Nah, he wasn't even in the viewfinder, let alone in the picture."

"You look frustrated."

"Tired."

"Maybe tired and frustrated. You didn't get her."

"All things come to those who wait. And if you wait long enough, you die so it doesn't matter anyway."

"Love that optimistic attitude."

The front door opened, Rina came in, Hannah tugging at her arm, giving one of her famous four-year-old lectures.

She saw her father and Hannah jumped into his arms. "Daddy! We fed the horses!"

"That's great."

"They ate a lot. Their tummies were reeeeal full."

"Good to have a full tummy."

Rina brushed his lips. "You're home. How wonderful!" She looked at her stepdaughter. "How's the game going?"

"I'm leaving with Joachim."

"Are you coming back for dinner?"

"Not tonight, Rina. But thank you." She went back into the kitchen.

Decker plopped his younger daughter on top of his shoulders. Hannah said, "We found garbage outside, Daddy."

He turned to Rina. "Is that good or bad?"

"Garbage is packing peanuts. She collects them, then glues them onto paper for her artwork. I wonder if Warhol started this way."

"So it's a good thing to find garbage."

"Very good."

"I found four garbages," Hannah continued.

"Wonderful, Hannah Rosie. I'm very proud of you." Decker paused. "If Cindy came with Joachim . . . who's the girl in our kitchen?"

"Allison Berg. She goes to the yeshiva's high school with the boys—I mean, the girls' section of the boys' school . . . I'm getting this wrong—"

"Rina, I know that the boys and girls are in separate classes." A smile formed on Decker's lips. "Obviously not that separate. Sammy bring her?"

"No, Jacob did."

"*Jacob?*" Decker grinned. "No wonder he was so motivated to move."

"Behave yourself."

"Why? That never got me anywhere."

The kitchen door opened and out came the wordsmiths. Sammy held the car keys. "I'm taking everyone home. Be back in around a half hour."

"No longer, Shmuel," Rina said. "I'm sure your father's hungry."

"I can wait. But not too long." Decker held out his hand to Joachim. "Call me if you need anything."

"Got it."

"Half hour," Rina reiterated. Sammy nodded, then left with his brother, Allison, and Joachim.

Cindy removed the keys from her purse, kissed Hannah's baby-soft thigh. "Couldn't you just eat her—"

"Noooo, don't eat me."

"It's a metaphor, kid." Cindy smiled. "Gotta go . . . oh, Grandma called."

"What did she want?" Decker asked, anxiously.

Cindy chuckled. "The message was for Rina, Daddy. She said she's bringing her own corn, squash, green beans, and pumpkin for Thanksgiving dinner next week. So don't waste your money and buy them."

"That's a direct quote?" Rina said.

"Indeed it is." Cindy blew a kiss to Hannah. The tot touched her fingers to pouty lips and returned the gesture. Waving, Cindy walked out the door.

Decker waited a moment, then said, "We have groceries here. Do you know how much a pumpkin weighs?"

"She probably grew the vegetables in her garden," Rina said. "If it makes her feel good and useful to bring them, I say, more power to her."

"Agreed."

Silence.

Rina said, "I'm sure if anything was serious, she would have told us by now."

"Not true. She could be on her deathbed and say straight-faced that everything was fine."

"Then there's nothing we can do."

Decker nodded, helpless and anxious.

Though upset, Rina spoke in a cheery voice. "Good news. Your brother's wife called this morning. Randy managed to trade shifts so they're all coming out as well. Looks like we'll have a full house next week."

Decker said, "Oh, happy days!"

"They're your relatives!" Rina took off her coat, put it in the closet. "Also, I invited Marge for dinner. She said she'd love to come, but she already promised Scott Oliver that she'd have Thanksgiving with him. So I was kind of stuck. I invited him, too."

"Why don't we just open up a mission and dish out turkey to indigents?"

"It's not a bad idea. Giving a little charity when we have so much."

"Saint Rina."

She whacked him gently. "And while you're feeling so ebullient, I might as well tell you that we've received a counter offer—"

"So fast?"

"He's motivated."

"I'm sure he is. He found a sucker—"

"Peter—"

"Did he come down?"

"He split the difference—"

"It's too much!"

"Peter—"

"All right, just give me the papers and I'll sign the damn thing." He remembered he was holding Hannah. "The darn thing. I'll sign the *darn* thing. How about a video, pumpkin?"

The child's face lit up. "I want to watch *Wonderful World of Bugs*. You watch it with me, Daddy?"

Decker stifled a groan. She'd seen the tape a hundred times, feasting with delight on such gruesome visuals as a hill of ants devouring dead beetles and a Venus flytrap snaring its unsuspecting victim in cold blood. "I'll come watch in a few minutes. First I want to talk to Mommy, okay?"

"Okay."

"Take off her coat, Peter. I don't want her to get overheated."

"Yeah, yeah." Decker set up the machine, placed the child—sans jacket—in front of the boob tube, waited for the ominous theme music to start. As soon as it did, Hannah squealed with joy. Then came the credits with pictures. The child sang out, "There's the beetle. And there's the mill-i-pede. Oh, Daddy, the little praying mantis. He's so *cute*—"

"I'll be right back, sweetie—"

"Look, Daddy, the hissing cockroach!"

"Lovely, Hannah. I'll come watch in a minute." Decker went into the kitchen where Rina was putting the finishing touches on dinner. He said, "That child is strange."

"She likes bugs. You should be delighted she isn't squeamish."

"Thrilled."

Rina regarded her husband. "It didn't go well, did it?"

"On the contrary, the bust went very well. We took a nasty kid off the streets and that's very good."

Rina paused, "And Jeanine?"

Decker shrugged. "God works in mysterious ways. Who am I to judge?"

"So she's a lost cause?"

Decker said, "I have a glimmer of hope. Ballistics is running a gun we picked up at the bust. I want to see if it matches any of the strays we bagged at Estelle's. I don't expect anything." He paused. "I never expect anything. That way, I'm rarely disappointed."

Slowly, Marge walked into Decker's office. He hung up the phone, offered her a seat and a newspaper. "She's taking it on the road."

"Pardon?"

"To wit: Today's sports section. The wheelchair tournament was so successful, she's taking it on the road with Wade." Decker waited a beat. "The article refers to Wade as her *fiancé*. Think I should send him a card?"

"Not unless it's for sympathy."

Decker laughed softly. "Anyway, you're just the woman I was looking for. You're coming over on Thursday, aren't you?"

"Of course. What can I bring?"

"You're bringing Scott. I think that's enough—"

"Pete, what could I do—"

"Nah, I'm just teasing you. Bring some flowers."

Decker looked her in the eye. "Before you come, let's get one thing straight. My mother's going to be there—"

"Really?" Marge grinned. "This should be very interesting—"

"And my brother," Decker said. "You or Scotty breathe a word of anything that has to do with my youth, your jobs are on the line."

Marge laughed, then grew serious. Tossed the paper on his desk.

"What?" Decker asked.

She said, "Not the kind of news you were hoping for before a holiday, but . . . Ballistics called. They couldn't find anything—"

Decker hit his desk. "They couldn't have tested everything! Not *that* fast."

"No, they just picked out a couple of random samples—"

"A *couple* of random samples—"

"Pete—"

"A *couple*? As in *two*?"

"Maybe a few more than that—"

"Marge, we recovered over a hundred bullets."

She sighed. "Look, Scott and I worked our butts off. Pressured them to move for us especially because of the holiday week. This was the best we could do."

Decker counted to ten. "You did great. I couldn't have done any better."

"Pete, we can press it. But I don't know how much good it'll do. You know how slowly the wheels turn over there."

Decker nodded. The state crime labs were in sorry shape—backlogged and understaffed. Innocent people languished in jail, hardcase criminals were prematurely released because the labs didn't have the manpower to process the evidence fast enough for court-date trials. A case like Estelle's—two months old with an established perpetrator—was very low priority.

Decker said, "We've got time. We can wait for them to finish the job."

"Good, 'cause it's likely to take months, maybe years."

Decker cursed under his breath. "Maybe we should consider a private lab."

"Believe it or not, I checked into it. It's really expensive. I just don't have that kind of money lying around."

Decker thought of his newly purchased shack lying on a small plot of forest grounds. Unless he got it together, it was going to remain a shack. "Neither do I."

"Time to move on." Marge shrugged. "We tried our best. Nothing else we can do."

"We can wait for a miracle."

Marge chuckled, "Sure. Let's wait for a miracle. Won't cost me money, I can't get pregnant from it, and most important, it won't put any fat on my hips."

❧40

Fixed in front of the TV—the Macy's Thanksgiving Day Parade—Hannah was captivated by a dinosaur float that breathed out dry-ice smoke. She kept trying to convince everyone around that the dinosaur wasn't real. But there was too much commotion in the room, and her tiny voice was blighted by adult drone.

Rina kissed her forehead.

"He's not real," Hannah said.

"No, he's not real."

"He's pretend."

"Yes, honey."

"Not real."

Rina smiled, rubbed her temples. Lots of people. Peter's parents, Randy, his wife, Lurene, and their three school-aged children. Plus Clark—Randy's seventeen-year-old son from his first marriage. Clark, Sam and Jacob, were slouched across the living-room furniture, tossing a football back and forth. Lurene was out in the orchard with her kids, picking oranges.

Lyle Decker walked into the dining room, studying a blueprint as he stood in front of the TV. His burly body completely obscured Hannah's view of her beloved dinosaur. She shrieked out, "I can't see, I can't see."

Rina gently moved her father-in-law away from the screen. "Why don't you sit outside on the patio, Dad?"

"Where?" he yelled out.

"Come." Rina held his arm, led him out the side door into the backyard. A bricked patio held a round umbrella table and six plastic chairs. "Have a seat here. It's quiet and comfortable. You want some more coffee?"

"Coffee?"

"Yes, coffee. I've just brewed a fresh pot—"

"I'll take a cup of coffee."

"Great." Rina started to walk away.

Lyle said, "Where's Peter?"

"He's in the barn with Randy—"

"Where?"

"Over there in the barn, Dad. You want me to get him for you?"

"When are we going to the house?"

"Do you mean the new house?"

"Yeah. The new house." Lyle held up the blueprint. "This house."

"I think Peter was planning on taking you there in about a half hour."

"Before the game then?"

"Yes, before the game. I know you like the game."

Lyle laughed heartily. "What's Thanksgiving without turkey and the game?"

"Not much," Rina smiled. Such a sweet, sweet man, with twinkly blue eyes, a round, red face and thin, silver hair. He announced, "I found the sewer line."

It took a moment for Rina to switch gears. "Oh. That's great. Is the bathroom going to be a problem?"

"Nah!" Again the laughter. "We should be able to knock it out in no time."

Rina's smile was genuine. "I'll get you the coffee."

"I'd *love* a cup of coffee."

"Right away." She came into the kitchen through the back door. Ida Decker was basting an eighteen-pound stuffed tom turkey with seasoned broth. Pete's mother was tall and bony, her knobby hands made even more gnarled by persistent, long-standing arthritis. Short gray hair framed a noble face which was long and aristocratic. High cheekbones, wide-set, midnight blue eyes. A very handsome woman. She held her mouth tight, lips pressed together. Lips that rarely expressed emotion, let alone love. But lips that never gossiped and never complained.

Rina asked, "How's it looking, Mom?"

"It'll pass muster."

"Dad wants another cup of coffee—"

"He's already had three."

"It's decaf."

"The heart's not the problem. It's the stomach. Too much acid."

Rina said, "I'll make him herbal tea if you're concerned."

"He hates tea," Ida snorted, waved her hand in the air. "Oh, give him the coffee. It *is* a holiday. You want to check the pies in the other oven for me, Rina? They're no good if they're overcooked. Like eating rubber."

Rina opened the door to the twin side of her double oven. "They look perfect! The crust is golden, the filling has set but is still moist." She took one out. "A-one—"

"They may look perfect but I don't know how they'll taste. I usually make my pies with evaporated milk."

"I'm sure they'll be fine—"

"Never made pies with Mocha Mix before."

"I'm sure these will be the best ever."

"Well, we'll see."

Rina took the pies out of the oven, then poured a cup of coffee. "I'll just take this out to Dad."

Ida let out another small snort and started noodling with the candied yams. Rina returned outside. At the moment, Peter and Randy were standing over their father's shoulders as Lyle pointed out details in the blueprint, lecturing about structural beams. Ginger had fallen asleep under the table. Since both Randy and Peter were adopted, they held no physical resemblance to each other except for their stature. Peter was the taller of the duo, but topping six two, Randy was no tiny toon. The man was barrel-chested with short legs and long arms. He had short black hair, a wide forehead, and a ruddy complexion. Big brown eyes that sparkled. A coarse black mustache sat over his upper lip.

Lyle had moved on to floor joists.

Rina set down the coffee cup.

Randy said, "That looks good."

"I'll get you a cup."

"I'll get it," Decker said.

Randy smiled. "She got you trained, bro?"

Decker shot him a hard look, then slipped his arm around his wife's shoulders. Whispered, "Let's walk the *long* way."

Rina nodded enthusiastically. Randy shouted out, "Cream and sugar, Peter."

"No prob." With Ginger on his heels, Decker and his wife returned to the house via the side door, into the dining room. Ida had perched Hannah on her lap, both of them entranced by the floats. Ginger sniffed Hannah, then Ida. The old woman gave him a gentle tap on her nose.

"Down."

To Decker's surprise, the dog obeyed. "Never works for me."

"That's because he don't take you seriously." Ida looked away from the TV, announced, "Poor Hannah. Just sitting here. She wasn't getting a lick of attention."

Rina nodded. "Thanks for helping out."

Hannah said, "I like the birdies, Grandma. They're flying high in the sky."

Ida's instant smile was very real but very brief. She kissed her granddaughter's cheek. "Wouldn't you just love to go fly with them, Hannie? Just go over the sun and visit the moon and stars?"

Hannah pondered the statement. "Could Mommy go, too?"

Ida bit back a smile. " 'Course Mommy could come."

Rina said, "You have some dreams, Mom?"

Ida scowled, "Just trying to amuse my granddaughter. Might want to baste the turkey. And glaze it, too. You know how to glaze it with a little sugar syrup and orange juice?"

"Sure." Rina went into the kitchen. Decker made his move. He said, "How you doing, Mom? You all right?"

"Of course I'm all right." Ida answered. "Why shouldn't I be all right?"

"So you're feeling fine?"

"Stop repeating yourself!"

Hannah said, "Look at that doggie balloon, Grandma."

"Now I like that one. What kind of dog is that, Peter?"

"Looks like a spaniel of some sort."

"Don't look like any dog I've ever seen."

"Artistic license."

Ida snorted. Decker used that as his exit line, joined his wife in the kitchen. He leaned against the counter. "*How* many days are they staying?"

Rina looked up from the oven, closed the door, and stood. "Think of us as Norman Rockwell with an edge."

Decker looked at the ceiling. "Is she giving you a hard time?"

"No, she's just angry that she can't use evaporated milk for her pies."

"I'm sor—"

"I'm teasing, Peter." Rina paused. "Actually, she's doing a bang-up job in the kitchen. She moves well for seventy-five."

Decker sighed. "I see her taking pills. She tell you what that's all about?"

Rina shook her head. "I'm watching her, Peter. Making sure she's not overdoing it. And I think she's smarter about it than she lets on. Sitting down with Hannah. She knows how to pace herself."

"So you think something's wrong?"

"Nothing obvious. Whatever it is, she's not going to tell us if we push. And she seems happy to be here . . . thrilled with Hannah. And I'm the first to admit that the feeling is mutual. Hannah loves her."

From the dining room, Randy shouted, "Where's the coffee?"

Ida told him to pipe down.

Decker rolled his eyes, brought in the coffee cup, and slapped his brother's gut. "What am I? Your friggin' maid?"

Randy broke into laughter.

"Hush up, the lot of you," Ida said. "Can't you see the child is trying to watch."

They piled into the living room. Decker said, "Take it outside, boys!"

Instead, Sammy hurled a fast one to Randy, his *kippah* nearly flying off his head. Randy shot it back to Decker, who caught it easily. Decker said, "What are you *doing*?"

Randy relieved him of the ball, smacked Decker back. "Loosen up." He lobbed it to Jacob.

The doorbell rang.

Marge and Oliver. She was carrying a huge bouquet of fall-colored mums. "We're a little early."

Decker looked at his watch. More like two hours early. "Hey, glad you could make it. We're not doing much."

Jacob threw the ball to Oliver, who buzzed it to Clark, the boy's long blond bangs hanging over his eyes. The teen threw it back to Sammy.

Decker said, "Guys, take it *outside*!"

"C'mon," Randy said. "Let's get a game going. We'll choose up sides." He offered his hand to Oliver. "Randy Decker."

"Scott Oliver."

"You look like one of us."

"Got the look, huh?"

"Got the look. Let me guess. GTA?"

"No, Homicide."

"Ah, one of my brother's dicks—"

Oliver broke into laughter. "Never knew he had more than one."

Randy guffawed out loud. Decker said, "Glad you're having fun."

Sam lobbed the ball back to Clark, who threw a bullet to his father. It missed Peter's head by an inch. Decker said, *"Outside! Now!"*

Randy smiled. "You in, Peter?"

"Yeah, yeah, in a minute. Just get out of here. And take the dog."

Randy whistled to Ginger. The setter came in a flash.

Marge handed the flowers to Decker, said, "I'm in."

Randy said, "You?"

Oliver said, "She's not my wife, she's my partner."

"Ah, sorry." Randy held out his hand. "Randy Decker."

"Yeah, the Narc in Miami. Marge Dunn—"

"So *you're* the famous Marge? Nice to meet you." Randy shook her hand vigorously. "You play forward, I can play defense. Are you coming, Dad?"

"I thought we were going to the house." Lyle was disappointed.

"In about a half hour, Dad," Decker said.

"Let's go outside, Dad," Randy said. "You'll be on my team. You can help me with defense—"

"Randy!" Decker scolded. "He's seventy-seven—"

"I'll take care of it. Don't worry. Are you coming or not?"

Decker showed him an armful of flowers. "I got to put these in a vase."

Randy patted his brother's butt. "I didn't know you were so *inclined*."

Decker was about to swear but realized his father was in the room. "I'll be there in a minute."

When they had all left, Decker dropped onto the couch. "Blessed *silence*!"

His solitude was short-lived. The front door opened.

"Cindy!" Decker exclaimed.

"Hi there." Cindy looked at the mums. "How sweet. For me?"

Decker said, "They're actually from Marge—"

"I'm kidding, Daddy." Cindy paused, noticing her father's off-kilter expression. "You look shell-shocked."

Decker didn't answer.

Cindy relieved her father of the flora. She said, "Maybe I should put those in a vase for you."

"That would be great." Decker blinked several times. "It's all coming back to me."

"What?" Cindy asked.

"Why I moved out of state." Decker focused his eyes

on his daughter. "I thought you were with your mom today."

"They're going to a friend's at six for the dinner. I told her I'd be back before then."

"Did she know you were coming here?"

"I think so. But she was smart enough not to ask."

"Good for Jan." Suddenly, Decker embraced his daughter, then moved away.

"What was that for?" Cindy said, smiling.

"For being you. For helping me out like you did."

Cindy looked away. "Sorry I couldn't do more—"

"You did plenty. We got a great bust."

"What's happening with Carey?"

"Ten to twenty-five. He'll be eligible for parole in four and a half years—"

"That's outrageous!" Cindy shrieked.

Decker shrugged. "It's not a slap on the wrist. I've had worse outcomes."

"Considering what he probably did, it's a horrid miscarriage of justice."

"We can't prosecute on a 'probably.' After a couple of months on the street, you'll learn that quickly enough." Decker swallowed hard. "I'm very *proud* of you. You're a wonderful daughter, a fine human being, and you'll make a great cop—"

"Oh, God, don't *start*." Cindy's eyes started to water.

Decker laughed, "You gotta control that leaky tap of yours."

"I know, I know." Cindy wiped her eyes. "It's terrible."

"No, it's not terrible." Decker kissed his daughter's cheek. "But it's not a desirable asset for a cop."

She showed him the flowers. "I'll just go put these in water."

"While you're there, say hello to Grandma."

"Grandma's *here*?"

"In the flesh. Along with Randy, Lurene, and your cousins. They're out playing football. Why don't you join them?"

"Think I'll pass. Rather grump with Grandma."

Decker laughed and so did Cindy. She stood on her toes, kissed her father. "I love you."

"I love you, too."

Gently, she hit him over the head with the flowers, then headed for the kitchen. Once again, Decker was alone. He took a deep breath in, then let it out slowly.

Repeated the inhalation . . . the exhala—

The damn doorbell!

He swung open the door, eyes growing in circumference as he regarded the visitor. Then he gave him a bear hug but not too hard. Because the man was as thin as a piece of hay, his sport coat hanging on his body like a zoot suit. His hair had been braided tightly, his beard neatly combed and smelling like pine needles.

Abel broke the embrace, leaned against his cane. "Don't you look like a million bucks."

"Green and wrinkled," Decker answered. "I don't believe . . . to what do I owe this unexpected surprise? Are you trying to mooch a holiday meal or something?"

"More like the or something."

Decker continued to look at him. "What's wrong? Are you in trouble?"

Abel smiled. "Not this time. Actually, I've been working, found a temporary job."

"Really? Doing what?"

"Know that big wheelchair tennis tournament that went down 'bout two weeks ago?"

Decker tried to keep his face flat. "Of course. It was for the victims of the Estelle's massacre."

"Yeah, that was some horrific thing, wasn't it?"

"Horrific is a good adjective, yes." Decker paused. "How'd you get involved with the tournament?"

Abel hit his false leg. "Through the network. I heard they were hiring gimps. Sounded like it was an easy way to pick up some spare change. Lots of food, too. The woman . . . Jeanine Garrison . . . man, she catered one party after another. 'Course, we peons weren't invited to the festivities. But there was always plenty of leftover grub. Her beau, Wade Anthony, he brought us the leavings the next day.''

"Considerate of him.''

"Yeah. If it had been up to her, she would have pitched it in the garbage. She is one interesting lady.''

"Yes, she is.''

"And beautiful, too.''

"Yes.''

Abel stroked his beard. "Actually, she's kinda the reason why I'm here, doc.''

A long, long pause.

"Oh?'' Decker said.

Abel shifted his weight on his cane. Decker hit his forehead. "Where are my manners? Come in. Sit down.''

"I'm all right. Let me just get this off my chest . . . 'bout this Jeanine. You know when you're doing manual labor, no one pays you too much mind. Certain people think that when you work with your hands, it means you don't have a brain. They talk freely . . . like you're not there. So you pick up a thing or two especially when people fight. . . .''

Another pause.

"Go on,'' Decker urged.

"This woman, Jeanine Garrison. You know Jeanine t'all?''

"I've met her.''

"Wade Anthony is her beau now. But before that . . . I mean to tell you that this gal has all sorts of admirers. Big admirers, little admirers, old ones and *young* ones, too. Specifically a kid named Malcolm Carey. You know the name?''

Decker stared at Abel's face. It revealed nothing. With great effort, he kept his voice even. "Yes, I know the name.''

Abel nodded. "He'd come around to see her—on the sly.''

"Interesting. Why on the sly?''

"Probably Jeanine wanted it that way. Even so . . . us termites . . . we'd hear things . . . see things. Like a stolen kiss. He was mighty fond of the lady.''

Abel paused.

"Fond is too weak a word. He was smitten. She, on the other hand, was nervous when he was around. Told him it was dangerous to talk to her. Still, whenever Mal would come sneaking in, Jeanine would talk to him."

"Know what they talked about?" Decker asked.

"Don't know what they said when they talked in low voices. But oftentimes things got heated. Ended up with her saying something like: 'It'll work out, but it takes time. You've got to have patience.' Clandestine talk. You'd think they were making a drug deal."

Again, Abel shifted his weight. A million thoughts flooded Decker's brain. Though tense and nervous, he refrained from barraging Abel with questions. His old friend's style was slow and casual. Best to keep it that way. Decker said, "Sure you don't want to sit?"

"No, I'm fine, thanks. You really look good."

"You look too thin. We've got to feed you."

"In a minute. Got a little more to tell you."

"Sure."

Abel cleared his throat. "I read in the paper that Malcolm Carey was arrested in a big drug bust."

"Yep."

"Your case?" Abel asked.

"Yes. That's why I know the name."

"Ah . . ." Abel paused. "Thing is . . . I felt kinda sorry for the kid. 'Cause it sounded to me like he was taking the fall for someone."

"Taking the fall?"

"All this talk about him needing patience. Then the next thing the kid knows, he's bagged. I was wondering just how did the police find out about that drug party?"

"A tip," Decker said.

"By whom?"

"It wasn't Jeanine."

"Sure about that?"

"Yes."

"So you know who tipped you?"

"I know who tipped Narc, yes."

Abel paused, tapped his only foot. "And you're sure they received just the *one* tip?"

Heat coursed through Decker's body.

Just the *one* tip.

The tip had come through Narcotics. Niels never identified the sex of the caller.

Why . . . *why* would Joachim have called *Narcotics* when he had been given *Decker*'s number, had been given *Oliver*'s number, had been given *Marge*'s number?

In fact, Joachim *did* call Marge.

Kid's thorough, she had said.

It was clear as a bell. Joachim didn't call Narc. There had been two phone calls made. Two phone calls, two tips. One had been from Joachim to Marge.

And Jeanine had tipped Narcotics.

Using Malcolm Carey as an ally, Jeanine had set up both Harlan Manz to take the fall for Estelle's and Sean Amos to take the fall for David Garrison. Then—in the end—she had set up Malcolm himself, tipping Narc to the dope party.

Unbelievable. Incredible. It defied logic.

It was evil.

It was Jeanine.

He wiped his mouth with his fingers, rubbed his neck.

"Thinkin' 'bout something, Pete?" Abel asked.

"An interesting theory."

Abel nodded. "Thing is, Pete. Even though the kid's a punk, I kinda felt sorry for him. You know how I feel sorry for the underdog."

"You got a kind heart, Abel."

"See, I really think he was set up—"

"You heard someone make a phone call maybe?"

"Well, maybe if you look up the phone records of a certain public phone booth I'm gonna tell you about, you might find a call that went into Narc."

"Interesting."

Abel rocked on his feet. "Actually, that's not the only reason I'm here. See, I just come back from jail, Pete. Paid the kid a visit—"

"*What*—"

"Kid didn't want to see me till I told the jailer that I had a message for him from Jeanine."

"Did you?"

"Of sorts. But not the kind of message he wanted to hear. See, I told Mal my theory, Pete. Told him how I thought Jeanine set him up. The boy wasn't pleased. Told me to stick it where the sun don't shine—"

"Sounds like Malcolm."

"Yeah, I was about to leave. Then I delivered the kid my *real* message from Jeanine—a photograph from Tuesday's paper of Jeanine and Wade, announcing their engagement."

Abel laughed.

"Kid went absolutely apeshit. My opinion is that Jeanine made the boy some promises. Promises that she didn't keep. Promises that she never had any intention of keeping. And that's why she set him up."

"What kind of promises, Abel?"

"Romantic promises *if* he agreed to do certain things."

"*What* certain things?"

Abel shrugged. "To be patient and wait. If he'd do his time nice and quiet, then she'd wait for him. And he agreed to it. What can I say? Sometimes a man does strange things for a beautiful woman. Especially if that man is a teenage boy with a constant boner who thinks he's in love. He just might go through all sorts of shit."

Abel cleared his throat.

"But once the bubble's been burst, and it's clear the boy ain't gonna live happily ever after . . . that's another story. I showed Mal the article and the boy's demeanor changed considerably. He started screaming that he was framed, started asking for a lawyer, just spouting off all kinds of things—"

"*What* kind of things?"

"Talking about Jeanine's brother, David, for one thing. How she popped him with a needle. Talking about the murders at Estelle's—saying very different things from the official story. I told him . . . I told him, 'Mal, my friend, it looks like you been had. Might as well grow some donkey ears and a tail and bray 'cause you've just been made into an ass.' ''

Decker's heart sank. "Why'd you tell him *that*?"

"Because it was the truth."

No one spoke.

"Boy was real upset," Abel said. "Man, I told him not to get mad. I told him to get *even*. Then I thought of you. Mentioned your name. Son of a gun, he said you were responsible for the bust. You were the reason he was in the clink in the first place—"

"Shit—"

"Wait a minute. Just hold on. I told him you weren't the reason, I told him *Jeanine* was the reason. I told him you had clout with the DA . . . which wasn't hard for him to believe, being as you sent him to jail. I suggested he talk to you . . . about David Garrison . . . about Estelle's."

Silence.

Decker took a breath, let it out. "Is he willing?"

"Yeah, he's willing. Says he's got some interesting names for you. Names and dates and letters: Things like notes from Jeanine to Harlan Manz. Apparently, Malcolm was in Manz's apartment right after the murders at Estelle's, cleared the place of some interesting mementos. Notes from Jeanine. Also some audiotapes. Stuff he hid, just in case. Tapes where she says stuff you'd be interested in."

Decker could feel his body float. "When would he like to speak with me?"

"I b'lieve right now."

"*Now*?"

"Boy is fighting mad at the moment, Pete. Don't think it would be wise for him to cool off—"

"I'll get my jacket." Decker tried to keep his thoughts coherent. "I've got some of my detectives on the case here at the house—"

"Don't think it would be wise to overwhelm the boy, Pete. Let's make it the two of us. We can reminisce about old days on the ride over."

"Fine. Just let me find Ri—" Decker stopped talking.

Rina was a few feet away, her head down, blushing scarlet.

Decker said, "How long have you been standing there?"

"Long enough to hear."

Decker blew out air. "You remember Abel?"

"Of course." Rina held out her hand to him. "So, you two are on your way to County?"

Decker nodded.

"For how long?"

"Whatever it takes, Rina. I can't let this opportunity—"

"Of course."

Decker ran his hand through his hair. "I can't tell Oliver and Marge about this. Not just yet. Make excuses for me. Tell them . . . God, I can't use work as an excuse—"

"You can use me, doc," Abel said. "They know I'm a needle in your rear. Tell them I needed your help."

"Good idea," Rina said.

Decker patted Abel's shoulder. "You're a good friend, Abe."

"Likewise, I'm sure."

Rina said, "I'll keep the turkey warm."

"You already do that every night." Decker smiled, but it was wistful. "I'm never around when you need me."

"Nonsense. Besides I don't need you now. Go."

"You're crying. I'm so sorry—"

"No, no, no!" Rina wiped her eyes. "I'm not crying. I was peeling onions." She looked at Abel. "Of course you'll stay for dinner afterward. Whenever it is. Even if it's two in the morning. And don't say no. I'm very persistent."

"I figured as much. I'd love dinner, Mrs. Decker."

"It's Rina."

Decker slipped on his jacket, made sure he had his official identification and his gun. "Let's move it."

Abel held the door open for him. Before he left, he turned around, winked at Rina.

She winked back, dammed back tears. One day Peter would figure it out. By then, it would all be past. She watched them peel rubber, zoom off in Peter's Porsche. Closing the door, she went back into the kitchen to baste the turkey.

❧41

And it came to pass at midnight.

A line from the Passover Seder. Decker didn't know why it had flashed into consciousness since the holiday was still months away. Guess it had something to do with the magic of the witching hour: the first ticks of a new day so promising with hope. It had been a long night, replete with frantic activity and never-ending paperwork. Maybe there would even be a payoff.

He brought the Volare to a stop at a red light. A deserted intersection. He looked around, charged through the light. From the backseat, Oliver chuckled.

Decker said, "Hell with it. I'm tired. Just let some punk uniform *try* to stop me."

"The man is on a mission." Marge sat shotgun, nervously sipped cold coffee from a paper cup. "You lost out on a great meal, Pete. Never seen so much variety. Rina outdid herself."

"Rina and Mom are a deadly combination."

Oliver grinned. "Mom's got a bit of a 'tude, don't she?"

"Watch your mouth."

"Hey, I behaved myself." He turned to Marge for support. "Didn't I behave?"

"You were a very good boy."

Decker felt his stomach growl. "So I'll have leftovers. Sometimes that's better. The flavors are blended." Anxiously, he tapped the wheel of the car. "Just want to finish up and call it a night."

Marge slapped the warrant against her knee. "I can't believe we're actually *doing* this."

"It's long overdue," Decker said.

"More than overdue, Deck," Oliver stated. "It's *weird*! Abel popping up . . . like pulling a rabbit from a hat."

"*Deus ex machina.*" Decker licked his lips. "Providence. What else could it be? Abel hasn't worked even a *part*-time job in years."

Oliver said, "Okay. I can see him working this job, doing something for the tournament. After all, your friend's a gimp—"

"An amputee," Decker corrected.

"A lame-o." Oliver was undeterred. "Okay. So he worked the tournament. I still don't understand *why* he took an interest in a bit player like Malcolm Carey."

"Lord only knows," Decker said. "Abel always had an eye for the bizarre."

But his own explanation didn't sit well. Something was off. *Way* off! But he couldn't concentrate on that now. More important things to do.

They rode for a few moments in smothering silence. The minutes before an arrest were always tense. Time elongated, time contracted. Everyone on edge, overly focused. The blackness of night seemed bright and shiny, reflective roadway surfaces slick with mist.

Marge spoke in a tight voice. "You should have let Scott and me handle Malcolm, Pete. That way, you could have eaten with your family."

"Carey asked for me specifically. I didn't want to take the chance—"

"I know how particular perps can be," Marge cut him off. "But you didn't have to lie."

Decker knew she was hurt by the exclusion. He should have taken both Marge and Scott into his confidence. But everything had been so rushed. He tried to keep his voice even. "I was thinking expedience. I brought you both in as soon as I could."

"I know," Marge said. "I'm just sulking." A sigh. "I would have *loved* to have been there."

"At least you had a good meal."

"A fantastic meal," Oliver expounded. "You know your brother's a real funny guy. Not at all a stiff."

Not like you was the implication. Decker laughed, too exhausted to be insulted. "Glad you found a soul mate."

"He does remind me of me. Kinda a fuckup. I got the feeling you've pulled him out of some rough spots."

"What can I say? He's my bro."

Oliver said, "You got Randy, you got me, you got Marge, you got Abel. You just love the strays, don'tcha, rabbi?"

"I beg your pardon," Marge said, stiffly.

Decker smiled. The chitchat eased the gripping tension. A beat. Then Marge said, "Unbelievable that Jeanine thought she could work around Malcolm."

"With him in the hole, she had at *least* four-plus years breathing room."

"But she had to figure that Carey would find out about the engagement," Marge persisted.

"Jails keep you isolated. Malcolm was completely dependent on Jeanine for outside news."

"They get newspapers," Oliver said.

"Obviously Carey didn't read the social section because Abel's revelation came as a total shock. He was still under the delusion that she intended to wait for him. Because that's what she told him: Behave yourself and I'll wait."

Marge said, "Carey could have learned about the engagement from Sean Amos."

"Amos wouldn't dare to go *near* Carey. Kid's been handed an undeserved reprieve. Even *he's* not stupid enough to spit in Lady Luck's eye." Decker smoothed his mustache. "Jeanine was Carey's eyes to the outside world. As long as she strung him along, he remained quiet."

"Idiot that he is," Oliver said.

"Idiot that he *was*," Decker said. "He thought he was in love."

"How'd he get involved with Jeanine in the first place?"

Oliver asked. "Through Amos or Greenvale?"

"Both actually," Decker said. "Carey happened to be at Greenvale one day when Jeanine and Sean were playing tennis together. Sean introduced them. Mal was smitten. Or in his words . . . 'Fuck, I had the hots for her.' Talked at great length about the boner she gave him."

Oliver smiled. "He's still a kid."

"A kid but a lethal one."

A pause.

Marge said, "Who approached Mal to do Estelle's? Sean or Jeanine?"

"Sean had nothing to do with Estelle's or Garrison. He was just a dumb dupe."

"Like Manz?"

"Yep." Decker tried to relax his shoulders. "According to Carey, Jeanine approached him to shoot up the restaurant. Now his word isn't worth a damn. But he does have tapes to back him up."

Oliver said, "I haven't heard them yet. You have Jeanine soliciting Carey to shoot up Estelle's?"

"No such luck. But Carey's tapes have them talking about the shootings. Lots of details. We'll go over them at great length in the morning."

Another drawn silence. This time Decker broke it.

"Carey told me that Jeanine had been thinking about popping her parents for a long time. When they met, she was working on Harlan, trying to get him irate enough to go in and blast the place. Of course, she was failing miserably. Harlan was a fuck-up, but no killer. It was Carey's idea to use Harlan as a dupe. Jeanine got him mad enough to charge into Estelle's and confront the management . . . specifically the manager who fired him months earlier. Mal followed on Harlan's heels, went inside and just *sprayed* the place, leaving a dead Manz to take the blame."

A pause. Marge squeezed her empty coffee cup. "Jeanine and Mal. What a pair."

Decker said, "Two really . . . *evil* people who found each other. It's true that Estelle's was Jeanine's idea. But Carey jumped at the opportunity. I think he liked shooting people.

You'll note that even though he wanted Jeanine, he demanded payment for the job. Carey *wanted* to be a hit man . . . talked about how being a ninja was a time-honored, noble profession. Incredible how far we've fallen as a society."

"But shooting up Estelle's was *Jeanine*'s idea," Marge said.

"Yes. I guess it just took her a while to find an acceptable cast of characters. The woman was right about one thing. She was one hell of an organizer."

Marge asked, "Did Jeanine ever state *why* she wanted to kill her parents?"

"Money, Dunn! Why else?" Oliver cleared his throat. "Carey probably did it for money too. What'd you say she gave him? Something like thirty grand in bearer bonds."

"Thirty-five." Decker cleared his throat. "Carey liked the money. Matter of fact, I think popping David Garrison was also Malcolm's call and he did it for money. Of course, he really liked Jeanine and wanted to impress her. The one thing Carey never factored into the equation was Jeanine's genuine affection for Wade Anthony. Since Anthony was a paraplegic, Carey didn't view him as a romantic threat. But later, Carey began to suspect things. Especially since Sean kept complaining about the two of them. Even so, Carey couldn't seriously believe that Jeanine would marry a guy stuck in a wheelchair."

Oliver said, "At some point, Mal must have felt Anthony's threat. We did find all those pictures of Wade and his daily schedule at the bust. Looks like he was planning a hit to me."

"I can believe it. Kid was stricken with bloodlust."

"And he'd probably try to pin it on Sean," Marge added. "Just like he did with David Garrison."

"Makes sense."

Decker felt himself clutching the wheel and relaxed his fingers.

"I guess Jeanine figured she could string Mal along until he lost interest in her. But when Wade came into the picture, she accelerated her plans. She knew Mal would drop a dime if she bailed out on him so soon. So she got rid of him. Making the call to Narc to get him busted.''

Oliver shook his head. ''Carey's a dumbshit. By going state's witness on Estelle's, he ain't going to lessen his own jail time.''

''Not by a minute.''

''It'll probably screw up his parole, make him serve an even longer sentence.''

''No doubt.''

Marge said, ''At least this way he can't be prosecuted for Estelle's.''

''Dunn, without Carey turning state's witness and his tapes, the state *has* no case. All he did was create a mess for himself.''

''Teenagers are impulsive,'' Marge said. ''They don't think things through.''

''C'mon. Had to be more to it.''

Decker said, ''You never craved revenge?''

''Not if it screwed me blue.''

''A sane man,'' Marge said.

Decker said, ''Lucky for us that Carey wasn't so sane. And like Marge said, lucky that he was impulsive. Because at that point, more than anything, Carey craved *revenge*. And you know what, Scott? When he spoke about the big get-even with her, I can tell you that old Mal and I were of one mind.''

The condo was set atop undulating hillside that peered out into city lights, and looked down into deep sweeps of lush canyons. The air was wet and sweet-scented; a gentle breeze rustled through the brush. A lovely setting to plan a mass murder.

Instinctively, Decker felt for his gun. Never could tell what was on the other side of the door. But he didn't anticipate trouble. He nodded to the others; they walked up to the building. A twenty-four-hour doorman sat at a desk behind locked glass doors. He was heavyset and moved with effort. His face was moon-shaped and registered surprise when confronted by the badges of the midnight posse.

Slowly, he unlocked the doors, let them cross the threshold. He was wary but cooperative.

"Should I ring Ms. Garrison?"

"No," Decker said. "But I want you to come up with us."

"All right."

"Unlock her door if necessary."

Pink permeated the doorman's face. "I don't know if I can do that."

Oliver said, "Surely you don't want us to break it down."

"All the noise," Marge added. "Plus it's not an easy thing to do."

The doorman looked over his shoulder as if trying to spot a hidden ally. "Well, all right. I guess . . ." He nodded.

Decker said, "Can you tell me if Ms. Garrison has any visitors at the moment?"

"Just Mr. Anthony."

Decker pushed the elevator button. "Let's go."

The ride up to the penthouse was stone silent. The elevator stopped. They got out. Decker took a deep breath, balled his hands into fists. The rap on Jeanine's door was rapid and loud.

Waiting.

Nothing.

Decker tried again. Firmer. Louder.

Shuffling noises. Stomping noises. Seconds later, Garrison's voice asking who it was. She spoke in an angry tone.

Decker said, "Police, Ms. Garrison! Open up now!"

"Of all the *nerve*!" The door swung open. Jeanine dressed in black sweats, a rosy face damp with perspiration. Beads of moisture were resting above her upper lip, tendrils of blond hair cascading across her cheeks and down her shoulders.

Obvious what she had been doing.

A male voice emanated from the other room, asked what was going on. Her livid face glaring upward. "Just *who* the hell do you think you are?"

Decker said, "Jeanine Holly Garrison, you are under arrest for the murder of—"

Immediately the door flew at Decker's face. He blocked it with his shoulder, shoved it back open. She was waiting for him, her arm raised high above her shoulder, a furious open palm arcing downward to smack his face. He caught her wrist in midair and set it firmly behind her back. Brought the other wrist down and around and cuffed her hands together.

Once restrained, Jeanine melted. She burst into unrestrained sobs, water exploding from her eyes.

At last! Decker thought. *Genuine tears! Camus would have been proud.*

Jeanine wailed out, "But you have no *right*!"

Decker said, "Ms. Garrison, this is America. Everyone has rights. Now let me tell you some of yours."

"If you're asking me about a smoking gun, I'm going to tell you no, nothing yet. These things take time, Romulus."

Rukmani was talking through a white paper face mask. Head down, she was peering into a sea of tissue and viscera, probing at something red and squishy with a metal instrument. Six hours ago, Trent Minors was puking over Britanny's face. Now the young girl had been literally reduced to flesh and bones.

Again, Rukmani spoke . . . almost muttering. Poe could barely understand her. "Can you take a break?"

"A break?"

"Yes. Like in a coffee break. Or a tea break?"

She looked up, covering the dissected body with a tarp. "Is the smell bothering you?"

"A little." Poe snapped his fingers as his eyes swept across the steel room of death. They eventually settled upon Rukmani, dressed in surgical blues. Wrapped up like an anorectic mummy. He said, "It's hard to talk in here."

"C'mon." She untied her mask and snapped off her gloves. "But only for five minutes. I don't like to leave my bodies unattended."

"Thanks." He kissed her cheek. She stank from formaldehyde.

Together they boarded a two-person, staff-only elevator. Staff only.

As if a morgue would be teaming with visitors.

They took the lift to the third floor. Her office was immediately to the right—about the size of a coffin, but it had a ceiling and a lockable door, and it was all her own. A standard issue desk and a couple of chairs. A wall of bookshelves held medical tomes and pictures of her two grown children: twenty-five-year-old daughter, Shoba, a sophomore at Harvard Medical School, and twenty-seven-year-old Michael, a resident in radiology at Barnes Hospital in St. Louis.

Married in the old country, Rukmani had given birth to her son two weeks past her sixteenth birthday. The untimely death of her much older, mercantile husband, a hidden cache of rainy day money, and a couple of American relatives gave her a new life in the States. In the States, she wasn't judged by her caste or her in-laws. In the States, she wasn't forced to avoid the sun to keep her Indian complexion as Anglo-light as possible. Probably the reason why she moved to Vegas. At the moment, Ruki was nutmeg brown.

"Sit." All business. She said, "What specifically do you want to know?"

"Bullet holes?"

"Not yet."

"Stab wounds?"

"None so far."

Poe felt ill. "She died while this monster was gouging out her eyeball?"

"Not necessarily."

Poe drummed her desktop and waited.

Rukmani said, "There are other ways to murder besides stabbing and shooting." She made an imaginary needle with her finger and stuck it in the crook of her arm.

Poe said, "He ODed her first?"

"Or at least sedated her. That's my guess."

"You found something in her veins."

"Bloodwork hasn't come back yet." Rukmani put her hands over his to quiet his fidgeting. Then she propped her elbows on her desk and leaned her face against her hands. "You look tired. Did you sleep at all?"

"An hour at my desk this morning. What about you?"

"About four hours." A pause. "Come to my place tonight. I'll cook you dinner. If your face drops in mulligatawny, I won't say a word."

"Sounds wonderful, but I'm probably going to pull another all-nighter."

"Romulus, you can't work effectively on an hour's sleep."

She was right. He said, "Nothing happens in this town before dark. I'll grab a couple of hours of sleep before I go out again."

Rukmani looked grave. "Why don't you live in a normal house?"

"I like where I live. It's very quiet."

"It doesn't have running water or electricity."

"Modern conveniences are highly overrated—"

"At least get a box spring for the mattress."

"I couldn't get it through the door frame."

"So get a bigger door, for godsakes—"

"Why are you pissed at me? You know I'd love to come for dinner, spend the night with you engaged in wild, passionate lovemaking. Do you think I'm doing this by *choice?*"

Again, Rukmani was quiet.

Poe said, "Why do you think she was sedated while he was . . . you know . . . flaying her?"

"The evenness of the gouges. Almost ruler perfect parallel lines. If she had been awake, she would have been thrashing about, lines would have been squiggly."

"What about if he bound her?"

"Even so, she could have squirmed unless he had her head in a vice. Even with millimeters worth of motion, there would have been waves or chinks in the lines. The rakes were almost . . . surgical in their precision."

"Someone from the medical profession?"

"Or a farmer."

Poe made a sour face. "So she was either sedated or dead when he . . . attacked her."

"There was evidence of fresh bleeding into the depressions. I'd say she was sedated. Very heavily sedated. Alive but unconscious. She probably never felt a thing." She gave him a weak smile. "Small comfort."

He thought about her words. "That could say something about the killer."

"Like what?"

"He's a control freak. Wants her completely defenseless so he can do his thing. Doesn't want to leave anything up to chance."

"Or maybe he has sensitive ears and doesn't like screaming."

Poe pondered her statement. "You may have something there."

"Sensitive ears?"

"He doesn't like to hear screaming because he doesn't do torture for torture sake."

"Just enjoys raking human flesh?" Rukmani shook her head. "I suppose a boy needs a hobby."

Poe talked as much to himself as he did to Rukmani. "He likes killing. He likes . . . dressing his victim in a certain fashion. But like a hunter with his prey. Hunters don't get their kicks out of torturing animals. They like clean kill shots. One big *bam* and the animal keels over. The thrill is the hunt."

"And the head on the wall afterward," Rukmani stated. "Something they can brag about. Maybe that's what she was. A trophy kill."

"She wasn't dressed or displayed like a trophy." Poe paused. "Of course, I got to her after she'd been in a windstorm. Who knows what she looked like before?"

Rukmani said, "I should be getting back."

Poe said, "Do you have a fix as to what kind of instrument made the gouges?"

"I was hoping you wouldn't ask me that."

"Go on."

"I've found flakes of metal lodged where it touched bone

. . . consistent with a rake or some kind of tool. But I've also found bits of tooth enamel.''

"Consistent with biting."

"No bite marks, Rom. More like . . . methodical tearing at the victim with the teeth." She looked away. "There was something very animalistic about this death. Like he was . . . eating her—''

"Oh Christ!"

"More like grazing—''

"This is truly nauseating.''

Rukmani scratched at her hair tucked under a scrub cap. "This has not been an easy autopsy. It's going to take weeks before I come to anything definitive." She stood. "I've really got to go."

Poe got up as well. "I can't entice you for a quick lunch at my place?"

"*Lunch*?"

"Well, lunch and munch.''

"Rukmani laughed, then hit his shoulder. "I'd love to but I got this corpse—''

"Aha! Okay for you to refuse me, but—''

"Rom, you leave a body exposed for more than a short period of time, it screws up every—''

"When it's *your* ox that's being gored—'' Poe stopped talking. "Why did I say that?"

Rukmani smiled with fatigue. "My place, tomorrow night?

"It's a deal.''

"We are really too busy. We never see each other."

"Guess that makes us a true ideal American couple.''

"If we're going to lapse into mindless treadmilling and burnout, we might as well get married.''

"Name a date.''

She waved him off, then kissed his cheek. "Mind if I don't walk you out? Britanny Newel is calling my name.''

Poe snapped his fingers. "You actually think of her as Britanny Newel?''

"You bet, I do. She had a name in her life. I'll be damned if I take it away in death.''